The Real Adventure

The Real Adventure

Henry Kitchell Webster

MINT EDITIONS

The Real Adventure was first published in 1916.

This edition published by Mint Editions 2021.

ISBN 9781513283517 | E-ISBN 9781513288536

Published by Mint Editions®

 MINT
EDITIONS

minteditionbooks.com

Publishing Director: Jennifer Newens
Design & Production: Rachel Lopez Metzger
Project Manager: Micaela Clark
Typesetting: Westchester Publishing Services

Contents

BOOK I
THE GREAT ILLUSION

I

A Point of Departure

"Indeed," continued the professor, glancing demurely down at his notes, "if one were the editor of a column of—er advice to young girls, such as I believe is to be found, along with the household hints and the dress patterns, on the ladies' page of most of our newspapers—if one were the editor of such a column, he might crystallize the remarks I have been making this morning into a warning—never marry a man with a passion for principles."

It drew a laugh, of course. Professorial jokes never miss fire. But *the* girl didn't laugh. She came to with a start—she had been staring out the window—and wrote, apparently, the fool thing down in her note-book. It was the only note she had made in thirty-five minutes.

All of his brilliant exposition of the paradox of Rousseau and Robespierre (he was giving a course on the French Revolution), the strange and yet inevitable fact that the softest, most sentimental, rose-scented religion ever invented, should have produced, through its most thoroughly infatuated disciple, the ghastliest reign of terror that ever shocked the world; his masterly character study of the "sea-green incorruptible," too humane to swat a fly, yet capable of sending half of France to the guillotine in order that the half that was left might believe unanimously in the rights of man; all this the girl had let go by unheard, in favor, apparently, of the drone of a street piano, which came in through the open window on the prematurely warm March wind. Of all his philosophizing, there was not a pen-track to mar the virginity of the page she had opened her note-book to when the lecture began.

And then, with a perfectly serious face, she had written down his silly little joke about advice to young girls.

There was no reason in the world why she should be The Girl. There were fifteen or twenty of them in the class along with about as many men. And, partly because there was no reason for his paying any special attention to her, it annoyed him frightfully that he did.

She was good-looking, of course—a rather boyishly splendid young creature of somewhere about twenty, with a heap of hair that had, in spite of its rather commonplace chestnut color, a sort of electric vitality about it. She was slightly prognathous, which gave a humorous lift to her otherwise sensible nose. She had good straight-looking, expressive eyes, too, and a big, wide, really beautiful mouth, with square white teeth in it, which, when she smiled or yawned—and she yawned more luxuriously than any girl who had ever sat in his classes—exerted a sort of hypnotic effect on him. All that, however, left unexplained the quality she had of making you, whatever she did, irresistibly aware of her. And, conversely, unaware of every one else about her. A bit of campus slang occurred to him as quite literally applicable to her. She had all the rest of them faded.

It wasn't, apparently, an effect she tried for. He had to acquit her of that. Not even, perhaps, one that she was conscious of. When she came early to one of his lectures—it didn't happen often—the men, showed a practical unanimity in trying to choose seats near by, or at least where they could see her. But while this didn't distress her at all—they were welcome to look if they liked—she struck no attitudes for their benefit. A sort of breezy indifference—he selected that phrase finally as the best description of her attitude toward all of them, including himself. When she was late, as she usually was, she slid unostentatiously into the back row—if possible at the end where she could look out the window. But for three minutes after she had come in, he knew he might as well have stopped his lecture and begun reciting the Greek alphabet. She was, in the professor's mind, the final argument against coeducation. Her name was Rosalind Stanton, but his impression was that they called her Rose.

The bell rang out in the corridor. He dismissed the class and began stacking up his notes. Then:

"Miss Stanton," he said.

She detached herself from the stream that was moving toward the door, and with a good-humored look of inquiry about her very expressive eyebrows, came toward him. And then he wished he hadn't called her. She had spoiled his lecture—a perfectly good lecture—and his impulse had been to remonstrate with her. But the moment he saw her coming, he knew he wasn't going to be able to do it. It wasn't her fault that her teeth had hypnotized him, and her hair tangled his ideas.

"This is an idiotic question," he said, as she paused before his desk, "but did you get anything at all out of my lecture except my bit of facetious advice to young girls about to marry?"

She flushed a little (a girl like that hadn't any right to flush; it ought to be against the college regulations), drew her brows together in a puzzled sort of way, and then, with her wide, boyish, good-humored mouth, she smiled.

"I didn't know it was facetious," she said. "It struck me as pretty good. But—I'm awfully sorry if you thought me inattentive. You see, mother brought us all up on the Social Contract and The Age of Reason, things like that, and I didn't put it down because. . ."

"I see," he said. "I beg your pardon."

She smiled, cheerfully begged his and assured him she'd try to do better.

Another girl who'd been waiting to speak to the professor, perceiving that their conversation was at an end, came and stood beside her at the desk—a scrawny girl with an eager voice, and a question she wanted to ask about Robespierre; and for some reason or other, Rosalind Stanton's valedictory smile seemed to include a consciousness of this other girl—a consciousness of a contrast. It might not have been any more than that, but somehow, it left the professor feeling that he had given himself away.

He was particularly polite to the other girl, because his impulse was to act so very differently.

There is nothing cloistral about the University of Chicago except its architecture. The presence of a fat abbot, or a lady prioress in the corridor outside the recitation room would have fitted in admirably with the look of the warm gray walls and the carven pointed arches of the window and door casements, the blackened oak of the doors themselves.

On the other hand, the appearance of the person whom Rose found waiting for her out there, afforded the piquant effect of contrast. Or would have done so, had the spectacle of him in that very occupation not been so familiar.

He was a varsity half-back, a gigantic blond young man in a blue serge suit. He said, "Hello, Rose," and she said, "Hello, Harry." And he heaved himself erect from the wall he had been leaning against and reached out an immense hand to absorb the little stack of note-books she carried. She ignored the gesture, and when he asked for them said she'd carry them herself. There was a sort of strategic advantage in having your own note-books under your own arm—a fact which no one appreciated better than the half-back himself.

He looked a little hurt. "Sore about something?" he asked.

She smiled widely and said, "Not a bit."

"I didn't mean at me necessarily," he explained, and referred to the fact that the professor had detained her after he had dismissed the class. "What'd he try to do—call you down?"

There was indignation in the young man's voice—a hint of the protector aroused—of possible retribution.

She grinned again. "Oh, you needn't go back and kill him," she said.

He blushed to the ears. "I'm sorry," he observed stiltedly, "if I appear ridiculous." But she went on smiling.

"Don't you care," she said. "Everybody's ridiculous in March. You're ridiculous, I'm ridiculous, he"—she nodded along the corridor—"he's plumb ridiculous."

He wasn't wholly appeased. It was rather with an air of resignation that he held the door for her to go out by. They strolled along in silence until they rounded the corner of the building. Here, ceremoniously, he fell back, walked around behind her and came up on the outside. She glanced up and asked him, incomprehensibly, to walk on the other side, the way they had been. He wanted to know why. This was where he belonged.

"You don't belong there," she told him, "if I want you the other way. And I do."

He heaved a sigh, and said "Women!" under his breath. *Mutabile semper*! No matter how much you knew about them, they remained incomprehensible. Their whims passed explanation. He was getting downright sulky.

As a matter of fact, he did her an injustice. There was a valid reason for her wanting him to walk on the other side. What gave the appearance of pure caprice to her request was just her womanly dislike of hurting his feelings. There was a small boil on the left side of his neck and when he walked at her left hand, it didn't show.

"Oh, don't be fussy," she said. "It's such a dandy day."

But the half-back refused to be comforted. And he was right about that. A woman never tells you to cheer up in that brisk unfeeling way if she really cares a cotton hat about your troubles. And a candid deliberate self-examination would have convinced Rose that she didn't, in spite of the sentimentally warm March wind that was blowing her hair about. She was less moved by the half-back's sorrows this morning than at any time during the last six months. She'd hardly have minded the boil before today.

Six months ago, he had been a very wonderful person to her. There had been a succession of pleasant—of really thrilling discoveries. First, that he'd rather dance with her than with any other girl in the university. (You're not to forget that he was a celebrity. During the football season, his name was on the sporting page of the Chicago papers every day—generally in the head-lines when there was a game to write about, and Walter Camp had devoted a whole paragraph to explaining why he didn't put him on the first all-American eleven but on the second instead—a gross injustice which she had bitterly resented.)

There was a thrill, then, in the discovery that he liked her better than other girls, and a greater thrill in the subsequent discovery that she had become the basis of his whole orientation. It was her occupations that left him leisure for his own; his leisure was hers to dispose of as she liked; his energy, including his really prodigious physical prowess, to be directed toward any object she thought laudable. Six months ago she would not have laughed—not in that derisive way at least—at the notion of his going back and beating up the professor.

There had been a thrill, too, in their more sentimental passages. But at this point, there developed a most perplexing phenomenon. The idea that he wanted to make love to her, really moved and excited her; set her imagination to exploring all sorts of roseate mysteries. The first time he had ever held her hand—it was inside her muff, one icy December day when he hadn't any gloves on—the memory of the feel of that big hand, and of the timbre of his voice, left her starry-eyed with a new wonder. She dreamed of other caresses; of wonderful things that he should say to her and she should say to him.

But here arose the perplexity. It was her imagination of the thing that she enjoyed rather than the thing itself. The wonderful scenes that her own mind projected never came true. The ones that happened were disappointing—irritating, and eventually and unescapably, downright disagreeable to her. There was no getting away from it, the ideal lover of her dreams, whose tenderness and chivalry and devotion were so highly desirable, although he might wear the half-back's clothes and bear his face and name, was not the half-back. She might dote on his absence, but his presence was another matter.

The realization of this fact had been gradual. She wasn't fully conscious of it, even on this March morning. But something had happened this morning that made a difference. If she'd been ascending an imperceptible gradient for the last three months, today she had come to a recognizable step up and taken it. Oddly enough, the thing had happened back there in the class-room as she stood before the professor's desk and caught his eye wavering between herself and the scrawny girl who wanted to ask a question about Robespierre. There had been more than blank helpless exasperation in that look of his, and it had taught her something. She couldn't have explained what.

To the half-back she attributed it to the month of March. "You're ridiculous, I'm ridiculous, he's ridiculous." That was about as well as she could put it.

She and the half-back had walked about a hundred yards in silence. Now they were arriving at a point where the path forked.

"You're elegant company this morning, I must say," he commented resentfully.

Again she smiled. "I'm elegant company for myself," she said, and held out her hand. "Which way do *you* go?" she asked.

A minute later she was swinging along alone, her shoulders back, confronting the warm March wind, drawing into her good deep chest, long breaths. She had just had, psychically speaking, a birthday.

She played a wonderful game of basket-ball that afternoon.

II

BEGINNING AN ADVENTURE

I t was after five o'clock when, at the conclusion of the game and a cold shower, a rub and a somewhat casual resumption of her clothes, she emerged from the gymnasium. High time that she took the quickest way of getting home, unless she wanted to be late for dinner.

But the exhilaration of the day persisted. She felt like doing something out of the regular routine. Even a preliminary walk of a mile or so before she should cross over and take the elevated, would serve to satisfy her mild hunger for adventure. And, really, she liked to be a little late for dinner. It was always pleasanter to come breezing in after things had come to a focus, than to idle about for half an hour in that no-man's-land of the day, when the imminence of dinner made it impossible to do anything but wait for it.

So, with her note-books under her arm and her sweater-jacket unfastened, at a good four-mile swing, she started north. In the purlieus of the university she was frequently hailed by friends of her own sex or the other. But though she waved cheerful responses to their greetings, she made her stride purposeful enough to discourage offers of company. They all seemed young to her today. All her student activities seemed young. As if, somehow, she had outgrown them. The feeling was none the less real after she had laughed at herself for entertaining it.

She noticed presently that it was a good deal darker than it had any right to be at this hour, and the sudden fall of the breeze and a persistent shimmer of lightning supplied her with the explanation. When she reached Forty-seventh Street, the break of the storm was obviously a matter of minutes, so she decided to ride across to the elevated—it was another mile, perhaps—rather than walk across as she had meant to do. She didn't in the least mind getting wet, providing she could keep on moving until she could change her clothes. But a ten-mile ride in the elevated, with water squashing around in her boots and dripping out of her hair, wasn't an alluring prospect.

She found quite a group of people waiting on the corner for a car, and the car itself, when it came along, was crowded. So she handed her nickel to the conductor over somebody's shoulder, and moved back to the corner of the vestibule. It was frightfully stuffy inside and most of the newly received passengers seemed to agree with her that the platform was a pleasanter place to stay; which did very well until the next stop, where half a dozen more prospective passengers were waiting. They were in a hurry, too, since it had begun in very downright fashion to rain.

The conductor had been chanting, "Up in the car, please," in a perfunctory cry all along. But at this crisis, his voice got a new urgency. "Come on, now," he proclaimed, "you'll have to get inside!"

From the step the new arrivals pushed, the conductor pushed, and finally he was able to give the signal for starting the car. The obvious necessity of making room for those who'd be waiting at the next corner, kept him at the task of herding them inside and the sheep-like docility of an American crowd helped him.

Regretfully, with the rest, Rose made her way to the door.

"Fare, please," he said sharply as she came along.

She told him she had paid her fare, but for some reason, perhaps because he was tired at the end of a long run, perhaps because he saw some one else he suspected of being a spotter, he elected not to believe her.

"When did you pay it?" he demanded.

"A block back," she said, "when all those other people got on."

"You didn't pay it to me," he said truculently. "Come along! Pay your fare or get off the car."

"I paid it once," she said quietly, "and I'm not going to pay it again." With that she started forward toward the door.

He reached out across his little rail and caught her by the arm. It was a natural act enough—not polite, to be sure, by no means chivalrous. Still, he probably put into his grip no more strength than he thought necessary to prevent her walking by into the car.

But it had a surprising result—a result that normally would not have happened. Yet, on this particular day, it could not have happened differently. It had been a red-letter day from the beginning, from no assignable cause an exciting joyous day, and the thrill of the hard fast game, the shower, the rub, the walk, had brought her up to what engineers speak of as a "peak."

Well, the conductor didn't know that. If he had, he would either have let the girl go by, or have put a good deal more force into his attempt to stop her. And the first thing he knew, he found both his wrists pinned in the grip of her two hands; found himself staring stupidly into a pair of great blazing blue eyes—it's a wrathful color, blue, when you light it up—and listening uncomprehendingly to a voice that said, "Don't dare touch me like that!"

The episode might have ended right there, for the conductor's consternation was complete. If she could have walked straight into the car, he would not have pursued her. But her note-books were scattered everywhere and had to be gathered up, and there were two or three of the passengers who thought the situation was funny, and laughed, which did not improve the conductor's temper.

Rose was aware, as she gathered up her note-books, of another hand that was helping her—a gloved masculine hand. She took the books it held out to her as she straightened up, and said, "Thank you," but without looking around for the face that went with it. The conductor's intentions were still at the focal point of her mind. They were, apparently, unaltered. He had jerked the bell while she was collecting her note-books and the car was grinding down to a stop.

"You pay your fare," he repeated, "or you get off the car right here."

"Right here" was in the middle of what looked like a lake, and the rain was pouring down with a roar.

She didn't hesitate long, but before she could answer a voice spoke—a voice which, with intuitive certainty, she associated with the gloved hand that had helped gather up her note-books—a very crisp, finely modulated voice.

"That's perfectly outrageous," it said. "The young lady has paid her fare."

"Did you see her pay it?" demanded the conductor.

"Naturally not," said the voice. "I got on at the last corner. She was here then. But if she said she did, she did."

It seemed to relieve the conductor to have some one of his own sex to quarrel with. He delivered a stream of admonition somewhat sulphurously phrased, to the general effect that any one whose concern the present affair was not, could, at his option, close his jaw or have his block knocked off.

Rose hadn't, as yet, looked round at her champion. But she now became aware that inside a shaggy gray sleeve which hung beside her, there was a sudden tension of big muscles; the gloved hand that had helped gather up her note-books, clenched itself into a formidable fist. The thought of the sort of thud that fist might make against the overactive jaw of the conductor was pleasant. Still, the thing mustn't be allowed to happen.

She spoke quickly and decisively. "I won't pay another fare, but of course you may put me off the car."

"All right," said the conductor.

The girl smiled over the very gingerly way in which he reached out for her elbow to guide her around the rail and toward the step. Technically, the action constituted putting her off the car. She heard the crisp voice once more, this time repeating a number, "twenty-two-naught-five," or something like that, just as she splashed down into the two-inch lake that covered the hollow in the pavement. The bell rang twice, the car started with a jerk, there was another splash, and a big gray-clad figure alighted in the lake beside her.

"I've got his number," the crisp voice said triumphantly.

"But," gasped the girl, "but what in the world did you get off the car for?"

It wasn't raining. It was doing an imitation of Niagara Falls, and the roar of it almost drowned their voices.

"What did I get off the car for!" he shouted. "Why, I wouldn't have missed it for anything. It was immense! It's so confounded seldom," he went on, "that you find anybody with backbone enough to stick up for a principle. . ."

He heard a brief, deep-throated little laugh and pulled up short with a, "What's the joke?"

"I laughed," she said, "because you have been deceived." And she added quickly, "I don't believe it's quite so deep on the sidewalk, is it?" With that she waded away toward the curb.

He followed, then led the way to a lee-wall that offered, comparatively speaking, shelter.

Then, "Where's the deception?" he asked.

On any other day, it's probable she'd have acted differently; would have paid some heed, though a bit contemptuously, perhaps, to the precepts of ladylike behavior, in which she'd been admirably grounded. The case for reticence and discretion was a strong one. The night was dark; the rain-lashed street deserted; the man an utterly casual stranger—why, she hadn't even had a straight look into his face. His motive in getting off the car was at least dubitable. Even if not sinister, it could easily be unpleasantly gallant. A man might not contemplate doing her bodily harm, and still be capable of trying to collect some sort of sentimental reward for the ducking he had submitted himself to.

HENRY KITCHELL WEBSTER

Her instinct rejected all that. The sound of his voice, the general—atmosphere of him had been exactly right. And then, he'd left undone the things he ought not to have done. He hadn't tried to take hold of her arm as they had splashed along through the lake to the curb. He hadn't exhibited any tenderly chivalrous concern over how wet she was. And, today being today, she consigned ladylike considerations to the inventor of them, and gave instinct its head.

She laughed again as she answered his question. "The deception was that I pretended to do it from principle. The real reason why I wouldn't pay another fare, is because I had only one more nickel."

"Good lord!" said the man.

"And," she went on, "that nickel will pay my fare home on the elevated. It's only about half a mile to the station, but from there home it's ten. So you see I'd rather walk this than that."

"But that's dreadful," he cried. "Isn't there. . . Couldn't you let me. . ."

"Oh," she said, "it isn't so bad as that. It's just one of the silly things that happen to you sometimes, you know. I didn't have very much money when I started, it being Friday. And then I paid my subscription to *The Maroon* . . ." She didn't laugh audibly, but without seeing her face, he knew she smiled, the quality of her voice enriching itself somehow. . . "And I ate a bigger lunch than usual, and that brought me down to ten cents. I could have got more of course from anybody, but ten cents, except for that conductor, would have been enough."

"You will make a complaint about that, won't you?" he urged. "Even if it wasn't on principle that you refused to pay another fare? And let me back you up in it. I've his number, you know."

"You deserve that, I suppose," she said, "because you did get off the car on principle. But—well, really, unless we could prove that I did pay my fare, by some other passenger, you know, they'd probably think the conductor did exactly right. Of course he took hold of me, but that was because I was going right by him. And then, think what I did to him!"

He grumbled that this was nonsense—the man had been guilty at least of excessive zeal—but he didn't urge her, any further, to complain.

"There's another car coming," he now announced, peering around the end of the wall. "You will let me pay your fare on it, won't you?"

She hesitated. The rain was thinning. "I would," she said, "if I honestly wouldn't rather walk. I'm wet through now, and it'll be pleasanter to—walk a little of it off than to squeeze into that car. Thanks, really very, very much, though. Don't *you* miss it." She thrust out her hand. "Good-by!"

"I can't pretend to think you need an escort to the elevated," he said. "I saw what you did to the conductor. I haven't the least doubt you could have thrown him off the car. But I'd—really like it very much if you would let me walk along with you."

"Why," she said, "of course! I'd like it too. Come along."

III

FREDERICA'S PLAN AND
WHAT HAPPENED TO IT

At twenty minutes after seven that evening, Frederica Whitney was about as nearly dressed as she usually was ten minutes before the hour at which she had invited guests to dinner—not quite near enough dressed to prevent a feeling that she had to hurry.

Ordinarily, though, she didn't mind. She'd been an acknowledged beauty for ten years and the fact had ceased to be exciting. She took it rather easily for granted, and knowing what she could do if she chose, didn't distress herself over being lighted up, on occasions, to something a good deal less than her full candle-power. To Frederica at thirty—or thereabout—the job of being a radiantly delightful object of regard lacked the sporting interest of uncertainty; was almost too simple a matter to bother about.

But tonight the tenseness of her movements and the faint trace of a wire edge in the tone in which she addressed the maid, revealed the fact that she wished she'd started half an hour earlier. Even her husband discovered it. He brought in a cigarette, left the door open behind him and stood smiling down at her with the peculiarly complacent look that characterizes a married man of forty when he finds himself dressed beyond cavil in the complete evening harness of civilization, ten minutes before his wife.

She shot a glance of rueful inquiry at him—"Now what have *you* come fussing around for?" would be perhaps a fair interpretation of it—and asked him what time it was, in the evident hope that the boudoir clock on her dressing-table had deceived her. It had, but in the wrong direction.

"Seven twenty-two, thirty-six," he told her. It was a perfectly harmless passion he had for minute divisions of time, but tonight it irritated her. He might have spared her that thirty-six seconds.

She made no comment except with her eyebrows, but he must have been looking at her, for he wanted to know, good-humoredly, what all the excitement was about.

"You could go down as you are and not a man here tonight would know the difference. And as for the women—well, if they have something on you for once, they'll be all the better pleased."

"Don't try to be knowing and philosophical, and—Havelock Ellish, Martin, dear," she admonished him, pending a minute operation with an infinitesimal hairpin. "It isn't your lay a bit. Just concentrate your mind on one thing, and that's being nice to Hermione Woodruff. . ."

She broke off for a long stare into her hand-glass; then finished, casually, ". . . and on seeing that Roddy is."

He asked, "Why Rodney?" in a tone that matched hers; looked at her, widened his eyes, said "Huh!" to himself and, finally, shook his head. "Nothing to it," he pronounced.

She said, "Nothing to what?" but abandoned this position as untenable. She despatched the maid with the key to the wall safe in her husband's room. "Why isn't there?" she demanded. "Rodney won't look at young girls. They bore him to death—and no wonder, because he freezes them perfectly brittle with fright. But Hermione's really pretty intelligent. She can understand fully half the things he talks about and she's clever enough to pretend about the rest. She's got lots of tact and skill, she's good-looking and young enough—no older than I and I'm two years younger than Roddy. She'll appreciate a real husband, after having been married five years to John Woodruff. And she's rich enough, now, so that his wild-eyed way of practising law won't matter."

"All very nice and reasonable," he conceded, "but somehow the notion of Rodney Aldrich trying to marry a rich widow is one I'm not equal to without a handicap of at least two cocktails." He looked at his watch again. "By the way, didn't you say he was coming early?"

She nodded. "That's what he told me this morning when I telephoned him to remind him that it was tonight. He said he had something he wanted to talk to me about. I knew I shouldn't have a minute, but I didn't say so because I thought if he tried to get here early, he might miss being late."

They heard, just then, faint and far-away, the ring of the door-bell, at which she cried, "Oh, dear! There's some one already."

"Wait a second," he said. "Let's see if it's him."

The paneled walls and ceiling of their hall were very efficient sounding-boards and there was no mistaking the voice they heard speaking the moment the door opened—a voice with a crisp ring to it that sounded always younger than his years. What he said didn't matter, just a cheerful greeting to the butler. But what they heard the butler say to him was disconcerting.

"You're terribly wet, sir."

Frederica turned on her husband a look of despair.

"He didn't come in a taxi! He's walked or something, through that rain! Do run down and see what he's like. And if he's very bad, send him up to me. I can imagine how he'll look."

She was mistaken about that though. For once Frederica had overestimated her powers, stimulated though they were by the way she heard her husband say, "Good lord!" when the sight of his brother-in-law burst on him.

"Praise heaven you can wear my clothes," she heard him add. "Run along up-stairs and break yourself gently to Freddy."

She heard him come squudging up the stairs and along the hall, and then in her doorway she saw him. His baggy gray tweed suit was dark with the water that saturated it. The lower part of his trousers-legs, in irregular vertical creases, clung dismally to his ankles and toned down almost indistinguishably into his once tan boots by the medium of a liberal stipple of mud spatters. Evidently, he had worn no overcoat. Both his side pockets had been, apparently, strained to the utmost to accommodate what looked like a bunch of pasteboard-bound note-books, now far on the way to their original pulp, and lopped despondently outward. A melancholy pool had already begun forming about his feet.

The maddening, but yet—though she hadn't much room for any other emotion—touching thing about the look of him, was the way his face, above the dismal wreck, beamed good-humored innocent affection at her. It was a big featured, strong, rosy face, and the unmistakable intellectual power of it, which became apparent the moment he got his faculties into action, had a trick of hiding, at other times, behind a mere robust simplicity.

"Good gracious!" he said. "I didn't know you were going to have a party."

It seemed though, he didn't want to make an issue of that. He hedged. "I know you said something about a birthday cake, but I thought it would just be the family. So instead of dressing, I thought I'd walk down from home. It takes about the same time. And then it came on to rain, so I took a street-car—and got put off."

It appeared from the way she echoed his last two words that she wanted an explanation. He was painting with a large brush and a few details got obliterated.

"Got into a row with the conductor, who wanted to collect two fares for one ride, so I walked over to the elevated—and back, and here I am."

"Yes, here you are," said Frederica.

She didn't mean anything by that. Already she was making up her mind what she would do with him. His own suggestion was that he should decamp furtively by the back stairs, the sound of new arrivals to the dinner party warning him that the other way of escape was barred. Waiters could be instructed to rescue his hat for him, and he could toddle along down-town again.

She didn't give him time to complete the outline of this masterly stratagem. "Don't be impossible, Rod," she said. "Don't you even know whose birthday party this is?"

He looked at her, frowned, then laughed. He had a great big laugh.

"I thought it was one of the kid's," he said.

"Well, it isn't," she told him. "It's yours. And those people down there were asked to meet you. And you've got just about seven minutes to get presentable in. Go into Martin's bathroom and take off those horrible clothes. I'll send Walters in to lay out some things of Martin's."

She came up to him and, at arm's length, touched him with cautious finger-tips. "And do, please, there's a dear boy," she pleaded, "hurry as fast as you can, and then come down and be as nice as you can"—she hesitated—"especially to Hermione Woodruff. She thinks you're a wonder and I don't want her to be disappointed."

"The widdy?" he asked. "Sure I'll be nice to her."

She looked after him rather dubiously as he disappeared in the direction of her husband's room.

She'd have felt safer about him if he had seemed more subdued as a result of his escapade. There was a sort of hilarious contentment about him that filled her with misgivings.

Well, they were justified!

But the maddening thing was, she had afterward to admit, that the disaster had been largely of her own contriving. She had been caught in the net of her own stratagem—hoist by her own petard.

She had made it a six-couple dinner in order to insure that the talk should be by twos rather than general, and she had spent a good half-hour over the place-cards, getting them to suit her.

Hermione had to be on Martin's right hand, of course. She was just back in the city after an absence of years, and everybody was rushing her. She put Violet Williamson, whom Martin was always flirting with in a harmless way, on his left, and Rod to the right of Hermione. At Rodney's right, she put a girl he had known for years and cared nothing whatever about, and then Howard West—who probably wasn't interested in her either, but would be polite because he was to everybody. Frederica herself sat between Carl Leaventritt of the university—a great acquisition, since whatever you might think of him as an empirical psychologist, there was no doubt of his being an accomplished diner-out—and Violet's husband, as he vociferously proclaimed himself, John Williamson, an untired business man who, had their seasons coincided, could have enjoyed a ball game in the afternoon and stayed awake at the opera in the evening. Doctor Randolph's pretty wife she slid in between Leaventritt and Howard West, and, in happy ignorance of what the result was going to be, she put Randolph himself between Violet and Alice West. He was a young, up-to-the-minute mind and nerve doctor.

It was an admirable plan all right, the key-note of it being, as you no doubt will have observed, the easy unforced isolation of Rodney and the rich widow. Before that dinner was over, they ought to be old friends.

And, for a little while, all went well. Rodney came down almost within the seven minutes she had allowed him, looking much less dreadful than she had expected, in her husband's other dress suit, and not forgetful, it appeared, of the line of behavior she had enjoined on him; namely, that he was to be nice to Hermione Woodruff.

From her end of the table, she saw them apparently safely launched in conversation over the hors-d'oeuvre, took a look at them during the soup to see that all was still well, then let herself be beguiled into a conversation with John Williamson, whom she liked as well as Martin did Violet. She never thought of the objects of her matrimonial design again until her ear was caught by a huge seven-cornered word in her brother's voice. He couldn't be saying it to Hermione; no, he was leaning forward, shouting at Doctor Randolph, who apparently knew what he meant and was getting visibly ready to reply in kind.

According to Violet Williamson's account, given confidentially in the drawing-room afterward, it was really Hermione's fault. "She just wouldn't let Rodney alone—would keep talking about crime and Lombroso and psychiatric laboratories—I'll bet she'd got hold of a paper of his somewhere and read it. Anyway, at last she said, 'I believe Doctor Randolph would agree with me.' He was talking to me then, but maybe that isn't why she did it. Well, and Rodney straightened up and said, 'Is that Randolph, the alienist!' You see he hadn't caught his name when they were introduced. And that's how it started. Hermione was game—I'll admit that. She listened and kept looking interested, and every now and then said something. Sometimes they'd take the trouble to smile and say 'Yes, indeed!'—politely, you know, but other times they wouldn't pay any attention at all, just roll along over her and smash her flat—like what's his name—Juggernaut."

"You don't need to tell me that," said Frederica. "All I didn't know was how it started. Didn't I sit there and watch for a mortal hour, not able to do a thing? I tried to signal to Martin, but of course he wasn't opposite to me and. . ."

"He did all he could, really," Violet answered her. "I told him to go to the rescue, and he did, bravely. But what with Hermione being so miffy about getting frozen out, and Martin himself being so interested in what they were shouting at each other—because it was frightfully interesting, you know, if you didn't have to pretend you understood it—why, there wasn't much he could do."

In the light of this disaster, she was rather glad the men lingered in the dining-room as long as they did—glad that Hermione had ordered her car for ten and took the odd girl with her. She made no effort to resist the departure of the others, with reasonable promptitude, in their train. When, after the front door had closed for the last time, Martin released a long yawn, she told him to run along to bed; she wanted to talk with Rodney, who was to spend the night while his own clothes were drying out in the laundry.

"Good night, old chap," said Martin in accents of lively commiseration, "I'm glad I'm not in for what you are."

IV

Rosalind Stanton Doesn't Disappear

Rodney found a pipe of his that he kept concealed on the premises, loaded and lighted it, sat down astride a spindling little chair that looked hardly up to his weight, settled his elbows comfortably on the back of it, and then asked his sister what Martin had meant—what was he in for?

Frederica, curled up in a corner of the sofa, finished her own train of thought aloud, first.

"She's awfully attractive, don't you think? His wife, I mean. Oh, James Randolph's, of course." She turned to Rodney, looked at him at first with a wry pucker between her eyebrows, then with a smile, and finally answered his question. "Nothing," she said. "I mean, I was going to scold you, but I'm not."

"Why, yes," he admitted through his smoke. "Randolph's wife's a mighty pretty woman. But I expect that lets her out, doesn't it?"

Frederica shook her head. "She's a good deal of a person, I should say, on the strength of tonight's showing. She kept her face perfectly through the whole thing—didn't try to nag at him or apologize to the rest of us. I'd like to know what she's saying to him now."

Then, "Oh, I was furious with you an hour ago," she went on. "I'd made such a nice, reasonable, really beautiful plan for you, and given you a tip about it, and then I sat and watched you in that thoroughgoing way of yours, kicking it all to bits. But somehow, when I see you all by yourself, this way, it changes things. I get to thinking that perhaps my plan was silly after all—anyhow, it was silly to make it. The plan was, of course, to marry you off to Hermione Woodruff."

He turned this over in his deliberate way, during the process of blowing two or three smoke rings, began gradually to grin, and said at last, "That was some plan, little sister. How do you think of things like that? You ought to write romances for the magazines, that's what you ought to do."

"I don't know," she objected. "If reasonableness counted for anything in things like that, it was a pretty good plan. It would have to be somebody like Hermione. You can't get on at all with young girls. As long as you remember they're around, you're afraid to say anything except milk and water out of a bottle that makes them furious, and then if you forget whom you're talking to and begin thinking out loud, developing some idea or other, you—simply paralyze them.

"Well, Hermione's sophisticated and clever, she's lived all over the place; she isn't old yet, and she was a brick about that awful husband of hers—never made any fuss—bluffed it out until he, luckily, died. Of course she'll marry again, and I just thought, if you liked the idea, it might as well be you."

"I don't know," said Rodney, "whether Mrs. Woodruff knows what she wants or not, but I do. She wants a run for her money—a big house to live in three months in the year, with a flock of servants and a fleet of motor-cars, and a string of what she'll call cottages to float around among, the rest of the time. And she'll want a nice, tame, trick husband to manage things for her and be considerate and affectionate and amusing, and, generally speaking, Johnny-on-the-spot whenever she wants him. If she has sense enough to know what she wants in advance, it will be all right. She can take her pick of dozens. But if she gets a sentimental notion in her head—and I've a hunch that she's subject to them—that she wants a real man, with something of his own to do, there'll be, saving your presence, hell to pay. And if the man happened to be me. . . !"

Frederica stretched her slim arms outward. Thoughtful-faced, she made no comment on his analysis of the situation, unless a much more observant person than Rodney might have imagined there was one in the deliberate way in which she turned her rings, one at a time, so that the brilliant masses of gems were inside, and then clenched her hands over them.

He had got up and was ranging comfortably up and down the room.

"I know I look more or less like a nut to the people who've always known us—father's and mother's friends, and most of their children. But I give you my word, Freddy, that most of them look like nuts to me. Why, they live in curiosity shops—so many things around, things they have and things they've got to do, that they can't act or think for fear of breaking something.

"Why a man should load himself up with three houses and a yacht, a stable of motor-cars, and God knows what besides, when he's rich enough to buy himself real space and leisure to live in, is a thing I can't figure out on any basis except of defective intelligence. I suppose they're equally

HENRY KITCHELL WEBSTER

puzzled about me when I refuse a profitable piece of law work they've offered me, because I don't consider it interesting. All the same, I get what I want, and I'm pretty dubious sometimes whether they do. I want space—comfortable elbow room, so that if I happen to get an idea by the tail, I can swing it around my head without knocking over the lamp."

"It's a luxury though, Rod, that kind of spaciousness, and you aren't very rich. If you married a girl without anything. . ."

He broke in on her with that big laugh of his. "You've kept your sense of humor pretty well, sis, considering you've been married all these years to a man as rich as Martin, but don't spring remarks like that, or I'll think you've lost it. If a man can't keep an open space around him, even after he's married, on an income, outside of what he can earn, of ten or twelve thousand dollars a year, the trouble isn't with his income. It's with the content of his own skull."

She gave a little shiver and snuggled closer into a big down pillow.

"You will marry somebody, though, won't you, Roddy? I'll try not to nag at you and I won't make any more silly plans, but I can't help worrying about you, living alone in that awful big old house. Anybody but you would die of despondency."

"Oh," he said, "that's what I meant to talk to you about! I sold it today—fifty thousand dollars—immediate possession. Man wants to build a printing establishment there. You come down sometime next week and pick out all the things you think you and Harriet would like to keep, and I'll auction off the rest."

She shivered again and, to her disgust, found that her eyes were blurring up with tears. She was a little bit slack and edgy today, anyhow.

But really there was something rather remorseless about Rodney. It occurred to her that the woman he finally did marry would need to be strong and courageous and rather insensitive to sentimental fancies, to avoid a certain amount of unhappiness.

What he had just referred to in a dozen brisk words, was the final disappearance of the home they had all grown up in. Their father, one of Chicago's great men during the twenty great years between the Fire and the Fair, had built it when the neighborhood included nearly all the other big men of that robust period, and had always been proud of it. There was hardly a stone or stick about it that hadn't some tender happy association for her. Of course for years the neighborhood had been impossible. Her mother had clung to it after her husband's death, as was of course natural.

But when she had followed him, a year ago now, it was evident that the old place would have to go. Rodney, who had lived alone with her there, had simply stayed on, since her death, waiting for an offer for it that suited him. Frederica had known that, of course—had worried about him, as she said, and in her imagination, had colored his loneliness to the same dismal hue her own would have taken on in similar circumstances.

All the same, his curt announcement that the long-looked-for change had come, brought up quick unwelcomed tears. She squeezed them away with her palms.

"You'll come to us then, won't you?" she asked, but quite without conviction. She knew what he'd say.

"Heavens, no! Oh, I'll go to a hotel for a while—maybe look up a little down-town apartment, with a Jap. It doesn't matter much about that. It's a load off, all right."

"Is that," she asked, "why you've been looking so sort of—gay, all the evening—as if you were licking the last of the canary's feathers off your whiskers?"

"Perhaps so," he said. "It's been a pretty good day, take it all round."

She got up from the couch, shook herself down into her clothes a little, and came over to him.

"All right, since it's been a good day, let's go to bed." She put her hands upon his shoulders. "You're rather dreadful," she said, "but you're a dear. You don't bite my head off when I urge you to get married, though I know you want to. But you will some day—I don't mean bite my head off—won't you, Rod?"

"When I see any prospect of being as lucky as Martin—find a girl who won't mind when I turn up for dinner looking like a drowned tramp, or kick her plans to bits, after she's tipped me off as to what she wants me to do. . ."

Frederica took her hands off, stepped back and looked at him. There was an ironical sort of smile on her lips.

"You're such an innocent," she said. "You've got an idea you know me—know how I treat Martin. Roddy, dear, a girl's brother doesn't matter. She isn't dependent on him, nor responsible for him. And if she's rather sillily fond of him, she's likely to spoil him frightfully. Don't think the girl you marry will ever treat you like that."

"But look here!" he exclaimed. "You say I don't know you, whom I've lived with off and on for thirty years—don't know how you'd treat me if you were married to me. How in thunder am I going to know about the girl I get engaged to, before it's too late?"

"You won't," she said. "You haven't a chance in the world."

"Hm!" he grunted, obviously struck with this idea. "You're giving the prospect of marriage new attractions. You're making the thing out—an adventure."

She nodded rather soberly. "Oh, I'm not afraid for you," she said. "Men like adventures—you more than most. But women don't. They like to dream about them, but they want to turn over to the last chapter and see how it's going to end. It's the girl I'm worried about. . . Oh, come along! We're talking nonsense. I'll go up with you and see that they've given you pajamas and a tooth-brush."

She had accomplished this purpose, kissed him good night, and under the hint of his unbuttoned waistcoat and his winding watch, turned to leave the room, when her eye fell on a heap of damp, warped, pasteboard-bound note-books, which she remembered having observed in his side pockets when he first came in. The color on the pasteboard binding had run, and as they lay on the drawn linen cover to the chiffonier, she went over and picked them up to see how much damage they'd done. Then she frowned, peered at the paper label that had half peeled off of the topmost cover, and read what was written on it.

"Who," she asked with considerable emphasis, "is Rosalind Stanton?"

"Oh," said Rodney very casually, behind the worst imitation of a yawn she had ever seen, "oh, she got put off the car when I did."

"That sounds rather exciting," said Frederica behind an imitation yawn of her own—but a better one. "Going to tell me about it?"

"Nothing much to tell," said Rodney. "There was a row about a fare, as I said. The conductor was evidently solid concrete above the collar-bone, and didn't think she'd paid. And she grabbed him and very nearly threw him out into the street—could have done it, I believe, as easily as not. And he began to talk about punching somebody's head. And then, we both got put off. So, naturally, I walked with her over to the elevated. And then I forgot to give her her note-books and came away with them."

"What sort of looking girl?" asked Frederica. "Is she pretty?"

"Why, I don't know," said Rodney judicially. "Really, you know, I hardly got a fair look at her."

Frederica made a funny sounding laugh and wished him an abrupt "good night."

She was a great old girl, Frederica—pretty wise about lots of things, but Rodney was inclined to think she was mistaken in saying women didn't like adventures. Take that girl this afternoon, for example. Evidently she was willing to meet one half-way. And how she'd blazed up when that conductor touched her! Just the memory of it brought back something of the thrill he had felt when he saw it happen.

"You're a liar, you know," remarked his conscience, "telling Frederica you hadn't had a good look at her."

On the contrary, he argued, it was perfectly justifiable to deny that a look as brief as that, was good. He wouldn't deny, however, that the thing had been a wholly delightful and exhilarating little episode. That was the way to have things happen! Have them pop out of nowhere at you and disappear presently, into the same place.

"Disappear indeed!" sneered his conscience. "How about those note-books, with her name and address on every one. And there's another lie you told—about forgetting to give them to her!"

He protested that it was entirely true. He had gone into the station with the girl, shaken hands with her, said good night, and turned away to leave the station, unaware—as evidently she was—that he still had her note-books under his arm. But it was equally true that he had discovered them there, a good full second before the girl had turned the corner of the stairs—in plenty of time to have called her back to the barrier, and handed them over to her.

"All right, have it your own way," said Rodney cheerfully, as he turned out the light.

V

The Second Encounter

Portia Stanton was late for lunch; so, after stripping off her jacket and gloves, rolling up her veil and scowling at herself in an oblong mahogany-framed mirror in the hall, she walked into the dining-room with her hat on. Seeing her mother sitting alone at the lunch table, she asked, "Where is Rose?"

"She'll be down presently, I think," her mother said. "She called out to me that she'd only be a minute, when I passed her door. Does your hat mean you're going back to the shop this afternoon?"

Portia nodded, pulled back her chair abruptly and sat down. "Oh, don't ring for Inga," she said. "What's here's all right, and she takes forever."

"I thought that on Saturday. . ." her mother began.

"Oh, I know," said Portia, "but Anne Loomis telephoned she's going to bring Dora Wild around to pick out which of my three kidney sofas she wants for a wedding present. That girl I've got isn't much good, and besides, I think there's a chance that Dora may give me her house to do. Her man's stupidly rich, they say, and richly stupid, so the job ought to be worth eating a cold egg for."

You'd have known them for mother and daughter anywhere, and you'd have had trouble finding any point of resemblance in either of them to the Amazonian young thing who had so nearly thrown a street-car conductor into the street the night before. Their foreheads were both narrow and rather high, their noses small and slightly aquiline, and both of them had slender fastidious hands.

The mother's hair was very soft and white, and the care with which it was arranged indicated a certain harmless vanity in it. There was something a little conscious, too, about her dress—an effect difficult to describe without exaggeration. It was not bizarre nor "artistic," but you would have understood at once that its departures from the prevailing mode were made on principle. If you took it in connection with a certain resolute amiability about her smile, you would be entirely prepared to hear her tell Portia that she was reading a paper on Modern Tendencies before the Pierian Club this afternoon.

A very real person, nevertheless, you couldn't doubt that. The marks of passionately held beliefs and eagerly given sacrifices were etched with undeniable authenticity in her face.

Once you got beyond a catalogue of features, Portia presented rather a striking contrast to this. Her hair was done—you could hardly say arranged—with a severity that was fairly hostile. Her clothes were bruskly cut and bruskly worn, their very smartness seeming an impatient concession to necessity. Her smile, if not ill-natured—it wasn't that—was distinctly ironic. A very competent, good-looking young woman, you'd have said, if you'd seen her with her shoulder-blades flattened down and her chest up. Seeing her today, drooping a little over the cold lunch, you'd have left out the adjective young.

"So Rose didn't come down this morning at all," Portia observed, when she had done her duty by the egg. "You took her breakfast up to her, I suppose."

Mrs. Stanton flushed a little. "She didn't want me to; but I thought she'd better keep quiet."

"Nothing particular the matter with her, is there?" asked Portia.

There was enough real concern in her voice to save the question from sounding satirical, but her mother's manner was still a little apologetic when she answered it.

"No, I think not," she said. "I think the mustard foot-bath and the quinine probably averted serious consequences. But she was in such a state when she came home last night—literally wet through to the skin, and blue with cold. So I thought it wouldn't do any harm. . ."

"Of course not," said Portia. "You're entitled to one baby anyway, mother, dear. Life was such a strenuous thing for you when the rest of us were little, that you hadn't a chance to have any fun with us. And Rose is all right. She won't spoil badly."

"I'm a little bit worried about the loss of the poor child's note-books," said her mother. "I rather hoped they'd come in by the noon mail. But they didn't."

"I don't believe Rose is worrying her head off about them." said Portia.

The flush in her mother's cheeks deepened a little, but it was no longer apologetic.

"I don't think you're quite fair to Rose, about her studies," she said. "The child may not be making a brilliant record, but really, considering the number of her occupations, it seems to me she does very well. And if she doesn't seem always to appreciate her privilege in getting a college education, as seriously as she should, you should remember her youth."

"She's twenty," said Portia bluntly. "You graduated at that age, and you took it seriously enough."

"It's very different," her mother insisted. "And I'm sure you understand the difference quite well. Higher education was still an experiment for women then—one of the things they were fighting for. And those of us by whom the success of the experiment was to be judged. . ."

"I'm sorry, mother," Portia interrupted contritely. "I'm tired and ugly today, and I didn't mean any harm, anyway. Of course Rose is all right, just as I said. And she'll probably get her note-books back Monday." Then, "Didn't she say the man's name was Rodney Aldrich?"

"I think so," her mother agreed. "Something like that."

"It's rather funny," said Portia. "It's hardly likely to have been the real Rodney Aldrich. Yet, it's not a common name."

"The *real* Rodney Aldrich?" questioned her mother. But, without waiting for her daughter's elucidation of the phrase, she added, "Oh, there's Rose!"

The girl came shuffling into the room in a pair of old bedroom slippers. She had on a skirt that she used to go skating in, and a somewhat tumbled middy-blouse. Her hair was wopsed around her head anyhow—it really takes one of Rose's own words to describe it. As a toilet representing the total accomplishment of a morning, it was nothing to boast of. But, if you'd been sitting there, invisibly, where you could see her, you'd have straightened up and drawn a deeper breath than you'd indulged in lately, and felt that the world was distinctly a brighter place to live in than it had been a moment before.

She came up behind Portia, whom she had not seen before that day, and enveloped her in a big lazy hug.

"Back to work another Saturday afternoon, Angel?" she asked commiseratingly. "Aren't you ever going to stop and have any fun?" Then she slumped into a chair, heaved a yawning sigh and rubbed her eyes.

"Tired, dear?" asked her mother. She said it under her breath in the hope that Portia wouldn't hear.

"No," said Rose. "Just sleepy." She yawned again, turned to Portia, and, somewhat to their surprise, said: "Yes, what do you mean—the *real* Rodney Aldrich? He looked real enough to me. And his arm felt real—the one he was going to punch the conductor with."

"I didn't mean he was imaginary," Portia explained. "I only meant I didn't believe it was the Rodney Aldrich—who's so awfully prominent;

either somebody else who happened to have the same name, or somebody who just—said that was his name."

"What's the matter with the prominent one?" Rose wanted to know. "Why couldn't it have been him?"

Portia admitted that it could, so far as that went, but insisted on an inherent improbability. A millionaire, a member of one of the oldest families in the city—a social swell, the brother of that Mrs. Martin Whitney whose pictures the papers were always publishing on the slightest excuse—wasn't likely to be found riding in street-cars, in the first place, and the improbability reached a climax during a furious storm like that of last night, when, if ever during the year, the real Rodney Aldrich would be saying, "Home, James," to a liveried chauffeur, and sinking back luxuriously among the whip-cord cushions of a palatial limousine.

I hasten to say that these were not Portia's words; all the same, what Portia did say, formed a basis for Rose's unspoken caricature.

"Millionaires have legs," she said aloud. "I bet they can walk around like anybody else. However, I don't care who he is, if he'll send back my books."

Portia went back presently to the shop, and it wasn't long after that that her mother came down-stairs clad for the street, with her *Modern Tendencies* under her arm in a leather portfolio.

It had turned cold overnight, and there was a buffeting gusty wind which shook the windows and rattled the stiff branches of the trees. Her mother's valedictory, given with more confidence now that Portia was out of the house, was a strong recommendation that Rose stay quietly within doors and keep warm.

The girl might have palmed off her own inclination as an example of filial obedience, but she didn't.

"I was going to, anyway," she said. "Home and fireside for mine today."

Ordinarily, the gale would have tempted her. It was such good fun to lean up against it and force your way through, while it tugged at your skirts and hair and slapped your face.

But today, the warmest corner of the sitting-room lounge, the quiet of the house, deserted except for Inga in the kitchen, engaged in the principal sporting event of her domestic routine—the weekly baking; the fact that she needn't speak to a soul for three hours, a detective story just wild enough to make little intervals in the occupation of doing nothing at all—presented an ideal a hundred per cent. perfect.

She hadn't meant to go to sleep, having already slept away half the morning, but the author's tactics in the detective story were so flagrantly unfair, he was so manifestly engaged trying to make trouble for his poor anemic characters instead of trying to solve their perplexities, that presently she tossed the book aside and began dreaming one of her own in which the heroine got put off a street-car in the opening chapter.

The telephone bell roused her once or twice, far enough to observe that Inga was attending to it, so when the front door-bell rang, she left that to Inga, too—didn't even sit up and swing her legs off the couch and try, with a prodigious stretch, to get herself awake, until she heard the girl say casually:

"Her ban right in the sitting-room."

So it fell out that Rodney Aldrich had, for his second vivid picture of her,—the first had been, you will remember, when she had seized the conductor by both wrists, and had said in a blaze of beautiful wrath, "Don't dare to touch me like that!"—a splendid, lazy, tousled creature, in a chaotic glory of chestnut hair, an unlaced middy-blouse, a plaid skirt twisted round her knees, and a pair of ridiculous red bedroom slippers, with red pompons on the toes. The creature was stretching herself with the grace of a big cat that has just been roused from a nap on the hearth-rug.

If his first picture of her had been brief, his second one was practically a snap-shot, because at sight of him, she flashed to her feet.

So, for a moment, they confronted each other about equally aghast, flushed up to the hair, and simultaneously and incoherently, begging each other's pardon—neither could have said for what, the goddess out of the machine being Inga, the maid-of-all-work. But suddenly, at a twinkle she caught in his eye, her own big eyes narrowed and her big mouth widened into a smile, which broke presently into her deep-throated laugh, whereupon he laughed too, and they shook hands, and she asked him to sit down.

VI

THE BIG HORSE

It's too ridiculous," she said. "Since last night, when I got to thinking how I must have looked, wrestling with that conductor, I've been telling myself that if I ever saw you again, I'd try to act like a lady. But it's no use, is it?"

He said that he, too, had hoped to make a better impression the second time than the first. That was what he brought the books back for. He had hoped to convince her that a man capable of consigning a half-drowned girl to a ten-mile ride on the elevated, instead of walking her over to his sister's, having her dried out properly, and sent home in a motor, wasn't permanently and chronically as blithering an idiot as he may have seemed. It was a great load off of his mind to find her alive at all.

She gave him a humorously exaggerated account of the prophylactic measures her mother had submitted her to the night before, and she concluded:

"I'm awfully sorry mother's not at home—mother and my sister Portia. They'd both like to thank you for—looking after me last night. Because really, you did, you know."

"There never was anything less altruistic in the world," he assured her. "I dropped off of that car solely in pursuit of a selfish aim. And I didn't come out here today to be thanked, either. I mean, of course, I'd enjoy meeting your mother and sister very much, but what I came for was to get acquainted with you."

He saw her glance wander a little dubiously to the door. "That is," he concluded, "if you haven't something else to do."

She flushed and smiled. "No, it wasn't that," she said, "I was trying to make up my mind whether it would be better to ask you to wait here ten minutes while I went up and made myself a little more presentable. . . I mean, whether you'd rather have me fit to look at, or have me like this and not be bored by waiting. It's all one to me, you see, because even if I did come down again presentable, you'd know—well, that I wasn't that way naturally."

Whereupon he laughed out again, told her that a ten-minute wait would bore him horribly, and that if she didn't mind, he much preferred her natural.

"All right," she said, and went on with the conversation where she had interrupted it.

"Why, I'm nobody much to get acquainted with," she said. "Mother's the interesting one—mother and Portia. Mother's quite a person. She's Naomi Rutledge Stanton, you know."

"I know I ought to know," Rodney said, and her quick appreciative smile over his candor rewarded him for not having pretended.

"Oh," she said, "mother's written two or three books, and lots of magazine articles, about women—women's rights and suffrage, and all that. She's been—well, sort of a leader ever since she graduated from college, back in—just think!—1870, when most girls used to have—accomplishments—'French, music, and washing extra,' you know."

She said it all with a quite adorable seriousness and his gravity matched hers when he replied:

"I would like to meet her very much. Feminism's a subject I'm blankly ignorant about."

"I don't believe," she said thoughtfully, "that I'd call it feminism in talking to mother about it, if I were you. Mother's a suffragist, but"—there came another wave of faint color along with her smile—"but—well, she's awfully respectable, you know."

She didn't seem to mind his laughing out at that, though she didn't join him.

"What about the other interesting member of the family," he asked presently, "your sister? Which is she, a suffragist or a feminist?"

"I suppose," she said, "you'll call Portia a feminist. Anyway, she smokes cigarettes. Oh, can't I get you some? I forgot!"

He had a case of his own in his pocket, he said, and got one out now and lighted it.

"Why," she went on, "Portia hasn't time to talk about it much. You see, she's a business woman. She's a house decorator. I don't mean painting and paper-hanging. She tells you what kind of furniture to buy, and then sells it to you. Portia's terribly clever and awfully independent."

"All right," he said. "That brings us down to you. What are you?"

She sighed. "I'm sort of a black sheep, I guess. I'm just in the university. But I'm to be a lawyer."

Whereupon he cried out "Good lord!" so explosively that she fairly jumped.

Then he apologized, said he didn't know why her announcement should have taken him like that, except that the notion of her in court trying a case—he was a lawyer himself—seemed rather startling.

She sighed. "And now I suppose," she said, "you'll advise me not to be. Portia won't hear of my being a decorator. She says there's nothing in it any more; and my two brothers—one's a professor of history and the other's a high-school principal—say, 'Let her do anything but teach.' One of mother's great friends is a doctor, and she says, 'Anything but medicine,' so I suppose you'll say, 'Anything but law.'"

"Not a bit," he said. "It's the finest profession in the world."

But he said it off the top of his mind. Down below, it was still engaged with the picture of her in a dismal court room, blazing up at a jury the way she had blazed up at that street-car conductor. It was a queer notion. He didn't know whether he liked it or not.

"I suppose," she hazarded, "that it's awfully dull and tiresome, though, until you get way up to the top."

That roused him. "It's awfully dull when you do get to the top, or what's called the top—being a client caretaker with the routine law business of a few big corporations and rich estates going through your office like grist through a mill. I can't imagine anything duller than that. That's supposed to be the big reward, of course. That's the bundle of hay they dangle in front of your nose to keep you trotting straight along without trying to see around your blinders."

He was out of his chair now, tramping up and down the room. "You're not supposed to discover that it's interesting. You're pretty well spoiled for their purposes if you do. The thing to bear in mind, if you're going to travel their road, is that a case is worth while in a precise and unalterable ratio to the amount of money involved in it. If you question that axiom at all seriously, you're lost. That's what happened to me."

He pulled up with a jerk, looked at her and laughed. "If my sister Frederica were here," he explained, "she would warn you, out of a long knowledge of my conversational habits, that now was the time for you to ask me,—firmly, you know,—if I'd been to see Maude Adams in this new thing of hers, or something like that. In Frederica's absence, I suppose it's only fair to warn you myself. Have you been to see it? I haven't."

She smiled in a sort of contented amusement and let that do for an answer to his question about Maude Adams. Then the smile transmuted itself into a look of thoughtful gravity and there was a long silence which, though it puzzled him, he made no move to break.

At last she pulled in a long breath, turned straight to him and said, "I wish you'd tell me what *did* happen to you."

And under the compelling sincerity of her, for the next two hours and a half, or thereabouts, he did—told it as he had never told it before—talked as Frederica, who thought she knew him, had never heard him talk.

He told her how he had started at the foot of the ladder in one of the big successful firms of what he called "client caretakers," drawing up bills and writs, rounding up witnesses in personal injury suits, trying little justice-shop cases—the worst of them, of course, because there was a youngster just ahead of him who got the better ones. And then, dramatically, he told of his discovery amid this chaff, of a real legal problem—a problem that for its nice intricacies and intellectual suggestiveness, would have brought an appreciative gleam to the eye of Mr. Justice Holmes, or Lord Mansfield, or the great Coke himself. He told of the passionate enthusiasm with which he had attacked it, the thrilling weeks of labor he had put on it. And then he told her the outcome of it all; how the head of the firm, an old friend of his father, had called him in and complimented him on the work that he had done; said it was very remarkable, but, unfortunately, not profitable to the firm, the whole amount involved in the case having been some twenty dollars. They were only paying him forty dollars a month, to be sure, but they figured that forty dollars practically a total loss and they thought he might better go to practising law for himself. In other words, he was fired.

But the thing that rang through the girl's mind like the clang of a bell—the thing that made her catch her breath, was the quality of the big laugh with which he concluded it. He didn't ask her to be sorry for him. He wasn't sorry for himself one bit,—nor bitter—nor cynical. He didn't even seem trying to make a merit of his refusal to acquiesce in that sordid point of view. He just dismissed the thing with a cymbal-like clash of laughter and plunged ahead with his story.

He told her how he'd got in with an altruistic bunch—the City Homes Association; how, finding him keen for work that they had little time for, the senior legal counselors had drawn out and let him do it. And from the way he told of his labors in drafting a new city building ordinance, she felt that it must have been one of the most fascinating occupations in the world, until he told her how it had drawn him into politics—municipal, city council politics, which was even more thrilling, and then how, after an election, a new state's attorney had offered him a position on his staff of assistants.

In a sense, of course, it was true that he had, as Frederica would have put it, forgotten she was there—had forgotten, at least, who she was. Because, if he had remembered that she was just a young girl in the university, he would hardly, as he tramped about the room expounding the practise of criminal law in the state's attorney's office, have characterized the state's attorney himself as a "damned gallery-playing mountebank," nor have described the professions and the misdeeds of some of the persons he prosecuted in blunt Anglo-Saxon terms she had never heard used except in the Bible.

The girl knew he had forgotten, and her only discomfort came from the fear that the spell might be broken and he remember suddenly and be embarrassed and stop.

In the deeper sense—and she was breathlessly conscious of this too—he hadn't forgotten she was there. He was telling it all because she was there—because she was herself and nobody else. She knew, though how she couldn't have explained,—with that intuitive certainty that is the only real certainty there is,—that the story couldn't have been evoked from him in just that way, by any one else in the world.

At the end of two years in the state's attorney's office, he told her, he figured he had had his training and was ready to begin.

"I made just one resolution when I hung out my shingle," he said, "and that was that no matter how few cases I got, I wouldn't take any that weren't interesting—that didn't give me something to bite on. A lot of my friends thought I was crazy, of course—the ones who came around because they liked me, or had liked my father, to offer me nice plummy little sinecures, and got told I didn't want them. Just for the sake of looking successful and accumulating a lot of junk I didn't want, I wasn't going to asphyxiate myself, have strings tied to my arms and legs like a damned marionette. I wasn't willing to be bored for any reward they had to offer me. It's cynical to be bored. It's the worst immorality there is. Well, and I never have been."

It wasn't all autobiographical and narrative. There was a lot of his deep-breathing, spacious philosophy of life mixed up in it. And this the girl, consciously, and deliberately, provoked. It didn't need much. She said something about discipline and he snatched the word away from her.

"What is discipline? Why, it's standing the gaff—*standing* it, not submitting to it. It's accepting the facts of life—of your own life, as they happen to be. It isn't being conquered by them. It's not making masters of them, but servants to the underlying things you want."

She tried to make a reservation there—suppose the things you wanted weren't good things.

But he wouldn't allow it.

"Whatever they are," he insisted, "your desires are the only motive forces you've got. No matter how fine your intelligence is, it can't ride anywhere except on the backs of your own passions. There's no good lamenting that they're not different, and it's silly to beat them to death and make a merit of not having ridden anywhere because they might have carried you into trouble. Learn to ride them—control them—spur them. But don't forget that they're *you* just as essentially as the rider is."

It was with a curiously relaxed body, her chin cradled in the crook of her arm that lay along the back of the couch, her eyes unfocused on the window, that the girl listened to it.

Primarily, indeed, she wasn't exactly listening. Much of the narrative went by almost unheard. Much of the philosophy she hardly tried to understand. What was constantly present and more and more poignantly vivid with every five minutes that ticked away on the banjo clock, was a consciousness of the man himself, the driving power of him, the boisterous health and freshness and confidence. She was conscious, too, of something formidable—carelessly exultant in his own strength. She got to thinking of the flight of a great bird wheeling up higher and higher on his powerful wings.

He had caught her up, too, and was carrying her to altitudes far beyond her own powers. He might drop her, but if he did, it wouldn't be through weakness. At what he said about riding on the backs of one's own passions, her imagination varied the picture so that she saw him galloping splendidly by.

At that, suddenly and to her consternation, she felt her eyes flushing up with tears. She tried to blink them away, but they came too fast.

Presently he stopped short in his walk—stopped talking, with a gasp, in the middle of a sentence, and looked into her face. She couldn't see his clearly, but she saw his hands clench and heard him draw a long breath. Then he turned abruptly and walked to the window and for a mortal endless minute, there was a silence.

At last she found something—it didn't matter much what—to say, and the conversation between them, on the surface of it, was just what it had been for the first ten minutes after he had come in. But, paradoxically, this superficial commonplaceness only heightened the tensity of the thing that underlay it. Something had happened during that moment while he stood looking into her tear-flushed eyes; something momentous, critical, which no previous experience in her life had prepared her for.

And it had happened to him, too. The memory of his silhouette as he stood there with his hands clenched, between her and the window, would have convinced her, had she needed convincing.

The commonplace thing she had found to say met, she knew, a need that was his as well as hers, for breathing-space—for time for the recovery of lost bearings. Had he not felt it as well as she—she smiled a little over this—he wouldn't have yielded. The man on horseback would have taken an obstacle like that without breaking the stride of his gallop.

What underlay her quiet meaningless chat, was wonder and fear, and more deeply still, a sort of cosmic contentment—the acquiescence of a swimmer in the still irresistible current of a mighty river.

It was distinctly a relief to her when her mother came in and, presently, Portia. She introduced him to them, and then dropped out of the conversation altogether. As if it were a long way off, she heard him retailing last night's adventure and expressing his regret that he hadn't taken her to Frederica (that was his sister, Mrs. Whitney) to be dried out, before he sent her home.

She was aware that Portia stole a look at her in a puzzled penetrating sort of way every now and then, but didn't concern herself as to the basis of her curiosity. She knew that it was getting on toward their dinner-time, but didn't disturb herself as to the effect Inga's premonitory rattlings out in the dining-room might have on her guest. As a matter of fact, they had none whatever.

She smiled once widely to herself, over a thought of the half-back. The man here in the room with her now, chatting so pleasantly with her mother, wouldn't ask for favors—would accept nothing that wasn't offered as eagerly as it was sought.

It wasn't until he rose to go that she aroused herself and went with him into the hall. There, after he'd got into his overcoat and hooked his stick over his arm, he held out his hand to her in formal leave-taking.

Only it didn't turn out that way. For the effect of that warm lithe grip flew its flag in both their faces.

"You're such a wonder!" he said.

She smiled. "So are y-you." It was the first time she had ever stammered in her life.

When she came back into the sitting-room, she found Portia inclined to be severe.

"Did you ask him to come again?" she wanted to know.

Rose smiled. "I never thought of it," she said.

"Perhaps it's just as well," said Portia. "Did you have anything at all to say to him before we came home, or were you like that all the while? How long ago did he come?"

"I don't know," said Rose behind a very real yawn. "I was asleep on the couch when he came in. That's why I was dressed like this." And then she said she was hungry.

There wasn't, on the whole, a happier person in the world at that moment.

Because Rodney Aldrich, pounding along at five miles an hour, in a direction left to chance, was not happy. Or, if he was, he didn't know it. He couldn't yield instantly, and easily, to his intuitions, as Rose had done. He felt that he must think—felt that he had never stood in such dire need of cool level consideration as at this moment:

But the process was impossible. That fine instrument of precision, his mind, that had, for many years, done without complaint the work he gave it to do, had simply gone on a strike. Instead of ratiocinating properly, it presented pictures. Mainly four: a girl, flaming with indignation, holding a street-car conductor pinned by the wrists; a girl in absurd bedroom slippers, her skirt twisted around her knees, her hair a chaos, stretching herself awake like a big cat; a girl with wonderful, blue, tear-brimming eyes, from whose glory he had had to turn away. Last of all, the girl who had said with that adorable stammer, "So are y-you," and smiled a smile that had summed up everything that was desirable in the world.

It was late that night when his mind, in a dazed sort of way, came back on the job. And the first thing it pointed out to him was that Frederica had undoubtedly been right in telling him that, though they had lived together off and on for thirty years, they didn't know each other. The pictures his memory held of his sister, covered no such emotional range as these four. Did Martin's? It seemed absurd, yet there was a strong intrinsic probability of it.

Anyway, it was a remark Frederica had made last night that gave him something to hold on by. Marriage, she had said, was an adventure, the essential adventurousness of which no amount of cautious thought taken in advance could modify. There was no doubt in his mind that marriage with that girl would be a more wonderful adventure than any one had ever had in the world.

All right then, perhaps his mind had been right in refusing to take up the case. The one tremendous question,—would the adventure look promising enough to her to induce her to embark on it?—was one which his own reasoning powers could not be expected to answer. It called simply for experiment.

So, turning off his mind again, with the electric light, he went to bed.

VII

How It Struck Portia

It was just a fortnight later that Rose told her mother she was going to marry Rodney Aldrich, thereby giving that lady a greater shock of surprise than, hitherto, she had experienced in the sixty years of a tolerably eventful life.

Rose found her neatly writing a paper at the boudoir desk in the little room she called her den. And standing dutifully at her mother's side until she saw the pen make a period, made then her momentous announcement, much in the tone she would have used had it been to the effect that she was going to the matinée with him that afternoon.

Mrs. Stanton said, "What, dear?" indifferently enough, just in mechanical response to the matter-of-fact inflection of Rosalind's voice. Then she laid down her pen, smiled in a puzzled way up into her daughter's face, and added, "My ears must have played me a funny trick. What did you say?"

Rose repeated: "Rodney Aldrich and I are going to be married."

But when she saw a look of painful incomprehension in her mother's face, she sat down on the arm of the chair, slid a strong arm around the fragile figure and hugged it up against herself.

"I suppose," she observed contritely, "that I ought to have broken it more gradually. But I never think of things like that."

As well as she could, her mother resisted the embrace.

"I can't believe," she said, gripping the edge of her desk with both hands, "that you would jest about a solemn subject like that, Rose, and yet it's incredible! . . . How many times have you seen him?"

"Oh, lots of times," Rose assured her, and began checking them off on her fingers. "There was the first time, in the street-car, and the time he brought the books back, and that other awful call he made one evening, when we were all so suffocatingly polite. You know about those times. But three or four times more, he's come down to the university—he's great friends with several men in the law faculty, so he's there quite a lot, anyway—but several times he's picked me up, and we've gone for walks, miles and miles and miles, and we've talked and talked and talked. So really, we know each other awfully well."

"I didn't know," said her mother in a voice still dull with astonishment, "that you even liked him. You've been so silent—indifferent—both times he was here to call. . ."

"Oh, I haven't learned yet to talk to him when any one else is around," Rose admitted. "There's so little to say, and it doesn't seem worth the bother. But, truly, I do like him, mother. I like everything about him. I love his looks—I don't mean just his eyes and nose and mouth. I like the shape of his ears, and his hands. I like his big loud voice"—her own broadened a little as she added, "and the way he swears. Oh, not at me, mother! Just when he gets so interested in what he's saying that he forgets I'm a lady.

"And I like the way he likes to fight—not with his fists, I mean, necessarily. He's got the most wonderful mind to—wrestle with, you know. I love to start an argument with him, just to see how easy it is for him to—roll me in the dirt and walk all over me."

The mother freed herself from the girl's embrace, rose and walked away to another chair. "If you'll talk rationally and seriously, my dear," she said, "we can continue the conversation. But this flippant, rather—vulgar tone you're taking, pains me very much."

The girl flushed to the hair. "I didn't know I was being flippant and vulgar," she said. "I didn't mean to be. I was just trying to tell you—all about it."

"You've told me," said her mother, "that Mr. Aldrich has asked you to marry him and that you've consented. It seems to me you have done so hastily and thoughtlessly. He's told you he loves you, I've no doubt, but I don't see how it's possible for you to feel sure on such short acquaintance."

"Why, of course he's told me," Rose said, a little bewildered. "He can't help telling me all the time, any more than I can help telling him. We're—rather mad about each other, really. I think he's the most wonderful person in the world, and"—she smiled a little uncertainly—"he thinks I am. But we've tried to be sensible about it, and think it out reasonably. We're both strong and healthy, and we like each other. . . I mean—things about each other, like I've said. So, as far as we can tell, we—fit. He said he couldn't guarantee that we'd be happy; that no pair of people could be sure of that till they'd tried. But he said it looked to him like the most wonderful, magnificent adventure in the world, and asked if it looked to me like that, and I said it did. Because it's true. It's the only thing in the world that seems worth—bothering about. And we both think—though, of course, we can't be sure we're thinking straight—that we've got a good chance to make it go."

HENRY KITCHELL WEBSTER

Even her mother's bewildered ears couldn't distrust the sincerity with which the girl had spoken. But this only increased the bewilderment. She had listened with a sort of incredulous distaste she couldn't keep her face from showing, and at last she had to wipe away her tears.

At that Rose came over to her, dropped on the floor at her knees and embraced her.

"I guess perhaps I understand, mother," she said. "I didn't realize—you've always been so intellectual and advanced—that you'd feel that way about it—be shocked because I hadn't pretended not to care for him and been shy and coy"—in spite of herself, her voice got an edge of humor in it—"and a startled fawn, you know, running away, but just not fast enough so that he wouldn't come running after and think he'd made a wonderful conquest by catching me at last. But a man like Rodney Aldrich wouldn't plead and protest, mother. He wouldn't *want* me unless I wanted him just as much."

It was a long time before her mother spoke and when she did, she spoke humbly—resignedly, as if admitting that the situation she was confronted with was beyond her powers.

"It's the one need of a woman's life, Rose, dear," she said, "—the corner-stone of all her happiness, that her husband, as you say, 'wants' her. It's something that—not in words, of course, but in all the little facts of married life—she'll need to be reassured about every day. Doubt of it is the one thing that will have the power to make her bitterly unhappy. That's why it seems to me so terribly necessary that she be sure about it before it's too late."

"Yes, of course," said Rose. "But that's true of the man, too, isn't it? Otherwise, where's the equality?"

Her mother couldn't answer that except with a long sigh.

Strangely enough, it wasn't until after Rose had gone away, and she had shut herself up in her room to think, that any other aspect of the situation occurred to her—even that there was another aspect of it which she'd naturally have expected to be the first and only critical one.

Ever since babyhood Rose had been devoted, by all her mother's plans and hopes, to the furtherance of the cause of Woman, whose ardent champion she herself had always been. For Rose—not Portia—was the devoted one.

The elder daughter had been born at a time when her own activities were at their height. As Portia herself had said, when she and her two brothers were little, their mother had been too busy to—luxuriate in them very much and during those early and possibly suggestive years, Portia had been suffered to grow up, as it were, by herself. She was not neglected, of course, and she was dearly loved. But when, for the first time since actual babyhood, she got into the focal-plane of her mother's mind again, there was a subtle, but, it seemed, ineradicable antagonism between them, though that perhaps is too strong a word for it. A difference there was, anyway, in the grain of their two minds, that hindered unreserved confidences, no matter how hard they might try for them. Portia's brusk disdain of rhetoric, her habit of reducing questions to their least denominator of common sense, carried a constant and perfectly involuntary criticism of her mother's ampler and more emotional style—made her suspect that Portia regarded her as a sentimentalist.

But Rose, with her first adorable smile, had captured her mother's heart beyond the possibility of reservation or restraint. And, as the child grew and her splendid, exuberant vitality and courage and wide-reaching, though not facile, affection became marked characteristics, the hope grew in her mother that here was a new leader born to the great Cause. It would need new leaders. She herself was conscious of a side drift to the great current, that threatened to leave her in a backwater. Or, as she put it to herself, that threatened to sweep over the banks of righteousness and decorum, and inundate, disastrously, the peaceful fields.

She couldn't expect to have the strength to resist this drift herself, but she had a vision of her daughter rising splendidly to the task. And for that task she trained her—or thought she did; saw to it that the girl understood the Eighteenth Century Liberalism, which, limited to the fields of politics and education, and extended to include women equally with men, was the gospel of the movement she had grown up in. With it for a background, with a university education and a legal training, the girl would have everything she needed.

She expected her to marry, of course. But in her day-dreams, it was to be one of Rose's converts to the cause—won perhaps by her advocacy at the bar, of some legal case involving the rights of woman—who was to lay his new-born conviction, along with his personal adoration, at the girl's feet.

Certainly Rodney Aldrich, who, as Rose outrageously had boasted, rolled her in the dust and tramped all over her in the course of their arguments, presented a violent contrast to the ideal husband she had selected. Indeed, it should be hard to think of him as anything but the rock on which her whole ambition for the girl would be shattered.

It was strange she hadn't thought of that during her talk with Rose!

Now that the idea had occurred to her she tried hard to look at the event that way and to nurse into energetic life a tragic regret over the miscarriage of a lifetime's hope. It was all so obviously what she ought to feel. Yet the moment she relaxed the effort, her mind flew back to a vibration between a hope and a fear: the hope, that the man Rose was about to marry would shelter and protect her always, as tenderly as she herself had sheltered her; the terror—and this was stronger—that he might not.

That night, during the process of getting ready for bed, Rose put on a bath-robe, picked up her hair brush and went into Portia's room. Portia, much quicker always about such matters, was already on the point of turning out the light, but guessing what her sister wanted, she stacked her pillows, lighted a cigarette, climbed into bed and settled back comfortably for a chat.

"I hope," Rose began, "that you're really pleased about it. Because mother isn't. She's terribly unhappy. Do you suppose it's because she thinks I've—well, sort of deserted her, in not going on and being a lawyer—and all that?"

"Oh, perhaps," said Portia indifferently. "I wouldn't worry about that, though. Because really, child, you had no more chance of growing up to be a lawyer and a leader of the 'Cause' than I have of getting to be a brigadier-general."

Rose stopped brushing her hair and demanded to be told why not. She had been getting on all right up to now, hadn't she?

"Why, just think," said Portia, "what mother herself had gone through when she was your age; put herself through college because her father didn't believe in 'higher education'—practically disowned her. She'd taught six months in that awful school—remember?—she was used to being abused and ridiculed. And she was working hard enough to have killed a camel. But you! . . . Why, Lamb, you've never really *had* to do anything in your life. If you felt like it, all right—and equally all right if you didn't. You've never been hurt—never even been frightened. You wouldn't know what they felt like. And the result is. . ."

Portia drew in a long puff, then eyed her cigarette thoughtfully through the slowly expelled smoke. "The result is," she concluded, "that you have grown up into a big, splendid, fearless, confiding creature that it's perfectly inevitable some man like Rodney Aldrich would go straight out of his head about. And there you are."

A troubled questioning look came into the younger sister's eyes. "I've been lazy and selfish, I know," she said. "Perhaps more than I thought. I haven't meant to be. But. . . Do you think I'm any good at all?"

"That's the real injustice of it," said Portia; "that you are. You've stayed big and simple. It couldn't possibly occur to you now to say to yourself, 'Poor old Portia! She's always been jealous because mother liked me best, and now she's just green with envy because I'm going to marry Rodney Aldrich.'"

She wouldn't stop to hear Rose's protest. "I know it couldn't," she went on. "That's what I say. And yet there's more than a little truth in it, I suppose. Oh, I don't mean I'm sorry you're going to be happy—I believe you are, you know. I'm just a little sorry for myself. Curious, anyway, to see where I've missed all the big important things you've kept. I've been afraid of my instincts, I suppose. Never able to take a leap because I've always stopped to look, first. I'm too narrow between the cheek-bones, perhaps. Anyhow, here I stay, grinding along, wondering what it's all about and what after all's the use. . . While you, you baby! are going to find out."

What Rose wanted to do was to gather her sister up in her arms and kiss her. But the faint ironic smile on Portia's fine lips, the twist of her eyebrows, the poise of her body as she sat up in bed watching the blue-brown smoke rising in a straight thin line from her diminishing cigarette, combined to make such a demonstration altogether impossible.

"Mother thinks, I guess," she said, to break the silence, "that I ought to have looked a little longer. She thinks Rodney would have 'wanted' me more, if I hadn't thrown myself at him like that."

Portia extinguished her cigarette in a little ash-tray, and began unpacking her pillows before she spoke. "I don't know," she said at last. "It's been said for a long time that the only way to make a man want anything very wildly, is to make him think it's desperately hard to get. But I suspect there are other ways. I don't believe you'll ever have any trouble making him 'want' you as much as you like."

The color kept mounting higher and higher in the girl's face during the moment of silence while she pondered this remark. "Why should

I—make him want me?—Any more than... I think that's rather—horrid, Portia."

Portia gave a little shiver and huddled down into her blankets. "You don't put things out of existence by deciding they're horrid, child," she said. "Open my window, will you? And throw out that cigarette. There. Now, kiss me and run along to bye-bye. And forget my nonsense."

VIII

Rodney's Experiment

The wedding was set for the first week in June. And the decision, instantly acquiesced in by everybody, was that it was to be as quiet— as strictly a family affair—as possible. The recentness of the death of Rodney's mother gave an adequate excuse for such an arrangement, but the comparative narrowness of the Stantons' domestic resources enforced it. Indeed, the notion of even a simple wedding into the Aldrich family left Portia rather aghast.

But this feeling was largely allayed by Frederica's first call. Being a celebrated beauty and a person of great social consequence didn't, it appeared, prevent one from being human and simple mannered and altogether delightful to have about. She was so competent, too, and intelligent (Rose didn't see why Portia should find anything extraordinary in all this. Wasn't she Rodney's sister?) that her conquest of the Stanton family was instantaneous. They didn't suspect that it was deliberate.

Rodney had made his great announcement to her, characteristically, over the telephone, from his office. "Do you remember asking me, Freddy, two or three weeks ago, who Rosalind Stanton was? Well, she's the girl I'm going to marry."

She refused to hear a word more in those circumstances. "I'm coming straight down," she said, "and we'll go somewhere for lunch. Don't you realize that we can't talk about it like this? Of course you wouldn't, but it's so."

Over the lunch table she got as detailed an account of the affair as Rodney, in his somnambulistic condition, was able to give her, and she passed it on to Martin that evening as they drove across to the north side for dinner.

"Well, that all sounds exactly like Rodney," he commented. "I hope you'll like the girl."

"That isn't what I hope," said Frederica. "At least it isn't what I'm most concerned about. I hope I can make her like me. Roddy's the only brother I've got in the world, and I'm not going to lose him if I can help it. That's what will happen if she doesn't like me."

Frederica was perfectly clear about this, though she admitted it had taken her fifteen minutes or so to see it.

"All the way down-town to talk to Rodney," she said, "I sat there deciding what she ought to be like—as if she were going to be brought up to me to see if she'd do. And then all at once I thought, what good would it do me to decide that she wouldn't? I couldn't change his relation to her one bit. But, if she decides I won't do, she can change his relation to me pretty completely. It's about the easiest thing a wife can do.

"Well, I'm going to see her, and her mother and sister—that's the family—tomorrow. And if they don't like me before I come away and think of me as a nice sort of person to be related by marriage to, it won't be because I haven't tried. It will be because I'm just a naturally repulsive person and can't help it."

As it happened though, she forgot all about her resolution almost with her first look at Rose. Rodney's attempts at description of her had been well meaning; but what he had prepared his sister for, unconsciously of course, in his emphasis on one or two phases of their first acquaintance, had been a sort of slatternly Amazon. But the effect of this was, really, very happy; because when a perfectly presentably clad, well-bred, admirably poised young girl came into the room and greeted her neither shyly nor eagerly, nor with any affectation of ease, a girl who didn't try to pretend it wasn't a critical moment for her but was game enough to meet it without any evidences of panic— when Frederica realized that this was the Rose whom Rodney had been telling her about, she fell in love with her on the spot.

Amazingly, as she watched the girl and heard her talk, she found she was considering, not Rose's availability as a wife for Rodney, but Rodney's as a husband for her. It was this, perhaps, that led her to say, at the end of her leave-taking, just as Rose, who had come out into the hall with her, was opening the door:

"Roddy has been such a wonderful brother, always, to me, that I suspect you'll find him, sometimes, being a brother to you. Don't let it hurt you if that happens."

The most vivid of all the memories that Frederica took away with her from that memorable visit was the smile with which Rose had answered that remark. She had her chauffeur stop at the first drug store they came to and called up Rodney on the telephone, just because she was too impatient to wait any longer for a talk with him.

"I'm simply idiotic about her," she told him. "I know, now, what you meant when you were trying to tell me about her smile. She looked at me like that just as I was leaving, and my throat's tight with it yet. She's such a darling! Don't be too much annoyed if I put my oar in once in a while, just to see that you're treating her properly."

She walked into his office one morning a few days later, dismissed his stenographer with a nod, and sat down in the just vacated chair. She was sorry, she said, but it was the only way she had left, nowadays, of getting hold of him. Then she introduced a trivial, transparent little errand for an excuse, and, having got it out of the way, inquired after Rose. What had the two of them been doing lately?

"Getting acquainted," he said. "It's going to be an endless process, apparently. Heavens, what a lot there is to talk about!"

"Yes," Frederica persisted, "but what do you do by way of being—nice to her?" And as he only looked puzzled and rather unhappy, she elucidated further. "What's your concession, dear old stupid, to the fact that you're her lover—in the way of presents and flowers and theaters and things?"

"But Rose isn't like the rest of them," he objected. "She doesn't care anything about that sort of thing."

Whereat Frederica laughed. "Try it," she said, "just for an experiment, Roddy. Don't ask her if she wants to go, ask her to go. Get tickets for one of the musical things, engage a table for dinner and for supper, at two of the restaurants, and send her flowers. Do it handsomely, you know, as if ordinary things weren't good enough for her. Oh, and take our big car. Taxis wouldn't quite be in the picture. Try it, Roddy, just to see what happens."

He looked thoughtful at first, then interested, and at last he smiled, reached over and patted her hand. "All right, Freddy," he said. "The handsome thing shall be done."

The result was that at a quarter past one A.M., a night or two later, he tipped the carriageman at the entrance to the smartest of Chicago's supper restaurants, stepped into Martin's biggest limousine, and dropped back on the cushions beside a girl he hardly knew.

"You wonder!" he said, as her hand slid into his. "I didn't know you could shine like that. All the evening you've kept my heart in my throat. I don't know a thing we've seen or eaten—hardly where we've been."

"I do," she declared, "and I shall never forget it. Not one smallest thing about it. You see, it's the first time anything like it ever happened to me."

He exclaimed incredulously at that—wanted to know what she meant.

He felt the weight of her relaxed contented body, as she leaned closer to him—felt her draw in a long slow sigh. "I don't know whether I can talk sense tonight or not," she said, "but I'll try. Why, I've been quite a lot at the theater, of course, and two or three times to the restaurants. But never—oh, as if I belonged like that. It always seemed a little wrong, and extravagant. And then, it's never lasted. After the theater, or the dinner, I've walked over to the elevated, you know. So this has been like—well, like flying in a dream, without any bumps to wake me up. It sort of goes to my head just to be sitting here like this, floating along home. Only—only, I wish it was to our home, Rodney, instead of just mine."

"You darling!" he said. And, presently: "I'll tell you what we'll do tomorrow, if you'll run away from your dressmaker. We'll go and buy a car for ourselves. It's ridiculous I didn't get one long ago. Frederica's always been at me to. You see, mother wouldn't have anything but horses, and I sold those, of course, when she died. I've meant to get a car, but I just never got round to it."

A small disagreeable voice, hermetically sealed in one of the remoter caverns of him, remarked at this point that he was a liar. A motor-car, it pointed out, was one of the things he had always denounced as a part of the useless clutter of existence that he refused to be embarrassed with. But it didn't speak with much conviction.

She picked up his hand and brushed her lips softly against the palm of it. "You're so wonderful to me," she said. "You give me so much. And I—I have so little to give back. And I want to—I want to give you all the world." And then, suddenly, she put her bare arm around his neck, drew his face to hers and kissed him.

It was the first time she had ever begun a caress like that.

IX

AFTER BREAKFAST

For their honeymoon, Martin had loaned them his camp up in northern Wisconsin—uncut forest mostly, with a river and a lot of little lakes in it. There were still deer and bear to be shot there, there was wonderful fishing, and, more to the point in the present instance, as fine a brand of solitude as civilization can ask to lay its hands on. It was modified, and mitigated too, by a backwoods family—a man and his wife, a daughter or two, and half a dozen sons, who lived there the year round, of course; so that by telegraphing two or three days in advance, you could be met by a buckboard at the nearest railroad station for the twenty-five-mile drive over to the camp. You could find the house itself (a huge affair, decorously built of logs, as far as its exterior manifestations went, but amply supplied on the interior with bathrooms, real beds and so forth) opened and warmed and flavored with the odor of fried venison steak. Also, there was always a boy to paddle a canoe for you, or saddle a horse, if you didn't feel like doing it for yourself.

Rodney and Rose spent a night in this establishment, then rigged up an outfit for camping of a less symbolistic sort, and repaired to an island out in the lake, where for two weeks they lived gorgeously, like the savages they both, to a very considerable extent, really were.

But, at the end of this fortnight, a whipping north wind, with a fine penetrating rain in its teeth, settled down for a three-days' visit, and drove them back to adequate shelter. One rainy day in an outdoor camp is a good thing; a second requires fortitude; a third carries the conviction that it has been raining from the first day of Creation and will keep on till the Last Judgment, and if you have anywhere to go to get dry, you do.

Of course the storm blew itself away when it had accomplished its purpose of driving them from their island paradise, but they didn't go back to it. Two weeks of camp-fires, hemlock boughs and blankets, had given them an appreciation for sleeping between smooth sheets, and coming down to a breakfast that was prepared for them. And one morning Rose came into the big living-room to find Rodney lounging there, in front of the fire, with a book.

It wasn't the first time he had done that. But always before, on seeing her come in, he had chucked the book away and come to meet her. This time, he went on reading.

She moved over toward him, meaning to sit down on the arm of his chair, cuddle her arm around his neck, and at the same time, discover what it was that so absorbed him. But half-way across the room, she changed her mind. He hadn't even reached out an unconscious hand toward her. He went on reading as if, actually, he were alone in the room. Evidently, too, it was a book he'd brought with him—a formidable-looking volume printed in German—she got near enough to see that. So she picked up an old magazine from the table, and found a chair of her own, smiling a little in anticipation of the effect this maneuver would have.

She opened the magazine at random, and, presently, for the sake of verisimilitude, turned a page. Rodney was turning pages as regularly as clockwork. It was a silly magazine! She wished she'd found something that really could interest her. It was getting harder and harder to sit still. He couldn't be angry about anything, could he? No, that was absurd. There hadn't been the slightest trace of a disagreement between them. She wouldn't go on pretending to read, anyhow, and she tossed the magazine away.

She had meant it to fall back on the table. But she put more nervous force than she realized into the toss, so that it skittered across the table and fell on the floor with a slap.

That roused him. He closed his book—on his finger, though—looked around at her, stretched his arms and smiled. "Isn't this great?" he said.

It wasn't a sentiment she could echo quite whole-heartedly just then, so she asked him what he meant—wasn't what great.

"Oh, this," he told her. "Being like this."

"Sitting half a mile apart this way," she asked, "each of us reading our own book?"

She didn't realize how completely provocative her meaning was, until, to her incredulous bewilderment, he said enthusiastically, "Yes! exactly!"

He wasn't looking at her now, but into the fire, and he rummaged for a match and relighted his pipe before he said anything more. "Being permanent, you know," he explained, "and—well, our real selves again."

She tried hard to keep her voice even when she asked, "But—but what have we been?"

And at that he laughed out. "Good heavens, what haven't we been! A couple of transfigured lunatics. Why, Rose, I haven't been able to see straight, or think straight, for the last six weeks. And I don't believe you have either. My ideas have just been running in circles around you. How I ever got through those last two cases in the Appellate Court, I don't see. When I made an argument before the bench, I was—talking to you. When I wrote my briefs, I was writing you love-letters. And if I'd had sense enough to realize my condition, I'd have been frightened to death. But now—well, we've been sitting here reading away for an hour, without having an idea of each other in our heads."

By a miracle of self-command, she managed to keep control of her voice. "Yes," she said. "That—that other's all over, isn't it?"

"I wouldn't go so far as to say that," he demurred around a comfortable yawn. "I expect it will catch us again every now and then. But, in the main, we're sane people, ready to go on with our own business. What was it you were reading?"

"I don't believe I'll read any more just now," she said. "I think I'll go out for a walk." And she managed to get outside the room without his discovering that anything was wrong.

It was, indeed, her first preoccupation, to make sure he shouldn't discover the effect his words had had on her—to get far enough away before the storm broke so that she could have it out by herself. The crowning humiliation would be if he came blundering in on her and asked her what was the matter.

She fled down the trail to the little lake, ran out a canoe, caught up a paddle and bent a feverish energy to the task of getting safely around into the shelter of a fir-grown point before she let herself stop, as she would have said, to think. It wasn't really to think, of course. Not, that is, to interpret out to the end of all its logical implications, the admission he had so unconsciously made to her that morning.

She had never seriously been hurt or frightened, Portia had said weeks ago. And when she said it, it was true. She was both hurt and frightened now, and the instinct that had urged her to fly was as simple and primitive as that which urges a wounded animal to hide.

Indeed, if you could have seen her after she had swung her paddle inboard, sitting there, gripping the gunwales with both hands, panting, her wide eyes dry, you might easily have thought of some defenseless wild thing cowering in a momentary shelter, listening for the baying of pursuing hounds.

He didn't love her any more, that was what he had said. For what was the thing he had so cheerfully described himself as cured of, what were the symptoms he had enumerated as if he had been talking about a disease—the obsession with her, the inability to get her further away than the middle ground of his thoughts, and then only temporarily; the necessity of saying everything he said and doing everything he did, with reference to her; the fact that his mind could focus itself sharply on nothing in the world but just herself?—What was all that but the veritable description, though in hostile terms, of the love he had promised to feel for her till death should—part them; of the very love she felt for him, this moment stronger than ever?

Recurrent waves of the panic broke over her, during which she would catch up her paddle again and drive ahead, blindly, without any conscious knowledge of where she was going. And in the intervals, she drifted.

The relief of tears didn't come to her until she saw, just ahead, the island where, for two paradisiacal weeks, she and Rodney had made their camp. Here she beached her canoe and went ashore; crept into a little natural shelter under a jutting rock, where they had lain one day while, for three hours, a violent unheralded storm had whipped the lake to lather. The heap of hemlock branches he had cut for a couch for them was still there.

At the end of half an hour, she observed with a sort of apathetic satisfaction, that the weather conditions of their former visit were going to be repeated now—a sudden darkness, a shriek of wind, a wild squall flashing across the surface of the little lake, and a driving rain so thick that small as the lake was, it veiled the shore of it.

She watched it for an hour before it occurred to her to wonder what Rodney would be doing—whether he'd have discovered her absence from the house and begun to worry about her. She told herself that he wouldn't—that he'd sit there until he finished his book, or until they called him for lunch, without, as he himself had boasted that morning, a thought of her entering his mind.

She wept again over this notion, luxuriating rather, it must be confessed, in the pathos of it, until she caught herself in the act and, disgustedly, dried her eyes. Of course he'd worry about her. Only there was nothing either of them could do about it until the storm should be over; then she'd paddle back to the house as fast as she could and set his mind at rest.

Suddenly she sat erect, looked, rubbed her eyes, looked again, then sprang to her feet and went out into the driving rain. A spot of white, a larger one of black, two moving pin-points of light, was what she saw. The white was Rodney's shirt, the black the canoe, the pin-points the reflection from the two-bladed paddle as, recklessly, he forced his way with it into the teeth of the storm. He wanted her, after all.

So, with a racing heart and flushed cheeks, she watched him. It was not until he had come much nearer that she went white with the realization of his danger—not until she could see how desperately it needed all his strength and skill to keep his little cockle-shell from broaching to and being swamped.

She went as far to meet him as she could—out to the end of the point, and then actually into the water to help him with the half-filled boat.

They emptied it and hauled it up on the beach. Then, looking up at him a little tremulously, between a smile and tears, she saw how white he was, caught him in her arms and felt how he was trembling.

"I thought you were gone," he said, but couldn't manage any more than that because of a great shuddering sob that stopped him.

"Don't!" she cried. "Don't.—Oh, my dear! I didn't know!"

Presently, back in the shelter again, she drew his head down on her breast and held him tight.

Logically, of course, the situation wasn't essentially changed. It couldn't be a part of their daily married routine that he should think he'd lost her and come through perils to the rescue. When the storm had blown over and they'd come back to the house—still more, when after another few weeks they'd gone back to town, he'd still have a world of his own to withdraw into, a business of his own to absorb him, and she, with no world at all except the one he was the principal inhabitant of, would be left outside. But you couldn't have expected her to think of that while she held him, quivering, in her arms.

BOOK II
LOVE AND THE WORLD

I

The Princess Cinderella

When the society editor of "America's foremost newspaper," as in its trademark it proclaims itself to be, announced that the Rodney Aldriches had taken the Allison McCreas' house, furnished, for a year, beginning in October, she spoke of it as an ideal arrangement. As everybody knew, it was an ideal house for a young married couple, and it was equally evident that the Rodney Aldriches were an ideal couple for it.

In the sense that it left nothing to further realization, it was an ideal house; an old house in the Chicago sense, built over into something very much older still—Tudor, perhaps—Jacobean, anyway—by a smart young society architect who wore soft collars and an uptwisted mustache, and who, by a perfectly reciprocal arrangement which almost deserves to be called a form of perpetual motion, owed the fact that he was an architect to his social position, and maintained his social position by being an architect.

He had cooperated enthusiastically with Florence McCrea, not only in the design of the house, but in the supplementary matters of furniture, hangings, rugs and pictures, with the effect that the establishment presented the last politely spoken word in things as they ought to be. The period furniture was accurate almost to the minute, and the arrangement of it, the color schemes and the lighting, had at once the finality of perfection and the perfection of finality. If you happened to like that sort of thing, it was precisely the sort of thing you'd like.

The same sort of neat, fully acquired perfection characterized the McCreas' domestic arrangements. Allison McCrea's income, combined with his wife's, was exactly enough to enable them to live in this house and entertain on the scale it very definitely prescribed, just half the time. Every other year they went off around the world in one direction or another, and rented their house furnished for exactly enough to pay all their expenses. They had no children, and his business, which consisted in allowing his bank to collect his invariable quarterly dividends for him and credit them to his account, offered no obstacle to this arrangement.

On the alternate years, they came back and spent two years' income living in their house.

Florence was an old friend of Rodney's and it was her notion that it would be just the thing he'd want. She made no professions of altruism—admitted she was fussy about whom she rented her darling house to, and that Rodney and his wife would be exactly right. Still, she didn't believe he could do better. They'd have to have some sort of place to live in, in the autumn. It would be such a mistake to buy a lot of stuff in a hurry and find out later that they didn't want it! The arrangement she proposed would leave him an idyllically untroubled summer—nothing to fuss about, and provide. . . Well, Rodney knew for himself what the house was—complete down to the cork-screws.

Even the servant question was eliminated. "Ours are so good," Florence said, "that the last time we rented the house, we put them in the lease. I wouldn't do that with you, of course, but I know they'll be just what you want." And six thousand dollars a year was simply dirt cheap.

To clinch the thing, Florence went around and saw Frederica about it. And Frederica, after listening, non-committally, dashed off to the last meeting of the Thursday Club (all this happened in June, just before the wedding) and talked the matter over with Violet Williamson on the way home, afterward.

"John said once," observed Violet, "that if he had to live in that house, he'd either go out and buy a plush Morris chair from feather-your-nest Saltzman's, and a golden oak sideboard, or else run amuck."

Frederica grinned, but was sure it wouldn't affect Rodney that way. He'd never notice that there *wasn't* a golden oak sideboard with a beveled mirror in it. As for Rose, she thought Rose would like it—for a while, anyway. Of course it wasn't forever. But this wasn't the point. It was something else she had to get an unprejudiced opinion on, "simply because in this case my own isn't trustworthy. I'm so foolish about old Roddy, that I can't be sure I haven't—well, caught being mad about Rose from him. It all depends, you see, on whether Rose is going to be a hit this winter or not. If she is, they'll want a place just like that and it would be a shame for her to be bothered and unsettled when she might have everything all oiled for her. But of course if she doesn't—go (and it all depends on her; Rodney won't be much help)—why, having a house like that might be pretty sad. So, if you're a true friend, you'll tell me what you think."

"What I really think," said Violet, "—of course I suppose I'd say this anyway, but I do honestly mean it—is that she'll be what John calls a 'knock-out.' To be sure, I've only met her twice, but I think she's absolutely thrilling. She's so perfectly simple. She's never—don't you know—*being* anything. She just is. And she thinks we're all so wonderful—clever and witty and beautiful and all that—just honestly thinks so, that she'll make everybody feel warm and nice inside, and they'll be sure to like her. Of course, when she gets over feeling that way about us. . ."

"She's got a real eye for clothes, too," said Frederica. "We've been shopping. Well then, I'm going to tell Rodney to go ahead and take the house."

Rose was consulted about it of course, though consulted is perhaps not the right word to use. She was taken to see it, anyway, and asked if she liked it, a question in the nature of the case superfluous. One might as well have asked Cinderella if she liked the gown the fairy godmother had provided her with for the prince's ball.

It didn't occur to her to ask how much the rent would be, nor would the fact have had any value for her as an illuminant, because she would have had no idea whether six thousand dollars was a half or a hundredth of her future husband's income. The new house was just a part—as so many of the other things that had happened to her since that night when Rodney had sent her flowers and taken her to the theater and two restaurants in Martin's biggest limousine had been parts—of a breath-arresting fairy story.

It takes a consciousness of resistance overcome to make anything feel quite real, and Rose, during the first three months after their return to town in the autumn, encountered no resistance whatever. It was all, as Frederica had said, oiled. She was asked to make no effort. The whole thing just happened, exactly as it had happened to Cinderella. All she had to do was to watch with wonder-wide eyes, and feel that she was, deliciously, being floated along.

The conclusion Frederica and Violet had come to about her chance for social success was amply justified by the event, and it is probable that Violet had put her finger on the mainspring of it. One needn't assume that there were not other young women at the prince's ball as beautiful as Cinderella, and other gowns, perhaps, as marvelous as the one provided by the fairy godmother. The godmother's greatest gift, I should say, though the fable lays little stress on it, was a capacity for unalloyed delight. No other young girl, beautiful as she may have been, if she were accustomed to driving to balls in coaches and having princes ask her to dance with them, could possibly have looked at that prince the way Cinderella must have looked at him.

While a sophisticated woman can affect this sort of simplicity well enough to take in the men, the affectation is always transparently clear to other women and they detest her for it. But it was altogether the real thing with Rose, and they knew it and took to her as naturally as the men did.

So it fell out that what with the Junior League, the woman's auxiliary boards of one or two of the more respectably elect charities, the Thursday Club and The Whifflers (this was the smallest and smartest organization of the lot—fifteen or twenty young women supposed to combine and reconcile social and intellectual brilliancy on even terms. They met at one another's houses and read scintillating papers about nothing whatever under titles selected generally from *Through the Looking-glass* or *The Hunting of the Snark*)—what with all this, her days were quite as full as the evenings were, when she and Rodney dined and went to the opera and paid fabulous prices to queer professionals, to keep themselves abreast of the minute in all the new dances.

But it wasn't merely the events of this sort, sitting in boxes at the opera and going to marvelous supper dances afterward, that had this thrilling quality of incredibility to Rose. The connective tissue of her life gave her the same sensation, perhaps even more strongly.

Portia had been quite right in saying that she had never *had* to do anything; the rallying of all her forces under the spur of necessity was an experience she had never undergone. And it was also true that her mother, and for that matter, Portia herself had spoiled her a lot—had run about doing little things for her, come in and shut down her windows in the morning, and opened the register, and on any sort of excuse, on a Saturday morning, for example, had brought her her breakfast on a tray.

But these things had been favors, not services—never to be asked for, of course, and always to be accepted a little apologetically. She never knew what it was really to be served, until she and Rodney came back from their camp in the woods. The whole mechanism of ringing bells for people, telling them, quite courteously of course, but with no spare words, precisely what she wanted them to do and seeing them, with no words at all of their own, except the barest minimum required to indicate respectful acquiescence—carrying out these instructions, was in its novelty, as sensuously delightful a thing to her feelings as the contact with a fine fabric was to her finger-tips.

"I haven't," Rose, in bed, told Rodney one morning, "a single, blessed, mortal thing to do all day." Some fixture scheduled for that morning had been moved, she went on to explain, and Eleanor Randolph was feeling seedy and had called off a little luncheon and matinée party. So, she concluded with a deep-drawn sigh, the day was empty.

"Oh, that's too bad," he said with concern. "Can't you manage something. . . ?"

"Too bad!" said Rose in lively dissent. "It's too heavenly! I've got a whole day just to enjoy being myself;—being"—she reached across to the other bed for his hand, and getting it, stroked her cheek with it—"being my new self. You've no idea how new it is, or how exciting all the little things about it are. State Street's so different now—going and getting the exact thing I want, instead of finding something I can make do, and then faking it up to look as much like the real thing as I could. Portia used to think I faked pretty well. It was the one thing she really admired about me, because she couldn't do it herself at all. But I never was—don't you know?—right.

"And then when I was going anywhere, I'd figure out the through routes and where I'd take transfers, and how many blocks I'd have to walk, and what kind of shoes I'd have to wear. And coming home in time for dinner always meant the rush hour, and I'd have to stand. And it simply never occurred to me that everybody else didn't do it that way. Except"—she smiled—"except in Robert Chambers' novels and such."

It wasn't necessary to see Rose smile to know she did it. Her voice, broadening out and—dimpling, betrayed the fact. This smile, plainly enough, went rather below the surface, carried a reference to something. But Rodney didn't interrupt. He let her go on and waited to inquire about it later.

"So you see," she concluded, "it's quite an adventure just to say—well, that I want the car at a quarter to eleven and to tell Otto exactly where I want him to drive me to. I always feel as if I ought to say that if he'll just stop the car at the corner of Diversey Street, I can walk."

He laughed out at that and asked her how long she thought this blissful state of things would last.

"Forever," she said.

But presently she propped herself up on one elbow and looked over at him rather thoughtfully. "Of course it's none of it new to you," she said—"not the silly little things I've been talking about, nor the things we do together—oh, the dinners, and the dances, and the operas. Do you sort of—wish I'd get tired of it? Is it a dreadful bore to you?"

"So long as it doesn't bore you," he said; "so long as you go on—shining the way you do over it, and I am where I can see you shine"—he got out of his bed, sat down on the edge of hers, and took both her hands—"so long as it's like that, you wonder," he said, "well, the dinners and the operas and all that may be piffle, but I shall be blind to the fact."

She kissed his hands and told him contentedly that he was a darling. But, after a moment's silence, a little frown puckered her eyebrows and she asked him what he was so solemn about.

Well, he had told her the truth. The edge of excitement in his voice would have carried the irresistible conviction to anybody, that the thing he had said was, without reserve, the very thing he meant. But precisely as he said it, as if, indeed, the thing that he had said were the detonating charge that fires the shell, he felt the impact, away down in the inner depths of him, of a realization that he was not the same man he had been six months ago. Not the man who had tramped impatiently back and forth across Frederica's drawing-room, expounding his ideals of space and leisure—open, wind-swept space, for the free range of a hard, clean, athletic mind. Not the man who despised the clutter of expensive junk—"so many things to have and to do, that one couldn't turn around for fear of breaking something." That man would have derided the possibility that he could ever say this thing that he, still Rodney Aldrich, had just said to Rose—and meant.

To that man, the priceless hour of the day had always been precisely this one, the first waking hour, when his mind, in the enjoyment of a sort of clairvoyant limpidity, had been wont to challenge its stiffest problems, wrestle with them, and whether triumphant or not, despatch him to his office avid for the day's work and strides ahead of where he had left it the night before.

He spent that hour very differently now. He spent all his hours, even the formal working ones, differently. And the terrifying thing was that he hadn't resisted the change, hadn't wanted to resist, didn't want to now, as he sat there looking down at her—at the wonderful hair which framed her face and, in its two thick braids, the incomparable whiteness of her throat and bosom—at the slumberous glory of her eyes.

So, when she asked him what he was looking so solemn about, he said with more truth than he pretended to himself, that it was enough to make anybody solemn to look at her. And then, to break the spell, he asked her why she had laughed a little while back, over something she had said about Robert W. Chambers' novels.

"I was thinking," she said, "of the awful disgrace I got into yesterday, with somebody—well, with Bertram Willis, by saying something like that. I'll have to tell you about it."

Bertram Willis, it should be said, was the young architect with the upturned mustaches and the soft Byronic collars, who had done the house for the McCreas. And I must warn you to take the adjective young, with a grain of salt. Youth was no mere accident with him. He made an art of it, just as he did of eating and drinking and love-making and, incidentally, architecture. He was enormously in demand, chiefly perhaps, among young married women whose respectability and social position were alike beyond cavil. He never carried anything too far, you see. He was no pirate—a sort, rather, of licensed privateer. And what made him so invincibly attractive— after you had granted his other qualities, that is—was that he professed himself, among women, exceedingly difficult to please, so that attentions from him, even of a casual sort, became *ex hypothesi* compliments of the first order. If he asked you, in his innocently shameless way, to belong to his *hareem*, you boasted of it afterward;—jocularly, to be sure, but you felt pleased just the same. The thing that had given the final cachet of distinction to Rose's social success that season, had been the fact that he had shown a disposition to flirt with her quite furiously.

Rose didn't need to tell her husband that, of course, because he knew it already, as he also knew that Willis had asked her to be one of the Watteau group he was getting up for the charity ball (the ball was to be a sumptuously picturesque affair that year), nor that he had been spending hours with her over the question of costumes—getting as good as he gave, too, because her eye for clothes amounted to a really special talent.

All that Rodney didn't know, was about the conversation the two of them had had yesterday afternoon at tea-time.

Rose, intent on telling him all about it, had postponed the recital while she made up her own mind as to how she should regard the thing herself; whether she ought to have been annoyed, or seriously remonstrant, or whether the smile of pure amusement which had come so spontaneously to her lips, had expressed, after all, an adequate emotion.

The look in her husband's face made an end of all doubts, reduced the episode of yesterday to its proper scale. Married to a man who could look at her like that, she needn't take any one else's looks or speeches very seriously. It was at this angle that she told about it.

"Why," she said, "of course he's always talked to me as if I were about six—sixteen, anyway, no older than that, and the names he makes up to call me are simply too silly to repeat. But I never paid any attention, because—well, everybody knows he's that way to everybody. 'Flower face' was one of his favorites, but there were others that were worse. Well, yesterday he brought around some old costume plates, but he wouldn't let me look at them without coming round beside me and—holding my hand, so that didn't work very well. And then he got quite solemn and said I'd—given him the only real regret of his life, because he hadn't seen me until it was too late."

"I didn't know," said Rodney, "that he ever let obstacles like husbands bother him."

"That's what I thought he meant at first," said Rose, "but it wasn't. He didn't mean it was too late because of my being married to you. He meant too late because of him. He couldn't love me, he said, as I deserved, because he'd been in love so many times before, himself.

"And then, of course, just when I should have been looking awfully sad and sympathetic, I had to go and grin, and he wanted to know why, and I said, 'Nothing,' but he insisted, you know, so then I told him.

"Well, it was just what I said to you a while ago—that I didn't know any men ever talked like that except in books by Hichens or Chambers—why do you suppose they're both named Robert?—and he went perfectly purple with rage and said I was a savage. And then he got madder still and said he'd like to be a savage himself for about five minutes; and I wanted to tell him to go ahead and try, and see what happened, but I didn't. I asked him how he wanted his tea, and he didn't want it at all, and went away."

As she finished, she glanced up into his face for a hardly-needed reassurance that the episode looked to him, as it had looked to her, trivial. Then, with a contented little sigh, for his look gave her just what she wanted, she sat up and slid her arms around his neck.

"How plumb ridiculous it would have been," she said, "if either of us had married anybody else."

If Rodney, that is, had married a girl who'd have taken Bertram Willis seriously; or if she had married a man capable of thinking the architect's attentions important.

II

The First Question and an Answer to It

B ut within a day or two, when a conversation overheard at a luncheon table recalled the architect to her mind, a rather perplexing question propounded itself to her. Why had it infuriated him so—why had he glared at her with that air of astounded incredulity, on discovering that she wasn't prepared to take him seriously? There could be only one answer to that question. He could not have expected Rose to be properly impressed and fluttered, unless that were the effect he was in the habit of producing on other women. These others, much older that Rose all of them (because no débutantes were ever invited to belong to the *hareem*), these new, brilliant, sophisticated friends her marriage with Rodney had brought her, did not, evidently, regard the dapper little architect with feelings anything like the mild, faintly contemptuous mirth that he had roused so spontaneously and irresistibly in Rose. Every one of them had a husband of her own, hadn't she? And they were happily married, too. Well, then. . . !

She found Violet Williamson in Frederica's box at the Symphony concert one Friday afternoon, and took them both home to tea with her afterward. And when the talk fairly got going, she tossed her problem about Bertie Willis and his *hareem* into the vortex to see what would come of it.

It was always easy to talk with Frederica and Violet, there was so much real affection under the amusement they freely expressed over her youth and inexperience and simplicity. They always laughed at her, but they came over and hugged her afterward.

"I'm turned out of the *hareem*," she said, apropos of the mention of him, "in disgrace."

Violet wanted to know whatever in the world she had done to him. "Because, he's been positively—what do you call it?—dithyrambic about you for the last three months."

"I laughed," Rose acknowledged; "in the wrong place of course."

The two older women exchanged glances.

"Do you suppose it's ever been done to him before," asked Frederica, "in the last fifteen years, anyway?" And Violet solemnly shook her head.

"But why?" demanded Rose. "That's what I want to know. How can any one help thinking he's ridiculous. Of course if you were alone on a desert island with him like the Bab Ballad, I suppose you'd make the best of him. But with any one else that was—real, you know, around. . ."

Only a very high vacuum—this was the idea Rose seemed to be getting at—might be expected, *faute de mieux*, to tolerate Bertie. So if you found him tolerated seriously in a woman's life, you couldn't resist the presumption that there was a vacuum there.

"Don't ask me about him," said Frederica. "He never would have anything to do with me; said I was a classic type and they always bored him stiff. But Violet, here. . ."

"Oh, yes," said Violet, "I lasted one season, and then he dropped me. He beat me to it by about a minute. All the same—oh, I can understand it well enough. You see, what he builds on is that a woman's husband is always the least interesting man in the world. Oh, I don't mean we don't love them, or that we want to change them—permanently, you know. Take Frederica and me. We wouldn't exchange for anything. Yet, we used to have long arguments. I've said that Martin was more— interesting, witty, you know, and all that, than John. And Frederica says John is more interesting than Martin. Oh, just to talk to, I mean. Not about anything in particular, but when you haven't anything else to do."

She paused long enough to take a tentative sip or two of boiling hot tea. But the way she had hung up the ending to her sentence, told them she wasn't through with the topic yet.

"It's funny about that, too," she went on, "because really, we see each other so much and have known each other so long, that I know Martin's—repertory, about as well as Frederica. I mean, it isn't like Walter Mill, when he was just back from the Legation at Pekin, or even like Jimmy Wallace, who spends half his time playing around with all sorts of impossible people—chorus-girls and such, and tells you queer stories about them. There's something besides the—familiarness that makes husbands dull. And that's what makes Bertie amusing."

"Oh, of course," said Frederica, "everybody likes to flirt—whether they have to or not."

"Have to?" Rose echoed. She didn't want to miss anything.

Frederica hesitated. Then, rather tentatively, began her exegesis.

"Why, there are a lot of women—especially of our sort, I suppose, who are always. . . well, it's like taking your own temperature—sticking a thermometer into their mouths and looking at it. They think they

HENRY KITCHELL WEBSTER

know how they ought to feel about certain things, and they're always looking to see if they do. And when they don't, they think their emotional natures are being starved, or some silly thing like that. And of course, if you're that way, you're always trying experiments, just the way people do with health foods. In the end, they generally settle on Bertie. He's perfectly safe, you know—just as anxious as they are not to do anything really outrageous. Bertie keeps them in a pleasant sort of flutter, and maybe he does them good. I don't know.—Drink your tea, Violet. We've got to run."

That was explicit enough anyway. But it didn't solve Rose's problem—broadened and deepened it rather, and gave it a greater basis of reality. It was silly, of course, always to be asking yourself questions. But after all, you didn't question a thing that wasn't questionable. There had been no necessity for a compromise between romance and reality in her own case. She hadn't any need of a thermometer. Why had they?

Of course she knew well enough that marriage was not always the blissful transformation it had been for her. There were unhappy marriages. There were such things in the world as unfaithful husbands and brutal drunken husbands, who had to be divorced. And equally, too, there were cold-blooded, designing, mercenary wives. (In the back of her mind was the unacknowledged notion that these people existed generally in novels. She knew, of course, that those characters must have real prototypes somewhere. Only, it hadn't occurred to her to identify them with people of her own acquaintance.) But the idea had been that, barring these tragic and disastrous types, marriage was a state whose happy satisfactoriness could, more or less, be taken for granted.

Oh, there were bumps and bruises, of course. She hadn't forgotten that tragic hour in the canoe last summer. There had, indeed, been two or three minor variants on the same theme since. She had seen Rodney drop off now and again into a scowling abstraction, during which it was so evident he didn't want to talk to her, or even be reminded that she was about, that she had gone away flushed and wondering, and needing an effort to hold back the tears.

These weren't frequent occurrences, though. Once settled into what apparently was going to be their winter's routine, they had so little time alone together that these moments, when they came, had almost the tension of those that unmarried lovers enjoy. They were something to look forward to and make the delicious utmost of.

So, until she got to wondering about Bertie, Rose's instinctive attitude toward the group of young to middle-aged married people into which her own marriage had introduced her, was founded on the assumption that, allowing for occasional exceptions, the husbands and wives felt toward each other as she and Rodney did—were held together by the same irresistible, unanalyzable attraction, could remember severally, their vivid intoxicating hours, just as she remembered the hour when Rodney had told her the story and the philosophy of his life.

Bertie, or rather the demand for what Bertie supplied, together with Frederica's explanation of it, brought her the misgiving that marriage was not, perhaps, even between people who loved each other,— between husbands who were not "unfaithful" and wives who were not "mercenary"—quite so simple as it seemed.

The misgiving was not very serious at first—half amused, and wholly academic, because she hadn't, as yet, the remotest notion that the thing concerned, or ever could concern, herself; but the point was, it formed a nucleus, and the property of a nucleus is that it has the power of attracting to itself particles out of the surrounding nebulous vapor. It grows as it attracts, and it attracts more strongly as it grows.

An illustration of this principle is in the fact that, but for the misgiving, she would hardly have asked Simone Gréville what she meant by saying that though she had always supposed the fundamental sex attraction between men and women to be the same in its essentials, in all epochs and in all civilizations, her acquaintance with upper-class American women was leading her to admit a possible exception.

Since that amiable celestial, Wu Ting Fang, made his survey of our western civilization and left us wondering whether after all we had the right name for it, no one has studied our leisured and cultivated classes with more candor and penetration than this great Franco-Austrian actress. She had ample opportunities for observation, because during the first week of her tour the precise people who count the most in our informal social hierarchy took her up and, upon examination, took her in. Playing in English as she did, and with an American supporting company, she did not make a great financial success (the Continental technique, especially when contrasted so intimately with the one we are familiar with does not attract us), but socially she was a sensation. So during her four weeks in Chicago, while she played to houses that couldn't be dressed to look more than a third full, she was enormously in demand for luncheons, teas, dinners, suppers, Christmas bazaars, charity dances and so on. (If it had only been possible to establish a scale of fees for these functions, her manager used to reflect despairingly, he might have come out even after all.) Any other sort of engagement melted away like snow in the face of an opportunity of meeting Simone Gréville.

Rose had met her a number of times before the incident referred to happened, but had always surveyed the lioness from afar. What could she, whose acquaintance with Europe was limited to one three-months trip, undertaken by the family during the summer after she graduated from high school, have to say to an omniscient cosmopolite like that?

So she hung about, within ear-shot when it was possible, and watched, leaving the active duties of entertainment to heavily cultured illuminati like the Howard Wests, or to clever creatures like Hermione Woodruff and Frederica, and Constance Crawford, whose French was good enough to fill in the interstices in Madame Gréville's English.

She was standing about like that at a tea one afternoon, when she heard the actress make the remark already quoted, to the effect that American women seemed to her to be an exception to what she always supposed to be the general law of sex attraction.

It was taken, by the rather tense little circle gathered around her, as a compliment; exactly as, no doubt, Gréville intended it to be taken. But her look flashed out beyond the confines of the circle and encountered a pair of big luminous eyes, under brows that had a perplexed pucker in them. Whereupon she laughed straight into Rose's face and said, lifting her head a little, but not her voice:

"Come here, my child, and tell me who you are and why you were looking at me like that."

Rose flushed, smiled that irresistible wide smile of hers, and came, not frightened a bit, nor, exactly, embarrassed; certainly not into pretending she was not surprised, and a little breathlessly at a loss what to say.

"I'm Rose Aldrich." She didn't, in words, say, "I'm just Rose Aldrich." It was the little bend in her voice that carried that impression. "And I suppose I was—looking that way, because I was wishing I knew exactly what you meant by what you said."

Gréville's eyes, somehow, concentrated and intensified their gaze upon the flushed young face; took a sort of plunge, so it seemed to Rose, to the very depths of her own. It was an electrifying thing to have happen to you.

"*Mon dieu*," she said, "*j'ai grande envie de vous le dire*." She hesitated the fraction of a moment, glanced at a tiny watch set in a ring upon the middle finger of her right hand, took Rose by the arm as if to keep her from getting away, and turned to her hostess.

"You must forgive me," she said, "if I make my farewells a little soon. I am under orders to have some air each day before I go to the theater, and if it is to be done today, it must be now. I am sorry. I have had a very pleasant afternoon.—Make your farewells, also, my child," she concluded, turning to her prisoner, "because you are going with me."

There was something Olympian about the way she did it. The excuse was made, and the regret expressed in the interest of courtesy, but neither was insisted on as a fact, nor was seriously intended, it appeared, even to disguise the fact, which was simply that she had found something better worth her while, for the moment, than that tea. It occurred to Rose that there wasn't a woman in town—not even terrible old Mrs. Crawford, Constance's mother-in-law, who could have done that thing in just that way; no one who felt herself detached, or, in a sense, superior enough, to have done it without a trace of self-consciousness, and consequently without offense. An empress must do things a good deal like that.

The effect on Rose was to make complete frankness seem the easiest thing in the world. And frankness seemed to be the thing called for. Because no sooner were they seated in the actress' car and headed north along the drive, than she, instead of answering Rose's question, repeated one of her own.

"I ask who you are, and you say your name—Rose something. But that tells me nothing. Who are you—one of them?"

"No, not exactly," said Rose. "Only by accident. The man I married is—one of them, in a way. I mean, because of his family and all that. And so they take me in."

"So you are married," said the French woman. "But not since long?"

"Six months," said Rose.

She said it so with the air of regarding it as a very considerable period of time that Gréville laughed.

"But tell me about him then, this husband of yours. I saw him perhaps at the tea this afternoon?"

Rose laughed. "No, he draws the line at teas," she said. "He says that from seven o'clock on, until as late as I like, he's—game, you know—

willing to do whatever I like. But until seven, there are no—well, he says, siren songs for him."

"Tell me—you will forgive the indiscretions of a stranger?—how has it arrived that you married him? Was it one of your American romances?"

"It didn't seem very romantic," said Rose. "I mean not much like the romantic stories you read, and of course one couldn't make a story about it, because there was nothing to tell. We just happened to get acquainted, and we knew almost straight off that we wanted to marry each other, so we did. Some people thought it was a little—headlong, I suppose, but he said it was an adventure anyway, and that people could never tell how it was going to come out until they tried. So we tried, and—it came out very well."

"It 'came out'?" questioned the actress.

"Yes," said Rose. "Ended happily, you know."

"Ended!" Madame Gréville echoed. Then she laughed.

Rose flushed and smiled at herself. "Of course I don't mean that," she admitted, "and I suppose six months isn't so very long. Still you could find out quite a good deal. . ."

"What is his affair?" The actress preferred asking another question, it seemed, to committing herself to an answer to Rose's unspoken one. "Is he one of your—what you call tired business men?"

"He's never tired," said Rose, "and he isn't a business man. He's a lawyer—a rather special kind of lawyer. He has other lawyers, mostly, for his clients, he's awfully enthusiastic about it. He says it's the finest profession in the world, if you don't let yourself get dragged down into the stupid routine of it. It certainly sounds thrilling when he tells about it."

The actress looked round at her. "So," she said, "you follow his work as he follows your play? He talks seriously to you about his affairs?"

"Why, yes," said Rose, "we have wonderful talks." Then she hesitated. "At least we used to have. There hasn't seemed to be much—time, lately. I suppose that's it."

"One question more," said the French woman, "and not an idle one—you will believe that? *Alors!* You love your husband. No need to ask that. But how do you love him? Are you a little indulgent, a little cool, a little contemptuous of the grossness of masculine clay, and still willing to tolerate it as part of your bargain? Is that what you mean by love? Or do you mean something different altogether—something vital and strong and essential—the meeting of thought with thought, need with need, desire with desire?"

"Yes," said Rose after a little silence, "that's what I mean."

She said it quietly, but without embarrassment and with full meaning; and as if conscious of the adequacy of her answer, she forbore to embroider on the theme. There was a momentary silence, while the French woman gazed contemplatively out of the open window of the limousine, at a skyscraping apartment building which jutted boldly into a curve of the parkway they were flying along.

"That's a beauty, isn't it?" said Rose, following her gaze. "Every apartment in that building has its own garage that you get to with an elevator."

The actress nodded. "You Americans do that;" she said, "better than any one else in the world. The—surfaces of your lives are to marvel at."

"But with nothing inside?" asked Rose. "Is that what you mean? Is—that what you mean about—American women, that you said you'd tell me?"

Madame Gréville took her time about answering. "They are an enigma to me," she said, "I confess it. I have never seen such women anywhere, as these upper-class Americans. They are beautiful, clever, they know how to dress. For the first hour, or day, or week, of an acquaintance, they have a charm quite incomparable. And, up to a certain point, they exercise it. Your *jeunes filles* are amazing. All over the world, men go mad about them. But when they marry. . ." She finished the sentence with the ghost of a shrug, and turned to Rose. "Can you account for them? Were you wondering at them, too, with those great eyes of yours? *Alors*! Are we puzzled by the same thing? What is it, to you, they lack?"

Rose stirred a little uneasily. "I don't know very much," she said. "I don't know them well at all, and of course I shouldn't criticize. . ."

"Ah, child," broke in the actress, "there you mistake yourself. One must always criticize. It is by the power of criticism and the courage of criticism, that we have become different from the beasts."

"I don't know," said Rose, "except that some of them seem a little dissatisfied and restless, as if—well, as if they wanted something they haven't got."

"But do they truly want it?" Madame Gréville demanded. "I am willing to be convinced, but myself, I find of your women of the aristocrat class, the type most characteristic is"—she paused and said the thing first to herself in French, then translated—"is a passive epicure in sensations; sensations mostly mental, irritating or soothing—a

HENRY KITCHELL WEBSTER

pleasant variety. She waits to be made to feel; she perpetually—tastes. One may demand whether it is that their precocity has exhausted them before they are ripe, or whether your Puritan strain survives to make all passion reprehensible, or whether simply they have too many ideas to leave room for anything else. But, from whatever cause, they give to a stranger like me, the impression of being perfectly frigid, perfectly passionless. And so, as you say, of missing the great thing altogether.

"A few of your women are great, but not as women, and of second-rate men in petticoats, you have a vast number. But a woman, great by the qualities of her sex, an artist in womanhood, I have not seen."

"Oh, I wish," cried Rose, "that I knew what you meant by that!"

"Why, regard now," said the actress. "In every capital of Europe—and I know them all—wherever you find great affairs—matters of state, diplomacy, politics—you find the influence of women in them; women of the great world, sometimes, sometimes of the half-world; great women, at all events, with the power to make or ruin great careers; women at whose feet men of the first class lay all they have; women the tact of whose hands is trusted to determine great matters. They may not be beautiful (I have seen a faded little woman of fifty, of no family or wealth, whose salon attracted ministers of state), they haven't the education, nor the liberties that your women enjoy, and, in the mass, they are not regarded—how do you say?—chivalrously. Yet there they are!

"And why? Because they are capable of great passions, great desires. They are willing to take the art of womanhood seriously, make sacrifices for it, as one must for any art, in order to triumph in it."

Rose thought this over rather dubiously. It was a new notion to her—or almost new. Portia had told her once she never would have any trouble making her husband "want" her as much as she liked. This idea of making a serious art of your power to attract and influence men, seemed to range itself in the same category.

"But suppose," she objected, "one doesn't want to triumph at it? Suppose one wants to be a—person, rather than just a woman?"

"There are other careers indeed," Madame Gréville admitted, "and one can follow them in the same spirit, make the sacrifices—pay the price they demand. *Mon dieu!* How I have preached. Now you shall talk to me. It was for that I took you captive and ran away with you."

For the next half-hour, until the car stopped in front of her house, Rose acted on this request; told about her life before and since her marriage to Rodney, about her friends, her amusements—anything that came into her mind. But she lingered before getting out of the car, to say:

"I hope I haven't forgotten a single word of your—preaching. You said so many things I want to think about."

"Don't trouble your soul with that, child," said the actress. "All the sermon you need can be boiled down into a sentence, and until you have found it out for yourself, you won't believe it."

"Try me," said Rose.

"Then attend.—How shall I say it?—Nothing worth having comes as a gift, nor even can be bought—cheap. Everything of value in your life will cost you dear; and some time or other you'll have to pay the price of it."

It was with a very thoughtful, perplexed face that Rose watched the car drive away, and then walked slowly into her house—the ideal house that had cost Florence McCrea and Bertie Willis so many hours and so many hair-line decisions—and allowed herself to be relieved of her wraps by the perfect maid, who had all but been put in the lease.

The actress had said many strange and puzzling things during their ride; things to be accepted only cautiously, after a careful thinking out. But strangest of all was this last observation of hers; that there was nothing of worth in your life that you hadn't to pay a heavy price for.

Certainly it contradicted violently everything in Rose's experience, for everything she valued had come to her precisely as a gift. Her mother's and Portia's love of her, the life that had surrounded her in school and at the university, the friends; and then, with her marriage, the sudden change in her estate, the thrills, the excitement, the comparative luxuries of the new life. Why,—even Rodney himself, about whom everything else swung in an orbit! What price had she paid for him, or for any of the rest of it? It was all as free as the air she breathed. It had come to her without having cost even a wish. Was Rodney's love for her, therefore, valueless? No, the French woman was certainly wrong about that.

III

WHERE DID ROSE COME IN

However, it was one thing to decide that this was so, and quite another thing to dismiss the preposterous idea from her mind. There was still an hour before she need begin dressing for the Randolph dinner, but as she had already had her tea and there was nothing else to do, she thought she might as well go about it. It might help her resist a certain perfectly irrational depression which the talk with the actress, somewhat surprisingly, had produced. And besides, if she were all dressed when Rodney came home, she'd be free to visit with him while he dressed—to sit and watch him swearing at his studs, and tell him about the events of her day, including their climax in the ride with the famous Simone Gréville. And he'd come over every now and then and interrupt himself and her with some sort of unexpected caress—a kiss on the back of her neck, or an embrace that would threaten her coiffure—and this vague, scary, nightmarish sort of feeling, which for no reasonable reason at all seemed to be clutching at her, would be forgotten.

It was a queer sort of feeling—a kind of misgiving, in one form or another, as to her own identity—as if all the events since her marriage were nothing but a dream of Rose Stanton's, from which, with vague painful stirrings, she was just beginning to wake. Or, again, as if for all these months, she had been playing a part in a preposterously long play, on which the curtain was, presently, going to be rung down. She wished Rodney would come—hoped he wouldn't be late, and finally sat down before the telephone with a half-formed idea of calling him up and reminding him that they were dining with the Randolphs.

Just as she laid her hand upon the receiver, the telephone bell rang. It was Rodney calling her.

"Oh, that you, Rose?" he said. "I shan't be out till late tonight. I've got to work."

She wanted to know what he meant by late.

"I've no idea," he said. "Ten—twelve—two. I've got to get hold of something, but I've no idea how long it will take."

"But, Roddy, dearest," she protested. "You have to come home. You've got the Randolphs' dinner."

"Oh, the devil!" he said. "I forgot all about it. But it doesn't make a bit of difference, anyway. I wouldn't leave the office before I finished this job, for anybody short of the Angel Gabriel."

"But what shall we do?" she asked despairingly.

"I don't know," said Rodney. "Call them up and tell them. Randolph will understand."

"But,"—it was absurd that her eyes should be filling up and her throat getting lumpy over a thing like this,—"but what shall I do? Shall I tell Eleanor *we* can't come, or shall I offer to come without you?"

"Lord!" he said, "I don't care. Do whichever you like. I've got enough to think about without deciding that. Now do hang up and run along."

"But, Rodney, what's happened? Has something gone wrong?"

"Heavens, no!" he said. "What is there to go wrong? I've got a big day in court tomorrow and I've struck a snag, and I've got to wriggle out of it somehow, before I quit. It's nothing for you to worry about. Go to your dinner and have a good time. Good-by."

The click in the receiver told her he had hung up. The difficulty about the Randolphs was managed easily enough. Eleanor was perfectly gracious about it and insisted that Rose should come by herself.

She was completely dressed a good three-quarters of an hour before it was time to start, and after pretending for fifteen interminable minutes to read a magazine, she chucked it away and told her maid to order the car at once. If she drove straight down-town, she could have a ten-minute visit with Rodney and still not be late for the dinner. She was a little vague as to why she wanted it so much, but the prospect was irresistible.

If any one had accused her of feeling very meritorious over not having allowed herself to be hurt at his rudeness to her or annoyed at the way he had demolished their evening's plans, and of hoping to make him feel a little contrite by showing him how sweet she was about it, she might, with a rueful grin, have acknowledged a tincture of truth about the charge; but she didn't discover it by herself. As she dreamed out the little scene, riding down-town in the car, she'd come stealing up behind him as he sat, bent wearily over his book, and clasp her hands over his eyes and stroke the wrinkles out of his forehead. He'd give a long sigh of relaxation, and pull her down on the chair-arm and tell her what it was that troubled him, and she'd tell him not to worry—it was surely coming out all right. And she'd stroke his head a little longer and offer not to go to the dinner if he wanted her to stay, and he'd say, no, he was better already, and then she'd give him a good-by kiss and steal away, and be the life of the party at the Randolphs' dinner, but her thoughts would never leave him. . .

She knew she was being silly of course, and her beautiful wide mouth smiled an acknowledgment of the fact, even while her checks flushed and her eyes brightened over the picture. Of course it wouldn't come out exactly like that.

Well, it didn't!

She found a single elevator in commission in the great gloomy rotunda of the office building, and the watchman who ran her up made a terrible noise shutting the gate after he had let her out on the fifteenth floor. The dim marble corridor echoed her footfalls ominously, and when she reached the door to his outer office and tried it, she found it locked. The next door down the corridor was the one that led directly into his private office, and here the light shone through the ground-glass.

She stole up to it as softly as she could, tried it and found it locked, too, so she knocked. Through the open transom above it, she heard him say "Hell!" in a heartfelt sort of way, and heard his chair thrust back. The next moment he opened the door with a jerk.

His glare of annoyance changed to bewilderment at the sight of her, and he said:

"Rose! Has anything happened? What's the matter?" And catching her by the arm, he led her into the office. "Here, sit down and get your breath and tell me about it!"

She smiled and took his face in both her hands. "But it's the other way," she said. "There's nothing the matter with me. I came down, you poor old boy, to see what was the matter with you."

He frowned and took her hands away and stepped back out of her reach. Had it not been for the sheer incredibility of it, she'd have thought that her touch was actually distasteful to him.

"Oh," he said. "I thought I told you over the phone there was nothing the matter!—Won't you be awfully late to the Randolphs'?"

"I had ten minutes," she said, "and I thought. . ."

She broke off the sentence when she saw him snap out his watch and look at it.

"I know there's something," she said. "I can tell just by the way your eyes look and the way you're so tight and—strained. If you'd just tell me about it, and then sit down and let me—try to take the strain away. . ."

Beyond a doubt the strain was there. The laugh he meant for a good-humored dismissal of her fears, didn't sound at all as it was intended to.

"Can't you tell me?" she repeated.

"Good heavens!" he said. "There's nothing to tell! I've got an argument before the Court of Appeals tomorrow and there's a ruling decision against me. It is against me, and it's bad law. But that isn't what I want to tell them. I want some way of making a distinction so that I can hold that the decision doesn't rule."

"And it wouldn't help," she ventured, "if you told me all about it? I don't care about the dinner."

"I couldn't explain in a month," he said.

"Oh, I wish I were some good," she said forlornly.

He pulled out his watch again and began pacing up and down the room.

"I just can't stand it to see you like that," she broke out again. "If you'll only sit down for five minutes and let me try to get that strained look out of your eyes. . ."

"Good God, Rose!" he shouted. "Can't you take my word for it and let it alone? I'm not ill, nor frightened, nor broken-hearted. I don't need to be comforted nor encouraged. I'm in an intellectual quandary. For the next three hours, or six, or however long it takes, I want my mind to run cold and smooth. I've got to be tight and strained. That's the way the job's done. You can't solve an intellectual problem by having your hand held, or your eyes kissed, or anything like that. Now, for God's sake, child, run along and let me forget you ever existed, for a while!"

And he ground his teeth over an impulse that all but got the better of him, after she'd shut the door, to follow her out into the corridor and pull her up in his arms and kiss her face all over, and to consign the Law and the Prophets both, to the devil.

HENRY KITCHELL WEBSTER

IV

Long Circuits and Short

James Randolph was a native Chicagoan, but his father, an intelligent and prosperous physician, with a general practise in one of the northern suburbs, afterward annexed to the city, did not belong to the old before-the-fire aristocracy that Rodney and Frederica, and Martin Whitney, the Crawfords and Violet Williamson were born into. The medical tradition carried itself along to the third generation, when James made a profession of it, and in him, it flowered really into genius. From the beginning his bent toward the psychological aspect of it was marked and his father was sympathetic enough to give it free sway. After graduating from one of the Chicago medical colleges he went to Johns Hopkins, and after that to Vienna, where he worked mostly under Professor Freud.

It was in Vienna that he met Eleanor Blair. She, too, was a native of Illinois, but this fact cut a very different figure in her life from that which it cut in his. Her grandfather, a pioneer, forceful, thrifty and probably rather unscrupulous, had settled on the wonderfully fertile land at a time when one had almost to drive the Indians off it. He had accumulated it steadily to the day of his death and died in possession of about thirty thousand acres of it. It was in much this fashion that a feudal adventurer became the founder of a line of landed nobility, but the centrifugal force of American life caused the thing to work out differently. His son had an eastern college education, got elected to Congress, as a preliminary step in a political career, went to Washington, fell in love with and married the beautiful daughter of an unreconstructed and impoverished southern gentleman. She detested the North, and as her love for the South found its expression in passionate laments over its ruin, uncomplicated by any desire to live there, she spent more and more of her time—her husband's faint wishes becoming less and less operative with her until they ceased altogether—in one after another of the European capitals.

So Eleanor, two generations away from the fertile soil of central Illinois, was as exotic to it as an orchid would be in a New England garden. Two or three brief perfunctory visits to the land her income came from, and to the relatives who still lived upon it, became the substitute for what, in an older and stabler civilization, would have been the dominant tradition in her life.

She must have been a source of profound satisfaction to large numbers of French, Italian, Austrian and English persons, to whose eminent social circles her mother's wealth and breeding gained admittance, by embodying for them, with perfect authenticity, their notion of the American girl. She was rich, beautiful, clever in a rather shallow, "American" way, she had a will of her own, and was indulged by her mother with an astounding amount of liberty; she was audacious, yet with a tempering admixture of cool shrewdness, which kept her out of the difficulties she was always on the brink of.

Kept her out of them, that is, until, in Vienna, as I have said, she met James Randolph. That she fell in love with him is one of those facts which seem astonishing the first time you look at them, and inevitable when you look again. Physically, a sanguine blond, with a narrow head, a forward thrusting nose, and really blue eyes, his dominating spiritual quality was the sort of asceticism which proclaims not weak anemic desires, but strong unruly ones, curbed in by the hand of a still stronger will. He was highly imaginative, as a successful follower of the Freudian method must be. He was capable of the gentlest sympathy, and of the most relentless insistence. And he thought, until he met Eleanor Blair, that he was, indisputably, his own master.

The wide social gulf between them—between a beautiful American heiress with the entry into all circles of aristocratic society, except the highest, and an only decently pecunious medical student, caught both of them off their guard. The utter unlikelihood of anything coming of such an acquaintance as theirs, was just the ambush needed to make it possible for them to fall in love. They would, probably, have attracted each other anywhere. But, in a city like Vienna, where all the sensuous appurtenances of life are raised to their highest power, the attraction became irresistible.

He did resist as long as he could—successfully, indeed, to the point of holding himself back from asking her to marry him, or even explicitly from making love to her. But the thing shone through his deeply-colored emotions, like light through a stained-glass window. And when she asked him to marry her, as she did in so many words—pleaded her homesickness for a home she had never known, and a loneliness she had suddenly become aware of, amid would-be friends and lovers, who could not, not one of them, be called disinterested, his resistance melted like a powder of April snow.

It was the only serious obstacle she had to overcome. The terms of her father's will left her share of the income of the estate wholly at her disposal. And so, in spite of her mother's horrified protest, they were married, and not long afterward, her mother, who was still a year or two on the sunny side of fifty, gratified her aristocratic yearnings by marrying a count herself.

The Randolphs came back to America and, somewhat against Eleanor's wishes, settled in Chicago. With her really very large income, her exotic type of beauty and her social skill, she was probably right in thinking she could have made a success anywhere. One of the larger eastern cities—preferably New York or Washington, would have suited her better. But Chicago, he said, was where he belonged and where his best chance for professional success lay, and she yielded, though without waiving her privilege of making a more or less good-humored grievance of it. However, she found the place much more tolerable than riding into and out of it on the train a few times had led her to expect.

She knew a few people of exactly the right sort and she neatly and almost painlessly detached her husband from his old Lake View associations. She looked out a house in precisely the right neighborhood, and furnished it to combine the splendor of her income with the simple austerity of his profession in just the right proportions. She trailed her game with unfailing precision, never barked up the wrong tree, could distinguish a goat from a sheep as far as she could see one, and in no time at all had won the exact position she wanted.

Her attitude toward her husband (you have already had a sample of it at Frederica's famous dinner, where Rodney was supposed to take the preliminary steps toward marrying Hermione Woodruff) attracted general admiration, and it was fortified, of course, by the story of their romantic marriage. It was conceded she had done a very fine and splendid thing in marrying the man she loved, settling down to live with him on so comparatively simple and modest a scale, and devoting herself so whole-heartedly to his career. She had an air—and it wasn't consciously assumed, either—of living wholly with reference to him, which people found exceedingly engaging. (A cynic might observe at this point that the same quality in a homely unattractive woman would fail of producing this effect.)

Indeed, he had much to be grateful for. But for the fact that his wife was accepted without reserve, a man whose principal preoccupation was with matters of sex psychology, who was said to cure hysterical and neurasthenic patients by the interpretation of their dreams, would have been regarded askance by the average run of common-sense, golf-playing men of affairs. Even his most miraculous cures would be attributed to the imaginary nature of the disease, rather than to the skill of the physician.

Not even his wife's undeniable charm could altogether efface this impression from the mind of this sort of man. But though his way of turning the theme of a smoking-room story into a subject for serious scientific discussion might make you uncomfortable, you couldn't meet James Randolph and hear him talk, without respecting him. He was attractive to women (it amounted almost to fascination with the neurotic type), and to men of high intelligence, like Rodney, he was a boon and a delight. And the people who liked him least were precisely those most attracted by his wife. Anyhow, no one refused an invitation to their dinners.

Rose's arrival at this one—a little late, to be sure, but not scandalously—created a mild sensation. None of the other guests were strangers, either, on whom she could have the effect of novelty. They were the same crowd, pretty much, who had been encountering one another all winter—dancing, dining and talking themselves into a state of complete satiety with one another. They'd split up pretty soon and branch out in different directions—the Florida east coast, California, Virginia Hot Springs and so on, and so galvanize their interest in life and in one another. At present they were approaching the lowest ebb.

But when Rose came into the drawing-room—in a wonderful gown that dared much, and won the reward of daring—a gown she'd meant to hold in reserve for a greater occasion, but had put on tonight because she had felt somehow like especially pleasing Rodney—when she came in, she reoxygenated the social atmosphere. She won a moment of complete silence, and when the buzz of talk arose again, it was jerky—the product of divided minds and unstable attentions.

She was, in fact, a stranger. Her voice had a bead on it which roused a perfectly unreasoning physical excitement—the kind of bead which, in singing, makes all the difference between a church choir and grand opera. The glow they were accustomed to in her eyes, concentrated itself into flashes, and the flush that so often, and so adorably, suffused her face, burnt brighter now in her cheeks and left the rest pale.

And these were true indices of the change that had taken place within her. From sheer numb incredulity, which was all she had felt as she'd walked away from Rodney's office door, and from the pain of an intolerable hurt, she had reacted to a fine glow of indignation. She had found herself suddenly feeling lighter, older, indescribably more confident. That dinner was to be gone through with, was it? Well, it should be! They shouldn't suspect her humiliation or her hurt. She was conscious suddenly of enormous reserves of power hitherto unsuspected—a power that could be exercised to any extent she chose, according to her will.

Her husband, James Randolph reflected, had evidently either been making love to her, or indulging in the civilized equivalent of beating her; he was curious to find out which. And having learned from his wife that Rose was to sit beside him at the table, he made up his mind that he would make her tell him.

He didn't attempt it, though, during his first talk with her—confined himself rigorously to the carefully sifted chaff which does duty for polite conversation over the same hors-d'oeuvres and entrées, from one dinner to the next, the season round. It wasn't until Eleanor had turned the table the second time, that he made his first gambit in the game.

"No need asking you if you like this sort of thing," he said. "I would like to know how you keep it up. You have the same things said to you seven nights a week and you make the same answers—thrust and parry, carte and tierce, buttons on the foils. It can't any of it get anywhere. What's the attraction?"

"You can't get a rise out of me tonight," said Rose. "Not after what I've been through today. Madame Gréville's been talking to me. She thinks American women are dreadful dubs,—or she would if she knew the word—thinks we don't know our own game. Do you agree with her?"

"I'll tell you that," he said, "after you answer my question. What's the attraction?"

"Don't you think it would be a mistake," said Rose, "for me to try to analyze it? Suppose I did and found there wasn't any! You aren't supposed to look a gift horse in the mouth, you know."

"Is that what's the matter with Rodney?" he asked. "Is this sort of"—a gesture with his head took in the table—"caramel diet, beginning to go against his teeth?"

"He had to work tonight," Rose said. "He was awfully sorry he couldn't come."

She smiled just a little ironically as she said it, and exaggerated by a hair's breadth, perhaps, the purely conventional nature of the reply.

"Yes," he observed, "that's what we say. Sometimes it gets us off and sometimes it doesn't."

"Well, it got him off tonight," she said. "He was pretty impressive. He said there was a ruling decision against him and he had to make some sort of distinction so that the decision wouldn't rule. Do you know what that means? I don't."

"Why didn't you ask him?" Randolph wanted to know.

"I did and he said he could explain it, but that it would take a month. So of course there wasn't time."

"I thought," said Randolph, "that he used to talk law to you by the hour."

The button wasn't on the foil that time, because the thrust brought blood—a bright flush into her cheeks and a sudden brightness into her eyes that would have induced him to relent if she hadn't followed the thing up of her own accord.

"I wish you'd tell me something," she said. "I expect you know better than any one else I could ask. Why is it that husbands and wives can't talk to each other? With people who live the way we do, it isn't that they've worn each other out, because they see no more of each other, hardly, than they do of the others. And it isn't that they're naturally more uninteresting to each other than the rest of the people they know. Because then, why did they marry each other in the first place, instead of any one of the others who are so easy to talk to afterward? Imagine what this table would be if the husbands and wives sat side by side! Would Eleanor ever be able to turn it so that they talked that way?"

"That's a fascinating speculation," he said. "I wish I could persuade her some time to indulge the wild eccentricity of trying it out."

"Well, why?" she demanded.

"Shall I try to say something witty," he asked, "or do you want it, as near as may be, absolutely straight?"

"Let's indulge," she said, "in the wild, eccentricity of talking straight."

The cigarettes came around just then, and he lighted one rather deliberately, at one of the candles, before he answered.

"I am under the impression," he said, "that husbands and wives can talk exactly as well as any other two people. Exactly as well, and no better. The necessary conditions for real conversation are a real interest in and knowledge of a common subject; ability on the part of both to contribute something to that subject. Well, if a husband and wife can meet those terms, they can talk. But the joker is, as our legislative friend over there would say," (he nodded down the table toward a young millionaire of altruistic principles, who had got elected to the state assembly) "the joker is that a man and a woman who aren't married, and who are moderately attracted to each other, can talk, or seem to talk, without meeting those conditions."

"Seem to talk?" she questioned.

"Seem to exchange ideas mutually. They think they do, but they don't. It's pure illusion, that's the answer."

"I'm not clever, really," said Rose, "and I don't know much, and I simply don't understand. Will you explain it, in short words,"—she smiled—"since we're not married, you know?"

He grinned back at her. "All right," he said, "since we're not married, I will. We'll take a case. . ." He looked around the table. "We'll be discreet," he amended, "and take a hypothetical case. We'll take Darby and Joan. They encounter each other somewhere, and something about them that men have written volumes about and never explained yet, sets up—you might almost call it a chemical reaction between them—a physical reaction, certainly. They arrest each other's attention—get to thinking about each other, are strongly drawn together.

"It's a sex attraction—not quite the oldest and most primitive thing in the world, but nearly. Only, Darby and Joan aren't primitive people. If they were, the attraction would satisfy itself in a direct primitive way. But each of them is carrying a perfectly enormous superstructure of ideas and inhibitions, emotional refinements and capacities, and the sex attraction is so disguised that they don't recognize it. Do you know what a short circuit is in electricity?"

"I think so," said Rose, "but you'd better not take a chance. Tell me that, too."

"Why," he said, "the juice that comes into your house to light it and heat the flat-irons and the toaster, and so on, comes in by one wire and goes out by another. Before it can get out, it's got to do all the work you want it to do—push its way through the resistance of fine tungsten filaments in your lamps and the iron wires in your heaters that get white hot resisting it. When it's pushed its way through all of them and done the work you want it to do, it's tired out and goes away by the other wire. But if you cut off the insulation down in the basement, where those two wires are close together, and make it possible for the current to jump straight across without doing any work, it will take the short circuit instead of the long one and you won't have any lights in your house. Now do you see what I mean?

"Darby and Joan are civilized. That is to say, they're insulated. The current's there, but it's long-circuited. The only expression it's got is through the intelligence,—so it lights the house. Absence of common knowledge and common interests only adds to the resistance and makes it burn all the brighter. Naturally Darby and Joan fall victims to the very dangerous illusion that they're intellectual companions. They think they're having wonderful talks. All they are doing, is long-circuiting their sex attraction. Well, marriage gives it a short circuit. Why should the current light the lamps when it can strike straight across? There you are!"

"And poor Joan," said Rose, after a palpable silence, but evenly enough, "who has thought all along that she was attracting a man by her intelligence and her understanding, and all that, wakes up to find that she's been married for her long eyelashes, and her nice voice—and her pretty ankles. That's a little hard on her, don't you think, if she's been taking herself seriously?"

"Nine times in ten," he said, "she's fooling herself. She's taken her own ankles much more seriously than she has her mind. She's capable of real sacrifices for them—for her sex charm, that is. She'll undergo a real discipline for it. Intelligence she regards as a gift. She thinks the witty conversation she's capable of after dinner, on a cocktail and two glasses of champagne, or the bright letters she can write to a friend, are real exercises of her mind—real work. But work isn't done like that. Work's overcoming something that resists; and there's strain in it, and pain and discouragement."

In her cheeks the red flared up brighter. She smiled again—not her own smile—one at any rate that was new to her.

"You don't 'solve an intellectual problem' then;" she quoted, "'by having your hand held, or your eyes kissed?'"

Whereupon he shot a look at her and observed that evidently he wasn't as much of a pioneer as he thought.

She did not rise to this cast, however. "All right;" she said, "admitting that her ankles are serious and her mind isn't, what is Joan going to do about it?"

"It's easier to say what she's not to do," he decided, after hesitating a moment. "Her fatal mistake will be to despise her ankles without disciplining her mind. If she will take either one of them seriously, or both for that matter—it's possible—she'll do very well."

He could, no doubt, have continued on the theme indefinitely, but the table turned the other way just then and Rose took up an alleged conversation with the man at her right which lasted until they left the table and included such topics as indoor golf, woman's suffrage, the new dances, Bernard Shaw, Campanini and the Progressive party; with a perfectly appropriate and final comment on each.

Rose didn't care. She was having a wonderful time—a new kind of wonderful time. No longer gazing, big-eyed like little Cinderella at a pageant some fairy godmother's whim had admitted her to, but consciously gazed upon; she was the show tonight, and she knew it. Her low, finely modulated voice so rich in humor, so varied in color, had tonight an edge on it that carried it beyond those she was immediately speaking to and drew looks that found it hard to get away again. For the first time in her life, with full self-consciousness, she was producing effects, thrilling with the exercise of a power as obedient to her will as electricity to the manipulator of a switchboard.

She was like a person driving an aeroplane, able to move in all three dimensions. Pretty soon, of course, she'd have to come back to earth, where certain monstrously terrifying questions were waiting for her.

Madame Gréville's final apothegm had suggested one of them. Was all she valued in the world just so much fairy gold that would change over night into dry leaves in her treasure chest because she had never earned it—paid the price for it that life relentlessly exacts for all we may be allowed to call ours?

Her tragi-comic scene with Rodney suggested another. What was her value to him? Was she something enormously desirable when he wanted his hand held and his eyes kissed, but an infernal nuisance when serious matters were concerned? A fine and luxurious dissipation, not dangerous unless recklessly indulged in, but to be kept strictly in her place? Before her talk with Randolph she'd have laughed at that.

But did the horrible plausibility of what he had said actually cover the truth? Did she owe that first golden hour with Rodney, his passionate thrilling avowal of his life's philosophy, to nothing deeper in herself than her unconscious power of rousing in him an equally unconscious, primitive sex desire? Was the fine mutuality of understanding she had so proudly boasted to her mother clear illusion? Now that the short circuit had been established, would the lights never burn in the upper stories of their house again? Turned about conversely the question read like this: Was the thing that had, in Randolph himself, aroused his vivid interest in the subject—well, nothing more than the daring cut of her gown, the gleam of her jewels, the whiteness of her skin. . . ?

Those questions were waiting for her to come back to earth; and they wouldn't get tired and go away. But for the present the knowledge that they were there only made the aeroplane ride the more exhilarating.

She was called to the telephone just as she was on the point of starting reluctantly for home, and found Rodney on the wire. He told her that he had got hold of the thing he was looking for, but that there were still hours of work ahead of him while he was fortifying himself with necessary authorities. He wouldn't come home tonight at all, he said. When his work was finished, he'd go to the club and have a Turkish bath and all the sleep he had time for. When he got through in court tomorrow afternoon, he'd come home.

It was all perfectly reasonable—it was to her finely tuned ear just a shade too reasonable. It had been thought out as an excuse. Because it wasn't for the Turkish bath nor the extra hour's sleep that he was staying away from home. It was herself he was staying away from. He wanted his mind to stay cold and taut, and he was afraid to face the temptation of her eyes and her soft white arms. And in the mood of that hour, it pleased her that this should be so—that the ascetic in him should pay her the tribute of fear.

Afterward, of course, she felt like lashing herself for having felt like that and for having replied, in a spirit of pure coquetry, in a voice of studied, cool, indifferent good humor:

"That's a good idea, Roddy. I'm glad you're not coming back. Good night."

V

Rodney Smiled

I t was with a reminiscent smile that Rose sat down before her telephone the next morning and called a number from memory. Less than a year ago, it had been such a thrilling adventure to call the number of that fraternity house down at the university and ask, in what she conceived to be a businesslike way, for Mr. Haines. And then, presently, to hear the voice of the greatest half-back the varsity had boasted of in years, saying in answer to her "Hello, Harry," "Hello, Rose."

It was really less than a year, and yet it was so immensely long ago, judged by anything but the calendar, that the natural way to think of him was as a married man with a family somewhere and faint memories of the days when he was a student and used to flirt with a girl called Rose something—Rose Stanton, that was it!

It was during one of the interminable waking hours of last night that she had thought of the half-back as a person who might be able, and willing, to do her the service she wanted, and she had spent a long while wondering how she could get track of him. Then the logic of the calendar had forced the conviction on her, that he was, in all probability still at the university, dozing through recitations, or lounging about the corridors, in a blue serge suit and a sweater with a C on it, waiting for some other girl to come out of her class-room; and that between the hours of ten-fifteen and eleven, it was altogether likely that she'd find him again, as she had so many times in the past, at his fraternity house, going through the motions of getting up an eleven o'clock recitation. It was absurd enough now to find herself calling the old number and asking again for Mr. Haines. The dreamlike unreality of it grew stronger, when the voice that answered said, "Just a minute," and then bellowed out his old nickname—"Hello, Tiny! Phone!" and, after a wait, she heard his own very deep bass.

"Hello. What is it?"

"Hello, Harry," she said. "This is Rose Aldrich. Do you remember me?—Rose Stanton, you know."

The ensuing silence was so long, that she said "Hello" again to make sure that he was still there.

"Y—yes," he said. "Of—of course I haven't forgotten. I—I only. . . I. . ."

She wondered what he was so embarrassed about, but to save the situation, she interrupted.

"Are you going to be awfully busy this afternoon? Because, if you aren't, there's something you can do for me. You're in the law school this year, aren't you?"

"Yes," he said. "Of course I'm not busy at all."

"It'll take quite a little while," she warned him, "an hour or so, and I don't want to interfere with anything you've got to do."

Again he assured her that he hadn't anything.

"Well, then," she said rather dubiously, because his voice sounded still so constrained and unnatural, "I'll come down in the car and pick you up about half past one. Is that all right?"

"Yes," he said. "Yes, of course. Thank you very much."

Had inclination led Rose to do a little imaginative thinking about the half-back, from his own point of view, she might, without much trouble, have approximated the cause of his embarrassment.

Here is a poor but honest young man, who has devoted himself, heart, brain and good right arm, to the service of a beautiful young fellow student at the university. They must wait for each other, of course, until he can graduate and get admitted to the bar and make a success that will enable him to support her as she deserves to be supported. The girl declines to wait. A much older man—a great, trampling brute of a man, possessed of wealth and fame, and a social altitude positively vertiginous—asks her to marry him. She, woman-weak, yields to the temptation of all the gauds and baubles that go with his name, and marries him. Indeed, few young men at the university ever have as valid an excuse for becoming broken-hearted misogynists as the half-back. He would he faithful, of course, though she was not. And some day, years later, it might he, she would come hack broken-hearted to him, confess the fatal mistake that she had made; seek his protection, perhaps, against the cruelties of the monster she had come to hate. He would forgive her, console her—in a perfectly moral way, of course—and for a while, they would just be friends. Then the wicked husband would conveniently die, and after long years, they could find happiness.

It made a very pretty idea to entertain during the semi-somnolent hours of dull lectures and while he was waiting for the last possible moment to leap out of bed in the morning and make a dash for his first

HENRY KITCHELL WEBSTER

recitation. Written down on paper, the imaginary conversation between them would have filled volumes.

But to be called actually to the telephone—she had telephoned to him a thousand times in the dream—and hear her say, just as in the dream she had said—"This is Rose; do you remember me?" was enough to make even his herculean knees knock together. To be sure her voice wasn't choked with sobs, but you never could tell over the telephone.

What did she want to do? Confront her husband with him, perhaps, this very afternoon, and say, "Here is the man I love?" And what would he do then? He'd have to back her up, of course—and until his next mouth's allowance came in, he had only a dollar and eighty-five cents in the world!

Rose couldn't have filled in all the details, of course, but she might have approximated the final result. Indeed, I think she had done so, unconsciously, by half past one, when her car stopped in front of the fraternity house and, instantaneously, like a cuckoo out of a clock, the half-back appeared. He was portentously solemn, and Rose thought he looked a little pale.

"Get in," she said holding out a hand to him. "I'm going to take you down-town to do an errand for me—well, two errands, really. My, but it's a long time since I've seen you!"

She didn't look tragic, to be sure—not as if there were livid bruises underneath her furs. And nothing about the manner of her greeting suggested that she was on the point of sobbing out a plea to be forgiven. Still, what did she mean by an errand? It might be anything.

"You see," she explained, "I happened to remember that you were going to begin studying law this year, and that you were just the person who wouldn't mind doing what I want."

"Divorce!" thought the half-back with a shudder.

"I want you," she went on, "to tell me just how you begin studying law—what text-books you get, and where you get them. I want you to come along and pick them out for me. You see, I've decided to study it myself."

It was a fact that the half-back was enormously relieved. But it was a brutal derisive fact—an unescapable one. He wasn't heart-broken over the dashing of a suddenly raised hope. He was, in his heart of hearts, saying, "Thank the Lord!"

If he had been pale before, he was red enough now. He felt ridiculous and irritable.

"Your husband knows all that a great deal better than I, of course," he said.

"Yes, of course," Rose was thoughtless enough to admit, "but you see, I don't want him to know." She flushed a little herself. "It's going to be a—surprise for him," she said.

"And, after we've got the books," she went on, "I want you to do something else. He's making an argument in court today, and I want to go and hear him. Only—I'm so ignorant, you see, I don't know how to do it and I didn't want to tell him I was going. So you're to find out where the court room is and how to get me in. Now, tell me all about everything and what's been happening since I went away. I saw you made the all-American last fall, and meant to write you a note about it, but I didn't get a chance. That was great!"

But even at this new angle, the talk didn't run smoothly. Because, precisely as the half-back forgot his terrors and the hopes that had prompted them, and the absurdity of both—precisely as he began to feel, after all, that it was a very superb and grown-up thing to be a familiar friend of a married woman with a limousine and a respectful chauffeur, and wonderful clothes and an air of taking them all for granted—precisely as he made up his mind to this, he became so very mature, and wise and blasé, modeled his manners and his conversation so strictly on John Drew in his attempt to rise to the situation, that the schoolboy topics she suggested froze on his tongue. So that, by the time he had picked out the books for her and seen them stowed away in the car, and then had telephoned Rodney's office to find what court he was appearing before, and finally taken her up to the eighth floor in the Federal Building and left her there, she was, though grateful, distinctly glad to be rid of him.

What heightened this feeling was that just as she caught herself smiling a little, down inside, over his callow absurdity, she reflected that a year ago they had been equals; that, as far as actual intelligence went, he was no doubt her equal today—her superior, perhaps. He'd gone on studying and she hadn't. Except for the long-circuited sex attraction that Doctor Randolph had been talking about last night, he was as capable of being an intellectual companion to her husband as she was. That idea stung the red of resolution into her cheeks. She would study law. She'd study it with all her might!

She was successful in her project of slipping into the rear of the court room without attracting her husband's attention, and for two hours and a half, she listened with mingled feelings, to his argument. A good part of the time she was occupied in fighting off, fiercely, an almost overwhelming drowsiness. The court room was hot of course, the glare from the skylight pressed down her eyelids; she hadn't slept much the night before. And then, there was no use pretending that she could follow her husband's reasoning. Listening to it had something the same effect on her as watching some enormous, complicated, smooth-running mass of machinery. She was conscious of the power of it, though ignorant of what made it go, and of what it was accomplishing.

The three stolid figures behind the high mahogany bench seemed to be following it attentively, though they irritated her bitterly, sometimes, by indulging in whispered conversations. Toward the end, though, as Rodney opened the last phase of his argument, one of them, the youngest—a man with a thick neck and a square head—hunched forward and interrupted him with a question; evidently a penetrating one, for the man sitting across the table from Rodney looked up and grinned, and interjected a remark of his own.

"I simply followed the cases cited in *Aldrich on Quasi Contracts*," he said. "I have a copy of the work here, in case Mr. Aldrich didn't bring one along himself, which I'd be glad to submit to the Court."

Rose gasped. It was his own book they were quoting against him.

"I propose to show," said Rodney, "if the Court please, that an absolutely vital distinction is to be made between the cases cited in the section of *Aldrich on Quasi Contracts*, which my honorable opponent refers to, and the case before the Court."

Then the other judges spoke up. They knew the cases, it appeared, and didn't want to look at the book, but it was clear that they were skeptical about the distinction. For five minutes the formal argument was lost in swift flashing phrases in which everybody took a part. Rodney was defending himself against them all. And Rose, in an agony because she couldn't understand it, was reminded, grotesquely enough, of the Gentleman of France, or some other of the sword-and-cloak heroes of her girlhood, defending the head of the stairway against the simultaneous assault of half a dozen enemies. And then suddenly it was over. The judges settled back again, the argument went on.

At half past four, the oldest judge, who sat in the middle, interrupted again to tell Rodney, with what seemed to Rose brutally bad manners, what time it was.

"If you can finish your argument in fifteen minutes, Mr. Aldrich, we'll hear you out. If it's going to take longer than that, the Court will adjourn till tomorrow morning."

"I don't think I shall want more than fifteen minutes," said Rodney, and he went on again.

And, presently, he just stopped talking and began stacking up his notes. The oldest judge mumbled something, everybody stood up and the three stiff formidable figures filed out by a side door. It was all over.

But nothing had happened!

Rose had been looking forward, you see, to a driving finish; to a dramatic summoning of reserves, a mighty onslaught. And at the end of it, as from the umpire at a ball game, to a decision. She had expected to leave the court room in the blissful knowledge of Rodney's victory or the tragic acceptance of his defeat. In her surprise over the failure of this climax to materialize, she almost neglected to make her escape before he discovered her there.

One practical advantage she had gained out of what was, on the whole, a rather unsatisfactory afternoon. When she had gone home and changed into the sort of frock she thought he'd like and come downstairs in it in answer to his shouted greeting from the lower hall, she didn't say, as otherwise she would have done, "How did it come out, Roddy? Did you win?"

In the light of her newly-acquired knowledge, she could see how a question of that sort would irritate him. Instead of that, she said: "You dear old boy, how dog tired you must be! How do you think it went? Do you think you impressed them? I bet you did."

And not having been rubbed the wrong way by a foolish question, he held her off with both hands for a moment, then hugged her up and told her she was a trump.

"I had a sort of uneasy feeling," he confessed, "that after last night— the way I threw you out of my office, fairly, I'd find you—tragic. I might have known I could count on you. Lord, but it's good to have you like this! Is there anywhere we have got to go? Or can we just stay home?"

He didn't want to flounder through an emotional morass, you see. A firm smooth-bearing surface, that was what, for every-day use, he wanted her to provide him with; lightly given, casual caresses that could be accepted with a smile, pleasantness, a confident security that she wouldn't be "tragic." And on the assumption that she couldn't walk beside him on the main path of his life, it was just and sensible. But it wasn't good enough for Rose.

So the very next morning, she stripped the cover off the first of the books the half-back had picked out for her, and really went to work. She bit down, angrily, the yawns that blinded her eyes with tears; she made desperate efforts to flog her mind into grappling with the endless succession of meaningless pages spread out before her, to find a germ of meaning somewhere in it that would bring the dead verbiage to life. She tried to recall the thrill in Rodney's voice when he had told her, on that wonderful wind-swept afternoon, that the law was the finest profession in the world. Also, he had told her, he'd never been bored with it—it was immoral to be bored. It was a confession of defeat, anyway, she could see that. And she wouldn't—she absolutely would not be defeated.

In a variety of moods which included everything except real hope and confidence, she kept the thing up for weeks—didn't give up indeed, until Fate stepped in, in her ironic way, and took the decision out of her hands. She was very secretive about it; developed an almost morbid fear that Rodney would discover what she was doing and laugh his big laugh at her. She resisted innumerable questions she wanted to propound to him, from a fear that they'd betray her secret.

She even forbore to ask him about the case—it was The Case in her mind—the one she knew about, and as she struggled along with her heavy text-books, and a realization grew in her mind of the countless hours of such struggling on his part which must have lain behind his ability to make that argument that day, the thing accumulated importance to her. How could he, under the suspense of waiting for that decision, concentrate his mind on anything else?

She discovered in the newspaper one day, a column summary of court decisions that had been handed down, and though The Case wasn't in it, she kept, from that day forward, a careful watch—discovered where the legal news was printed, and never overlooked a paragraph. And at last she found it—just the bare statement "Judgment affirmed." Rodney, she knew, had represented the appellant. He was beaten.

For a moment the thing bruised her like a blow. She had never succeeded in entertaining, seriously, the possibility that it could end otherwise than in victory for him. She read it again and made sure. She remembered the names of both parties to the suit, and she knew which side Rodney was on. There couldn't be any mistake about it. And the certainty weighed down her spirits with a leaden depression.

And then, all at once, in the indrawing of a single breath, she saw it differently. Now that it had happened—and she couldn't help its happening—didn't it give her, after all, the very opportunity she wanted? She remembered what he had said the night he had turned her out of his office. He wasn't sick or discouraged. He was in an intellectual quandary that couldn't be solved by having his hand held or his eyes kissed.

She saw now, that that had been just enough. She couldn't help him out of his intellectual quandaries—yet. But under the discouragement and lassitude of defeat, couldn't she help him? She remembered how many times she had gone to him for help like that. In panicky moments when the new world she had been transplanted into seemed terrible to her; in moments when she feared she had made hideous mistakes; and, most notably, during the three or four days of an acute illness of her mother's, when she had been brought face to face with the monstrous, incredible possibility of losing her, how she had clung to him, how his tenderness had soothed and quieted her—how his strength and steady confidence had run through her veins like wine!

He had never come to her like that. She knew now it was a thing she had unconsciously longed for. And tonight she'd have a chance! Oddly enough, it turned out to be the happiest day she'd known in a long while. There was a mounting excitement in her, as the hours passed—a thrilling suspense. Perhaps, after all, it wasn't going to be necessary to grind through all those law-books in order to win the place beside him that she wanted. If she could comfort him—mother him in his defeat and discouragement—hold him fast when his world reeled around him, that would be the basis of a better companionship than mere ability to chop legal logic with him. She could he content with the shallow sparkle of the stream of their life together, if it deepened, now and then, into still pools like this.

She resisted the impulse to call him up on the telephone, and a stronger one to go straight to him at his office. She'd wait until he came home to her. She had been feeling wretched lately—headachy, nervous, sickish;—probably, she thought, from staying in the house too much and bending over her heavy law-books. Perhaps she had strained her eyes. But today these discomforts were forgotten. Every little while she straightened up and stood at an open window drawing in long breaths. He should see her at her best tonight—serene—triumphant. The pallor of her cheeks he had commented on lately, shouldn't be there to trouble him.

For two hours that afternoon, she listened for his latch-key, and when at last she heard it she stole down the stairs. He didn't shout her name from the hall, as he often did. He didn't hear her coming, and she got a look at his face as he stood at the table absently turning over some mail that lay there. He looked tired, she thought.

He saw her when she reached the lower landing, but for just a fraction of a second his gaze left her and went back to the letter he held in his hand, as if to satisfy himself it was of no importance before he tossed it away. Then he came to meet her.

"Oh!" he said. "I thought you were going to be off somewhere with Frederica this afternoon. It's been a great day. I hope you haven't spent the whole of it indoors. You're looking great, anyway. Come here and give me a kiss."

Because she had hesitated, a little perplexed. Did he mean not to tell her—to "spare" her, as he'd have said? The kiss she gave had a different quality from those that ordinarily constituted her greetings, and the arms that went round his neck, didn't give him their customary hug. But they stayed there.

"You poor dear old boy!" she said. And then, "Don't you care, Roddy!"

He returned the caress with interest, before he seemed to realize the different significance of it. Then he pushed her away by the shoulders and held her where he could look into her face.

"What do you mean?" he asked. "Don't care about what?"

It didn't seem like bravado—like an acted out pretense, and yet of course it must be.

"Don't," she said. "Because I know. I've known all day. I read it in the paper this morning."

From puzzled concern, the look in his face took on a deeper intensity. "Tell me what it is," he said very quietly. "I don't know. I didn't read the paper this morning. Is it Harriet?" Harriet was his other sister—married, and not very happily, it was beginning to appear, to an Italian count.

A revulsion—a sort of sick misgiving took the color out of Rose's cheeks.

"It isn't any one," she said. "It's nothing like that. It's—it's that case." Her lips stumbled over the title of it. "It's been decided against you. Didn't you know?"

For a moment his expression was simply the absence of all expression whatever. "Good lord!" he murmured. Then, "But how the dickens did you know anything about it? How did you happen to see it in the paper? How did you know the title of it?"

"I was in the court the day you argued it," she said unevenly. "And when I found they printed those things in the paper, I kept watch. And today. . ."

"Why, you dear child!" he said. And the queer ragged quality of his voice drew her eyes back to his, so that she saw, wonderingly, that they were bright with tears. "And you never said a word, and you've been bothering your dear little head about it all the time. Why, you darling!"

He sat down on the edge of the table, and pulled her up tight into his arms again. She was glad to put her head down—didn't want to look at his face; she knew that there was a smile there along with the tears.

"And you thought I was worrying about it," he persisted, "and that I'd be unhappy because I was beaten?" He patted her shoulder consolingly with a big hand. "But that's all in the day's work, child. I'm beaten somewhere nearly as often as I win. And really, down inside, leaving out a little superficial pleasure, I don't care a damn whether I win or lose. A man couldn't be any good as a lawyer, if he did care, any more than a surgeon could be any good if he did. You've got to keep a cold mind or you can't do your best work. And if you've done your best work, there's nothing to care about. I honestly haven't thought about the thing once from that day to this. Don't you see how it is?"

He couldn't see how it was, that was plain enough. What he very reasonably expected was that after so lucid an explanation, she would turn her wet face up to his, with her old wide smile on it. But that was not what happened at all. Instead, she just went limp in his arms, and the sobs that shook her seemed to be meeting no resistance whatever. It wasn't like her to work herself up in that way over trifles, either; yet, surely a trifle was all this could be called—a laughable mistake he couldn't help loving her for, or a touching demonstration of affection that he couldn't help smiling at. Either way you took it, it was nothing to make a scene about. Where was her sense of humor? That was the thing to do—get her quiet first, and then persuade her to laugh at the whole affair with him.

He was saved from carrying out this program by the fact that Rose, of her own accord, anticipated him. At least she controlled, rather suddenly, her sobs, sat up, wiped her eyes and, after a fashion, smiled. Not at him, though; resolutely away from him, he might almost have thought—as if she didn't want him to see.

"That's right," he said, craning round to make sure that the smile was there. "Have a look at the funny side of it."

She winced at that as from a blow and pulled herself away from him. Then she controlled herself and, in answer to his look of troubled amazement, said:

"It's all right. Only it happens that you're the one who d-doesn't know how awfully funny it really is." Her voice shook, but she got it in hand again. "No, I don't mean anything by that. Here! Give me a kiss and then let me wash my face."

And for the whole evening, and again next morning until he left the house, she managed to keep him in the only half-questioning belief that nothing was the matter.

It was about an hour after that, that her maid came into her bedroom, where she had had her breakfast, and said that Miss Stanton wanted to see her.

VI

The Damascus Road

It argued no real lack of sisterly affection that Rose didn't want to see Portia that morning. Even if there had been no other reason, being found in bed at half past ten in the morning by a sister who inflexibly opened her little shop at half past eight, regardless of bad weather, backaches and other potentially valid excuses, was enough to make one feel apologetic and worthless. Rose could truthfully say that she was feeling wretched. But Portia would sit there, slim and erect, in a little straight-backed chair, and whatever perfunctory commiseration she might manage to express, the look of her fine eyebrows would be skeptical. Justly, too. Rose could never deny that. Not so long as she could remember the innumerable times when she had yielded to her mother's persuasions that she was over-tired and that a morning in bed was just what she needed. Portia, so far as she could remember, had never been the subject of these persuasions.

But this was only the beginning of Rose's troubles today. She was paying the price of yesterday's exaltation and her spirits had sunk down to nowhere. What a fool's paradise yesterday had been with its vision of her big self-sufficient husband coming to her for mothering because he had lost a law-suit! What a piece of mordant irony it was, that she should have found herself, after all her silly hopes, sobbing in his arms, while he comforted her for her bitter disappointment over not being able to comfort him! She had told the truth when she said he was the one, really, who didn't know how funny it was.

Well, and wasn't her other effort just as ridiculous? If ever he found her heap of law-books and learned of the wretched hours she had spent trying to discover what they were all about in the hope of promoting herself to a true intellectual companionship with him, wouldn't he take the discovery in exactly the same way—be touched by the childish futility of it and yet amused at the same time—cuddle her indulgently in his arms and soothe her disappointment;—and then urge her to look at the funny side of it? He must know hundreds of practising lawyers. Were there a dozen out of them all whose minds had the power to stimulate and bring into action the full powers of his own?

Well then, what was the use of trying? If James Randolph was right—and it seemed absurd to question it—she had just one charm for her husband—the charm of sex. To that she owed her hours of simulated companionship with him, his tenderness for her, his willingness to make her pleasures his own. To that she owed the extravagantly pretty clothes he was always urging her to buy—the house he kept her in—the servants he paid to wait on her. Well then, why not make the best of it?

Only, if she went on much longer, feeling sick and faded like this, she'd have nothing left to make the most of, and then where would she be?

Oh, she was getting maudlin, and she knew it! And when she got over feeling so weak and giddy, she'd brace up and be herself again. But for the present, she didn't feel like seeing Portia.

But Rose's shrinking from a talk with Portia that morning was a mild feeling compared with Portia's dread of the impending talk with Rose. Twice she had walked by the perfect doorway of the McCrea house before she entered it; ostensibly to give herself a little more time to think—really, because she shrank from the ordeal that awaited her in there.

Her sister's ménage had been a source of irritation to Portia ever since it was established, though a deeper irritation was her own with herself for allowing it to affect her thus. Rose's whole-hearted plunge into the frivolities of a social season, her outspoken delight in it, her finding in it, apparently, a completely satisfactory solution to the problem of existence, couldn't fail to arouse Portia's ironic smile. This was the sort of vessel her mother had freighted with her hopes! This was the course she steered.

She had fought this feeling with a bitter self-contempt. The trouble with her was, she told herself in icy self-communings, that she envied Rose her happiness, her opportunities, her husband—even her house. Why should all that wonderful furniture have been wasted on Rose, to whom a perfect old Jacobean gate-legged table was nothing but a surface to drop anything on that she wanted out of her hands? Why should a man of Rodney's powerful intelligence waste his time on her frivolous amusements, content, apparently, just to sit and gaze at her, oblivious of any one else who might happen to be about? She knew that she, Portia, out of her disciplined experience of life, and her real eagerness for knowledge of it, was better able to challenge the attention of his mind than Rose. And yet she had never really got it. She remained half invisible to him—some one to be remembered with a start, after an interval of oblivion, and treated considerately—even affectionately, for that matter—as Rose's sister!

They had been seeing each other with reasonable frequency all winter. The Aldriches had Portia and her mother in to a family dinner pretty often, and always came out to Edgewater for a one-o'clock dinner with the Stantons on Sunday. The habit was for Rose to come out early in the car and take them to church, while Rodney walked out later, and turned up in time for dinner.

Mrs. Stanton had taken a great liking to Rodney. His manner toward her had just the blend of deference and breezy unconventionality that pleased her. So, while Portia would worry through the dinner, for fear it wouldn't be cooked well enough, or served well enough, not to present a sorry contrast to the meals her guests were accustomed to, her mother would sit beaming upon the pair with a contentment as unalloyed as if Rose were the acknowledged new leader of the great Cause and her husband her adoring convert, as they had been in her old day-dream.

As far as Rodney went, the dream might have been true, for he showed an unending interest in the Woman Movement—never tired of drawing from his mother-in-law the story of her labors and the exposition of her beliefs. Sometimes he argued with her playfully in order to get her started. More often, and as far as Portia could see, quite seriously, he professed himself in full accord with her views.

After this had been going on for about so long, Rose would yawn and stretch and sit down on the arm of her mother's chair, begin stroking her hair and offering her all manner of quaint unexpected caresses. And then, pretty soon, Rodney's attention to the subject would begin to wander and at last flag altogether and leave him stranded, gazing and unable to do anything but gaze, at the lovely creature—the still miraculous creature, who, when he got her home again, would come and sit on the arm of his chair like that! When this happened, Portia found it hard to stay in the room.

Until Mrs. Stanton's terrifying illness along in January, these meetings constituted the whole of the intercourse between the families. Rose had done her best to carry Portia with her, to some extent at least, into her new life—to introduce her to her new friends and make her, as far as might be, one of them. And in this she was seconded very amiably, by Frederica. But Portia had put down a categorical veto on all these attempts. She hadn't the inclination nor the energy, she said, and her mother needed all the time she could spare away from her business. Once, when Rose pressed the matter, she gave a more genuine reason. Rose's new friends, she said, would regard her introduction to them solely as a bid for business. She didn't want them coming around to her place to buy their wedding presents "in order to help out that poor old maid sister of Rose Aldrich's." She was getting business enough in legitimate ways.

Sometimes she told herself that if Rose had really wanted her, she'd have pressed the matter harder—wouldn't have given up unless she was clutching with real relief at an excuse that let her out of an embarrassment. But at other times she accused herself of having acted in a petty snobbish spirit in declining the chance not only for pleasant new friendships, especially Frederica's, but for a closer association with her sister. Well, the thing was done now, and the question certainly never would rise again.

The reason why it couldn't arise again was what Portia came to tell Rose this morning. She hoped she'd be able to tell it gently— provide Rose with just the facts she'd have to know, and get away without letting any other facts escape, so that afterward she'd have the consolation of being able to say to herself, "That was finely done." All her life, she told herself, she had been doing fine things grudgingly, mutilating them in the doing. If she weren't very careful, that would happen this morning. If she could have known the truth and made her resolution, and confided it to Rose during the first hours of her mother's illness, when the fight for life had drawn them together, it would not have been hard. But with the beginning of convalescence, when Rose, with an easy visit and a few facile caresses, could outweigh in one hour, all of Portia's unremitting tireless service during the other twenty-three, and carry off as a prize the whole of her mother's gratitude and affection, the old envy and irritation had come back threefold.

Rose greeted her with a "Hello, Angel! Why didn't you come right up? Isn't it disgraceful to be lying around in bed like this in the middle of the morning?"

"I don't know," said Portia. "Might as well stay in bed, if you've nothing to do when you get up." She meant it to sound good-humored, but was afraid it didn't. "Anyhow," she added after a straight look into Rose's face, "you look, this morning, as if bed was just where you ought to be. What's the matter with you, child?"

"Nothing," said Rose, "—nothing that you'd call anything at any rate."

Portia smiled ironically. "I'm still the same old dragon, then," she said. And then, with a gesture of impatience, turned away. She hadn't meant to begin like that. Why couldn't she keep her tongue in control!

"I only meant," said Rose very simply, "that you'd say it was nothing, if it was the matter with you. I've seen you, so many times, get up looking perfectly sick and, without any breakfast but a cup of black coffee, put on your old mackintosh and rubbers and start off for the shop, saying you were all right and not to bother, that I knew that was what you'd say now, if you felt the way I do."

"I'm sorry," said Portia. "I might have known that was what you meant. I wonder if you ever want to say ugly things and don't, or if it's just that it never occurs to you to try to hurt anybody. I didn't mean to say that either. I've had a rather worrying sort of week."

"What is it?" said Rose. "Tell me about it. Can I help?"

"No," said Portia. "I've thought it over and it isn't your job." She got up and went to the window where Rose couldn't see her face, and stood looking out. "It's about mother," she concluded.

Rose sat up with a jerk. "About mother!" she echoed. "Has she been ill again this week? And you haven't let me know! It's a shame I haven't been around, but I've been busy"—her smile reflected some of the irony of Portia's—"and rather miserable. Of course I was going this afternoon."

"Yes," said Portia, "I fancied you'd come this afternoon. That's why I wanted to see you alone first."

"Alone!" Rose leaned sharply forward. "Oh, don't stand there where I can't see you! Tell me what it is."

"I'm going to," said Portia. "You see, I wasn't satisfied with old Murray. That soothing bedside manner of his, and his way of encouraging you as if you were a child going to have a tooth pulled, drove me nearly wild. I thought it was possible, either that he didn't understand mother's case, or else that he wouldn't tell me what he suspected. So a week ago today, I got her to go with me to a specialist. He made a very thorough examination, and the next day I went around to see him." Her voice got a little harder and cooler. "Mother'll never be well, Rose. She's got an incurable disease. There's a long name for it that I can't remember. What it means is that her heart is getting flabby—degenerating, he called it. He says we can't do anything except to retard the progress of the disease. It may go fast, or it may go slowly. That attack she had was just a symptom, he said. She'll have others. And by and by, of course, a fatal one."

Still she didn't look around from the window. She knew Rose was crying. She had heard the gasp and choke that followed her first announcement of the news, and since then, irregularly, a muffled sound of sobbing. She wanted to go over and comfort the young stricken thing there on the bed, but she couldn't. She could feel nothing but a dull irresistible anger that Rose should have the easy relief of tears, which had been denied her. Because Portia couldn't cry.

"He said," she went on, "that the first thing to do was to get her away from here. He said that in this climate, living as she has been doing, she'd hardly last six months. But he said that in a bland climate like Southern California, in a bungalow without any stairs in it, if she's carefully watched all the time to prevent excitement or over-exertion, she might live a good many years.

"So that's what we're going to do. I've written the Fletchers to look out a place for us—some quiet little place that won't cost too much, and I've sold out my business. I thought I'd get that done before I talked to you about it. I'll give the house here to the agent to sell or rent, and as soon as we hear from the Fletchers, we'll begin to pack. Within a week, I hope."

Rose said a queer thing then. She cried out incredulously, "And you and mother are going away to California to live! And leave me here all alone!"

"All alone with the whole of your own life," thought Portia, but didn't say it.

"I can't realize it at all," Rose went on after a little silence. "It doesn't seem—possible. Do you believe the specialist is right? They're always making mistakes, aren't they—condemning people like that, when the trouble isn't what they say? Can't we go to some one else and make sure?"

"What's the use?" said Portia. "Suppose we did find a man who said it probably wasn't so serious as that, and that she could probably live all right here? We shouldn't know that he was right—wouldn't dare trust to that. Besides, if I drag mother around to any more of them, she'll know."

Rose looked up sharply. "Doesn't she know?"

"No," said Portia in that hard even voice of hers. "I lied to her of course. I told her the doctor said her condition was very serious, and that the only way to keep from being a hopeless invalid would be to do what he said—go out to California—take an absolute rest for two or three years—no lectures, no writing, no going about.

"You know mother well enough to know what she'd do if she knew the truth about it. She'd say, 'If I can never be well, what's the use of prolonging my life a year, or two, or five; not really living, just crawling around half alive and soaking up somebody else's life at the same time?' She'd say she didn't believe it was so bad as that anyway, but that whether it was or not, she'd go straight along and live as she's always done, and when she died, she'd be dead. Don't you know how it's always pleased her when old people could die—'in harness,' as she says?"

Her voice softened a little as she concluded and the tenseness of her attitude, there at the window, relaxed. The ordeal, or the worst of it, was over; what she had meant to say was said, and what she had meant not to say, if hinted at once or twice, had not caught Rose's ear. She turned for the first time to look at her. Rose was drooping forlornly forward, one arm clasped around her knees, and she was trying to dry her tears on the sleeve of her nightgown. The childlike pathos of the attitude caught Portia like the surge of a wave. She crossed the room and sat down on the edge of the bed. She'd have come still closer and taken the girl in her arms but for the fear of starting her crying again.

"Yes," Rose said. "That's mother. And I guess she's right about it. It must be horrible to be half alive;—to know you're no use and never will be. Only I don't believe it will be that way with her. I believe you told her the truth without knowing it. It's just a feeling, but I'm sure of it. She'll get strong and well again out there. You'll think so, too, when you get rested up a little.—You're so frightfully tired, poor dear. It makes me sick to think what a week you've had. And that you've gone through it all alone;—without ever giving Rodney and me a chance to help. I don't see why you did that, Portia."

"Oh, I saw it was my job," Portia said, in that cool dry way of hers. "It couldn't work out any other way. It had to be done and there was no one else to do it. So what was the use of making a fuss? It was easier, really, without, and—I didn't want any extra difficulties."

"But all the work there must have been!" Rose protested. "Selling your shop, and all. How did you ever manage to do it?"

"That was luck, of course," Portia admitted. "Do you know that Craig woman? You may have met her. She's rather on the fringe of your set, I believe. She's got a good deal of money and nothing to do, and I think she's got a fool notion that it'll be *chic* to go 'into trade.' She came and

HENRY KITCHELL WEBSTER

offered to buy me out a month ago, and of course I wouldn't listen. But just by luck she called me up again the very day I went to talk to the specialist. I asked for twenty-four hours to think it over, and by that time I'd made up my mind. I got a very good price from her, really. She bought the whole thing; lease, stock and good-will."

It wasn't more than a very subconscious impression in the back of Rose's mind, that Portia must be pretty callous and cold to have been able on the very day of the doctor's sentence to look as far ahead as that, and to drive a good bargain on the next—awfully efficient, anyway. "I wish I was more like you," she said.

But she didn't want to be questioned as to just what she meant by it and, aware that Portia had just shot a queer searching look at her, she changed the subject, or thought she did.

"Anyway, I'm glad it worked out so well for you," she went on; "selling the shop so easily, and all. And I believe it'll do you as much good as mother. Getting a rest. . . You do need it. You're worked right down to the bones. And out there where it's warm and bright all the time, and you don't have to get up in the dark any more winter mornings and wade off through the slush to the street-car. . . And a nice little bungalow to live in—just you and mother. . . I—I sort of wish I was going too."

Portia laughed—a ragged, unnatural sounding laugh that brought a look of puzzled inquiry from Rose.

"Why, nothing," Portia explained. "It was just the notion of your leaving Rodney and all you've got here—all the wonderful things you have to do—for what we'll have out there. The idea of your envying me is something worth a small laugh, don't you think?"

Rose's head drooped lower. She buried her face in her hands. "I do envy you," she said. There was a dull muffled passion in her voice. "Why shouldn't I envy you? You're so cold and certain all the time. You make up your mind what you'll do, and you do it. I try to do things and just make myself ridiculous. Oh, I know I've got a motor and a lot of French dresses, and a maid, and I don't have to get up in the morning, because, as you say, I have nothing else to do—and I suppose that might make some people happy."

"You've got a husband," said Portia in a thin brittle voice. "That might count for something, I should think."

"Yes, and what good am I to him?" Rose demanded. "He can't talk to me—not about his work or anything like that. And I can't help him any way. I'm something nice for him to make love to, when he feels like doing it, and I'm a nuisance when I make scenes and get tragic. And that's all. That's—marriage, I guess. You're the lucky one, Portia."

The silence had lasted a good while before Rose noticed that there was any special quality about it—became aware that since the end of her outburst—of which she was ashamed even while she yielded to it, because it represented not what she meant, but what, at the moment, she felt—Portia had not stirred; had sat there as rigidly still as a figure carved in ivory.

Becoming aware of that, she raised her head. Portia wasn't looking at her, but down at her own clenched hands.

"It needed just that, I suppose," she heard her older sister say between almost motionless lips. "I thought it was pretty complete before, but it took that to make it perfect—that you think I'm the lucky one—lucky never to have had a husband, or any one else for that matter, to love me. And lucky now, to have to give up the only substitute I had for that."

"Portia!" Rose cried out, for the mordant alkaline bitterness in her sister's voice and the tragic irony in her face, were almost terrifying. But the outcry might never have been uttered for any effect it had.

"I hoped this wouldn't happen," the words came steadily on, one at a time. "I hoped I could get this over and get away out of your life altogether without letting it happen. But I can't. Perhaps it's just as well—perhaps it may do you some good. But that's not why I'm doing it. I'm doing it for myself. Just for once, I'm going to let go! You won't like it. You're going to get hurt."

Rose drew herself erect and a curious change went over her face, so that you wouldn't have known she'd been crying. She drew in a long breath and said, very steadily, "Tell me. I shan't try to get away."

"A man came to our house one day to collect a bill," Portia went on, quite as if Rose hadn't spoken. "Mother was out, and I was at home. I was seventeen then, getting ready to go to Vassar. Fred was a sophomore at Ann Arbor, and Harvey was going to graduate in June. You were only seven—I suppose you were at school. Anyhow, I was at home, and I let him in, and he made a fuss. Said he'd have us black-listed by other grocers, if it wasn't paid.

"It was the first I ever knew about anything like that. I knew we weren't rich, of course—I never had quite enough pocket money. But the idea of an old unpaid grocery bill made me sick. I talked things over with mother the next day—told her I wasn't going to college—said I was going to get a job. I got her to tell me how things stood, and she did, as well as she could. The boys were getting their college education out of the capital of father's estate, so that the income of it was getting smaller. She had meant that I should do the same. But the income wasn't really big enough to live on as it was.

"Mother could earn money of course, lecturing and writing, but money wasn't one of the things she naturally thought about, and when there was something big and worth while to do, she plunged in and did it whether it was going to pay her anything or not. And there were you coming along, and mother wasn't so very strong even then, and I—well, I saw where I came in.

"I got mother to let me run all the accounts after that, and attend to everything. And I got a job and began paying my way within a week."

"If I had a thing like that to remember," said Rose unsteadily, "I'd never forget to be proud of it so long as I lived!"

"I wish I could be proud of it," said Portia. "But, like everything else I do, I spoiled it. I knew that mother was doing a big fine work worth doing—worth my making a sacrifice for, and I wanted to make the sacrifice. But I couldn't help making a sort of grievance of it, too. In all these years I've always made mother afraid of me—always made her feel that I was, somehow, contemptuous of her work and ideas. That's rather a strong way of putting it, perhaps. But I've seen her trying to hide her enthusiasms from me a little, because of my nasty way of sticking pins in them.

"Oh, of course in a way I was making the enthusiasms possible—I knew that. She never could have gone on as she did if she'd been nagged at all the time for money. Big ideas are always more important to her than small facts, but without some narrow-minded, literal person to look after the facts her ideas wouldn't have had much chance. I grubbed away until I got things straightened out, so that her income was enough to live on—enough for her to live on. I'd pulled her through. But then. . ."

"But then there was me," said Rose.

"I thought I was going to let you go," Portia went on inflexibly. "You'd got to be just the age I was when I went to work, and I said there was no reason why you shouldn't come in for your share. If things had happened a little differently, I'd have told mother how matters stood and you'd have got a job somewhere and gone to work. But things didn't come out that way—at least I couldn't make up my mind to make them—so you went to the university. I paid for that, and I paid for your trousseau, and then I was through."

Rose was trembling, but she didn't flinch. "Wh—what was it," she asked quietly, "what was it that might have been different and wasn't? Was it—was it somebody you wanted to marry—that you gave up so I could have my chance?"

Portia's hard little laugh cut like a knife. "I ought to believe that," she said. "I've told myself so enough times. But it's not true. I wonder why you should have thought of that—why it occurred to you that a cold-blooded fish like me should want to marry?"

Rose didn't try to answer. She waited.

"You have always thought me cold," Portia said. "So has mother. I'm not, really. I'm—the other way. I don't believe there ever was a girl that wanted love and marriage more than I. But I didn't attract anybody. I was working pretty hard, of course, and that left me too tired to go out and play—left me a little cross and acid most of the time. But I don't believe that was the whole reason. It wouldn't have worked out that way with you. But nobody ever saw me at all. The men I was introduced to forgot me—were polite to me—got away as soon as they could. They were always craning around for a look at somebody else. The few men—the two or three who weren't like that, weren't good enough. But a man did want me to marry him at last, and for a while I thought I would. Just—just for the sake of marrying somebody. He wasn't much, but he was some one. But I knew I'd come to hate him for not being some one else and I couldn't make up my mind to it. So I took you on instead.

"I stopped hoping, you see, and tried to forget all about it—tried to crowd it out of my life. I said I'd make my work a substitute for it. And, in a way, I succeeded. The work opened up and got more interesting as it got bigger. It wasn't just selling four-dollar candlesticks and crickets and blue glass flower-holders. I was beginning to get real jobs to do—big jobs for big people, and it was exciting. That made it easier to forget. I was beginning to think that some day I'd earn my way into the open big sort of life that your new friends have had for nothing.

"And then, a week ago, there came the doctor and cut off that chance. Oh, there's no way out, I know that! That's the way the pattern was cut, I suppose, in the beginning. I've always suspected the cosmic Dressmaker of having a sense of humor. Now I know it. I'm the lucky one who isn't going to have to wade through the slush any more. I'm to go out to southern California and live in a nice little bungalow and be a nurse for five or ten years, and then I'm going to be left alone in genteel poverty, without an interest in the world, and too tired to make any. And I'll probably live to eighty.

"And yet,"—she leaned suddenly forward, and the passion that had been suppressed in her voice till now, leaped up into flame—"and yet, can you tell me what I could have done differently? I've lived the kind of life they preach about—a life of noble sacrifice. It hasn't ennobled me. It's made me petty—mean—sour. It's withered me up. Look at the difference between us! Look at you with your big free spaciousness— your power of loving and attracting love! Why, you even love me, now, in spite of all I've said this morning. I've envied you that—I've almost hated you for it.

"No, that's a lie. I've wanted to. The only thing I could ever hate you for, would be for failing. You've got to make good! You've had my share as well as yours—you're living my life as well as yours. I'm the branch they cut off so that you could grow. If you give up and let the big thing slip out of your hands the way you were talking this morning, because you're too weak to hold it and haven't pluck enough to fight for it. . ."

"Look at me!" said Rose. The words rang like a command on a battle-field.

Portia looked. Rose's blue eyes were blazing. "I won't do that," she said very quietly. "I promise you that." Then the hard determination in her face changed to something softer, and as if Portia's resistance counted no more than that of a child, she pulled her sister up in her arms and held her tight. And so at last Portia got the relief of tears.

VII

How the Pattern Was Cut

Through the two weeks that intervened before Portia and her mother left for the West, Rose disregarded the physical wretchedness—which went on getting worse instead of better—and dismissed her psychical worries until she should have time to attend to them. She helped Portia pack, she presented a steady cheerful radiance of optimism to her mother, that never faltered until the last farewells were said.

Just how she'd take up the fight again for the great thing Portia had adjured her not to miss, she didn't know. She supposed she'd go back to her law-books—at any rate until she could work out something better.

But the pattern, it seemed, was cut differently. She went to the doctor's office the day after Portia took her mother away, and discovered the cause of her physical wretchedness. She was pregnant.

VIII

A Birthday

Rodney heard young Craig, who deviled up law for him, saying good night to the stenographer; glanced at his watch and opened the door to his outer office.

"You may go home, Miss Beach," he said. "I'm staying on for a while but I shan't want you." Then, to the office boy: "You, too, Albert."

He waited till he heard them go, then went out and disconnected his own desk telephone, which the office boy, on going home, always left plugged through; went back into his inner office again and shut the door after him.

There was more than enough pressing work on his desk to fill the clear hour that remained to him before he had to start for home. But he didn't mean to do it. He didn't mean to do anything except drink down thirstily the sixty minutes of pure solitude that were before him; to let his mind run free from the clutch of circumstance. That hour had become a habit with him lately, like—he smiled at the comparison—like taking a drug. When something happened that forced him to forego it, he felt cheated—irrationally irritable. He was furtive about it, too. He never corrected Rose's assumption that the thing which kept him late at the office so much of the time nowadays was a press of work. He even concealed the fact that he pulled his telephone plug, by sticking it back again every night just before he left.

He tried to laugh that guilty feeling out of existence. But he couldn't. He knew too well whence it sprang. He knew whom he was stealing that hour from. It wasn't the world in general he intrenched himself against. It was his wife. The real purpose of that sixty minutes was to enable him to stop thinking and feeling about her.

It was not that she had faded for him—become less the poignant, vivid, irresistible thing he had first fallen in love with. Rather the contrary. The simple rapture of desire that had characterized the period of their engagement and the first months of their marriage, had lost something—not so much, either—of its tension. But it had broadened—deepened into something more compelling, more pervasive—more, in his present mood, formidable.

She hadn't seemed quite well, lately, nor altogether happy, and he had not been able to find out why. He had attributed it at first to the shock occasioned by her mother's illness and her departure with Portia to California, but this explanation seemed not to cover the ground. Why couldn't she have talked freely with him about that? Inquiries about her health, attempts—clumsily executed, no doubt—to treat her with special tenderness and guard her against overexertion, only irritated her, drove her to the very edge of her self-control—or over it. She was all right, she always said. He couldn't force confidences from her of course. But her pale face and eyes wide with a trouble in them he could not fathom stirred something deeper in him than the former glow and glory had ever reached.

And there was a new thing that gripped him in a positively terrifying way—a realization of his importance to her. The after-effect of her invasion of his office the night of the Randolphs' dinner and of his learning of the tremulous interest with which she had afterward followed the case he was then working on, had been very different from his first irritation and his first amusement.

He had discovered, too, one day—a fortnight or so ago, in the course of a rummage after some article he had mislaid, a heap of law-books that weren't his. He had guessed the explanation of them, but had said nothing to Rose about it—had found it curiously impossible to say anything. If only she had taken up something of her own! It seemed as essentially a law of her being to attempt to absorb herself in him, as it was a law of his to resist that absorption of himself in her.

But resistance was difficult. The tendency was, after his perfectly solid, recognizable duties had been given their places in the cubic content of his day, that Rose should fill up the rest. It was as if you had a bucket half full of irregularly shaped stones and filled it up with water. And yet there was a man in him who was neither the hard-working, successful advocate, nor Rose's husband—a man whose existence Rose didn't seem to suspect. (Was there then in her no woman that corresponded to him?) That man had to fight now for a chance to breathe.

He got a pipe out of a drawer in his desk, loaded and lighted it, stretched his arms, and sat down in his desk chair. In the middle of his blotter was a stack of papers his stenographer had laid there just before she went out. On top of the heap was a memorandum in her handwriting, and mechanically he read it.

"Please ask Mrs. Aldrich about this bill," it read. "The work done seems to be the same that was paid for last month."

The rest of the month's bills lay beneath, all neatly scheduled and totaled; and the total came to more than three thousand dollars. He damned them cordially and moved them over to one side.

But the mood of quiet contentment he had, for just a moment, captured, had given place to angry exasperation. He felt like a bull out in a ring tormented by the glare and the clamor and the flutter of little red flags.

There was nothing ruinous about his way of living. Including his inherited income with what he could earn, working the way he had been working lately, he could meet an expenditure of thirty-six thousand dollars a year well enough. It meant thinking about his fees of course, seeing to it that the work he undertook was profitable as well as interesting. Only, declared the man who was not Rose's husband, it was senseless—suffocating! Rodney tried, with an athletic sweep of his will, to crowd that train of thought out of his mind as, with his hand, he had swept the papers that gave rise to it.

He leaned his elbows on the cleared blotter and propped up his chin on his fists. The thing exactly in front of his eyes was his desk calendar. There was something familiar about the date—some subconscious association that couldn't quite rise to the surface. Was there something he had to do today, that he'd forgotten? No, Miss Beach would have reminded him of anything except a social engagement. And he distinctly remembered that Rose had said this morning that the evening was clear. And yet, surely. . . Then, with a grunt of relief and amusement, he got it. It was his birthday! Another mile-stone.

Where had he been, what had he been doing a year ago today? It would be interesting if he could manage to remember.

A year ago—why, good lord! That was the day it had all begun. He'd sold the old house that day and then had started to walk over to Frederica's for dinner, and got caught in the rain and taken a street-car. He had heard a vibrant young voice say, "Don't dare touch me like that," and, turning, had seen the blazing glorious creature who held the conductor pinned by both wrists. That had been Rose—his Rose; whom he was spending these sixty minutes out of the twenty-four hours trying to forget about!

And that was only a year ago. It was curiously hard to realize. Their identities had shifted so strangely—his own as well as hers. Well, and in what direction had, he changed? How did he compare—the man who sat here now, with the man who had unhesitatingly jumped off the car to follow a new adventure—the man who had turned up water-logged at Frederica's dinner and made hay of her plan to marry him off to Hermione Woodruff?

They had had a great old talk that night, Frederica and he, he remembered. He remembered what he had talked about, and he smiled grimly over the recollection—space and leisure; the defective intelligence that trapped men into cluttering their lives with useless junk; so many things to have and to do that they couldn't turn around without breaking something. Had he been a fool then, or was he a fool now? Both, perhaps. But how old Frederica must have grinned over the naiveté of him. Which of the two of him in her candid opinion would be the better man?

He believed he could answer that question. Oh, he was succeeding all right—increasing his practise, making money, getting cautious—prudent; he didn't bolt the track any more. And the quality of his work was good, he couldn't quarrel with that. Only, the old big free dreams that had glorified it, were gone. He was in harness, drawing a cart; following a bundle of hay.

He sprang impatiently to his feet, thrust back his chair so violently as he did so that it tipped over with a crash. The one really footling, futile, fool thing to do, was what he was doing now—lamenting his old way of life and making no effort to recapture it! Let him either accept the situation, make up his mind to it and stop complaining, or else offer it some effective resistance—sweep the flummery out of his life—clear decks for action.

Well, and that was the most asinine consideration of all. Because of course he couldn't do one thing or the other. As long as the man who wasn't Rose's husband remained alive in him, he'd protest—struggle—clamor for his old freedom. And yet, as long as the million tiny cords that bound hum, Gulliver-like, went back to Rose, talk of breaking them was sophomoric foolishness. He'd better go home!

The building was pretty well deserted by now, and against the silence he heard the buzzer in his telephone switchboard proclaiming insistently that some one was trying to get him on the telephone. His hour of recollection hadn't been a success, but the invasion of it irritated him none the less. He thought at first he wouldn't answer. He didn't care who was on the wire. He didn't want to talk to anybody. But no one can resist the mechanical bell-ringers they use in exchanges nowadays—the even-spaced ring and wait, ring and wait, so manifestly incapable of discouragement. At the end of forty-five seconds, he snatched open his door, punched the jack into its socket, caught up the head-piece, and bellowed, "Hello!" into the dangling transmitter.

And then the look of annoyance in his face changed to one of incredulous pleasure. "Good God!" he said. "Is that you, Barry Lake? Are you here in Chicago? And Jane, too? How long you going to be here? . . . Lord, but that's immense!"

And five minutes later he was calling Rose on the wire. "Rose, listen to this! Barry Lake and his wife are here. He just called up. They got in from New York at five o'clock, and I've asked them out to dinner. Barry Lake and Jane! What's the matter? Can't you hear me? . . . Why, they're about the best friends I've got. The magazine writer, you know, and his wife. And they're coming out to dinner—coming right out. I told them not to dress. I'll come straight home myself—get there before they do, I guess. . . Why, Rose, what's the matter? Aren't you well? Look here! If you're below par, and don't feel like having them come, I can call it off and go over to the hotel and dine with them. . . You'd rather we came out to the house? You're sure? Because they won't mind a bit. I can take them to a restaurant or anywhere. . . All right, if you're sure it won't be too much for you. I'll be home in fifteen minutes. Lord, but it was good to hear old Barry's voice again! I haven't seen him for over a year. You're sure you'd rather? . . . All right. Good-by."

But he sat there frowning in a puzzled sort of way for half a minute after he'd pulled the plug. Rose's voice had certainly sounded queer. He was sure she hadn't planned anything else for tonight. He distinctly remembered her saying just before he left for the office that they'd have the evening to themselves. And it was incredible that she minded his bringing home two old friends like the Lakes on the spur of the moment, to take pot-luck. Oh, well, you couldn't tell about people's voices over the telephone. There must have been something funny about the connection.

An opportune taxi just passing the entrance to his office building as he came out, enabled him to better the fifteen minutes he'd allowed for getting home. But in spite of this he found Rose rather splendidly gowned for her expected guests.

"Good gracious!" he cried excitedly. "What did you do that for? I thought I told you over the phone the Lakes weren't going to dress."

"I was—dressed like this when you telephoned," Rose said. "And I was afraid there wouldn't be time to change into anything else."

"We weren't going anywhere, were we?" he asked. "There's nothing I've forgotten?"

"No," she said, "we weren't going anywhere."

"And you dressed like that just for a—treat for me?"

She nodded. "Just for you," she said. "Roddy, who are the Lakes? Oh, I know his articles, I think! But where were they friends of yours, and when?"

"Why, for years, until they moved to New York. They used to live here. I know I must have told you about them. I was always having dinner with them—either out in Rogers Park, where they lived, or at queer, terrible little restaurants down-town. They were always game to try anything, once. He's the longest, leanest, angularest, absent-mindedest chap in the world. And just about the best. And his wife fits all his angles. She's a good chap, too. That's the way you have to think of her. They're a great pair. She writes, too. Oh, you're sure to like them! They're going to be out here for months, he says. He's going to specialize in women, and he's come back here where they've got the vote and all, to make headquarters. Lord, but it's great! I haven't had a real talk with anybody since he went away, over a year ago!"

Then, at the sound of the bell, he cried out, "There they are!" and dashed down into the hall ahead of the parlor maid, as eagerly as a schoolboy anticipating a birthday present.

Rose followed more slowly, and by the time she had reached the landing she found him slapping Barry on the back and shaking both hands with Jane, and trying to help both of them out of their wraps at once.

The last thing she could have thought of just then, was of making, for herself, an effective entrance on the scene. But it worked out rather that way. The three of them, Rodney and the Lakes, at the foot of the stairs, in the clothes they had been working and traveling in all day, looked up simultaneously and saw Rose, gowned for a treat for Rodney, on the first landing; a wonderful rose-colored Boucher tapestry (guaranteed authentic by Bertie Willis) on the wall behind her for a background, and the carved Gothic newel-post bringing out the whiteness of the hand that rested upon it. The picture would have won a moment's silence from anybody. And Barry and Jane simply gazed at her wide-eyed.

Rodney was the first to speak. "It's really the Lakes, Rose. I couldn't quite believe it till I saw them. And the lady on the landing," he went on, turning to his guests, "is really my wife. It's all a little incredible, isn't it?"

When the greetings were over and they were on the way up-stairs again, he said: "I told Rose we weren't going to dress, but she explained she didn't put on this coronation robe for you, but for a treat for me before I telephoned, and hadn't time to change back."

And when Jane cried out, as they entered the drawing room, "Good heavens, Rodney, what a house!" he answered: "It isn't ours, thank God! We rented it for a year in a sort of honeymoon delirium, I guess. We don't live up to it, of course. Nobody could, but the woman who built it. But we do our damnedest."

The gaiety in his voice clouded a little as he said it, and his grin, for a moment, had a rueful twist. But for a moment only. Then his untempered delight in the possession of his old friends took him again and, with the exception of one or two equally momentary cloud-shadows, lasted all evening.

They talked—heavens how they talked! It was like the breaking up of a log-jam. The two men would rush along, side by side, in perfect agreement for a while, catching each other's half expressed ideas, and hurling them forward, and then suddenly they'd meet, head on, in collision over some fundamental difference of opinion, amid a prismatic spray of epigram. Jane kept up a sort of obbligato to the show, inserting provocative little witticisms here and there, sometimes as Rodney's ally, sometimes as her husband's, and luring them, when she could, into the quiet backwaters of metaphysics, where she was more than a match for the two of them. Jane could juggle Plato, Bergson and William James, with one hand tied behind her. But when she incautiously ventured out of this domain, as occasionally she did—when, for example, she confessed herself in favor of a censorship of the drama, she was instantly demolished.

"The state's got no business with morals," said Barry.

"That's the real cause of most of our municipal corruption," said Rodney. "A city administration, for instance, is corrupt exactly in ratio to its attempt to be moral. The more moral issues you import into politics—gambling, prostitution, Sunday closing, censored movies, and the rest—the more corrupt and helpless and inefficient your government will be." And, between them, for the next half-hour, they kept on demonstrating it until the roar of their heavy artillery fairly drove Jane from her trenches.

But all this was preliminary to the main topic of the evening, which got launched when Rodney seized the advantage of a pause to say:

"A series of articles on women, eh! What are you going to do to them?"

With that the topic of feminism was on the carpet and it was never thereafter abandoned. "Utopia to Brass Tacks," was the slogan Barry's chief had provided him with, he said. We were about the end of the heroic age of the movement, the age of myths and saints and prophecies. A transition was about due to smaller, more immediate things. The quality of the leaders would probably change. The heroines of the last three or four decades, women like Naomi Rutledge Stanton, to take a fine type of them.

"She's my mother," said Rose.

Barry Lake's aplomb was equal to most situations, but it failed him here; for a moment he could only stare. The contrast between the picture in his mind's eye, of the plain, square-toed, high-principled and rather pathetic champion of the Cause—pathetic in the light of what she hoped from it—facing indifference and ridicule with the calm smile of one who has climbed her mountain and looked into the promised land,—between that and the lovely, sensitive, sensuous creature he was staring at, was enough to stagger anybody. He got himself together in a moment, said very simply and gravely how much he admired her and how high a value, he believed, the future would put on her work; then he picked up his sentence where Rose had broken it.

The heroines and the prophets were going to be replaced, he believed, by leaders much more practical and less scrupulous, and the movement would follow the leaders. As far as politics went, he not only looked for no millennium, but for a reaction in the other direction. There'd be more open graft, he thought.

Rose asked him if he meant that he thought women were less honest than men.

"It isn't a lack of old-fashioned honesty that makes a man a grafter," he said. "It's seeing the duties and privileges of a public office in a private and personal way, instead of in a public, impersonal one; being kind to old friends who need a helping hand, and grateful to people who've held out helping hands to you. Well, and women have been trained for hundreds of years to see things in that private and personal way, and to exalt the private and personal virtues. Just as they've been trained to stick to rule of thumb methods that more or less work, rather than to try experiments. So, on the whole, I think their getting the vote will mean that politics will be crookeder and more reactionary than they've been in a good many years. All the same I'm for it, because it's a part of democracy, and I'm for democracy all the way. Not because you get good government out of it; you don't. You get as good as you deserve, and in the long run I think a society that has to deserve as good a government as it gets, grows stronger and healthier than one that gets a better government than it deserves."

"That old tory radical over there," said Jane, with a nod at Rodney, "has been grinning away for half an hour without saying a word. I'd like to know what you think about it."

"'Tory radical'?" questioned Rose.

"That's what Barry calls him," Jane explained. "He's so conservative about the law that he calls Blackstone an upstart and a faker, but the things he'd do, when it comes, down to cases—on good old common law principles, of course, would make the average Progressive's hair curl. Why, when people were getting excited over Roosevelt's recall of judicial decisions—remember?—Rodney was for abolishing the Bill of Rights altogether."

"What's the Bill of Rights?" asked Rose.

Jane headed Rodney off. "Oh, life, liberty and property without due process of law," she said. "Neither of these men has any opinion of rights. The only natural inalienable right you've got, they say, is to take what you can get and keep it until somebody stronger than you, that you can't run away from, catches you. What you call your individual rights are just what society has made and doesn't for the moment need, to keep itself going. If it does need them, it takes them back. Only, of course, it has got to keep itself going. If it doesn't, people get up and kick it to bits and start again." She turned to Rodney. "But what do you think about it, really? What Barry's been talking about, I mean. Are you for it?"

"For what?" Rodney wanted to know.

"For what women want," said Jane. "Economic independence, equality, easy divorce—all the new stuff."

"I'm not against it," Rodney said, "any more than I'm against tomorrow being Tuesday. It's going to be Tuesday whether I like it or not. But that conviction keeps me from crusading for it very hard.

What I'm curious about is how it's going to work. When they get what they want, do you suppose they're going to want what they get?"

"I knew there was something deadly about your grin," said Jane. "What are you so cantankerous about?"

"Why, the thing," said Rodney, "that sours my naturally sweet disposition is this economic independence. I've been hearing it at dinner tables all winter. When I hear a woman with five hundred dollars' worth of clothes on—well, no, not on her back—and anything you like in jewelry, talking about economic independence as if it were something nice—jam on the pantry shelf that we men were too greedy to let them have a share of—I have to put on the brakes in order to stay on the rails.

"We men have to fight for economic independence from the time we're twenty, more or less, till the time we die. It's a sentence to hard labor for life; that's what economic independence is. How does that woman think she'd set about it, to make her professional services worth a hundred dollars a day—or fifty, or ten? What's she got that has a market value? What is there that she can capitalize? She's got her physical charm, of course, and there are various professions besides the oldest one, where she can make it pay. Well, and what else?"

"She can bear children," said Jane. "She ought to be paid well for that."

"You're only paid well," Rodney replied, "for something you can do exceptionally well, or for something that few people can do at all. As long as the vast majority of women can bear children, the only women who could get well paid for it would be those exceptionally qualified, or exceptionally proficient. This is economics, now we're talking. Other considerations are left out. No, I tell you. Economic independence, if she really got it—the kind of woman I've been talking about—would make her very, very sick."

"She'd get over being sick though, wouldn't she," said Rose, "after a while? And then, don't you think she'd be glad?"

Rodney laughed. "The sort of woman I've been talking about," he said, "would feel, when all was said, that she'd got a gold brick."

Rose poured his coffee with a steady hand. They were in the library by now.

"If that's so," she said, "then the kind of woman you've been talking about has already got a profession—the one you were just speaking of as—as the oldest. As Doctor Randolph says, she's cashed in on her ankles. But maybe you're mistaken in thinking she wouldn't choose something else if she had a chance. Maybe she wouldn't have done it, except because her husband wanted her to and she was in love with him and tried to please. You can't always tell."

It was almost her first contribution to the talk that evening. She had asked a few questions and said the things a hostess has to say. The other three were manifestly taken by surprise—Rodney as well as his guests.

But surprise was not the only effect she produced. Her husband had never seen her look just like that before (remember, he had not been a guest at the Randolphs' dinner on the night he had turned her out of his office), the flash in her eyes, the splash of bright color in her cheeks.

Barry saved him the necessity of trying to answer, by taking up the cudgels himself. Rodney didn't feel like answering, nor, for the moment, like listening to Barry. His interest in the discussion was eclipsed for the moment, by the thrill and wonder of his wife's beauty.

He walked round behind her chair, on the pretext of getting his coffee cup, and rested his hand, for an instant, on her bare shoulder. He was puzzled at the absence of response to the caress. For there was none, unless you could call it a response that she sat as still as ivory until he took his hand away. And looking into her face, he thought she had gone pale. Evidently though, it was nothing. Her color came back in a moment, and for the next half-hour she matched wits with Barry Lake very prettily.

When Jane declared that they must go, her husband protested.

"I haven't managed yet to get a word out of Rodney about any of his things. He dodged when I asked him how his Criminal Procedure Reform Society was getting on, and he changed the subject when I wanted to know about his model Expert Testimony Act." He turned on Rodney. "But there's one thing you're not going to get out of. I want to know how far you've come along with your book on Actual Government. It was a great start you had on that, and a bully plan. I shan't let you off any details. I want the whole thing. Now."

"I've had my fling," said Rodney, with a sort of embarrassed good humor. "And I don't say I shall never have another. But just now, there are no more intellectual wild-oats for me. What I sow, I sow in a field and in a furrow. And I take good care to be on hand to gather the crop. Model Acts and Reform of Procedure! Have you forgotten you're talking to a married man?"

On learning their determination to walk down-town, he said he'd go with them part of the way. Would Rose go, too? But she thought not.

"Well, I can't pretend to think you need it," he admitted. Then, turning to the Lakes: "You people must spend a lot of evenings with us like this. You've done Rose a world of good. I haven't seen her look so well in a month of Sundays."

IX

A DEFEAT

The gown that Rodney had spoken of apologetically to the Lakes as a coronation robe, was put away; the maid was sent to bed. Rose, huddled into a big quilted bath-robe, and in spite of the comfortable warmth of the room, feeling cold clear in to the bones—cold and tremulous, and sure that when she tried to talk her teeth would chatter—sat waiting for Rodney to come back from seeing the Lakes part way home.

It was over an hour since they had gone, but she was in no hurry for his return. She wanted time for getting things straight before he came—for letting the welter subside and getting the two or three essentials clear in her mind. She hadn't cried a tear.

The old Rose would have cried—the Rose of a month ago, before that devastating, blinding scene with Portia, and what had happened since. She even managed to smile a little satirically, now, over the way that child would have taken it. Here it was their first anniversary of the day—the great day in their two lives—their birthday, as well as his! And he'd forgotten it! He had remained oblivious that morning, in spite of all the little evocative references she had made. She hadn't let herself be hurt about that—not much, anyway; had managed to smile affectionately over his masculine obtuseness, as if it had meant no more to her than it would have, say, to Frederica. She had impressed him strongly, though—or tried to—with the idea that the evening was to be kept clear just for their two selves. And then she had arranged a feast—a homely little feast that was to culminate in a cake with a hedge of little candles around the edge for his birthday, and a single red one in the center, for theirs.

Well, and that was only part of it. She had planned, when the cake should have come in, all lighted up, and the servants had gone away and the other lights had been put out,—she had planned to tell him her great news. She hadn't told him yet, though it was over a fortnight since her visit to the doctor.

She had no reasoned explanation of her postponement of it. The instinct that led her to keep it wholly to herself, was probably one of the reflections of that morning with Portia. She was still in a penitential mood when she went to the doctor—a mood which the contemplation of Portia's frustrated life and her own undeservedly happy one, had bitten deep into her soul. It was a mood that nothing but pain could satisfy. The only relief she could get during that fortnight of packing and leave-taking, came in flogging herself to do hard things—things that hurt, physically and literally, I mean; that made her back ache and cramped the muscles of her arms. Her spiritual aches were too contemptible to pay any attention to.

Conversely, in that mood, the thing she couldn't endure, that made her want to scream, was precisely what, all her life, she had taken for granted; tenderness, concern, the smoothing away of little difficulties for which the people about her had always sacrificed themselves. That mood made it hard to go to the doctor. But, after she had fainted dead away twice in one morning, a saving remnant of common sense—the reflection that if there were anything organically wrong with her, it would be a poor trick to play on Rodney, not to take remedial measures as soon as possible—dictated the action.

When the doctor told her what had happened, she was a little bewildered. She hadn't, in her mind, any prepared background for the news. She and Rodney had decided at the beginning not to have any children for the first year or two—in view of Rose's extreme youth, the postponement seemed sensible—and the decision once made, neither of them had thought much more about it.

Rodney's vigorously objective mind had always been so fully occupied with things as they were that it found little leisure for speculation on things as they might be. The day's work was always so vividly absorbing to him that day-dreams never got a chance. His sex impulses had always been crowded down to the smallest possible compass, not because he was a Puritan, but because he was, spiritually and mentally, an athlete. He had never thought of marriage as a serious possibility, Frederica's efforts to the contrary notwithstanding, until, in a moment of bewilderment, he found himself head over ears in love with Rose Stanton. That this emotion had been able to fight its way into the fortress of his life spoke volumes for the power and the vitality of it. Once it got inside, it formed a part of the garrison of the fort. And, just as the contemplation of marriage had had to wait until there was a Rose Stanton to make it concrete and irresistible, so the contemplation of fatherhood would have to wait for a concrete fact to drive it home.

With certain important differences, Rose was a good deal like him. She had never had time to dream much. The pretending games of childhood—playing with dolls, playing house—had never attracted her away from more vigorous and athletic enterprises. A superb physique gave her an outlet for her emotional energy, so that she satisfied her wants pretty much as she became aware of them. And, conversely, she remained unaware of possibilities she had not, as yet, the means to realize.

They were both rather abnormally normal about this. Persons of robust emotions seldom think very much about them. The temperament that cultivates its emotional soil assiduously, warms it, waters it and watches anxiously for the first sprouts, gets a rather anemic growth for its pains. Which of these facts is cause and which effect, one need not pretend to say: whether it is a lack of vitality in the seed that prompts the instinct of cultivation, or whether it is the cultivation that prevents a sturdy growth. But, feeble as the results of cultivation may be, they produce at least the apparent advantage of running true to form. The thing that sprouts in cultivated soil will be what was planted there—will be, at all events, appropriate.

But in Rose's penitential mood, and in the absence of a prepared background, it was the processes of her pregnancy rather than the issue of it, that got into the foreground of her mind. She was in for an experience now that no one could call trivial. She had months of misery ahead of her, she assumed, reasoning from the one she had just gone through with, surmounted by hours of agony and peril that even Portia wouldn't deny the authenticity of.

Well, she was glad of it; glad she was going to be hurt. She could get back some of her self-respect, she thought, by enduring it all, first the wretchedness, then the pain, with a Spartan fortitude. There would he a sort of savage satisfaction in marching through all her miseries with her head up.

She couldn't do that if Rodney knew. He wouldn't let her. He'd want to care for her, comfort her, pack her in cotton-wool. And there was a terrible yearning down in her heart, to let him. For just that reason, he mustn't be told.

But, as the sharp edges of this mood wore off, she saw a little more justly. Already he suspected something. She caught, now and again, a puzzled, worried, almost frightened look in his face. It was a poor penance that others had to share. So, at the end of her feast tonight, when the candles were lighted and the servants gone away, she'd tell him. And, oh, what a comfort it would be to have him know!

That was the moment she was waiting for when he telephoned that he was bringing the Lakes out for dinner. The old Rose might well have cried.

But now, as she sat trembling in front of her little boudoir fire, the door open behind her so that she'd surely hear him when he came in, the disappointment and the hurt that had clutched at her throat when she turned from the telephone, were wholly forgotten. As I said, she hadn't shed a tear.

The situation she was confronted with now was beyond tears. Portia's stinging words went over and over through her mind. "If you let the big thing slip out of your hands because you haven't the pluck to fight. . ." and her own, "I promise I won't do that." It would mean a fight. She must keep her head.

She gave a last panicky shiver when she heard his latch-key, then pulled herself together.

"Come in here, Roddy," she called, as he reached the head of the stairs. "I want to talk about something."

He had hoped, evidently, to find her abed and fast asleep. His cautious footfalls on the stairs made clear his intention not to waken her.

"Oh, I'm sorry," he said, pausing in the doorway to her dressing-room, but not coming in. "I didn't know you meant to sit up for me. If I'd known you were waiting, I'd have come back sooner. But we got to talking and we were at the hotel before we knew it, and it was so long since I'd seen them. . ."

"I haven't minded," she told him. "I've been glad of a chance to think. But now. . . Oh, please come in and shut the door!"

He did come in, but with manifest reluctance, and he stayed near the door in an attitude of arrested departure.

"It's pretty late," he protested with a nonchalance that rang a little flat. "You must be awfully tired. Hadn't we better put off our pow-wow?"

She understood well enough. The look in her face, some uncontrolled inflection in the voice she had meant to keep so even, had given her away. He suspected she was going to be "tragic." If he didn't look out, there'd be a "scene."

"We can't put it off," she said. "I let you have your talk out with the Lakes, but you'll have to talk with me now."

"We spent most of the time talking about you, anyway," he said pleasantly. "They're both mad about you. Barry says you've got a fine mind."

She laughed at that, a little raggedly. Whereupon Rodney looked hurt and protested against this imputation of insincerity against his friend.

"When you know him better," he said, "you will see he couldn't say a thing like that unless he meant it."

"Oh, he meant it, all right," said Rose. And she added incomprehensibly, "It isn't his fault, of course. It's just the way the world's made."

She had been in good looks tonight, she knew; hurt, humiliated, confronted with a crisis, she had rallied her powers just as she had done at the Randolphs' dinner. She had been aware of the color in her cheeks, the brightness in her eyes, the edge to her voice. Each of the two men had responded to the effect she produced. Barry had talked with her all the last part of the evening—brilliantly, eagerly, and had come away saying she had a fine mind. Her husband had come across to her and put his hand on her bare shoulder. And the two of them had responded to an identical impulse, although they translated it so differently—one over the long circuit, the other over the short.

Lacking the clue, Rodney, of course, didn't understand. The look in Rose's eyes softened suddenly.

"Don't mind, dear;" she said. "I'm truly glad if they liked me. It will make things a lot easier."

At that his eyes lighted up. "Do you seriously think any one could resist you, you darling?" he said. "You were a perfect miracle tonight, when they were here. But now, like this. . ." He came over to her with his arms out.

But she cried out "Don't!" and sprang away from him. "Please don't, Roddy—not tonight! I can't stand it to have you touch me tonight!"

He stared at her, gave a shrug of exasperation, and then turned away. "You *are* angry about something then," he said. "I thought so when I first came in. But I honestly don't know what it's about."

"I'm *not* angry," she said as steadily as she could. She mustn't let it go on like this. They were getting started all wrong somehow. "You didn't want me to touch you, the night when I came to your office, when you were working on that case. But it wasn't because you were angry with me. Well, I'm like that tonight. There's something that's got to be thought out. Only, I'm not like you. I can't do it alone. I've got to have help. I don't want to be soothed and comforted like a child, and I don't want to be made love to. I just want to be treated like a human being."

"I see," he said. Very deliberately he lighted a cigarette, found himself an ash-tray and settled down astride a spindling little chair. (It was lucky for Florence McCrea's peace of mind that she didn't see him do it.) "All right," he said. "Now, come on with your troubles." He didn't say "little troubles," but his voice did and his smile. The whole thing would probably turn out to be a question about a housemaid, or a hat.

Rose steadied herself as well as she could. She simply mustn't let herself think of things like that. If she lost her temper she'd have no chance.

"We've made a horrible mistake," she began. "I don't suppose it's either of our faults exactly. It's been mine in a way of course, because it wouldn't have happened if I hadn't been—thoughtless and ignorant. I might have seen it if I'd thought to look. But I didn't—not really, until tonight."

He wanted to know what the mistake was. He was still smiling in good-humored amusement over her seriousness.

"It's pretty near everything," she said, "about the way we've lived— renting this house in the first place."

He frowned and flushed. "Good heavens, child!" he said. "Can't you take a joke? I didn't mean anything by what I said about the house— except that—well, it is a precious, soulful, sacred—High Church sort of house, and we're not the sort of people, thank God—I'll say it again— who'd have built it and furnished it for ourselves. You *aren't* right, Rose. You're run down and very tired and hypersensitive, or you wouldn't have spent an evening worrying over a thing like that."

"You can make jokes about a thing that's true," she persisted. "And it's true that you've hated the way we've lived—the way this house has made us live.—No, please listen and let me talk. I can't help it if my voice chokes up. My mind's just as cool as yours and you've got to listen. It isn't the first time I've thought of it. It's always made me feel a little unhappy when people have laughed about the 'new leaf' you've turned over; how 'civilized' you've got, learning all the new dances and going out all the time and not doing any of the—wild things you used to do. In a joking sort of way, people have congratulated me about it, as if it were some sort of triumph of mine. I haven't liked it, really. But I never stopped to think out what it meant."

"What it does mean," he said, with a good deal of attention to his cigarette, "is that I've fallen in love with you and married you and that things are desirable to me now, because I am in love with you, that weren't desirable before. And things that were desirable before, are less so. I don't see anything terrible about that."

"There isn't," she said, "when—when you're in love with me."

He shot a frowning look at her and echoed her phrase interrogatively. She nodded.

"Because you aren't in love with me all the time. And when you aren't, you must see what I've done to you. You must—hate me for what I've done to you. I remember the first day we ever talked—when you laughed at my note-books. You talked about people who wore blinders and drew a cart and followed a bundle of hay. That's what I've made you do."

His face flushed deep. He sprang to his feet and threw his cigarette into the fire. "That's perfectly outrageous nonsense," he said. "I won't listen to it."

"If it weren't true," she persisted, "you wouldn't be excited like that. If I hadn't known it before, I'd have known it when I saw you with the Lakes. You can give them something you can't give me, not with all the love in the world. I never heard about them till tonight—not in a way I'd remember. And there are other people—you spoke of some of them at dinner—who are living here, that you've never mentioned to me before. You've tried to sweep them all out of your life; to go to dances and the opera and things with me. You did it because you loved me, but it wasn't fair to either of us, Roddy. Because you can't love me all the time. I don't believe a man—a real man—*can* love a woman all the time. And if she makes him hate her when he doesn't love her, he'll get so he hates loving her."

"You're talking nonsense!" he said again roughly. He was pacing the room by now. "Stark staring nonsense!"

Of course the reason it caught him like that was simply that it echoed so uncannily the things that went through his own head sometimes in his stolen hours of solitude—thoughts he had often tried, unavailingly, to stamp out of existence.

"I'd like to know where you get that stuff. Is it from James Randolph? He's dangerous, that fellow. Oh, he's interesting, and I like him, but he's a cynic. He doesn't want anybody to be happier than he is. But what may be true of him, isn't true of me. I've never stopped loving you since the first day we talked together. And I should think I'd done enough to prove it."

"That's it," she said. "You've done too much. And you're so sorry for me when you don't love me, that it makes you do all the more."

She had found another joint in his armor. She was absolutely clairvoyant tonight, and this time he fairly cried out, "Stop it!"

Then he got himself together and begged her pardon. "After all, I don't see what it comes to," he said. "I don't know what we're fighting about tonight. You're saying you think we ought to do more playing around with the Lakes and people like that; not spend all our time with the Casino set, as we have done this winter. Well, that may be good sense. I've no objection certainly."

"Well, then," she said, "that's settled—that's one thing settled. But there's something else. Oh, it all comes to the same thing, really. Roddy,"—she had to gulp and draw a long breath and steady herself before this—"Roddy, how much money have you got, and how much are we spending?"

"Oh, good lord!" he cried. "*Please* don't go into that now, Rose. It's after one o'clock, and you're worn to a frazzle. If we've got to go into it, let's do it some other time, when we can be sensible about it."

"When I am, you mean?"

"Yes," he said.

"Well, I'm sensible now. I can't help it if my—voice chokes and my eyes fill up. That's silly, of course, but down in my mind, I don't believe I've ever been as sensible as I am right now. And I've had the nerve to ask—I don't know when I will again—and I know you won't bring the subject up by yourself. I've been trying to for ever so long. But money's always seemed the one thing I couldn't b-bear to talk about with you.

"You see, when I first told mother and Portia about you—about how you helped me with the conductor that night, I told them your name, and Portia said she didn't think it could be you, because you were a millionaire. I supposed she knew. Anyway, I didn't think very much about it. You yourself,—just being with you and hearing you talk, were so much more important. After we got engaged, and you began doing all sorts of lovely things for me, I enjoyed it of course. But it was just something that went with you. After we were married and took this house. . . Well, I knew, of course, I hadn't married you for money, but I thought it would sound sort of queer and prying to ask questions about it; because I hadn't anything."

HENRY KITCHELL WEBSTER

He had looked up two or three times and drawn in his breath for a protest, but apparently he couldn't think of anything effective to say. Now though, he cried out, "Rose! Please!"

But she went steadily on. "You were always so dear about it. You never let me feel like a beggar, and—well, it was the easy way, and I took it. I got worried once during the winter when I heard the Crawfords talking. All those people were millionaires, I'd supposed. They were going on at a dinner here, one night, about being awfully hard up, and I began to wonder if we were. I spent a week trying to—get up my courage to ask you about it. But then Constance got a new necklace on her birthday, and they went off to Palm Beach the next week, so I persuaded myself it was all a joke. The thing's come up again several times since, but never so that I couldn't side-step it some way, until tonight. But tonight—oh, Roddy. . . !" Her silly ragged voice choked there and stopped and the tears brimmed up and spilled down her cheeks. But she kept her face steadfastly turned to his.

"That's what I said about being married and not sowing wild oats, I suppose," he said glumly. "It was a joke. Do you suppose I'd have said it if I meant it?"

"It wasn't only that," she managed to go on. "It was the way they looked at the house; the way you apologized for my dress; the way you looked when you tried to get out of answering Barry Lake's questions about what you were doing. Oh, how I despised myself! And how I knew you and they must be despising me!"

"The one thing I felt about you all evening," he said, with the patience that marks the last stage of exasperation, "was pride. I was rather crazily proud of you."

"As my lover you were proud of me," she said. "But the other man—the man that's more truly you—was ashamed, as I was ashamed. Oh, it doesn't matter! Being ashamed won't accomplish anything. But what we'll *do* is going to accomplish something."

"What do you mean to do?" he asked.

"I want you to tell me first," she said, "how much money we have, and how much we've been spending."

"I don't know," he said stubbornly. "I don't know exactly."

"You've got enough, haven't you, of your own. . . I mean, there's enough that comes in every year, to live on, if you didn't earn a cent by practising law? Well, what I want to do, is to live on that. I want to live however and wherever we have to to live on that—out in the suburbs somewhere, or in a flat, so that you will be free; and I can work—be some sort of help. Barry and the others—your real friends, that you really care about, won't mind. And as long as we want to get rid of the other people anyway, that's the way to do it."

"You can wash the dishes and scrub the floors," he supplemented, "and I can carry my lunch to the office with me in a little tin box." He looked at his watch. "And now that the thing's reduced to an absurdity, let's go to bed. It's getting along toward two o'clock."

"You don't have to get to the office till nine tomorrow morning," said Rose. "And I want to talk it out now. And I don't think I said anything that was absurd."

The devil of it was she hadn't. The precise quality about her suggestions that pointed and barbed them, was their fantastic logic. It would be ridiculous—impossible—to uproot their life as she wanted it done. One simply couldn't do such a thing. Serious discussion of it was preposterous. But to explain why. . . ! He was apt enough at explanations generally. This one seemed to present difficulties.

"I shouldn't have called it absurd," he admitted after a rather long silence. "But it's exaggerated and unnecessary. I don't care to make a public proclamation that I'm not able to support you and run our domestic establishment in a way that we find natural and agreeable;—and that I've been a fool to try. The situation doesn't call for it. You've made a mountain out of an ant-hill. When our lease is up, if we think this house is more than we want, we can find something simpler."

"But we'll begin economizing now," she pleaded; "change things as much as we can, even if we do have to go on living in this house. It won't hurt me a bit to work, and you could go back to your book. We'd both be happier, if I were something besides just a drag on you."

"Discharge a couple of maids, you mean," he asked, "and sweep and make beds and that sort of thing yourself?"

"I don't know exactly how we'd do it," she said. "That's why I said I needed your help in figuring it out. Something like that, I suppose. Sweeping and making beds isn't very much, but it's something."

"The most we could save that way," he said, "would be a few hundred dollars a year. It wouldn't be a drop in the bucket. But everything would run at cross-purposes. You'd be tired out all the time—you're that pretty much as it is lately, we'd have to stop having people in; you'd be bored and I'd be worried. When you start living on a certain scale, everything about your life has to be done on that scale. Next October, as I said, when the lease on this house runs out, we can manage, perhaps, to change the scale a little. There you are! Now do stop worrying about it and let's go to bed."

But she sat there just as she was, staring at the dying fire, her hands lying slack in her lap, all as if she hadn't heard. The long silence irked him. He pulled out his watch, looked at it and began winding it. He mended the fire so that it would be safe for the night; bolted a window. Every minute or two, he stole a look at her, but she was always just the same. Except for the faint rise and fall of her bosom, she might have been a picture, not a woman.

At last he said again, "Come along, Rose, dear."

"It'll be too late in October," she said. "That's why I wanted to decide things tonight. Because we must begin right away." Then she looked up into his face. "It will be too late in October," she repeated, "unless we begin now."

The deep tense seriousness of her voice and her look arrested his full attention.

"Why?" he asked. And then, "Rose, what do you mean?"

"We're going to have a baby in October," she said.

He stared at her for a minute without a word, then drew in a deep breath and pressed his hands against his eyes. All he could say at first was just her name. But he dropped down beside her and got her in his arms.

"So that's it," he said raggedly at last. "Oh, Rose, darling, it's such a relief! I've been so terrified about you—so afraid something had gone wrong. And you wouldn't let me ask, and you seemed so unhappy. I'd even thought of talking to Randolph. I might have guessed, I suppose. I've been stupid about it. But, you darling, I understand it all now."

She didn't see just what he meant by that, but she didn't care. It was such a wonderful thing to stop fighting and let the tension relax, cuddle close into his embrace, and know nothing in the world but the one fact that he loved her; that their tale of golden hours wasn't spent—was, perhaps, illimitable. She was even too drowsily happy to think what he meant when he said a little later:

"So now you won't let anything trouble you, will you, child? And if queer worrying ideas get into your head about the way we live, and about being a drag on me and making me hate you, you'll laugh at them? You'll be able to laugh, because you'll know why they're there."

It wasn't until the next day that she recalled that remark of his and analyzed it. It meant, of course, that she was beaten; that her first fight for the big thing had been in vain. There would be no use, for the present, in renewing the struggle. He'd taken the one ground that was impregnable. So long as he could go on honestly interpreting every plea of hers for a share in the hard part of his life as well as in the soft part of it, for a way of life that would make them something more than lovers—as wholly subjective to herself, the inevitable accompaniment of her physical condition—the pleas and the struggles would indeed be wasted. She'd have to wait.

X

The Door That Was to Open

She would have to wait. Accepted, root and branch, as Rose was forced by her husband's attitude to accept it, a conclusion of that sort can be a wonderful anodyne. And so it proved in her ease. Indeed, within a day after her talk with Rodney, though it had ended in total defeat, she felt like a person awakened out of a nightmare. There had taken place, somehow, an enormous letting-off of strain—a heavenly relaxation of spiritual muscles. It was so good just to have him know; to have others know, as all her world did within the next week!

Ultimately nothing was changed, of course. The great thing that she had promised Portia she wouldn't fail in getting—the real thing that should solve the problem, equalize the disparity between her husband and herself and give them a life together in satisfying completeness beyond the joys of a pair of lovers;—that was still to be fought for.

She'd have to make that fight alone. Rodney wouldn't help her. He wouldn't know how to help her. Indeed, interpreting from the way he winced under her questions and suggestions, as if they wounded some essentially masculine, primitive element of pride in him, it seemed rather more likely that he'd resist her efforts—fight blindly against her. She must be more careful about that when she took up the fight again; must avoid hurting him if she could.

She hadn't an idea on what lines the fight was to be made. Perhaps before the time for its beginning, a way would appear. The point was that for the present, she'd have to wait—coolly and thoughtfully, not fritter her strength away on futile struggles or harassments.

The tonic effect of that resolution was really wonderful. She got her color back—I mean more than just the pink bloom in her cheeks—and her old, irresistible, wide slow smile. She'd never been so beautiful as she was during the next six months.

People who thought they loved her before—Frederica for example, found they hadn't really, until now. She dropped in on Eleanor Randolph one day, after a morning spent with Rose, simply because she was bursting with this idea and had to talk to somebody. That was very like Frederica.

She found Eleanor doing her month's bills, but glad to shovel them into her desk, light up a cigarette, and have a chat; a little rueful though, when she found that Rose was to be the subject of it.

"She's perfectly wonderful," Frederica said. "There's a sort of look about her. . ."

"Oh, I know," Eleanor said. "We dined there last night."

"Well, didn't it just—get you?" insisted Frederica.

"It did," said Eleanor. "It also got Jim. He was still talking about her when I went to sleep, about one o'clock. I don't a bit blame him for being perfectly maudlin about her. As I say, I was a good deal that way myself, though a half-hour's steady raving was enough for me. But poor old Jim! She isn't one little bit crazy about him, either—unfortunately."

"*Un*fortunately!" thought Frederica. This was rather illuminating. The Randolphs' love-match had been regarded as establishing a sort of standard of excellence. But when you heard a woman trying to arrange subsidiary romances for her husband, or lamenting the failure of them, it meant, as a rule, that things were wearing rather thin. However, she dismissed this speculation for a later time, and went back to Rose.

"I had been worrying about her, too;" she said. "Rodney was so funny about her. *He* was worried, I could see that. And he means the best in the world, the dear. But he could be a dreadful brute, just in his simplicity. Oh, I know! He and I were always rather special pals—more than Harriet. But no man ever learned less from his sisters,—about women, I mean. He's always been so big and healthy and even-minded, you couldn't tell him anything, except what you could print right out in black and white. So when you were feeling edgy and blue and miserable you either kept out of his way or kept your troubles to yourself. He was always easy to fool—there was that about it. If you wiped your eyes and blew your nose, he always thought you had a cold. Which is all very nice about a brother; but in a husband. . ."

Something that Eleanor did with her shoulders, the way she blew out her smoke and twisted her mouth around, caught Frederica's eye. "What did you mean by that?" she asked. "Oh, I know you didn't say anything."

Eleanor got up restlessly, squared the cushions on her *chaise longue*, tapped her cigarette ash into a receiver and said that Rose was happy enough now, anyway, if looks were anything to go by; hesitated again, and finally answered Frederica's question.

"Why," she said, "whenever I hear a woman miaouling about being misunderstood, I always want to tell her she doesn't know her luck. Wait till she marries a man who really does understand—too well. Let her see how she likes it, whenever she turns loose and gets—going a little, to have him look interested, as if he were taking notes, and begin asking questions that are—a little too intelligent. How does she think it'll feel never to know, *never*—I mean that, that she isn't being—experimented on!"

It was a rather horrible idea, Frederica didn't try to deny it. But not being understood wasn't very agreeable either. What did they want then?

Eleanor laughed. "Did you ever think," she asked, "that one of these regular stage husbands would be rather satisfactory? Terribly particular, you know, and bossy and domineering. The kind that discovers a letter or a handkerchief or sees you going into some other man's 'rooms' and gets frightfully jealous, and denounces you without giving you a chance to explain, and drags you round by the hair and threatens to kill you? And then discovers—in the last act, you know,—that you were perfectly innocent all the while, and repents all over the place and begs you to forgive him and take him back; and you do? Do you suppose any of the men we know would be capable of acting like that? Don't you think we'd like it if they were? Not if they really did those things, perhaps, but if we thought they might?"

Frederica was amused, but didn't think there was much to that. Of course, if the play was very thrilling, and you liked the leading man, you might build yourself into the romance somehow. But when it came to the real thing. . .

"No, there is something in it," Eleanor insisted. "There's something you can't get in any other way. Whom do you think I'd pick," she asked suddenly, "for the happiest wife I know? Edith Welles. Yes, really. Oh, I know, her husband's a slacker and no real good to anybody. And he goes out every now and then and drinks too much and doesn't know just what happens afterward. But he always comes back and wants to be forgiven. And he thinks she's an angel,—which she is—and he thinks he isn't worthy to put on her rubbers—which he isn't, and—well, there you are! She knows she's *got* him, somehow.

"But you take Jim. I can get my way with him always. I can outmaneuver him every time. He's positively simple about things, unless they happen to strike him—professionally. But there's always something that gets away. Something I'm no nearer now than I was the day I first saw him. And I sometimes think that if there were—something horrible I had to forgive him for—if I could get something on him as they say. . . It's rather fun, isn't it, sometimes, just to let your mind go wild and see where you bring up. Awful rot, of course. Can you stop for lunch?"

Frederica thought she couldn't; must run straight along. But the talk had been amusing. "Only—you won't mind?—don't spring any of that stuff on Rose. She's just a child, really you know, and entitled to any illusions that Rodney leaves; especially these days."

"You, as an old hen fussing about your new chicken!" Eleanor mocked. "Wait till you can look the part a little better, Frederica, dear. But really, I'm harmless. Talk to Jim and Rodney and those fearful and wonderful Lakes of his. They were there, and—well, you ought to have heard the talk. I thought I was pretty well hardened, but once or twice I gasped. Jim's pretty weird when he gets going, but that Barry Lake has a sort of—surgical way of discussing just *anything*, and his wife's as bad. Oh, she's awfully interesting, I'll admit that, and she's as crazy about Rose as any of the rest of us, which is to her credit.

"We never got off women all the evening. Barry Lake had their history down from the early Egyptians, and Jim had an endless string of pathological freaks to tell about. And then Rodney came out strong for economic independence, only with his own queer angle on it of course. He thought it would be a fine thing, but it wouldn't happen until the men insisted on it. When a girl wasn't regarded as marriageable unless she had been trained to a trade or a profession, then things would begin to happen. I think he meant it, too, though he was more than usually outrageous in his way of putting things.

"Well, and all the while there sat Rose, taking it all in with those big eyes of hers, smiling to herself now and then; saying things, too, sometimes, that were pretty good, though nobody but Jim seemed to understand, always, just what she meant. They've talked before, those two. But she didn't mind—anything; no more embarrassed than as if we'd been talking embroidery stitches. You don't need to worry about her. And she absolutely seemed to like Jane Lake."

Frederica did worry. Seriously meditated running in on Rodney before she went home to lunch and giving him a tip that a young wife in Rose's condition wanted treating a little more carefully. It was not for prudential reasons that she decided against doing it. She was perfectly willing to

HENRY KITCHELL WEBSTER

have her head bitten off in a good cause. But she knew Rodney down to the ground; knew that it was utterly impossible for him, whatever his previous resolutions might be, to pull up on the brink of anything. Once you launched a topic that interested him, he'd go through with it. So the only thing that would do any good would be to ban the Lakes and James Randolph completely. And Rodney, if persuaded to do that—he would in a minute, of course, if he thought it would be good for Rose—would be incapable of concealing from her why he had done it; which would leave matters worse than ever.

The only outcome, then, of her visit to Eleanor and her subsequent cogitations, was that Martin, when he came home that night, found her unusually affectionate and inclined to be misty about the eyes. "I'm a—lucky guy, all right"—this was her explanation,—"being married to you. Instead of any of the others."

He was a satisfactory old dear. He took her surplus tenderness as so much to the good, and didn't bother over not knowing what it was all about.

Eleanor was right in her surmise that Rose had really taken a fancy to Jane Lake. She was truly—and really humbly—grateful to Jane, in the first place, for liking her, finding her, in Jane's own phrase, "worth while," and her ideas worth listening to. Because here was something, you see, that she could take at its face value. There was no long-circuited sex attraction to discount everything, in Jane's case. But she had another reason.

Rodney, it seemed, had told the Lakes about the prospective baby the very morning after he'd learned the news himself, and Jane—this was perfectly characteristic of her—had come straight up to see Rose about it; even before Frederica. And about the first thing she said was:

"Which do you want—a boy or a girl?"

Rose looked puzzled, then surprised. "Why," she said at last, "I don't believe I know."

"It's funny about that," said Jane. "The one thing I was frightened about—the first time, you know—was that it might be a girl. I think Barry really wanted a girl, too. He does now, and we're going to try to have one, though we can't rightly afford it. But I'm just primitive enough—I'm a cave person, really—to have felt that having a girl, at least before you had a boy, would be a sort of disgrace. Like the Hindoo women in Kipling. But don't you really care?"

"Why, the queer thing is," said Rose, who had been in a daze ever since Jane's first question, "that I hadn't thought of it as anything at all but—It. Hardly that, really. I've known how miserable I've been, and that there were things I must be careful not to do,—and, of course, what was going to happen. But that when it was all over there'd be a baby left,—a—a son or a daughter, why, that's. . ."

Her surprise had carried her into a confidence that her budding friendship for Jane was hardly ripe for, and she pulled up rather suddenly. "I didn't know you had any children," she concluded, by way of avoiding a further discussion of the marvel just then. "Are they here with you now?"

Jane explained why they were not. They weren't babies any more, two husky little boys of five and three, and they were rejoicing in the care of a grandmother and a highly competent nurse. "One of those terribly infallible people, you know. Oh, I don't like it. I get a night letter every morning, and, of course, if one of them got the sniffles I'd be off home like a shot. I'd like to be a regular domestic mother; not let another soul but me touch them (Jane really believed this) but you see we can't well afford it. Barry pays me five dollars a day for working for him. I scout around and dig up material and interview people for him—I used to be a reporter, you know. He'd have to hire somebody, and it might better be me and keep the money in the family. Because the nurse who takes my place doesn't cost near so much as that. All the same, as I say, I don't half like it. You can preach the new stuff till you're black in the face, but there's no job for a woman like taking care of her own children."

Rose listened to all this, as well as to Jane's subsequent remarks, with only so much attention as was required to keep her guest from suspecting that she wasn't really listening at all. Jane didn't stay long. She had to go out and earn Barry's five dollars—she'd lose her job if she didn't, so she said, and Rose was presently left alone to dream, actually for the first time, of the wonders that were before her.

What a silly little idiot she'd been not to have seen the thing for herself! She'd been, all the while, beating her head against blind walls when there was a door there waiting to open of itself when the time came. Motherhood! There'd be a doctor and a nurse at first, of course, but presently they'd go away and she'd be left with a baby. Her own baby! She could care for him with her own hands, feed him—her joy reached an ecstasy at this—feed him from her own breast.

That life which Rodney led apart from her, the life into which she had tried with such ludicrous unsuccess to effect an entrance, was nothing to this new life which was to open before her in a few short

HENRY KITCHELL WEBSTER

months now. Meanwhile, she not only must wait; she could well afford to.

That was why she could listen with that untroubled smile of hers to the terrible things that Rodney and James Randolph and Barry Lake and Jane got into the way of hurling across her dinner table, and to the more mildly expressed but equally alkaline cynicisms of Jimmy Wallace.

(Jimmy was dramatic critic on one of the evening papers, as well as a bit of a playwright. He was a slim, cool, smiling, highly sophisticated young man, who renounced all privileges as an interpreter of life in favor of remaining an unbiased observer of it. He never bothered to speculate about what you ought to do;—he waited to see what you did. He knew, more or less, everybody in the world,—in all sorts of worlds. He was, for instance, a great friend of Violet Williamson's and Bella Forrester's and was, at the same time, on terms of avuncular confidence with Dotty Blott of the Globe chorus. And he was exactly the same man to the three of them. He fitted admirably in with their new circle.)

Well, in the light of the miraculous transformation that lay before her Rose could listen undaunted to the tough philosophizings her husband and Barry Lake delighted in as well as to the mordant merciless realities with which Doctor Randolph and Jimmy Wallace confirmed them. She wasn't indifferent to it all. She listened with all her might.

If there was anything in prenatal influence, that baby of hers was going to be intelligent!

XI

An Illustration

So far as externals went, her life, that spring, was immensely simplified. The social demands on her, which had been so insistent all winter, stopped almost automatically. The only exception was the Junior League show in Easter week, for which she put in quite a lot of work. She was to have danced in it.

This is an annual entertainment by which Chicago sets great store. All the smartest and best-looking of the younger set take part in it, in costumes that would do credit to Mr. Ziegfeld, and as much of Chicago as is willing and able to pay five dollars a seat for the privilege is welcome to come and look. Delirious weeks are spent in rehearsal, under a first-class professional director, audience and performers have an equally good time, and Charity, as residuary legatee, profits by thousands.

Rose dropped in at a rehearsal one day at the end of a solid two hours of committee work, found it unexpectedly amusing, and made a point thereafter of attending when she could. Her interest was heightened if not wholly actuated by some things Jimmy Wallace had been telling her lately about how such things were done on the real stage.

He had written a musical comedy once, lived through the production of it, and had spent a hard-earned two-weeks vacation trouping with it on the road, so he could speak with authority. It was a wonderful Odyssey when you could get him to tell it, and as she made a good audience she got the whole thing—what everybody was like, from the director down, how the principals dug themselves in and fought to the last trench for every line and bit of business in their parts, and sapped and mined ahead to get, here or there, a bit more;—how insanely hard the chorus worked. . .

The thing got a sociological twist eventually, of course, when Jane wanted to know if it were true, as alleged by a prominent woman writer on feminism, that the chorus-girls were driven to prostitution by inadequate pay. Jimmy demolished this assertion with more warmth than he often showed. He didn't know any other sort of job that paid a totally untrained girl so well. There were initial requirements, of course. She had to have reasonably presentable arms and legs and a rudimentary sense of rhythm. But it took a really accomplished stenographer, for instance, to earn as much a week as was paid the average chorus-girl. The trouble was that the indispensable assets in the business were not character and intelligence and ambition, but just personal charms.

Rose grinned across at Rodney. "That's like wives, isn't it?" she observed.

"And then," Jimmy went on, "the work isn't really hard enough, except during rehearsals, to keep them out of mischief." Rose smiled again, but didn't press her analogy any further. "But a girl who's serious about it, who doesn't have to be told the same thing more than once, and catches on, sometimes, without being told at all,—why, she can always have a job and she can be as independent as anybody. She can get twenty-five dollars a week or even as high as thirty. It's surprising though," he concluded, "considering what a bunch of morons most of them are, that they work as well as they do; turn up on time for rehearsals and performances, even when they're feeling really seedy, stand the awful bawling out they get every few minutes—because some directors are downright savages—and keep on going over and over a thing till they're simply reeling on their pins, without any fuss at all."

"They can always lose their job," said Barry. "There's great merit in that."

The latter part of this conversation was what she was to remember afterward, but the thing which impressed Rose at the time, and that held her for hours looking on at the League show rehearsals, was what Jimmy had told her about the technical side of the work of production, the labors of the director, and so on.

The League was paying their director three hundred dollars a week, and by the end of the third rehearsal Rose decided that he earned it. The change he could make, even with one afternoon's work, in the effectiveness, the carrying power, of a dance number was astonishing. It wasn't at all a question of good taste. There stood Bertie Willis simply awash with good taste and oozing suggestions whose hopeless futility was demonstrated, even to him, the moment an attempt was made to put them into effect. The director was concerned with matters of fact. There were ascertained methods of getting a certain range of effects and he knew what they were and applied them—as well as the circumstances admitted. He was working under difficulties, poor chap! Rose, enlightened by Jimmy Wallace, could see that. A man habituated to bawling at a girl, when the spirit so moved him, "Here, you Belmont! What do you think you're trying to do? You try sleeping at night and staying awake at rehearsal. See how it works!"—accustomed to the liberty of saying things like that, and then finding himself under the necessity of swallowing hard and counting ten, and beginning with an—"I think, if you don't mind. . . !" was in a hard case.

Bertie Willis had his usefulness here. Sometimes Rose heard the director whisper hoarsely, "For God's sake, don't let her do that! She *can't* do that!" and then Bertie would intervene and accomplish wonders by diplomacy.

But it must be wonderfully exhilarating, Rose thought, to know exactly why that girl was ridiculous and what to do to make her look right. And to be able to sell your knowledge for three hundred dollars a week. This was the sort of thing Rodney did, when one came to think of it. She wondered whether he could sell his special sort of knowledge for as much. That must be: the sort of possession Simone Gréville had had in mind when she said that nothing worth having could be bought cheap. Neither Rodney nor the director had found his specialty growing on a bush!

But her specialty, which in her life was to fill the place a knowledge of stage dancing filled in the director's, was to come in a different way. You paid a price, of course, for motherhood, in pain and peril, but it remained a miraculous gift, for all that.

XII

What Harriet Did

S he must wait for her miracle. As the weeks and months wore away, and as the season of violent and high-frequency alternations between summer and winter, which the Chicagoan calls spring, gave place to summer itself, Rose was driven to intrench herself more and more deeply behind this great expectation. It was like a dam holding back waters that otherwise would have rushed down upon her and swept her away.

The problems went on mounting up behind the dam, of course. All the minor luxuries of their way of living, which had been so keen a delight to her during the first unthinking months of their married life; all the sumptuous little elaborations of existence which she had explored with such adventurous delight, had changed—now that she knew they had been bought by the abridgment of her husband's freedom, by the invasion of the clear space about himself which he had always so jealously guarded—into a cloud of buzzing stinging distractions.

And they were the harder to bear now that she recognized how hard they were going to be to drive away. It would have to be effected without wounding Rodney's primitive masculine pride—without convicting him of being an inadequate provider.

The baffling thing about him was that he had, quite unconsciously and sincerely, two points of view. His affection for her, his wife, lover, mistress, was a lens through which he sometimes looked out on the world. As she refracted the facts of life for him they presented themselves in the primitive old-fashioned way.

But there was another window in his soul through which he saw life with no refractions whatever; remorselessly, logically. Looking through the window, as he did when he talked to Barry Lake, or James Randolph, he saw life as a mass of unyielding reciprocities. You got what you paid for. You paid for what you got. And he saw both men and women—though chiefly women—tangling and nullifying their lives in futile efforts to evade this principle; looking for an Eldorado where something was to be had for nothing; for panaceas; for the soft without the hard.

He was perfectly capable of seeing and describing an abstract wife like that in blistering terms that would make an industrious street-walker look almost respectable by comparison. But when he looked at Rose, he saw her through the lens, as some one to be loved and desired,—and prevented, if possible, from paying anything.

Somehow or other those two views must be reconciled before a life of real comradeship between them was possible; before the really big thing she had promised Portia to fight for could be anything more than a tormenting dream.

Would the miracle solve this? It must. It was the only thing left to hope for. In the shelter of the great dam she could wait serene.

And then came Harriet, and the pressure behind the dam rose higher.

Rose had tried, rather unsuccessfully, to realize, when during the earlier days of her marriage she had heard Harriet talked about, that there was actually in existence another woman who occupied, by blood anyway, the same position toward Rodney and herself that Frederica did. She felt almost like a real sister toward Frederica. But without quite putting the notion into words, she had always felt it was just as well that Harriet was an Italian *contessa* four thousand miles away. Rodney and Frederica spoke of her affectionately, to be sure, but their references made a picture of a rather formidably correct, seriously aristocratic sort of person. Harriet had always had, Rose could see, a very effective voice in the family councils. She hadn't much of a mind, perhaps; Rodney described it once as a small, well oiled, easy running sort of mind that stitched away without misgivings, to its conclusions. Rodney never could have been very fond of her. But she had something he knew he lacked, and in matters which he regarded as of minor importance—things that he didn't consider worth bothering much about one way or the other—he'd submit to her guidance, it appeared, without much question.

She had written, on the occasion of Rodney's marriage, a letter to Rose, professing with perfect adequacy, to give her a sisterly welcome into the family. But Rose felt pretty sure (a fragment of talk she overheard, an impatient laugh of Rodney's, and Frederica's "Oh, that's Harriet of course," had perhaps suggested it) that the *contessa* regarded Rodney's marriage as a *mésalliance*. She had entertained this notion the more easily because at that time what Harriet thought—whatever Harriet might think—seemed a matter of infinitesimal importance.

HENRY KITCHELL WEBSTER

She'd discovered, along in the winter sometime, that Harriet's affairs were going rather badly. Neither Rodney nor Frederica had gone into details. But it was plain enough that both of them were looking for a smash of some sort. It was in May that the cable came to Frederica announcing that Harriet was coming back for a long visit. "That's all she said," Rodney explained to Rose. "But I suppose it means the finish. She said she didn't want any fuss made, but she hinted she'd like to have Freddy meet her in New York, and Freddy's going. Poor old Harriet! That's rather a pill for her to swallow, if it's so. We must try to cheer her up."

She didn't seem much in need of cheering up, Rose thought, when they first met. All that showed on the *contessa's* highly polished surface was a disposition to talk humorously over old times with her old friends, including her brother and sister, and a sort of dismayed acquiescence in the smoky seriousness, the inadequate civilization, the sprawling formlessness of the city of her birth, not excluding that part of it which called itself society.

In broad strokes, you could describe Harriet by saying she was as different as a beautiful woman could be from Frederica. She wasn't so beautiful as Frederica, to be sure, but together they made a wonderfully contrasted pair—Harriet almost as perfect a brunette type as Frederica was a blonde, and got up with her ear-rings and her hair and all to look rather exotic. Her speech, too, and the cultivated things she could do with her shoulders, carried out the impression. She had a trick—when she wanted to be disagreeable an ill-natured observer would have said— of making remarks in Italian and then translating them.

She wasn't disagreeable though—not malicious anyway, and the very hard finish she carried, had been developed probably as a matter of protection. She must have been through a good deal in the last few years. She'd had two children stillborn, for one thing, and she was frankly afraid to try it again. She never wanted any sympathy from anybody. If it came down to that, she'd prefer arsenic. She resisted Rose's rather poignant charm, as she resisted any other appeal to her emotions. With the charm left out, Rose was simply a well meaning, somewhat insufficiently civilized young person, the beneficiary, through her marriage with Rodney, of a piece of unmerited good fortune. She didn't in the least mean to be unkind to her, however, and didn't dream that she was giving Rose an inkling how she thought of her.

Her manner toward this new member of the family was studiously affectionate. She avoided being either disagreeable or patronizing. Rose could see, indeed, how carefully she avoided it. She knew, too, that Frederica saw the same thing and tried to compensate for it by a little extra affectionateness. She even thought—though perhaps this was mere self-consciousness—that she detected a trace of the same thing in Rodney.

The tie of blood is a powerful thing. Rose had never realized before how powerful. With Harriet's arrival, she became aware of the Aldrich family as a sodality—something she didn't belong to and never could. It was quite true, as Frederica had said, that she and Rodney had always been special pals. Harriet fitted into the family on the other side of Frederica from her brother. She was a person with a good deal of what one calls magnetism, and she attracted Frederica toward herself—made her, when she was about, a somewhat different Frederica. She even attracted Rodney a little in the same way.

The time of the year (it was after the end of the social season) made it natural for them to be together a good deal. And of course Harriet's return, after an absence of years, made them seek such meetings. The result was that Rose, at the end of almost a year of marriage, got her first real taste of lonesomeness. When the four of them were together, Rose felt like an outsider intruding on intimates. They didn't mean her to feel that way—made a distinct effort, Rodney and Frederica, anyway, to prevent her feeling that way; which of course only pointed it. They had old memories to talk about; old friendships. They had, like all close knit families, a sort of shorthand language to talk in. If Rose came into the room where they were, she'd often be made aware that the current subject of the conversation had been dropped and a new one was getting started; or else there'd be laborious explanations.

It wouldn't have mattered—not so much anyway, if Rose had had a similar sodality of her own to fall back on—a mass of roots extending out into indigenous soil. But Rose, you see, had been transplanted. Her two brothers were hardly more than faint memories of her childhood. One was a high-school principal down in Pennsylvania; the other a professor of history at one of the western state universities. Both of them had married young and had been very much married—on small incomes—ever since. The only family she had that counted, was her mother and Portia. And they were gone now to California.

She had had a world of what she called friends, of course, of her own age, at the high school and at the university. But her popularity in those circles, her easy way of liking everybody, and her energetic preoccupation with things to do, had prevented any of these friendships from biting in very deep. None of them had been solidly founded enough to withstand the wavelike rush of Rodney Aldrich into her life. She had gone over altogether into her husband's world. The world that had been her own, hadn't much more existence, except for her mother and sister out in California, than the memory of a dream.

But it took Harriet's arrival to make her realize this. And the realization, when it was pressed home particularly hard, brought with it moments of downright panic. Everything—everything she had in the world, went back to Rodney. Except for him, she was living in an absolute vacuum. What would happen if the stoutly twisted cable that bound her to him should be broken, as the cable that bound Harriet to her husband was, apparently, broken? What would she have then of which she could say, "This much is mine"? Well, she'd have the child. That would be, partly at least, hers.

But Harriet's contribution to Rose's difficulties, to the mounting pressure behind the dam, was destined to be more serious—more actual, anyway—before very long.

The question where Rose and Rodney were going to live after their lease on the McCrea house ended, had begun to press for an answer. October first was when the lease expired and it wasn't far from the date at which they expected the baby. Rose wouldn't be in any condition for house hunting during the hot summer months. Things would have to be settled somehow before then. A heavy calendar of important cases had kept Rodney from giving as much attention to the problem as he himself felt it needed. He had delighted Rose with the suggestion that they go out into the country somewhere. Not the real country of course, but up along the shore, where the train service was good and the motor a possible alternative.

They spent some very lovely afternoons during the early days of the emerging spring, cruising about looking at possible places. They talked of building at first, but long before they could make up their minds what they wanted it had become too late for that, and they shifted to the notion of buying an old place somewhere and remodeling it. One reason why they made no more progress was because they were looking for such different things. Rodney wanted acres. He'd never gardened a bit, and never would; was an altogether urban person, despite the physical energy which took him pounding off on long country walks. But when he heard there was a tract just west of Martin Whitney's, up at Lake Forest, that could be had at a bargain—thirty-five thousand dollars—he let his eye rove over it appreciatively. And Frank Crawford and Howard West knew of advantageous sites, also, on which to expatiate with convincing enthusiasm. The kind of house you'd have to build on that sort of place would cost you an easy thirty thousand more.

Rose didn't even yet know much about money, to be sure, but she knew enough to be aghast at all that. What she tried to make Rodney look for was a much more modest establishment—a yard big enough to hold a tennis court, perhaps, and a house, well, that could be added to as they needed room.

Neither of them stuck very close to the main point on these expeditions. They always had too good a time together—more like a pair of children on a picnic than serious home-hunters, and they frittered a good deal of time away that they couldn't well afford.

This was the situation when Harriet took a hand in it. It was a situation made to order for Harriet to take a hand in. She'd sized it up at a glance, made up her mind in three minutes what was the sensible thing for them to do, written a note to Florence McCrea in Paris, and then bided her opportunity to put her idea into effect. She went out cruising with Rose in the car two or three times, looking at places, but gave her no indications that she felt more than the most languid interest in the problem. She could seem less interested in a thing without being quite impolite, than any one Rose knew.

When she got Florence McCrea's answer to her letter, she took the first occasion to get Rodney off by himself and talk a little common sense into him.

"What about where to live, Rodney?" she asked. "Made up your mind about it yet? I suppose you know how many months there are between the first of June and the first of October."

"We haven't got much of anywhere," he admitted. "We know we want to live in the country, that's about all."

"Out in the country just as winter's getting started?" she asked. "Settling into a new place—Rose with a new baby—everybody else back in town;—simply no *chance* of keeping servants? Roddy, old man, you're entitled to be a babe in the woods, of course. Any man is who does the kind of work you do. But it is time some one with a little common sense straightened you out about this."

Harriet couldn't be sure from the length of time he took seeing that his pipe was properly alight, whether he altogether liked this method of approach or not.

"Common sense always was a sort of specialty of yours, sis," he said at last, "and straightening out. You were always pretty good at it." Then, out of a cloud of his own smoke, "Fire away."

"Well, in the first place;" she said, "remodeling is the slowest work in the world, and the fussiest. And you can't just tell an architect, with a wave of the hand, to go ahead. You have to do your own fussing, which would drive you crazy. If you had your house today, you'd be lucky if the paint was dry and the thing was fit to move into by the first of September. And next September, if it's blazing hot, won't be exactly the time for Rose to go ramping around trying to buy furniture for a whole establishment—because you haven't a stick yourselves, of course—and getting settled in, hiring servants, getting the thing going. You can't be sure you'll have till the first of October. Things like that don't always happen exactly as they are expected to. But suppose you have good luck and manage it. Then where are you? Out in the woods somewhere at the beginning of winter, just when you ought to be settled comfortably somewhere in town.

"Oh, I know it's all very poetic, sitting in front of a roaring fire of logs, while the wind bangs the shutters, and that sort of thing, Rose singing to the baby and all. But you're not an Arcadian one bit. Neither is she, really, and you'll simply perish out there, both of you, and be back in town before the holidays.

"Rose oughtn't to be in town this summer. But she'll have to be to put this through. She ought to be down at York Harbor, or one of those Cape Cod places, instead of in this horrible smoky hole. Because she's not so very fit, really do you think? Bit moody, I'd say."

"But good lord, Harriet, we've got to get out of here anyway, in October. And that means we've got to have some sort of place to get into. It is an awkward time, I'll admit."

"No, you haven't," she said. "You can stay right here another six months, if you like. I've heard from Florence. I met her in Paris in April, and found she wasn't a bit keen to come back and take this house on. Their securities have gone down again, and they're feeling hard-up. Florence has got an old barn of an *atelier*, and she's puttering around in the mud thinking she's making statuary. Well, when I found how things stood here, I wrote and asked her if she'd lease for six months more if she got the chance, and she wrote back and simply grabbed at it. All you've got to do is to send her a five-word cable and you're fixed. Then, next spring, when your troubles are over, and you know what you want, you can look out a place up the shore and have the summer there."

Rodney smoked half-way through his pipe before he made any comment on this suggestion.

"This house isn't just what we want," he said. "In the first place, it's damned expensive."

Harriet shrugged her shoulders, found herself a cigarette and lighted it; picked up one of Florence's poetry books and eyed the heavily tooled binding with a satirical smile before she replied. She could feel him looking at her, and she knew he'd wait till she got ready to go on.

"I'd an idea there was that in it," she said at last. "Freddy said something. . . Rose had been talking to her." Then after another little silence, and with a sudden access of vehemence, "You don't want to go and do a regular *fool* thing, Roddy. You're getting on perfectly splendidly. You'll be at the head of the bar out here in ten years, if you keep on. Frank Crawford was telling me about you the other day. You've settled down, and we thought you never would. It was a corking move, your taking this house, just because it made you settle down. You can earn forty thousand dollars next year, just with your practise, if you want to. But if you pull up and go to live in a barn somewhere, and stop seeing anybody—people that count, I mean. . ."

Rodney grunted. "You're beyond your depth, sis," he said. "Come back where you don't have to swim. The expense isn't a capital consideration, I'll admit that. Now go on from there."

"That's like old times," she observed with a not ill-humored grimace. "I wonder if you talk to Rose like that. Oh, I know the house is rather solemn and absurd. It's Florence herself all over, that's the size of it, and I suppose you are getting pretty well fed up with it. But what does that matter for six months more? Heavens! You won't know where you're living. But the place is comfortable, and there's room in it for nurses and all and the best doctor in town in the line you'll want, is right around the corner. And, as I say, when your troubles are over and you know what you want. . ."

He pocketed his pipe and got up out of this chair.

"There's something in it," he admitted. "I'll think it over."

HENRY KITCHELL WEBSTER

"Better cable Florence as soon as you can," she advised. "She'll want to know. . ."

Rose protested when the plan for living six months more in Florence McCrea's house was broached to her. She made the best fight she could. But Harriet's arguments, re-stated now by Rodney with full conviction, were too much for her. When she broke down and cried, as she couldn't help doing, Rodney soothed and comforted her, assured her that this notion of hers about the expensiveness of it all, was just a notion—obsession was the word he finally came to—which she must struggle against as best she could. She'd see things in a truer proportion afterward.

Then it came out that he had made all his plans for a long summer vacation. There was no court work in July and August anyway. He was going to carry her off to a quiet little place out on Cape Cod that he knew about, and just luxuriate in her; have her all to himself—not a soul they knew about them. They would lie about in the sands all day, building air castles. If she got tired of him, any person she wanted to see should be telegraphed for forthwith. The one thing she had to bear in mind was that she was to be happy and not bother about things; leave everything to him.

This plan was carried out, and in a paradise, made up of blue sea, white sands, warm sun and Rodney—Rodney always there, and queerly content to drowse away the time with her, she almost forgot the great dam and the pressure of the waters that had mounted up behind it. Was it an obsession just as Rodney said? Would she find when it was all over and she rallied herself for the great endeavor, that there was, after all, no battle to be fought—nothing but a baby at her breast?

XIII

FATE PLAYS A JOKE

Traveling bars flowing along parallel, black and white; the white ones incandescent;—and a small helpless harried thing struggling to keep in the shadow of the black ones, or to regain it again across the pitiless zone of white that the little helpless thing called pain.—Traveling bars flowing along endlessly.

And then a great ball whirling in planetary space, half dark, half incandescent white, having for its sole inhabitant, the small harried thing that struggled to keep in the dark out of the glare of that pitiless white pain.—One watched its struggles from a long way off—like God.—But the ball whirled drunkenly and it made one sick to look.—And then a supervening chaos—no longer a ball but still whirling, reeling, tottering. Rectangles of light, which, had they kept still, would have been windows—a mirror.

And then, very fine and small and weak, something that knew it was Rose Stanton—Rose Stanton lying in a bed with people about her. She let her eyes fall heavily shut again lest they should discover she was there and want her to speak or think.

The bars came back, but the whiteness of them was no longer so white, and slowly they faded out. Then, for a long time, nothing. Then sounds, movements—soft, skilful, disciplined sounds and movements. And, presently, a hand—a firm powerful hand, that picked up and supported a heavy limp wrist—Rose Stanton's wrist—and two sensitive finger-tips that rested lightly on the upper surface of it. After that, an even measured voice—a voice of authority, whose words no doubt made sense, only Rose was too tired to think what the sense was:

"She's out of the ether now, practically. That's a splendid pulse. She's doing the best thing she can, sleeping like that. It's been a thoroughly normal delivery from the beginning. Oh, a long difficult one, I'll admit. But there's nothing now, that you could want better than what you've got."

And then another voice, utterly unlike Rodney's and yet unmistakably his—a ragged voice that tried to talk in a whisper but couldn't manage it; broke queerly.

"That's all right," it said. "But I'll find it easier to believe when. . ."

She must see him—must know what it meant that he should talk like that. With a strong physical effort, she opened her eyes and tried to speak his name.

She couldn't; but some one must have been watching and seen, because a woman's voice said quickly and quietly, "Mr. Aldrich."

And the next moment, vast and towering, and very blurred in outline, but, like his voice, unmistakable, was Rodney—her own big strong Rodney. She tried to hold her arms up to him, but of course she couldn't.

And then he shortened suddenly. He had knelt down beside her bed, that was it. And she felt upon her palm, the pressure of his lips, and his unshaven cheek, and on her wrist, a warm wetness that must be—tears.

Why was he crying? What had happened? She must try to think.

It was very hard. She didn't want to think, but she must. She must begin with something she knew. She knew who she was. She was Rose—Rodney's Rose. Here was his mouth down close to the pillow saying her name over and over and over again. And she was in her own bed. But what had happened? She must try to remember. She remembered something she had said—said to herself over and over again an illimitable while ago. "It's coming. The miracle's beginning." What had she meant by that?

And then she knew. The urgency of a sudden terror gave her her voice.

"Roddy," she said. "There was going to be a—baby. Isn't there?"

Something queerly like a laugh broke his voice when he answered. "Oh, you darling! Yes. It's all right. That isn't why I'm crying. It's just because I'm so happy."

"But the baby!" she persisted. "Why isn't it here?"

Rodney turned and spoke to some one else. "She wants to see," he said. "May she?"

And then a woman's voice (why, it was the nurse, of course! Miss Harris, who had come last night) said in an indulgent soothing tone, "Why, surely she may. Wait just a minute."

But the wait seemed hours. Why didn't they bring the baby—her baby? There! Miss Harris was coming at last, with a queerly bulky, shapeless bundle. Rodney stepped in between and cut off the view, but only to slide an arm under mattress and pillow and raise her a little so that she could see. And then, under her eyes, dark red and hairy against the whiteness of the pillow, were two small heads—two small shapeless masses leading away from them, twitching, squirming. She stared, bewildered.

"There were twins, Rose," she heard Rodney explaining triumphantly, but still with something that wasn't quite a laugh, "a boy and a girl. They're perfectly splendid. One weighs seven pounds and the other six."

Her eyes widened and she looked up into his face so that the pitiful bewilderment in hers was revealed to him.

"But the *baby!*" she said. Her wide eyes filled with tears and her voice broke weakly. "I wanted a baby."

"You've got a baby," he insisted, and now laughed outright. "There are two of them. Don't you understand, dear?"

Her eyes drooped shut, but the tears came welling out along her lashes. "Please take them away," she begged. And then, with a little sob she whispered, "I wanted a baby, not those."

Rodney started to speak, but some sort of admonitory signal from the nurse silenced him.

The nurse went away with her bundle, and Rodney stayed stroking her limp hand.

In the dark, ever so much later, she awoke, stirred a little restlessly, and the nurse, from her cot, came quickly and stood beside her bed. She had something in her hands for Rose to drink, and Rose drank it dutifully.

"Is there anything else?" the nurse asked.

"I just want to know," Rose said; "have I been dreaming, or is it true? Is there a baby, or are there twins?"

"Twins, to be sure," said the nurse cheerfully. "The loveliest, liveliest little pair you ever saw."

"Thank you," said Rose. "I just wanted to know."

She shut her eyes and pretended to go to sleep. But she didn't. It was true then. Her miracle, it seemed somehow, had gone ludicrously awry.

HENRY KITCHELL WEBSTER

XIV

THE DAM GIVES WAY

She began getting her strength back very fast after the next two or three days, but this queer kink in her emotions didn't straighten out. She came to see that it was absurd—monstrous almost, but that didn't help. Instead of a baby, she had given birth to two. They were hers of course, as much as one would have been. Only, her soul, which had been waiting so ecstatically for its miracle—for the child which, by making her a mother, should supply what her life needed—her soul wouldn't—couldn't accept the substitution. Those two droll, thin voiced, squirming little mites that were exhibited to her every morning, were as foreign to her, as detached from her, as if they had been brought into the house in a basket.

There was a certain basis of reason back of this. At some time, during those early hours of misty half-consciousness, it had been decided that two children would be too much for her to attempt to nurse.

She had a notion that this idea hadn't originated with the doctor, though it was he who had stated it to her with the most plausible firmness. Rodney had backed the doctor up, firmly, too. Rose was only a girl in years—why, just a child herself; hadn't had her twenty-second birthday yet; the labor had been long, she was very weak, the children were big and vigorous, and she couldn't hope to supply them both for more than a very few weeks, anyway. And, at this time of year, as the doctor said, there was no difficulty to be apprehended from bottle feeding. It would be better on all accounts.

Still, it didn't sound exactly like Roddy's idea either.

When Harriet came in for the first time to see her, Rose knew. Harriet was living here now, running the house for Rodney, while Rose was laid up. Doing it beautifully well, too, through all the confusion of nurses and all. Not the slightest jar or creak of their complex domestic machinery ever reached Rose in the big chamber where she lay. Harriet said:

"I think you're in great luck to have had two at once; get your duty to posterity done that much sooner. And, of course, you couldn't possibly be expected to nurse two great creatures like that."

Rose acquiesced. What was the use of struggling against so formidable a unanimity? She would have struggled though, she knew, but for that queer trick Fate had played her. Her heart ached, as did her breasts. But that was for the lips of the baby—the baby she hadn't had!

When she found that struggling with herself, denouncing herself for a brute, didn't serve to bring up the feelings toward the twins that she knew any proper mother ought to have, she buried the dark fact as deep as she could, and pretended. It was only before Rodney that the pretense was necessary. And with him, really, it was hardly a pretense at all. He was such a child himself, in his gleeful delight over the possession of a son and a daughter, that she felt for him, tenderly, mistily, luminously, the very emotion she was trying to capture for them—felt like cradling his head in her weak arms, kissing him, crying over him a little.

She wouldn't have been allowed to do that to the babies anyway. They were going to be terribly well brought up, those twins; that was apparent from the beginning. They had two nurses all to themselves, quite apart from Miss Harris, who looked after Rose: one uncannily infallible person, omniscient in baby lore—thoroughgoing, logical, efficient, remorseless as a German staff officer; and a bright-eyed, snub-nosed, smart little maid, for an assistant, who boiled bottles, washed clothes, and, at certain stated hours, over a previously determined route, at a given number of miles per hour, wheeled the twins out, in a duplex perambulator, which Harriet had acquired as soon as the need for it had become evident.

Miss Harris was to go away to another case at the end of the month. But Mrs. Ruston (she was the staff officer) and Doris, the maid, were destined, it appeared, to be as permanent as the babies. But Rose had the germ of an idea of her own about that.

They got them named with very little difficulty. The boy was Rodney, of course, after his father and grandfather before him. Rose was a little afraid Rodney would want the girl named after her, and was relieved to find he didn't. There'd never in the world be but one Rose for him, he said. So Rose named the girl Portia.

They kept Rose in bed for three weeks; flat on her back as much as possible, which was terribly irksome to her, since her strength and vitality were coming back so fast. The irksomeness was added to by a horrible harness largely of whalebone. Rose got the notion, too, that the purpose of all this was not quite wholly hygienic. Harriet had said once: "You know the most distinguished thing about you, Rose, dear—

about your looks, I mean—is that lovely boyish line of yours. It will be a perfect crime if you let yourself spread out."

This wasn't the sort of consideration to make the inactivity any easier to endure. She might have rebelled, had it not been for that germinant idea of hers. It wouldn't do, she saw, in the light of that, to give them any excuse for calling her unreasonable.

At the end of this purgatorial three weeks, she was carried to a chair and allowed to sit up a little, and by the end of another, to walk about—just a few steps at a time of course. One Sunday morning, Rodney carried her up-stairs to the nursery to see her babies bathed. This was a big room at the top of the house which Florence McCrea had always vaguely intended to make into a studio. But, in a paralysis of indecision as to what sort of studio to make it (book-binding, pottery and art weaving called her about equally) she had left the thing bare.

Rodney had given Harriet *carte blanche* to go ahead and fit it up before he and Rose came back from the seashore, and the layette was a monument to Harriet's thoroughgoing practicality. There had been a wild day of supplementing of course, when it was discovered that there were two babies instead of one.

The room, when they escorted Rose into it, was a terribly impressive place. The spirit of a barren sterile efficiency brooded everywhere. And this appearance of barrenness obtained despite the presence of an enormous number of articles; a pair of scales, a perfect battery of electric heaters of various sorts; rows of vacuum jars for keeping things cold or hot; a small sterilizing oven; instruments and appliances that Rose couldn't guess the uses or the names of. Mrs. Ruston, of course, was master of them all, and Doris flew about to do her bidding, under a watchful and slightly suspicious eye. (Doris was the sort of looking girl who might be suspected of kissing a tiny pink hand when no one was looking.)

Rose surveyed this scene, just as she would have surveyed a laboratory, or a factory where they make something complicated, like watches. That's what it was, really. Those two pink little objects, in their two severely sanitary baskets, were factory products. At precise and unalterable intervals, a highly scientific compound of fats and proteids was put into them. They were inspected, weighed, submitted to a routine of other processes. And in all the routine, there was nothing that their mother, now they were fairly born, was wanted for. Indispensable to a certain point, no doubt. But after that rather the other way about—an obstacle to the routine instead of a part of it.

Rose kept these ideas to herself and kept her eye on young Doris; listened to the orders she got; and studied alertly what she did in the execution of them.

Rodney had a lovely time watching the twins bathed. He stood about in everybody's way, made what he conceived to be alluring noises, in the perfectly unsuccessful attempt to attract the infants' attention, and finally, when the various processes were complete, on schedule, like a limited train, and the thermometrically correct bottles of food were ready, one for each baby, he turned suddenly to his wife and said: "Don't you want to—hold them, Rose?" She'd have held a couple of glowing brands in her arms for him, the way he had looked and the way he had said it.

A stab of pain went through her and tears came up into her eyes. "Yes, give them to me," she started to say.

But Mrs. Ruston spoke before she could frame the words. It was their feeding hour, she pointed out; a bad time for them to be excited, and the bottles were heated exactly right.

By that time Rose's idea had flowered into resolution. She knew exactly what she was going to do. But she mustn't jeopardize the success of her plan by trying to put it into effect too soon.

She waited patiently, reasonably, for another fortnight. Harriet by that time had gone off to Washington on a visit, taking Rodney's heartfelt thanks with her. Rose expressed hers just as warmly, and felt ashamed that they were so unreal. She simply mustn't let herself get to resenting Harriet! At the end of the fortnight, the doctor made his final visit. Rose had especially asked Rodney to be on hand to hear his report when the examination was over. Rose and the doctor found him waiting in the library.

"He says," Rose told her husband, "that I'm perfectly well." She turned to the doctor for confirmation, "Don't you?"

The doctor smiled. "As far as my diagnostic resources go, Mrs. Aldrich, you are perfectly well."

Rodney was pleased of course, and expressed this feeling fervently. But he looked across at his glowing radiant wife, with a touch of misgiving.

"What are you trying to put over on me?" he asked.

"Not a thing," said Rose demurely. "I thought you'd be glad to know that I needn't be kept in cotton-wool any more, and that you'd feel surer of it if he told you."

"I feel surer that you've got something up your sleeve," he said. And, to the doctor: "I don't imagine that in saying my wife is perfectly well, you mean to suggest an absence of all reasonable caution."

The doctor took the hint, expatiated largely; it was always well to be careful—one couldn't, in fact, be too careful. The human body at best, more especially the—ah—feminine human body, was a delicate machine, not to be abused without inviting serious consequences. He was even a little reproachful about it.

"But there's no more reason, is there," Rose persisted, "why I should be careful than why any other woman should—my nurse-maid for example? Is she any healthier than I am?"

It was indiscreet of the doctor to look at her before he answered. Her eyes were sparkling, the color bright in her cheeks; unconsciously, she had flattened her shoulders back and drawn a good deep breath down into her lungs. The doctor smiled a smile of surrender and turned back to Rodney. "I'll confess," he said, "that in my experience, Mrs. Aldrich is almost a *lusus naturae*—a perfectly sound, healthy woman."

Rose smiled widely and contentedly on the pair of them. "That's more like it," she said to the doctor. "Thanks very much."

But after he had gone, she did not spring anything on Rodney, as he fully expected she would. She took him out for a tramp through the park in the dusk of a perfect autumn afternoon, and went to a musical show with him in the evening. She might have been, as far as he could see, the Rose of a year ago. She had the same lithe boyish swing. She even wore, though he didn't know it, the same skirt for their walk in the park that she had worn on some of their tramps before they were married. And when they had had their evening at the theater, and a bite of supper somewhere, and come home, she let him drop off to sleep without a word that would explain her insistence on getting a clean bill of health from the doctor.

But the next morning, while Doris was busy in the laundry, she found Mrs. Ruston in the nursery and had a talk with that lady, which was destined to produce seismic upheavals.

"I've decided to make a little change in our arrangements, Mrs. Ruston," she said. "But I don't think it's one that will disturb you very much. I'm going to let Doris go—I'll get her another place, of course—and do her work myself."

Mrs. Ruston compressed her lips, and went on for a minute with what she was doing to one of the twins, as if she hadn't heard.

"Doris is quite satisfactory, madam," she said at last. "I'd not advise making a change. She's a dependable young woman, as such go. Of course I watch her very close."

"I think I can promise to be dependable," Rose said. "I don't know much about babies, of course, but I think I can learn as well as Doris. Anyhow, I can wheel them about and wash their clothes and boil bottles and things as well as she does. For the rest, you can tell me what to do just as you tell her."

Mrs. Ruston took a considerably longer interval to digest this reply. "Then you're meaning to give the girl her notice at once, madam?" she asked.

"I'm not going to give her notice at all," said Rose. "I'm going to find her another place. I shan't have any trouble about it though. As you say, she's a very good nurse-maid, and she's a pleasant sort of a human being besides. But as soon as I can find her another place, I'm going to take over her work."

To this last observation it became evident that Mrs. Ruston meant to make no reply at all. She gave Rose some statistical information about the twins instead, in which Rose showed herself politely interested and presently withdrew.

It soon appeared, however, that though Mrs. Ruston might be slow and sparing of speech, she was capable of acting with a positively Napoleonic dash. Rodney wore a queer expression all through dinner, and when he got Rose alone in the library afterward, he explained it. Mrs. Ruston had made her two-hour constitutional that afternoon into an opportunity for calling on him at his office. She had given him notice, contingently. She made it an inviolable rule of conduct, it appeared, never to undertake the care of two infants without the assistance of a nurse-maid. She was a conscientious person and she felt she couldn't do justice to her work on any other basis. Rose had informed her of her intention to dispense with the services of the nurse-maid, without engaging any one else to take her place. If Rose adhered to this intention, Mrs. Ruston must leave.

It was some sort of absurd misunderstanding, of course, Rodney concluded and wanted to know what it was all about.

"I did say I meant to let Doris go," Rose explained, "but I told her I meant to take Doris' job myself. I said I thought I could be just as good a nurse-maid as she was. I said I'd boil bottles and wash clothes and take Mrs. Ruston's orders exactly as if I were being paid six dollars a week and board for doing it. And I meant it just as literally as I said it."

He was prowling about the room in a worried sort of way, before she got as far as that.

"I don't see, child," he exclaimed, "why you couldn't leave well enough alone! If it's that old economy bug of yours again, it's nonsense. You'd save, including board, about ten dollars a week. And it would work out one of two ways: If you didn't do all the maid's work. Mrs. Ruston would have a real grievance. She's right about needing all the help she gets. If you did do it, it would mean that you'd work yourself sick.—Oh, I know what the doctor said, but that's all rot, and he knew it. You had him hypnotized. You'd have to give up everything for it—all your social duties, all our larks together. Oh, it's absurd! You, to spend all your time doing menial work—scrubbing and washing bottles, to save me ten dollars a week!"

"It isn't menial work," Rose insisted. "It's—apprentice work. After I've been at it six months, learning as fast as I can, I'll be able to let Mrs. Ruston go and take *her* job. I'll be really competent to take care of my own children. I don't pretend I am now."

"I don't see why you can't do that as things are now. She'll let you practise bathing them and things like that, and certainly no one would object to your wheeling them out in the pram. But the nurse-maid would be on hand in case. . ."

"I'm to take it on then," said Rose, and her voice had a new ring in it—the ring of scornful anger—"I'm to take it on as a sort of polite sentimental amusement. I'm not to do any real work for them that depends on me to get done. I'm not to be able to feel that, even in a bottle-washing sort of way, I'm doing an indispensable service for them. They're not to need me for anything, the poor little mites! They're to be something for me to have a sort of emotional splurge with, just as"—she laughed raggedly—"just as some of the wives you're so fond of talking about, are to their husbands."

He stared at her in perfectly honest bewilderment. He'd never seen her like this before.

"You're talking rather wild I think, Rose," he said very quietly.

"I'm talking what I've learned from you," she said, but she did get her voice in control again. "You've taught me the difference between real work, and the painless imitation of it that a lot of us women spend our lives on—between doing something because it's got to be done and is up to you, and—finding something to do to spend the time.

"Oh, Rodney, *please* try to forget that I'm your wife and that you're in love with me. Can't you just say: 'Here's A, or B, or X, a perfectly healthy woman, twenty-two years old, and a little real work would be good for her'?"

She won, with much pleading, a sort of troubled half-assent from him. The matter might be borne in mind. It could be taken up again with Mrs. Ruston.

But Mrs. Ruston was adamant. Under no conceivable circumstances could she consent to regard her employer's wife as a substitute for her own hired assistant. There were other nurses though, to be got. Somewhere one could be found, no doubt, who'd take a broader view.

Given a fair field, Rose might have won a victory here. But, as Portia had said once, the pattern was cut differently. There was a sudden alarm one night, when her little namesake was found strangling with the croup. There were seven terrifying hours—almost unendurable hours, while the young life swung and balanced over the ultimate abyss. The heroine of those hours was Mrs. Ruston. It was her watchfulness that had been accessible to the first alarm—her instant doing of the one right thing that stemmed the first onrush. That the child lived was clearly creditable to her.

Rose made another effort even after that, though she knew she was beaten in advance. She waited until the storm had subsided, until the old calm routine was reestablished. Then, once more, she asked for her chance.

But Rodney exploded before she got the words fairly out of her mouth.

"No," he shouted, "I won't consider it! She's saved that baby's life. Another woman might have, but it's more likely not. You'll have to find some way of satisfying your whims that won't jeopardize those babies' lives. After that night—good God, Rose, have you forgotten that night?—I'm going to play it safe."

Rose paled a little and sat ivory still in her chair. There were no miracles any more. The great dam was swept away.

XV

The Only Remedy

The sudden flaw of passion that had troubled the waters of Rodney's soul, subsided, spent itself in mutterings, explanations, tending to become at last rather apologetic. He said he didn't know why her request had got him like that. It had seemed to him for a moment as if she didn't realize what the children's lives meant to them—almost as if she didn't love them. He knew that was absurd, of course.

Her own rather monstrous comments on these observations had luckily remained unspoken. What if she did lose a child as a result of her effort to care for it herself? She could bear more children. And what chance had she to love them? Where was the soil for love to take root in, unless she took care of them herself? These weren't really thoughts of hers—just a sort of crooked reflection of what he was saying off the surface of a mind terribly preoccupied with something else.

She was in the grip of an appalling realization. This moment—this actually present moment that was going to last only until she should speak for the next time, or move her eyes around to his face—was the critical moment of her life. She had, for just this moment, a choice of two things to say when next she should speak—a choice of two ways of looking into his face. A mountaineer, standing on the edge of a crevasse, deciding whether to try to leap across and win a precarious way to the summit, or to turn back and confess the climb has been in vain, is confronted by a choice like that. If ever the leap was to be made, it must be made now. The rainbow bridge across the crevasse, the miracle of motherhood, had faded like the mist it was composed of.

She was a mother now. Yet her relation to her husband's life was the same as that of the girl who had gone to his office the night of the Randolphs' dinner. And no external event—nothing that could *happen* to her (remember that even motherhood had "happened" in her case) could ever transmute that relation into the thing she wanted. If the alchemy were to be wrought at all, it would be by the act of her own will—at the cost of a deliberately assumed struggle. There was nothing, any more, to hope from waiting. The thing that whispered, "Wait! Tomorrow—some tomorrow or other, it may be easier! Wait until, for yourself, you've thought out the consequences,"—that was the voice of cowardice. If she turned back, down the easier path, tonight, it must be under no delusion that she'd ever try to climb again, or find a pair of magic wings that would carry her, effortless, to what she wanted.

Well, then, she had her choice. One of two things she might do now. It was in her power to look up at him and smile, and say: "All right, Roddy, old man, I'll stop being disagreeable. I won't have any more whims." And she could go to him and clasp her hands behind his head and feel the rough pressure of his cheeks against the velvety surfaces of her forearms, and kiss his eyes and mouth; surrender to the embrace she knew so well would follow.

She could make, after a fashion, a life of that. She had no fear but it would last. Barring incalculable misfortunes, she ought to be able to keep her looks and her charm for him, unimpaired, or but little impaired, for twenty years—twenty-five, with care. For the rich, the resources of modern civilization would almost guarantee that. Well, twenty-five years would see Rodney through his fifties. She needn't, barring accident, have any more children. He'd probably be content with two; especially as they were boy and girl.

The other man in him—the man who wasn't her lover—would struggle of course. Except when she was by, the lover would probably have a bad time of it. She'd have to find some amusing sort of occupation to enable her to forget that. But when she was there, it would be strange if she and her lover together couldn't, most of the time, keep the other man locked up where he wouldn't disturb them much.

Lived without remorse or misgivings, played magnificently for all it was worth, as she could play it—she knew that now—it would be a rather wonderful life. They must be decidedly an exceptional pair of lovers, she thought. Certainly Madame Gréville's generalization about Americans did not apply to them, and she was coming to suspect it did apply to the majority of her friends. She could have that life—safely, surely, as far as our poor mortality can be sure of anything. She had only to reach out her hands.

But if, instead, she took the leap. . . !

"Roddy. . ." she said.

He was slumped down in a big easy chair at the other side of the table, swinging a restless foot; drumming now and then with his fingers. It was many silent minutes since the storm of reproach with which he had repelled her plea for a part in the actual responsible care of her children had died away. He had spoken with unnecessary vehemence, he knew. He had admitted that—said he was sorry, as well as he could without withdrawing from his position. But he had been met by that most formidable of all weapons—a blank silence—an inscrutable face. Some sort of scene was inevitable, he knew. And he sat there waiting for it. She had been hurt. She was undoubtedly very angry.

He thought he was ready for anything. But just the way she spoke his name, startled—almost frightened—him, she said it so quietly, so—tenderly.

"Roddy," she said, "I want you to come over here and kiss me, and then go back and sit down in that chair again."

He went a little pale at that. The swing of his foot was arrested suddenly. But, for a moment, he made no move—just looked wonderingly into her great grave eyes.

"Something's going to happen," she went on, "and before it's over, I'm afraid it's going to hurt you terribly—and me. And I want the kiss for us to remember. So that we'll always know, whatever happens afterward, that we loved each other." She held out her arms to him. "Won't you come?"

He came—a man bewildered—bent down over her and found her lips; but almost absently, out of a daze.

"No, not like that," she murmured. "In the old way."

There was a long embrace.

"I wouldn't do it," she said, "I don't believe I'd have the courage to do it, if it were just me. But there's some one else—I've made some one a promise. I can't tell you about that. Now please go back and sit over there where you were, where we can talk quietly.—Oh, Roddy, I love you so!—No, please go back, old man! And—and light your pipe. Oh, don't tremble like that! It—it isn't a tragedy. It's—for us, it's the greatest hope in the world."

He went back to his chair. He even lighted his pipe as she asked him to, and waited as steadily as he could for her to begin.

But she couldn't begin while she looked at him. She moved a little closer to the table and leaned her elbow on it, shaded her eyes with one hand, while the other played with the stump of a pencil that happened to be lying there.

"Do you remember. . ." she began, and it was wonderful how quiet and steady her voice was. There was even the trace of a smile about her wonderful mouth. "Do you remember that afternoon of ours, the very first of them, when you brought home my note-books and found me asleep on the couch in our old back parlor? Do you remember how you told me that one's desires were the only motive power he had? One couldn't ride anywhere, you said, except on the backs of his own passions? Well, it was a funny thing—I got to wondering afterward what my desires were, and it seemed I hadn't any. Everything had, somehow, come to me before I knew I wanted it. Everything in the world, even your love for me, came like that.

"But I've got a passion now, Rodney. I've had it for a long while. It's a desire I can't satisfy. The thing I want, and there's nothing in the world that I wouldn't give to get it, is—well, your friendship; that's a way of saying it."

What he had been waiting to hear, of course, she didn't know. But she knew by the way he started and stared at her, that it hadn't been for that. The thing struck him, it seemed, as a sort of grotesquely irritating anti-climax.

"Gracious Heaven!" he said. "My friendship! Why, I'm in love with you! That's certainly a bigger thing. Go back to your geometry, child. The greater includes the less, doesn't it?"

"I don't know whether it's a bigger thing or not," she said. "But it doesn't include the other. Love's just a sort of miracle thing that happens to you. You don't have it because you deserve it. The person I made that promise to would have earned it, if any one could. But it doesn't come that way. It's like lightning. It strikes or else it doesn't. Well, it struck us. But friendship—there's this about it. You can't get it any way in the world, except just by earning it. Nobody can give it to you, no matter how hard he tries. So when you've got it, you can always say, 'There's something that I'm entitled to—something that's mine.' Your love isn't mine any more than the air is. I never did anything to earn it.

"And that's why it can't satisfy me.—Because it doesn't, Roddy. It hasn't for ever so long. It's something wonderful that's—*happened* to me. It's the loveliest thing that ever happened to anybody. And just because it's so wonderful and beautiful, I can't bear to—well, this is hard to say—I can't bear to use it to live on. I can't bear to have it mixed up in things like millinery bills and housekeeping expense. I can't bear to see it become a thing that piles a load of hateful obligations on your back. I could live on your friendship, Roddy; because your friendship would mean that somehow I was earning my way, but I can't live on your love;

any more than you could on mine. Won't you—won't you just try to think for a moment what that would mean to you?"

Now that he had sensed the direction her talk was headed in, even though he hadn't even vaguely glimpsed the point at which she was going to bring up, he made it much harder for her to talk to him. He was tramping up and down the room, stopping and turning short every now and then with a gesture of exasperation, or an interruption that never got beyond two or three words and broke off always in a sort of frantic speechlessness.

She knew he couldn't help it. Down underneath his mind, controlling utterly its processes, was a ganglion of instincts that were utterly outraged by the things she was saying to him. It was they and not his intelligence she had to fight. She must be patient, as gentle as she could, but she must make him listen.

"You've got my friendship!" he cried out now. "It's a grotesque perversion of the facts to say you haven't."

She smiled at him as she shook her head. "I've spent too many months trying to get it and seeing myself fail—oh, so ridiculously!—not to know what I am talking about, Roddy."

And then, still smiling, rather sadly, she told what some of the experiments had been—some of her attempts to break into the life he kept locked away from her and carry off a share of it for herself.

"I was angry at first when I found you keeping me out," she said, "angry and hurt. I used to cry about it. And then I saw it wasn't your fault. That's how I discovered friendship had to be earned."

But her power to maintain that attitude of grave detachment was about spent. The passion mounted in her voice and in her eyes as she went on.

"You thought it was because of my condition, as you called it, that my mind had got full of wild ideas;—the wild idea that I wasn't really and truly your wife at all, but only your mistress, and that I was pulling you down from something free and fine that you had been, to something that you despised yourself for being and had to try to deny you were. Those were the obsessions of a pregnant woman, you thought—something she was to be soothed and coddled into forgetting. You were wrong about that, Roddy.

"I did have an obsession, but it wasn't the thing you thought. It was an obsession that kept me quiet, and contented and happy, and willing to wait in spite of everything. The obsession was that none of those things mattered because a big miracle was coming that was going to change it all. I was going to have a job at last—a job that was just as real as yours—the job of being a mother."

Her voice broke in a fierce sharp little laugh over the word, but she got it back in control again.

"I was going to have a baby to feed out of my own body, to keep alive with my own care. There was going to be responsibility and hard work, things that demanded courage and endurance and sacrifice. I could earn your friendship with that, I said. That was the real obsession, Roddy, and it never really died until tonight. Because of course I have kept on hoping, even after I might have seen how it was. But the babies' lives aren't to be jeopardized to gratify my whims. Well, I suppose I can't complain. It's over, that's the main thing.

"And now, here I am perfectly normal and well again—as good as ever. I've kept my looks—oh, my hair and my complexion and my figure. I could wear pretty clothes again and start going out to things now that the season's begun, just as I did a year ago. People would admire me, and you'd be pleased, and you'd love me as much as ever, and it would all be like the paradise it was last year, except for one thing. The one thing is that if I do that, I'll know this time what I really am. Your mistress, Roddy; your legal, perfectly respectable mistress,— and a little more despicable rather than less, I think, because of the adjectives."

"I've let that word go by once," he said quietly, but with a dangerous light of anger in his eyes. "I won't again. It's perfectly outrageous and inexcusable that you should talk like that, and I'll ask you never to do it again."

"I won't," she flashed back at him, "if you'll explain why I'm not exactly what I say." And after ten seconds of silence, she went on.

"Why, Roddy, I've heard you describe me a hundred times. Not the you that's my lover. The other you; talking all over the universe to Barry Lake. You've described the woman who's never been trained nor taught nor disciplined; who's been brought up soft, with the bloom on, for the purpose of making her marriageable; who's never found her job in marriage, who doesn't cook, nor sew, nor spin, nor even take care of her own children; the woman who uses her sex charm to save her from having to do hard ugly things, and keep her in luxury. Do you remember what you've called her, Roddy? Do you remember the word you've used? I've used a gentler word than that.

"Oh, you didn't know, you poor blind boy, that I was the woman you were talking about. You never saw it at all. But I am. I was brought up like that.—Oh, not on purpose. Dear old mother! She wasn't trying to make me into a prostitute any more then you are trying to make me into your mistress. You both love me, that's all. It's just an instinct not to let anything hurt me, nor frighten me, nor tire me, nor teach me what work is. She thought she was educating me to be a lawyer so that when the time came, I could be one of the leaders of the woman movement just as she'd been. And all the while, without knowing it, she was educating me to be the sort of person you'd fall in love with—something precious and expensive—something to be taken care of.

"I didn't understand any of that when you married me, Roddy; it was just like a dream to me—like a fairy story come true. If any one had told me a year ago, that I should ever be anything but perfectly happy in your love for me, I'd have laughed at him. I remember telling Madame Gréville that our marriage had turned out well—ended happily. And she did laugh. That was before I'd begun to understand. But I do understand now. I know why it was you could talk to me, back in those days before we were married, about anything under the sun—things ten thousand miles above my head; what it was that fooled me into thinking we were friends as well as lovers. I know why you've never been able to talk to me like that since. And I know—this is the worst of all, Roddy,—this is the piece of knowledge that makes it impossible—I know what a good mistress I could make. I know I could make you love me whether you wanted to or not; whether I loved you or not. I could make other men love me, if I could make up my mind to do it—make them tell me all their hopes and dreams, and think I had a fine mind and a wonderful understanding. Oh, it's too easy—it's too hatefully easy!

"Do you know why I told you that? Because if you believe it and understand it, you will see why I can't go on living on your love. Because how can you be sure, knowing that my position in the world, my friends—oh, the very clothes on my back, and the roof over my head, are dependent on your love,—how are you going to be sure that my love for you is honest and disinterested? What's to keep you from wondering—asking questions? Love's got to be free, Roddy. The only way to make it free is to have friendship growing alongside it. So, when I can be your partner and your friend, I'll be your mistress, too. But not—not again, Roddy, till I can find a way. I'll have to find it for myself. I'll have to go. . ."

She broke down there over a word she couldn't at first say, buried her face in her arms and let a deep racking sob or two have their own way with her. But presently she sat erect again and, with a supreme effort of will, forced her voice to utter the word.

"I've got to go somewhere alone—away from you, and stay until I find it. If I ever do, and you want me, I'll come back."

XVI

Rose Opens the Door

The struggle between them lasted a week—a ghastly week, during which, as far as the surface of things showed, their life flowed along in its accustomed channels. It was a little worse than that, really, because the week included, so an ironic Fate had decreed, Thanksgiving Day and a jolly family party at Frederica's, with congratulations on the past, plans for the future. And Rose and Rodney, as civilized persons will do, kept their faces, accepted congratulations, made gay plans for the twins; smiled or laughed when necessary—somehow or other, got through with it.

But at all sorts of times, and in all sorts of places when they were alone together, the great battle was renewed; mostly through the dead hours of the night, in Rose's bedroom, she sitting up in bed, he tramping up and down, shivering and shuddering in a big bath-robe. It had a horrible way of interrupting itself for small domestic commonplaces, which in their assumption of the permanency of their old life, their blind disregard of the impending disaster, had an almost unendurable poignancy. A breakfast on the morning of an execution is something like that.

The hardest thing about it all for Rose—the thing that came nearest to breaking down her courage—was to see how slowly Rodney came to realize it at all. He was like a trapped animal pacing the four sides of his cage confident that in a moment or two he would find the way out, and then, incredulously, dazedly, coming to the surmise that there was no way out. She really meant to go away and leave him—leave the babies; go somewhere where his care and protection could not reach her! She was actually planning to do it—planning the details of doing it! By the end of one of their long talks, it would seem to her he had grasped this monstrous intention and accepted it. But before the beginning of the next one, he seemed to manage somehow to dismiss the thing as an impossible nightmare.

An invitation came in from the Crawfords for a dance at the Blackstone, the fifth of December, and he said something about accepting it.

"I shan't be here then, Roddy, you know," she said.

He went completely to pieces at that, as if the notion of her going away had never really reached his mind before.

The struggle ranged through the widest possible gamut of moods. They had their moments of rapturous love—passionate attempts at self-surrender. They had long hours of cool discussion, as impersonal as if they had been talking about the characters out of a book instead of about themselves. They had stormy nerve-tearing hours of blind agonizing, around and around in circles, lacerating each other, lashing out at each other, getting nowhere. They had moments of incandescent anger.

He tried, just once, early in the fight, to take the ground he had taken once before; that she was irresponsible, obsessed. There was a fracture somewhere, as James Randolph's jargon had it, in her unconscious mind. She didn't let him go far with that. He saw her blaze up in a splendid burst of wrath, as she had blazed once—oh, an eternity ago, at a street-car conductor. Her challenge rang like a sword out of a scabbard.

"We'll settle that before we go any further," she said. "Telephone for James Randolph, or any other alienist you like. Let him take me and put me in a sanatorium somewhere and keep me under observation as long as he pleases, until he's satisfied whether I'm out of my mind or not. But unless you're willing to do that, don't call me irresponsible."

He grew more reasonable as a belief in her complete seriousness and determination sobered him. He made desperate efforts to recover his self-control—to get his big, cool, fine mechanism of a mind into action. But his mind, to his complete bewilderment, betrayed him. He'd always looked at Rose before, through the lens of his emotions. But now that he forced himself to look at her through the non-refracting window from which he looked at the rest of the world, she compelled him again and again to admit that she was right.

"Why shouldn't I be right?" she said with a woebegone smile. "These are all just things I've learned from you."

After a long and rather angry struggle with himself, he made up his mind to a compromise, and in one of their cooler talks together, he offered it.

"We've both of us pretty well lost our sense of proportion, it seems to me," he said. "This whole ghastly business started from my refusing to let Mrs. Ruston go and get a nurse who'd allow you to be your own nurse-maid. Well, I'm willing to give up completely on that point. You can let Mrs. Ruston go as soon as you like and get a nurse who'll meet with your ideas."

"You're doing that," said Rose thoughtfully, "rather than let me go away. That's the way it is, isn't it?"

"Why, yes, of course," he admitted. "I was looking at things from the children's point of view, and I thought I was right. From their point of view, I still think so."

She drew in a long sigh and shook her head. "It won't do, Roddy. Can't you see you're giving way practically under a threat—because I'll go away if you don't? But think what it would mean if I did stay, on those terms. The thing would rankle always. And if anything did happen to one of the babies because the new nurse wasn't quite so good, you'd never forgive me—not in all the world.

"And," she added a little later, "that would be just as true of any other compromise. I mean like going and living in a flat and letting me do the housework—any of the things we've talked about. I can say I am going away, don't you see, but I couldn't say I'd go away—*unless* . . . I couldn't use that threat to extort things from you without killing our whole life dead. Can't you see that?"

His mind infuriated him by agreeing with her—goaded him into another passionate outburst during which he accused her of bad faith, of being tired of him, anxious to get away from him—seizing pretexts. But he offered no more compromises. The thing he fell back on after that was a plea for delay. The question must be decided coolly; not like this. Let them just put it out of their minds for a while, go on with the old routine as if nothing threatened it and see if things didn't work somewhat better—see if they weren't, after all, better friends than she thought.

"If I were ill, Roddy," she said, "and there was an operation talked about; if they said to you that there was something I might drag along for years, half alive, without, but that if I had it, it would either kill or cure, you wouldn't urge delay. We'd decide for or against it and be done. It's—it's taking just all the courage I've got to face this thing now that I am excited—now that I've thought it out and talked it out with you—now that I've got the big hope before my eyes. But to wait until I was tangled in the old routine and the babies began to get a little older and more—human, so that they knew me, and then do it in cold blood! I couldn't do that. We'd patch up some sort of a life, pretending a little, quarreling a little, and when my feelings got especially hurt about something, I'd try to make myself think, and you, that I was going away. And we'd both know down inside that we were cowards."

He protested against the word, but she stuck to it.

"We're both afraid now," she insisted. "That's one of the things that makes us so cruel to each other when we talk—fear. The world's a terrible place to me, Roddy. I've never ventured out alone in it; not a step. A year ago, I don't think I'd have been so frightened. I didn't know then—I'd never really thought about it—what a hard dangerous thing it is, just to earn enough to keep yourself alive. I haven't any illusions now that it's easy—not after the things I've heard Barry Lake tell about. But sometimes I think you're more afraid than I; and that you've got a more intolerable thing to fear—ridicule—an intangible sort of pitying ridicule that you can't get hold of; guessing at the sort of things people will say and never really quite knowing. And we have each got the other's fear to suffer under, too.—Oh, Roddy, Roddy, don't hate me too bitterly. . . ! But I think if we can both endure it, stand the gaff, as you said once, and know that the other's standing it, too, perhaps that'll be the real beginning of the new life."

Somehow or other, during their calmer moments toward the end, practical details managed to get talked about—settled after a fashion, without the admission really being made on his part that the thing was going to happen at all.

"I'd do everything I could of course, to make it easier," she said. "We could have a story for people that I'd gone to California to make mother a long visit. You could bring Harriet home from Washington to keep house while I was gone. I'd take my trunks, you see, and really go. People would suspect of course, after a while, but they'll always pretend to believe anything that's comfortable—anything that saves scenes and shocks and explanations."

"Where would you go, really?" he demanded. "Have you any plan at all?"

"I have a sort of plan," she said. "I think I know of a way of earning a living."

But she didn't offer to go on and tell him what it was, and after a little silence, he commented bitterly on this omission.

"You won't even give me the poor satisfaction of knowing what you're doing," he said.

"I'd love to," she said, "—to be able to write to you, hear from you every day. But I don't believe you want to know. I think it would be too hard for you. Because you'd have to promise not to try to get me back—not to come and rescue me if I got into trouble and things went badly and I didn't know where to turn. Could you promise that, Roddy?"

He gave a groan and buried his face in his hands. Then:

"No," he said furiously. "Of course I couldn't. See you suffering and stand by with my hands in my pockets and watch!" He sprang up and seized her by the arms in a grip that actually left bruises, and fairly shook her in the agony of his entreaty. "Tell me it's a nightmare, Rose," he said. "Tell me it isn't true. Wake me up out of it!"

But under the indomitable resolution of her blue eyes, he turned away. This was the last appeal of that sort that he made.

"I'll promise," she said presently, "to be sensible—not to take any risks I don't have to take. I'll regard my life and my health and all, as something I'm keeping in trust for you. I'll take plenty of warm sensible clothes when I go; lots of shoes and stockings—things like that, and if you'll let me, I'll—I'll borrow a hundred dollars to start myself off with. It isn't a tragedy, Roddy,—not that part of it. You wouldn't be afraid for any one else as big and strong and healthy as I."

Gradually, out of the welter of scenes like that, the thing got itself recognized as something that was to happen. But the parting came at last in a little different way from any they had foreseen.

Rodney came home from his office early one afternoon, with a telegram that summoned him to New York to a conference of counsel in a big public utility case he had been working on for months. He must leave, if he were going at all, at five o'clock. He ransacked the house, vainly at first, for Rose, and found her at last in the trunk-room—dusty, disheveled, sobbing quietly over something she held hugged in her arms. But she dried her eyes and came over to him and asked what it was that had brought him home so early.

He showed her the telegram. "I'll have to leave in an hour," he said, "if I'm to go."

She paled at that, and sat down rather giddily on a trunk. "You must go," she said, "of course. And—Roddy, I guess that'll be the easiest way. I'll get my telegram tonight—pretend to get it—from Portia. And you can give me the hundred dollars, and then, when you come back, I'll be gone."

The thing she had been holding in her hands slipped to the floor. He stooped and picked it up—stared at it with a sort of half awakened recognition.

"I f—found it," she explained, "among some old things Portia sent over when she moved. Do you know what it is? It's one of the note-books that got wet—that first night when we were put off the street-car. And—and, Roddy, look!"

She opened it to an almost blank page, and with a weak little laugh, pointed to the thing that was written there:

"'March fifteenth, nineteen twelve!' Your birthday, you see, and the day we met each other."

And then, down below, the only note she had made during the whole of that lecture, he read: "Never marry a man with a passion for principles."

"That's the trouble with us, you see," she said. "If you were just an ordinary man without any big passions or anything, it wouldn't matter much if your life got spoiled. But with us, we've got to try for the biggest thing there is. Oh, Roddy, Roddy, darling! Hold me tight for just a minute, and then I'll come and help you pack."

BOOK III
THE WORLD ALONE

I

The Length of a Thousand Yards

Here's the first week's rent then," said Rose, handing the landlady three dollars, "and I think you'd better give me a receipt showing till when it's paid for. Do you know where there's an expressman who would go for a trunk?"

The landlady had tight gray hair, a hard bitten hatchet face, and a back that curved through a forty-degree arc between the lumbar and the cervical vertebræ, a curve which was accentuated by the faded longitudinal blue and white stripes—like ticking—of the dress she wore. She had no charms, one would have said, of person, mind or manner. But it was nevertheless true that Rose was renting this room largely on the strength of the landlady. She was so much more humanly possible than any of the others at whose placarded doors Rose had knocked or rung. . . !

For the last year and a half, anyway since she had married Rodney Aldrich, the surface that life had presented to her had been as bland as velvet. She'd never been spoken to by anybody except in terms of politeness. All the people she encountered could be included under two categories: her friends, if one stretches the word to include all her social acquaintances, and, in an equally broad sense, her servants; that is to say, people who earned their living by doing things she wanted done. Her friends' and her servants' manners were not alike, to be sure, but as far as intent went, they came to the same thing. They presented, whatever passions, misfortunes, dislikes, uncomfortable facts of any sort might lie in the background, a smooth and practically frictionless, bearing surface. A person accustomed to that surface develops a soft skin. This was about the first of Rose's discoveries.

To be looked at with undisguised suspicion—to have a door slammed in her face as the negative answer to a civil question, left her at first bewildered, and then enveloped in a blaze of indignation. It was perhaps lucky for her that this happened at the very beginning of her pilgrimage. Because, with that fire once alight within her, Rose could go through anything. The horrible fawning, leering landlady whom she had encountered later, might have turned her sick, but for that fine steady glow. The hatchet-faced one she had finally arrived at, made no protestations of her own respectability, and she seemed, though rather reluctantly, willing to assume that of her prospective lodger. She was puzzled about something, Rose could see; disposed to be very watchful and at no pains to conceal this attitude.

Well, she'd probably learned that she had to watch, poor thing! And, for that matter, Rose would probably have to do some watching on her own account. And, if the fact was there, why bother to keep up a contradictory fiction. So Rose asked for a receipt.

The matter of the trunk was easily disposed of. Rose had a check for it. It was at the Polk Street Station. There was a cigar and news stand two blocks down, the landlady said, where an expressman had his headquarters. There was a blue sign out in front: "Schulz Express"; Rose couldn't miss it.

The landlady went away to write out a receipt. Rose closed the door after her and locked it.

It was a purely symbolistic act. She wasn't going to change her clothes or anything, and she didn't particularly want to keep anybody out. But, in a sense in which it had never quite been true before, this was her room, a room where any one lacking her specific invitation to enter, would be an intruder—a condition that had not obtained either in her mother's house or in Rodney's.

She smiled widely over the absurdity of indulging in a pleasurable feeling of possession in a squalid little cubby-hole like this. The wall-paper was stained and faded, the paint on the soft-wood floor worn through in streaks; there was an iron bed—a double bed, painted light blue and lashed with string where one of its joints showed a disposition to pull out. The mattress on the bed was lumpy. There was a dingy-looking oak bureau with a rather small but pretty good plate-glass mirror on it; a marble topped, black walnut wash-stand; a pitcher of the plainest and cheapest white ware standing in a bowl on top of it, and a highly ornate, hand-painted slop-jar—the sole survivor, evidently, of a much prized set—under the lee of it. The steep gable of the roof cut away most of one side of the room, though there would be space for Rose's trunk to stand under it, and across the corner, at a curiously distressing angle, hung an inadequate curtain that had five or six clothes hooks behind it.

In the foreground of the view out of the window, was a large oblong plateau—the flat roof of an extension which had casually been attached to the front of the building and carried it forward to the sidewalk over what had once been a small front yard. The extension had a plate-glass front and was occupied, Rose had noticed before she plunged into the little tunnel that ran alongside it and led to the main building, by a dealer in delicatessen. Over the edge of the flat roof, she could see the top third of two endless streams of trolley-cars, for the traffic in this street was heavy, by night, she imagined, as well as by day.

The opposite façade of the street, like the one of which her own wall and window formed a part, was highly irregular and utterly casual. There were cheap two-story brick stores with false fronts that carried them up a half story higher. There were little gable-ended cottages with their fronts hacked out into show-windows. There were double houses of brick with stone trimmings that once had had some residential pretensions. The one characteristic that they possessed in common, was that of having been designed, patently, for some purpose totally different from the one they now served.

The shops on the street level had, for the most part, an air of shabby prosperity. There was, within the space Rose's window commanded, a cheap little tailor shop, the important part of whose business was advertised by the sign "pressing done." There was a tobacconist's shop whose unwashed windows revealed an array of large wooden buckets and dusty lithographs; a shoe shop that did repairing neatly while you waited; a rather fly-specked looking bakery. There was a saloon on the corner, and beside it, a four-foot doorway with a painted transom over it that announced it as the entrance of the Bellevue Hotel.

The signs on the second-story windows indicated dentist parlors, the homes of mid-wives, ladies' tailors and dressmakers, and everywhere furnished rooms for light housekeeping to let.

The people who patronized those shops, who drank their beer at the corner saloon, who'd be coming hurriedly in the night to ring up the mid-wife, who smoked the sort of tobacco that was sold from those big wooden buckets; the people who lounged along the wide sidewalks, or came riding down-town at seven in the morning, and back at six at night, packed so tight that they couldn't get their arms up to hold by the straps in the big roaring cars that kept that incessant procession going in the middle of the street—they all inhabited, Rose realized, a world utterly different from the one she had left. The distance between the hurrying life she looked out on through her grimy window, and that which she had been wont to contemplate through Florence McCrea's exquisitely leaded casements, was simply planetary.

And yet, queerly enough, in terms of literal lineal measurement, the distance between the windows themselves, was less than a thousand yards. Less than ten minutes' walking from the mouth of the little tunnel alongside the delicatessen shop, would take her back to her husband's door. She had, in her flight out into the new world, doubled back on her trail. And, such is the enormous social and spiritual distance between North Clark Street and The Drive, she was as safely hidden here, as completely out of the orbit of any of her friends, or even of her friends' servants, as she could have been in New York or in San Francisco.

Having to come away furtively like this was a terrible countermine beneath her courage. If only she could have had a flourish of defiant trumpets to speed her on her way! But, done like that, the thing would have hurt Rodney too intolerably. His intelligence might be twentieth century or beyond. It might acquiesce in, or even enthusiastically advocate, a relation between men and women that hadn't existed, anyway since the beginning of the Christian Era; it might accept without faltering, all the corollaries pendent to that relation. But his actuating instincts, his psychical reflexes, stretched their roots away back to the Middle Ages. Under the dominance of those instincts, a man lost caste—became an object of contemptuous derision, if he couldn't keep his wife. It was bad enough to have another man take her away from him, but it was worse to have her go away in the absence of such an excuse; worst of all, to have her go away to seek a job and earn her own living.

Rose didn't know how long the secret could be kept. Wherever she went, whatever she did, there'd always be the risk that some one who could carry back the news to Rodney's friends, would recognize her. It was a risk that had to be taken, and she didn't intend to allow herself to be paralyzed by a perpetual dread of what might at any time happen. At the same time, she'd protect the secret as well as she could.

But there were two people it couldn't be kept from—Portia and her mother. Rose had at first entertained the notion of keeping her mother in the dark. It wasn't until she had spent a good many hours figuring out expedients for keeping the deception going, that she realized it couldn't be done. She had been writing her mother a letter a week ever since the departure to California—letters naturally full of domestic details that simply couldn't be kept up. The only possible deception would be a compromise with the truth and compromises of that sort are apt to be pretty unsatisfactory. They suggest concealments in every phase, and to an imaginative mind, are more terrifying, nine times in ten, than the truth you're trying to soften. Then, too, the story given out to Rodney's friends being that Rose was in California with her mother and Portia, left the chance always open for some contretemps which would lead to her mother's discovering the truth in a surprising and shocking way.

But the truth itself, confidently stated, not as a tragic ending, but as the splendid hopeful beginning of a life of truer happiness for Rose and her husband, needn't be a shock. So this was what Rose had borne down on in her letter to Portia. It wasn't a very long letter, considering how much it had to tell.

". . . I have found the big thing couldn't be had without a fight," she wrote. "You shouldn't be surprised, because you've probably found out for yourself that nothing worth having comes very easily. But you're not to worry about me, nor be afraid for me, because I'm going to win. I'm making the fight, somehow, for you as well as for myself. I want you to know that. I think that realizing I was living your life as well as mine, is what has given me the courage to start. . .

"I've got some plans, but I'm not going to tell you what they are. But I'll write to you every week and tell you what I've done and I want you to write to Rodney. I want to be sure that you understand this: Rodney isn't to blame for what's happened. I don't feel that I am, either, exactly. We're just in a situation that there's only one real way out of. I don't know whether he sees that yet or not. He's too terribly hurt and bewildered. But we haven't quarreled, and I believe we're further in love with each other than we've ever been before. I know I am with him. . .

"Break this thing to mother as gently as you like, but tell her everything before you stop. . ."

This letter written and despatched, she had worked out the details of her departure with a good deal of care. In her own house, before her servants, she had tried to act—and she felt satisfied that her attempt was successful—just as she would have done had her pretended telegram really come from Portia. She had packed, looked up trains, made a reservation. She had called up Frederica and told her the news. The train she had selected left at an hour and on a day when she knew Frederica wouldn't be able to come and see her off. Frederica had come down to the house of course to say good-by to her, and carrying her pretense through that scene, that had for her so much deeper and more poignant a regret than she dared show—because she really loved Frederica—was, next to bidding the twins good-by, the hardest thing she had to go through with. Lying and pretending were always terribly hard for Rose, and a lie to any one she was fond of, almost impossible. The only thing that enabled her to see it through, was the consideration that she was doing it for Rodney. He'd probably tell Frederica what had happened in time, but Rose was determined that he should have the privilege of choosing his own time for doing it.

Her bag was packed, her trunk was gone, her motor waiting at the door to take her to the station, when the maid Doris brought the twins home from their airing. This wasn't chance, but prearrangement.

"Give them to me;" Rose said, "and then you may go up and tell Mrs. Ruston she may have them in a few minutes."

She took them into her bedroom and laid them side by side on her bed. They had thriven finely—justified, as far as that went, Harriet's decision in favor of bottle feeding. Had she died back there in that bed of pain, never come out of the ether at all, they'd still be just like this—plump, placid, methodical. Rose had thought of that a hundred times, but it wasn't what she was thinking of now.

The thing that caught her as she stood looking down on them, was the wave of sudden pity. She saw them suddenly as persons with the long road all ahead of them, as a boy and a girl, a youth and a maid, a man and a woman. They were destined to have their hopes and loves, fears, triumphs, tragedies perhaps. The boy there, Rodney, might have to face, some day, the situation his father confronted now; might have to come back into an empty home, and turn a stiff inexpressive face on a coolly curious world. Little Portia there might find herself, some day, gazing with wide seared eyes, at a life some unexpected turn of the wheel of Fate had thrust her, all unprepared, into the midst of. Or it might be her fate to love without attracting love—to drain all the blood out of her life in necessary sacrifices; to wither that some one else might have a chance to grow. Those possibilities were all there before these two solemn, staring, little helpless things on the bed. What toys of Chance they were!

She'd never thought of them like that before. The baby she had looked forward to—the baby she hadn't had—had never been thought of that way either. It was to be something to provide her, Rose, with an occupation; to enable her to interpret her life in new terms; to make an alchemic change in the very substance of it. The transmutation hadn't taken place. She surmised now, dimly, that she hadn't deserved it should.

"You've never had a mother at all, you poor little mites," she said. "But you're going to have one some day. You're going to be able to come to her with your troubles, because she'll have had troubles herself. She'll help you bear your hurts, because she's had hurts of her own. And she'll be able to teach you to stand the gaff, because she's stood it herself."

For the first time since they were born, she was thinking of their need of her rather than of her need of them and with that thought, came for the first time, the surge of passionate maternal love that she had waited for, so long in vain. There was, suddenly, an intolerable ache in her heart that could only have been satisfied by crushing them up against her breast; kissing their hands—their feet.

Rose stood there quivering, giddy with the force of it. "Oh, you darlings!" she said. "But wait—wait until I deserve it!" And without touching them at all, she went to the door and opened it. Mrs. Ruston and Doris were both waiting in the hall.

"I must go now," she said. "Good-by. Keep them carefully for me." Her voice was steady, and though her eyes were bright, there was no trace of tears upon her cheeks. But there was a kind of glory shining in her face that was too much for Doris, who turned away and sobbed loudly. Even Mrs. Ruston's eyes were wet.

"Good-by," said Rose again, and went down composedly enough to her car.

She rode down to the station, shook hands with and said good-by to Otto, the chauffeur, allowed the porter to carry her bag into the waiting-room. There she tipped the porter, picked up the bag herself, and walked out the other door; crossed over to Clark Street and took a street-car. At Chicago Avenue she got off and walked north, keeping her eye open for placards advertising rooms to let. It was at the end of about a half mile that she found the hatchet-faced landlady, paid her three dollars, and locked her door, as a symbol, perhaps, of the bigger heavier door that she had swung to and locked on the whole of her past life.

Amid all the welter of emotions boiling up within her, grief was not present. There was a very deep-reaching excitement that sharpened all her faculties; that even made her see colors more brightly and hear fainter sounds. There was an intent eagerness to get the new life fairly begun. But, strangest of all, and yet so vivid that even its strangeness couldn't prevent her being aware of it, was a perfectly enormous relief. The thing which, when she had first faced it as the only thoroughfare to the real life she so passionately wanted, had seemed such a veritable nightmare, was an accomplished fact. The week of acute agony she had lived through while she was forcing her sudden resolution on Rodney had been all but unendurable with the enforced contemplation of the moment of parting which it brought so relentlessly nearer. There had been a terror, too, lest when the moment actually came, she couldn't do it. Well, and now it had come and gone! The surgery of the thing was over. The nerves and sinews were cut. The thing was done. The girl who stood there now in her three-dollar room was free; had won a fresh blank page to write the characters of her life upon.

She felt a little guilty about this. What heartless sort of a monster must she be to feel—why, actually happy, at a moment like this? She ought to be prone on the bed, her face buried in the musty pillow, sobbing her heart out.

But presently, standing there, looking down on the lumpy bed, she smiled widely instead, over the notion of doing it as a sort of concession to respectability. She had got her absolution from Rodney himself out of the memory of their first real talk together. Discipline, he'd said, was accepting the facts of life as they were. Not raising a lamentation because they weren't different. The only way you had of getting anywhere was by riding on the backs of your own passions. Well, her great ride was just beginning!

Rose dusted the mirror with a towel—a reckless act, as she saw for herself, when she discovered she was going to have to use that towel for a week—and took an appraising look at herself. Then she nodded confidently—there was nothing the matter with her looks—and resumed her ulster, her rubbers and her umbrella, for it was the kind of December day that called for all three. Her landlady could stick the receipt under the door, she reflected, as she locked it.

Two blocks down the street, she found, as predicted, the cigar store with the blue sign, "Schulz Express," and left her trunk check there with her address and fifty cents. Then, putting up her umbrella, and glowingly conscious that she was saving a nickel by so doing, she set off down-town afoot to get a job. She meant to get it that very afternoon. And, partly because she meant to so very definitely, she did.

I don't mean to say that getting a job is a purely volitional matter. There is the factor of luck, always large of course, though not quite so large as a great many people suppose, and the factor of intelligence. Rose's intelligence had been in pretty active training for the last year. Ever since her talk with Simone Gréville had set her thinking, she had been learning how to weigh and assess facts apart from their emotional nebulæ. She'd taught herself how to look a disagreeable or humiliating fact in the face as steadily and as coolly as she looked at any other fact.

She had accumulated a whole lot of facts about women in industry from Barry Lake and Jane. She knew the sort of job and the sort of pay that the average untrained woman gets. She knew some of the reasons why the pay was so miserably, intolerably small. She knew about the vast army of young women who weren't expected to be fully self-supporting, who counted on marrying comfortably enough some day, and accepted board and lodging at home as one of the natural laws of existence. But who, if they wanted pocket money, pretty enough clothes to make them attractive enough for men to want to marry; who, if they wanted to escape the stupid drudgery of housework at home, had to go to work. They'd rather get eight dollars a week than six, of course, or ten than eight. But as long as even six was velvet (cotton-backed velvet, one might say) they'd take that, cheerfully oblivious to the fact, as naturally one might expect them to be, that by taking six, they established a standard at which a girl who had to earn her own living simply couldn't live.

Rose knew exactly what would happen to her if she went to one of the big State Street department stores and asked for a job. Jane had been trying some experiments lately, and stating her results with convincing vivacity at their little dinners afterward. There was no thoroughfare there.

She knew too, what sort of life she'd have to face if she offered herself out in the West Side factory district as a cracker packer, a chocolate dipper, a glove stitcher; any of those things. You got a sort of training, of course, at any one of these trades. You learned to develop a certain uncanny miraculous speed and skill in some one small operation, as remorseless and unvaried as the coming into mesh and out again of two cogs in a pair of gears. But the very highest skill could just about be made to keep you alive, and it led to nothing else. You wore out your body and asphyxiated your soul.

Rose didn't mean to do that. She was holding both body and soul in trust. The penitential mood that had resulted from her talk with Portia was utterly gone. She wasn't looking for hurts. Deliberately to impose tortures on herself was as far from her intent as shirking any of the inevitable trials that should come to her in the course of the day's work. The only way she could see to a life of decent self-respecting independence lay through some sort of special training—business training, she thought. She'd begin by learning to be a stenographer—a cracking good stenographer. Miss Beach had begun that way. She had a real job.

Only, Rose had first to get a job that would pay for her training; and not only pay for it, but leave time for it; a problem which might have seemed like the problem of lifting yourself by your boot straps, if it hadn't been for Jimmy Wallace—Jimmy with his talk about chorus-girls.

The trouble with that profession, Jimmy had said, was that the indispensable assets in it were not industry, intelligence, ambitions, but a reasonably presentable pair of arms and legs (a good-looking face would surely come in handy too) and a rudimentary sense of rhythm. Another demoralizing thing about it, he had said, was the fact that the work wasn't hard enough, except during rehearsal, to keep its votaries out of mischief.

When the notion first occurred to her that these statements of Jimmy's might some day have an interest for her that was personal rather than academic, she had dismissed it with a shrug of good-humored amusement. It wasn't until her idea of leaving Rodney and going out and making a living and a life for herself had hardened into a fixed resolution, and she had begun serious consideration of ways and means, that she called it back into her mind. There was no use blinking the facts. The one marketable asset she would possess when she walked out of her husband's house, was simply—how she looked.

Well then, if that was all you had, there was no degradation in using it until you could make yourself the possessor of something else. And the merit of this particular sort of job, for her, lay precisely in the thing that Jimmy had cited as its chief disadvantage—it left you abundant leisure. You might occupy that leisure getting into mischief—no doubt most chorus-girls did. But there was nothing to prevent your using it to better advantage.

With this in mind, on the Sunday before Rose went away, she had studied the dramatic section of the morning paper with a good deal of care and was rewarded by finding among the news notes, an item referring to a new musical comedy that was to be produced at the

Globe Theater immediately after the Christmas holidays. *The Girl Upstairs* was the title of it. It was spoken of as one of the regular Globe productions, so it was probable that Jimmy Wallace's experience with the production of an earlier number in the series would at least give her something to go by. The thing must be in rehearsal now.

Granted that she was going to be a chorus-girl for a while, she could hardly find a better place than one of the Globe productions to be one in. According to Jimmy Wallace, it was a decent enough little place, and yet it possessed the advantage of being spiritually as well as actually, west of Clark Street. Rodney's friends were less likely to go there, and so have a chance of recognizing her, than to any other theater in the city, barring of course the flagrantly and shamelessly vulgar ones of the purlieus.

Among her older friends of school and college days, the chances were of course worse. But even if she were seen on the stage by people who knew her, even though they were to say to each other that that girl looked surprisingly like Rose Aldrich, this would be a very different thing from full recognition. She would be well protected by the utter unlikelihood of her being in such a place; by the absence of anybody's knowledge that she had flown off at a tangent from the orbit of Rodney's world. Then, too, she'd be somewhat disguised no doubt, by make-up. Of course with all those considerations weighed at their full value, there remained a risk that she would be fully discovered and recognized. But it was a risk that couldn't be avoided, whatever she did.

She entertained for a while, the notion of taking Jimmy Wallace into her confidence—he had as many depositors of confidences on his books, as a savings bank, and he was just as safe. It was altogether likely that he could get her a job out of hand. He was still on the best of terms with the Globe people, and he was a really influential critic. But even if he didn't get her a job outright, he could at least tell her how to set about getting one for herself—where to go, whom to ask for, the right way to phrase her request, which makes such an enormous difference in things of that kind.

But she wasn't long in abandoning the notion of appealing to Jimmy at all. The corner-stone of her new adventure must be that she was doing things for herself; that she was through being helped, having ways smoothed for her, things done for her. If she owed her first job even indirectly to Jimmy, all the rest of her structure would be out of plumb. Whatever success she might have would be tainted by the misgiving that but for somebody else's help, she might have failed. Rose Stanton who had rented that three-dollar room was going to be beholden to nobody!

The news item in the paper gave her really all she needed. It told her that a production was in rehearsal and it mentioned the name of the director, John Galbraith, referring to him as one of the three most prominent musical-comedy directors in the country; imported from New York at vast expense, to make this production unique in the annals of the Globe, and so forth.

They hadn't rehearsed Jimmy's piece, she knew, in the theater itself, but in all sorts of queer out-of-the-way places—in theaters that happened for the moment to be "dark," in dance-halls; pretty much anywhere. This was because there was another show running at the time at the Globe. She had looked in the theater advertisements to see whether a show was running there now. Yes, there was. Well, that gave her her formula.

When she asked at the box office at the Globe Theater, where they were rehearsing *The Girl Up-stairs* today, the nicely manicured young man inside, answered automatically, "North End Hall."

Evidently Jimmy Wallace couldn't have phrased the question better himself. But the quality of the voice that asked it had, even to his not very sensitive ear, an unaccustomed flavor. So, almost simultaneously with his answer, he looked up from his finger-nails and shot an inquiring glance through the grille.

What he saw betrayed him into an involuntary stare. He didn't mean to stare; he meant to be respectful. But he was surprised. Rose, in the plainest suit that she could hope would seem plausible to her servants for a traveling costume to California, an ulster and a little beaver hat with a quill in it, had no misgivings about looking the part of a potentially hard-working young woman renting a three-dollar room on North Clark Street and seeking employment in a musical-comedy chorus. A realization that her neat black seal dressing-case wasn't quite in the picture, helped to account for the landlady's puzzlement about her. But it hadn't been introduced in evidence here. And yet the young man behind the grille seemed as surprised as the landlady.

He repeated his answer to her question with the lubricant of a few more words and a fatuous sort of smile. "I believe they rehearse in the North End Hall this afternoon."

Rose couldn't help smiling a little herself. "I'm afraid," she said, "I'll have to ask where that is."

"Not at all," said the young man idiotically, and he told her the address; then cast about for a slip of paper to write it down on, racking his thimbleful of brains all the while to make out who she could be. She wasn't one of the principals in the company. They'd all reported and he hadn't heard that any of them was to be replaced.

"Oh, you needn't write it," said Rose. "I can remember, thank you." She gave him a pleasant sort of boyish nod that didn't classify at all with anything in his experience, and walked out of the lobby.

He stared after her almost resentfully, feeling all mussed up, somehow, and inadequate; as if here had been a situation that he had failed signally to make the most of. He sat there for the next half-hour gloomily thinking up things he might have said to her.

II

THE EVENING AND THE MORNING
WERE THE FIRST DAY

With her umbrella over her shoulder, Rose set sail northward again through the rain, absurdly cheered; first by the fact that the opening skirmish had distinctly, though intangibly, gone her way; secondly by the small bit of luck that North End Hall would be, judging by its number on North Clark Street, not more than a block or two from her three-dollar room.

The sight of the entrance to it gave her a pang of misgiving. A pair of white painted doors opened from the street level upon the foot of a broadish stair which took you up rather suddenly; there was space enough between the foot of the stair and the doors for a ticket-window, but it was too small to be called a lobby; an arc lamp hung there though, and two more—all three were extinct—hung just outside. What gave the place its air of vulgarity, a suggestion of being the starting and finishing point for lewd, drink sodden revels, she couldn't determine. It did suggest this plainly. But, in the light of what Jimmy Wallace had told her, she didn't think it likely there'd be any reveling to speak of at rehearsal.

At the head of the stairway, tilted back in a kitchen chair beneath a single gas-jet whose light he was trying to make suffice for the perusal of a green newspaper, sat a man, under orders no doubt, to keep intruders away.

Rose cast about as she climbed for the sort of phrase that would convince him she wasn't an intruder. She would ask him, but in the manner of one who seeks a formal assurance merely, if this was where they were rehearsing *The Girl Up-stairs*. Three steps from the top, she changed her tactics, as a result of a glance at his unshaven face. The thing to do was to go by as if he weren't there at all—as if, for such as she, watchmen didn't exist. The rhythmic pounding of feet and the frayed chords from a worn-out piano, convinced her she was in the right place.

HER STRATAGEM SUCCEEDED, BUT NOT without giving her a bad moment. The man glanced up and, though she felt he didn't return

HENRY KITCHELL WEBSTER

to his paper again, he made no attempt to stop her. But right before her was another pair of big white doors, closed with an effect of permanence—locked, she suspected. A narrower door to the left stood open, but over it was painted the disconcerting legend "Bar," flanked on either side, to make the matter explicit even to the unlearned, by pictorial representations of glasses of foaming beer. She hadn't time to deliberate over her choice. The watchman's eyes were boring into her back. If she chose wrong, or if she visibly hesitated, she knew she'd hear a voice say, "Here! Where you going!"

She caught a quick breath, turned to the left and walked steadily through the narrower door into the bar. It proved to be a deserted, shrouded, sinister-looking place, with an interminable high mahogany counter at one side, and with a lot of little iron tables placed by pairs, their tops together, so that half of them had their legs in the air. Its lights were fled, its garlands dead all right, but there wasn't anything poetic about it. However, there was another open door at the far end of the room, through which sounds and light came in. And the watchman hadn't interfered with her. Evidently she had chosen right.

She paused for a second steadying breath before she went through that farther door, her eyes starry with resolution, her cheeks, just for the moment, a little pale. If the comparison suggests itself to you of an early Christian maiden about to step out into an arena full of wild beasts, then you will have mistaken Rose. The arena was there, true enough. But she was stepping out into it with the intention of, like Androcles, taming the lion.

The room was hot and not well lighted—a huge square room with a very high ceiling. In the farther wall of it was a proscenium arch and a raised stage somewhat brighter than the room itself, though the stained brick wall at the back, in the absence of any scenery, absorbed a good deal of the light. On the stage, right and left, were two irregular groups of girls, with a few men, awkwardly, Rose thought, disposed among them. All were swaying a little to mark the rhythm of the music industriously pounded out by a sweaty young man at the piano—a swarthy, thick young man in his undershirt. There were a few more people, Rose was aware without exactly looking at any of them, sprawled in different parts of the hall, on sofas or cushioned window-seats.

It was all a little vague to her at first, because her attention was focused on a single figure—a compact, rather slender figure, and tall, Rose thought—of a man in a blue serge suit, who stood at the exact center of the stage and the extreme edge of the footlights. He was counting aloud the bars of the music—not beating time at all, nor yielding to the rhythm in any way; standing, on the contrary, rather tensely still. That was the quality about him, indeed, that riveted Rose's attention and held her as still as he was, in the doorway—an exhilarating sort of intensity that had communicated itself to the swaying groups on the stage. You could tell from the way he counted that something was gathering itself up, getting ready to happen. "Three. . . Four. . . Five. . . Six. . . Seven. . . *Now!*" he shouted on the eighth bar, and with the word, one of the groups transformed itself. One of the men bowed to one of the girls and began waltzing with her; another couple formed, then another.

Rose watched breathlessly, hoping the maneuver wouldn't go wrong;—for no reason in the world but that the man, there at the footlights, was so tautly determined that it shouldn't.

Determination triumphed. The number was concluded to John Galbraith's evident satisfaction. "Very good," he said. "If you'll all do exactly what you did that time from now on, I'll not complain." Without a pause he went on, "Everybody on the stage—big girls—all the big girls!" And, to the young man at the piano, "We'll do *Afternoon Tea*." There was a momentary pause then, filled with subdued chatter, while the girls and men re-alined themselves for the new number—a pause taken advantage of by an exceedingly blond young man to scramble up on the stage and make a few remarks to the director. He was the musical director, Rose found out afterward. Galbraith, to judge from his attitude, gave his colleague's remarks about twenty-five per cent. of his attention, keeping his eye all the while on the chorus, to see that they got their initial formation correctly. Rose looked them over, too. The girls weren't, on an average, extravagantly beautiful, though, with the added charm of make-up allowed for, there were no doubt many the audiences would consider so. What struck Rose most emphatically about them, was their youth and spirit. How long they had been rehearsing this afternoon she didn't know. But now, when they might have gone slack and silent, they pranced and giggled instead and showed a disposition to lark about, which evidently would have carried them a good deal further but for the restraining presence of the director. They were dressed in pretty much anything that would allow perfect freedom to their bodies; especially their arms and legs; bathing suits mostly, or middy-blouses and bloomers. Rose noted this with satisfaction. Her old university gymnasium costume would do perfectly. Anything, apparently, would do, because as her eye adjusted itself to details, she discovered romper suits, pinafores, chemises, overalls—all equally taken for granted. There weren't nearly so many chorus men as girls. She couldn't be sure just how many there were, because they couldn't be singled out. As they wore no distinctly working costume, merely took off their coats, waistcoats and collars, they weren't distinguishable from most of the staff, who, with the exception of the director, garbed themselves likewise.

Galbraith dismissed the musical director with a nod, struck his hands together for silence, and scrutinized the now motionless group on the stage.

"We're one shy," he said. "Who's missing?" And then answered his own question: "Grant!" He wheeled around and his eyes searched the hall.

Rose became aware for the first time, that a mutter of conversation had been going on incessantly since she had come in, in one of the recessed window-seats behind her. Now, when Galbraith's gaze plunged in that direction, she turned and looked too. A big blonde chorus-girl was in there with a man, a girl, who, with twenty pounds trained off her, and that sulky look out of her face, would have been a beauty. She had roused herself with a sort of defiant deliberation at the sound of the director's voice, but she still had her back to him and went on talking to the man.

"Grant!" said John Galbraith again, and this time his voice had a cutting edge. "Will you take your place on the stage, or shall I suspend rehearsal until you're ready?"

For answer she turned and began walking slowly across the room toward the door in the proscenium that led to the stage. She started walking slowly, but under Galbraith's eye, she quickened her pace, involuntarily, it seemed, until it was a ludicrous sort of run. Presently she emerged on the stage, looking rather artificially unconcerned, and the rehearsal went on again.

But just before he gave the signal to the pianist to go ahead, Galbraith with a nod summoned a young man from the wings and said something to him, whereupon, clearly carrying out his orders, he vaulted down from the stage and came walking toward the doorway where Rose was still standing. The director's gaze as it flashed about the hall, had evidently discovered more than the sulky chorus-girl.

The young man wasn't intrinsically formidable—a rather limp, deprecatory sort, he looked. But, as an emissary from Galbraith, he quickened Rose's heart-beat a trifle. She smiled though as she made a small bet with herself that he wouldn't be able to turn her out, even in his capacity of envoy.

But he didn't come straight to Rose; deflected his course a little uncertainly, and brought up before a woman who sat in a folding chair a little farther along the wall.

Rose hadn't observed her particularly before, though she was aware that one of the "big girls" who had responded promptly to Galbraith's first call for them, had been talking to her when Rose came in, and she had assumed her to be somebody connected with the show; at least with an unchallengeable right to watch its rehearsals. But she had corrected this impression even before she had heard what John Galbraith's assistant said to the woman and what she said to him; for she drew herself defensively erect when she saw him turn toward her, assumed a look of calculated disdain; tapped a foot inadequately shod for Chicago's pavements in December, although evidently it had experienced them— gave, on the whole, as well as she could, an imitation of a duchess being kept waiting.

But the limp young man didn't seem disconcerted, and inquired in so many words, what her business was. The duchess said in a harsh high voice with a good deal of inflection to it, that she wanted to see the director; a very partic'lar friend of his, she assured the young man, had begged her to do so. "You'll have to wait till he's through rehearsing," said the young man, and then he came over to Rose.

The vestiges of the smile the duchess had provoked were still visible about her mouth when he came up. "May I wait and see Mr. Galbraith after the rehearsal?" she asked. "If I won't be in the way?"

"Sure," said the young man. "He won't be long now. He's been rehearsing since two." Then, rather explosively, "Have a chair."

He struck Rose as being a little flustered and uncertain, somehow, and he now made a tentative beginning of actually bringing a chair for her.

"Oh, don't bother," said Rose, and now she couldn't help smiling outright. "I'll find one for myself."

But, whenever he had begun rehearsing, it was evident that John Galbraith didn't mean to stop until he got through, and it was a long hour that Rose sat there in a little folding chair similar to the one occupied by the duchess; an hour which, in spite of all her will could do, took some of the crispness out of her courage. It was all very well to reflect with pitying amusement on the absurdities of the duchess. But it was evident the duchess was waiting with a purpose like her own. She meant to get a job in the chorus. Her rather touching ridiculousness as a human being wouldn't stand in her way. It was likely that she had had dozens of jobs in choruses before, knew exactly what would be wanted of her, and was confident of her ability to deliver it.

As Rose's heart sank lower with the dragging minutes she even took into account the possibility that the duchess had spoken the truth about John Galbraith's "partic'lar friend." Just the mention of a name might settle the whole business. Then her spirits went down another five degrees. Here she had been assuming all along that there was a job for either of them to get! But it was quite likely there was not. The chorus looked complete enough; there was no visible gap in the ranks crying aloud for a recruit.

When at last, a little after six o'clock, Galbraith said, "Quarter to eight, everybody," and dismissed them with a nod for a scurry to what were evidently dressing-rooms at the other side of the ball, the ship of Rose's hopes had utterly gone to pieces. She had a plank to keep herself afloat on. It was the determination to stay there until he should tell her in so many words that he hadn't any use for her and under no conceivable circumstances ever would have.

The deprecatory young man was talking to him now, about her and the duchess evidently, for he peered out into the hall to see if they were still there; then vaulted down from the stage and came toward them.

The duchess got up, and with a good deal of manner, went over to meet him. Rose felt outmaneuvered here. She should have gone to meet him herself, but a momentary paralysis kept her in her chair. She didn't hear what the duchess said. The manner of it was confidential, in marked protest against the proximity of a handful of other people—the blond musical director, the thick pianist in his undershirt, a baby-faced man in round tortoise-shell spectacles, three or four of the chorus people, each of whom had serious matters to bring before the director's attention.

But all the confidences, it seemed, were on the side of the duchess. Because, when John Galbraith answered her, his voice easily filled the room. "You tell Mr. Pike, if that's his name, that I'm very much obliged to him, but we haven't any vacancies in the chorus at present. If you care to, leave your name and address with Mr. Quan, the assistant stage manager; then if we find we need you, we can let you know."

He said it not unkindly, but he exercised some power of making it evident that as he finished speaking, the duchess, for him, simply ceased to exist. Anything she might say or do thereafter, would be so much effort utterly wasted.

The duchess drew herself up and walked away.

And Rose? Well, the one thing she wanted passionately to do just then, was to walk away herself out of that squalid horrible room; to soften her own defeat by evading the final sledge-hammer blow. What he had said to the duchess licensed her to do so. If there were no vacancies. . . But she clenched her hands, set her teeth, pulled in a long breath, and somehow, set herself in motion. Not toward the door, but toward where John Galbraith was standing.

But before she could get over to him, the pianist and the musical director had got his attention. So she waited quietly beside him for two of the longest minutes that ever were ticked off by a clock. Then, with disconcerting suddenness, right in the middle of one of the musical director's sentences, he looked straight into her face and said: "What do you want?"

She'd thought him tall, but he wasn't. He was looking on a perfect level into her eyes.

"I want a job in the chorus," said Rose.

"You heard what I said to that other woman, I suppose?"

"Yes," said Rose, "but. . ."

"But you thought you'd let me say it to you again."

"Yes," she said. And, queerly enough, she felt her courage coming back. She managed the last "yes" very steadily. It had occurred to her that if he'd wanted merely to get rid of her, he could have done it quicker than this. He was looking her over now with a coolly appraising eye.

"What professional experience have you had?" he asked.

"I haven't had any."

He almost smiled when she stopped there.

"Any amateur experience?" he inquired.

"Quite a lot," said Rose; "pageants and things, and two or three little plays."

"Can you dance?"

"Yes," said Rose.

HENRY KITCHELL WEBSTER

He said he supposed ballroom dancing was what she meant, whereupon she told him she was a pretty good ballroom dancer, but that it was gymnastic dancing she had had in mind.

"All right," he said. "See if you can do this. Watch me, and then imitate me exactly."

In the intensity of her absorption in his questions and her own answers to them, she had never given a thought to the bystanders. But now as they fell back to give him room, she swept a glance across their faces. They all wore smiles of sorts. There was something amusing about this—something out of the regular routine. A little knot of chorus-girls halted in the act of going out the wide doors and stood watching. Was it just a hoax? The suppressed unnatural silence sounded like it. But at what John Galbraith did, one of the bystanders guffawed outright.

It wasn't pretty, the dance step he executed—a sort of stiff-legged skip accompanied by a vulgar hip wriggle and concluding with a straight-out sidewise kick.

A sick disgust clutched at Rose as she watched—an utter revulsion from the whole loathly business. She could scrub floors—starve if she had to. She couldn't do the thing he demanded of her here out in the middle of the floor, in her street clothes, without the excuse of music to make it tolerable—and before that row of leering faces.

"Well?" he asked, turning to her as he finished. He wasn't smiling at all.

"I'm not dressed to do that," she said.

"I know you're not," he admitted coolly, "but it can be done. Pick up your skirts and do it as you are,—if you really want a job."

There was just a faint edge of contempt in that last phrase and, mercifully, it roused her anger. A blaze kindled in her blue eyes, and two spots of vivid color defined themselves in her cheeks.

She caught up her skirts as he had told her to do, executed without compromise the stiff-legged skip and the wriggle, and finished with a horizontal sidewise kick that matched his own. Then, panting, trembling a little, she stood looking straight into his face.

The first thing she realized when the processes of thought began again was that even if there had been a hoax, she was not, in the event, the victim of it. The attitude of her audience told her that. Galbraith was staring at her with a look that expressed at first, clear astonishment, but gradually complicated itself with other emotions—confusion, a glint of whimsical amusement. That gleam, a perfectly honest, kindly one, decided Rose to take him on trust. He wasn't a brute, however it might suit his purposes to act like one. And with an inkling of how her blaze of wrath must be amusing him, she smiled slowly and a little uncertainly, herself.

"We've been rehearsing this piece two weeks," he said presently, looking away from her when he began to talk, "and I couldn't take any one into the chorus now whom I'd have to teach the rudiments of dancing to. I must have people who can do what I tell them. That's why a test was necessary. Also, from now on, it would be a serious thing to lose anybody out of the chorus. I couldn't take anybody who had come down here—for a lark."

"It's not a lark to me," said Rose.

Now he looked around at her again. "I know it isn't," he said. "But I thought when you first came in here, that it was."

With that, Rose understood the whole thing. It was evidently a fact that despite the plain little suit, the beaver hat, the rough ulster she was wearing, she didn't look like the sort of girl who had to rely on getting a job in the chorus for keeping a roof over her head. Looks, speech, manner—everything segregated her from the type. It was all obvious enough, only Rose hadn't happened to think of it. It accounted, of course, for the rather odd way in which the landlady, the ticket-seller at the Globe, and meek little Mr. Quan, the assistant stage manager, all had looked at her, as at some one they couldn't classify. John Galbraith, out of a wider experience of life, had classified her, or thought he had, as a well-bred young girl who, in a moment of pique, or mischief, had decided it would be fun to go on the stage. The test he had applied wasn't, from that point of view, unnecessarily cruel. The girl he had taken her for, would, on being ordered to repeat that grotesque bit of vulgarity of his, have drawn her dignity about her like a cloak, and gone back in a chastened spirit to the world where she belonged.

A gorgeous apparition came sweeping by them just now, on a line from the dressing-room to the door—a figure that, with regal deliberation, was closing a blue broadcloth coat, trimmed with sable, over an authentic Callot frock. The Georgette hat on top of it was one that Rose had last seen in a Michigan Avenue shop. She had amused herself by trying to vizualize the sort of person who ought to buy it. It had found its proper buyer at last—fulfilled its destiny.

"Oh, Grant!" said John Galbraith.

HENRY KITCHELL WEBSTER

The queenly creature stopped short and Rose recognized her with a jump, as the sulky chorus-girl. Dressed like this, her twenty pounds of surplus fat didn't show.

Galbraith walked over to her. "I shan't need you any more, Grant." He spoke in a quiet impersonal sort of way, but his voice had, as always, a good deal of carrying power. "It's hardly worth your while trying to work, I suppose, when you're so prosperous as this. And it isn't worth my while to have you soldiering. You needn't report again."

He nodded not unamiably, and turned away. Evidently she had ceased to exist for him as completely as the duchess. She glared after him and called out in a hoarse throaty voice, "Thank Gawd I don't *have* to work for you."

He'd come back to Rose again by this time, and she saw him smile. "When you do it," he said over his shoulder, "thank Him for me too." Then to Rose: "She's a valuable girl; had lots of experience; good-looking; audiences like her. I'm giving you her place because as long as she's got those clothes and the use of a limousine, she won't get down to business. I'd rather have a green recruit who will. I'm hiring you because I think you will be able to understand that what you feel like doing isn't important and that what I tell you to do is. The next rehearsal is at a quarter to eight tonight. Give your name and address to Mr. Quan before you go. By the way, what is your name?"

"Rose Stanton," she said. "But. . ." She had to follow him a step or two because he had already turned away. "But, may I give some other name than that to Mr. Quan?" He frowned a little dubiously and asked her how old she was. And even when she told him twenty-two, he didn't look altogether reassured.

"That's the truth, is it? I mean, there's nobody who can come down here about three days before we open and call me a kidnaper, and lead you away by the ear?"

"No," said Rose gravely, "there's no one who'll do that."

"Very good," he said. "Tell Quan any name you like."

The name she did tell him was Doris Dane.

It was a quarter to seven when she came out through the white doors into North Clark Street. The thing that woke her out of a sort of daze as she trudged along toward her room in the unrelenting rain was a pleasurable smell of fried onions; whereupon she realized that she was legitimately and magnificently hungry. In any other condition, the dingy little lunch-room she presently turned into, would hardly have invited her. But the spots on the frayed starchy table-cloth, the streakiness of the glasses, the necessity of polishing knife and fork upon her damp napkin, couldn't prevent her doing ample justice to a small thick platter of ham and eggs, and a plate of thicker wheat-cakes.

It occurred to her as she finished, that a quarter to eight probably meant the hour at which the rehearsal was to begin. She'd have to be back at the hail at least fifteen minutes earlier, in order to be dressed and ready. She had no time to waste; would even have to hurry a little.

She didn't try to explore for the reason why this discovery pleased her so much. It was enough that it did. She flew along through the rain to her tunnel, charged up the narrow stair, and in the unlighted corridor outside her room, collided with her trunk. Well, it was lucky it had come anyway. She tugged it into her room after she had lighted the gas.

You might have seen, if you had been there to see, just a momentary hesitation after she'd got her trunk key out of her purse before she unlocked it. It was a sort of Jack-in-the-box, that trunk. Would the emotions with which she'd packed it, spring out and clutch her as she released the hasp? The saving factor in the situation was that it was a quarter past seven. In fifteen minutes she must be back at North End Hall, getting ready to go to work at her job. Suppose she hadn't found a job this afternoon? The thought turned her giddy.

She plunged into her trunk, rummaged out a middy-blouse, a pair of black silk bloomers, and her gymnasium sneakers, rolled them all together in a bundle, got into her rubbers and her ulster again, and—I'm afraid there is no other word for it—fled.

She was one of the first of the chorus to reach the hail and she had nearly finished putting on her working clothes before the rest of them came pelting in. But she didn't get out quickly enough to miss the sensation that was exciting them all—the news that Grant had been dropped. A few of them were indignant; the rest merely curious. The indignant ones allowed themselves a license in the expression of this feeling that positively staggered Rose; made use in a quite matter-of-fact way of words she had supposed even a drunken truck-man would have attempted to refrain from in the presence of a woman. She made a discovery afterward, that there were many girls in the chorus who never talked like that; and among those who did, the further distinction between those who used vile language casually, or even jocularly, and those who were driven to it only by anger. But for these first few minutes in the dressing-room, she felt as if she had blundered into some foul pit abysmally below the lowest level of decency.

One of the girls advanced the theory that Grant hadn't finally been dropped; it was absurd that she should be. She was one of the most popular chorus-girls in Chicago. The director was merely trying to scare her into doing better work for him. She'd come back, all right. She had reasons of her own, this girl intimated, for wanting to work, despite the possession of French clothes and the use of a limousine. Her "friend," it seemed, needed to be taught some sort of lesson. Grant would come around before tomorrow night, and eat enough humble pie to induce Galbraith to take her back.

If this theory were sound, and it had a dreadful plausibility to Rose, her only chance for keeping her job would be to do as well as Grant could do, tonight, in this very first rehearsal; and she went out on the stage in a perfect agony of determination. She must see everything, hear everything; put all she knew and every ounce of energy she had, into the endeavor to make John Galbraith forget that she was a recruit at all.

The intensity of this preoccupation was a wonderful protection to her. It kept away the sick disgust that had threatened her in the dressing-room; prevented her even glancing ahead to a future that would, had she taken to guessing about it, utterly have overwhelmed her. The intensely illuminated present instant kept her mind focused to its sharpest edge.

It is true that before she had been working fifteen minutes, she had forgotten all about Grant and the possibility of her return. She'd even forgotten her resolution not to let John Galbraith remember she was a recruit. Indeed, she had forgotten she was a recruit. She was nothing at all but just a reflection of his will. She'd felt that quality strongly in him even behind his back during the afternoon rehearsal. Now, on the stage in front of him, she was completely possessed by it.

She didn't know she was tired, panting, wet all over with sweat. Really, of course, she was pretty soft, judged by her own athletic standards. She hadn't done anything so physically exacting as this for over a year. But she had the illusion that she wasn't *doing* anything now; that she was just a passive plastic thing, tossed, flung, swirled about by the driving power of the director's will. It wouldn't have surprised her if the chairs had danced for him.

It couldn't of course have occurred to her that she was producing her own effect on the director; she couldn't have surmised that he was driving his rehearsal at a faster pace and with a renewed energy and fire because of the presence, there in the ranks of his chorus, of a glowing, thrilling creature who devoured his intentions half formed, met them with a blue spark across the poles of their two minds.

She realized, when the rehearsal was over, that it had gone well and that it couldn't have gone so if her own part had been done badly. She hesitated a moment after he'd finally dismissed them with a nod, and an, "Eleven o'clock tomorrow morning, everybody," from a previously formed intention of asking him if she'd do. But she felt, somehow, that such a question would be foolish and unnecessary.

He had marked her hesitation and shot her a look that she felt followed her as she walked off, and she heard him say to the world in general and in a heartfelt sort of way, "Good God!" But she didn't know that it was the highest encomium he was capable of, nor that it was addressed to her.

She carried away, however, a glow that saw her back to her room, and through the processes of unpacking and getting ready for bed, though it faded swiftly during the last of these. But when the last thing that she could think of to do had been done, when there was no other pretext, even after a desperate search for one, that could be used to postpone turning out her light and getting into bed, she had to confess to herself that she was afraid to do it. And with that confession, the whole pack of hobgoblin terrors she had kept at bay so valiantly since shutting her husband's door behind her, were upon her back.

Here she was, Rose Aldrich, in a three-dollar-a-week room on North Clark Street, having deserted her husband and her babies—a loving honest husband, and a pair of helpless babies not yet three months old—to become a member of the chorus in a show called *The Girl Up-stairs!* Was there a human being in the world, except herself, who would not, as the most charitable of possible explanations, assume her to be mad? Could she herself, seeing her act cut out in silhouette like that, be sure she wasn't mad? Hysterical anyway, the victim of her own rashly encouraged fancies, just as Rodney had so often declared she was? Oughtn't she to have let James Randolph explore the subconscious part of her mind and find the crack there must be in it, that could have driven her to a crazy act like this?

It didn't matter now. She couldn't go back. She never could go back after the things she had said to Rodney, until she had made good those fantastic theories of hers. Probably he wouldn't want her to come back even then. He'd find out where she was of course—what she was doing. Why had she been such a fool, going away, as not to have gone far enough to be safe? He'd feel that she'd disgraced him. Any man would. And he'd never forgive her. He'd divorce her, perhaps. He'd have a right to, if she stayed away long enough. And, without her there, with nothing of her but memories—tormenting memories, he'd perhaps fall in love with some one else—marry some one else. And her two babies would call that unknown some one "mother." She must have been crazy! She'd thought she didn't love them. That had been a delusion anyway. Her heart ached for them now—an actual physical ache that almost made her cry out. And for Rodney himself, for his big strong arms around her! Would she ever feel them again?

She told herself this was a nightmare—something to be fought off, kept at bay. But how did that help her now, when the armor must be laid aside? Sometime or other she must turn out that light and lie down in that bed, defenseless. She had never in her life asked more of her courage than when, at last, she did that thing. There were nine hours then ahead of her before eleven o'clock and the next rehearsal.

III

Rose Keeps the Path

Rose rehearsed twice a day for a solid week without forming the faintest conception of who "the girl" was or why she was "the girl up-stairs." She didn't know what sort of scene it was for instance that they burst in on through the space marked by two of the little folding chairs brought up from the floor of the dance-hall for the purpose. The group of iron tables borrowed from the bar and set solidly together in the upper right-hand corner of the stage whenever they rehearsed a certain one of their song numbers, might with equal plausibility represent a mountain in Arizona, the front veranda of a house or a banquet table in the gilded dining-hall of some licentious multi-millionaire. They got up on the insecure thing and tried to dance; that was all she knew.

During the entire period, and for that matter, right up to the opening night she never saw a bar of music except what stood on the piano rack, nor a written word of the lyrics she was supposed to sing. Rose couldn't sing very much. She had a rather timorous, throaty little contralto that contrasted oddly with the fine free thrill of her speaking voice. But nobody had asked her what her voice was, nor indeed, whether she could sing at all. She picked up the tunes quickly enough, by ear, but the words she was always a little uncertain about.

It all seemed too utterly haphazard to be possible, but Rose decided not to ask any of the authorities about this, because, while the possibility of Grant's return dangled over her head, she didn't want to remind anybody how green she was. But she finally questioned one of her colleagues in the chorus about it, and was told that back at the beginning of things, they had had their voices tried by the musical director, who had conducted three or four music rehearsals before John Galbraith arrived. They had never had any music to sing from but there had been half a dozen mimeograph copies of the words to the songs, which the girls had put their heads together over in groups of three or four, and more or less learned. What had become of this dope, and whether it was still available for Rose in case she were animated by a purely supererogatory desire to study it, the girl didn't know.

She was a pale-haired girl, whom Rose thought she had heard addressed as Larson, and she had emerged rather slowly as an individual personality, out of the ruck of the chorus; a fact in her favor, really, because the girls who had first driven themselves home to Rose through the shell of her intense preoccupation with doing what John Galbraith wanted, had been the vividly and viciously objectionable ones. The thing that had prompted her to sit down beside Larson and, with this question about how one learned the words to the songs, take her first real step toward an acquaintance, was an absence of any strong dislike, rather than the presence of a real attraction.

She made a surprising discovery when the girl, with a friendly pat on the sofa beside her, for an invitation to her to sit down, began answering her question. She was a real beauty. Or, more accurately, she possessed the constituent qualities of beauty. She was pure English eighteenth century; might have stepped down out of a Gainsborough portrait. Dressed right, and made up a little, with her effects legitimately heightened (and warned not to speak), she could have gone to the Charity Ball as the Honorable Mrs. Graham, and Bertie Willis would have gone mad about her. Only you had to look twice at her to perceive that this was so; and what she lacked was just the unanalyzable quality that makes one look twice.

Her speaking voice would have driven Bertie mad, too—foaming, biting mad. It was disconcertingly loud, in the first place, and it came out upon the promontories of speech with a flat whang that fairly made you jump. Its undulations of pitch gave you something the same sensation as riding rapidly over a worn-out asphalt pavement in a five-hundred-dollar automobile; unforeseen springs into the air, descents into unexpected pits. Her grammar wasn't flagrantly bad, though it had, rather pitiably, a touch of the genteel about it. But now, when she spoke to Rose, and with the lassitude of fatigue in her voice besides, Rose heard something friendly about it.

"I don't know what you should worry about any of that stuff for," she said. "How you sing or what you sing don't make much difference."

Rose admitted that it didn't seem to. "But you see," she said (she hadn't had a human soul to talk to for more than a week and she had to make a friend of somebody); "you see, I've just got to keep this job. And if every little helps, as they say, perhaps that would."

The girl looked at her oddly, almost suspiciously, as if for a moment she had doubted whether Rose had spoken in good faith. "You've got as good a chance of losing your job," she said, "as Galbraith has of losing his."

"I don't worry about it," said Rose, "when I'm up there on the stage at work. It's too exciting. And then, I feel somehow that it's going all right. But early in the morning, I get to imagining all sorts of things. He's so terribly sudden. The girl whose place I got,—she hadn't any warning, you know. It just happened."

The Larson girl gave a decisive little nod. Not so much, it seemed, in assent to what Rose had just said, but as if some question in her own mind had been answered.

"You'll get used to that feeling," she said. "You've got to take a chance anyway, so why worry? We can work our heads off, but if the piece is a fliv the opening night, they'll tack up the notice, and there we'll be with two weeks' pay for eight weeks' work, and another six weeks' work for nothing in something else if we're lucky enough to get it."

This was a possibility Rose hadn't thought of. "But—that isn't fair!" she said.

The other girl laughed grimly. "Fair!" she echoed. "What they want to print that word in the dictionary for, I don't see. Because what it means don't exist. Not where I live, anyway. But what's the good of making a fuss about it? We've got to take our chance like everybody else."

"I don't believe this piece will fall, though," said Rose. "I don't think Mr. Galbraith would let it. I think he's a perfect wonder, don't you?"

The Larson girl looked at her again. "He's supposed to be about the best in the business," she said, "and I guess he is." She added, "Dave tells me he's going to put you with us in the sextette."

Dave was the thick pianist, and Rose had found him in the highest degree obnoxious. He seemed to occupy an indeterminate social position in their ship's company, between the forecastle, which was the chorus, and the quarter-deck, which comprised Galbraith (you might call him the pilot), the baby-faced man with the tortoise-shell spectacles, reputed to be the author, two awesome intermittent gentlemen identified in the dressing-room as the owners of the piece, and the musical director, together with one or two more as yet unclassified. The principals, when they should appear, would, Rose assumed, belong on the quarter-deck too. The social gap between this afterguard and Rose and her colleagues in the chorus, was not so very wide, but it was abysmally deep. Nevertheless, the pianist, buoyed up

HENRY KITCHELL WEBSTER

on the wings of a boundless effrontery, seemed to manage to remain unaware of it.

He had started rehearsals with this piece, it appeared, as a chorus-man, and had become a pianist, thanks to the interposition of Fate (the real pianist had fallen suddenly and desperately ill), and to his own irresistible assurance that he could do anything. He could keep time and he hit perhaps a third of the notes right.

The chorus liked him. The girls all called him Dave, seemed to appreciate his notion of humor, and accepted his hugs and pawings as a matter of course. But he took his jokes, his familiarities, and his apparently impregnable self-esteem, upon the quarter-deck—slapped the author on the back now and then, and had even been known to address John Galbraith as "Old man." Incidentally, he hung about within ear-shot during conferences of the powers, freely offered his advice, and brought all sorts of interesting tidbits of gossip and prophecy back to the chorus.

His announcement that Rose was going to be put into the sextette was entitled to consideration, even though it couldn't be banked on. There were three mediums and three big girls in the sextette. (Olga Larson was one of the mediums and so needn't fear replacement by Rose, who was a big girl.) Besides appearing in two numbers as a background to one of the principals, they had one all to themselves, a fact which constituted them a sort of super-chorus. Galbraith used to keep them for endless drills after the general rehearsal was dismissed.

But the intimation that Rose was to be promoted to this select inner circle, didn't, as it first came to her, give her any pleasure. Somehow, as Larson told her about it, she could fairly see the knowing greasy grin that would have been Dave's comment on this prophecy. And in the same flash, she interpreted the Larson girl's look, half incredulous, half satirical, and her, "You've got as good a chance of losing your job as Galbraith has of losing his."

"I haven't heard anything about being put in the sextette," she said quietly, "and I don't believe I will be."

"Well, I don't know why not." There was a new warmth in the medium's voice. Rose had won a victory here, and she knew it. "You've got the looks and the shape, and you can dance better than any of the big girls, or us mediums, either. And if he doesn't put that big Benedict lemon into the back line where she belongs, and give you her place in the sextette, it will be because he's afraid of her drag."

Rose forbore to inquire into the nature of the Benedict girl's drag. Whatever it may have been, John Galbraith was evidently not afraid of it, because as he dismissed that very rehearsal, calling the rest of the chorus for twelve the following morning, and the sextette for eleven, he told Rose to report at the earlier hour. And a moment later, she heard Dave say to the big show girl named Vesta Folsom (some one with a vein of playful irony must have been responsible for this christening), "Well, maybe I didn't call that turn."

"You're the original wise guy, all right," Vesta admitted. "You're Joseph to all the sure things."

Barring Olga Larson, the chorus was probably unanimous, Rose reflected, in looking at it like that. They accounted for her having got a job in the first place at Grant's expense, and a promotion so soon thereafter to the sextette, by assuming that John Galbraith had a sentimental interest in her. Whether his reward had been collected in advance, or was still unpaid, was an interesting theme for debate. But that, past or present, the reward was his actuating motive, it wouldn't occur to anybody to question.

There was no malice in this. Rose didn't lose caste with any of them on account of it. But a chorus-girl is the most sentimental person in the world. If there's anybody who really believes that love makes the world go round, she is that one. It's love that actuates men to deeds of heroism or of crime; it's love that makes men invest good money in musical comedies; love that makes stars out of her undeserving sisters in the chorus; love that is always waiting round the corner to open the door to wealth and fame for her.

So when Grant came back and ate her humble pie in vain, and later, when Benedict was relegated to a place in the back line, the natural explanation was that Galbraith was crazy about the new girl.

Of course it set Rose all ablaze with wrath when she became aware of this. It was precisely because she had rebelled against the theory that love was what made the world go round, that she was here in the chorus. Had she been content to let it make her world go round, she never would have left Rodney. The only way she had of refuting the assumption in this case would be by making good so demonstrably and instantaneously, that they'd be compelled to see that her promotion had been inevitable.

It was in this spirit, with blazing cheeks and eyes, that she attacked the next morning's rehearsal. She was only dimly aware of Benedict out in the hall in front, viperishly waiting for the arrival of one of the owners to make an impassioned plea for reinstatement. Her tears or her tantrums were matters of supremely little importance. But that John Galbraith should see that he had promoted her on merit and on nothing but merit, mattered enormously.

Lacking the clue, he watched her in a sort of amused perplexity. Her way of snatching his instructions, her almost viciously determined manner of carrying them out, would have been natural had she been working under the spur of some stinging rebuke, instead of under the impetus of an unexpected promotion.

"Don't make such hard work of it, Dane," he said at last. "You're all right, but have a little fun out of it. There are eight hundred people out there," he waved his arm out toward the empty hall, "who have paid their hard-earned money to feel jolly and have a good time. If you go on looking like that, they'll think this piece was produced by Simon Legree."

There came the same gleaming twinkle in his eye that had disarmed her resentment once before, and as before, she found herself feeling rather absurd. What mattered the microcephalic imaginings of greasy Dave and his friends among the chorus? John Galbraith wasn't the sort of man to get infatuated with a chorus-girl. The gleam in his eye was enough, all by itself, to make that plain.

So, flushing up a little, she grinned back at him, gave him a nod of acquiescence, and fell back to her place for the beginning of the next evolution.

"If she smiles like that," thought John Galbraith, "she'll break up the show." At the end of the rehearsal, he said to her, "You're doing very well indeed, Dane. If I could have caught you ten years ago, I could have made a dancer out of you."

It was a very real, unqualified compliment, and as such Rose understood it. Because, by a dancer, he meant something very different from a prancing chorus-girl. The others giggled and exchanged glances with Dave at the piano. They didn't understand. To them, the compliment seemed to have been delivered with the left hand. And somehow, an amused recognition of the fact that they didn't understand, as well as of the fact that she did, flashed across from John Galbraith's eyes to hers.

"Just a minute," he said as they all started to leave the stage, and they came back and gathered in a half-circle around him. "We'll rehearse the first act tonight with the principals. You six girls are supposed to be young millionairesses, very up-to-date-bachelor-girl type, intimate friends of the leading lady, who is a multi-millionairess that's run away from home. You've all got a few lines to say. Go to Mr. Quan and get your parts and have them up by tonight."

At half past four that afternoon, when the regular chorus rehearsal was over, Rose asked John Galbraith if she might speak to him for a minute. He had one foot on a chair and was in the act of unlacing his dancing shoes, so he seemed to be, for him, comparatively permanent. He had a disconcerting way, she had noticed, of walking away on some business of his own in the middle of other people's sentences, intending to come back, no doubt, in time to hear the end of them, but forgetting to.

"Fire away," he said, looking around at her over his shoulder. Then, with reference to the blue-bound pair of sides she held in her hand, "What's the matter? Isn't the part fat enough for you?"

"Fat enough?" Rose echoed inquiringly. "Oh, you mean long enough." She smiled in good-humored acknowledgment of his joke, and let that do for an answer.

John Galbraith hadn't been sure that it would be a joke to Rose. He'd been a musical-comedy producer so long that no megalomaniacal absurdity could take him by surprise. There were chorus-girls no doubt in this very company, who, on being promoted to microscopic parts, would be capable of complaining because they weren't bigger.

"All the same," said Rose, "I'm afraid I've got to tell you that I can't take this, and to ask you to put me back into the regular chorus."

He wasn't immune to surprise after all, it seemed. He straightened up in a flash and stared at her. "What on earth are you talking about?" he asked.

"If I have words to say, even only a few, wouldn't anybody who happened to be in the audience, know who I was?—I mean if they knew me already."

"Of course they would. What of it?"

"I told you," said Rose, "the day you gave me a job, that it wasn't a lark. I had to begin earning my own living suddenly, and without any training for it at all, and this seemed to be the best way. That's—all true, and it's true that no one could come and, as you say, lead me away by the ear. Nobody's responsible for me but myself. But there are people who'd be terribly shocked and hurt if they found out I'd gone on the stage. They know I'm earning my own living, but they don't know how I'm doing it. I thought that as just one of the chorus, made up and all, I'd be safe. But with these lines to say. . ."

"Now listen to me," said John Galbraith; "listen as hard as you can. Because when I've done talking, you will have to make up your mind. In the first place you wouldn't be 'safe,' as you said, even in the chorus. A make-up isn't a disguise. You will be rouged and powdered, your eyelashes blackened, your lips reddened and so on, not to make you look different, but to keep you looking the same under the strong lights. You're not the sort of person to escape notice. That's the reason I made up my mind to hire you before I knew you could dance. I saw you standing back there in the doorway. You've got the quality about you that makes people see you. That's one of your assets.

"So, if you're ashamed of being recognized in this business, you'd better get out of it altogether. On the other hand, it seems to me that if you've got to earn your living, it's nobody's business but your own how you do it. You're the one who'll go hungry if you don't earn it, not these friends of yours. So, if it seems a legitimate way of earning a living to you, if you don't feel disgraced or degraded by being in it, you'd better forget your friends and go ahead. You've made an excellent start; you've earned a legitimate promotion. It will mean that instead of getting twenty dollars a week when the show opens, you will get twenty-five. It's a long time since I've given a person without experience a chance like that. I gave it to you because you seemed ambitious and intelligent—the sort who'd see me through. But if you aren't ambitious, if the game doesn't look worth playing to you, and you aren't willing to play it for all it's worth—why, good as you are, I don't want you at all. So that's your choice!"

His manner wasn't quite so harsh as his words, but it convinced her that he meant every one of them right to the foot of the letter.

She couldn't answer for a moment. She hadn't guessed that the choice he was going to offer her would be between taking the little part he had given her and playing it for all it was worth, defiant of Rodney's feelings and of the scandal of the Lake Shore Drive—and going back to her three-dollar room this afternoon, out of a job and without even a glimmering chance of finding another.

"Take your time," he said. "I don't want to be a brute about it, but look here! Try to see it my way for a minute. Here are my employers, the owners of this piece. They're putting thousands of dollars into the production of it. They've hired me to make that production a success. Well, I don't know about other games, but this game's a battle. If we win, it will be because we put every bit of steam and every bit of confidence we've got into it and *make* it win. That goes for me, and for the principals, and right down through to the last girl in the chorus. Every night there'll be a new audience out there that you will have to fight—shake up out of the grouch they get when they pay for their tickets; persuade to laugh and loosen up and come and play with you.

"Will you be able to do your share, do you suppose, if you're slinking around, afraid of being recognized? We don't care whether your pussy-cat friends get their fur rubbed the wrong way or not. The only thing we care about is putting this show across. Well, if you feel the way we do about it, if you can make it the one thing you do care about, too—why, come along. Let the pussy-cats go. . ." He finished with a snap of his fingers.

"The only one that really matters isn't a pussy-cat," said Rose, with a reluctant wide smile, "and—he'd agree with you altogether, if he didn't know you were talking to me. And I'm really very much obliged to you."

"You will come along then?"

"Yes," said Rose, "I'll come."

"No flutters?" questioned Galbraith. "No eleventh-hour repentance?"

"No," said Rose, "I'll see it through."

John Galbraith went away satisfied. Rose had the same power that he had, of making a simple unemphatic statement irresistibly convincing. When she said that she would go through, he knew that unless struck by lightning, she would. But there had been something at once ironic and tender about the girl's smile, when she had spoken of the only one who really mattered, that he couldn't account for. Who was the only one that really mattered, anyway? Her husband? He didn't think it likely. Young women who quarreled with their husbands and ran away from them to go on the stage, wouldn't, as far as his experience went, be likely to smile over them like that. More probably a brother—a younger brother, perhaps, fiercely proud as such a boy would be of such a sister.

She certainly had sand, that girl. He was mighty glad his bluff that he would put her out of the chorus altogether, unless she took the little part in the sextette, had worked. He'd have felt rather a fool if she had called it.

Of course the thing that had got Rose was the echo, through everything John Galbraith had said, of Rodney's own philosophy; his dear, big, lusty, rather remorseless way. And now again, as before when she had left him, it was his view of life that was recoiling upon his own head.

She was really grateful to Galbraith. What had she left Rodney for, except to build a self for herself; to acquire, through whatever pains might be the price of it, a life that didn't derive from him; that was, at the core of it, her own? Yet here, right at the beginning of her pilgrimage, she'd have turned down the by-path of self-sacrifice; have begun ordering her life with reference to Rodney, rather than herself, if John Galbraith hadn't headed her back.

IV

The Girl With the Bad Voice

The Girl Up-stairs had quite a miscellaneous lot of plot; indeed a plot fancier might have detected nearly all the famous strains in its lineage. Its foci were Sylvia Huntington, the beautiful multi-millionairess, and Richard Benham, nephew of Minim, the Cosmetic King and head of the Talcum Trust. Sylvia, tired of being sought for her wealth, and yearning to be loved for herself alone, has run away to Bohemia and installed herself in an attic over a studio occupied by two penniless artists, one a poet, the other a musician. Only they aren't penniless any more, having leaped to wealth and fame with an immensely successful musical comedy they have just written. And, like Nanki Poo, the musician isn't really a musician, but is the talented, rebellious nephew of the Cosmetic King, none other than Dick Benham himself, a truant from his tyrannical uncle's determination to make him into a rouge and talcum salesman. He falls in love with Sylvia, not knowing her as Sylvia, of course, but only as the girl up-stairs, a poor little wretch to whom in the goodness of his heart, he is giving singing lessons. And she falls in love with him, knowing him neither as Dick Benham, nor as the successful composer (because his authorship of the musical comedy has been kept a secret from her), but only as a poor struggling musician. Poor Dick's affections are temporarily led astray by the mercenary seductions of the leading lady in his opera, who has learned the secret of his true identity and vast wealth, and means to marry him under the cloak of disinterested affection. He gets bad advice from his poet friend, too, who has dishonorable designs on the girl up-stairs and so warns Dick against throwing himself away on a nobody, of, possibly, doubtful virtue. It is, of course, essential to Sylvia that Dick should ask her to marry him before he learns who she really is, in order that she may be sure it isn't for her wealth that he is seeking her.

This was the general lie of the land, though the thing was complicated, of course, by minor intrigues, as for instance in the first act, when Minim, the uncle, came to inquire of the successful composer what his terms would be for introducing a song into his opera, extolling the merits of Minim's newest brand of liquid face-powder. Then there was the comic detective, whom Sylvia's frantic father had given the job of finding her, and who, considering that he was the typical idiot detective of musical comedy, came unaccountably close to doing it.

Then in the second act, there was the confusion produced by the fact that Dick and his poet friend gave a midnight party on the roof, unaware of the fact that Sylvia made it a practise, during these hot nights, to crawl out from her attic, on to this same roof and sleep there. And on this particular night, she had invited her six bachelor-girl friends, who were in her confidence, to come and share its hospitalities with her. The mutual misunderstandings, by this time piled mountain high, were projected into the third act by the not entirely unprecedented device of a mask ball in the palatial Fifth Avenue mansion of Sylvia's father, in celebration of her return home—a ball whose invitation list was precisely coincident, even down to the detective, with the persons who had appeared in the first two acts. One minute before the last curtain, Dick and Sylvia manage to thread their way out of the tangle of scandal and misconception, and satisfy each other as to the disinterested quality of their mutual adoration, falling into each other's arms just as the curtain starts down.

It was not, of course, until after a good many rehearsals that Rose could have given a connected account of it like that. They worked for three hours on this first occasion, merely getting through the first act—a miserable three hours, too, for Rose, owing to a little misfortune that befell her right at the beginning.

The glow of determination Galbraith had inspired her with, to put her own shoulder to the wheel and do her very topmost best, for the one great desideratum, the success of the show, had kept her studying her little handful of lines long after she supposed she knew them perfectly. They weren't very satisfactory lines to study—just the smallest of conversational small change, little ejaculations of delight or dismay, acquiescence or dissent. But the trouble with them was, they were, for the most part, exactly the last expressions that a smart young woman of the type she was supposed to represent would use.

So, remembering what Galbraith had said about everybody down to the last chorus-man doing the best he knew for the success of the show, Rose sought him out, for a minute, just before the rehearsal began, and asked if she might change two of her lines a little.

Galbraith grinned at her, turned and beckoned to the baby-faced man in spectacles who stood a dozen paces away. "Oh, Mr. Mills!" he called. "Can you come over here a minute?"

"He's the author," Galbraith then explained to Rose, "and we can't change this book of his without his permission."

Then, "This is Miss Dane of the sextette," he said to Mills, "and she tells me she'd like to make one or two changes in her lines."

It didn't need a sensitive ear to detect a note of mockery in this speech, though Galbraith's face was perfectly solemn. But the face of the author went a delicate pink all over, and his round eyes stared. "My God!" he said.

The exclamation was explosive enough to catch the ear of an extremely pretty young woman who stood near by with her hands in her pockets. She wore a Burberry raglan and an entirely untrimmed soft felt hat, and she came over unceremoniously and joined the group.

"Miss Devereux," said the author, with hard-fetched irony, "here's a chorus-girl in perfect agreement with you. She's got about six lines to say, and she wants to change two of them."

"What are your changes, Dane?" Galbraith asked.

Queerly enough, the curt seriousness of his speech was immensely grateful to her—suggested that she perhaps hadn't been, wholly anyhow, the object of his derision before.

"I only thought," said Rose, "that if instead of saying, 'My gracious, Sylvia!' I said, 'Sylvia, *dear!*' or something like that, it would sound a little more natural. And if I said, 'I *do* wish, Sylvia' instead of, 'I wish to goodness, Sylvia. . .'"

She had said it all straight to the author.

"I suppose," he said, sneering very hard, "that your own personal knowledge of the way society women talk is what leads you to believe that your phrases are better than mine?"

"Yes," said Rose, serenely matter-of-fact, "it is."

Sarcasm is an uncertain sort of pop-gun. You never can tell from which end it's going to go off.

"I don't know," said Miss Devereux, turning now a deadly smile on him, "whether Miss—what's-her-name—agrees with me or not. But, do you know, I agree with her."

"Oh, I don't care a *damn!*" said Mr. Harold Mills. "Go as far as you like. I don't recognize the piece now. What it'll be when you—butchers get through with it. . . !" He flung out his hands and stalked away.

"Go find Mr. Quan," said Galbraith to Rose, "and tell him to mark those changes of yours in the book. Tell him I said so."

It was, though, a pretty unsatisfactory victory. Everybody was grinning; for the tale spread fast, and while Rose knew it wasn't primarily at her, her sensations were those of a perfectly serious, well-meaning child, in adult company, who, in all innocence has just made a remark which, for some reason incomprehensible to him, has convulsed one member of it with fury, and the others with laughter. More or less she could imagine where the joke lay. Harold had evidently been quarreling with pretty much all of the principals, over more or less necessary changes in his precious text, until everybody was rather on edge about it, loaded and primed for all sorts of explosions; when, cheerfully along came Rose, a perfectly green young chorus-girl, unsuspectingly carrying the match for the mine, or the straw for the camel, whichever way you wanted to put it.

She wouldn't have minded the way she had blundered into the focus of public attention, if, in other particulars, the rehearsal had been going well with her. Unluckily, though, she started off wrong foot foremost in the very first of their numbers, with a mistake that snarled up everything and brought down an explosion of wrath from Galbraith. Even if she'd been trying, he groaned, to make mistakes, he didn't see how she'd managed that one. But the real nightmare didn't begin till the first of her scenes with Sylvia, where she had to talk.

She'd said her lines over about a thousand times apiece, and practised their inflection and phrasing in as many ways as she could think of, but she had neglected to memorize her cues. Not altogether, of course; she thought she'd learned them, but they were terribly scanty little cues anyway, just a single word, usually, and never more than two, and nothing short of absolutely automatic memorization was any good. So she sat serene through a five-second stage wait while Quan frantically spun the pages of his book to find the place—he ought to have been following of course, but he'd yielded to the temptation of trying to do something else at the same time and had got lost—and then dry-throated, incapable of a sound for a couple of seconds more—hours they seemed—after she had been identified as the culprit who had failed to come in on a cue.

The sight of the author out in the hall invoking his gods to witness that this girl who had presumed to change his lines, was an idiot incapable of articulate speech, brought her out of her daze. But even then she couldn't get anything quite right. There seemed to be no golden mean between the bellow of a fireman and a tone which

Galbraith assured her wouldn't be audible three rows back. And when they came to one of the lines she'd been allowed to change, in her panic over the thing, she mixed the two versions impartially together into a sputter of words that meant nothing at all, whereupon the author, out at the back of the hall, laughed maniacally.

She would have gone on stuttering at it until she got it straight, if Galbraith hadn't put her out of her misery by striding over, snatching the book from Quan, and reading the line himself. She hadn't anything more to say in the first act, and she managed to get through the rest of the song numbers without disaster, if equally without confidence or dash. She felt as limp as if she had been boiled and put through the clothes-wringer. And when, as he dismissed the rehearsal Galbraith told her to wait a minute, she expected nothing less than ignominious reduction to the ranks.

"That matter of putting your voice over, Dane," he said, to her amazement quite casually, "is just a question of thinking where you want it to go. If you'll imagine a target against the back wall over there, and will your voice to hit it, whatever direction you're speaking in, and however softly you speak, you will be heard. If you forget the target and think you're talking to the person on the stage you're supposed to be talking to, you won't be heard. Say your lines over to me now, without raising your voice or looking out there. But keep the target in mind."

Rose said all the lines she had in the whole three acts. It didn't take a minute. He nodded curtly. "You've got the idea." He added, just as she turned away, "You were quite right to suggest those changes. They're an improvement."

That rehearsal marked the nadir of Rose's career at the Globe. From then on, she was steadily in the ascendent, not only in John Galbraith's good graces, which was all of course that mattered. She won, it appeared, a sort of tolerant esteem from some of the principals, and even the owners themselves spoke to her pleasantly.

They entertained her vastly, now that a confidence in her ability to do her own part left her leisure to look around a bit. The contrast between the two leading women, Patricia Devereux, who played the title part, and little Anabel Astor, who played the mercenary seductress, was a piquant source of speculation. As far as speech and manners went, Miss Devereux might have been a born citizen of the world Rose had been naturalized into by her marriage with Rodney; in fact, she reminded her rather strikingly of Harriet. She was cool, brusk, hard finished, and, as was evident from Galbraith's manifest satisfaction with her, thoroughly workmanly and competent. Yet she never seemed really to work in rehearsal. She gave no more than a bare outline of what she was going to do. But the outline, in all its salient angles, was perfectly indicated. She rehearsed in her ordinary street clothes, with her hat on, and as often as not, with a wrist-bag in one hand. She neither danced, sang, nor acted. But she had her part letter perfect before any of the other principals. She never missed a cue, and though she sang off the top of her voice, and let the confines of a very scant little tailor skirt mark the limits of her dancing, she sang her songs in perfect tempo and always made it completely clear to Galbraith and the musical director, just how much of the stage in every direction, her dances were going to occupy and precisely the *tempi* at which they were to be executed. In a word, if her work had no more emotional value than a mechanical drawing, it did have the precision of one.

Rose mightn't have appreciated tins, had she not seen and admired Miss Devereux from the front in a production she and Rodney had been two or three times to see the season before.

Little Anabel Astor presented as striking a contrast to all this as it would be possible to imagine. She, too, had attained a good deal of celebrity in the musical-comedy world—was to be one of the features of the cast. She'd come up from the ranks of the chorus. She'd been one of the ponies, years ago, in some of George M. Cohan's productions, and she was still just a chorus-girl. But a chorus-girl raised to the third, or fourth, or, if you like, the *n*th power. She had an electric grin, and a perfectly boundless vitality, which she spent as freely on rehearsals as on performances. She always dressed for rehearsals just as the chorus did, in a middy-blouse and bloomers, and she worked as hard as they did, and even more ungrudgingly.

She was a pretty little thing, with nothing very feminine about her—even her voice had a harsh boyish quality—and she never looked prettier to Rose than when, her face flushed with an hour's honest toil, she would wipe the copious sweat of it off with her sleeve, and panting, look up with a smile at John Galbraith and an expectant expression, waiting for his next command, which reminded Rose of the look of a terrier alert for the stick his master means to throw for him. Her speech was unaffectedly that of a Milwaukee Avenue gamin, and it served adequately and admirably as a vehicle for the expression of her emotions and ideas.

She formed her likes and dislikes with a complete disregard of the social or professional importance of the objects of them. She took an immediate liking to Rose; gave her some valuable hints on dancing, took to calling her "dearie" before the end of the second rehearsal and, with her arm around her, confided to her in terms of blood-curdling profanity, her opinion of Stewart Lester, the tenor, who played the part of Dick Benham in the piece.

The queer thing was that she and Patricia were on the best of terms. They didn't compete, that was it, Rose supposed, and they were both good enough cosmopolites to bridge across the antipodal distances between their respective traditions and environments. Patricia hated the tenor as bitterly as Anabel. And, in her own way, she was as pleasantly friendly to Rose. There were no endearments or caresses, naturally, but her brusk nods of greeting and farewell seemed to have real good feeling behind them.

The men principals—this was rather a surprise to Rose—weren't nearly so pleasant nor so friendly. Most of them professed to be totally unaware of her existence and the one or two who showed an awareness—Freddy France, who played the comic detective, was chief of these offenders—did it in a way that brought the fighting blood into her cheeks.

My astronomical figure for the expression of Rose's rise in her profession is, in one important particular, misleading. There was nothing precalculable about it, as there is about the solemn swing of the stars. The impetus and direction of Rose's career derived from two incidents that might just as well not have happened—two of the flukiest of small chances.

The first of these chances concerned itself with Olga Larson and her bad voice. Olga, as I think I have told you, was one of the sextette. And, oddly enough, she owed her membership in this little group of quasi principals, to her voice and nothing else. Because it was a bad voice only when she talked. When she sang, it had a gorgeous thrilling ring to it that made Patricia Devereux, when she heard it, clench her hands and narrow her eyes. She'd never been taught what to do with it, but then, for what Galbraith wanted of her she needed no teaching. Her ear was infallible; let her hear a tune once and she could reproduce it accurately, squarely up to time, squarely, always, in the middle of the pitch. When she opened her rather dainty-looking mouth and sang, she could give you across the footlights the impression that at least four first-class sopranos were going uncommon strong. She hadn't a salient or commonplace enough sort of beauty to have singled her out from the chorus and she was no better a dancer than passable. But none of the girls who would be picked out by a committee of automobile salesmen as the prettiest and the best dancers in the chorus could sing a note, and the sextette would have been dumb without her voice.

It was natural enough that Patricia didn't like it. She owed her own position as a leading light-opera soprano to the cultivation to its highest possible perfection of a distinctly second-rate voice, to a precise knowledge of its limitations and to a most scrupulous economy in its effects. Inevitably, then, the raw splendors that Olga Larson dispensed so prodigally gave Patricia the creeps.

Inevitably, too, without any conscious malice about it, she made up her clear, hard little mind the moment she heard Olga talk, that she was utterly impossible for the sextette. "Really, my dear man," she told Galbraith after the first rehearsal, "you'll have to find some one else. American audiences will stand a good deal, I know, in the way of atrocious speech, but positively she'll be hooted. They'll all sound frightful enough, especially because that Dane girl, if that's her name, talks like a lady, but this one. . . !" She gave a cruelly adequate little imitation of Olga's delivery of one of her lines. "Like some one who doesn't know how, trying to play the slide trombone," she commented.

Galbraith couldn't pretend that she exaggerated the horrors of it, but explained why the girl was indispensable. The explanation didn't please Patricia any too well, either.

"Sing!" she cried hotly. "But she sings detestably!"

"No doubt," Galbraith admitted, "but she makes a great big noise always on the right note, and that's what that bunch of penny whistlers can't do without. Give her a little time," he concluded diplomatically, "and I'll try to teach her."

"It can't be taught," said Patricia. "That's too much even for you."

So it happened that when Rose came out of her own nightmare, got her breath and found leisure to look around, she found some one else whose troubles weren't so transitory. The little scene in the first act, between Sylvia and the sextette, was held up again and again, endlessly, it seemed to Rose,—and what must it have seemed to the poor victim?— while Galbraith bellowed Larson's lines after her, sometimes in grotesque imitation of her own inflections, sometimes in what was meant as a pattern for her to follow. The girl whose ear was so wonderfully sensitive to pitch and rhythm, was simply deaf, it seemed, to the subtleties of inflection. She reduced Galbraith to helpless wrath, in her panic, by mistaking now and again, his imitations for his models. The chorus tittered; the spectators suffocated their guffaws as well as they could. Patricia grew more and more acutely and infuriatingly ironic all the while.

Evidently Galbraith didn't mean to be a brute about it. He began every one of these tussles to improve her reading of a line, with a gentleness that would have done credit to a kinder-gartener. But, after three attempts, each more ominously gentle and deliberate than the last, his temper would suddenly fly all to pieces. "—No—no—no!" he would roar at her, and the similes his exasperation would supply him with, for a description of what her speech was like, were as numerous as the acids in a chemical laboratory; and they all bit and burned just as hard.

Rose looked on with rather tepid feelings. She sympathized with Galbraith on the whole. The poor man was doing his best; and the girl, queerly, didn't seem to care. She confronted him in a sort of stockish stupidity, saying her lines, when he told her to try again, with the same frightful whang he was doing his best to correct, so that he was justified, Rose felt, in accusing her of not trying, or even listening to him.

It was in the dressing-room one night, after one of these rehearsals, that she caught a different view of the situation. She sat down on a bench to unlace her shoes and looked straight into Olga Larson's face—a face sunken with a despair that turned Rose cold all over. The tearless tragic eyes were staring, without recognition, straight into Rose's own. It must be with faces like this that people mounted the rails on the high bridge in Lincoln Park, intent on leaving a world that had become intolerable. Packed in all around her in the inadequate dressing-room, the other girls were chattering, squealing, scrambling into their clothes, as unaware of her tense motionless figure, as if it had been a mere inanimate lump. She couldn't have been more alone if she had been sitting out on the rock of Juan Fernandez.

Rose invented various pretexts to delay her own dressing until the other girls were gone. She could no more have abandoned that hopeless creature there, than she could have left a person drowning. When they had the room to themselves, she sat down on the bench beside her.

"You're all right," she said, feeling rather embarrassed and inadequate and not knowing just how to begin. "I'm going to help you."

"It's always like this," the girl said. "It's no use. He'll put me back in the chorus again."

"Not if I can help it," Rose said. "But the first thing to do is to put on your clothes. Then we'll go out and get something to eat."

Even that little beginning involved a struggle—a conscious exertion of all the power Rose possessed. She learned, for the first time, what the weight of an immense melancholy inertia like that can be. The girl was like one paralyzed. She was willing enough to talk. She told Rose the whole story of her life; not as one making confidences to a friend; rather with the curious detachment of a melancholy spectator discussing an unfortunate life she had no concern with.

She knew how good her voice was, and, equally, how badly it needed training. She'd had, always, a passionate desire to sing and a belief in her possibilities. If she could get a chance, she could succeed. She'd undergone heartbreaking privations, trying to save money enough out of her earnings at one form of toil after another, to take lessons. But, repeatedly, these small savings had, by some disaster, been swept away: stolen once, by a worthless older brother; absorbed on another occasion by her mother's fatal illness. Two years ago she had drifted into the chorus, but had been altogether unlucky in her various ventures. She wasn't naturally graceful—had been slow learning to dance. Again and again, she'd been dropped at the end of three or four weeks of rehearsal (gratuitous of course) and seen another girl put in her place. When this hadn't happened, the shows she had been in had failed after a few weeks' life.

When Galbraith had put her into the sextette in *The Girl Up-stairs*, a hope, just about dead, had been awakened. She'd at last learned to dance well enough to escape censure and she had seen for herself how indispensable her singing voice was to the group. And then it had appeared she'd have to talk! And, inexplicably to herself, her talking wasn't right. The thing had just been another mirage. It was hopeless. Galbraith would put her back into the chorus—drop her, likely enough, altogether.

The thing that at first exasperated Rose and later, as she came vaguely to understand it, aroused both her pity and her determination, was the girl's strange, dully fatalistic acquiescence in it all. The sort of circumstances that in Rose herself set the blood drumming through her arteries, keyed her will to the very highest pitch, quickened her brain, made her feel in some inexplicable way, confident and irresistible, laid on this girl a paralyzing hand. It wasn't her fault that she didn't meet her difficulties half-way with a vicious, driving offensive—rout them, demoralize them. It was her tragedy.

"All right," Rose apostrophized them grimly. "This time you're up against me."

"Look here!" she said to Olga, when the story was told (this was across the table in the dingy lunch-room where, as Doris Dane, she had had her first meal, and most of her subsequent ones), "look here, and listen to what I'm going to tell you. I know what I'm talking about. You're going to learn to say your lines before tomorrow's rehearsal, so that Mr. . . So that Galbraith won't stop you once." (This was a trick of speech that came hard to Rose, but she was gradually learning it.) "We're going up to my room now, and I'm going to teach you. We've got lots of time. Rehearsal tomorrow isn't till twelve o'clock. You're going to stay in the sextette, and when the piece opens, you're going to make a hit."

She hesitated a moment, then added in the same blunt matter-of-fact way, "You're one of the most beautiful women in Chicago. Did you know that? Dressed right and with your hair done right, you could make them stare. Have you finished your coffee? Then come along. Here! Give me your part. You don't want to lose it."

For the girl, pitiably, almost ludicrously, was staring at Rose in a sort of somnambulistic daze. She hadn't been hypnotized, but she might about as well have been, for any real resistance her mind, or her will, could offer to her new friend's vibrant confidence.

She went with Rose up to the little three-dollar room. Rose put her into a chair, sat down opposite her, took the first phrase of her first speech, and said it very slowly, very quietly, half a dozen times. That was at half past eleven o'clock at night. By midnight, Olga could say those first three words, if not to Rose's complete satisfaction, at least a lot better. She went on and finished the sentence. They worked straight through the night, except that two or three times the girl broke down; said it was hopeless. She got up once and said that she was going home, whereupon Rose locked the door and put the key in her stocking. She sulked once, and for fifteen minutes wouldn't say a word. But by seven o'clock in the morning, when they went back to the lunch-room and ate an enormous breakfast, Olga's sluggish blood was fired at last. It was a profane thought, but you *could* take the Fatal Sisters by the hair and coerce a change in the pattern they were weaving.

And Rose, by that time, by the plain brute force of necessity, was a teacher of phonetics. She'd discovered how she made sounds herself and had, with the aid of a hand mirror, developed a rough-

and-ready technique for demonstrating how it was done. She remembered, with bitter regret, a course she had dozed through at the university, dreaming about the half-back, which, had she only listened to the professor instead, would be doing her solid service now. Had there been other courses like that, she wondered vaguely? Had the education she had spent fifteen years or so on an actual relation to life after all? It was a startling idea.

She walked Olga out to the park and back at seven-thirty, and at eight they were up in her room again. They raided the delicatessen at eleven o'clock, and made an exiguous meal on the plunder. And at twelve, husky of voice, but indomitable of mind, they, with the others, confronted Galbraith upon the stage in North End Hall.

"Do you suppose," Olga said during the preliminary bustle of getting started, "that he's put any one else in my part already?"

It was a fear Rose had entertained, but had avoided suggesting to her pupil.

"I don't believe so," she said. "If he has, I'll talk to him."

"No, you won't!" said Olga. "I'll talk to him myself."

There was a ring to that decision that did Rose's heart good. It took a long time to get that northern blood on fire, but when you did, you could count on its not going cold again overnight.

It got pretty exciting of course, as the scene between Sylvia and the sextette drew near, and when it came, Rose could hardly manage her own first line—hung over it a second, indeed, before she could make her voice work at all, and drew a sharp look of inquiry from Galbraith. But on Olga's first cue, her line was spoken with no hesitation at all, and in tone, pitch and inflection, it was almost a phonographic copy of the voice that had served it for a model.

There was a solid two seconds of silence. For once in her life Patricia Devereux had missed a cue!

John Galbraith had been an acrobat as well as a dancer, and he was quick on his feet. He had just turned, unexpectedly, an intellectual somersault, but he landed cleanly and without a stagger. "Come, Miss Devereux," he said, "that's your line." And the scene went on.

But when, about four o'clock that afternoon, the rehearsal was over, Galbraith called Olga out to him and allowed himself a long incredulous stare at her. "Will you tell me, Larson," he asked, "why in the name of Heaven, if you could do that, you didn't do it yesterday?"

"I couldn't do it yesterday," she said. "Dana taught me."

"Taught you!" he echoed. "Beginning after last night's rehearsal? . . . Dane!" he called to Rose, who had been watching a little anxiously to see what would happen.

"You've learned it very well indeed," he said with a nod of dismissal to Olga, as Rose came up. "Don't try to change it. Stick to what you've got."

Then, to Rosa, "Larson tells me you taught her. How did you do it?"

"Why, I just—taught her," said Rosa. "I showed her how I said each line, and I kept on showing her until she could do it."

"How long did it take you—all night?"

"All the time there's been since last rehearsal," said Rosa, "except for three meals."

"Good God!" said Galbraith. "Devereux said it couldn't be done, and I agreed with her. Well, live and learn. Look here! Will you teach the others—the other four in the sextette? I'll see you're paid for it."

"Why, yes,—of course," said Rose, hesitating a little.

"Oh, I don't mean overnight," he said, "but mornings—between rehearsals—whenever you can."

"I wasn't thinking of that," said Rose. "I was just wondering if they'd want to be taught—I mean, by another chorus-girl, you know."

"They'll want to be taught if they want to keep their jobs," said Galbraith. And then, to her astonishment, and also perhaps to his, for the thing was radically out of the etiquette of the occasion, he reached out and shook hands with her. "I'm very much obliged to you," he said.

V

Mrs. Goldsmith's Taste

If there was a profession in the world which Rose had never either idly or seriously considered as a possible one for herself, that of a teacher was it. And yet, the first money she ever earned in her life was the twenty dollars the management paid her for teaching the other four girls in the sextette to say their lines. She was a born teacher, too. And the born teacher is a rare bird.

One must know something in the first place, of course, before one can teach it—a fact that has resulted in the fitting of an enormous number of square pegs into round holes. Most of the people in the world who are trying to teach, are those whose aptitude is for learning. But the scholar's temper and the teacher's are antipodal; a salient, vivid personality that can command attention, the unconscious will to conquer—to enforce (a very different thing from the wish to do these things) that is the *sine qua non* for a real teacher. And that, of course, was Rose all over.

Those four sulky, rather supercilious chorus-girls, coming to Rose under a threat of dismissal, for lessons in the one last thing that a free-born American will submit to dictation about, might not want to learn, nor mean to learn, but they couldn't help learning. You couldn't be unaware of Rose and, being aware of her, you couldn't resist doing things as she wanted you to.

Informally, too, she taught them other things than speech. "Here, Waldron!" Galbraith would say. "This is no cake-walk. All you've got to do is to cross to that chair and sit down in it like a lady. Show her how to do it, Dane." And Rose, with her good-humored disarming smile at the infuriated Waldron, would go ahead and do it.

I won't pretend that she was a favorite with the other members of the sextette, barring Olga. But she managed to avoid being cordially hated, which was a very solid personal triumph.

I have said that there were two small incidents destined to have a powerful influence at this time, in Rose's life. One of them I have told you about—the chance that led her to teach Olga Larson to talk. The other concerned itself with a certain afternoon frock in a Michigan Avenue shop.

The owners of *The Girl Up-stairs* were very inadequately experienced in the business of putting on musical comedies. Galbraith spoke of them as amateurs, and couldn't, really, have described them better. Your professional gambler—for musical-comedy producing is an especially sporting form of gambling and nothing else—assesses his chances in advance, decides coolly whether they are worth taking or not, and then, with a steely indifference awaits the event. The amateur, on the contrary, is always fluttering between an insane confidence and a shuddering despair; between a reckless disregard of money and a foolish attempt to save it. It had been in one of their hot fits that the owners of *The Girl Up-stairs* had retained Galbraith. The news item Rose had read had not exceeded truth in saying that he was one of the three greatest directors in the country. They couldn't have got him out to Chicago at all but for the chance that he was, just then, at the end of a long-time contract with the Shumans and holding off for better terms before he signed a new one. The owners were staggered at the prices they had to pay him, at that, but they recovered and were still blowing warm when they authorized him to engage Devereux, Stewart, Astor and McGill (McGill was the chief comedian, the Cosmetic King) for all of these were high-priced people.

But by the time the question of costumes came up, they were shivering in a perfect ague of apprehension. Was there no limit to the amount they were to be asked to spend? This figure that Galbraith indicated as the probable cost of having a first-class brigand in New York design the costumes and a firm of pirates in the same neighborhood execute them, was simply insane. New York managers might be boobs enough to submit to such an extortion, but they, believe them, were not. Many of the costumes could be bought, ready made, on State Street or Michigan Avenue. Some of the fancy things could be executed by a competent wardrobe mistress, if some one would give her the ideas. And ideas—one could pick them up anywhere. Mrs. Goldsmith, now,—she was the wife of the senior of the two owners—had splendid taste and would be glad to put it at their service. There was no reason why she should not at once take the sextette down-town and fit them out with their dresses.

Galbraith shrugged his shoulders, but made no further complaint. It was, he admitted, as they had repeatedly pointed out, their own money. So a rendezvous was made between Mrs. Goldsmith and the sextette for Lessing's store on Michigan Avenue at three o'clock on an afternoon when Galbraith was to be busy with the principals. He might manage to drop in before they left to cast his eye over and approve the selection.

It was with some rather uncomfortable misgivings that Rose set out to revisit a part of town so closely associated with the first year of her married life. The particular shop wasn't, luckily, one that she had patronized in that former incarnation. But it was in the same block with a half dozen that were, and she hadn't been east of Clark Street since the day Otto had driven her to the Polk Street Station.

The day was cold and blustery—a fact that she was grateful for, as it gave her an excuse for wearing a thick white veil, which was almost as good as a mask. It was with a rather breathless excitement that persisted in feeling like guilt—her heart wouldn't have beaten any faster, she believed, if she had just robbed a jewelry store and were walking away with the swag in her pocket—that she debouched out of Van Buren Street, around the corner of the Chicago Club, and into the avenue. Unconsciously, she had been expecting to meet every one she knew, beginning with Frederica, in the course of the two blocks or so she had to walk. Very naturally, she didn't catch even a glimpse of any one she even remotely knew. Suppose there should be any one in the store! But this, she realized, wasn't likely.

It wasn't a really smart shop. It paid an enormous rent there in that neighborhood in order to pretend to be, and the gowns on the wax figures in its windows, were taken on faith by pleasurably scandalized pedestrians as the very latest scream of fashion. The prices on these confections were always in the process of a violent reduction, as large exclamatory placards grievously testified. The legend eighty-eight dollars crossed out in red lines, with thirty-nine seventy-five written below, for a sample. The most exclusive smartness for the economy-loving multitude. This was the slogan.

Rose, arriving promptly at the hour agreed on, had a wait of fifteen minutes before any of her sisters of the sextette, or Mrs. Goldsmith arrived. She told the suave manager that she was waiting for friends, but this didn't deter him from employing a magnificent wave of the hand to summon one of the saleswomen and consigning Rose almost tenderly, to her care. He didn't know her, but he knew that that ulster of hers had come straight over from Paris, had cost not less than two hundred dollars, and had been selected by an excellently discriminating eye; and that was enough for him.

"I don't want anything just now," Rose told the saleswoman. But she hadn't, in these few weeks of Clark Street, lost the air of one who will buy if she sees anything worth buying. In fact, the saleswoman thought, correctly, that she knew her and was in for a shock a little later when Mrs. Goldsmith and the other five members of the sextette arrived.

Meanwhile, she showed Rose the few really smart things they had in the store—a Poiret evening gown, a couple of afternoon frocks from Jennie, and so on. There wasn't much, she admitted, it being just between seasons. Their Palm Beach things weren't in yet.

Rose made a few appreciative, but decidedly respect-compelling comments, and faithfully kept one eye on the door.

The rest of the sextette arrived in a pair and a trio. One of them squealed, "Hello, Dane!" The saleswoman got her shock on seeing Rose nod an acknowledgment of this greeting and just about that time, they heard Mrs. Goldsmith explaining who she was and the nature of her errand, to the manager. The necessary identifications got themselves made somehow. They weren't in any sense introductions, everybody in the store felt that plainly. Mrs. Goldsmith was touching the skirts of musical comedy with a very long pair of tongs. There was absolutely no connection, social or personal, between herself and the young persons who were to wear the frocks she was going to buy.

She stood them up and stared at them through her eye-glasses, discussed their various physical idiosyncrasies with candor, and, one by one, packed them off to try on haphazard selections from the mounds which three industrious saleswomen piled up before her. You couldn't deny her the possession of a certain force of character, for not one of the six girls uttered a word of suggestion or of protest.

And the sort of gowns she was exclaiming over with delight and ordering put into the heap of possibilities, were horrible enough to have drawn a protest from the wax figures in the windows. The more completely the fundamental lines of a frock were disguised with sartorial scroll-saw work, the more successful this lady felt it to be. An ornament, to Mrs. Goldsmith, did not live up to its possibilities, unless it in turn were decorated with ornaments of its own; like the fleas on the fleas on the dog.

It is a tribute to one of the qualities that made John Galbraith a successful director, that Rose spent a miserable half-hour worrying over these selections of the wife of the principal owner of the show, feeling she ought to put up some sort of fight and hardly deterred by the patent futility of such a course. To rest her esthetic senses from the delirium of fussiness that was giving Mrs. Goldsmith so much pleasure, she began thinking about that Poiret frock—the superb simple audacity of it! It had been made by an artist who knew where to stop. And he had stopped rather incredibly soon. Just suppose. . . And then her eyes lighted up, gazed thoughtfully out the window across the wind-swept desert of the avenue, and, presently she grinned—widely, contentedly.

For the next hour and a half, during the intervals of her own trying on, she entertained herself very happily with the day-dream that she herself had a commission to design the costumes for *The Girl Up-stairs*. She had always done that more or less, she realized, when she went to musical-comedy shows with Rodney, especially when they were badly costumed. But this time she did it a good deal more vividly, partly because her interest in the piece was more intense, partly because her imagination had a blank canvas to work on.

All the while, like Sister Anne in the tower, she kept one eye on the door and prayed for the arrival of John Galbraith.

He came in just as Mrs. Goldsmith finished her task—just when, by a process of studious elimination, every passable thing in the store had been discarded and the twelve most utterly hopeless ones—two for each girl—laid aside for purchase. The girls were despatched to put on the evening frocks first, and were then paraded before the director.

He was a diplomat as I have said (possibly I spoke of him before as an acrobat. It comes to the same thing), and he was quick on his feet. Rose, watching his face very closely, thought that for just a split second, she caught a gleam of ineffable horror. But it was gone so quickly she could almost have believed that she had been mistaken. He didn't say much about the costumes, but he said it so promptly and adequately that Mrs. Goldsmith beamed with pride. She sent the girls away to put on the other set—the afternoon frocks, and once more the director's approbation, though laconic, was one hundred per cent. pure.

"That's all," he said in sudden dismissal of the sextette. "Rehearsal at eight-thirty."

Five of them scurried like children let out of school, around behind the set of screens that made an extemporaneous dressing-room, and began changing in a mad scramble, hoping to get away and to get their dinners eaten soon enough to enable them to see the whole bill at a movie show before the evening's rehearsal.

But Rose didn't avail herself of her dismissal—remained hanging about, a couple of paces away from where Galbraith was talking to Mrs. Goldsmith. The only question that remained, he was telling her, was whether her selections were not too—well, too refined, genteel, one might say, for the stage. Regretfully he confessed he was a little afraid they were. It needed a certain crudity to withstand the glare of the footlights and until these gowns had been submitted to that glare, one couldn't be sure.

He wasn't looking at her as he talked, and presently, as his gaze wandered about the store, it encountered Rose's face. She hadn't prepared it for the encounter, and it wore, hardly veiled, a look of humorous appreciation. His sentence broke, then completed itself. She turned away, but the next moment he called out to her, "Were you waiting for me, Dane?"

"I'd like to speak to you a minute," she said, "when you have time."

"All right. Go and change your clothes first," he said.

Out of the tail of her eye as she departed, she saw him shaking hands with the owner's wife and thanking her effusively for her help. Incidentally, he was leading her toward the door as he did it. And at the door, he declined an offer to be taken anywhere he might want to go in her electric.

She found the other girls on the point of departure. But Olga offered to wait for her.

"No, you run along," Rose said. "I've some errands and I don't feel like seeing a movie tonight, anyway."

Olga looked a little odd about it, but hurried along after the others.

A saleswoman—the same one the manager assigned to Rose under the misconception which that smart French ulster of hers had created when she came into the store—now came around behind the screen to gather up the frocks the girls had shed.

"Will you please bring me," said Rose, "that Poiret model you showed me before the others came in? I'll try it on."

The saleswoman's manner was different now and she grumbled something about its being closing time.

"Then, if you'll bring it at once. . ." said Rose. And the saleswoman went on the errand.

Five minutes later, Galbraith from staring gloomily at the mournful heap of trouble Mrs. Goldsmith had left on his hands, looked up to confront a vision that made him gasp.

"I wanted you to see if you liked this," said Rose.

"If I liked it!" he echoed. "Look here! If you know enough to pick out things like that, why did you let that woman waste everybody's time with junk like this? Why didn't you help her out?"

"I couldn't have done much," Rose said, "even if my offering to do anything hadn't made her angry—and I think it would have. You see, she's got lots of taste, only it's bad. She wasn't bewildered a bit. She knew just what she wanted and she got it. It's the badness of these things she likes. And I thought. . ." She hesitated a little over this. "I thought as long as they couldn't be good, perhaps the next best thing would be to have them as bad as possible. I mean that it would be easier to throw them all out and get a fresh start."

He stared at her with a frown of curiosity. "That's good sense," he said. "But how did you come to think of it?—Oh, I don't mean that!" he went on impatiently. "Why should you bother to think of it?"

Her color came up perceptibly as she answered. "Why—I want the piece to succeed, of course. I was awfully miserable when I saw the sort of things she was picking out and I spent half an hour trying to think what I could do about it. And then I saw that the best thing I could do, was nothing."

"You didn't do nothing though," he said. "That thing you've got on is a start."

Rose turned rather suddenly to the saleswoman. "I wish you'd get that little Empire frock in maize and corn-flower," she said. "I'd like Mr. Galbraith to see that, too." And the saleswoman, now placated, bustled away.

"This thing that I've got on," said Rose swiftly, "costs a hundred and fifty dollars, but I know I can copy it for twenty. I can't get the materials exactly of course, but I can come near enough."

"Will you try this one on, miss?" asked the saleswoman, coming on the scene again with the frock she had been sent for.

"No," said Rose. "Just hold it up."

Galbraith admitted it was beautiful, but wasn't overwhelmed at all as he had been by the other.

"It's not quite so much your style, is it? Not drive enough?"

"It isn't for me," said Rose. "It's for Olga Larson to wear in that *All Alone* number for the sextette."

"Why Larson especially?" he asked. "Except that she's a friend of yours."

"She isn't," said Rose, "particularly. And anyway, that wouldn't be a reason. But—did you ever really look at her? She's the one really beautiful woman in the company."

"Larson?" said John Galbraith incredulously.

And Rose, with a flush and a smile partly deprecatory over her presumption in venturing to say such things to a formidable authority like the director, and partly the result of an exciting conviction that she was right, told him her mind on the subject, while Galbraith, half fascinated, half amused, listened.

"I don't happen to remember the portrait of the Honorable Mrs. Graham that you speak about," he said, "but I won't deny that you may be right about it."

It was well after closing time by now—a fact that the manager, coming to reinforce the saleswoman, contrived, without saying so, to indicate.

"Put on your street things," said Galbraith bruskly. "I'll wait."

VI

A Business Proposition

Why, this was what I wanted to say," said Rose, taking up the broken conversation as he pulled the shop door to behind him. She didn't go out on to the sidewalk, but lingered in the recessed doorway. "I thought if you'd let me fake that evening frock for twenty dollars, and then buy the little Empire one for Olga Larson—it's only eighty—that the two would average just about what Mrs. Goldsmith was paying for the others."

"Why not fake the other one too?" he asked.

"It couldn't be done," said Rose decisively. "There's no idea in it, you see, that just jumps out and catches you. It gets its style from being so—reserved and so just exactly right. And of course that's true of the girl herself. She's perfect, just about. But it's a perfection that it's awfully easy to kill. She kills it herself by the way she does her hair."

Buzzing around in the back of John Galbraith's mind was an unworded protest against the way Rose had just killed her own beauty with a thick white veil so nearly opaque that all it let him see of her face was an intermittent gleam of her eyes. Keenly aware—a good deal more keenly aware than he was willing to admit—of the sort of splendor which, but for the veil, he'd be looking at now, a splendor which nothing short of a complete mask could hide, he was not quite in the mood to wax enthusiastic over a beauty so fragile as that of the girl they had been talking about. There was a momentary silence, broken again, by Rose.

"Of course, you'll want to take a look at her for yourself, before you decide," she said; "but I'm pretty sure you'll see it." She put a cadence of finality into her voice. The business between them was over, it said, and all she was waiting for was a word of dismissal, to nod him a farewell and go swinging away down the avenue. Still he didn't speak, and she moved a little restlessly. At last:—

"Do you mind crossing the street?" he asked abruptly. "Then we can talk as we walk along." She must have hesitated, because he added, "It's too cold to stand here."

"Of course," she said then. All that had made her hesitate was her surprise over his having made a request instead of giving an order.

Galbraith turned her north on the vast empty east sidewalk—a highway in itself broader than many a famous European street, and they walked a little way in silence.

No observant Chicagoan, Rose reflected, need ever yearn for the wastes of the Sahara when a desire for solitude or the need of privacy came upon him. The east side of Michigan Avenue was just as solitary and despite the difficulty of getting across to it, really a good deal more accessible. The west side was one unbroken glow of light and though the Christmas crowds had thinned somewhat with the closing of the shops, they were still thick enough to have made it difficult for two people to walk and talk together. A quadruple stream of motors, bellowing warnings at one another, roaring with suddenly opened throttles, squealing under sudden applications of the brake, occupied the roadway and served more than the mere distance would have done, to isolate the pair that had the east sidewalk all to themselves.

He couldn't be looking for a better place to talk than this, Rose thought. Why didn't he begin? Probably he'd got started thinking about something else. A motor coming along near the curb emitted a particularly wanton bellow, and she saw him jump like a nervous woman, then stand still and glare after the offender. He must be feeling specially irritable tonight, she thought.

It was a good diagnosis. And his irritation had, for him, a most unusual cause. Chorus-girls, principals, owners, authors, costumers, were frequently the objects of his exasperated dissatisfaction. But tonight the person he was out of all patience with was himself. He couldn't make up his mind what he wanted to do. Or rather, knowing what he wanted to do, he couldn't make up his mind to do it. It was this indecision of his that had produced the silence while he and Rose had stood in the entrance to Lessing's store. The only resolution he had come to there had been not to allow her to say good night to him and walk away. But now that she was striding along beside him, he couldn't make up his mind what to say to her.

A more self-conscious man would have forgiven himself his indecision from recognizing the real complexities of the case. He was, to begin with, an artist—almost a great artist. And a universal characteristic of such is a complete detachment from the materials in which they work—a sort of remorselessness in the use of anything that can contribute to their complete expression. The raw materials of John

HENRY KITCHELL WEBSTER

Galbraith's art were paint and canvas, fabrics, tunes, men and women. It was an axiom in his experience, that any personal feeling—any sort of human relation with one of the units in the mosaic he was building—was to be avoided like the plague. His professional and personal contempt for a colleague capable of a love-affair with a woman in a company he was directing, would be inexpressible—unfathomable. Of course when a man's job was finished—and this sort of job nearly always did finish on the opening night—why, after that, his affairs were his own affair.

In a word: he ordered his life on the perfectly sound masculine instinct for keeping his work and his sex emotions in separate water-tight compartments. Rose was a working member of his production, and it was therefore flagrantly impossible that his relation with her should be other than purely professional.

And yet there had been something intangibly personal from the very first, about every one of their broken momentary conversations—almost about every meeting of their eyes. It had disturbed him the first time he had ever seen her smile. He remembered the occasion well enough. She had just finished executing the dance step—the almost inexcusably vulgar little dance step he had ordered her to do as a condition of getting the job she said she wanted—had turned on him blazing with indignation; but right in the full blaze of it, at something she must have seen, and understood, in his own face, in deprecation of her own wrath, she had, slowly and widely, smiled.

And then the way she worked for him in rehearsal! He'd seen girls work hard before—desperately, frantically hard, under the fear that they weren't good enough to hold their jobs. That wasn't the spirit in which this girl worked. She seemed possessed by a blazing determination that the results he wanted should he obtained. It seemed she couldn't devour his intentions quickly enough, and her little unconscious nod of satisfaction after he had corrected a mistake and she felt sure that now she knew exactly what he wanted, was like nothing in his previous experience.

The wonderful thing about it was that she carried that eagerness beyond the confines of her own job. And she put it to good effect too. She had taken that Larson girl and, by the plain force of personal dominance, made her talk right. Well, why? That was the question. Who was she anyway? Where had she come from? Who was "the only person who really mattered" to her—the person who wasn't a pussy-cat?

He had tried hard to convince himself that these were all professional questions. It was true they had a bearing on the more important and perfectly legitimate question whether he had, in this altogether extraordinary personality, discovered a new star. He had, during the last quarter century, discovered a number—one or two of them authentically of the first magnitude.

It would have simplified matters immensely if he could have seen Rose in this category. But the stubborn fact was, he couldn't. She couldn't sing a bit, and marked as her natural talent was for dancing, she hadn't begun young enough ever to master the technique of it. That left acting; but he doubted if she could ever go very far at that. Salient as her personality was, she hadn't the instinct for putting it over. Or, if she had it, she distrusted it. She was handicapped, too, by her sense of humor. A real star in the egg, wouldn't have stopped in the middle of that first fine blaze of wrath he'd seen, to join him in smiling at it. A real actress wouldn't have spent her energies teaching another woman to talk, nor persuading him to buy another woman a beautiful frock. The focus had to be sharper than that. The only way you got the drive it took to spell your name in electric lights, was by subordinating everything else to the projection of yourself, treating your surroundings, with irresistible conviction, merely as a background. This girl could never do that.

Yet the notion wouldn't leave his mind that she could do something, and do it more than commonly well. She must have an instinct of her own for effects to enable her to understand so instantaneously what he was trying to do. And once in a while, especially lately, he'd seen, over some experiment of his, a flash of dissent across her eager face which gave him the preposterous idea that by asking her—asking a chorus-girl!—he might get a suggestion worth thinking about.

Certainly she had helped him in another way, there was no doubt of that. That sextette, thanks to her teaching, would be the smartest, best mannered bunch of chorus-girls that had adorned a production of his in a long, long time.

And here, perhaps, he came closer than anywhere else to an understanding of the source of the girl's attraction for him. John Galbraith could remember the time when, a nameless little rat of a cockney, he had slept under London bridges, opened cab doors for half-pence, carried links on foggy nights. By the clear force of genius he had made his way up from that;—from throwing cart-wheels for the amusement of the queues waiting at the pit entrances of theaters, from the ribald knock-about of East End halls, from the hilarity of Drury

Lane pantomimes. Professionally his success was a solid indubitable thing. If he weren't actually preeminent in his special field, at least there was no one who was accorded a preeminence over him.

But another ambition, quite apart from the professional one, was hardly so well satisfied. From the time of his very earliest memories he had felt a passionate admiration for good breeding, and a consuming envy of the lucky unconscious possessors of it. Since ten years old, he had been possessed by the great desire to be acknowledged a gentleman. There was nothing of vulgar veneer about this. It was the real interior thing he wanted; that invisible yet perfectly palpable hall-mark which without explanations or credentials, classified you. His profession had not brought him in contact more than very infrequently with people of this sort, and his personal interests never could be made to do so with results perfectly satisfactory to himself. There it was,—the thing those lucky elect possessed without a thought or an effort. It was an indestructible possession, apparently, too. You couldn't throw it away. Dissipation, dishonesty, even a total collapse that brought its victim down to the sink that he himself had sprouted from, seemed powerless to efface that hall-mark.

He learned to suppose that if it were indestructible, it was also unattainable, though perhaps he himself failed of attaining it only in the consciousness of having failed—in the inability to stop trying for it, straining all his actions through a sieve in the effort to conform to a standard not his own.

Well, this girl, whose own life must have collapsed under her in a peculiarly cruel and dramatic fashion so that she had had to come to him and ask him for a job in the chorus—she had the hall-mark. She had besides a lot of the qualities that traditionally went with it, but often didn't. She was game—game as a fighting-cock. What must it not have meant to her to come down into that squalid dance-hall in the first place and submit to the test he had subjected her to! How must the dressing-room conversation of her colleagues in the chorus have revolted and sickened her? What must it mean to her to take his orders—sharp rasping orders, with the sting of ridicule in the tail of them when they had to be repeated;—to be addressed by her last name like a servant? Why, this very afternoon, how must she have felt, standing there like a manikin, ordered to put on this dress and that, by a fussy fat woman who wouldn't have touched her with tongs? But from not one of these experiences had he ever seen her flinch or protest. Oh, yes, she was game, and she was simple, as they always were; a fine type of the real thing.

And, somehow, he felt, she treated him as if he were hall-marked too. He hadn't much to go by—absurdly little things really. But, after all, it was the little things that counted;—a fine distinction in the cadence of a voice, in the sort of nod of greeting or farewell one gave. She never nodded at him in that curt telegraphic sort of way without warming him up a bit inside.

And all the while he was a director and she was a chorus-girl and an unyielding etiquette of their respective professions forbade a word of human intercourse between them! He had violated it, as both of them had been aware, when he shook hands with her and thanked her for having taught Olga Larson to talk. And just because he recognized quite well how necessary the barrier was in all but one out of a thousand cases, its existence in this one case baffled and irritated him.

Up to the hour when he had turned into Lessing's store this afternoon, for a look at the dresses Mrs. Goldsmith had been picking out for the sextette, this feeling of baffled curiosity and of irritation over the etiquette that forbade his satisfying it, would have summed up, adequately enough, all the emotions he was conscious of toward the girl. His professional admiration for her was another thing of course—a perfectly legitimate thing. But with her appearance from behind the screen, in that French evening gown—a gown she wore with the indescribable air of belonging in it—with all her vibrant, irregular, fascinating, eupeptic beauty fully revealed, his mood of impatient acquiescence had fallen away. The basis of his feeling toward her shifted in a manner that James Randolph wouldn't have had a moment's difficulty in explaining, although Galbraith didn't understand it himself.

The thing he was conscious of was, when she made that offer to copy this gown herself for twenty dollars and so leave him leeway for the purchase of the Empire frock for Olga—offering to go to that trouble not for herself or her friend, but to further the accomplishment of what he wanted; namely, the success of his production—what he was conscious of then, was an overpowering desire to make a confidante of her; to talk matters out with her, show her some of the major strategy of the game that he had to consider, and find out how the thing would look to her.

It was all against the rules, of course. But to this case—the one in a thousand certainly, in ten thousand maybe—the rules manifestly did not apply.

HENRY KITCHELL WEBSTER

If it hadn't been for that opaque white veil, the glow of light and eagerness in her face would probably have conquered his resistance finally and for good, while they stood there in the entry to the store. As it was, he was still hanging on a dead center as they walked down the east side of the avenue together.

Ahead of them, and to the right, over in Grant Park, was the colossal municipal Christmas tree, already built, and getting decorated against the celebration of Christmas Eve, now only two days away.

"Shall we rehearse on Christmas Day?" Rose asked.

He came out of his preoccupation a little vaguely. "Why, yes. Yes, of course," he said absently. Then, coming a little further, and with a different intonation, he went on: "We're really getting pressed for time, you see. And the opening won't wait for anybody. It's hard luck though, isn't it?"

"I suppose it is, for the others;" Rose said, "but—I'm glad."

It wouldn't have needed so sensitive an ear as his to catch the girl's full meaning. Christmas—this Christmas, the first since that mysterious collapse of her life, whose effect he had seen, but whose cause he couldn't guess—was going to be a terrible day for her. She had dreaded lest it should be empty. He wanted to say, "You poor child!" But—this was the simple fact—he was afraid to.

There was another momentary silence, and again Rose broke it.

"Do you think you'll be able to convince Mrs. Goldsmith," she asked, "that her gowns don't look well on the stage?"

"Probably not," he said in quick relief. Rose had decided the issue for herself; brought up the very topic he'd wanted to bring up; got him off his dead center at last. Back of Rose, of course, was the municipal Christmas tree with its power of suggesting a lot of ideas she must fight out of her mind.

"Certainly not," he went on, "if you're right about her, and I fancy you are, that her taste isn't negative, but bad, and that it's the very hideousness of the things she likes. No, she won't be convinced, and if I know Goldsmith, he'll say his wife's taste is good enough for him. So if we want a change, we've a fight on our hands."

The way he had unconsciously phrased that sentence startled him a little.

"The question is," he went on, "whether they're worth making a fight about. Are they so bad as I think they are?"

"Oh, yes," said Rose. "They're dowdy and fourth-class and ridiculous. Of course I don't know how many people in the audience would know that."

"And I don't care." said John Galbraith with a flash of intensity that made her look round at him. "That's not a consideration I'll give any weight to. When I put out a production under my name, it means it's the best production I can make with the means I've got. There may be men who can work differently; but when I have to take a cynical view of it and try to get by with bad work because most of the people out in front won't know the difference, I'll retire. I'm only fifty and I've got ten or fifteen good years in me yet. But before I'll do that, I'll go out to my little farm on Long Island and raise garden truck."

There was another momentary silence, for the girl made no comment at all on this statement of his *credo*. But he felt sure, somehow, that she understood it and there was nothing deprecatory about the tone in which, presently, he went on speaking.

"Of course a director's got only one weapon to use against the owners of a show, when it comes down to an issue, and that's a threat to resign unless they let him have his way. I've used that twice in this production already, and I can see one or two places coming where I may have to use it again. So, if there's any way of throwing out those costumes without giving them their choice between getting new ones or getting a new director, I'd like to find it. Would it be possible, do you think, to get better ones that would also be cheaper? That argument would bring Goldsmith around in a hurry. It's ridiculous, of course, but that's the trouble with making a production for amateurs. You spend more time fighting them, than you do producing the show."

"I don't believe," said Rose, "that you could get better ready-made costumes a lot cheaper; at least, not enough to go around, and in a hurry. Of course every now and then, you can pick up a tremendous bargain— some imported model that's a little extreme, or made in trying colors, that they want to get rid of and will sell almost for whatever you'll pay. But the two or three we might be able to find, wouldn't help us much."

"And I suppose," he said dubiously, "it's out of the question getting them any other way than ready-made; that is, and cheaper too."

The only sign of excitement there was in the girl's voice when she answered, was a sort of exaggerated matter-of-factness. Oh, yes, there was besides a wire edge on it, so that the words came to him through the cold air with a kind of ringing distinctness.

"I could design the costumes and pick out the materials," she said, "but we'd have to get a good sewing woman—perhaps more than one, to get them done."

He wasn't greatly surprised. Perhaps the notion that she might suggest something of the sort was responsible for the tentative dubious way in which he had said he supposed it couldn't be done.

But Rose, at the sound of her own voice and the extraordinary proposition it was uttering, was astonished clear through. She hadn't had the remotest idea of saying such a thing a moment or two before. What had suggested it, she couldn't have told. That day-dream perhaps, that she had amused herself with while Mrs. Goldsmith was making up the tale of her atrocities. Perhaps it had been just the suggestions speaking in the tone, not the words, of John Galbraith's voice—that he hoped she'd offer something like that.

Anyway, whatever it was that presented the idea to her, the thing that seized on it and spoke it aloud was an instinct that didn't need to stop and think—an instinct that realized indeed, if this isn't too far-fetched a way of putting it, that its only chance lay in escaping into the open ahead of the slower-footed processes of thought. If she hadn't spoken instantly like that, it's perfectly clear she wouldn't have spoken at all. But, having heard her own voice say the words, she resolved, in spite of her fright—because she was frightened—to back them up.

"You've had—experience in designing gowns, have you?" Galbraith asked.

"Only for myself," she admitted. "But I know I can do that part of it."

And she wasn't telling more than the truth! The confident excitement that possessed her, gave a stronger assurance than any amount of experience could have done.

"But,"—she reverted to the other part of the plan—"I'm not a good sewer. I'd have to have somebody awfully good, who'd do exactly what I told her."

"Oh, that can be managed;" he said a little absently, and with what struck Rose as a mere man's ignorance of the difficulties of the situation. Expert sewing women didn't grow on every bush. But at the end of a silence that lasted while they walked a whole block, he convinced her that she had been mistaken.

"I was just figuring out the way to work it," he said then, explaining his silence. "I shall tell Goldsmith and Block (Block was the junior partner in the enterprise) that I've got hold of a costumer who agrees to deliver twelve costumes satisfactory to me, at an average of say, twenty per cent less than the ones Mrs. Goldsmith picked out. If they aren't satisfactory, it's the costumer's loss and we can buy these that

Mrs. Goldsmith picked out, or others that will do as well, at Lessing's. I think that saving will be decisive with them."

"But do you know a costumer?" Rose asked.

"You're the costumer," said Galbraith. "You design the costumes, buy the fabrics, superintend the making of them. As for the woman you speak of, we'll get the wardrobe mistress at the Globe. I happen to know she's competent, and she's at a loose end just now, because her show is closing when ours opens. You'll buy the fabrics and you'll pay her. And what profit you can make out of the deal, you're entitled to. I'll finance you myself. If they won't take what we show them, why, you'll be out your time and trouble, and I'll be out the price of materials and the woman's labor."

"I don't think it would be fair," she said, and she found difficulty in speaking at all because of a sudden disposition of her teeth to chatter— "I don't think it would be fair for me to take all the profit and you take all the risk."

"Well, I can't take any profit, that's clear enough," he said; and she noticed now a tinge of amusement in his voice. "You see, I'm retained, body and soul, to put this production over. I can't make money out of those fellows on the side. But you're not retained. You're employed as a member of the chorus. And so far, you're not even being paid for the work you're doing. As long as you work to my satisfaction there on the stage, nothing more can be asked of you. As for the risk, I don't believe it's serious. I don't think you'll fall down on the job, and I don't believe Goldsmith and Block will throw away a chance to save some money."

At the end of another silence, for Rose was speechless here, he went on expanding the plan a little further. And if the assurances he gave her were essentially mendacious, he himself wasn't exactly aware that they were. It had often happened in productions of his, he said—and this much was true—that to save time or to accomplish some result he wanted, he put up a little of his own money for something and trusted to a prosperous event for getting it back. It was clearly for the good of the show that the costumes for the sextette should be better than the ones Mrs. Goldsmith had picked out. The only alternative way of getting them, to a knock-down and carry-away fight with Goldsmith and Block, which, even if it were successful, would weaken the effect of his next ultimatum, was the plan he now proposed to Rose. She needn't regard the money he put up as in any sense a personal loan to her. They were simply cooperating for the good of the enterprise. If her work turned out to be valuable, it was only right she should be paid for it.

And then he pressed her for an immediate decision. The job would be a good deal of a scramble at best, as the time was short. If she agreed to it, he'd get in touch with the wardrobe mistress at the Globe, tonight. As for the money, he had a hundred dollars or so in his pocket, which she could take to start out with.

Of course the only lie involved in all this was the warp of the whole fabric; that he was doing it, impersonally, for the success of the show. And that might well enough have been true. Only in this case, it definitely wasn't. He was doing it because it would establish a personal connection, the want of which was becoming so tormenting a thing to his soul, between himself and this girl whom he had to order about on the stage and call by her last name, or rather by a last name that wasn't hers—an imagination-stirring, question-compelling, warm human creature, who, up to now, had been as completely shut away from him as if she had been a wax figure in a show-window.

They had reached the Randolph Street end of the avenue, and a policeman, like Moses cleaving the Red Sea, had opened the way through the tide of motors for a throng of pedestrians bound across the viaduct to the Illinois Central suburban station.

"Come across here," said Galbraith taking her by the arm and stemming this current with her. "We've got to have a minute of shelter to finish this up in," and he led her into the north lobby of the public library. The stale baked air of the place almost made them gasp. But, anyway, it was quiet and altogether deserted. They could hear themselves think in here, he said, and led the way to a marble bench alongside the staircase.

Rose unpinned her veil and, to his surprise, because of course she was going out in a minute, put it into her ulster pocket. But, curiously enough, the sight of her face only intensified an impression that had been strong on him during the last part of their walk—the impression that she was a long way off. It wasn't the familiar contemplative brown study, either. There was an active eager excitement about it that made it more beautiful than ever he had seen it before. But it was as if she were looking at something he couldn't see—listening to words he couldn't hear.

"Well," he said a little impatiently, "are you going to do it?"

At that the glow of her was turned fairly on him. "Yes," she said, "I'm going to do it. I suppose I mustn't thank you," she went on, "because you say it isn't anything you're doing for me. But it is—a great thing for me—greater than I could tell you. And I won't fail. You needn't be afraid."

Inexplicably to him (the problem wouldn't have troubled James Randolph) the very completeness with which she made this acknowledgment—the very warmth of the hand-clasp with which she bound the bargain, vaguely disappointed him—left him feeling a little flat and empty over his victory.

He found his pocketbook and counted out a hundred and twenty dollars, which he handed over to her. She folded it and put it away in her wrist-bag. The glow of her hadn't faded, but once more it was turned on something—or some one—else. It wasn't until he rose a little abruptly from the marble bench, that she roused herself with a shake of the head, arose too, and once more faced him.

"You're right about our having to hurry," she said. "Don't you suppose that some of the department stores on the west side of State Street would still be open—on account of Christmas, you know?"

"I don't know," he said. "Very likely. But look here!" He pulled out his watch. "It's after seven already. And rehearsal's at eight-thirty. You've got to get some dinner, you know."

"Dinner doesn't take long at the place where I go," she reminded him. "But if I can get one or two things now—I don't mean the materials— why, I can get a start tonight after the rehearsal's over."

"I don't like it," he said glumly. "Oh, I know, it's a rush job and you'll have to work at it at all sorts of hours. If only you. . . If I could just ease up a bit on your rehearsals! Only, you see, the sextette would he lost without you. Look here! There's nothing life or death about this, you know. You don't want to forget that you've got a limit, and crowd the late-at-night and early-in-the-morning business too hard. Think where we'd be if you turned up missing on the opening night!"

"I shan't do that," she said absently almost, and not in his direction. Then, with another little shake, bringing herself back to him with a visible effort: "If you only knew what a wonderful thing it's going to be, to have something for late at night and early in the morning. . ."

Before he could find the first one of the words he wanted, she had given him that curt farewell nod which, so inexplicably, from the first had stirred and warmed him, and turned away toward the door.

And she had never seen what was fairly shining in his face; no more than she had heard the thing that rang so eagerly in his voice through the thin disguise of an impersonal, director-like concern that she shouldn't impair her health so far as to spoil her for the sextette!

VII

The End of a Fixed Idea

She couldn't of course have missed a thing as plain as that but for a complete preoccupation of thought and feeling that would have left her oblivious to almost anything that could happen to her. Galbraith himself had detected this preoccupation, but he would have been staggered had he known its intensity. He had likened it in his own thoughts, to an effect that might have been caused by the presence with her of another person whom he could neither see nor hear. And that, had he believed it seriously, would have been an almost uncannily correct guess.

The flaming vortex of thoughts, hopes, desires which enveloped her, was so intense as almost to evoke a sense of the physical presence of the subject of them—of that big, powerful-minded, clean-souled husband of hers, who loved her so rapturously, and who had driven her away from him because that rapture was the only thing he would share with her.

She had been living, since that day of his departure for New York, when she had felt the last of his strong embraces, a life that fell into two hemispheres as distinct from each other as tropic night from day. One half of it had been lighted and made tolerable by the exactions of her new job. "What you feel like doing isn't important, and what I tell you to do is," John Galbraith had said to her on the day this strange divided life of hers had begun. And this lesson, taken to heart, had spelt salvation to her—for half of the time; for as many hours of the day as he went on telling her to do something. Those hours, in a way almost incredible to herself when they were over, had been almost happy—would have been altogether happy, but for the stain that soaked through in memory and in anticipation, from the other half of her days.

But when evening rehearsal was over and she came back to her room and had to undress and put out her light and relax her mind for sleep, letting the terrors that came to tear at her do their unopposed worst, then the girl who sang and danced and was so nearly happy snatching John Galbraith's intentions half formed, and executing them in the thrill of satisfaction over work well done, became an utterly unreal, incredible person—the mere figment of a dream that couldn't— couldn't possibly recur again even as a dream; the only self in her that had any actual existence was Rodney Aldrich's wife and the mother of his children, lying here in a mean bed, or looking with feverish eyes out of the window in a North Clark Street rooming house, in a torment of thwarted desire for him that was by no means wholly mental or psychical.

And what was he doing now in her absence? Was he in torment, too; shaken by gusts of uncontrollable longing for her; fighting off nightmare imaginings of disasters that might be befalling her? Or was he happy, drinking down in great thirsty drafts the nectar of liberty which her incursion into his life had deprived him of? She didn't know which of these alternatives was the more intolerable to her.

And the twins! Were they, the fine lusty little cherubs she had parted from that day, smiling up with growing recognition into other faces— Mrs. Ruston's and the maid Doris'? Or might there have been, since the last information relayed by Portia, a sudden illness? Might it be that there was going on now, in that house not a thousand yards away, another life-and-death struggle like the one which had made an end of all her hopes for the efficacy of her miracle?

The only treatment for hobgoblins like that was plain endurance. This was a part of a somber sobering discovery that Rose had made during the first few days of her new life. Courage of the active sort she'd always had. The way she went up to North End Hall and wrested a job that didn't strictly exist, from John Galbraith, was an example of it. When it was a question of blazing up and doing something, she had rightly counted on herself not to fail. This was what she'd foreseen when she promised Portia that she would fight for the big thing.

But that part of the battle of life had to consist just in doing nothing, enduring with a stiff mouth and clenched hands assaults that couldn't be replied to, was a fact she hadn't foreseen. What a child she had always been! Rodney, Portia, everybody who amounted to anything, must have learned that lesson of sheer endurance long ago.

The queerly incredible quality of the lighted half of her life—the half that John Galbraith's will galvanized into motion—prevented any afterglow from illuminating and making tolerable the dark half. No achievement of her days—not even teaching the sextette to talk—had the power to give her, in her nights, a sense of progress, or to lessen the necessity for that sheer dumb endurance which was the only weapon she had. Because she was in the fetters of a fixed idea.

Of course it was only by virtue of the possession of a fixed idea—a purpose as rigid in its outlines as the steel frame of a sky-scraper—that she had been able to force herself to leave Rodney and set out in pursuit of a job that would make a life of her own a possible thing. You are already acquainted with the outlines of that purpose. She lacked the special training which alone could make any sort of self-respecting life possible. The only thing she had to capitalize when she left her husband's house, was the thing which had got her into it—her sex charm. The only excuse for capitalizing that again was that it would make it possible for her to acquire a special training in some other field. Stenography, she had thought vaguely, would be the first round of the ladder. Until this production opened and she began drawing a salary, she couldn't really begin doing the thing she had set out to do.

Consequently, anything that seemed like progress during her day's work for Galbraith—any glow of triumph she came away with after meeting and conquering some difficulty—must be pure illusion.

It was all perfectly logical and it was all perfectly false. She had been growing really, in strides, from day to day, since that first day of all when, after hearing the director tell another woman that there were no vacancies in the chorus, she had forced herself to go up and ask him for a job. She had been disciplining herself under Rodney's own definition of the term. Discipline, he had said, was standing the gaff—standing it, not submitting to it; accepting the facts of your own life as they happened to be! Not making masters of them, but servants to the underlying thing you wanted.

And if only she could have believed her own vision, the outlines of the underlying thing she wanted were beginning to appear, as in a half developed negative. It hadn't been from a cold sense of duty, or from a cold fear of losing her job, that she had thrown herself into the accomplishment of John Galbraith's wishes, or had felt that almost fierce desire that some effect he was trying for and that she understood, should get an objective validity. It hadn't been out of pure altruism that she'd spent those twelve solid hours compelling Olga Larson to talk better. She might have felt sorry for the girl—might have loaned her money, comforted her; but she wouldn't have locked her in her room and beaten down her sullen opposition, set her afire with her own vitality, except that it was a thing that had to be done for the good of the show.

In short, she was, to fall back on Rodney's phrase again, for the first time driving herself with the motive power of her own desires—riding the back of a hitherto unsuspected passion. But the binding force of that fixed idea of hers had been sufficient all along to keep up the delusion of unreality about the real half of her life and to make the nightmare half of it seem true.

It wasn't until she heard herself telling John Galbraith that she could design those costumes for him, and in a flame of suddenly kindled excitement, resolved to make that unexpected promise good, that the fetters of her false logic fell away from her.

The truth of the matter, the wonderful, almost incredible truth, kept coming up brighter and clearer as she walked silently along beside him down the avenue. The real beginning of the pilgrimage that was to carry her back into her husband's life, wasn't a thing that had to be waited for. It could begin now! No, the truth was better than that; it had begun already! Because if John Galbraith had come to her house a month ago, when she was casting about so desperately for a way of earning a living, and had offered her the chance just as he had offered it tonight, she'd have declined it. She wouldn't have known what he wanted. She'd rightly have said that the thing was utterly beyond her powers. Tonight she knew what he wanted and she was utterly confident of her ability to give it to him.

And the one word that blaze of confidence spelled for her in letters of fire, was her husband's name. This chance that had been offered her was a ladder that would enable her to climb part of the way back to him. Her accomplishment of this first breathlessly exciting task would be a thing, when it was achieved, that she could recount to him—well, as man to man. Her success, if she succeeded—and the alternative was something she wouldn't contemplate—would compel the same sort of respect from him that he accorded to a diagnosis of James Randolph's, or an article of Barry Lake's.

Since she had left his house and begun this new life of hers, she had, as best she could, been fighting him out of her thoughts altogether. She had shrunk from anything that carried associations of him with it. Outside the hours of rehearsal (and how grateful she always was when they protracted themselves unduly) she had walked timidly, like a child down a dim hallway with black yawning doorways opening out of it, in a dread which sometimes reached the intensity of terror, lest reminders of the man she loved should spring out upon her. That all thoughts and memories of him must necessarily be painful, she had taken for granted.

But with this sudden lighting up of hope, which took place within her when she made John Galbraith that astonishing offer and he accepted it, she flung the closed door wide and called her husband back into her thoughts—greeted the image of him passionately, in an almost palpable embrace. This hard thing that she was going to do, which had, to common-sense calculation, so many chances of disaster in it—this thing that meant sleepless nights, and feverishly active days, was an expression simply of her love for him; a sacrificial offering to be laid before the shrine of him in her heart. Well, it was no wonder then that to John Galbraith she had seemed preoccupied and far away, nor that amid the surging thoughts and memories of her lover, coming in like a returning tide, she should have been deaf to a meaning in the director's tones that any one of the stupid little flutterers in the chorus would instantly have understood.

A man with a volcanic incandescence within him such as was now afire in Rose, is utterly useless until it subsides—totally incapable, at least, of any sort of creative or imaginative work. Until the fire can be, by one means or another and for the time being, put out, he has no energies worth mentioning, to devote to anything else. And, just as no woman can understand the cold austerities of the cell into which a man must retire in order to give his finer faculties free play, so no man can possibly understand, although objective evidence may compel him to admit and chronicle it as a fact, that a woman borne along as Rose was, upon an irresistible tide of passions, memories and hopes, which all but made her absent husband actually visible to her, could at the same time, be seeing visions of her accomplished work and laying plans—limpid practicable plans, for their realization.

This is, perhaps, one of the few, and certainly one of the most fundamental chasms of cleavage between the two sexes; a chasm bridged by habit invariably, because some sort of thoroughfare has to exist, bridged, too, more rarely, by intellectual understanding. But never bridged, I think, between two persons strongly masculine and feminine respectively, by an instinctive sympathy. To each, the other's way of life must always be mysterious, and at times exasperating or a little contemptible.

To the woman, with the finely constant impenetration of love through all her spiritual life, the man's uncontrollable blaze and his alternate coldness, seem fitful—weak—brutish, almost unworthy of a creature with a soul.

To the man who knows the value of his phases of high austerity and understands quite well the price at which he obtains them, the woman who fails to understand the necessity or to appreciate the mood seems sentimental and a little unworthy.

Well, the fact that Rose's heart was racing and her nerves were tingling with a newly welcomed sense of her lover's spiritual presence, did not prevent her flying along west on Randolph Street and south again on the west side of State, with a very clearly visualized purpose. She had forgotten to replace her veil, but at that hour it didn't matter. The west side of State Street, anyway, is almost as far from the east as North Clark Street is from the Drive.

As she came abreast of the first of the big department stores which line the west side of this thoroughfare, she saw that her surmise had been correct. It was open. Throngs of weary shoppers were crowding out, and a very respectable stream of them were forcing their way in. She told an exhausted floor-walker that she wanted to buy a dressmaking form. And, spent as he was, he reflected a little of her own animation in his unusually precise reply; had, indeed, a little of it left over for his next inquirer.

Something automatic in her mind took charge of Rose and delivered her, presently, unconscious of intervening processes, at the counter where the forms were sold. She selected what she wanted instantly, and counted out the money from her own purse. She didn't have to dip into John Galbraith's hundred and twenty dollars for this.

"Address?" inquired the saleswoman preparing to make out her sales-slip. Then, as Rose didn't answer instantly, she looked up frowning into her face. "You want it sent, don't you?" she added.

The question was rhetorical, because with its standard, the thing stood five feet high and weighed twenty-five pounds.

A frown of perplexity in Rose's face gave way to her own wide smile. "I guess I'll have to take it with me," she said. Because as near Christmas as this, the thing mightn't be delivered for two days.

"Take it with you?" the woman echoed, aghast.

"Have it wrapped up," said Rose decisively, "and put my name on it—Mrs. . ." She checked herself with another smile. She had nearly said, "Mrs. Rodney Aldrich." But the mistake didn't hurt as it would have hurt yesterday. "Doris Dane," she went on. "And have it sent down to the main entrance. I'll be there as soon as it is. Do you know where I can buy paper cambric?" But she had to get that information from another floor-walker.

Paper cambric seemed to have more of a bearing upon the approach of Christmas Day than dressmaking forms, though just what the connection was, Rose couldn't make out. There was a crowd at the counter, anyhow. It was five minutes before she could get waited on. But once she caught a saleswoman's eye, her purchase was quickly made. She bought three bolts: one of black, one of white, and one of a washed-out blue. Once more she counted out the money, and this time, "I'll take it with me," she said.

Strong as she was, the immense bundle was almost more than she could carry. But she managed to make her way at last to the main entrance, where, under the incredulous eye of the doorman, she found a porter waiting with her dressmaking form.

"That's mine," she said. "Doris Dane is the name on it." Then, to the doorman as the porter made off, "Will you get me a cab?"

But this particular store had, quite naturally, no facilities for doing a carriage business, a fact which the doorman laconically explained.

"All right," said Rose dumping her heavy bundle beside the dressmaking form. "You won't mind keeping an eye on this for a minute, will you?" She didn't actually smile, but there was in her face a humorous appreciation of the fact that a mountain like this wouldn't be hard to watch.

The doorman grinned back at her. "Sure I will," he said. "I'm sorry I can't leave the door to get you a cab."

Rose hailed one that happened to be passing, a creaking, mud-bespattered disreputable affair with a driver to match, and briskly drove a bargain with him. He announced when she told him the address that the fare would be a dollar and a half. She offered him seventy-five cents, which he, with the air of a disillusioned optimist in a bitter world, accepted. "Christmas, too!" he muttered ironically.

"Oh, come," said Rose, grinning up at him. "How many tired people have you given free rides to today, on the strength of that?"

"All right, miss; I don't complain," he said. He did, though, but humorously, when Rose, assisted by a page boy the doorman had impressed for her, carried the dressmaker's form and the other heavy bundle out to the curb. He declared the form should go as another passenger (its semi-human shape was clearly visible through the wrappings) and that the other bundle ought to have a van. All the same, when at her destination Rose had paid him, he came down, voluntarily from the box—voluntarily but with a sort of reluctance—and carried the form up to her room for her.

Also, rather incredibly, he refused an extra quarter she had ready for him when he had completed this service. "Just to show no ill feelings," he said, and he told her where his stand was and gave himself a little recommendation: "Honest and reliable."

Here in her close little room, the suggestion of an alcoholic basis for this generosity obtruded itself, but Rose didn't care. She wished him a merry Christmas and waved him off with a smile.

It was now after eight o'clock. Rehearsal was at eight-thirty and she had had nothing to eat since noon. But she stole the time, nevertheless, to tear the wrappings off her "form" and gaze on its respectable nakedness for two or three minutes with a contemplative eye. Then, reluctantly—it was the first time she had left that room with reluctance—she turned out the light and hurried off to the little lunch-room that lay on the way to the dance-hall.

She never again, in the active practise of her profession, knew anything quite like the ensuing seventy-two hours. Every stimulus was, of course, abnormally heightened. There was the novelty, the thrilling sense of adventure that missed being fear only through an inexplicable confidence of success. And then, anyway, her imagination was a virgin field that had never been cropped, and the luxurious fertility of it was amazing.

It was during that first rehearsal, which she so narrowly missed being late for, that she got the general schemes for both sets of costumes. That there must be a general scheme she had decided at once. The sextette was a unit; none of the members of it ever appeared without the others, and it would be immensely more effective, she perceived, if this fact were expressed somehow in the costumes. Not by means of a stupid uniformity, of course. The effect she wanted was subtler than that. But if each one of the six costumes that these girls first appeared in could be made somehow to express the same thing in a different way—not only in different, though harmonious, colors, but in different, though related, forms—the effect produced by the six of them together would be immensely greater than the sum of their individual effects.

This, of course, wasn't what Rose said to herself. She just wanted a scheme, and with ridiculous ease, she got it. She didn't even get it. There it was staring at her. And the other scheme for the evening frocks was knocking at the door, too, eager to get in the moment she could give it a chance. She began studying the girls for their individual peculiarities of style. Each one of the costumes she made was going to be for a particular girl, suited, without losing its place in the general plan, to the enhancement of her special approximation to beauty.

At last, when a shout from Galbraith aroused her to the fact that she had missed an entrance cue altogether, in her entranced absorption in these visions of hers, and had caused that unpardonable thing, a stage wait, she resolutely clamped down the lid upon her imagination and, until they were dismissed, devoted herself to the rehearsal.

But the pressure kept mounting higher and higher and she found herself furiously impatient to get away, back to her own private wonderland, the squalid little room down the street, that had three bolts of cambric in it and a dressmaker's manikin—the raw materials for her magic!

Rose couldn't draw a bit. Her mother's fine contempt for ladylike accomplishments had even intervened in the high-school days to prevent her taking a free-hand course required in the curriculum, during which you spent weeks making a charcoal study of a bust of Demosthenes. But this lack never even occurred to Rose as a handicap. She hadn't the faintest impulse to make a beginning by putting a picture down on paper and making a dress of it afterward. She went straight at her materials, or the equivalent of her materials, as a sculptor goes at his clay. She couldn't have told just why she had bought those three shades of paper cambric.

"I'm really awfully obliged to you for having explained it to me," she told Burton, the portrait painter long afterward.

"I see!" he had exclaimed, on the occasion of an initiatory visit to her workroom. "You design these things in their values first, just the way the old masters used to paint. Once you get the values in, you can project them in any colors that will leave your value scale true."

And Rose, as she said, was really grateful to him for telling her what it was she had been doing all the while, just as Monsieur Jourdain was grateful for the information that he had been talking prose all his life and never known it.

What she had felt, of course, at the very outset, was the need of something to indicate roughly the darks and lights in her design. And, short of the wild extravagance of slashing into the fabrics themselves and making her mistakes at their expense, she could think of nothing better than the scheme she chose.

She came to the conclusion afterward that even apart from the consideration of expense, her own plan was better. You got more vigor somehow, into the actual construction of the thing, if you could make it express something quite independently of color and texture.

Rehearsal was dismissed a little early that first night, and she was back in her room by eleven. Arrived there, she took off her outer clothes, sat down cross-legged on the floor, and went to work. When at last, with a little sigh, and a tremulously smiling acknowledgment of fatigue, she got up and looked at her watch, it was four o'clock in the morning. She'd had one of those experiences that every artist can remember a few of in his life, when it is impossible for anything to go wrong; when each tentative experiment accomplishes not only its purpose, but another unsuspected purpose as well; when the vision miraculously betters itself in the execution; when the only difficulty is that which the hands have in the purely mechanical operation of keeping up.

She was destined later, of course, even during the achievement of this first success, to learn the comparative rarity of those hours. Though, as she looked back on it afterward, the whole of this first job seemed to have been done with a kind of miraculous facility she couldn't account for.

And all through those five hours, fast as her mind flew, utterly absorbed as it seemed to be, she never once lost the consciousness of the almost palpable presence of Rodney Aldrich there in the room with her. Once she laughed outright over the memory of a girl who had tried to win her husband's friendship by studying law. Fancy Rodney trying to study costumes! But he would understand what it meant to conceive them and the sort of work it took, once they were conceived, to project them as something objective to herself—something that had to challenge expert opinion; meet the exactions of criticism. He'd understand the thrill, too, of seeing them come up for judgment—the triumph of getting them accepted and paid for.

And, in the confidence born of that understanding, he'd be able to offer for her to understand, the fundamentals of his own work. Not the dry husks of technical considerations. What did they amount to anyway, except as they formed the boundaries of the live thing he meant? But the live thing itself—the thing that spelled challenge and work and victory for him,—that thing, since at last she'd grown to deserve it, he'd give her. Freely, fully,—just because he couldn't help giving it.

Tired as she was, she could hardly bear to stop work. The half finished thing on the manikin lured her on from one moment to another. It was really insane not to stop. She must get up at seven-thirty, three hours or so from now, in order to get to the shops ahead of the crowds and begin the selection of her fabrics. At last, with a single movement of resolution she turned out the gas and undressed, or rather, finished undressing, in the dark, amid a litter of pins and paper cambric.

And now, for the first time in this squalid, mean little room, the dark had balm in it, became a fragrant miracle, obliterating the harsh actualities of her immediate yesterdays and tomorrows, winging her spirit for a breathless flight straight to the end she sought,—to the time when the long pilgrimage before her should be accomplished.

What a wonderful thing Rodney's cool firm friendship would be! Worth anything, anything in the world it might cost to win it. But. . . But. . .

She drew in a long unsteady breath and pressed her cooling hands down upon her face.

What a thing his love would be, when it should come, free of its tasks and obligations; no longer in the treadmill making her world go round, but given its wings again!

VIII

Success—and a Recognition

There is a kaleidoscopic character about the events of the ten days or so preceding the opening performance of most musical comedies which would make a sober chronicle of them seem fantastically incredible; and this law of Nature made no exception in the case of *The Girl Up-stairs*. There were rehearsals which ran so smoothly and swiftly that they'd have done for performances; there were others so abominably bad that the bare idea of presenting the mess resulting from six weeks' toil, before people who had paid money to see it, was a nightmare.

As the nervous pressure mounted, people took to exploding all over the place in the most grotesquely inconceivable ways and from totally unpredictable causes. Freddy France, who played the comic detective (like most comedians he had no sense of humor whatever and treated his "art" with a sort of sacrificial solemnity), developed delusions of persecution, proclaimed himself the victim of a conspiracy to which the owners, the author, Galbraith and most of the principals were parties, and finally, when the director cut out a little scene that he had two feeble jokes in, reached up unexpectedly and hit McGill on the nose, flung his part on the stage, stamped on it and left the theater. Quan read his lines in a painstaking manner for two days and then, after a three-hour session in the Sherman House bar, Freddy was induced to come back.

Stewart Lester, one day, at the end of a long patient effort of Galbraith's to improve his acting (he acted like a tenor; one needn't say more than that), licked his thin red lips, and in a feline fury, announced his indifference as to whether the management accepted his resignation or that of Miss Devereux. As long as she insisted on treating her vis-à-vis like a chorus-man, she'd perhaps be happier if a chorus-man were given the part; and he would he only too happy, in case the management agreed with her, to make the substitution possible. Whereupon Miss Devereux remarked that even having been a failure in grand opera didn't necessarily assure a man success in musical comedy, and that possibly a chorus-man would be an improvement. Galbraith had a long private conference with each of them—the fact that they would not speak at all off stage guaranteed him against their comparing notes as to what he'd said—and while the thing he effected could not be called a reconciliation, it amounted to a sort of armed truce. They went through their love scenes without actually scratching and biting.

Even little Anabel Astor, whose good humor for a long time had seemed invincible, tempestuously left the stage one day in the middle of one of her scenes with her dancing partner, and could be heard sobbing loudly in the wings through all that remained of that rehearsal.

Queer things began happening to the plot, resulting sometimes from the violent transposition of song numbers from one act to another, sometimes from the interpolation of songs or specialties. Two or three scenes, which the author regarded with special pride and was prepared to die in the defense of, were pronounced by Galbraith to be junk. He had made superhuman efforts, he told Goldsmith and Block, to put a little life into them, and had demonstrated that this miracle was impossible of performance. They were dead and they'd got to be buried before they became, to the olfactory sense, any more unpleasant.

There was an ominous breathlessness in the air after this ultimatum had been delivered, and at the next rehearsal, when the director announced the cut of six solid pages of manuscript, the voice of the author was heard from back of the hall proclaiming in a hollow Euripidean bellow that it was all over. He was going to his lawyer to get an injunction against the production of the piece.

Of all the persons directly, or even remotely, affected by this nerve-shattering confusion, Rose was perhaps the least perturbed. The only thing that really mattered to her, was the successful execution of those twelve costumes. The phantasmagoria at North End Hall was a regrettable, but necessary, interruption of her more important activities. The interruption didn't interfere so seriously as at first she thought it would. The routine of rehearsal as Galbraith developed it, began with special scenes—isolated bits that needed modification or polishing. The general rehearsals, taking this act or that and going through with it from beginning to end, and involving, of course, the presence of everybody in the company, didn't, as a rule, begin till three in the afternoon; sometimes till as late as five. Of course when they did begin, they lasted until all hours.

But the labors of the chorus, and even of the sextette, shrank very much in proportion to the work of the principals. Nearly all the changes that were made were in the direction of compressing the chorus and giving the principals more room. So that for long stretches of time, during which, dressed in her working clothes and curled up in one of the remoter of the cushioned window-seats, but ready to answer a summons to the stage as promptly as a fireman, she could let her mind run without interruption on the solution of some of her own problems, and then be ready when she went back to her room, to fall into bed and asleep (the two acts had become practically simultaneous) secure in the possession of a clearly thought out program for the morrow.

She wakened automatically at half past seven and was down-town by half past eight, to do whatever shopping the work of the previous day revealed the need of. The fact that it was, for the greater part, John Galbraith's money she was spending (she had managed to put in a little herself by calculating down to a fine point the necessary margin for existence) worked to her advantage in these operations. She could not, but for that fact, have forced herself to hunt down bargains so persistently nor to keep the incidental expense for findings and such, so low.

At nine-thirty in the morning—an unheard of hour in the theater—the watchman at the Globe let her in the stage door, and Rose had half an hour before the arrival of the wardrobe mistress and her assistant, for looking over the work done since she had left for rehearsal the day before.

She liked this quiet, cavernous old barn of a place down under the Globe stage; liked it when she had it to herself before the two sewing women came and later, when, with a couple of sheets spread down on the floor she cut and basted according to her cambric patterns, keeping ahead of the flying needles of the other two. After her own little room, the mere spaciousness of it seemed almost noble. She even liked it, when, about half past one in the afternoon, on matinée days, the chorus-girls of the show now drawing to the end of its run, began dawdling in, passing shrill jokes with Bill Flynn, the fireman, rummaging through the mail in the letter-box, casually unfastening their clothes all the while, preliminary to kimonos and make-up, gathering in little knots about the sewing-machines and exclaiming in profane delight over the costumes. She wondered at herself, sometimes, for having ceased to mind their language, their shameless way of going half-clad, their general atmosphere of moth-like worthlessness—and then laughed at herself for wondering!

How would her own quality be finer, her soul a more ample thing, for the keeping, on one of the shelves of it, of a pot of carefully preserved horror? If she could succeed with these costumes, her success, she hoped, would lead her directly into the business of designing other costumes for the stage. And if she became a professional stage costumer, this rather loose, ramshackle, down-at-the-heel morality of back-stage musical comedy would be a permanent fact in her life, just as the dustiness of law-books and the stuffiness of court rooms were permanent facts in Rodney's.

As the work went on, her confidence in the success of this initiatory venture became less ecstatic and more reasonable. A few of the costumes were finished and, seen on live models (a couple of girls in the chorus in the Globe show had volunteered to try on) were, if Rose knew anything at all about clothes, without doubt or qualification, good.

She had had just one really bad quarter of an hour over them, and that, back on Christmas Day as it happened, was when Galbraith, having detained her after he had dismissed the rehearsal, asked to see her sketches.

"Sketches!" she echoed, perplexed.

"Oh, I don't mean regular water-colored plates," he said. "Just whatever rough drafts of the things you will have put down on paper to start yourself off with. It's simple curiosity, you understand."

"But," she gasped, "I haven't put anything down on paper—not anything at all! I don't know how to draw."

And now he was perplexed in turn. How could one design a costume without drawing a picture of it?

She explained her working method to him; though not, she felt, very successfully. She was perhaps a bit flustered, and he didn't seem to be giving her his complete attention—seemed to be covering up, with the pretense of listening, a strong interior abstraction.

This was again a good diagnosis as far as it went. Only it didn't dig in far enough for even the faintest surmise as to what the nature of his abstraction was.

"I could bring the patterns down here. Or, if you had time, you could come up to my room and see them. But I'm afraid you couldn't tell much from that, because they're all taken apart, you see, and they're just in paper cambric and not the right colors."

What the man was struggling for—it had been his sole reason for detaining her in the first place—was some sort of opening that would make it seem natural to tell her he hoped her Christmas Day had not been too intolerably unhappy; to shake hands with her and wish her luck—assure her in one way or another, that she had in him a friend she could bring her troubles to—any sort of troubles. He'd made up his mind to do this when the Christmas rehearsal should he over, as long ago as the night of their walk down the avenue. This resolution had been reinforced by the look he had caught in her face when she came up to rehearsal this afternoon—a rather misty, luminous, exalted look,—a little lack of definition about her eyelids suggesting there had been tears there.

This was good observation like her own of him. But, again like hers, in its failure to get the central clue, it only mislead him, the worse. If he could have guessed that she had been having a Christmas celebration of her own that day; that there had been unwrapped and displayed, three little presents she had bought the day before; one for her husband, and one for each of her two babies, and that, just before starting for rehearsal, she had wrapped them up and put them into her trunk to await the day when they could be given, it might have altered matters somewhat.

The thing that finally made it clearly impossible for Galbraith to express anything at all of this feeling which he, in good faith, called friendship for her, was her alternative offer—if he had time, to take him up to her room for a look at the patterns.

If she's seen him as anything at all but starkly her employer and her financier; if she's had the faintest glimmer of him as one who held for her any personal feelings whatever, she never would have suggested as an alternative to her bringing the patterns here to rehearsal, his coming up to her room for a look at them.

The thing of all others that irritated Galbraith was the possession of a divided mind. Just now, disappointed as he was, almost to the point of pain, though he wouldn't acknowledge to himself that it went as far as that, over the evident fact that his relation to the girl, in spite of their partnership, was exactly what it had been from the beginning, he was still aware that if he'd got the opening he wanted, had managed another of those warm lithe hand-clasps with her, and had got the notion across to her that he wanted her to make a friend of him and a confidant, he'd be going away now, afterward, under the painful misgiving that he was a bit of an old fool. The product of all this irritation was, however, that he declined Rose's offer of a view of her patterns rather bruskly.

"It was just curiosity, as I said. Go along your own way and don't worry about me. You will be all right."

Rose couldn't feel much conviction behind this expression of confidence, and she went away, as I have said, in a sort of panic. Was she all wrong, after all? Couldn't you design stage costumes except by making pictures of them? She knew what he meant by water-colored plates. She'd seen them framed in the lobbies at musical shows she'd been to with Rodney. That was how costume designers worked, was it? Well she knew she never could do anything like that.

But her fears only lasted until she got back to her room and caught a reassuring look at the pattern that was assembled on the form. After all, the pictures in the lobby weren't so important as the costumes on the stage. And as for Galbraith—well, if he didn't expect too much of her, that was all the better.

In keeping with the good luck which had attended everything that happened in connection with this first venture of hers, she was able to tell Galbraith that both sets of costumes were done and ready to try on, on the very day he announced that the next rehearsal would be held at ten tomorrow morning at the Globe. It might very easily have happened, of course, that Rose's enterprise, together with Galbraith's partnership in it, had become known here or there, got passed on from one to another, with modifications and embellishments according to fancy, and grown to be a monument of scandal and conjecture. But nothing is more capricious than the heat-lightning of gossip, and it just chanced that, up to the morning of Rose's little triumph, no one beyond Galbraith and Rose herself even suspected the identity with Dane of the chorus, of the costumer who was to submit, on approval, gowns for the sextette. The fact, of course, was bound to come out on the day the company moved over for rehearsals to the Globe, and the event was very happily dramatized for Rose, by her ability to let the costumes appear first and her authorship of them only after their success was beyond dispute.

She persuaded the girls to wait until all six were dressed in the afternoon frocks and until she herself had had a chance to give each of them a final inspection and to make a few last touches and readjustments. Then they all trooped out on the stage and stood in a row, turned about, walked here and there, in obedience to Galbraith's instructions shouted from the back of the theater.

It was dark out there and disconcertingly silent. The glow of two cigars indicated the presence of Goldsmith and Block in the middle of a little knot of other spectators.

The only response Rose got—the only index to the effect her labors had produced—was the tone of Galbraith's voice. It rang on her ear a little sharper, louder, and with more of a staccato bruskness than the directions he was giving called for. And it was not his practise to put more cutting edge into his blade, or more power behind his stroke, than was necessary to accomplish what he wanted. He was excited, therefore. But was it by the completeness of her success or the calamitousness of her failure?

"All right," he shouted. "Go and put on the others."

There was another silence after they had fled out on the stage again, clad tins time in the evening gowns—a hollow heart-constricting silence, almost literally sickening. But it lasted only a moment. Then, "Will you come down here, Miss Dane?" called Galbraith.

There was a slight, momentary, but perfectly palpable shock accompanying these words—a shock felt by everybody within the sound of his voice. Because the director had not said, "Dane, come down here." He had said, "Will you come here, Miss Dane?" And the thing amounted, so rigid is the etiquette of musical comedy, to an accolade. The people on the stage and in the wings didn't know what she'd done, nor in what character she was about to appear, but they did know she was, from now on, something besides a chorus-girl.

Rose obediently crossed the runway and walked up the aisle to where Galbraith stood with Goldsmith and Block, waiting for her. She was still feeling a little numb and empty.

Galbraith, as she came up, held out a hand to her. "I congratulate you, Miss Dane," he said. "They're admirable. With all the money in the world, I wouldn't ask for anything handsomer."

Before she could say anything in reply, he directed her attention, with a nod of the head, to the partners, and walked away. Rose gasped at that. She'd never thought beyond him—beyond the necessity of pleasing him; and that he'd carry the details of the business through with Goldsmith and Block, she'd taken for granted. Now, here she was chucked into the water and told to swim. She'd never in her life, of course, tried to sell anything. What her mind first awoke to was that the partners were looking rather blank. Block, indeed, let his eyes follow the retreating Galbraith with a momentary look of outraged astonishment. Her wits, quickened by the emergency, interpreted the look. Galbraith, chucking her into the water indeed, had thrown her a life-preserver—the tip that her wares were good.

Goldsmith, quicker and shrewder than his junior, was already smiling politely. "They really are very good," he said. "If they are not too expensive for us, we'll consider buying them."

"They'll be," said Rose, "the twelve of them, four hundred and sixty-five dollars." She had something the same feeling of astonishment on hearing herself say this, that she'd had when she heard herself telling Galbraith that she'd design the costumes. Something or other had spoken without her will—almost without her knowledge. She had one figure clearly etched in her brain; that was the one hundred and ninety dollars she must pay back to Galbraith; and she'd put in fifty of her own. There was also a matter of twenty dollars or so still to be paid to the wardrobe mistress and her assistant. But this four hundred and sixty-five dollars had simply come out of the air.

Block pursed his lips and emitted a fine thin whistle of astonishment.

Goldsmith heaved a sigh. "My dear young lady," he protested. "The inducement held out to us to wait for these costumes of yours, was that they were to be cheap. But four hundred and sixty-five dollars is ridiculous! That's a lot of money."

"Quite a lot less," said Rose, "than the ones Mrs. Goldsmith picked out came to. They were just over six hundred." Goldsmith smiled indulgently. "By the figures on the tags, yes," he said. "But would we have paid that, do you think? Those figures represent what they'd like to get from people who buy one apiece. But from us, buying twelve. . ." He shrugged his shoulders expressively.

Well, this was reasonable and no doubt true and it left Rose rather aghast. She turned away toward the stage with the best appearance of indifference she could muster. Her mind was making an agonized effort to add up one hundred and ninety, fifty and twenty. But in the excitement of the moment it simply balked—rejected the problem altogether. She didn't think that the total came to much over three hundred dollars, but she couldn't be sure. And then there was, sticking burr-like, somewhere, the consciousness of another hundred unaccounted for in this total. Until she could discover what the gowns had actually cost her, she couldn't say anything. Therefore, she just stood where she was and said nothing whatever.

Goldsmith cleared his throat. "Really," he said in an intensely aggrieved tone, "you must try to see it from our point of view. This production's cost us thousands of dollars. If we bankrupt ourselves before the opening night it will be a bad business for everybody.

You ought to see that. The costumes are very nice, I admit that. But remember we took a chance on it. We waited for them with the idea that you'd cooperate with us in saving money."

Rose made a last frantic struggle to induce her figures to add up, but they were getting more meaningless every minute.

There was another moment of silence. Then Block took up the refrain with variations. But just as he began to speak, a brilliantly luminous ray of light struck Rose. She could have answered Goldsmith's arguments—would have done so, but for her preoccupation with that trifling sum in arithmetic. But it was incomparably better tactics not to answer at all. Because if she could answer their arguments, they in turn could answer hers. She'd be a child in their hands once she began to talk. But her silence disconcerted them—gave them nothing to go on. Well, then, she'd let them do the work and see what happened.

But suppose, through her stubborn insistence, they should refuse the costumes at any price! Well, the world wouldn't come to an end. She'd live through it somehow, and somehow she'd manage to repay Galbraith.

The partners went on talking alternately with symptoms of rising impatience.

"Oh, come," said Block at last, "we can't be all day about this! Your figure is out of all reason. If you'd said even four hundred now. . ."

"Oh, yes," said Goldsmith. "We want to be liberal. We appreciate you've done a good job. Say four hundred and I'll write you a check for it now." He took a small check-book and a fountain pen out of his pocket. "That's all right, eh?"

Rose made another effort at addition. A hundred and ninety, and fifty, and twenty, and the other ghostly hundred that wouldn't account for itself and yet insisted on coming in and mixing everything up. She turned on the two partners a look of perfectly genuine distress.

"If you'll let me go away and add it up. . ." she began.

Goldsmith's heart was touched. The costumes were a bargain at four hundred and sixty-five, and he knew it. There was an indescribable sort of dash to them that would lend tone to the whole production. And then the face of that pretty young girl who must have worked so desperately hard to make them and who was so obviously helpless at this bargaining game, would have moved a harder heart than his.

"Oh, all right!" he said. "We'll give in. Four hundred"—he began making out the check, but his hand hung over it a moment—"and fifty. How's that?"

Rose drew in a long breath. "That's all right," she said.

It was just as she turned away with the check made out to Doris Dane in her wrist-bag, that the mystery of that phantom hundred dollars solved itself. It was the hundred dollars she'd borrowed from Rodney and could now return to him!

Galbraith took the first chance he could make to shoot her a low-voiced question. "How much did you get?" he asked, and his face showed downright surprise when she told him. "That's a pretty fair price," he commented. "I was afraid they'd screw you way down on it, and I wanted to help you out, but. . ."

"Oh, you did," said Rose. "Telling me they were good. Of course you couldn't have done anything more. The first thing I want to do," she went on, "is to pay you back. But I don't know just how to do it. I can't go to the bank where they know me and—anyway, the name on the check isn't right."

He told her how easily that could be fixed. He'd take her to the bank he used here in town and identify her. Then she could pay him and deposit the balance to her own account. It was a bank where they didn't mind small accounts. That would be much better than carrying her money around with her where it could too easily be stolen.

He was very kind about it all and they put the program through that day. Yet she was vaguely conscious of a sense that he seemed a little chilled, as if something about the transaction unaccountably depressed him.

And indeed it was true that he'd have found his tendency to fall in love with her a good deal harder to resist if she'd shown herself more helpless in the hands of Goldsmith and Block. She'd actually driven a good bargain—an unaccountably good bargain! He wished he'd been on hand to see how she did it. Well, women were queer, there was no getting away from that.

But Goldsmith and Block came back the next day and drove, in turn, a good bargain of their own.

"You've certainly got a good eye for costumes, Miss Dane," Goldsmith said, "and here's a proposition we'd like to make. A lot of these other things we've got for the regular chorus don't look so good as they might. You'll be able to see changes in them that'll improve them maybe fifty per cent. Well, you take it on, and we'll begin paying you your regular salary now; you understand, twenty-five dollars a week, beginning today."

Rose accepted this proposition with a warm flush of gratitude. It indicated, she felt, that they were still friendly toward her, disposed of certain misgivings she'd experienced the night before, lest in driving, unwittingly, so good a bargain with them, she had incurred their enmity.

But, from the moment her little salary began, she found herself retained, body and soul, exactly as Galbraith himself was. They'd bought all her ideas, all her energy, all her time, except a few scant hours for sleep and a few snatched minutes for meals. She gave her employers, up to the time when the piece opened at the Globe, at a conservative calculation, about five times their money's worth. Even if she hadn't been in the company she'd have found something like two days' work in every twenty-four hours, just in the wardrobe room. Because the costumes were cheap and the frank blaze of borders, footlights and spots, pitilessly betrayed the fact. One set for the ponies was so hopelessly bad that the owners refused to accept them, and Rose, on the spur of the moment, made up a costume—they were uniform, fortunately—to replace them. The wardrobe mistress, with two assistants, and under Rose's intermittent supervision, managed somehow to get them made. And there wasn't a single costume, outside Rose's own twelve, that hadn't to be remodeled more or less.

On top of all that, the really terrible grind of rehearsals began; property rehearsals, curiously disconcerting at first, where instead of indicating the business with empty hands, you actually lighted the cigarette, picked up the paper knife, pulled the locket out from under your dress and opened it—and, in the process of doing these things, forgot everything else you knew; scenery rehearsals that caused the stage to seem small and cluttered up and actually made some of the evolutions you'd been routined in, impossible. At last and ghastliest, a dress rehearsal, which began at seven o'clock one night and lasted till four the next morning.

It would all have been so ludicrously easy, Rose used to reflect in despair, if, like the other girls in the sextette, she'd had only her own part in the performance to attend to—only to get into her costumes at the right time, be waiting in the wings for the cue, and then come on and do the things they'd taught her to do. But, between Goldsmith and Block, who were now in a state of frantic activity and full of insane suggestions, and the wardrobe mistress who was always having to be told how to do something, every minute was occupied. She would try desperately to keep an ear alert for what was happening on the stage, in order to be on hand for her entrances. But, in spite of her, it sometimes happened that she'd be snatched from something by a furious roar from Galbraith.

"Miss Dane!" And then, when she appeared, bewildered, contrite. "You *must* attend to the rehearsal. Those other matters can be attended to at some other time. If necessary, I can stop the rehearsal and wait till you're at liberty. But I can't pretend to rehearse and be kept waiting."

She never made any excuses; just took her place with a nod of acquiescence. But she often felt like doing as some of the rest of them did; felt it would be a perfectly enormous relief to shriek out incoherent words of abuse, burst into tears and sobs, and rush from the stage. Her position—her new position, she fancied, would entitle her to do that—once. And then the notion that she was saving up that luxurious possibility for some time when it would do the most good, would bring back her old smile. And Galbraith, lost in wonder at her already, would wonder anew.

They followed the traditions of the Globe in giving *The Girl Upstairs* its try-out in Milwaukee—four performances; from a Thursday to a Saturday night, with rehearsals pretty much all the time in between.

About all that this hegira meant to Rose was that she got two solid hours' sleep on the train going up on Thursday afternoon and another two hours on the train coming back on Sunday morning. She had domesticated herself automatically, in the little hotel across from the theater, and she had gone right on working just as she did at the Globe. Oddly enough, she didn't differentiate much between rehearsals and the performances. Perhaps because she was so absorbed with her labors off the stage; perhaps because the thoroughly tentative nature of everything they did was so strongly impressed on her.

The piece was rewritten more or less after every performance. They didn't get the curtain down on the first one until five minutes after twelve—for even an experienced director like Galbraith can make a mistake in timing—and the mathematically demonstrated necessity for cutting, or speeding, a whole hour out of the piece, tamed even the wild-eyed Mr. Mills. The principals, after having for weeks been routined in the reading of their lines and the execution of their business, were given new speeches to say and new things to do at a moment's notice—literally, sometimes, while the performance was going on. Ghastly things happened, of course. A tricky similarity of cues would betray somebody into a speech three scenes ahead; a cut would have the unforeseen effect of leaving somebody stranded, half-changed, in his dressing-room when his entrance cue came round; an actor would dry up, utterly forget his lines in the middle of a scene he could have repeated in his sleep—and the amazing way in which these disasters were retrieved, the way these people who hadn't, so far, impressed Rose very strongly with their collective intelligence, extemporized, righted the capsizing boat, kept the scene going—somehow—no matter what happened, gave her a new respect for their claims to a real profession.

This was the great thing they had, she concluded; the quality of coming up to the scratch, of giving whatever it took out of themselves to meet the need of the moment. They weren't—her use of this phrase harked back to the days of the half-back—yellow. If you'd walked through the train that took them back to Chicago Sunday morning, had seen them, glum, dispirited, utterly fagged out, unsustained by a single gleam of hope, you'd have said it was impossible that they should give any sort of performance that night—let alone a good one. But by eight o'clock that night, when the overture was called, you wouldn't have known them for the same people.

There is, to begin with, a certain magic about make-up which lends a color of plausibility to the paradoxical theory that our emotions spring from our facial expressions rather than the other way about. Certainly to an experienced actor, his paint—the mere act of putting it on and looking at himself in the glass as it is applied—effects for him a solution of continuity between his real self, if you can call it that, and his part; so that fatigues, discouragements, quarrels, ailments—I don't mean to say are forgotten; they are remembered well enough, but are given the quality of belonging to some one else. But beyond all that was the feeling, on the edge of this first performance, that they were now on their own. Harold Mills and the composer, Goldsmith and Block, John Galbraith, had done their best, or their worst, as the case might be. But their labors tonight would mean nothing to that rustling audience out in front. From now on it was up to the company!

The appearance, back on the stage, of John Galbraith in evening dress, just as the call of the first act brought them trooping from their dressing-rooms, intensified this sensation. He was going to be, tonight, simply one of the audience.

As a sample of the new spirit, Rose noted with hardly a sensation of surprise, that Patricia Devereux nodded amiably enough to Stewart

Lester and observed that she believed the thing was going to go; and that Lester in reply said, yes, he believed it was.

Rose herself was completely dominated by it. Her nerves—slack, frayed, numb, an hour ago—had sprung miraculously into tune. She not only didn't feel tired. It seemed she never could feel tired again. Not even, going back to her university days, on the eve of a class basketball game, or a tennis match, had she felt that fine thrill of buoyant confidence and adequacy quite so strongly!

It wasn't until along in the third act that the audience became, for her, anything but a colloid mass—something that you squeezed and thumped and worked as you did clay, to get into a properly plastic condition of receptivity, so that the jokes, the songs, the dances, even the spindling little shafts of romance that you shot out into it, could be felt to dig in and take hold. It never occurred to her to think of it with a plural pronoun; it was "it" simply, an inchoate monster, which was, as the show progressed, delightfully loosening up, becoming good-humored, undiscriminating, stupidly infatuate; laughing at things no human being would consider funny, approving with a percussive roar things not in the least good; a monster, all the same, whose approbation gave you an intense, if quite unreasoning, pleasure.

But, along in the third act, as I said, as she came down to the footlights with the rest of the sextette in their *All Alone* number, one face detached itself suddenly from the pasty gray surface of them that spread over the auditorium; became human—individual—and intensely familiar. Became the face, unmistakably, of Jimmy Wallace!

It is probable that of all the audience, only two men saw that anything had happened, so brief was the frozen instant while she stood transfixed. One of them was John Galbraith, in the back row, and he let his breath go out again in relief almost in the act of catching it. He guessed what had happened well enough—that she'd recognized one of those friends whose potential horror had made her willing to give up her promotion and her little part—the one she'd spoken of, perhaps, as the "only one that really mattered." But it was all right. She was going on as if nothing had happened.

The other man was Jimmy Wallace himself. He released, too, a little sigh of relief when he saw her off in her stride again after that momentary falter. But he hardly looked at the stage after that; stared absently at his program instead, and, presently, availed himself of the dramatic critic's license and left the theater.

But it wasn't to go to his desk and write his story (he was on an evening paper and so had no deadline staring him in the face) but to a quiet corner in his club, where he could, undistractedly, think.

From the moment of Rose's first appearance on the stage he had been tormented by a curiosity as to whether she was indeed Rose, or merely some one unbelievably like her. Because the fantastic impossibility that Rose Aldrich should be a member of the Globe chorus was reinforced by the fact that her gaze had traveled unconcernedly across his face a dozen times—his seat was in the fourth row, too—without the slightest flicker of recognition. Of course the way she stood there frozen for a second, when at last she did see him, settled that question. She was Rose Aldrich and she was in the Globe chorus!

But this certainty merely left him with a more insoluble perplexity on his hands; two, in fact—oh, half a dozen! What was she doing there? Did Rodney know? Well, those questions, and others in their train, could wait. But—what was he going to do about it?

As for Rose herself, it was a mere automaton that moved off in the dance and said the two or three lines that remained to her in the act as if nothing had happened, because all her mind and all her capacity for feeling were occupied and tested by something else.

Incredible as it seems, she had utterly overlooked Jimmy—overlooked the fact that, as a dramatic critic, he'd be certain to be present at the opening performance of *The Girl Up-stairs*—certain to be sitting close to the front, and certain, of course, to recognize her the moment she came on the stage. She hadn't even had him in mind when the fear lest some one of Rodney's friends might, for a lark, drop in at the Globe and recognize her, had led her to tell John Galbraith that she couldn't be in the sextette. Since that question had been settled, she'd hardly considered the possibility at all. And, during the three weeks before the opening, since she'd embarked on her career as a costumer, she literally hadn't given it a thought.

She had dreaded various things as the hour of the opening performance drew near—reasonable things like the failure of the piece to please, the reception of their offerings in a chilly silence intensified by contemptuous little riffles of applause. (She had been in audiences which had treated plays like that—taken her own part in the expression of chill disfavor, and she knew now she could never do it again.) She had dreaded unreasonable things, like the total failure of any audience to appear and the necessity of playing to empty rows as they had done in rehearsal;

nightmare things, like a total loss of memory, which should leave her stranded in the middle of a silent stage before a jeering audience. But it hadn't occurred to her to dread that the rise of the curtain would reveal to her any of the faces that belonged to a world which the last six weeks had already made to seem unreal.

So the sight of Jimmy Wallace had something the effect that a sudden awakening has on a somnambulist—bewilderment at first, and after that a sort of panic. Her first thought was that she must get word to him, somehow, before he left the theater. Unless she could do that, what was to prevent his going straight to Rodney, tonight, and telling him all about it? He was under no obligation not to do it. He was Rodney's friend quite as much as he was hers.

It didn't take her long to make up her mind though that he wouldn't do that. Jimmy was never precipitate. He'd give her a chance. Tomorrow morning would do. She could call him up at his office.

But as she began formulating her request and phrasing the preface of explanations she'd have to make before she'd be—well, entitled to ask a favor of him, she found herself in a difficulty. She didn't want to enter into a secret with him—with any man, this meant, of course—against Rodney. She couldn't think of any way of stating her reason for wanting her husband kept in the dark that didn't seem to slight him, belittle him, make him faintly ridiculous—like the pussy-cat John Galbraith had snapped his fingers at.

So she came, rather swiftly indeed, to the decision (she had arrived at it before Jimmy left the theater) that she wouldn't make any appeal to him at all. She'd do nothing that could lead him to think, either that she was ashamed of herself, or that she was afraid Rodney would be ashamed of her. In the absence of any appeal from her, mightn't he perhaps decide that Rodney was in her confidence and so say nothing about it? But even if he should tell Rodney. . .

In her conscious thoughts she went no further than that; didn't recognize the hope already beating tumultuously in her veins, that he would tell Rodney—that perhaps even before she got back to her dismal little room, Rodney, pacing his, would know.

It was so irrational a hope—so unexpected and so well disguised—that she mistook it for a fear. But fear never made one's heart glow like that.

That's where all her thoughts were when John Galbraith halted her on the way to the dressing-room after the performance was over.

IX

The Man and the Director

He said, "I want a talk with you," and she, thinking he meant then and there, glanced about for a corner where they'd be tolerably secure against the charging rushes of grips, property men and electricians, all racing against time to get the third act struck and the first one set and make their escape from the theater.

"Oh, I don't mean here in this bedlam," he explained with a tinge of impatience. And then his manner changed. "I'd like, for once, a chance to sit down with you where it's—quiet and we don't have to feel in a hurry." He added, a second later, answering a shade of what he took to be doubt or hesitation in her face, "You're frightfully tired I know. If you'd rather wait till tomorrow. . ."

"Oh, it wasn't that," said Rose. "I was just trying to think where a place was where one could be quiet and needn't hurry and where two people could talk."

He smiled. "You can leave that to me," he said. "That is, if you don't mind a restaurant and a little supper."

"Of course I don't mind," she said. "I'd like it very much."

He nodded. "Don't rush your dressing," he suggested, as he moved away. "I've got plenty to do."

The sextette dressed together in a sort of pen—big enough, because they had all sorts of room down under the old Globe stage, but so far as appointments went, decidedly primitive. The walls were of matched boards; there was a shelf two feet wide or so around three sides of it, to make a sort of continuous dressing-table; there were six mirrors, six deal chairs and a few hooks. These were for your street clothes. The stage costumes hung in neat ranks outside under the eye of the wardrobe mistress. When you wanted to put one on you went out and got it, and if the time allowed for the change were sufficient you took it back into your dressing-room. Otherwise you plunged into it just where you were. When you wanted to wash before putting on or after taking off your make-up you went to a row of stationary wash-bowls down the corridor.

All told it wasn't a place to linger in over the indulgence of day-dreams. But the first glimpse Rose caught, as she opened the door, in the mirror next her own, was the entranced face of Olga Larson. The other girls were in an advanced state of undress, intent on getting out as quickly as they could. They were all talking straight along, of course, but that didn't delay their operations a bit. They talked through the towels they were wiping off the make-up with, talked bent double over shoe-buckles, talked in little gasps as they tugged at tight sweaty things that didn't want to come off. And they made a striking contrast to Olga, who sat there just as she'd left the stage, without a hook unfastened, in a rapturous reverie, waiting for Rose.

In the instant before her entrance was noticed, Rose made an effort to shake herself together so that she should be not too inadequate to the situation that awaited her.

She was, of course, immensely pleased over Olga's little triumph.

(For it had been a triumph. Galbraith had persuaded Goldsmith and Block to buy the little Empire dress in maize and corn-flower; Rose had done her hair, and Olga had been allowed to sing, on the first *encore*, the refrain to *All Alone*, quite by herself. She'd gone up an octave on the end of it to a high A, which in its perfect clarity had sounded about a third higher and had brought down the house. Patricia had been furious, of course, but was at bottom too decent to show it much and had actually congratulated Olga when she came off. It looked as if she'd really got her foot on the ladder.)

Well, as I said, Rose was immensely pleased about it—for the girl, who certainly deserved a little good luck at last; for herself, whose judgment had been vindicated, and for the show, to the success of which the experiment had contributed. But she'd have been a good deal better pleased if Olga could have taken her success as simply her own, instead of being so adoringly grateful to Rose about it. Olga had been adoring her with a somewhat embarrassing intensity ever since the night she had locked her in her room and taught her to talk.

Rose had convicted herself here of a failure in human sympathy, and had done her best to correct it, without much avail. The stubborn fact was that, wishing Olga all the good fortune in the world, and being willing to take any amount of trouble to bring it about, she didn't particularly like her. And she flinched involuntarily, from the girl's more romantic and sentimental manifestations. This distaste had been heightened by the fact that along with Olga's adoration had gone a sense of proprietorship, with its inevitable accompaniment of jealousy.

Olga bridled every time she found Rose chatting with another member of the chorus, and when, up in Milwaukee, Patricia had invited her, along with Anabel, to come up to her room for a little supper after rehearsal, Olga had been sulky and injured for the whole of the next day.

It was something deeper in Rose than a mere surface distaste that made all this—the caresses, as well as the sulky exactions—repellent to her. And tonight, with her mind full of Rodney—full of that strange hope that disguised itself as fear, the repulsion was stronger than ever. She made an effort to conquer it. It would be a shame to throw a wet blanket on the girl's attempt to enjoy her triumph in her own way.

So Rose kissed her and told her how pleased she was, and good-humoredly forbore to disclaim, except as her wide smile did it for her, Olga's extravagant protestations of undying love and gratitude. Rose injected common-sense considerations where she could. Olga had better get out of that frock before she ruined it with grease paint, and unless she at least began to dress pretty soon she'd find herself locked up for the night in the theater.

"I wouldn't care," Olga said. "You'd be locked up, too. Because you aren't any further along than I am."

"I'm going to be, though," said Rose, "in about two minutes." The thought of what John Galbraith's disgust would be, in spite of his good-natured assurance she needn't hurry, if she really kept him waiting, set her at her task with flying fingers.

"There's no use hurrying," Olga commented on this burst of speed, "because you're going to wait for me. This is my night. We'll have a little table all by ourselves at Max's and then you'll come up and sleep with me tonight."

An instinct prompted Rose to defer the necessary negative to this suggestion until the last of the other girls, who was just then pinning on her hat, should have gone. When the door clicked, she said she was sorry but the plan couldn't be carried out.

Olga looked at her intensely. "I need you tonight," she said, "and if you care anything about me at all you'll come."

"I'd come if I could," said Rose, "but it can't be managed. I've promised to do something else."

Olga's face paled a little and her eyes burned. "So that's it, is it?" she said furiously. "You're going out with Galbraith." She went on to say more than that, but her meaning was plain at the first words.

Rose looked at her a little incredulous, quite cool, so far as her mind went (because, of course, Olga's accusation was merely grotesque) but curiously and most unpleasantly stirred, disgusted almost to the point of nausea. She stopped the tirade, not because she cared what the girl was saying, but because she couldn't stay in the room with a person making that sort of an exhibition of herself. It took no more than half a dozen words to accomplish this result. The mere fact that she spoke, after that rather long blank period of speechlessness, and the cold blaze of her blue eyes that accompanied her words, effected more than the words themselves. And then, in a tempest of tears and self-reproaches, Olga repented—a phase of the situation which was worse, almost, than the former one, because it couldn't be dealt with quite so summarily.

But Rose went on dressing as fast as she could all the while, and at last, long before Olga had begun putting on her street clothes, she was ready to go. With her hand on the door-latch she paused.

"I am going to have supper with Mr. Galbraith," she said. "He told me there was something he wanted to talk to me about." And with that she let herself out of the room, indifferent to the effect these last words of hers might produce.

She caught sight of Galbraith down at the end of the corridor waiting for her, but she paused a moment, pulled in a long breath and grinned at herself. In the state of mind she was in just then, divided between her impatience to get back to her own room where her thoughts could be free to run upon the one theme they welcomed, and her wrath and disgust over the scene Olga had just subjected her to, the poor man was in danger of having a pretty unsatisfactory sort of hour with her. She must brace up and really try to be nice to him.

So through all the preliminaries to the real talk which he'd said he wanted with her, she was consciously as cordial and friendly as she knew how to be. She said she hoped she hadn't kept him waiting too long, and when he apologized for taking her out through the stage door and the alley, with the explanation that the front of the house was by this time locked, she made a good-humored reference to the fact that the alley and the stage door were now her natural walk in life, and that it was just as well she shouldn't be spoiled with liberties.

He asked her if she had any preference as to where they went for supper, and the way she acknowledged, again with a smile, that she'd rather not go to Rector's, nor to any of the places over on Michigan Avenue, was an admission, in candid confidence, of the existence of another half of her life which she wished to keep, if possible, unentangled with this. She showed herself frankly pleased with the taxi he provided, sank back into her place in it with a sigh of clear satisfaction, and was, as far as he could see, completely incurious about the address he gave the chauffeur. The place he picked out was an excellent little chop-house in one of the courts south of Van Buren Street, a place little frequented at night—manned, indeed, after dinner, merely by the proprietor, one waiter and a man cook in the grille, and kept open to avoid the chance of disappointing any of the few epicurean clients who wouldn't eat anywhere else.

But neither the neighborhood nor the loneliness of the place got even so much as a questioning glance from Rose. She left the ordering of the supper to him, and assented with a nod to his including with it a bottle of sparkling Burgundy.

There is nothing quite so disconcerting as to be prepared to overcome a resistance and then to find no resistance there; to be ready with convincing arguments, and then not have them called for. This, very naturally, was the plight of John Galbraith.

Rose wasn't a child even on the day when she came and asked him for a job, and in the six weeks that had intervened since then she'd been dressing in the same room with chorus-girls—hearing the sort of things they talked about in the wings. Indeed, unless he was mistaken, she must have heard them linking her own name with his. His very special interest in her, and the way he'd shown it, promoting her to the sextette, and giving her a chance to design the costumes, was a thing they wouldn't have missed nor failed to put their own construction on. She must know then what their inferences would be from the fact of his asking her out to supper on the opening night.

What he'd been prepared to urge was that now that his connection with the enterprise had terminated, now that he was no longer a director and the representative of her employers, she should take him on trust simply as a friend. He was prepared to answer protests, to offer compromises—concessions to appearances. He'd expected her to exhibit some shyness of the taxi. According to his unconscious ideal of the situation she should have looked questioningly at him—hesitated, and then let him assure her that it was all right. She should have gasped a little when the car turned south in the dark little court below Van Buren Street, have shrunk a little at the isolation the emptiness of the restaurant enforced upon them, and declined, with something not far short of panic, her share of that bottle of Burgundy. Because all these flutters and questionings would just have opened the way for his assurances—perfectly honest assurances, too, as far as he knew—of the candor of his feelings and intentions toward her.

She needed a friend, that was plain enough, some one who had her best interests honestly at heart; some one who knew the pitfalls and the difficulties of this pilgrimage she'd so strangely set out on, and could advise her how to avoid them. That he was, potentially, that friend, he truly believed. And what better way could there be of convincing her of it than by persuading her to trust him, and then proving that her trust had not been misplaced?

But what was one to do—how was one to make a beginning when she trusted him without any persuasion? Trusted him as a matter of course, without the glimmer of any sort of emotion whatever; about as if he'd been—well, say, her brother-in-law!

He was at a loss for a peg to hang his definite sense of injury upon. He couldn't blame the girl for having trusted him, nor for proving so perfectly adequate to the unconventional situation he'd created. He couldn't reproach her, even in his thoughts, for the frankly expressed pleasure she took in the leisured dignity of the little restaurant, with its modestly sumptuous appointments (she even let him see that she appreciated the fineness of the napery and the handsomeness of the tableware; admitted, indeed, how sharply it contrasted with what she'd been used to lately), nor for the real appreciation she showed of the supper he selected.

But the moment he had been planning, counting on for days—weeks, if it came to that—with an excitement he couldn't deny, a tensity that had increased as the prospect of it drew nearer, was not exciting nor tense for her. If anything, she'd relaxed a little, as if the big moment of her day had passed—or, postponed by this affair of his, were still to come. Once or twice when her gaze detached itself from him and rested unfocused on the other side of the room, he saw little changes of expression go over her face that didn't relate to him at all. He simply wasn't in focus, that was the size of it. He had never seen her look lovelier, more completely desirable than she did right now, dressed as she was in her very simple street clothes and relaxed by the surrounding quiet and comfort and her own fatigue. And yet, all alone with him as she had so confidingly permitted herself to be, and near enough to reach with the bare stretching out of a hand, she'd never been further away nor seemed more unattainable.

As she came back from one of these momentary excursions she found him staring at her, and with a faint flush and a smile of contrition she pulled herself back, as it were, into his presence.

"I know you're tired," he said bruskly. "But I fancied you'd be tireder in the morning and I have to leave for New York on the fast train. So, you see, it was now or never." Strangely enough, that got her. She stared at him a little incredulous, almost in consternation.

"Do you mean you're going away?" she asked. "Tomorrow?"

"Of course," he said rather sharply. "I've nothing more to stay around here for." He added, as she still seemed not to have got it through her head. "My contract with Goldsmith and Block ended tonight, with the opening performance."

"Of course," she said in deprecation of her stupidity, "I didn't think you were going to stay indefinitely—as long as the show ran. And yet I never thought of your going away. It's always seemed that you were the show—or, rather, that the show was you; just something that you made go. It doesn't seem possible that it can keep on going with you not there."

The sincerity of that made it a really fine compliment—just the sort of compliment he'd appreciate. But—the old perversity again—the very freedom with which she said it spoiled it for him.

"I may be missed," he said—it was more of a growl really—"but I shan't be regretted. There's always a sort of Hallelujah chorus set up by the company when they realize I'm gone."

"I shall regret it very much," said Rose. The words would have set his blood on fire if she'd just faltered over them. But she didn't. She was hopelessly serene about it. "You're the person who's made this six weeks bearable and, in a way, wonderful. I never could thank you enough for the things you've done for me, though I hope I may try to some time."

"I don't want any thanks," he said. And this was completely true. It was something very different from gratitude that he wanted. But he realized how abominably ungracious his words sounded, and hastened to amend them. "What I mean is that you don't owe me any. Anything I've done that's worked out to your advantage was done because I believed it was to the advantage of the men who hired me—beginning with the afternoon when I first took you on in the chorus."

This didn't satisfy him either. Rose said nothing. He had indeed left her nothing to say. But there was a look of perplexity in her eyes—as if she were casting about for some stupidly tactless act or omission of her own to account for his surliness—that made him recant altogether.

"I don't know why in the world I should have said a thing like that!" he burst out. "It wasn't true. I've wanted to do things for you—wanted to do more than I could, and I want to still. You've done a lot to make this show go, as well as it did, in more ways than you know about. It wasn't for me, personally, that you did it. But all the same, I'm grateful. And it's to convince you of that that I asked you to come around here tonight."

She really lighted up over his praise, thanked him for it very prettily. But then, after a little silence, she went on reflectively, "It was, in a way, for you, personally, that I was working all the time. I don't know if I can explain that, though I think I understand it myself. But just because you wanted things so hard—you were so perfectly determined that something should happen in a certain way—I just *had* to help bring it about, or try to. It would have been exciting enough just to see that things were wrong and to watch them coming right. But taking hold one's self and helping a little to make them come right was—well, as I said, wonderful."

"Well," he said—and now he was brusk again—"I hope Goldsmith and Block are satisfied. They won't be; of course, unless the thing runs forty weeks. But that isn't what I want to talk about. I want to talk about you. I want to know what you're aiming at. I don't mean tomorrow or next week. You'll stay with this piece, I suppose, as long as the run lasts. But in the end, what's the idea? Do you want to be an actress?"

He had kept on going after that first question of his, because it was obvious the girl wasn't ready to answer. She seemed to be struggling to get the bearings of a perfectly new idea. At length she gave him the clue.

"It's that forty weeks," she said. "The notion of just going on—not changing anything or improving anything; doing the same thing over and over again for forty weeks, or even four, seems perfectly ghastly. And yet I suppose that's what everybody in the company is hoping for—just to keep going round and round like a horse at the end of a pole. What I'd like to do, now that this is finished, is—well, to start another."

His eyes kindled. "That's it," he said. "That's what I've felt about you all along. I suppose it's the reason I felt you never could be an actress. You see the thing the way I do—the whole fun of the game is getting the timing. Once it's got. . ." He snapped his fingers; and with an eager nod she agreed.

He was in focus now, there could he no doubt of that. But it didn't occur to him that it was the director who was in focus, not the man. The fact was that in evoking the director she'd banished the man—a triumph she wasn't to realize the importance of until a good deal later.

"Well, then, look here," he said. "I've an idea that I could use you to good advantage as a sort of personal assistant. There'll be a good deal of work just of the sort you did with the sextette, teaching people to talk and move about like the sort of folk they're supposed to represent. That's coming in more and more in musical comedies, the use of the chorus as real people in the story—accounting for their exits and entrances. It would be done more if we could teach chorus people to act human. Well, you can do that better than I; that's the plain truth. And then I think after you'd got my idea of a dance number you could probably rehearse it yourself, take some of that routine off my hands. Under this new contract of mine, that I expect to sign in a day or two, I'll simply have to have somebody. And then, of course, there's the costuming. That's a great game, and I've a notion, though of course I haven't a great deal to go by, that you could swing it. I think you've a talent for it.

"There you are! The job will be paid from the first a great deal better than what you've got here. And the costuming end of it, if you succeed, would run to real money. Well, how about it?"

"But," said Rose a little breathlessly—"but don't I have to stay here with *The Girl Up-stairs*? I couldn't just leave, could I?"

"Oh, I shan't be ready for you just yet anyway," he said. "I'll write when I am and by that time you'll be perfectly free to give them your two weeks' notice. By the way, haven't you some other address than care of the theater—a permanent address somewhere?"

"Care of Miss Portia Stanton," she told him, and as he got out his card and wrote it down, she added the California address. It recalled to his mind that she had told him her name was Rose Stanton on the day he had given her a job, and the memory diverted him for a moment. Then he pulled himself back.

"They'll be annoyed, of course—Goldsmith and Block. But, after all, you've given them more than their money's worth already. Well—will you come if I write?"

"It seems to be too wonderful to be true," she said. "Yes, I'll come, of course."

He sat there gazing at her in a sort of fascination. Because she was fairly lambent with the wonder of it. Her eyes were starry, her lips a little parted, and she was so still she seemed not even to be breathing. But the eyes weren't looking at him. Another vision filled them. The vision—oh, he was sure of it now!—of that "only one," whoever he was, that mattered.

He thrust back his chair with an abruptness that startled her out of her reverie, and the action, rough as it was, wasn't violent enough to satisfy the sudden exasperation that seized him. If he could have smashed the caraffe or something. . .

"I won't keep you any longer," he said. "I'll have them get a taxi and send you home."

She said she didn't want a taxi. If he'd just walk over with her to a Clark Street car. . . And she thanked him for everything, including the supper. But all the time he could see her trying, with a perplexity almost pathetic, to discover what she had done to change his manner again like that.

He was thoroughly contrite about it, and he did his best to recover an appearance of friendly good will. He didn't demur to her wish to be put on a car, and at the crossing where they waited for it, after an almost silent walk, he did manage to shake hands and wish her luck and tell her she'd hear from him soon, in a way that he felt reassured her.

But he kicked his way to the curb after the car had carried her off, and marched to his hotel in a sort of baffled fury. He didn't know exactly what had gone wrong about the evening. He couldn't, in phrases, tell himself just what it was he'd wanted. But he did know, with a perfectly abysmal conviction, that he was a fool!

X

The Voice of the World

If you were to accost the average layman, especially the layman who has, at one time or another, found his personal affairs, or those of his friends, casually illuminated by the straying search-light of newspaper notoriety, and put this hypothetical question to him: What chance would there be that a young married woman, who, in a social sense, really "belonged," could leave her husband for a musical-comedy chorus in the city he lived in, and escape having the fact chronicled in the daily press?—that layman would tell you that there was simply no chance at all. But if you were to put the same question to a person expert in the science of publicity—to an alumnus of the local room of any big city daily, you'd get a very different answer. Because your expert knows how many good stories there are that never get into the papers. He allows for the element of luck; he knows how vitally important it is that the right person should become aware of the fact at exactly the right time, in order that a simple happening may be converted into news.

Rose's "escapade"—that's how it would have been described—didn't get into the papers. Jimmy Wallace, of course, before the bar of his own conscience, stood convicted of high treason. There was no use arguing with himself that he was hired as a critic and not as a reporter. For, just as it is the doctor's duty to prolong, if possible, the life of his patient, or the lawyer's duty to defend his client, so it is the duty of every man who writes for a newspaper, to turn himself into a reporter when a story breaks under his eye. Jimmy ought that very night as soon as he had made sure of his facts, to have left a note on his city editor's desk informing him that Mrs. Rodney Aldrich was a member of the chorus in the new Globe show.

He didn't do it, even though he knew that a more troublesome accuser than his own conscience—namely, the city editor himself—would confront him, in case any of his colleagues on the other papers had happened to recognize her and, dutifully, had turned the story in. He read the other papers for the next twenty-four hours, rather more carefully than usual, and then with a sigh of relief, told his conscience to go to the devil. It was a well trained, obedient conscience, and it subsided meekly.

But his curiosity was neither meek nor accustomed to having its liberties interfered with, and it declined to leave the problem alone. Problem! It was a whole nest of problems. If you isolated one and worked out a tolerably satisfactory answer to it, you discovered that this answer made all the rest more fantastically impossible of solution than before. It actually began to cost him sleep! What made it harder to bear, of course, was the tantalizing possibility of finding out something by dropping in at the Globe during a performance, wandering back on the stage, where he was always perfectly welcome, going up and speaking to her and—seeing what happened. Something more or less illuminating would have to happen. Because, even in the extremely improbable case of her pretending she didn't know him, he'd then have something to go on. He dismissed this temptation as often as it showed its face around the corner of the door of his mind—dismissed it with objurgations. But it was a persistent temptation and it wouldn't stay away.

It was a real relief to him when Violet Williamson telephoned to him one day and asked him to come out to dinner. There'd be no one but herself and John, she said, and he needn't dress unless he liked. She'd been in New York for a fortnight and had only been back two days. He mustn't fail to come. There was a sort of suppressed excitement about Violet's voice over the telephone, which led him to suspect she might be able to throw some light on the enigma.

But light, it appeared, was what John and Violet wanted from him.

They were both in the library when he came in, and after the barest preliminaries in the way of greetings and cigarettes, and the swiftest summary of her visit to New York ("I stayed just long enough to begin being not quite so furious with John for not taking me there to live,") Violet made a little silence, visibly lighted her bomb, and threw it. "John and I went to the Globe last night to see *The Girl Up-stairs*," she said.

Jimmy carried his cocktail over to the fire, drew sharply on his cigarette to get it evenly lighted, and by that time had decided on his line.

"That's an amazing resemblance, isn't it?" he said.

"Resemblance fiddle-dee-dee!" said Violet.

John Williamson hunched himself around in his chair. "Well, you know," he protested to his wife, "that's the way I dope it out myself."

"Oh, *you!*" she said, with good-natured contempt. "You think you think so. Because you've always been wild about Rose ever since Rodney married her, you just won't let yourself think anything else. But Jimmy here, doesn't even think he thinks so. He knows better."

"They're the limit, aren't they?" said John in rueful appeal to his guest. "They not only know what you think, but what you think you think! It's a marvelous thing—feminine intuition."

"'Intuition,' nothing!" said Violet. Then she rounded on Jimmy.

"How much have you found out about her—this girl with the 'astonishing resemblance'?"

"Not very much," Jimmy confessed. "According to the program, her name is Doris Dane. I did ask Block about her. He's one of the owners of the piece. But he couldn't tell me very much. She's from out of town, he thinks, and he said something about her being a dressmaker. She did some work for them on the costumes. And she started in with this show as a chorus-girl. But Galbraith, the director, got interested in her, and put her into the sextette."

"Well, there we are," said John Williamson. "That settles it. Rose never was a dressmaker, that's a cinch."

Even Violet seemed a little shaken, and Jimmy was just beginning to congratulate himself on the skill with which he had modified what Block had told him about the costumes, when Violet began on him again.

"All right!" she said. "Where are we? You know quite a lot of people in that show, don't you?" This was a rhetorical question. It was notorious that Jimmy knew more or less everybody. So, without waiting for an answer, she went on, "Well, have you been behind the scenes there since the thing began?"

"No, I've not gone back," said Jimmy. "Why should I?"

"You haven't even been curious," she questioned, "to find out what a girl who looked and talked as much like Rose as that, was like?" She concluded, for good measure, with one more question voiced a little differently—more casually. "Have you happened to see Rodney lately?"

"Why, yes," Jimmy said unwarily. "I met him at the club the other day; only saw him for a minute or two. We had one drink."

"And did you happen to tell him," she asked, "about this dressmaker in *The Girl Up-stairs* who looked so wonderfully like Rose? Did you offer to take him round to see for himself?"

"I tell you there's nothing to that!" said John. He'd been caught in the same trap, it seemed. "What's the use of butting in? If anything has gone wrong with those two. . ."

"You've always said there hasn't," Violet interrupted.

"And you've said," he countered, "that you were sure there had. Well, then, if there's a chance of it, why run the risk, just for nothing?"

Jimmy, as it happened, had never heard even a suggestion that Rose and Rodney were on any other terms than those of perfect amity. He hoped they'd go on and tell him more. So to prevent their becoming suddenly discreet, he promptly changed the subject.

"I thought you had a taboo against the Globe," he said to Violet. "How did you happen to go there?"

"John went while I was in New York," she explained.

"He's—well, a regular fan, you know. He hasn't missed a show there in years. And he was *too* queer and absent-minded and fidgety for words, when I came back. I thought a bank must be going to fail, or something. And when he said, after dinner last night, that he felt like going to a musical show, of course I said I'd go with him. And when I found it was the Globe—he already had tickets—I was too—kind and sorry for him to make a fuss. Well, and then she came out on the stage, and I knew what it was all about."

"Where did you sit?" Jimmy asked.

"Fifth row," said John.

Violet hadn't got the bearing of Jimmy's question. "Oh, you couldn't mistake her," she said, "any more than you could in this room, now."

"Do you mean," John asked, "that she might have recognized us?"

"They can't," said Violet, "across the footlights,—can they?"

Jimmy nodded. "In a little theater like that," he said, "anywhere in the house. But it seems she didn't recognize you."

"Look here!" said Violet. "Don't you know, in your own mind, just as well as that you're standing there, that that was Rose Aldrich?"

Jimmy dropped down into a big chair. "Well," he said, "I'm willing to accept it as a working hypothesis."

"You men!" said Violet.

Dinner was announced just then, and the theme had to be dismissed until at last they were left alone with the dessert.

"What breaks me all up," Violet burst out, abandoning the pretense of picking over her walnuts, and showing, with a little outflung gesture, how impatient she had been to take it up, "what breaks me all up is how this'll hit Frederica. She just adores Rodney and she's been simply wonderful to Rose—for him, of course."

Neither of the men said anything, but she felt a little stir of protest from both of them and qualified the last phrase.

"Oh, she liked her for herself, too. We all did. We couldn't help it. But you haven't any idea, either of you, of even the beginning of what Frederica did for her—steered her just right, and pushed her just enough, and all the while seeming not to be doing a thing. Freddy's such a peach at that! And she's been so big-hearted about it; never even *felt* jealous. If it had been me, and I'd adored a brother like that, and he'd gone off and fallen in love with a girl nobody knew, just because he saw her in a wrestling-match with a street-car conductor, I'd have wanted, whatever I might have done, to—well, show her up. And yet, even after Rose had left him, for no reason at all, Freddy. . ."

"You're just guessing at all that, you know," her husband interrupted quietly. "You don't *know* a single thing about it."

"Well, what reason *could* Rose have for leaving him?" she flashed back. "Hasn't Rodney been perfectly crazy about her ever since he married her? Has he ever *seen* another woman the last two years? Or maybe you think he's been coming home drunk and beating her with a trunk-strap."

But John stuck to his guns. "You don't even know she's left him. The only thing you do know is that Bella Forrester met Frederica one day, about a week before Christmas, in the railway station at Los Angeles."

"Well, can you tell me any other reason," Violet demanded, "why Freddy should dash off alone to California, right in the middle of the holiday rush, without saying a word to anybody, and be back here in just a week; and not tell even *me* what she'd been doing, or where she'd been, so that if Bella hadn't written to me, I'd never have known about it at all? Is there any way of explaining that, except by supposing that Rose had quarreled with Rodney and left him and that Freddy was trying to get her to come back?"

Neither of the men could offer, on the spur of the moment, the alternative explanation she demanded. Indeed it would have taken a good deal of ingenuity to construct one. It was safer, anyway, just to go on looking incredulous.

There was silence for a minute or two, then Violet burst out again. "And then, after all Freddy had done, for Rose to come back here to Chicago, with all the other cities in the country where it wouldn't matter what she did, and start to be, of all things, a chorus-girl! It's just a"—she hesitated over the word, and then used it with an inflection that gave it its full literal meaning—"just a *dirty* trick. And poor Freddy, when she knows. . . !"

"I don't believe a word of it," said John Williamson. "I don't believe Doris Dane—if that's her name—is Rose, in the first place. And I don't believe Rose has had a quarrel with Rodney. But if she has, and if she's really there in that show. . . Well, I know Rose—not so well as I'd have liked to, but pretty well—and I know she's a fine girl and I know she's square. And if I ever saw a girl in love with her husband, she was. Well, and if she has done it, she's got a reason for it. Oh, I don't mean another woman or a trunk-strap, or any of the regular divorce court stuff. That's absurd, of course. And it may be, really, a fool reason. But you can bet it didn't look like that to her. She wouldn't have done it, admitting it's what she's done, unless she felt she had to."

"Oh, yes," said Violet, "I expect she's feeling awfully noble about it, and I'll admit she was in love with Rodney. And that makes it all the worse! If she'd fallen in love with some other man and run off with him—well, that isn't pretty, but it's happened before and people have got away with it. But this running away on account of some silly idea that she's picked up from that votes-for-women mother of hers, running away from a man like Rodney, too, just makes you sick."

Her husband didn't try to answer her, except with a regretful sigh. He recognized in the stinging contempt of his wife's words, the voice of their world. If Doris Dane of the sextette were really Rose—and in the bottom of his heart, despite his valiant pretense, he couldn't manage more than a feeble doubt of it—she had committed the unforgivable sin. Or so he thought, leaving out of his calculations one ingredient in the situation. She had done an unconventional thing for the sake of a principle!

"Well," said Jimmy Wallace after a while, heading the conversation away, as he was wont to do, from what might be an endless discussion of moral principles, "the purpose of this council of war is to decide what we are going to do about it. Are we going to tell Aldrich or his sister about the dressmaker who looks so much like his wife, and let them find out for themselves whether she is or not? Or are we going to make sure first by going back on the stage there and having a talk with her? Or are we just going to shut up about it—never have been to the Globe at all; or, in my case, never to have noticed the resemblance?"

"On the chance, you mean," John inquired, "that Rodney and Frederica never find out at all? How much does that chance amount to?"

"Well," said Jimmy, "the show's in its fourth week, and the story hasn't got into the papers yet. So the chances are now it won't. And you're about the only person in your crowd that makes a practise of going to the Globe. If you haven't heard any rumors it probably means that you two are the only ones who know, so far. People who knew her before she was married may have recognized her, to be sure, but they aren't likely to go around either to Aldrich or to Mrs. Whitney with the story. Of course there's always a big margin for the unforeseeable. But even at that, I think you might call it an even chance."

"That's what I vote for then," said John, "shut up."

"I certainly don't want to go back on the stage and talk to Rose," said Violet, "and I simply couldn't make myself tell either Rodney or Frederica. It would be just too ghastly! But there's another thing you haven't thought of. Suppose they both know already. I've got an idea they do."

This was a possibility they hadn't thought of, but the more they canvassed it, the likelier it grew.

"He acts as if he knew," Violet said, "now I come to think of it. Oh, I can't tell exactly why! Just the way he talks about her and—doesn't talk about her. And then there's Harriet. She came home from Washington and stayed three days with Frederica and then went away again. She kept house for him while Rose was laid up, and why shouldn't she be doing it now, except that she's perhaps spoken her mind a little too freely and Rodney doesn't want her around? There'd be no nonsense about Harriet, you could count on that."

"It would be like Rose," said John, "to tell him herself. It wouldn't be like her, when you come to think of it, to do anything else."

"Oh, yes, she'd tell him," said Violet. "If she had some virtuous woman-suffrage reason, she'd do more than tell him. She'd rub it in. Of course he knows. Well, what shall we do about that?"

"Same vote," said John Williamson; "shut up. Certainly if he knows, that lets us out."

But Violet wasn't satisfied. "That's the easiest thing, certainly," she said, "but I don't believe it's right. I think the people who know him best, ought to know—just a few, the people he still drops in on, like the Crawfords, and the Wests, and Eleanor and James Randolph; just so that they could—well, *not* know completely enough; so that they wouldn't, innocently, you know, say ghastly things to him. Or even, perhaps, do them, like making him go to musical shows, or talking about people who run away to go on the stage. There are millions of things like that that could happen, and if they know, they'll be careful."

Her husband wasn't very completely convinced, though she expounded her reasons at length, and urged them with growing intensity. But he'd never put a categorical veto upon her yet, and it wasn't likely he'd begin by trying to, now.

As for Jimmy Wallace, he was really out of it. But he went home feeling rather blue.

XI

The Short Circuit Again

It was, after all, out of that limbo that Jimmy had spoken of as the margin of the unforeseeable, that the blind instrument of Fate appeared. He was a country lawyer from down-state, who, for a client of his own, had retained Rodney to defend a will that presented complexities in the matter of perpetuities and contingent remainders utterly beyond his own powers. He'd been in Chicago three or four days, spending an hour or two of every day in Rodney's office in consultation with him, and, for the rest of the time, dangling about, more or less at a loose end. A belated sense of this struck Rodney when, at the end of their last consultation, the country lawyer shook hands with him and announced his departure for home on the five o'clock train.

"I'm sorry I haven't been able to do more," Rodney said,—"do anything really, in the way of showing you a good time. As a matter of fact, I've spent every evening this week here in the office."

"Oh, I haven't lacked for entertainment," the man said. "We hayseeds find the city a pretty lively place. I went to see a show just last night called *The Girl Up-stairs*. I suppose you've seen it."

"No," said Rodney, "I haven't."

"Well, the title's pretty raw, of course, but the show's all right. Nothing objectionable about it, and it was downright funny. I haven't laughed so hard in a year. Pretty tunes, too. I tried today to get some records of it but they didn't have any yet. If you want a real good time, you go to see it."

The client was working his way to the door all the while and Rodney followed him, so that the last part of this conversation took place in the outer office. Rodney saw the man off with a final hand-shake, closed the door after him and strolled irresolutely back toward Miss Beach's desk.

It was true, as he had told his client, that he had been spending most of his evenings lately in his office, and it was also true that he had an immense amount of work to do; he'd been taking it on rather recklessly during the last two months. But they'd been pretty sterile, those long solitary evening hours. He'd worked fitfully, grinding away by brute strength for a while, without interest, without imagination, and then, in a frenzy of impatience, thrusting the legal rubbish out of the way and letting the enigma of his great failure usurp, once more, his mind and his memories.

It had occurred to him to wonder, as he stood listening to his client's enthusiastic description of the show at the Globe, whether it would be possible, in any surroundings, for him, for an hour or two, to laugh and be jolly—and forget. It might be an experiment worth trying!

"Telephone over to the University Club," he said suddenly to Miss Beach, "and see if you can get me a seat for *The Girl Up-stairs*."

The office boy was out on an errand and in his absence the switchboard was Miss Beach's care.

"The—*The Girl Up-stairs*?" she repeated.

"That's what he said, isn't it?"

"Yes," she assented. "That's—the name of it."

He might have been expected, after giving an order like that, to go striding back into his private office and slam the door after him. It wasn't at all his way to keep a lingering hand on a task after he'd delegated it to some one else. But he didn't on this occasion act as she'd expected him to; remained abstractedly where he was while something turned itself over in his mind.

There was nothing urgent about his order of course, and it was natural enough that she should go on with her typing to the end of a sentence, or even of a paragraph. But he stayed on and on, and Miss Beach went steadily on with her typing. Finally he roused himself enough to look around at her.

"Go ahead and telephone," he said. "I want to find out if I can get a seat."

She arose obediently and moved over to the switchboard, then began fumbling with the directory.

"Good lord!" said Rodney. "You know the number of the University Club!"

Of course it was true she did. She called it up for him on an average of a dozen times a week. He was looking at her now with undisguised curiosity. She was acting, for a perfectly infallible machine like Miss Beach, almost queer. But she acted queerer the next moment. She laid down the directory, clasped her hands tight and pressed her lips together. Then, without looking around at him, she said:

"You don't want to go to see that show, Mr. Aldrich. It—it isn't good at all."

Rodney was more nearly amused than he had been in a month.

"You've been to see it?" he asked.

"Yes," she said, and managed to go on a little more naturally, "Mr. Craig took me. We had a bet on what the Supreme Court's decision would be in the Roderick case—theater tickets against two pounds of home-made fudge, and I won. And—that's where we went."

"And you didn't like it, eh?"

"No," she said.

By now he was grinning at her outright. "Vulgar?" he asked.

Her color had mounted again. "Yes," she said.

The notion of having his dramatic entertainment censored by a frail, prim little thing like Miss Beach tickled his burly sense of humor. "It would be a horrible thing if I should go to see anything vulgar, wouldn't it?" he observed. "But I think I'll take a chance. You go ahead and telephone."

At that she rose and, for the first time, faced him. To his amazement, he saw that she was in a perfect panic of embarrassment and fright. But, for some grotesque reason, she was determined, too. She was blushing up to the hair and her lips were trembling.

"Mr. Aldrich," she said, "you won't like that show. If—if you go, you'll be sorry."

While he was still staring at her, young Craig came bursting blithely out of his office, a bundle of papers in his hand and the pucker of a silent whistle still on his lips. "Oh, Miss Beach!" he said, and then stopped short, seeing that something had happened.

Rodney tried an experiment. "Craig," he said, "Miss Beach doesn't want me to buy a ticket for *The Girl Up-stairs*. She says I won't like it. Do you agree with her?"

A flare of red came up into the boy's face, and his jaw dropped. Then, as well as he could, he pulled himself together. "Yes, sir," he said, swung around and marched back into his own cubby-hole.

"You needn't telephone, Miss Beach," said Rodney curtly. And without another word he put on his hat and overcoat and left the office.

It was not a very profound emotion that drove him along; a violent superficial one, rather, like the gusty wrath which had precipitated the last phase of his great struggle with Rose—the time he told her he wouldn't jeopardize the children's lives to satisfy her whims. He was furiously impatient with the good intentions of his friends. He had been aware of a sort of unnatural gentleness about them ever since

Christmas; but either it had intensified during the last ten days, or else he had suddenly got more sensitive to it. The latter, most likely. And yet Violet Williamson's manner the last Sunday evening he had spent at her house, had stopped just short of a hushed voice and tiptoes. He'd been momentarily expecting her to offer him an egg-nog.

But this paroxysm of tact that had just broken out in his office was really too much. Of course they'd been talking him over, those two. It must have been amply obvious to them for a good while that there was something more than met the eye, about that long visit of his wife's to California. And it was nice and human of them to feel sorry for him. But that they should decide, because *The Girl Up-stairs* contained some rather coarsely derisive song, perhaps, about men whose wives run away from them, or something in the plot about a trip to California with a less honorable purpose than its ostensible one, that he should on no account be permitted to see the show, was ridiculous. He walked straight over to the club and told the man at the cigar counter to get him a ticket for tonight's performance.

It was then after five and he decided not to go back to the office before dinner. In fact, he might as well dine down here. So he went up to the lounge, armed himself with an evening paper against casual acquaintances, ordered a drink and dropped into a big leather chair.

But all his carefully contrived environment hadn't the power, it seemed, to shift the current of his thoughts. They went on dwelling on the behavior of Miss Beach and young Craig, which really got queerer the more one thought about it. It was hard to conceive of any allusion in the plot or the songs of a silly little musical comedy, pointed enough to account for Miss Beach's frantically determined effort to keep him away, or for the instantaneous flush that had leaped into young Craig's face. Because, after all, they didn't actually know that his great adventure had come to grief, and whatever either of them might have thought of the applicability of something that was said on the stage, to their employer's ease, it wouldn't have been a bit like either of them to discuss it with the other. In the absence of such a discussion, and the prevision of his going to the show, you couldn't account for young Craig's having caught the point instantly like that. And yet, what other explanation could there be? There was none, and there was an end of it!

Only it wasn't the end of it. The straying search-light of his memory picked up a moment during that last evening at the Williamsons'. The Crawfords had been there, and somebody else—a man he didn't know; and the stranger had said something, a harmless stupid remark enough, about the tired business man and the sort of musical-comedy he liked; whereupon both Constance and Violet had made a sort of concerted swoop and changed the subject almost violently. John Williamson made a practise of going to the Globe, he knew, but that John, who never spotted an allusion in his life, should have come home and passed the word along, and that all references to musical-comedy should therefore be taboo on Rodney's account, was simply fantastic.

But the fantasticality of an idea seemed, in his mood tonight, merely to give it the burr-like quality of sticking in his mind, holding on there with a hundred tiny barbs, despite his endeavors to pluck it out. It even occurred to him that the manner of the man at the cigar counter—the man he had just told to get him a ticket, had not been quite natural; had been a little exaggeratedly matter-of-fact. He always got his seats of that man, and the man always made some little encouraging remark, as, for example, that he'd heard it was a good show; or, more non-committally, that he hoped Mr. Aldrich would enjoy it. Tonight, certainly, he'd said nothing of the sort.

The absurdity of this consideration was simply intolerable. He flung down his paper and went into the adjoining room—a room full of tables of various sizes, and thronged, at this hour, with members getting up an appetite for dinner by the shortest route. The large round table nearest the door was preempted by a group of men he knew; some of them well, some only casually, and he came up with the intention of dropping into the one vacant chair. But just before the first of them caught a glimpse of him, his ear picked up the phrase, "*The Girl Up-stairs*." And then a lawyer named Gaylord looked up and recognized him. "Hello, Aldrich," he said, and Rodney would have sworn that the flash of silence that followed had a galvanic quality that wasn't given it merely by his own imagination. The others began greeting him, urging him to sit down and have a drink.

Rodney pulled in a long breath: "Didn't I hear some one talking about *The Girl Up-stairs*?" he asked. "Is it a good show? Shall I go to see it?"

The silence was even briefer this time.

Gaylord spoke through what would pass for a yawn. "I don't know," he said. "I haven't seen it."

One or two of the others shook their heads blankly. Finally somebody else said: "Just a regular Globe show, I guess. All right; but hardly worth bothering about."

HENRY KITCHELL WEBSTER

Once more they urged him to sit down and have a drink, but he said he was looking for somebody and walked away down the room and out the farther door.

He knew now that he was afraid. Yet the thing he was afraid of refused to come out into the open, where he could see it and know what it was. He still believed that he didn't know what it was, when he walked past the framed photographs in the lobby of the theater without looking at them and stopped at the box-office to exchange his seat, well down in front, for one near the back of the theater.

But when the sextette made their first entrance upon the stage, he knew that he had known for a good many hours.

He never stirred from his seat during either of the intermissions. But along in the third act, he got up and went out.

I doubt if ever a troglodytic ancestor of his had been as angry as Rodney was at that moment. Because, long before the pressure of the troglodyte's anger had mounted to the pressure of Rodney's, it would have relieved itself in action. He'd have descended on the scene, beating down any of the onlookers who might be fools enough to try to oppose his purpose, seized his woman and carried her off to his cave. Which is precisely and literally what Rodney, with every aching filament of nerve tissue in his body, most passionately wanted to do.

The knout that flogged his soul had a score of lashes, each with the sting of its own peculiar venom. Everybody who knew him, his closer friends, and his casual acquaintances as well, must have known, for weeks, of this disgrace. His friends had been sorry for him, with just a grain of contempt; his acquaintances had grinned over it with just a pleasurable salt of pity. "Do you know Aldrich? Well, his wife's in the chorus at the Globe Theater. And he doesn't know it, poor devil." That group at the round table at the club tonight. He could fancy their faces after he'd turned away.

Oh, but what did they matter after all? What did any of them matter? What did anything matter in the world, except that the woman he'd so whole-heartedly and utterly loved and lived for—the woman who'd left him with those protestations of the need of his friendship and respect, was there on that stage disporting herself for hire—and cheap hire at that, before this fatuous mass of humanity packed in all about him. They were staring at her, as the money they'd paid for admission entitled them to stare, licking their lips over her.

He hadn't had a moment's uncertainty that it was indeed she. Couldn't shelter himself, even for an instant, behind Jimmy Wallace's theory of an "amazing resemblance."

The others of their world had always known Rose as a person with a good deal of natural and quite unconscious dignity. She had never romped nor larked before any of them, and she conveyed the impression, not of refraining as a concession to good manners, but simply of being the sort of person who didn't, naturally, express herself in those ways. But in the interior privacies of their life together, she'd often shown herself, for him, a different Rose. She'd played with him with the abandon of a young kitten—romped and wrestled with him. And there'd been a deliciousness about this phase of her, which resided, for him, in the fact that it was kept for him alone.

But now, here on the stage of a cheap theater, she was parading that exquisite thing before the world! Along in the second act, where Sylvia's six friends come to spend the night with her and sleep out on the roof, there was a mad lark which brought up maddening memories. He felt that he must get his hands on her—shake her— beat her!

Yet, all the while, if any of his neighbors thought of him at all— became aware of him and wondered at him, it was only because he sat so still. And when the thing had become, at last, utterly unbearable, and he got up to go out, he managed to look at his watch first, quite in the manner of a "commuter" with anxieties about the ten-fifty-five train.

The northwest wind, which had been blowing icily since sundown, had increased in violence to a gale. But he strode out of the lobby and into the street, unaware of it. There must be a stage door somewhere, he knew, and he meant to find it. It didn't occur to him to inquire. He'd quite lost his sense of social being; of membership in a civilized society. He was another Ishmael.

It took him a long time to find that door, for, as it happened, he started around the block in the wrong direction and fruitlessly explored two alleys before he came on the right one. But he found it at last and pulled the door open. An intermittent roar of hand-clapping, increasing and diminishing with the rapid rise and fall of the curtain, told him that the performance was just over.

A doorman stopped him and asked him what he wanted.

"I want to see Mrs. Aldrich," he said, "Mrs. Rodney Aldrich."

"No such person here," said the man, and Rodney, in his rage, simply assumed that he was lying. It didn't occur to him that Rose would have taken another name.

He stood there a moment debating whether to attempt to force an entrance against the doorman's unmistakable intention to stop him, and decided to wait instead.

The decision wasn't due to common sense, but to a wish not to dissipate his rage on people that didn't matter. He wanted it intact for Rose.

He went back into the alley, braced himself in the angle of a brick pier and waited. He neither stamped his feet nor flailed his arms about to drive off the cold. He just stood still with the patience of his immemorial ancestor, waiting. Unconscious of the lapse of time, unconscious of the figures that presently began straggling out of the narrow door, that were not she.

Presently she came. A buffet of wind struck her as she closed the door behind her, and whipped her unbuttoned ulster about, but she did not cower under it, nor turn away—stood there finely erect, confronting it. There was something alert about her pose—he couldn't clearly see her face—that suggested she was expecting somebody. And then, not loud, but very distinctly:

"Roddy," she said.

He tried to speak her name, but his dry throat denied it utterance. He began suddenly to tremble. He came forward out of the shadow and she saw him and came to meet him, and spoke his name again.

"I saw you when you went out," she said. "I was afraid you mightn't wait. I hurried as fast as I could. I've—w-waited so long. Longer than you."

They were so near together now, that she became aware how he was trembling—shuddering fairly.

"You're c-cold," she said.

He managed at last to speak, and as he did so, reached out and took her by the shoulders. "Come home," he said. "You must come home."

At that she stepped back and shook her head. But he had discovered while his hands held her, that she was trembling, too.

The stage door opened again to emit a group of three of the ponies.

"My Gawd," one of them shrilled, "what a hell of a night!"

They stared curiously at Dane and the big man who stood there with her, then scurried away down the alley.

"We can't talk here," he said. "We must go somewhere."

She nodded assent and they moved off side by side after the three little girls, but slower. In an accumulation of shadows, half-way down the alley, he reached out for her arm. It might have begun as an automatic act—just an unconscious instinct to prevent her stumbling, there in the dark. But the moment he touched her, the quality of it changed. He gripped her arm tight and they both stood still. The next moment, and without a word, they moved on again. At the corner of the alley, they turned north. This was on Clark Street. Finally:

"Are you all right, Roddy? And the babies?" she managed to say. "It's a good many days since I've heard from Portia." And then, suddenly, "Was it because anything had gone wrong that you came?"

"I didn't know you were here until I saw you on the stage."

This was all, in words, that passed until they reached the bridge. But there needed no words to draw up, tighter and tighter between them, a singing wire of memories and associations; there was no need, even, of a prolonged contact between their bodies. He had let go her arm when they came out of the alley, and they walked the half-mile to the bridge side by side and in step, and except for an occasional brush of her shoulder against his arm, without touching.

But the Clark Street bridge, with a February gale blowing from the west down the straight reach of the river, is not to be negotiated lightly. Strong as they were, the force of the wind actually stopped them at the edge of the draw, caught Rose a little off her balance, turned her half around and pressed her up against him.

She made an odd noise in her throat, a gasp that had something of a sob in it, and something of a laugh.

For a moment—so vivid was the blaze of memory—he seemed veritably to be standing on another bridge (over the north branch of the Drainage Canal, of all places) with the last, leonine blizzard of a March, which had been treacherously lamblike before, swirling drunkenly about. He had been tramping for hours over the clay-rutted roads with a girl he had known a fortnight and had asked, the day before, to marry him. They had been discussing this project very sensibly, they'd have said, in the light of pure reason; and they were both unconscionably proud of the fact that since the walk began there had been nothing a bystander could have called a caress or an endearment between them. But there on the bridge, a buffet of the gale had unbalanced her, and she—with just that little gasping laugh—

had clutched at his shoulder. He had flung one arm around her and then the other. Without struggling at all she had held herself away for a moment, taut as a strung bow, her hands clutching his shoulders, her forearms braced against his chest; then, with the rapturous relaxation of surrender, her body went soft in his embrace and her arms slid round his neck; their faces, cool with the fine sleety sting of the snow, came together.

The vision passed. The wind was colder tonight than that March blizzard had been, and the dry groan of a passing electric car came mingled with the whine of it. Muffled pedestrians, bent doggedly down against it, jostled them as they went by.

He steadied her with a hand upon her shoulder, slipped round to the windward side, and linked his arm within hers. But it was a moment before they started on again. Their hands touched and, electrically, clasped. Like his, hers were ungloved. She'd had them in her ulster pockets.

"Do you remember the other bridge?" he asked.

Her answer was to press, suddenly—fiercely—the hand she held up against her breast. Even through the thickness of the ulster, he could feel her heart beat. They crossed the bridge, but the hand-clasp did not slacken when they reached the other side. Their pace quickened, but neither of them was conscious of it.

As for Rodney, he was not even conscious what street they were walking on, nor how far they went. He had no destination consciously in mind or any avowed plan or hope for what should happen when they reached it. Yet he walked purposefully and, little by little, faster. He looked about him in a sort of dazed bewilderment when she disengaged her hand and stopped, at last, at the corner of the delicatessen shop, beside the entrance to her little tunnel.

"Here's where I live," she said.

"Where you *live!*" he echoed blankly.

"Ever since I went away—to California. I've been right here—where I could almost see the smoke of your chimneys. I've a queer little room—I only pay three dollars a week for it—but—it's big enough to be alone in."

"Rose. . ." he said hoarsely.

A drunken man came lurching pitiably down the street. She shrank into the dark mouth of the passage and Rodney followed her, found her with his hands, and heard her voice, speaking breathlessly, in gasps. He hardly knew what she was saying.

"It's been wonderful. . . I know we haven't talked; we'll do that some other time, somewhere where we can. . . But tonight, walking along like that, just as. . . Tomorrow, I shall think it was all a dream."

"Rose. . ."

"Wh-what is it?" she prompted, at last.

"Let me in," he said. "Don't turn me away tonight! I—I can't. . ."

The only sound that came in answer was a long tremulously indrawn breath. But presently her hand took the one of his that had been clutching her shoulder and led him toward the end of the passage, where a faint light through a transom showed a door. She opened the door with a latch-key, and then, behind her, he made his way up two flights of narrow stairs, whose faint creak made all the sound there was. In the black little corridor at the top she unlocked another door.

"Wait till I light the gas," she breathed.

There was nothing furtive about their silence; it was the wonder, the magic of being together again, that made them steal forward like awed children.

Into an ugly, dingy, cramped, cold little room, with a rickety dresser and a lumpy bed and a grimy window, rattling fiercely in the gusts of wind that went whipping down the street. . . Into a palace of enchantment.

She left the gas turned low, took off her hat and ulster, pulled down the blind over the window and shut the door, hung up a garment that had been left flung over her trunk and dumped a bundle of laundry that had not been put away, into a bureau drawer. All the time he'd been watching her hungrily, without a word.

She turned and looked into his face, her eyes searching it as his were searching hers, luminously and with a swiftly kindling fire. Her lips parted a little, trembling. There was a sort of bloom on her skin that became more visible as the blood, wave on wave, came flushing in behind it. His vision of her swam suddenly away in a blur as his own eyes filled up with tears.

And then, with that little sob in her throat, she came to him. "Oh, Roddy. . . Roddy!" was all she said. With her own lithe arms she strained his embrace the tighter.

So far as the superstructures of their two lives were concerned,—the part of them that floated above the level of consciousness, the whole fabric of their thoughts and theories and ideals, that made them to their friends and to each other, and very largely to themselves, Rose and Rodney,—they were as far apart as on the day she had left his house. There hadn't been, since then, a word between them of argument or compromise. The great *impasse* was still unforced. He hadn't, as yet, shown that he could give her the friendship she demanded. She'd had no chance to tell him of any of the small triumphs and disciplines of her new life that she hoped would win it from him.

And as for Rodney, he was the same man who, an hour ago, in the theater, had raged and writhed under what he felt to be an invasion of his proprietary rights in her.

He wouldn't have defined it that way, to be sure, in a talk with Barry Lake. Would have denied, indeed, with the best of them, that a husband had any proprietary rights in his wife. But the intolerable sense of having become an object of derision, or contemptuous pity, of being disgraced and of her being degraded, through the appearance on the stage of a public theater, of a woman who was his wife; and through her exhibition, for pay, of charms he had always supposed would be kept for him, couldn't derive from anything else but just that. He'd waited there in the alley, full of bitter thoughts that were ready to leap forth in denunciations. He'd waited there, ready, he thought, to use actual physical force on her, in the unthinkable event of its becoming necessary, to drag her out of this pit where he had found her, back to his side again.

But somehow, when he had heard her speak his name, he'd begun to tremble. And when he had felt her trembling, too, the bitter phrases had died on his tongue and the thoughts that propelled them were smothered like fire under sand. And as he'd stood confronting her in her mean little room, his eyes searching her face, all he had been looking for was a sign of the hunger—the ages-old hunger—that was devouring him. And when he'd found it, that was enough for him. The great issue that was to be fought out between them remained intact, but the hunger had to be satisfied first.

It was hours later, in the very dead of the night, as he sat on the edge of the bed, with his back to her, that the old sense of outrage and degradation, almost as suddenly as it had left him, came back. And came back in a way that made it more intolerable than ever. For the clear flame of it had lost its clarity; the confidence that had fanned it was gone—the sense of his own rightness. The irresistible surge of passion that had carried him off, had destroyed that. The flame smoked and smoldered.

"Have you anything here," he asked her dully, "besides what will go in your trunk?"

It was the surliness of his tone, rather than the words themselves, that startled her.

"No," she said puzzled. "Of course not."

"Then let's throw them into it quickly," he said, "and we'll lock the thing up. Do you owe any rent?"

"Roddy!" she said. He heard her moving behind him. She struck a match and lighted the gas. Then came around in front of him and stared at him in frowning incredulity. "What do you mean?"

"I mean we're going to get out of this abominable place now—tonight. We're going home. We can leave an address for the trunk. If it never comes, so much the better."

Again all she could do was to ask him, with a bewildered stammer, what he meant. "Because," she added, "I can't go home yet. I've—only started."

"Started!" he echoed. "Do you think I'm going to let this beastly farce go any further?"

And with that the smoldering fire licked up into flame again. He told her what had happened in his office this afternoon; told her of the attitude of his friends, how they'd all known about it—undoubtedly had come to see for themselves, and, out of pity or contempt, hadn't told him. He told her how he'd felt, sitting there in the theater; why he'd waited at the stage door for her. He accused her, as with its self-engendered heat his wrath burned brighter, of having selected the thing to do that would hurt him worst, of having borne a grudge against him and avenged it.

It was the ignoblest moment of his life, and he knew it. The accusations he was making against her were nothing to those that were storing up in his mind against himself. The sense of rightness that would have made him gentle, had been carried away by the passion he'd shared with her, and he couldn't get it back.

He didn't look at her as he talked, and she didn't interrupt; said no word of denial or defense. The big outburst spent itself. He lapsed into an uneasy silence, got himself together again, and went on trying to restate his grievance—this time more reasonably, retracting a little. But under her continued silence, he grew weakly irritated again.

When at last she spoke, he turned his eyes toward her and saw a sort of frozen look in her dull white face that he had never seen in it before. Her intonation was monotonous, her voice scarcely audible.

"I guess I understand," she said. "I don't know whether I wish I was dead or not. If I'd died when the babies were born. . . But I'm glad I came away when I did. And I'm glad,"—she gave a faint shudder there at the alternative—"I'm glad I've got a job and that I can pay back that hundred dollars I owe you. I've had it quite a while. But I've kept it, hoping you might find out where I was and come to me, as you did, and that we might have a chance to talk. I thought I'd tell you how I'd earned it, and that you'd be a little—proud with me about it, proud that I could pay it back so soon."

She smiled a little over that, a smile he had to turn away from. But this tortured smile shriveled in the flame of passion with which she went on. "If I couldn't pay it back tonight, after this, I'd feel like killing myself, or like—going out and earning it in the streets. Because that's what you've made me tonight!"

He cried out her name at that, but she went on as if she hadn't heard; only calm again—or so one might have thought from the sound of her voice.

"I went away, you see, because I couldn't bear to have the love part of your life without a sort of friendly partnership in the rest of it. But I didn't know then that you could love me while you hated me, while you felt that I'd unspeakably degraded myself and disgraced you. So that while you loved me and had me in your arms, you felt degraded for doing it. I didn't know that till now.

"I suppose I'll be glad some day that it all happened; that I met you and loved you and had the babies, even though it's all had to end," she shuddered again, "like this."

It wasn't till he tried to speak that her apparent calm was broken. Then, with a sudden frantic terror in her eyes, she begged him, not to—begged him to go away, if he had any mercy for her at all, quickly and without a word. In a sort of daze he obeyed her.

The tardy winter morning, looking through her grimy window, found her sitting there, huddled in a big bath-robe, just as she'd been when he closed the door.

XII

"I'm All Alone"

The same grizzly dawn that looked in on Rose through the dim window of her room on Clark Street, saw Rodney letting himself in his own front door with a latch-key after hours of aimless tramping through deserted, unrecognized streets. He was in a welter of emotions he could no more have given names to than to the streets whose dreary lengths he had plodded.

The one thing that isolated itself from the rest, climbed up into his mind and there kept goading him into a weak helpless fury, was a jingling tune and a set of silly words that Rose and her sisters in the sextette had sung the night before: "You're all alone, I'm all alone; come on, let's be lonesome together." And then a line he couldn't remember exactly, containing, for the sake of the rhyme, some total irrelevancy about the weather, and a sickening bit of false rhyming to end up with, about loving forever and ever. The jingle of that tune had kept time to his steps, and the silly words had sung themselves over and over endlessly in his brain until the mockery of it had become absolutely excruciating. Except for that damnable tune, there was nothing in his mind at all. Everything else was synthesized into a dull ache, a hollow, gnawing, physical ache. But he'd endure that, he thought, if he could get rid of the diabolical malice of that tune. Perhaps if he stopped walking and just sat still it would go away.

That's why he went home, let himself in with his latch-key and made his way furtively to the library, where the embers of last night's fire were still warm. He had an hour at least before the servants would be stirring. He was terribly cold and pretty well exhausted, and the comfort of his big chair and the glow of the fire carried him off irresistibly into a doze—a doze that was troubled by fantastic dreams.

With the first early morning stirrings in the house, the sounds of opening doors here and there, the penetrating cry of one of the babies—muffled, to be sure, and a long way off, but still audible—he came broad awake again, but sat for a while staring about the room; at the wonderful ornate perfection of the Italian marble chimney-piece that framed the dying fire; at the tall carved chairs, the simple grandeur of the three-hundred-year-old table and the subdued richness, in the half light, of the tapestries that hung on the walls.

It was Florence McCrea's masterpiece, this room. But this morning its perfections mocked him with the ferocious irony of the contrast they presented to that other room—that unspeakably horrible room where he had left Rose. Details of its hideousness, that he hadn't been conscious of observing during the hours he had spent in it, came back to him, bitten out with acid clearness;—the varnished top of the bureau mottled with water stains, the worn splintered floor, the horrible hard blue of the iron bed, the florid pattern on the hand-painted slop-jar.

And that abominable room was where Rose was now! She was sitting, perhaps, just as he'd left her, with that look of frozen, dumb agony still in her face, while he sat here. . .

He sprang up in a sort of frenzy. The parlor maid would be in here any minute now, on her morning rounds, and would wish him a respectful good morning, and ask him what he wanted for breakfast. And then, with automatic perfection, would appear his coffee, his grapefruit, and the rest of it—all exactly right, the result of a perfect precalculation of his wishes. While Rose. . .

He put on his outdoor things and left the house, motivated now, for the first time in many hours, with a clear purpose. He'd go back to that room and get Rose out of it. He was incapable of planning how it should be done, but somehow—anyhow, it should be; that was all he knew!

But this purpose was frustrated the moment he reached Clark Street, by the realization that he hadn't an idea within half a mile at least, where the room was. Neither when he went into it with Rose, nor when he left it, had he picked up any sort of landmark. There was a passage, he remembered, leading back between two buildings, which projected to the sidewalk. But there were a dozen of these in every block.

A miserable little lunch-room caught his eye, displaying in its dingy windows, pies, oranges, big shallow pans of pork and beans. This was the sort of place Rose would have to come to, he reflected, for her breakfast. And with that thought—hardly the conscious hope that she would actually come to this place this morning—he turned in, sat down at a cloth spotted with coffee and catsup stains, and ordered his breakfast of a yawning waiter. He even forced himself, when it was brought in, to eat it. If it was good enough for Rose, wasn't it good enough for him?

And all the while he kept his eye on the street door, in the irrepressible, unacknowledged hope that the gods would be kind enough to bring her there.

But it was a mocking hope, he knew, and he didn't linger after he'd finished. He walked down-town to his office. It was still pretty early—not yet eight o'clock. Even his office boy wouldn't be down for three-quarters of an hour. He was safe, he found himself saying, for so long, anyway.

He sat down at his desk and stared bewildered at the stack of letters that lay there awaiting his signature. They were the very letters Miss Beach had been typing when he had told her to telephone to the club and get him a seat for *The Girl Up-stairs*, by way of passing a pleasant evening;—and had laughed at her when she protested. Oh, God!

He felt like a sort of inverted Rip Van Winkle—like a man who had been away twenty years—in hell twenty years!—and coming back found everything exactly as he had left it. As if, in reality, his absence had lasted only overnight.

He pulled himself together and began to read the letters, but interrupted himself before he'd gone far, to laugh aloud. The laugh startled him a little. He hadn't expected to do more than smile. But certainly it was worth a laugh, the solemn importance with which he'd dictated those letters; the notion that it mattered what he said, how he advised his clients in their bloodless, parchment-like affairs; that anything in all the files behind the black door of that vault represented more than the empty victories and defeats of a childish game. The dead smug orderliness of the place, with the infallible Miss Beach as its presiding genius, infuriated him. Clearly he couldn't stay here till he was better in hand than this.

He signed his letters without reading them, and scribbled a note to Craig that he'd been called out of town for a day or two on a matter of urgent personal business. He hadn't thought of actually going out of town until the note was written. But once he saw the statement in black and white, the notion of making it true, invited him. He'd run off to some small city where no curious eyes, animated by the knowledge that he was Rodney Aldrich whose wife had left him to become a chorus-girl, could steal glances at him. Where he needn't speak to any one from morning till night. Where he could really get himself together and think.

He added in a postscript to the note to Craig, instructions to call up his house and tell them he was out of town.

The thought cropped up in one of the more automatic sections of his brain, that for traveling he ought to have a bag, night things, fresh underclothes, and so on, and the routine method of supplying that need suggested itself to him; namely, to telephone to the house, have one of the maids pack his bag for him and send it down-town in the car. But just as he had rejected the notion of breakfasting at home, and had gone out to that miserable Clark Street lunch-room instead, so he rejected this. All the small civilized refinements of his way of life went utterly against his grain. They'd continue to be intolerable to him, he thought, as long as he had to go on envisaging Rose in that ghastly environment of hers.

He left his office and turned into one of the big department stores that backs up on Dearborn Street, where he bought himself a cheap bag and furnished it with a few necessaries. Then, leaving the store, simply kept on going to the first railway station that lay in his way. He chose a destination quite at random. The train announcer, with a megaphone, was calling off a list of towns which a train, on the point of departure, would stop at. Rodney picked one that he had never visited, bought a ticket, walked down the platform past the Pullmans, and found himself a seat in a coach.

He found a measure of relief in all this. It gave him the illusion, at least, of doing something. Or, more accurately, of getting ready to do something, while it liberated him from the immediate necessity of doing it. He'd go to a hotel in that town whose name was printed on his ticket, and hire a room; lock himself up in it, and then begin to think. Once he could get the engine of his mind to going, he'd be all right. There must be some right thing to do. Or if not that, at least something that was better to do than anything else. And when his mind should have discovered what that thing was, he'd have, he felt, resolution enough to go on and do it. Until he should find it, he was like a man shamed—naked, unable to encounter the most casual glance of any of the persons in his world who knew his shame. Once he was safe in that hotel room, the process of thinking could begin. He wouldn't have to hurry about it. He could take all the time he liked.

For the present, he was getting a queer sort of comfort out of what would ordinarily be labeled the discomforts of his surroundings: the fierce dry heat of the car, the smells—that of oranges was perhaps the strongest of these—the raucous persistence of the train butcher hawking his wares; and, most of all, in the very density of the crowd.

This is one of the comforts that many a member of the favored, chauffeur-driven, servant-attended class lives his life in ignorance of, the nervous relief that comes from ceasing, for a while, to be an isolated, sharply bounded, perfectly visible entity, and subsiding, indistinguishably, into a mere mass of humanity; in being nobody for a while. It was a want which, in the old days before his marriage, Rodney had often, unconsciously, felt and gratified. He had enjoyed being herded about, riding in crowded street-cars, working his way through the press in the down-town streets during the noon hour.

He was no more conscious of it now, but it was distinctly pleasant to him to be identified for the conductor merely by a bit of blue pasteboard with punch marks in it, stuck in his hat-band.

The pleasant torpor didn't last long, because presently, the rhythmic thud of the wheels began singing to him the same damned tune that had dogged his footsteps earlier that morning: "I'm all alone, you're all alone; come on, let's be lonesome together."

This was intolerable! To break it up, he bought a magazine from the train-boy and tried to read. But the story he lighted on concerned itself with a ravishingly beautiful young woman and an incredibly meritorious young man, and worked itself out, cleverly enough to be sure—which made it worse—upon the assumption that all that was needed for their supreme and permanent happiness was to get into each other's arms, which eventually they did.

Rose had been in his arms last night!

So the scorching treadmill round began again. But at last sheer physical exhaustion intervened and he fell heavily asleep. He didn't waken until the conductor took up his bit of pasteboard again, shook him by the shoulder, and told him that he'd be at his destination in five minutes.

Presently, in the hotel, he locked his door, opened the window and sat down to think.

XIII

FREDERICA'S PARADOX

Two days later, at half past eight in the morning, he walked in on Frederica at breakfast with her two eldest children. He had been able to count on this because the Whitneys had a certain pride in preserving some of the customs of the generation before them; at least Martin had, and Frederica's good-natured, rueful acquiescence gave her at once something to laugh at him a little about and a handy leverage for the extraction of miscellaneous concessions. It wasn't exactly a misdemeanor to be late to breakfast—it began promptly at eight o'clock—but it was distinctly meritorious not to be. Martin never was and he always left the house for his office at exactly eight-twenty. His chauffeur was trained to take just ten minutes trundling the big car down-town, and eight-thirty found him at his desk as invariably as it had found his father before him. It was all perfectly ritualistic, of course. There wasn't the slightest need for any of it.

A knowledge of the ritual, though, stood Rodney in good stead this morning. He liked Martin well enough—had really a traditional and vicarious affection for him. But he was about the last man he wanted to see today.

The children were a boy of ten, Martin, junior, and a girl, Ellen, of eight. There was a three-year-old baby, too, but his nurse looked after him. They had finished breakfast, but Frederica had a way of keeping them at the table for a little while every morning, chatting with her—oh, about anything they pleased. If it was a design for their improvement, they didn't suspect it. The talk broke off short when the three of them, almost simultaneously, looked up and saw Rodney in the doorway.

"Hello!" Frederica said, holding out a hand to him, but not rising. "Just in time for breakfast."

"Don't ring," he said quickly. "I've had all I want. My train got in an hour ago and I had a try at the station restaurant."

"Well, sit down anyway," said Frederica.

"Take this chair, Uncle Rod," said the boy in a voice of brusk indifference. "Excuse me, mother?" He barely waited for her nod and blundered out of the room.

The girl came round to Rodney's chair to offer him her hand and drop her curtsy; took a carnation from a bowl on the table and tucked it into his button-hole, slid her arm around his neck and kissed his cheek.

Both the children, Frederica was aware, had remarked something troubled and serious about their uncle's manner and each had acted on this observation in his own way. The boy, distressed and only afraid of showing it, had bolted from the room with a panicky assumption of indifference. The girl, though two years younger, was quite at ease in expressing her sympathy, and conscious of how decoratively she did it. (This was Frederica's analysis, anyhow. As is the wont of mothers, she liked the boy better.)

"I think Miss Norris is waiting for you, my dear."

"*Oui, maman*," said Ellen dutifully.

She was supposed to talk French all the morning, but somehow this particular observance of the régime irritated her mother a little and she rather visibly waited while Ellen quite adequately made her farewells to her uncle and gracefully left the room.

The tenseness of her attitude relaxed suddenly when the child was gone. She reached out a cool soft hand and laid it on one of Rodney's that rested limply on the table. There was rather a long silence—ten seconds perhaps. Then:

"How did you find out about it?" Rodney asked.

They were both too well accustomed to these telepathic short-cuts to take any note of this one. She'd seen that he knew, just with her first glance at him there in the doorway; and something a little tenderer and gentler than most of her caresses about this one, told him that she did. What it was they knew, went of course without saying.

"Harriet's back," she said. "She got in day before yesterday. Constance said something to her about it, thinking she knew. They've thought all along that you and I knew, too. Harriet was quick enough and clever enough to pretend she did and yet find out about it, all the same time. So that's so much to the good. That's better than having them find out we didn't know. Of course Harriet came straight to me. I'm glad it was Harriet Constance spoke to about it and not me. I'd probably have given it away. But Harriet never batted an eye."

"No," said Rodney, "Harriet wouldn't."

It was a certain dryness in his intonation rather than the words themselves Frederica answered.

"She'd do anything in the world for you, Roddy," she said, with a vaguely troubled intensity.

This time his mind didn't follow hers. For an instant he misunderstood her pronoun, then he saw what she meant.

"Harriet?—Oh, yes, Harriet's all right," he said absently.

She left his preoccupation alone for a minute or two, but at last broke in on it with a question. "How did you find out about it, Roddy? Who told you?"

"No one," he said in a voice unnaturally level and dry. "I went to see the show on the recommendation of a country client, and there she was on the stage."

"Oh!" cried Frederica—a muffled, barely audible cry of passionate sympathy. Then:

"Roddy," she demanded, "are you sure it's true? Are you absolutely sure that it's really Rose? Or if it is, that she's in her right mind—that she hasn't just wandered off as people do sometimes without knowing who they are?"

"There's nothing in that notion," he said. "It's Rose all right, and she knows what she's doing."

"You mean you've seen her off the stage—talked with her?"

He nodded.

She pulled in a long sigh of anticipatory relief.

"Well, then," she demanded, "what did she say? How did she explain how she *could* have done such a thing as that?"

"I didn't ask her to explain," said Rodney. "I asked her to come home, and she wouldn't."

"Oh, it's wicked!" she cried. "It's the most abominably selfish thing I ever heard of!"

He made a gesture of protest, but it didn't stop her.

"Oh, I suppose," she flashed, "she didn't *mean* any harm—wasn't just trying to do the cruelest thing she could to you. But it would be a little less infuriating if she had."

"Pull up, Freddy!" he said. Rather gently though, for him. "There's no good going on like that. And besides. . . You were saying Harriet would do anything in the world for me. Well, there's something *you* can do. You're the only person I know who can."

Her answer was to come around behind his chair, put her cheek down beside his, and reach for his hands.

"Let's get away from this miserable breakfast table," she said. "Come up to where I live, where we can be safely by ourselves; then tell me about it."

In front of her boudoir fire, looking down on her as she sat in her flowered wing chair, an enormously distended rug-covered pillow beside her knees waiting for him to drop down on when he felt like it, he began rather cautiously to tell her what he wanted.

"I'll tell you the reason why I've come to you," he began, "and then you'll see. Do you remember nearly two years ago, the night I got wet coming down here to dinner—the night you were going to marry me off to Hermione Woodruff? We had a long talk afterward, and you said, speaking of the chances people took getting married, that it wasn't me you worried about, but the girl, whoever she might be, who married me."

The little gesture she made admitted the recollection, but denied its relevancy. She'd have said something to that effect, but he prevented her.

"No," he insisted, "it wasn't just talk. There was something to it. Afterward, when we were engaged, two or three times, you gave me tips about things. And since we've been married. . . Well, somehow, I've had the feeling that you were on her side; that you saw things her way—things that I didn't see."

"Little things," she protested; "little tiny things that couldn't possibly matter—things that any woman would be on another woman's—side, as you say, about."

But she contradicted this statement at once. "Oh, I *did* love her!" she said fiercely. "Not just because she loved you, but because I thought she was altogether adorable. I couldn't help it. And of course that's what makes me so perfectly furious now—that she should have done a thing like this to you."

"All right," he said. "Never mind about that. This is what I want you to do. I want you to go to see her, and I want you to ask her, in the first place, to try to forgive me."

"What for?" Frederica demanded.

"I want you to tell her," he went on, "that it's impossible that she should be more horrified at the thing I did than I am myself. I want you to ask her, whatever she thinks my deserts are, to do just one thing for me, and that is to let me take her out of that perfectly hideous place. I don't ask anything else but that. She can make any terms she likes. She can live where or how she likes. Only—not like that. Maybe it's a deserved punishment, but I can't stand it!"

There was the crystallization of what little thinking he had managed to do in the two purgatorial days he'd spent in that down-state hotel—in the intervals of fighting off the torturing jingle of that tune, and the memory of the dull frozen agony he'd seen in Rose's face as he left her. No great result, truly. The mountain had labored and brought forth a mouse.

But reflect for a moment what Rodney's life had been; how gently, for all his buoyant theories about the acceptance of discipline, the world, in its material aspect at any rate, had dealt with him. How completely that boyish arrogance of his had been allowed to grow unbruised by circumstance. He'd always been rich, in the sense that his means had always been sufficient to his wants. He'd never in his life had an experience that even resembled Portia's with that old unpaid grocery bill. He'd enjoyed wearing shabby clothes, but he'd never worn them because he could afford no better. He'd always been democratic in the narrower social sense, but he'd never realized how easy that sort of democracy is and how little it means to a man never associated with persons who assert a social superiority over him. He'd always made a point of despising luxuries, to be sure. But it hadn't been brought to his attention at how high a level he drew the line between luxuries and mere decent necessities.

He wasn't then, near so much of a Spartan as he thought. His long association with the Lakes and their friends might, you'd think, have brought him the consolatory reflection that a woman who earned even a successful chorus-girl's wages, needn't be pitied too lamentably on the score of poverty; that Rose could, no doubt, have afforded a better room than that, if she'd wanted to. And that even a three-dollar room, a whole room that you hadn't to share with anybody, would—if the rent of it left you money enough to send out your clothes to the laundry and to buy adequate meals in restaurants—represent luxury—well, to more people than one likes to think about.

Rodney knew that well enough, of course. He'd read the Sage Foundation reports on housing; he was familiar with the results of the Pittsburgh Survey. But the person in question now, wasn't the Working Girl. It was his Rose!

Out of all the chaos of thought and feeling that had been boiling within him since the night he had gone with Rose to her room, there emerged, then, two outstanding ideas. One was that he had outraged her; the other that she simply couldn't be allowed to go on living as he had found her.

Frederica, naturally, was mystified. "That's absurd, of course, Roddy," she said gently. "You haven't done anything to Rose to be forgiven for."

"You'll just have to take my word for it," he said shortly. "I'm not exaggerating."

"But, Roddy!" she persisted. "You must be sensible. Oh, it's no wonder! You're all worn out. You look as if you hadn't slept for nights. I wish you'd sit down and be a little bit comfortable. But I *know* you're wrong about that!

"I went out to California with the idea that you might have been—well, awfully stupid about something and hurt Rose dreadfully without knowing it. I was perfectly ready to be—on her side, as you say. I thought we'd have a good talk and I'd find out what it was all about, and then come home and pack you out there yourself.

"Well, of course I didn't see Rose, and Portia wasn't very communicative. She'd always been a little stiff with me. I never managed to get her altogether. But she was clear enough about it at any rate, that Rose was more in love with you than ever and she didn't blame you for a thing. The thing that she seemed most anxious about was that her mother shouldn't blame you. Of course that took the wind out of my sails and I had to come back. So it's absurd for you to be talking as if she had a real reason for—detesting you."

"She hadn't, then," said Rodney, and he walked uneasily away to the window.

"Well, if you mean the other night, the only time you've seen her since, then it's all the more ridiculous. What if you were angry and lost your temper and hurt her feelings? Heavens! Weren't you entitled to, after what she'd done? And when she'd left you to find it out like that?"

"I tell you you don't know the first thing about it."

"I don't suppose you—beat her, did you?" It was too infuriating, having him meek like this!

His reply was barely audible. "I might better have done it."

Frederica sprang to her feet. "Well, then, I'll tell you!" she said. "I won't go to her. I'll go if you'll give me a free hand. If you'll let me tell her what I think of what she's done and the way she's done it—not letting you know—not giving you a chance. But go and beg her to forgive *you*, I won't.

"All right," he said dully. "You're within your rights, of course."

The miserable scene dragged on a little longer. Frederica cried and pleaded and stormed, without moving him at all. He seemed distressed at her grief, urged her to treat his request as if he hadn't made it; but he explained nothing, answered none of her questions.

It was an enormous relief to her, and, she fancied, to him, for that matter, when, after a premonitory knock at the door, Harriet walked in on them.

The situation didn't need much explaining, but Frederica summed it up while the others exchanged their coolly friendly greetings, with the statement:

"Rod's been trying to get me to go to Rose and say that it was all his fault, and I won't."

"Why not?" said Harriet. "What earthly thing does it matter whose fault it is? He can have it his fault if he likes."

"You know it isn't," Frederica muttered rebelliously.

Harriet seated herself delicately and deliberately in one of the curving ends of a little Victorian sofa, and stretched her slim legs out in front of her.

"Certainly I don't care whose fault it is," she said. "You never get anywhere by trying to decide a question like that. What I'm interested in is what can be done about it. It's not a very nice situation. Nobody likes it—at least I should *think* Rose would be pretty sick of it by now. She may have been crazy for a stage career, but she's probably seen that the chorus of a third-rate musical comedy won't take her anywhere.

"The thing's simply a mess, and the only thing to do, is to clear it up as quickly and as decently as we can—and it can be cleared up, if we go at it right. Only, for the love of Heaven, Freddy, before you let Rod go out of the house, give him a dose of veronal and pack him off to a quiet room up-stairs to sleep around the clock! The way he looks now, he's a proclamation of calamity across the street!"

She wasn't at all disturbed by the outburst this provoked from Rodney. Indeed, Frederica, from a glimpse she got of her face as she sat listening to his blistering denunciation of this apparently whole-hearted concern for appearances, and his passionate denial that they meant anything at all to him, suspected that her sister's words had been calculated to produce just this result. When it had subsided, Harriet's first words proved it.

"All right," she observed. "I knew you'd want to say that. Now, it's off your mind. Appearances do matter to Freddy and me, and of course they matter to you too, though you don't like to think so. They matter to all our kind of people. We're supposed to have been trained to take our medicine without making faces. If we've got cuts and sores and bruises, we cover them. We don't parade them as a bid for sympathy. We leave howling about rights and wrongs and soul-mates and affinities and 'ideals,' to the shabby sort of people who like to do that shabby sort of thing. According to our traditions, the decent thing to do is to shut up and keep your face and make it possible for other people to keep theirs. You're as strong for that as I am, really, Rod, and that's why I want you to back me up in the line I took with Constance. Pretend you've known all about what Rose was doing, and that you aren't ashamed of it. It would have been easier, of course, if she'd played fair with us at the start. . ."

"She did play fair," he interrupted. "She offered to tell me what she was going to do. I wouldn't let her."

Harriet's only commentary on this was a faint shrug.

"Anyhow," she went on, "the point is that once we begin pretending, everybody else will have to pretend to believe us. Of course the thing to do is to get her out of that horrible place as soon as we can. And I suppose the best way of doing it, will be to get her into something else—take her down to New York and work her into a small part in some good company. Almost anything, if it came to that, as long as it wasn't music. Oh, and have her use her own name, and let us make as much of it as we can. Face it out. Pretend we like it. I don't say it's ideal, but it's better than this."

"Her own name!" he echoed blankly. "Do you mean she made one up?"

Harriet nodded. "Constance mentioned it," she said, "but that was before I knew what she was talking about. And of course I couldn't go back and ask. Daphne something, I think. It sounded exactly like a chorus name, anyhow." And then: "Well, how about it? Will you play the game?"

"Oh, yes," he said with a docility that surprised Frederica. "I'll play it. It comes to exactly the same thing, what we both want done, and our reasons for doing it are important to nobody but ourselves."

She turned to Frederica.

"You too, Freddy?" she asked. "Will you give your moral principles a vacation and take Rod's message to Rose, even though you may think it's Quixotic nonsense?"

"I'll see Rose myself," said Rodney quietly.

It struck Frederica that if not his natural self, he had gone a long way at least, to recovering his natural manner. Telling Martin all about it that night, as she always told him about everything (because Martin was Frederica's discovery and her secret. No one else suspected, not even Martin himself, how intelligent and understanding he was, nor how luminous his simple remarks about complex situations could sometimes be), she adverted to a paradox which had often puzzled her in the past. Rodney was twice as fond of her as he was of Harriet, just as she was twice as fond of him as Harriet was. And yet, again and again, where her own love and sympathy had failed dismally to effect anything, Harriet's dry astringent cynicism would come along and produce highly desirable results.

"It seems as if it oughtn't to work out that way," she concluded. "You'd think that loving a person and feeling his troubles the way he feels them himself, ought to enable you to help him rather than just irritate. However, as long as it doesn't work that way with you. . ."

He reached out, took her by the chin, tilted her face back and kissed her expertly on the mouth. A rather horrifyingly familiar thing to do, one might think, to the Venus of Milo, or Frederica, or any one as simply and grandly beautiful as that. But she seemed to like it.

"No chance for the experiment," said Martin. "I shall never have any troubles while you're around."

XIV

The Miry Way

Rodney's docility didn't go to the length of the dose of veronal Harriet had recommended, but it did assent to a program that occupied the greater part of the day, including a Turkish bath, a good sleep, fresh clothes and the first decently cooked meal he had had since he'd dined at the club three days ago. When he turned into his office, about five o'clock, he was his own man again, perfectly capable of a greeting to Craig and Miss Beach which consigned the last scene between them here in the office to oblivion.

His fortitude was put to the test, too, during the first five minutes. In the stack of correspondence on his desk, to which Miss Beach directed his attention, was an unopened envelope addressed to him in Rose's handwriting. He couldn't restrain, of course, a momentary wild hope that she had written to tell him he was forgiven, or at least to offer him the chance of asking her forgiveness. But he paused to steel himself against this hope before looking to see what the thing contained.

It was well he did so, because there was nothing in it but a postal money-order for a hundred dollars; not an explanatory line of any sort. Of course the message it carried didn't need writing. It smarted like a slap across the face. Yet, down underneath the smart, he felt something that glowed more deeply, a feeling he couldn't have named or recognized, of pride in her courage.

He was badly in need of something to be proud of, too, for the next two days were full of humiliations. When he told Harriet and Frederica that he would see Rose himself, he hadn't any program for carrying out this intention. He didn't want to wait for her again at the stage door. There mustn't be anything about their next talk together to remind her of their last one, and it would be better if she could be assured in advance that she had nothing to fear from him. So the first thing to do was to write her a letter that would show her how he felt and how little he meant to ask. But before he could write the letter, he must learn her name.

He thought of Jimmy Wallace as a person who'd be able to help him out, here, but in the circumstances Jimmy was the last person he wanted to go to. There was no telling how much Jimmy might know about the situation already. The intolerable thought occurred to him that Rose might even have talked with Jimmy about going on the stage before she left his house. No, the person to see was the manager of the theater. He'd describe Rose to him and ask him who she was.

His attempt to carry out this part of his plan was disastrously unsuccessful. Theatrical managers no doubt cherish an ideal of courteous behavior. But, since ninety-nine out of a hundred of the strangers who ask for them at the box-office window, are actuated by a desire to get into their theaters without paying for their seats, they develop, protectively, a manner of undisguised suspicion toward all people who don't know them, and toward about three-quarters of those who pretend they do. It wasn't a manner Rodney was accustomed to, and it irritated him. Then, until he had got his request half stated, it didn't occur to him in what light the manager would be amply justified in regarding it. That notion, which he interpreted from a look in the manager's face, confused and angered him, and he stumbled and stammered, which angered him still more.

"We don't do that sort of thing in this theater," the manager said loudly (the conversation had taken place in the lobby of the theater, too) and turned away.

The grotesque improbability of the true explanation that the woman whose name he was inquiring about was his wife, silenced him and turned him away. It was fortunate for Rodney it did so. The thing would have made a wonderful story for the press agent, if he hadn't stopped just where he did.

He spent the rest of that evening, and a good part of the next day, trying to think of some alternative to waiting again at the stage door. But, except for the still inadmissible one of going to Jimmy Wallace, he couldn't think of one. So, at a quarter past seven that night, he stationed himself once more in the miserable alley, to wait for Rose. Seeing her before the show would, he thought, be an improvement on waiting till after it. The mere fact that they wouldn't have very long to talk, ought to reassure her that he didn't mean to take any advantages. He could show her how contrite he was, how little he meant to ask, and then leave it to her to select a place, at her own leisure and convenience, to talk over the terms of their treaty.

He waited from a quarter after seven to half past eight, but Rose didn't come. The thought that perhaps he hadn't taken his station early enough sent him back to another vigil at half past ten. At a quarter to twelve, his patience exhausted, he opened the stage door and told the doorman he was waiting for one of the girls in the sextette. The doorman informed him they had all gone home.

There was, unfortunately, no matinée the next day, and it was only by the exercise of all the will power he had, that he stayed in his office and did his work and waited for the hour of the evening performance. Then he went to the theater and bought a ticket. When the sextette made its first appearance on the stage, he saw that another girl than Rose was taking her part. He went out into the lobby, and once more sought the manager. But this time with a different air.

"Haven't you an office somewhere where we can talk?" he demanded. "This is important."

Evidently the manager saw it was, because he conducted him to a small room with a desk in it, half-way up the balcony stairs, and nodded him to a chair.

"There was a young woman in your company," Rodney said, "in the sextette. She isn't playing tonight. I want to know what her stage name is, and where she can be found. I assure you that it's of the first importance to her that I should find her."

The manager's manner was different, too. He looked perplexed and rather unhappy. But he didn't tell Rodney what he wanted to know.

"She's left the company," he said, "permanently. That's all I can tell you."

"Is she ill?" Rodney demanded.

The manager said not that he knew of, but this was all that was to be got out of him.

The thing that finally silenced Rodney and sent him away, was the reflection that the man might be withholding information about her, on Rose's own request.

He went away, sore, angry, discouraged. Jimmy Wallace seemed about the only hope there was. But he'd be damned if he'd go to Jimmy. Not yet, anyway. And then he thought of Portia!

She'd tell him. She'd have to tell him. Why hadn't he thought of her before? He'd write to her the message to Rose he'd tried to get Frederica to carry. No, he wouldn't do that! He'd go to her. And there was a chance. . . Why, there was the best kind of chance! Why hadn't he thought of it before? Why had he been such an idiot as to waste all these days!

It seemed almost certain he'd find Rose there with her. She'd felt—she couldn't have helped feeling after the things he'd said to her that ghastly night in the little North Clark Street room—that she couldn't go on. And stripped of her job like that, with nothing else to turn to, where should she go but home to her mother and sister? To the only friends and comforters she had in the world.

He'd send no word in advance of his coming. He'd just come up to the door of the little bungalow and ring the bell. And there was a chance that the person who'd come to answer it would be Rose herself.

The idea came to him all in a flash as he walked away from the theater, and his impulse from it was to jump into a taxicab and catch a ten-thirty train to the coast, that he had just time for. He denied the impulse as part of the discipline he'd been imposing on himself since his talk with Harriet, and went home instead. From now on he was going to act like a reasonable man, not like a distracted one.

He had his bag packed and his tickets bought the next morning, went to the office and put things in train to accommodate a week's absence, wrote a note to Frederica telling her of his discovery that Rose had left the company of *The Girl Up-stairs*, and of his hope of finding her in California with her mother and Portia; and when he settled himself in his compartment for the three-day ride he even had two or three books in his bag to pass the time with, as if it had been an ordinary journey. He didn't make much of them, it's true, but his honest attempt to, gave him the glimmering dawn of a discovery.

The cardinal principle of his life, if such a thing could be stated in a phrase, was self-expression through self-discipline. Well, his discovery was (it didn't come to much more than a surmise, it is true, but it was a beginning) that in his relations to Rose he'd never disciplined himself at all. The network of his instincts, passions, desires, that had involved her, had been allowed to grow unchecked, unscrutinized. He didn't begin to scrutinize them now. He was in no mind for the task. How could he undertake it until the fearful hope that he was actually on the way to her now should have been answered one way or the other!

It proved a vain hope. The person who answered his ring at the door of the little bungalow, on that wonderful sun-bathed, rose-scented morning (false auguries that mocked his disappointment and made it almost intolerable) was Portia.

She flushed at sight of him, then almost as quickly went pale. She stepped outside the door and closed it behind her before she spoke.

"I'm afraid I mustn't let mother know you're here," she said. "She's not been well these last days and she mustn't be excited. I don't want to let her suspect that things have changed or in any way gone wrong with Rose. I told her I was going out for a walk. Will you come with me?"

He nodded and did not even speak until they'd got safely away from the house. Then:

"I came out here," he said, "almost sure that I should find her. Isn't she here?"

"No," said Portia. Then she added with a sort of gasp, as if she'd tried to check her words in their very utterance, "Don't you know her better than that?"

"Do you know where she is?"

This question she didn't answer at all. They walked on a dozen paces in silence.

"Portia," he demanded, "is she ill? You'll have to tell me that."

Even this question she didn't answer immediately. "No," she said at last. "She's not ill. I'll take the responsibility of telling you that."

"You mean that's all you will tell me?" he persisted. "Why? On her instructions?"

"I think we'll have to sit down somewhere," said Portia. "Beside the road over there where it's shady."

"I got a letter from Rose yesterday," she said, after they'd been seated for a while. "She asked me in it not to go on writing you the little— bulletins that I'd been sending every week; not to tell you anything at all. So you see I've gone rather beyond her instructions in saying even as much as I have."

"And you," he asked quickly; "you mean to comply with a request like that?"

"I must," said Portia. "I can't do anything else."

He made no comment in words, but she interpreted his uncontrollable gesture of angry protest, and answered it.

"It's not a question of conscientious scruples; keeping my word, not betraying a confidence; anything like that. A year ago if she'd made such a request I'd have paid no attention to it. I'd have taken the responsibility of acting against her wishes, for her own good, if I happened to see it that way, without any hesitation at all. But Rose has shown herself so much bigger and stronger a person than I, and she's done a thing that would have been so splendidly beyond my courage to do that there's no question of my interfering. She's entitled to make her own decisions. So," she went on with a little difficulty, "I shan't betray her confidence nor disregard her instructions. But there's one thing I can do, one thing I can tell you, because it's my confidence, not hers."

The very obvious fact that her confidences were not of great moment to him, the way he sat there beside her in a glum abstraction through the rather long silence that followed her preface, made it easier for her to go on.

"You see," she said at last, "I'd always regarded Rose as a spoiled child. I'd loved her a lot, of course; but I'd despised her a little. At least I'd tried to, because I was jealous of her; of the big simple easy way she had—of making people love her. All the hard things came to me, I felt, and all the easy ones to her. And on the day I came to tell her about mother, and how we had to move out here—well, I was feeling sorrier for myself than usual. If you'll remember when that was and what her condition was (I didn't know about it then and neither did she) you'll understand my having found her terribly blue and unhappy. She talked discontentedly about her—failure with you and how she seemed to be nothing to you except. . . Well, she said she envied me. And that, as I was feeling just then, was too much for me. I lashed out at her; told her a lot of things she'd never known—about how we'd lived, and so on; things I'd done for her. I said she'd got my life to live as well as her own, and that if she failed with it I'd never forgive her. She made me a promise that she wouldn't, no matter how hard she had to fight for it."

"She spoke to me once of a promise," Rodney said dully, "but of course I didn't know what she meant."

Portia got to her feet. "I can't leave mother for very long," she said, "and I've some little errands at the shops before I can go back. So. . ."

"I see," he said. "I mustn't detain you any longer. I don't know, anyhow, that there's anything more to say."

"I'm sorry I can't—help you. You're entitled to—hate me, I think. Because it all goes back to that. I've been glad of a chance to tell you. And that makes me all the sorrier that I can't in any way make it up to you. But you see—don't you—how it is?"

"Yes," he said. "I see. I suppose, if it came to hating, that you're entitled to hate me. But there'll be no great satisfaction in that, I guess, for either of us." He held out his hand to her and with a painful sort of shy stiffness, she grasped it. "If Rose changes her instructions, or if you change your mind as to your duty under them, you'll let me know?"

She nodded. "Good-by," she said.

Rodney walked back to the railway station where he had checked his bag. In two hours he was on a train bound back to Chicago.

Various things occurred to him during the journey eastward that he might have said to Portia. He hadn't asked, for instance, whether Rose's embargo on news of herself to him had been made effective also in the other direction. Had she cut herself off from Portia's bulletins about himself and the babies? Could Portia have transmitted a message from him to Rose—the one Frederica had declined to take? But he felt in a way rather glad that he hadn't asked any more questions, nor offered any messages. He wasn't looking now for an intermediary between Rose and himself. He wanted Rose, and he meant to find her. His whole mind, by now, had crystallized into that hard-faceted, sharp-edged determination. The sore masculine vanity that had kept him from appealing to the man most likely to be able to help him was almost incredible now.

From the railway station in Chicago, the moment he got in, he telephoned Jimmy Wallace at his newspaper office. It was then about half past four in the afternoon. Jimmy couldn't leave for another hour, it seemed. It was his afternoon at home to press agents, and he always gave them till five-thirty to drop in. But he didn't think there were likely to be any more today, and if Rodney would come over. . .

Rodney got into a taxi and came, and found the critic at his shabby old desk under a green-shaded electric light, in the midst of a vast solitude, the editorial offices of an evening newspaper at that hour being about the loneliest place in the world. There was a rusty look about this particular local room, too, that made you wonder that any real news ever could emanate from it. Yet only this afternoon they had beaten the city in the announcement of the failure of the Mortimore-Milligan string of banks.

"I've come," said Rodney, finding a sort of fierce satisfaction in grasping the nettle as tightly as possible, "to see if you can tell me anything about my wife."

Jimmy may have felt a bit flushed and flustered, but the fact didn't show, and an imaginative insight he was in the habit of denying the possession of led him to draw most of the sting out of the situation with the first words he said.

"I'll tell you all I know, of course, but it isn't much. Because I haven't had a word with her since the last time I dined at your house, way back last September, I think it was. I saw her on the stage at the Globe, the opening night of *The Girl Up-stairs*, and I saw that she recognized me.

That's how I knew it was really she. And—well, I want you to know this! I haven't told anybody that she was there."

"You needn't tell me that," said Rodney. "I'm sure of it. But I'm glad you did tell me the other thing. But here's the situation: she's left that company; left it, I believe, as a result of a talk I had with her after I found her there, and I don't know where she is. The one thing I have got to do just now is to find her. I've asked at the theater, and they won't tell me. I imagine they're acting on her instructions. And as I don't even know the name she goes by I've found it pretty hard to get anywhere. I want you to help me."

"Her name there at the Globe was Doris Dane," said Jimmy, "and I imagine that unless she's left the show business altogether she'll have kept it; because it would be, in a small way, an asset. And, as she'll be easier to find if she has stayed in the business than if she hasn't, why, that's the presumption to begin on."

He lighted his pipe and lapsed into a thoughtful silence. "There are two things she may have done," he went on after a while. "She may have gone to New York, and in that case she's likely to have applied to the man who put on *The Girl* out here; that's John Galbraith. He took quite an interest in her, I understand; believed she had a future. But the other thing she may have done strikes me as a little more likely. How long ago was it you talked to her?"

"It's the better part of two weeks," said Rodney.

"Well," said Jimmy, "they sent out a Number Two company of *The Girl Up-Stairs* a week ago last Sunday night. If she had any reason for wanting to leave Chicago she might, I should think, have gone to them and asked them to let her go out on the road with that. They wouldn't have done it, of course, unless she'd convinced them that she was going to quit the Chicago company anyway. But if she had convinced them of that they'd have done it right enough. On the whole, that seems to me the likeliest place to look."

"Yes," said Rodney, "I think it is. Well, have you any way of finding out where the Number Two company is playing?"

Jimmy was rummaging in the litter of magazines on the top of his desk. He pulled one out and searched among the back pages of it for a moment.

"Here we are!" he said. "*The Girl Up-stairs*," and he began reading off the route. "They're playing tonight," he said, "at Cedar Rapids; tomorrow night in Dubuque."

"All right," said Rodney. "The next thing to find out is whether she's with the company. Who is there we can telephone to out there?"

"Why," said Jimmy, "I suppose we might raise the manager of the opera-house. They're at Cedar Rapids tonight, and we might get a good enough wire so that a proper name would be understood." He glanced at his watch. "But there's a quicker and surer and cheaper way, and that's to ask Alec McEwen. He's the press agent of the company here, and he'd be sure to know."

"He'd know," Rodney demurred, "but would he tell?"

"He'd tell me," said Jimmy.

"Can you find him?" Rodney wanted to know. "Where would he be at this time of day—at his office or his house?"

He hadn't any office nor any house, Jimmy said. "But since he's undoubtedly cleaned up the newspaper offices by now, on his weekly round," he concluded, "we can find him easily enough. I'll guarantee to locate him—within three bars. There'll be no one in to see me after this," he went on, slamming down the roll-top to his desk, getting up and reaching for his overcoat, "so we may as well go straight at it."

They walked down to the street entrance in silence. There Jimmy, with a nonchalance that rang a little flat on his own ear, pulled up and said:

"Look here! There's no need your trailing around on this job. Tell me where you will be in an hour and I'll call you up."

"Oh, I've nothing else to do," said Rodney, "and I'll be glad to go along."

They were at cross-purposes here. Jimmy didn't want him along. He had a hunch that Rodney wouldn't find little Alec very satisfactory, but he didn't know just how to say so. Rodney, on his part, strongly disrelished the notion of trailing the press agent from bar to bar. But he attributed the same distaste to Jimmy and felt it wouldn't be fair not to share it with him. There was, besides, a certain satisfaction in making his pride do penance.

Jimmy hadn't overestimated his knowledge of little Alec McEwen's orbit. They walked together to the corner of Clark and Randolph Streets and, working radially from there, in the third bar they found him.

Even before this, however, Rodney regretted that he hadn't let Jimmy do the job alone. He was not an habitué of the sumptuous bars of the Loop, and the voices of the men he found in them, the sort of men they were, and the sort of things they talked about found raw nerves all over him. On another errand, he realized, he wouldn't have minded. But it seemed as if Rose herself were somehow soiled by the necessity of visiting places like this in search of information about her.

The feeling he had come back with from that down-state town to which he had fled, that she was in a miry pit from which, at any cost, she must be saved, had been a good deal weakened during the ten days that had intervened since then. Her having sent back that hundred dollars; what Portia had said about her courage; Harriet's notion that a stage career, if properly managed, was something one could at least pretend not to be ashamed of; and, most lately, what Jimmy Wallace had said about the New York director who thought she had a future— all these things had contributed to the result.

But this pursuit, from one drinking bar to another, of the only man who could tell him where she was, was bringing the old feeling back in waves.

"Here we are," said Jimmy, as they entered the third place. It was a cramped cluttered room, thick with highly varnished, carved woodwork and upholstered leather. Its principal ornament was a nude Bouguereau in a red-draped alcove, heavily overlighted and fearfully framed; the sort of picture any one would have yawned at in a gallery, it acquired here, from the hard-working indecency of its intent, a weak salaciousness.

Rodney found himself being led up to a group in the far corner of the bar, and guessed rightly that the young man with the high voice and the seemingly permanent smile, who greeted Jimmy with a determined facetiousness, "Hello, old Top! Drunk again?" was the man they sought.

"Not yet," said Jimmy, "but I'm willing to help you along. What'll it be?" Then to Rodney: "This is Mr. Alexander McEwen, the leading liar among our local press agents." He added quickly: "You didn't come around this afternoon, so I suppose there's nothing stirring. How's business over at the Globe?"

"Immense," said Alec. "Sold out three times last week."

"Do you hear anything," Jimmy asked, "about the road company, what they're doing?"

"Rotten," said Alec. "But that don't worry Goldsmith and Block. They sold out their road rights to Block's brother-in-law."

"By the way," said Jimmy, "who's the girl in the sextette that's quit?"

"Doris Dane?" said little Alec. "Say no more. So you were on that lay, too, you old fox!" his smile widened as he looked round at Rodney, and his voice turned to a crow. "Trust this solemn old bird not to miss a bet.

She was some lady, all right! Why," he went on to Jimmy, "she has some sort of a row with her lover; big brute that used to lie in wait for her in the alley. You ought to hear the ponies go on about it. So she gets scared and goes to Goldsmith and gets herself sent out with the Number Two. And Goldsmith—believe me—crazy! He had his eye on it, too."

Jimmy finished his drink with a jerk. "Come along," he said to Rodney. "I don't like this place. Let's get out."

Rodney has never managed to forget little Alec McEwen. For weeks after that bar-room encounter he was haunted by the vision of the small bright prying eyes, the fatuously cynical smile, and by the sound of the high crowing voice. Little Alec became monstrous to him; impersonal, a symbol of the way the world looked at Rose, and he dreamed sometimes, half-waking dreams, of choking the life out of him. Not out of little Alec personally. He, obviously, wasn't worth it; but out of all the weakly venomous slander that he typified.

He managed a nod that seemed unconcerned enough, in response to Jimmy's suggestion, and followed him out to the sidewalk. The sort of florid rococo chivalry that would have "vindicated his wife's honor" by knocking little Alec down was an inconceivable thing to him. But the thing cut deep. He felt bemired. He wouldn't have minded that, of course, except that the miry way he'd trodden since he'd first gone to the stage door for Rose was the way she's taken ahead of him. He must overtake her and bring her back!

"I'm a thousand times obliged," he said in an even enough tone to Jimmy. "I'll find her at Dubuque, then, tomorrow."

"That's Wednesday," said Jimmy. "They may be playing a matinée, you know. She'll be there, right enough."

Then, to make the separation they both wanted come a little easier, he invented an errand over on State Street and nodded Rodney farewell. For the next half-hour he cursed himself with vicious heartfelt fluency for a fool. Mightn't he have known what little Alec McEwen would say?

XV

In Flight

Analyzing what little Alec McEwen actually said, disregarding the tone of his voice and the look in his eye; disregarding, indeed, the meaning he attached to his own words, and sticking simply to the words themselves, it would be difficult to bring home against him the charge of untruthfulness, or even of exaggeration.

Because it was in a simple panic that Rose, on the morning after Rodney's visit, had gone to Goldsmith and demanded to be transferred to the second company, which had started rehearsing as soon as a month of capacity business had demonstrated that the piece was a success.

Goldsmith was disgusted. Little Alec had been right about that, too. The unnaturalness of the request—for indeed it flew straight in the face of all traditions that a girl who might stay in Chicago if she liked, taking it easy and having a lot of fun, and rejoicing in the possession of a job that was going to last for months, should deliberately swap this highly desirable position for the hazards and discomforts of a second-rate road company, playing one-night stands over the kerosene circuit—was one too many for him. He demanded explanations without getting any. And as Jimmy Wallace had guessed, it was not until she'd convinced him that in no circumstances would she stay on in the Chicago company that he assented to the transfer. He didn't abandon his attempts to dissuade her until the very last moment. But neither his pictures of the discomforts of the road, nor his carefully veiled promises of further advancement if she stayed in Chicago, had the slightest effect on her. All that she wanted was to get away, and as quickly as she could!

The collapse of her courage was not quite the sudden thing it seemed. Forces she was vaguely aware had been at work, but didn't realize the seriousness of, had been undermining it steadily since the opening night when she recognized Jimmy Wallace in the audience, and when later she parted from Galbraith with his promise of a New York job as soon as he could get his own affairs ready for her.

Chief of these forces was the simple reaction of fatigue. Strong as she was, she had abused her strength somewhat during the last weeks of rehearsal; had taken on and triumphantly accomplished more than any one has a right to accomplish without calculating on replacing his depleted capital of energy afterward. It was her first experience with this sort of exhaustion, and she hadn't learned (indeed it is a lesson she never did fully learn) to accept the phase with philosophic calm as the inevitable alternate to the high-tension effective one.

She missed Galbraith horribly. She had, as she'd told him, personified the show as a mere projection of himself; he was it and it was he. Everything she said and did on the stage had continued, as it had begun in her very first rehearsal by being, just the expression of his will through her instrumentality. It was amazing to her that, with the core of it drawn out, the fabric should still stand; that the piece should go on repeating itself night after night, automatically, awakening the delighted applause of that queer foolish monster, the audience, just with its galvanic simulation of the life he had once imparted to it.

She was doing her own part, she felt at all events, in a manner utterly lifeless and mechanical. It was a stifling existence!

The most discouraging thing about it was that the others in the company seemed not to feel it in the same way. Anabel Astor for example: night after night she seemed to be born anew into her part with the rise of the first curtain; she fought and conquered and cajoled, and luxuriated in the approbation of every new audience, just as she had in the case of the first, and came off all aglow with her triumph, as if the thing had never happened to her before. And with the others, in varying degrees, even with the chorus people, the effect seemed to be the same.

But it was actually in the air, Rose believed, not merely in her own fancy, that she was failing to justify the promise she had given at rehearsal. Not alarmingly, to be sure. She was still plenty good enough to hold down her job. But the notion, prevalent, it appeared, before the opening, that she was one of those persons who can't be kept down in the chorus, but project themselves irresistibly into the ranks of the principals, was coming to be considered a mistake.

Galbraith, as was evident from his last talk with her, hadn't made that mistake. She remembered his having said she never could be an actress. That was all right of course. She didn't want to be. In a way, it was just because she didn't want to be that she couldn't be. But having it come home to her as it was doing now, in her own experience, made her all the more impatient to get out of the profession that wasn't hers and into the one that had beckoned her so alluringly.

It was just here that her disappointment was sharpest. The light that for a few weeks had flared up so brightly, showing a clear path of success that would lead her back to Rodney, had, suddenly, just when she needed it most, gone out and left her wondering whether, after all, it had been a true beacon or only fool's fire.

A resolution she came to within twenty-four hours after Galbraith left was that she would not wait passively for his letter summoning her to New York. She'd go straight to work (and fill in the disconcerting emptiness of her days at the same time) preparing herself for the profession of stage costume designing. She wasn't entirely clear in her mind as to just what steps this preparation should consist in, but the fact that Galbraith had once asked to see her sketches and had seemed amazed to learn that she hadn't any, gave her the hint that she might do well to learn to draw. She knew, of course, that she couldn't learn very much in the fortnight or so she supposed would elapse before Galbraith's letter came in, but she could learn a little. And anything to do that went in the right direction was better than blankly doing nothing.

Her first adventure in this direction was downright ludicrous, as she was aware without being able to summon the mood to appreciate it. The girls she'd known, back in the Edgewater days, who had ambitions to learn to draw went to the Art Institute. So Rose, summoning her courage for a sortie across the avenue, want there too, and felt, as she climbed the steps between the lions, a little the way Christian did in similar circumstances. After waiting a while she was shown into the office of an affable young man, with efficient looking eye-glasses and a keen sort of voice, and told him with admirable brevity that she wanted to learn to draw, as a preliminary to designing costumes.

He approved this ambition cordially enough and made it evident that the resources of the institute were entirely adequate to her needs. But then, just about simultaneously, she made the discovery that the course he was talking about was one of from three to five years' duration, and he, that the time immediately at her disposal amounted to something like a fortnight. They were mutually too completely disconcerted to do anything, for a moment, but stare at each other. When he found his breath he told her that he was afraid they couldn't do anything for her.

"There are places, of course, here in town (there's one right down the street) where they'll take you on for a month, or a week, or a day, if you like; let you begin working in oil in the life class the vary first morning, if you've a notion to. But we don't believe in that get-rich-quick sort of business. We believe in laying the foundation first."

His manner in describing the other sort of place had been so annihilating, his purpose in citing this horrible example was so plain, that he was justifiably taken aback when she asked him, very politely, to be sure, "Would you mind telling me where that other place is; the one down the street?"

He did mind exceedingly, and it is likely he wouldn't have done it if she'd been less extraordinarily good to look at and if there hadn't been, in her very expressive blue eyes, a gleam that suggested she was capable of laughing at him for having trapped himself like that. She wasn't laughing at him now, be it understood; had made her request with a quite adorable seriousness. Only. . .

He gave her the address of an art academy on Madison Street and thither at once she made her way, faintly cheered by the note on which her encounter with the young man had ended, but on the whole rather depressed by the thought of the five years he'd talked about.

They were more tactful at the new place. *Ars Longa est* was not a motto they paraded. They were not shocked at all at the notion of a young woman's learning as much as she could about drawing in two weeks. There was a portrait sketch class every morning; twenty minute poses. You put down as much as you could of how the model looked to you in that space of time, and then began again on something else. All the equipment Rose would need was a big apron, a stick of charcoal and a block of drawing paper; all of which were obtainable on the premises. She could begin this minute if she liked. It was almost as simple as getting on a pay-as-you-enter street-car.

This jumped with Rose's mood exactly, and she promptly fell to, with a momentary flare-up of the zest with which she had gone to work for Galbraith. But it was only momentary. She hadn't a natural aptitude for drawing, and her attempts to make the black lines she desperately dug and smudged into the white paper represent, recognizably, the object she was looking at failed so lamentably as to discourage her almost from the start.

She kept at it for the two weeks she'd contracted for, but at the end of that time she gave it up. She hadn't made any visible progress, and besides, she might be hearing from Galbraith almost any day now.

And when, four or five days later, her intolerable restlessness over waiting for a letter that didn't come, making up reasons why it hadn't come, one minute, and deciding that it never would, the next, drove her to do something once more, she set out on a new tack. If the ability to make fancy little water-colors of impossible-looking girls in only less impossible costumes were really an essential part of the business of designing the latter, then she'd have to set about learning, in a systematic way, to paint them; find out the proper way to begin, and take her time about it. Her two weeks at the academy had proved that it wasn't a knack that she could pick up casually. But there were books on costumes, she knew; histories of clothes, that went as far back as any sort of histories, with marvelous colored plates which gave you all the details. Bertie Willis had told her all about that when they were getting up their group for the Charity Ball. There were shelves of them, she knew, over at the Newberry Library. A knowledge of their contents would be sure to be valuable to her when Galbraith should set her to designing more costumes for him—if ever he did.

This misgiving, that she might never hear from him, that his plans had changed since their talk, so that he wasn't going to need any assistant, or that he had found some one in New York better qualified for the work, was, really, a little artificial. She encouraged it as a defense against another which was, in its insidious way, much more terrifying.

Would she ever be capable, again, of producing another idea in case it should be wanted? That one little flash of inspiration she'd had, that had resulted in the twelve costumes for the sextette—where had it come from? How had she happened on it? Wasn't it, perhaps, just a fluke that never could be repeated? During those wonderful days she had had antennæ out everywhere, bringing her impressions, suggestions from the unlikeliest objects. Now they were all drawn in and the part of her mind that had responded to them felt numb.

She ignored this sensation, or rather this absence of sensation, as well as she could; just as one might ignore the creeping approach of paralysis. She had an unacknowledged reason for going to the library and beginning that historic study of costumes. Certainly the sight of those quaint old plates ought to set her imagination racing again.

But it didn't work that way. She found herself poring over them, yawning herself blind over the French legends that accompanied them. (They were nearly all in French, these books, and though Rose had done two years' work in this language at the university and passed all her examinations, she found these technical descriptions of costumes frightfully hard to understand.) She stuck at it, though, for a long while, until one morning a comparison occurred to her that made her shut the folio with a slam. It had been in just this way, with just this dogged, blind, hopeless persistence, that, ages ago, in that former incarnation, she'd tried to study law!

This was too much for her. She walked out of the library with the best appearance of unconcern that she could muster,—it had been a near thing that she didn't break down and cry—and she did not go back. Probably it was just as well that Galbraith hadn't sent for her. She'd only have made a ghastly failure of it, if he had.

The background, of course, to all these endeavors and discouragements, or, to describe it more justly, the indivisible, all-permeating ether they floated about in, was, just as it had been in the time of her success—Rodney. The occupations, routine and otherwise, that she gave her mind to, might seem, in a way, to crowd him out of it, although not one of them was undertaken without some reference to him; the success of this, the failure of that, brought him nearer, put him farther away, like the children's game of *Warm and Cold*.

When she ran out of occupations that could absorb the conscious part of her mind, she did not even try to resist direct thoughts about him. She'd spent uncounted hours since that opening night, wondering if he knew where she was, inventing reasons why, knowing, he didn't come to her; explanations of the possibility of his still remaining in ignorance. She'd gone over and over again, the probable things that he would say, the things that she would say in reply, when he did come.

She was prepared for his anger. He was, she felt, entitled to be angry. But she felt sure she could get him to listen while she told him just why and how she had done it, and what she had done, and she had a sort of tremulous confidence that when the story was told, entire, his anger would be found to have abated, if not altogether to have disappeared. And afterward, when the shock had worn off, and he had had time to adjust himself to things, he'd begin to feel a little proud of her. They could commence—being friends. She'd constructed and let her mind dwell on almost every conceivable combination of circumstances, except the one thing that happened.

Only, as the active actual half of her life grew more discouraging, harder to steer toward any object that seemed worth attaining, her imaginary life with Rodney lost its grip on fact and reason; became roseate, romantic, a thinner and more iridescent bubble, readier to burst and disappear altogether at an ungentle touch.

So you will understand, I think, that the Rose, who incredulously heard him ask in that dull sullen tone, if she had anything besides what would go into her trunk; the Rose who got up and turned on the light for a look at him in the hope that the evidence of her eyes would belie that of her ears; the Rose he left shuddering at the window in that quilted dressing-gown, was not the Rose who had left him three months before and rented that three-dollar room and wrung a job out of Galbraith!

Dimly she was aware of this herself. At her best she wouldn't have lost her head, wouldn't have flown to pieces like that. If she'd kept any sort of grip on the situation, she might at least have averted a total shipwreck. She understood even on that gray morning, that the terrible things he'd said to her had been a mere outcry; the expression of a mood she had encountered before, though this was an extreme example of it.

But it was a long time before she went any further than that. The memory of the whole episode from the moment when he came up to her there in the alley and took her by the shoulders, until he closed her door upon himself four hours or so later, was so exquisitely painful that any reasoned analysis of it, any construction of potential alternatives to the thing that had happened, was simply impossible. The misgiving that with a little more courage and patience on her part, it might have terminated differently, only added to her misery.

She felt like a coward when she went to Goldsmith and demanded to be sent out on the road, and she experienced for a while, the utter demoralization of cowardice. The logic of the situation told her to stay where she was. If it were true, as she had fiercely told him that night, that their life together was ended, the whole fabric that they had woven for themselves rent clean across, then the only thing for her to do was to begin living now, as she had made an effort to do before, quite without reference to him, ordering her own existence as if he had ceased to exist; stick to whatever offered herself, Doris Dane, the best chance for success and advancement. She was, of course, seriously injuring Doris Dane's chances by going out on the road.

And, even with reference to Rodney, it was hard to see how her flight could help the situation. If what she'd done had really disgraced him in his own eyes and in those of his world, the disgrace was already complete. Acquiescing in that point of view, as by her flight she did, couldn't lighten it.

But all the power these considerations had, was to make her flight seem more ignominious. They were utterly incapable of preventing it.

A disinterested friend, had she boasted such a possession just then, might have pointed out for her comfort, that her rout was not complete. It was a retreat, but not a surrender. She hadn't become Rose Stanton again and gone back to Portia and her mother. Doris Dane, though badly battered, was still intact!

The first ten days of her life on the road had, on the whole, a distinctly restorative effect. I have never heard of a physician's recommending a course of one-night stands as a rest cure to nervously exhausted patients, but I am inclined to think the idea has its merits, for all that. Certainly the régime was, for a while, beneficial to Rose. The merit of it was that it offered some sort of occupation for practically all her time.

A typical day consisted in getting up in the morning at an hour determined for you either by the call posted on the bulletin board in the theater the night before, telling you what time you were to be at the railway station, or by the last moment at which you could get into the dining-room in the hotel. You ate all you could manage at breakfast, because lunch was likely to consist of a sandwich and an orange bought from the train butcher; with perhaps the lucky addition of a cup of coffee at some junction point where you changed trains. You lugged your suit-case down to the station, and had your arrival there noted by the manager, who, of course, bought all the tickets for the company. You needn't even bother to know where you were going, except out of idle curiosity. The train came along and you got a seat by yourself on the shady side, if you could; though the men being more agile, generally got there first.

The convention of giving precedence to the ladies, Rose promptly discovered, and with a sort of satisfaction, did not apply. Indeed, all the automatic small courtesies and services which, in any life she'd known, men had been expected to show to women, were here completely barred. A girl could let a man come up to her on a platform where they were all gathered waiting for the train, and casually slide an arm around her, without any one's paying the slightest attention to the act. But if, when the train came along, she permitted him to pick up her suit-case, carry it into the train and find a seat for her, there would be nods and glances.

Well, you got into the train and dozed and read a magazine (or both) and by and by, when everybody else did, you got up and got out. Perhaps you waited on a triangular railway platform for another train, or perhaps you trailed along in a procession, to a hotel. In the latter case, you got a meal and found out where the opera-house was.

There were various minor occupations that you slipped into the interstices of a day like this whenever they happened to come. You combed out and brushed your hair (a hundred strokes) which you were too tired to do at night after the performance and seldom waked up in time for in the morning. And, if you were wise, as Rose was, thanks to a tip from Anabel, and had emancipated yourself from the horror of overnight laundries by providing yourself with crêpe underclothes and dark little silk blouses, you got all the hot water you could beg of the chambermaid, and did the family wash in the bowl in your room, on an afternoon when you had a short jump and there was no matinée.

It was a life, of course, that abounded in what pass for hardships. There is no desolation to surpass that of the second-best hotel (rates two dollars a day), in a small middle western city, except the same kind of hotel in the same sort of city in the South. Bad air, bad beds and bad food are their staples and what passes for service seems especially calculated to encourage the victim to dispense with it as far as possible. The stages and dressing-rooms in the theaters were almost always dirty and were frequently overrun with rats. It was always cold and drafty back there, except when it happened to be suffocating. Also, the day's work by no means invariably concluded with even a half a bed in a two-dollar-a-day hotel. If there happened to be a train coming along at two o'clock in the morning, and also happened to be a chance to play a matinée in the town you were jumping to, you took your suit-case to the theater, lugged it from there after the performance, to the station, and spent an indefinite number of hours thereafter, in an air-tight waiting-room. Waiting, be it observed, for a chance to curl up in a seat in the day-coach, when the train came along.

But Rose didn't mind this very much. The rooms assigned to her and her roommate were fully as comfortable as the one she had lived in on Clark Street, and the meals, as a whole, were rather better than those her habitual lunch-room had provided. As for riding on the train: it gave you the sense of doing something and getting somewhere, without imposing the necessity either for judgment or for resolution. The real discomforts to Rose were not the material ones.

The piece had been, as she discovered during the one rehearsal she had attended in Chicago, deliberately cheapened and vulgarized for the road. The only one of the principals who had a shred of professional reputation, was a comedian named Max Webber, who played the part of the cosmetic king. He'd come up in vaudeville and his methods reeked of it. He was featured in the billing and he arrogated all the privileges of a real star. He was intensely and destructively jealous of any approbation he didn't himself arouse, even if it was manifested when he was not on the stage. He distended his part out of all reasonable semblance, and to the practical annihilation of the plot, by the injection into it of musty vaudeville specialties of his, which he assured the weak-kneed management were knock-outs. And his clowning and mugging made it impossible to play a legitimate scene with him, with any shadow of professional self-respect.

The result of this was that the girl who had rehearsed Patricia Devereux's part, an ambitious, well-equipped young woman who would have added much-needed strength to the cast, delivered an ultimatum during the last rehearsal but one, and on having her very reasonable demands rejected, walked out. Olga Larson, who had understudied Patricia ever since the Chicago opening, was given the part. The rest of the principals were either pathetic failures with lamentable stories of better days, or promising youngsters, like Olga herself, with no adequate training.

The chorus was similarly constituted. There were fifteen girls in it, including the sextette, now a trio, part of them worn-out veterans (one of these was the duchess—do you remember her?—who had applied to Galbraith for a job the day that Rose got hers) and the others green young girls, not more than sixteen or seventeen, some of them, who had never been on the stage before. It was one of these, a tiny, slim, black-haired little thing, who gave her name as Dolly Darling, but hadn't memorized it yet herself, obviously a runaway in quest of romantic adventure, whom Rose adopted as a permanent roommate.

Her doing so opened up the breach between herself and Olga Larson. It had existed, beneath the surface, ever since the night she had gone to supper with Galbraith. It wasn't that Olga believed Rose had taken Galbraith as a lover. She hadn't believed that even when she hurled the accusation against her. The wounding thing was that Rose seemed not to care whether she believed it or not; had met her tempestuous pleas for forgiveness and her offers of unlimited love and faith "whatever Rose might do and however things might look," with a cold distaste that hardly differed from the feeling she had shown in response to the tempest of angry accusation. She told Olga, to be sure, that everything was all right; that the thing for both of them to do, was to treat the quarrel as if it hadn't occurred.

This wasn't what Olga wanted at all. She wanted Rose as an emotional objective, to love passionately and be jealous of, and, for a moment now and then, hate, as a preliminary to another passionate reconciliation.

Rose had divined that this was so. Indeed, she understood it far better than Olga did, having had to evade one or two "crushes" of a similar sort while she was at the university. It was a sort of thing that went utterly against her instincts, and she was secretly glad that the quarrel on the opening night had given her a method of resisting this one that need not seem too utterly heartless.

Since the quarrel, Olga had been distant and dignified. She had a grievance (that Rose, pretending to forgive her confessed mistake, had really not done so) but she was bearing it bravely. Rose, when she could manage the manner, was good-humored and casual, and completely blind to the existence of the grievance Olga so nobly concealed. But Olga's wonderful good fortune, coming quite unheralded as it did, an advancement she had played with in her day-dreams, and never thought of as a realizable possibility, swept her out of her pose and carried her with a rush into Rose's arms.

This happened not a quarter of an hour after Rose had secured Goldsmith's consent to her own transfer to the Number Two company, and the first thing that registered on her mind was that she, who had taught Olga to talk, saved her her job, prevailed on Galbraith to dress her properly, and won her a chance for the space of that one song refrain, to make her individual appeal to the audience—Rose, who had done all this, was now going out as a chorus-girl in the company of which Olga was the leading woman. She didn't regret Olga's promotion, but she did wish, for herself, that she might have been spared just now, this ironic little cackle of laughter on the part of the malicious Goddess of Chance.

She was ashamed of the feeling—was she getting as small as that?—and, in consequence, she congratulated Olga a good deal more warmly than otherwise she would have done. But this warmer manner of hers opened Olga's flood-gates so wide, swamped her in such a torrent of sentiment, that Rose simply took to flight.

There was an element of real maternal pity in Rose's adoption of little Dolly Darling as her chum. Dolly was obviously as fragile and ephemeral as a transparent sand-fly. She had nothing that you could call a mind or a character, even of the most rudimentary sort. She knew nothing, except how to dance, and she knew that exactly as a kitten knows how to play with a ball of string; she dreamed of diamonds and wonderful restaurants and a sardonic hero nine feet tall with a straight nose and a long chin, who would clutch her passionately in his arms (there was no more real passion in her than there is in a soap-bubble) and murmur vows of eternal adoration in her ears.

She was a soap-bubble; that's the figure for her; just an iridescent reflection, wondrously distorted, of the tawdry life about her—a reflection, and then nothing!

But just the thin empty frailness of her, her gaiety in the face of perfectly inevitable destruction, appealed to Rose. She had Dolly in her pocket in five minutes, and before the end of the rehearsal, their treaty was signed and sealed. They were to be chums, bosom friends! The notion of it gave Rose the most spontaneous smile she'd had in days; the first one that hadn't had a bitter quirk in it.

When, down at the union station on Sunday morning, as they were leaving, Olga unfolded her plan that she and Rose should room together, Rose owned up to herself that there had been another element than maternal pity in her adoption of Dolly. She'd suspected that Olga would propose something of this sort, and she had fortified herself against it.

Olga was furious, of course, when she learned what Rose had done, and accused her, with a measure of justice, of having done it to be rid of her. If Rose didn't want to remain under this imputation, she could break with Dolly. When Rose refused to do this, Olga cut her off utterly; damned her, disowned her. They were the first pair in the company to begin not to speak.

As I said, the chief discomforts for Rose in those first ten days on the road, were not the material ones. Olga's absurd way of ignoring her, the fact that she attributed their quarrel, for the benefit of the company, to Rose's jealousy of her success; worst of all, the fact that Rose couldn't be sure she wasn't jealous of Olga's success, didn't feel at least, contemplating their reversed positions, more like a failure than she would have felt had the original girl kept the leading part,—all this contributed to a discomfort that did matter, that tormented, abraded, rankled.

It became the core of a sensation that she had turned cheap and shabby; that the distinction, which with her first entrance into this life, she had built up between herself and most of her colleagues, was breaking down; that her fiber was coarsening, her fine sensitiveness becoming calloused. It troubled her that she should feel so languid an indifference over the vulgarity of the piece, a vulgarity which, under Webber's infection, grew more blatant every day.

It was obvious to her that this quality was destroying whatever slim chance for success they had. The lines, with the new ugly twist that had been imparted to them, might draw a half dozen rude guffaws from different parts of the audience, but the chill disfavor with which they were received by the rest of the house, must, she felt, have been apparent to everybody. There seemed, though, to be a superstition that a laugh was a sacred thing; something to be fed carefully with more of the same thing that had originally produced it. This treatment was persisted in, despite the fact that the audiences shrank and shriveled and the box-office receipts, she gathered from the gossip of the company, hung just about at the minimum required to keep them going.

What troubled her was her own apathetic acceptance of it all. Just as her ear seemed to have grown dull to the offenses that nightly were committed against it on the stage, and to the leering response, which was all they ever got from across the footlights, so her spirit submitted tamely to the prospect of failure. She hardly seemed to herself the same person who had set to work in a blaze of eager enthusiasm, on the part she played so mechanically now.

She tried to reassure herself with the reflection that the tour meant nothing to her, except as it fell in with an ulterior purpose, and that it was actually serving that purpose well enough. She'd deliberately turned aside from the main channel of her new life to give mind and soul a rest they needed. When she'd got that rest and rallied her courage, she'd take a fresh start. She had, lying safely in the bank in Chicago, where Galbraith had taken her, something over two hundred dollars; for she'd lived thriftily during the Chicago engagement and had added a little every week to her nest-egg of profit from the costuming business. So she had enough to get her to New York and see her through the process of finding a new job. What sort of job it would be, she was still too tired to think, but she was sure she could find something.

Meantime, out there on the road, she was making no effort to save. She indulged in whatever small ameliorations to their daily discomforts her weekly wage would run to.

It was thus that matters stood with her, when, with the rest of the company, she arrived in Dubuque on a Wednesday morning, with an hour or so to spare before the matinée.

XVI

Anti-Climax

It was a beastly day. A gusty rain, whipping up from the south, by way of answer to the challenge of a heavy snowfall the day before, inflicted a combination of the rigors of winter, with a debilitating, disquieting hint of spring. The train, for which they had been routed out that morning at seven o'clock, had been blistering hot and the necessarily open windows had let in choking clouds of smoke.

The hotel was hot, too. Rose and Dolly, as soon as they had registered, went up to their room and washed off the stains of travel, as well as they could in translucent water that was the color of weak coffee. Then Rose, in a kimono, stretched out on the bed to make up some of the rest their early departure from Cedar Rapids had deprived her of. She did this methodically whenever opportunity offered, but without any great conviction.

Dolly, though she looked a bit hollow-eyed and much more in need of rest than Rose (for she hadn't any stamina at all. She was an under-nourished, and probably anemic little thing, and was always train-sick when their jumps began too early in the morning), went straight ahead with her toilet, tried to correct her pallor with a little too much rouge, and with the glaring falsehood that it was clearing up, put on the pathetic little fifteen-dollar suit that she religiously guarded for occasions.

She was very fidgety, a little bit furtive, and elaborately over-casual about all this; a fact to which Rose was, also a little artificially, oblivious.

Their partnership had not proved, from Dolly's point of view, at any rate, an unqualified success. They'd not been on the road three days before she'd begun to wonder whether she hadn't been hasty in the selection of her chum. Doris Dane was a very magnificent person, of course. She made the rest of the company, including the principals, look (this was a phrase Dolly had unguardedly used the day Rose first appeared at rehearsal) like a bunch of rummies. And of course it was an immense compliment to be singled out by an awe-inspiring person like that, for her particular chum. Only, once the compliment had been paid, its value as an abiding possession became a little doubtful. Awe is not a very comfortable sort of emotion to eat breakfast with.

Evidently the rest of the company felt that way about it, for Dane was not popular. She gave no handle for an active grievance, to be sure. She wasn't superior in the sense in which Dolly used the word. She didn't look haughty nor say withering things to people, nor tell passionately-believed stories designed to convince her hearers that her rightful place in the world was immensely higher than the one she now occupied. One didn't hear her exclaiming under some bit of managerial tyranny, that never, in the course of her whole life, had she been subjected to such an affront. But she had a blank, rather tired way of keeping silence when other people told stories like that, or made protests like that, which was subtly infuriating. The very fact that she never tried to impress the company, was presumptive evidence that the company didn't very greatly impress her. If their common feeling about her had ever crystallized into a phrase, its effect would have been, that all their affairs, personal and professional, past, present and to come, even those she shared with them, were not of sufficient importance to her ever to get quite the whole of her attention. It was a notion that irritated the women and frightened off the men. Probably nothing else could have kept a young woman of Rose's physical attractions from being, on a tour like that, with that sort of company, the object of, at least, experiments.

Men may consider these experiments worth trying in the face of a determined hostility on the part of the subject of them. The most rigorous primness of behavior does not daunt them, nor the assertion of an icily virtuous intangibility. But the sort of good-humored preoccupation that doesn't see them at all, that sees the pattern in the wall-paper behind their backs, that tries, half-heartedly, to be adequately courteous, is too much for them. And the more experienced they are in conquests, and the higher, on the basis of their own experience, they rate the irresistibility of their powers, the less of his particular sort of treatment they can stand. The mere sight of her, after the first day or two, was enough to give a professional "killer" like Max Webber, the creeps.

But Rose's manner not only kept the men away from herself. It kept them away from Dolly. Poor Dolly didn't know what the matter was, at first.

She had been told terrible stories by her mother and her elder brother, about the perils that beset young girls who ran away from good respectable homes. She had been told them with the misguided purpose of keeping her from running away from her own home, which was no doubt respectable, but was also deadly dull. She had run away and it was perils she was looking for. She didn't mean to succumb to them. None of the heroines of the only literature she knew—of the movies, that is to say—succumbed to perils. They were beset by the most terrific perils. It was over perils that they climbed to soul-entrancing heights of romance. It was because they were the almost certain victims of diabolical machinations, that wonderful heroes, with long eyelashes and curly hair, came to their rescue and clasped them in their arms and looked unutterable things into their eyes, just as the picture faded out.

Dolly had joined the chorus of a musical comedy, because that profession offered more alluring wares in the way of perils than any other that was open to her. And then she discovered that her calculations had gone awry. The impalpable shield her formidable friend carried with her, turned the perils aside. The little group of half-grown boys one sometimes found waiting at the stage door, never even spoke to Rose, and Dolly, in her company, partook of this unwelcomed immunity. As for the men in the company, Dolly found them letting her entirely alone.

She was bitterly unhappy at first about this, taking it as an indication of the insufficiency of her charms. But once she got the clue, she set about righting matters. She began taking tentative little strolls about the hotel lobbies by herself, and on her train journeys, when the motion and the odor of the men's pipes didn't make her too sick, she'd kneel upon a seat and look over the back of it into one of the perpetual poker-games they used to pass the time. It was astonishing how quickly she got results.

She wandered over to the cigar-stand at one of their hotels, one afternoon, a week before the arrival in Dubuque, to look at a rack of picture postcards. One of the chorus-men came over to buy some cigarettes. She felt him look at her, and she felt herself flush a little. And then he came a step closer to look at the postcards for himself, and sighed and said he wished he had somebody to send postcards to. He supposed she sent *him* one every day. Whereupon Dolly said she wasn't going to send him one today, anyway. They strolled across the lobby together and sat down in two of the wide-armed unsatisfactory chairs they have at such places; chairs that kept them so far apart they had to shout at each other. So, after a few minutes, it being a fine day, he suggested they go out for a walk. She had on her outdoor wraps and his overcoat lay across a chair.

She had already nodded acquiescence to his proposal, when she saw Rose coming in through the door.

"Wait," she whispered to him. "Don't come out with me. I'll wait outside." And with that she walked up to Rose and told her she was going out to get some cold cream.

Five per cent., perhaps, of the motive that prompted this maneuver, was what it pretended to be, a fear of Rose's disapprobation and a wish to avoid it. The other ninety-five per cent. of it was just instinctive love of intrigue.

The chorus-boy waited, blankly wooden enough to have attracted the suspicion of any eye less preoccupied than Rose's, until she had got around the curve of the stair. Then, joining Dolly on the pavement, he demanded to be told what it was all about.

Dolly, making up her little mystery as she went along, and making herself more interesting at every step, told him. They took a long walk, and by the time they got back to the hotel, they were in love. But they were separated by the malign influence of Dolly's friend. They developed a code of signals for circumventing her watchful eye. They slipped unsigned notes to each other.

So Dolly, on this blustering morning in Dubuque, fidgeting about the room, thinking up a perfectly unnecessary excuse for going out, to give to Rose, answered a knock at the door very promptly and took the folded bit of paper the bell-boy handed her, without listening to what he said, if indeed he said anything at all to her.

She carried it over to the window, turned her back to Rose, unfolded the bit of paper and read it; read it again, frowned in a puzzled way, and said:

"I didn't know there was anybody in the company named Rodney."

"What's his last name?" asked Rose. There was nothing in her tone that challenged Dolly's attention, though the quality of it would have caught a finer ear. And even if Dolly had looked up, she'd have seen nothing. Rose lay there just as she had been lying a moment ago. It would have needed a better observer than Dolly to see that she had stopped breathing.

"There ain't any last name," said Dolly. "He seems to think I'll know him by the first one." It pleased Dolly to make a parade of frankness about this note. She couldn't be sure Rose had been as oblivious as she seemed, to those the chorus-man had been sending her. This, to her rudimentary mind, seemed a good opportunity to allay Dane's

HENRY KITCHELL WEBSTER

suspicions. "See if you can make anything out of it," she said, and handed it over to Rose.

Rose got up off the bed and carried the note to the window. She stood there with it a long time.

"What's the matter?" said Dolly. "Can't you read his writing?"

"Yes," said Rose. "I know who he is. It's meant for me."

The tone, though barely audible, was automatic. It brushed Dolly away as if she had been a buzzing fly, and she felt distinctly aggrieved by it. That Dane, with all her loftily assumed indifference to men, even to a star like Max Webber, should get a note like that, and should have the nerve to betray no confusion over having her pretense thus confounded! Dolly had read the note thoroughly, and it had struck her as cryptic and suggestive in the extreme.

"I want to see you very much," it said, "and shall wait in the lobby unless you say impossible. I'll submit to any conditions you wish to make. No bad news."

It sounded like a code to Dolly.

Rose stood there a long time. When she turned around, Dolly saw she was pale. She'd crumpled the note tight in one palm, and her hands were trembling. Then, with great swiftness, she began to dress. But though her haste was evident, she didn't ask Dolly to help her; didn't seem to know, indeed, that she was in the room. It was no way for a friend to act!

The thing that had moved Rose to an extent that terrified her was that last phrase. The desire it showed to play fair with her; the unwillingness to take advantage of a fear his coming like that might have inspired her with. And then the way he had made it possible for her, with a single word, to send him away! And the restraint of that "I want to see you very much!" It wasn't like any Rodney she knew, to be humble like that. His humility stripped her of her armor. If he'd been imperious, exigent, she could have gone down to meet him with her head up. Suppose she found him broken, aged, with a dumb need for her crying out in his eyes, what would she do? What could she trust herself not to do? But just in human mercy to him she mustn't let him see she was wavering.

The Rose he was waiting for, there in the lobby, the only Rose he had been able to picture to himself for more than a fortnight of distressful days, was the Rose he'd last seen in that North Clark Street room; the Rose with a look of dumb frozen agony in her face. The one idea he'd clung to since starting for Dubuque, had been that he mustn't frighten her. She must see, with her first glance at him, that she had nothing to fear from a repetition of his former behavior. She must see that the brute in him—that was the way he put it to himself—was completely tamed.

Their meeting was a shock to both of them; an incredible mocking sort of anti-climax.

He was standing near the foot of the stairs when she came down, with a raincoat on, and a newspaper twisted up in his hands, and at sight of her, he took off his soft wet hat, and crunched it up along with the newspaper. He moved over toward her, but stopped two or three feet away. "It's very good of you to come," he said, his voice lacking a little of the ridiculous stiffness of his words, not much. "Is there some place where we can talk a little more—privately than here? I shan't keep you long."

"There's a room here somewhere," she said. "I noticed it this morning when we came in. Oh, yes! It's over there."

The room she led him to, was an appropriately preposterous setting for the altogether preposterous talk that ensued between them. It had a mosaic floor with a red plush carpet on it, two stained glass windows in yellow and green, flanking an oak mantel, which framed an enormous expanse of mottled purple tile, with a diminutive gas log in the middle. A glassy looking oak table occupied most of the room, and the chairs that were crowded in around it were upholstered in highly polished coffee-colored horse-hide, with very ornate nails. A Moorish archway with a spindling grill across the top, gave access to it. The room served, doubtless, to gratify the proprietor's passion for beauty. The flagrant impossibility of its serving any other purpose, had preserved it in its pristine splendor. One might imagine that no one had ever been in there, barring an occasional awed maid with a dust cloth, until Rodney and Rose descended on it.

"It's dreadfully hot in here," Rose said. "You'd better take off your coat." She squeezed in between the table and one of the chairs, and seated herself.

Rodney threw down his wet hat, his newspaper, and then his raincoat, on the table, and slid into a chair opposite her.

If only one of them could have laughed! But the situation was much too tragic for that.

"I want to tell you first," Rodney said, and his manner was that of a schoolboy reciting to his teacher an apology that has been rehearsed

HENRY KITCHELL WEBSTER

at home under the sanction of paternal authority, "I want to tell you how deeply sorry I am for. . . I want to say that you can't be any more horrified over what I did—that night than I am."

He had his newspaper in his hands again and was twisting it up. His eyes didn't once seek her face. But they might have done so in perfect safety, because her own were fixed on his hands and the newspaper they crumpled.

He didn't presume to ask her forgiveness, he told her. He couldn't expect that; at least not at present. He went on lamely, in broken sentences, repeating what he'd said, in still more inadequate words. He was unable to stop talking until she should say something, it hardly mattered what. And she was unable to say anything. There was a reason for this:

The thing that had amazed her by crowding up into her mind, demanding to be said, was that she forgave him utterly—if indeed she had anything more to forgive than he. She'd never thought it before. Now she realized that it was true. He was as guiltless of premeditation on that night as she. If he had yielded to a rush of passion, even while his other instincts felt outraged by the things she had done, hadn't she yielded too, without ever having tried to tell him certain material facts that might change his feeling? They'd both been victims, if one cared to put it like that, of an accident; had ventured, incautiously, into the rim of a whirlpool whose irresistible force they both knew.

She fought the realization down with a frantic repression. It wasn't—it couldn't be true! Why hadn't she seen it was true before? Why must the reflection have come at a moment like this, while he sat there, across the table from her in a public room, laboriously apologizing?

The formality of his phrases got stiffer and finally congealed into a blank silence.

Finally she said, with a gasp: "I have something to ask you to—forgive me for. That's for leaving you to find out—where I was, the way you did. You see, I thought at first that no one would know me, made up and all. And when I found out I would be recognizable, it was too late to stop—or at least it seemed so. Besides, I thought you knew. I saw Jimmy Wallace out there the opening night, and saw he recognized me, and—I thought he'd tell you. And then I kept seeing other people out in front after that, people we knew, who'd come to see for themselves, and I thought, of course, you knew. And—I suppose I was a coward—I waited for you to come. I wasn't, as you thought, trying to hurt you. But I can see how it must have looked like that."

He said quickly: "You're not to blame at all. I remember how you offered to tell me what you intended to do before you went away, and that I wouldn't let you."

Silence froze down on them again.

"I can't forgive myself," he said at last, "for having driven you out—as I'm sure I did—from your position in the Chicago company. I went back to the theater to try and find you, three days after—after that night, but you were gone. I've been trying to find you ever since. I've wanted to take back the things I said that night—about being disgraced and all. I was angry over not having known when the other people did. It wasn't your being on the stage. We're not so bigoted as that.

"I've come to ask a favor of you, though, and that is that you'll let me—let us all, help you. I can't—bear having you live like this, knocking about like this, where all sorts of things can happen to you. And going under an assumed name. I've no right to ask a favor, I know, but I do. I ask you to take your own name again, Rose Aldrich. And I want you to let us help you to get a better position than this; that is, if you haven't changed your mind about being on the stage; a position that will have more hope and promise in it. I want you to feel that we're—with you."

"Who are 'we'?" She accompanied that question with a straight look into his eyes; the first since they had sat down across this table.

"Why," he said, "the only two people I've talked with about it— Frederica and Harriet. I thought you'd be glad to know that they felt as I did."

The first flash of genuine feeling she had shown, was the one that broke through on her repetition of the name "Harriet!"

"Yes," he said, and he had, for about ten seconds, the misguided sense of dialectical triumph. "I know a little how you feel toward her, and maybe she's justified it. But not in this case. Because it was Harriet who made me see that there wasn't anything—disgraceful about your going on the stage. It was her own idea that you ought to use your own name and give us a chance to help you. She'll be only too glad to help. And she knows some people in New York who have influence in such matters."

During the short while she let elapse before she spoke, his confidence in the conviction-carrying power of this statement ebbed somewhat, though he hadn't seen yet what was wrong with it.

"Yes," she said at last, "I think I can see Harriet's view of it. As long as Rose had run away and joined a fifth-rate musical comedy in order to be on the stage, and as long as everybody knew it, the only thing to do was to get her into something respectable so that you could all pretend you liked it. It was all pretty shabby, of course, for the Aldriches, and in a way, what you deserved for marrying a person like that. Still, that was no reason for not putting the best face on it you could.—And that's why you came to find me!"

"No, it isn't," he said furiously. His elaborately assumed manner had broken down, anyway. "I came because I couldn't help coming. I've been sick—sick ever since that night over the way you were living, over the sort of life I'd—driven you to. I've felt I couldn't stand it. I wanted you to know that I'd assent to anything, any sort of terms that you wanted to make that didn't involve—this. If it's the stage, all right.—Or if you'd come home—to the babies. I wouldn't ask anything for myself. You could be as independent of me as you are here. . ."

He'd have gone on elaborating this program rather further but the look of blank incredulity in her face stopped him.

"I say things wrong," he concluded with a sudden humility that quenched the spark of anger in her eyes. "I was a fool to quote Harriet, and I haven't done much better in speaking for myself. I can't make you see."

"Oh, I can see plainly enough, Roddy," she said, with a tired little grimace that was a sorry reminder of her old smile. "I guess I see too well. I'm sorry to have hurt you and made you miserable. I knew I was going to do that, of course, when I went away, but I hoped that after a while, you'd come to see my side of it. You can't at all. You couldn't believe that I was happy in that little room up on Clark Street; that I thought I was doing something worth doing; something that was making me more nearly a person you could respect and be friends with. And, from what you've said just now, it seems as if you couldn't believe even that I was a person with any decent *self*-respect. The notion that I could blackmail your family into lending me their name and social position to get me a better job on the stage than I could earn! Or the notion that I could come back to your house and pretend to be your wife without even. . . !"

The old possibility of frank talk between them was gone. She couldn't complete the sentence.

"So I guess," she concluded after a silence, "that the only thing for you to do is to go home and forget about me as well as you can and be as little miserable about me as possible. I'll tell you this, that may make it a little easier: you're not to think of me as starving or miserable, or even uncomfortable for want of money. I'm earning plenty to live on, and I've got over two hundred dollars in the bank. So, on that score at least, you needn't worry."

There was a long silence while he sat there twisting the newspaper in his hands, his eyes downcast, his face dull with the look of defeat that had settled over it.

In the security of his averted gaze, she took a long look at him. Then, with a wrench, she looked away.

"You will let me go now, won't you?" she asked. "This is—hard for us both, and it isn't getting us anywhere. And—and I've got to ask you not to come back. Because it's impossible, I guess, for you to see the thing my way. You've done your best to, I can see that."

He got up out of his chair, heavily, tiredly; put on his raincoat and stood, for a moment, crumpling his soft hat in his hands, looking down at her. She hadn't risen. She'd gone limp all at once, and was leaning over the table.

"Good-by," he said at last.

She said, "Good-by, Roddy," and watched him walking across the lobby and out into the rain. He'd left his newspaper. She took it, gripped it in both hands, just as he'd done, then, with an effort, got up and mounted the stairs to her room. Dolly, fortunately, had gone out.

The violent struggle she had had to make during the last few moments in her effort to retain her self-control, had pretty well exhausted her. Only, had it been self-control, after all? That question shook her. Had she meant to be merciless to him like that; to send him away utterly discouraged in his sad humility, when the touch of an outreached hand would have changed the whole face of the world for him? Had she really been as noble as she felt while she was defending the impregnable righteousness of her position and so completely demolishing his?

She remembered a day when he had been beaten in a law-suit, and she had waited for him to come to her in his discouragement for help and comfort. It was thus he had come to her today. How helpless he was! What a boy he was!

Her memory flashed back over their not quite two years of life together and she realized that he had always been like that whenever his emotions toward her came into play. All his finely trained, formidable intelligence had always deserted him here. She remembered his having told her, the night he'd turned her out of his office, that his mind had to run cold. She hadn't really known what he meant. She saw now that her own mind didn't run cold, that it never really aroused itself except under the spur of strong emotion. So that just where he was most helpless, she was at her strongest. A victory over him in those circumstances, was about as much to feel triumphant over as one over a small child would be.

She realized now, more fully than before, what a crucifixion of his boyish pride it must have been to see her on the stage. It was no answer to say that with his intellectual concept of the ideal relations between men and women, he shouldn't have felt like that. Shouldn't have felt! The phrase was self-contradictory. Feelings weren't decorative abstractions which you selected according to your best moral and esthetic judgment out of an unlimited stock, and ordered wrapped and sent home. They were things that happened to you. In this case, two violently opposed feelings of terrible intensity had happened to him at once; had torn each other, and, in their struggle, had torn him. Justified or not, it was her act in leaving him, that had turned those feelings loose upon him. It was through her that he had suffered; that was plain enough. It must have been terribly plain to him.

And yet, despite the suffering she had caused him, he had crucified his pride again and come to find her; not with reproaches, with utter contrition and humility. The measures he'd suggested for easing their strained situation were, to be sure, maddeningly beside the mark. The fact that he'd offered them betrayed his complete failure to understand the situation. But it had cost him, evidently, as much pain to work them out and bring them to her, as if they had been the real solvents he took them for. And she had contemptuously torn them to shreds, and sent him away feeling like an unpardoned criminal. She hadn't drawn the sting from one of the barbs she'd planted in him, in her anger, before he'd left her in that North Clark Street room.

She didn't blame herself for the anger, nor for the panic of revulsion that had excited it. That was a feeling that had happened to her. What she did blame herself for was that, seeing them both now, as the victims of a regrettable accident (did she really regret it? Were it in her power to obliterate the memory of it altogether, as a child with a wet sponge can obliterate a misspelled word from a slate, would she do it? She dismissed that question unanswered.), she had allowed him to go away with his burden of guilt unlightened. She had done that, she told herself, out of sheer cowardice. She had been afraid of impairing the luster of her virtuously superior position.

Yet now, she protested, she was being as unfair to herself as she had been to him. What sort of situation would they have found themselves in, had she confessed her true new feelings about the love-storm that had swept over them, that night of the February gale? What good would protestations of love and sympathy for him do, if she had to go on denying him the tangible evidence and guarantee of these feelings?

She must deny them. Could she go home to him now, a repentant prodigal? Or even if, after hearing her story, he denied she was a prodigal; professed to see in it a reason for taking her fully into his life as his friend and partner? They might have a wonderful week together, living up to their new standard, professing all sorts of new understandings. But the thing wasn't to be for a week. It was for the rest of their lives. She'd never be able to feel that, in the bottom of his heart, he wasn't ashamed of her, as his world would say he ought to be. What satisfying guarantee could he ever give her that he wasn't ashamed? She couldn't think of any.

Oh, it was all hopeless! It didn't matter what you did. You didn't do things, anyway. They got done for you—and to you, by a blind force that masqueraded as your own will. The things she and Rodney had been saying to each other hadn't been the things they'd wanted to say. They'd been things wrung out between the rollers of a situation they hadn't produced and couldn't control.

What were they, the pair of them, but chips floating down the current; thrown together by one casual eddy, and parted by another! Half an hour ago, longing for each other unspeakably, they had been within hand's reach. Now, thanks to a few meaningless words, arguments, ideas—what was the good of ideas and words? Why couldn't they be like animals?—they were parted and she was clutching as a sole tangible memento of him, a rolled-up newspaper that she loved because she'd seen his strong lean hands gripping it.

She unrolled it and pressed it against her face, then laid it on her knee and smoothed out its rumpled folds and stroked it.

When Dolly came in a half-hour later, or so, to put on her other suit preparatory to the matinée, Rose opened up the paper and pretended to read. She was glad of the protection of it. As she felt just now, she didn't think she could stand Dolly's chatter without the intervention of some excuse for monosyllabic replies. She didn't notice that Dolly wasn't chattering. Mechanically she read the head-lines: *Mortimore Banks Crash*! She knew who Mortimore was. Once a powerful boss, now a discredited politician. He'd owned a whole string of banks, it appeared—along with the hitherto unheard of Milligan—whose solvency seemed to have evaporated along with the decay of his prestige.

She read without interest, but just because it was printed in black-faced type, a list of the banks in Chicago that the examiner had closed. But presently she turned back with a look a little more thoughtful, and read it again. The names of banks were so absurdly alike one never could tell. Presently she went over to her suit-case, rummaged in it, and produced a little bank-book. Then she dropped the book and the newspaper together into her bag and shut it.

She smiled a little cynically. Would she have refused Rodney's offer of help, she wondered, if she had known an hour ago, that the two hundred dollars she'd relied on so confidently to pull her out of this rut and give her a fresh start whenever she was ready to attempt it, were gone into the pockets of that fat-faced politician?

XVII

The End of the Tour

From Dubuque the company made a circuit northward into Wisconsin and Minnesota, swung around a loop and worked their way south again. Disaster stalked behind them all the way, casting its lengthening shadow before for them to walk in. On the very first salary day after Rodney's newspaper had informed Rose of her true financial situation, the manager doled out a little money on account to the more exigent members of the company, and remunerated the others with thanks, a nervous smile, and the rock-ribbed assurance that they'd get it all next week. The long jump they'd just taken, and a couple of bad houses (they were all bad, but the two he spoke of couldn't be called audiences at all, except by courtesy) had caused a temporary stringency.

Rose saw what the more experienced members of the company were doing, and knew that she ought to follow their example; keep after the manager for her money, hound him, appeal to him, invent fictitious needs, and then not spend a cent except what was absolutely wrung out of her by necessity, so that when the crash came, she wouldn't be left penniless. But she lacked the energy to do it. She was going through a passing phase of that same melancholy acquiescence in the decrees of Fate, which had been Olga Larson's permanent characteristic until Rose's own fire and a turn in the tide of fortune had roused her.

One little sequence of events springing directly from Rodney's visit to Dubuque, contributed largely to this result. The principal actor in it was Dolly.

Dolly's manner toward her had altered that very morning in Dubuque, though Rose, in her preoccupation, didn't mark the change for a day or two afterward. Then she saw that her frail little roommate had stopped chattering; that she no longer made nervous little excuses for leaving her, nor invented transparent little fibs to account for absences. She became, in her absurdly ineffectual little way, surly and defiant. She took to going about openly with her chorus-man, sharing his seat with him on the train, letting him carry her bag for her on the way to the hotel; and her manner toward Rose, when any of these manifestations fell beneath her eye, was one of uneasy challenge. Let

HENRY KITCHELL WEBSTER

Rose just try to remonstrate with her if she dared! She no longer came back to the hotel with Rose after the performances, took to turning up at their room at hours that grew steadily later and more outrageous, and while at first she stole in very quietly, undressed in the dark and tried to creep into bed without awakening her, she grew rapidly more brazen about it; turned on the light and undressed before the mirror, talked elaborately about nothing and laughed her high nervous little laugh without occasion.

It was not a lack of daring that kept Rose from asking the questions that were so patently waiting to be answered, or from making the remonstrances that Dolly's behavior so definitely invited. She knew she ought to stir herself up and do something. She had assumed, she knew, a measure of moral responsibility for the fluffy helpless little thing she had conquered so easily at first and taken for her chum. Of course remonstrances, moral lectures, scoldings, wouldn't accomplish anything. What the situation called for was a second conquest; a reassertion of her moral dominance over the girl. She would have to reconstruct the relation which, since the first week of their tour, she had, in her apathy, allowed to lapse. But that apathy had become too strong to break. She couldn't rouse herself from it. And, failing that, she kept silent; let Dolly go her ways.

But a fortnight after Dubuque, an incident occurred that even her acquiescent passivity couldn't ignore. There came a fine bright afternoon with no matinée and no washing or mending that needed to be done, when she suggested to Dolly that they go out for a good walk. Dolly didn't assent to the proposal, though the suggestion seemed to interest her.

"Where is there to walk to?" she asked. "These towns are all alike."

"I don't mean just a stroll around the town," Rose said. "Look here! I'll show you." She pointed from the window. "Across that bridge (they were playing one of the Mississippi River towns) and up to the top of that hill on the other side."

"Gee!" said Dolly. "That's miles."

"Do you good," said Rose.

"Are you going there anyway?" asked Dolly.

Rose nodded. "You'd better come along," she said. By turning on her full powers of persuasion, she might, she felt, have pulled Dolly along with her; swept her off and begun the reconquest she knew she ought to make. But somehow her will failed her. Dolly could come if she liked.

Dolly didn't refuse very decisively, but she watched Rose's preparations for departure without making any of her own. It wasn't until Rose, at the door, turned back to renew the invitation for the last time, that she said impatiently: "Oh, go along! I'll take a nap, I guess."

So Rose set out by herself.

The day proved colder than it looked; a fact that Rose tried to correct by walking more briskly. But when she got out on the bridge where the sharp wind got a full sweep at her, she saw it wasn't going to do. She'd be chilled to the bones long before she reached that hill and it would be colder coming back. She must go back for her ulster.

Fifteen minutes later, she tried the door of her room and found it locked. There was a moment of dead silence. But the realization that it hadn't been quite so silent the moment before, caused her to knock again. Then she heard the creak of the bed and the thud of Dolly's unshod feet on the floor, and then her steps coming toward the door.

"W—what—what is it?" Rose heard her ask.

"Let me in," said Rose. "Sorry I disturbed your nap, but I had to come back for my ulster."

Dolly was standing just at the other side of the door, she knew, but there was no sound of drawing the bolt. Only a long silence and then a sob.

"What's the matter?" Rose demanded. "Let me in."

"You *can't* come in!" said Dolly, and panic couldn't have spoken plainer than in her voice. "Oh, go away! What did you come back for? You said you were going to be gone hours. Go away!"

Out of a frozen throat Rose answered:

"All right. I'll go away." The situation was too miserably clear.

She went down to the lobby and a sudden giddiness caused her to drop down into the first chair she saw. She sat there for an hour, then went to the desk and told the clerk she wanted a room for that night by herself. She'd pay the extra price of it now.

The clerk took the money and selected a key from the rack. The look he saw in Rose's face silenced any comment, jocular or otherwise, that he might have made.

Rose went to her new room, took off her hat and jacket, and washed her face. When she heard the supper bell ringing down-stairs, she went back to her old room and knocked.

"Come in," said Dolly, and Rose entering, found her standing at the window looking out.

She had tried, while she sat down there in the lobby, and later in her own room, to think out what she'd say to Dolly when they next met. She hadn't been able to think of anything to say. She could think of nothing now. So, in silence, she began putting her smaller belongings into her half unpacked suit-case and laying the clothes that hung in the closet across a chair.

"So you're going to walk out on me are you?" said Dolly. Rose was aware that she'd been watching these proceedings.

"I'm going to have a room by myself for tonight," said Rose.

Dolly amazed her by flying into a sudden rage.

"Oh, you!" she said. "You make me sick. You're a hypocrite, that's what you are. Pretending to be so haughty and innocent, and then come spying back here, on purpose, and acting so shocked! You don't think I'm fit to live with, do you. Just because I've got a friend. You thought you was fit to live with me, all right, when you had two of them and wasn't straight with either."

Rose straightened up and looked at her. "What do you mean?" she demanded.

"That's right, go on with the bluff," said Dolly furiously. "But you can't bluff me. Larson put me wise to you that day in Dubuque, when that big guy—'Rodney'—came up to see you. He was one of them, and the fellow who put on the show in Chicago—what's his name?— Galbraith, was the other. You tried to play them both and got left."

"That's what Olga Larson told you?" asked Rose.

"You bet it's what she told me," said Dolly. "It's about half what she told me. And now you try to pull your high-and-mighty airs on me, just because Charlie and I are in love and ain't married yet. We're going to be. We're going into vaudeville as soon as this tour ends. He says the managers don't object to vaudeville teams being married. But we've got to wait till then, because theatrical managers won't have it. And yet you're walking out on me because you're too superior. . ."

"I don't feel superior," said Rose. "I'm sorry, that's all."

"Yes, you hypocrite!" said Dolly. "Go on and walk out on me. I'm glad of it."

Rose picked up her suit-case and the heap of clothes and left the room without another word.

She tried to be more astonished and indignant over Olga Larson's part in this affair than she really felt. It seemed so horribly cynical not to be surprised. But it was not cynicism; just an unconscious understanding of the fundamental processes of Olga's mind.

There was no malice in the story she had told Dolly, just after the two of them, looking through the Moorish archway in the hotel there in Dubuque, had seen Rose and Rodney deep in confidential talk. Olga had shown surprise and then, elaborately, tried to conceal it. She knew the man, all right, but hadn't expected him to follow Dane out here. Dolly told her about the note, and Olga's jealousy, which had been smoldering ever since the tour began, flared up again. Even in the days of their closest friendship—this was the way it looked to her distorted vision—Rose had never been frank with her. She had never mentioned a man named Rodney, nor even shown her a photograph. The only person Olga had known to be jealous of, was Galbraith. Her unacknowledged reason for inventing the calumny she recited so glibly for Dolly, was the hope that Dolly would go straight to Rose with it.

That couldn't fail, she thought, to break down Rose's attitude of icy indifference and precipitate a quarrel; and a quarrel was what she wanted. Because quarrels led to reconciliations. She wanted Rose to be angry with her and then forgive her, although the latter part of her hope was quite unconscious.

As I say, Rose understood. She didn't work the thing out in detail; didn't want to. But she knew that if she sought Olga out and demanded an explanation of the detestable things she'd said about her, the scene would terminate in a torrent of self-reproach from Olga, protestations of undying love, fondlings. . .

So Rose shuddered and said nothing. The only thing to do about the whole unspeakable business was, as far as possible, to disregard it.

It wasn't possible to disregard it utterly, because the story was evidently spread. She became conscious of a touch of contemptuous hostility on the part of everybody. Not on account of her moral derelictions, but because of her hypocrisy in pretending to a set of standards of breeding and behavior superior to those held by the rest of them.

Altogether it made complete and irresistible, a whole-souled loathing of the life. Her attempt to find a way to a career along this filthy stage-door alley must be confessed a total failure. She could never, she knew, nerve herself to look for another job in a musical-comedy chorus.

At the next overnight stop they made, Dolly went in to room with the duchess, and the duchess' former roommate, a fattish blonde girl with a permanent cold in the head, came in with her.

Somehow the days dragged along until the pursuing and long visible disaster finally overtook the company in Centropolis, Illinois (this is not the real name of the city, but it is no more flagrant a misnomer than the one it boasts). They played a matinée here and an evening performance, to two almost empty houses; that gave them the *coup de grace*.

There was no call posted on the bulletin board that night, and the next day, after a brisk exchange of telegrams with Chicago, the manager called the company together in one of the sample-rooms of the hotel and announced that the tour was off. He also announced, with a magnanimity that put far into the background the fact that he owed them all at least two weeks' salary, that everybody in the company would be provided with a first-class ticket for Chicago. There was nothing, except his scrupulous sense of honor, he managed to imply without saying it in so many words, to prevent his going off to Chicago all by himself and leaving them stranded here. But, though this might be good business, he was incapable of it. If they would all come down to the station at eleven o'clock, and sign a receipt discharging him from further obligations, he would see that their transportation was arranged for.

It was just after this that Rose caught a glimpse of Dolly shivering in a corner, weeping into a soiled pocket-handkerchief. The fat girl with a cold supplied her with the explanation.

Dolly's chorus-man, it seemed, had already departed on an earlier train to St. Louis, where he lived, without taking any leave of her at all.

Rose wanted to go over and try to comfort the child, but somehow she couldn't manage to. Sentimentalizing over her grief and disillusionment wouldn't do any good. The grief probably wasn't more than an inch deep anyway, and the illusions had been too tawdry to regret. As for doing anything, what was there one could do?

There wasn't much that Rose could do at any rate. Because after weeks of drifting, she'd come to a resolution.

She didn't go to the railway station to sign her receipt and get her ticket to Chicago. What was there in Chicago for her? She meant to stay, for the present, at any rate, in Centropolis. She checked her suit-case in the coat-room and, with a sensation of relief, watched the mournful company file away.

She had three dollars and some small change, and the day before her.

XVIII

The Conquest of Centropolis

Centropolis wasn't a very big town, but it had a wide, well paved street lined with stores, and a pleasant variety of gravel roads winding round hills that had neat and fairly prosperous-looking houses scattered over them. A rather dignified old court-house among the big trees of the Square proclaimed the place a county seat. It was a warm April day; the grass was green and the little leaves already were bursting out on the shrubbery.

Rose's idea was to stroll about a little and get her bearings first, and then go into one store after another on Main Street until she should find a job. She had no serious misgiving that she wouldn't get one eventually; before night, this was to say.

Her confidence sprang from two sources: one, that though inexperienced she knew she was intelligent, willing and attractive. People, she found, were apt to be disposed in her favor. The other source of her confidence was that she wasn't looking for much. She would take, for the present, anything that offered. Because any sort of work, even menial work, would be a relief after that nightmare tour. The weeks since she had left Chicago, especially the last two or three of them, seemed unreal, and the incidents of them as if they couldn't have happened. Anything that didn't involve associations with that detestable company, and the unspeakable piece they had played, would seem—well, almost heavenly. If she couldn't get a job in a store, she'd go and be a waitress at the hotel. She could make a pretty good waitress, she thought.

But her confidence was short-lived. She cut short her ramble about the streets because of the stares she attracted, and the remarks about herself that she couldn't ignore. Young men shouted at each other directing attention to her with a brutality of epithet that brought the blood to her cheeks. During all the time she had had that room on Clark Street in Chicago, through their rehearsals and that month of performances, she'd gone alone about the streets at all sort of hours, both in the theatrical part of the loop and in the district where she lived, without any molestation whatever. The small towns that she had visited with the company had been different of course. She'd been stared at in the streets and not infrequently addressed. She'd forgiven that because she was a member of the company. It was natural enough for people to stare at a girl they'd paid to see on the stage the night before, or were going to see tonight.

Now she discovered that the company had been an immense protection to her; had accounted for her, caused her to be taken, to a certain extent, for granted. The wild beast that comes to town with the circus, though an object of legitimate curiosity, does not excite the hostile and fearful speculation that he would if he were left behind after the circus had gone.

People got together in groups and nodded at her, pointed at her. A few of them leered, but more of them scowled. There seemed to be a sense of outrage that she hadn't left the town when the rest did.

There was a dry-goods store on the principal corner of the street, which she'd selected as she walked along as the place to begin her quest. She made a detour around two or three blocks in order to avoid retracing her steps down Main Street and slipped into the door of this establishment as unostentatiously as she could.

She was saved inquiring for the proprietor by the conviction that the rather dapper-looking gray-haired man who came blinking toward her in a near-sighted way as she paused in the main aisle, was he. He had a good deal of manner and was evidently proud of it. But he looked neither weak nor foolish.

"My name's Rose Stanton," she said as he came up. "I've come to see if I can get employment in your store."

His manner changed instantly. He came a step closer and stared at her with a surprise he didn't try to conceal.

"I haven't had any experience as a saleswoman," she went on, "and I know there's a lot to learn. But I'd work hard and learn as fast as. . ."

"Excuse me," he said, "but aren't you a member of that theatrical company that was here last night?"

The intensity with which he was staring at her made her look away and her eyes rested on a young man whose strong family likeness to the proprietor identified him for her as his son; he had come up and was waiting for a word with his father. At this question he stared at her too.

The older man whipped around on his son. "Clear out, Jim," he said sharply. And then to Rose: "You haven't answered my question."

"I was a member of that company," she said. "But. . ."

"We have no vacancy at present," he said sharply. "Good day."

She flinched a little but stood her ground. "I said I wasn't experienced as a saleswoman," she said, "but there are some things I know a good deal about—clothes and hats. . ."

He hadn't stayed to listen; had walked straight to the door and opened it. Reluctantly she followed him.

"There's no place," he said, "in this store, or I trust in the town either, for young women of your sort. Good day!"

Rose made five more applications for work on Main Street, all with the same result. Some of those who refused her were panicky about it; one threatened to have her put in jail. One looked knowing and after he had expressed in jocular though emphatic terms, his sense of her impossibility as a publicly acknowledged employee, intimated a desire to prosecute a personal acquaintance with her further.

She had left the first store incredulous rather than angry, under the impression that she had encountered a chance fanatic. It seemed impossible that anybody with a well-balanced mind, could treat her as if she carried contamination, merely because she had earned a living for a while in the chorus of a musical comedy. It was fortunate for her that her first applications were met by anger, rude discourtesy, and openly avowed suspicion, because this treatment roused in her, for the first time in months, a strong surge of indignation. Her blood came up after these encounters, nearer and nearer the boiling point. The man who smiled at her like a satyr, was shriveled by the blaze of her blue eyes, and was left, red-faced, blustering weakly after her.

When she walked back to the hotel along Main Street the lassitude that had so long held her half-paralyzed was gone. She was the old Rose again; the Rose whom Galbraith would have recognized.

She didn't know it. She was conscious of nothing but a hot determination that had not, as yet, even expressed itself in terms. It was just a newly kindled fire that warmed her shivering spirit; that made her fearless; in a quite unreasoning way, confident.

The only touch of self-conscious thought about her was a vague wonder at her long submission. What had she been doing all that while, drifting like that, letting herself be beaten like that, consenting to live amid the shabby degradations of the life that had surrounded her ever since the company had gone on the road? The sense of the unreality of those past weeks grew stronger. She felt like a person just waking out of a long troubled dream.

She mode her way among the loungers in the lobby of the hotel, not unmindful of their stares, but magnificently impervious to them; came up to the desk and told the clerk she wanted to see the proprietor.

"Nothing doing," said the clerk.

Then as he got the straight look of her eyes, he amended his speech a little.

"It won't do you any good to see him," he said sulkily.

"I'll see him, if you please," said Rose. "Will you have him called?"

The clerk hesitated. Stranded "actresses" weren't in the habit of talking like that. They always wanted to see the proprietor, they were always on the point of receiving an ample remittance from some generally distant place. They were often very queenly, incredibly outraged that their solvency should be questioned. But their voices never had the cool confident ring that this girl's voice had, nor the look in their eyes, the purposeful thrust.

He hesitated uncomfortably. Then his difficulty was solved for him.

"There he goes now," he said. "You can talk to him if you like."

The proprietor was sixty years old, perhaps; gray, stooped, stringy of neck. He had a short-cropped mustache, one corner of which he was always caressing with a protruding under-lip. He had a good shrewd pair of eyes, not altogether unkindly. Rose had seen him before, but hadn't known who he was.

He was making, just now, for a little office he had, that opened into the railed-off space behind the desk, and, by another door, into the corridor. He had another man with him, but it was evident that their business wasn't going to take long. The door into the corridor was left open behind them, and there Rose waited. When the other man came out, she stepped inside.

There was nothing kindly about the look the proprietor's eyes directed at her when he saw who she was. He looked up at her with a frown of resignation.

"So you didn't go to Chicago with the rest of the troupe?" he said. "That's where you made a mistake, I guess."

"I didn't want to go to Chicago," she said.

"I suppose," he drawled ironically, "you've written or telegraphed to some friends for money, and that it's surely coming, and that you want to stay here in my hotel on credit till it does. Well, there's not a chance in the world. The clerk could have told you that. I suppose he did."

"I haven't sent for money," said Rose. "There's no one I could send to. I've got to earn it for myself and I thought there was as good a chance to earn it here as in Chicago."

"Well, by God!" said the proprietor. "You've got your nerve with you at any rate. But I'll tell you, young woman, the town of Centropolis don't take kindly to the efforts of young women of your sort to make a living nor to the way they make it."

"You're wrong," said Rose, dangerously quiet, "if you think I mean to make a living in any other than a decent honest way. I have already asked for work in five places on Main Street and I have been refused as if I were the—sort of person you've just called me. I'm going to keep on until I find somebody in this town who's clean enough minded to recognize decency when he sees it. There are people like that, of course, even in Centropolis. I didn't come in here to borrow money of you, nor to ask for credit. I came to ask for a job as a waitress."

The proprietor stared at her. "Well," he said, "you are a new one on John Culver. I never got up against *your* game before."

"I haven't any game," said Rose. "I've told you the exact truth."

Culver twisted around uneasily in his chair and began biting thoughtfully on the end of a lead-pencil.

"Well," he said at last, "I'll take a chance. I'll tell you about a job I think you can get. Only it won't do you any good to use my name. If the man you go to comes to me, I can't tell him anything about you but what I know. His name's Albert Zeider and he's got a picture house three doors down the street. He's just put in a glass cage out in front, and he wants a pretty girl to sit in it and sell tickets. He hasn't been able to get anybody yet that filled the bill. So maybe he'd take a chance on you. Only, mind, don't tell him I recommended you."

"I won't," said Rose. "I won't go to him at all. I've walked the length of Main Street and back this morning, and I won't sit in Mr. Zeider's glass cage. I'll wash dishes or scrub floors, but I won't do that."

The proprietor flung out his hands with the air of a man of whom nothing more could be expected.

"Well, then," he said, "if you won't take a decent job that's offered to you. . ."

"It's not a decent job," said Rose. "Not for me; not for a girl who's looked on in this town as I am. I want work! Don't you understand?" Then, after a pause, "Won't you give it to me?"

"Well, I should say not," said John Culver. "Look here! What's the use? Suppose you are what you say. . ."

"You know I am," interrupted Rose.

"Well, I say, suppose it's true. What's the use? Do you think any decent store-keeper on Main Street would risk his reputation by giving a job to a stranded actress that had come here with a rotten show like the one you was with; or that I could have you in my dining-room? This is a respectable hotel, I tell you."

He broke off to wave his hand genially to a man who was walking slowly by the door on his way down to the dining-room.

"There!" he went on to Rose. "That's what I mean! That's Judge Granger of the Supreme Court of this state. He's come here regularly for meals, when he ain't in Springfield, for the last fifteen years. He's the biggest man in this county. Do you suppose he'd stand for it, if I asked him to give his order to a busted actress?"

"Would you stand for it if he did?" demanded Rose. "If he told you that I was all right and asked you to give me a job, would you do it?"

The proprietor laughed impatiently. "What's the good of talking nonsense?" he demanded. "Yes, I would, if that'll satisfy you. But you'd better take the next train for Chicago. And if. . ." He hesitated, stroked his mustache again with his under-lip, and went on,—"Oh, I suppose I'm a damned fool, but if a couple of dollars will help you out. . ."

"No, thank you," said Rose. "I'm going to see the judge." And she cut off John Culver's exclamation of protest by walking out of the office.

Rose went back to the desk, told the clerk she wanted dinner, and forestalled the objection she saw him preparing to make, by laying a dollar bill on the counter. He even hesitated a little over that, but he took it and gave her a quarter in change.

"That'll be all right," he said, and she went the way the judge had gone, down the corridor to the dining-room. A glance showed her where he sat, and without waiting for the assistance of the head waitress, she chose a chair near the door, facing it, and with her back to the judge.

Those were rather audacious tactics. Seventy-five cents, in the present state of her finances, was a good deal to squander on a meal. And the fact that she was openly stalking the judge might lead John Culver to give his honored patron a word of warning. But Rose didn't care. No tactics but the simplest and most direct appealed to her. When the judge finished his dinner, she would follow him to his office, wherever it might be, walk in with him, and demand a hearing. If he were forewarned, she would find some other way of getting access to him.

But, whether the proprietor was really ignorant of her plan, or whether the little scene with her in his office had shaken him so that he didn't care to try conclusions with her again, the judge was left to his fate. Rose followed him, unmolested, down the corridor and out into the street, across the road and up a flight of outside steps, to the second story of a brick building opposite.

He was fitting his key into the lock when she came up. And though he drew his eyebrows down into a frown as he looked at her, it seemed to be rather in the effort to make out who she was, than from any feeling of hostility. He asked her with a dry and rather affected judicial courtesy, what he could do for her.

"You can do me a service," said Rose, "that I don't think you will mind. Will you let me come in for about a minute and tell you what it is?"

His manner chilled a little, but his curt nod gave her permission to precede him into his office.

The outer room was bleak enough, furnished with three or four hard chairs, a table and an old black walnut desk with a typewriter on it. His secretary or stenographer was evidently still at dinner, because the room was empty.

The judge walked straight into an inner room and Rose followed him.

It was a big, rather fine-looking room, or so it looked to Rose after the places she had been seeing lately; evidently, from a beam across the middle of the ceiling, cut out of two. There was a fireplace with a fire in it, a big oak table and a number of easy chairs. There were two or three good rugs on the floor, and the walls were completely lined with books; the familiar buckram and leather-bound, red-labeled law-books that gave her memory a pang.

In these surroundings, the judge took on an added impressiveness, and he was not an unimpressive-looking man. He was not large. Nose, mouth and chin were small and rather fine, and he had the shape of head that is described as a scholar's. One might not have remarked it in the hotel dining-room, but in these surroundings, he looked altogether a judge.

But the effect of this on Rose was only to heighten her confidence. She hadn't used the dinner hour to think out what she'd say to him.

She'd been thinking of Rodney again. Somehow, just the rebirth of a sense of power in her, had brought the image of him back. She was throbbing with that sense now, and her thoughts of Rodney had given her an exhilarating idea. This man that she was about to confront was one whom Rodney had often confronted. It was before this man, on the bench of the Supreme Court, up at Springfield, that Rodney had made uncounted arguments. She would try to do as well as he did.

The judge was staring at her in growing perplexity. Who in the world could she be. What did she want? His very greatness in this little town made him accessible. It was so unthinkable a thing that any one should intrude upon his time frivolously. But this girl! She didn't belong in the town. Hadn't he seen her about the hotel yesterday, with that shabby theatrical troupe?

"You will please be brief," he said. "My time is limited."

"I'll be as brief as I can," said Rose.

He sat down in his desk chair, but she did not avail herself of the permission his half-hearted nod toward another chair accorded her; remained standing across the table from him.

"I came to Centropolis day before yesterday," said Rose, "with a theatrical company that failed. They went away this morning unpaid, with nothing but tickets to Chicago. I decided to stay here and try to get work. I applied for it at five places on Main Street this morning, and then went to Mr. Culver at the hotel. I asked him for a position as a waitress."

Already the judge was tapping his pencil.

"This doesn't concern me in the least," he said. "I have no possible employment for you. I can do nothing for you. Good day!"

"Employment isn't what I want from you," said Rose. "I'll come to what I do want in a minute."

It is safe to say that the judge hadn't been caught up with a round turn like that in years. He stared at her now in perfectly blank amazement.

"Mr. Culver," she went on, "told me why I hadn't been successful. He accused me of being the sort of person no decent employer would give work to, of being a person of bad character. I convinced him, I think, that I was not. Then he said that even though I were a perfectly honest, decent woman, he wouldn't dare put me in his dining-room. He cited you as the reason."

At that the judge suddenly went purple.

"Me!" he shouted.

The tension of Rose's body relaxed a little. A smile flickered just instantaneously over her mouth.

"He used you as an example," she explained. "He said that you were the most important person in the county; that your opinion counted for the most. He said that you were a regular patron of his hotel, and that you'd object seriously to giving your order, as he said, to a 'busted actress.'"

"That's perfectly unwarranted," fumed the judge. "Culver had no right to use my name like that. It's outrageous!"

"I hoped you'd feel that way," said Rose.

The judge pounded on the desk. "That's not what I mean. He had no right to drag me into it at all; into a miserable business like that."

"It is a miserable business," Rose assented. "It's a thoroughly contemptible business. But Mr. Culver didn't drag you into it deliberately. You were passing the door as we stood talking, and he used you for an illustration. But afterward he said that if you told him it was all right to give me a job, he would do it. That's what I have come up to ask you to do."

"That," said the judge, setting his teeth and breathing hard, "is the most monstrous piece of impudence I have ever heard of. On his part as well as yours. What have I to do with John Culver's waitresses?"

He wasn't expecting an answer to this question, but Rose had one ready for him.

"You've given him the idea, without meaning to most likely, that you wouldn't tolerate a girl among them who'd been earning her living on the stage. If that's just a stupid mistake of his, I'm asking you to tell him so."

"Well, I won't," said the judge. "The thing's preposterous. You're asking me for what amounts to a guarantee. In the first place, I don't know that you're not—after all—what you say you convinced Culver that you were not."

"I think you do," said Rose thoughtfully, with a steady look he angrily turned away from. "I think you knew, without any reason at all, just from your instinct and your experience in judging people. And if you don't know it that way, I think you can prove it to yourself by common sense. Do you think it likely that if a girl of my—appearance and—manners, had a mind to practise the—profession you've talked about, she would be here in Centropolis, fighting desperately like this, going through humiliations like this, for a chance to be a waitress in Mr. Culver's dining-room?"

She stopped there and took a good deep breath and waited. There was a solid minute of silence. The judge got up out of his chair and began pacing the room with short impatient steps. He stopped with a jerk two or three times, as if he were about to demolish her with speech, but always gave up the attempt before a word was spoken.

"Oh, I admit it's a hard case," he said at last. "You've apparently been a victim of circumstance. The people down in this part of the country are perhaps narrow. In the main it's a good sort of narrowness. It's better than the broadness of your cities. But in an isolated case it may work an injustice." Then he wheeled on her. "But I can't do anything for you. Can't you see that I can't do anything for you?"

"I don't see," said Rose, "why you can't do what I ask."

"Have it known," shouted the judge, "in this town and all over the county, and all over the Supreme Court district, as it would be in another week, that I had gone to John Culver and got a job in his hotel—the hotel where I go myself, three times a day—for a girl who got left behind by a stranded comic-opera company? Now can't you see? I'm coming up for re-election in two years."

Rose drew in a long sigh and for a moment drooped a little.

"Yes, I see," she said with a rueful little smile. They were afraid of him, and he was afraid of them.

"I'm sorry about it," said the judge. "If there's anything else I can do. . ." He put his hand tentatively in his pocket.

"No," Rose said, "that isn't what I want. Mr. Culver offered me two dollars to go away. I suppose you might offer me ten. But I'm not going. There is somebody in this town who isn't afraid of anybody, if I can only find out who that somebody is."

For a moment the judge looked annoyed; tried to collect his scattered dignity. But presently a twinkle lighted up in his eye. Then he smiled. "You might try Miss Gibbons," he said.

"Who is she?" Rose asked.

By now the judge was smiling broadly. Apparently there was something exquisitely humorous in the notion of an encounter between Rose and this lady he'd mentioned.

"She's lived," he said, "and practised gossip and millinery, for the last thirty years, up over the drug-store on the next corner. It's quite true that there's nobody in this tier of counties that she's afraid of. But I don't recommend her seriously. You will get small comfort out of her."

"All right," said Rose, "we'll see."

She walked straight from the judge's office to the stairs beside the drug-store on the next corner, which led up to Miss Gibbons' atelier. She walked fast, conserving as a precious thing that might ebb away from her, the warm feeling of indignant contempt her talk with the judge had inspired her with. He was the biggest man in this part of the state, was he! Why, he was a hollow man! A fabric of lath and plaster with no structural pillars inside! Well, if the rest of the town was afraid of him, she certainly wasn't afraid of the rest of the town.

She hadn't any thought of conciliating Miss Gibbons, of asking Miss Gibbons to give her a chance. She was going to give Miss Gibbons a chance to prove whether she was lath and plaster like the judge, or a real person with something besides her façade to hold her up.

So it wasn't at all in the manner of a disheartened applicant for work that she pushed open the glass door with *"Gibbons. Modes."* painted on it, and stepped inside.

A bell had rung somewhere in the distance as she opened the door, and there was no one in the room as she entered it. But she hadn't much time to look around—only long enough to get the impression that the place was somehow overflowing with hats—when another door opened, and a thin, gray-haired, tight little woman (she had a tight dress and tight hair, and her joints, when she moved, seemed to be tight, too) confronted her. She was unmistakably Miss Gibbons and in that first glance, Rose liked her. Her features were rather too big for her small face—a big nose not finely made, a wide thin-lipped mouth, and a long chin—and her eyes, looking very straight out through gold-rimmed spectacles, had a penetrating brightness about them that was a little formidable. It was not what one would call a good-natured face. But good-natured sentimentality was the last thing Rose was looking for.

"What can I do for you?" she asked. Her voice was as tight and brisk as the rest of her.

"I'm looking for a job," said Rose.

Miss Gibbons came a step closer and her bright look pierced a little more deeply.

"So!" she said. "You're the actress, are you?"

Rose smiled at that. "I'm not a real actress," she said, "but I'm who you mean. I was a chorus-girl with that company that broke down here."

"Why didn't you go away when the rest of them did?" the milliner demanded.

"I decided I didn't want to go on being a chorus-girl," said Rose, "and I thought there was as good a chance of getting other work here as in Chicago."

"That was a sort of fool idea, I guess, wasn't it?" Miss Gibbons suggested.

"It seems so, up to now," said Rose. "I spent the morning on Main Street without having any luck. I went to five places. . ."

"Five?" questioned Miss Gibbons. "I knew about Arthur Perkins and Sim Laidlaw and Tabby Parkes. Who were the other two?"

Rose couldn't enlighten her. She'd forgotten their names.

"I've had work offered to me," she went on, "or at least suggested. Mr. Culver at the hotel told me of a moving-picture place. . ."

"Where you could sit in that glass cage of Al Zeider's and sell tickets?" Miss Gibbons broke in. "Why didn't you take it?"

"I told Mr. Culver," said Rose, "that I'd already walked the length of Main Street and back, and that was enough for me."

"How did John Culver happen to say anything about that? How come it you were talking to him?"

"I'd asked him to hire me as a waitress," said Rose.

"And I reckon," said Miss Gibbons, "that he told you he kept a respectable hotel. He may have put some frills on it, but that's close enough to go on, isn't it?"

Rose nodded. In her relief at finding her situation so well understood, she was turning a little limp.

"Why did you come to me?" Miss Gibbons demanded. "He never would have thought of sending you here."

Rose braced up once more and told about her conversation with Judge Granger.

This time the milliner heard her through.

"And so the judge sent you to me," she said, when Rose had finished. "I suppose that was his fool idea of being funny. He thought it was a chance to get me poison mad."

Rose nodded a little wearily.

"Yes," she said, "I suppose that was it."

The milliner shot out a sharp glance at her. "Sit down," she said bruskly, and nodded to a chair.

Rose didn't much want to. Her instinct was to stay on her feet until she'd won her battle, and her fatigue only heightened it. But Miss Gibbons had given her an order rather than an invitation, and she obeyed it.

The older woman didn't sit down.

"Harvey Granger," she said thoughtfully, "will never forgive me as long as he lives, for not thinking he's a great man. That's just ridiculous, of course, because I know Harve. Years ago, you see,—so long ago that everybody's forgotten it—my father was the big man down in this part of the state. He was a circuit judge, when circuit judges amounted to something, and he was one of the best of them. But he was a fool about money and he got mixed up in things—and died. I was twenty-five years old then, and I took to hats.

"Well, Harve Granger was my father's law-clerk before father was elected judge. I used to see him night and morning. And, as I say, I know him all the way through. He knows I know him, and that's what he can't get over."

There was a little silence when she finished; a silence Rose's instinct told her not to break. Presently the little woman wheeled around on her.

"Well," she said, "you came to me anyway, though you saw the judge meant it for a joke. Why did you do that?"

"I don't know," said Rose. "I thought I would."

"And you haven't told me yet," said Miss Gibbons, "that you're really straight and respectable. What have you got to say about that?"

"Nothing much," said Rose. "I am straight and respectable. But I suppose a woman who wasn't would pretend to be. So you will have to decide about that for yourself."

"Hmph!" grunted Miss Gibbons. "I don't know why I asked a fool question like that, unless it's because, like the rest of them, I live in Centropolis. I know what you are, as well as you do yourself."

The words were brusk, and the inflection of them not much gentler, but they fell on Rose's heart like rain; like an unexpected warm little shower out of a brazen sky. She caught her breath, and, to her consternation, felt her eyes flushing up with tears. She hadn't realized the tension she had been under, until it was relaxed. She gave a shaky half-suppressed sob and then made a desperate effort to pull herself together.

"Now, look here!" said Miss Gibbons, in a tone harder and dryer than ever. "I'm not going to take you in and pay you wages just because you're a cat in a strange garret and don't know where to turn. I'm not even going to do it to spite Harve Granger. But, if you've got any sort of gumption about hats, I am going to do it, and the rest of this fool town can say what it likes and do what it pleases. So the thing for you to do is to quiet down sensibly and show me whether you can trim a hat."

It took Rose a few minutes to carry out the first part of this injunction. The rush of relief and gratitude and happiness shook her. Given *carte blanche* to design a special angel from Heaven to come down and give her just the comfort and encouragement she wanted, she couldn't have imagined one so good as Miss Gibbons,—with those keen straight-looking eyes that had observed her fellow citizens of Centropolis for the last half-century or so, not in vain; with her courageous common sense, and with that dry, cool, astringent manner, which lay with a pleasant healing sting on the lacerations of Rose's soul.

For a while she just sat still and tried to get the catch out of her breathing. At last, when she thought she could trust her voice not to break absurdly, she smiled and said:

"What sort of hat do you want me to trim? I mean, for what sort of person?"

"What sort of person!" echoed Miss Gibbons and gave Rose a rather keen look. "Why," she said, after hesitating a moment, "there's a silly old maid in this town. She ain't more than ten years younger than I am, but her hair's stayed sort of fluffy and yellow, and she's kept part of her looks, though not near as much of them as she thinks. She was a beautiful girl at twenty, I'll say that for her. None of these girls now compares with her. But she was a little too sure of herself and took too long deciding among the young men of this town, until all at once, she found that nobody wanted her. She's been trying ever since to show she doesn't care; and she pesters the life out of me twice a year trying to fit her out with a hat. I won't let her go around the streets looking like a giddy young fool, and that's what she's determined to do. So, if you can suit her *and* me, you will be doing pretty well."

The description made a picture for Rose. She saw the faded pathetic prettiness of the woman who'd looked too long and had been trying to pretend for the last fifteen years or so that she didn't care. And the picture in her mind's eye was surmounted by a hat; a hat that conceded some of the years Miss Gibbons had insisted on, and that her client was unwilling to acknowledge, and yet retained a sort of jauntiness.

She didn't know whether she could execute the thing she saw or not, out of the stock of materials at her disposal. But it hadn't cost her a thought or an effort to see the hat.

"All right," she said after a bit. "I'll see what I can do. If you'll show me where the things are. . ."

It was a much humbler sort of job, of course, designing a hat for a middle-aged village spinster, than making those dozen gowns for Goldsmith and Block had been. But this consideration never occurred to her. She found, and was not even amazed to find, the same thrill of exhilaration in conquering the small problem, that she had found in the larger one. She worked with the same swift unconscious economy of labor and materials.

At the end of two hours, she presented the result of her labors for the milliner's approval.

Miss Gibbons surveyed it with a smile of ironic appreciation.

"It isn't what I'd call a real finished job," she commented after a minute inspection of some of the details of Rose's sewing. "I wouldn't trust it in a high wind not to scatter all the way from here to the Presbyterian church. But it will certainly suit Agatha Stebbins."

She looked at it a while longer. "And I don't know," she concluded a little reluctantly, "as it'll look so all-mighty foolish on her, either. Will ten dollars a week suit you to begin on?"

"Yes," said Rose, "that will suit me very well indeed."

"All right," said Miss Gibbons. "That's settled. There's one more thing to settle now, and that's where you're going to live."

Rose contemplated this question a little blankly for a moment.

"Do you suppose," she said, "there's any place in this town where I *can* live; where they'd take a person like me? Or would it be all right, if you asked them?"

"Oh, I guess," said Miss Gibbons, "we could most likely find somebody. I'll think about it."

She gave Rose some work to do and didn't refer to the matter again till nearly six o'clock.

"I've been thinking," she said then, "that I've got room for a boarder myself. There's a little room back here that I don't use; there's a black girl does me out and cooks my dinner and supper, and I get my own breakfast. The girl could cook for two as well as one, and I guess I could feed you for two dollars a week. If that ain't satisfactory, you can just say so."

"Satisfactory!" said Rose, and once more her voice broke.

"All right," said Miss Gibbons hastily, "we'll say no more about it. That's settled. I'll send the girl to the hotel to get your bags."

JOHN GALBRAITH'S LETTER ASKING ROSE to report to him July first in New York, reached her via Portia, during the last week in June, and made an abrupt conclusion to her life at Centropolis.

Those weeks with Miss Gibbons in the millinery parlor, when she looked back on them afterward, set in as they were between that purgatorial winter and the first breathless months while she was establishing herself in New York, had a quality of happiness and peace, which she was wont to describe as heavenly.

She'd probably have taken to Miss Gibbons in any circumstance. But, coming into her life just when she did, the little woman was the shadow of a great rock to her. She was in a state, when she settled down in the milliner's spare back room over the drug-store, where all the warmer emotions seemed terrible to her. It was Rodney's love for her and hers for him, that had bruised and lacerated her; that had made the winter months a long torment, unmitigated during the last of them, by any form of adequate self-expression. The two parodies on love which had been thrust into her face just at the end, Olga Larson's inverted form of it toward herself, and Dolly's shabby little romance, had given her an absolute loathing for it. To her, in that condition, any expression of friendship that was warm and soft, and in the least sentimental, would have been almost unendurable to her. Miss Gibbons, in that acrid antiseptic way of hers, simply washed her soul in cold water and clothed it again in the garments of self-respect.

Her manner to Rose, even as their friendship ripened and grew more confident, never changed. Nor did the manner Rose adopted toward her. Their endless talks resulted in a good deal of self-revelation, but this was never direct. Miss Gibbons never again came as near to a confidential account of her life, as she did on that first afternoon, when she explained the thoroughness of her acquaintance with Judge Granger. And Rose never explained how it had happened that she was left at the mercy of the town of Centropolis by the failure of *The Girl Up-stairs* company. But she poured out for her friend a wealth of illustrative reminiscences, drawn from her childhood, her days at the university, her life on the stage; and though she was a good deal more reticent about it, she even touched on her married life with Rodney; at least, on the collateral incidents of it.

Miss Gibbons listened to all this with a hunger she didn't conceal, and this eagerness gave Rose a pretty vivid picture of the inner life the little woman had lived here in Centropolis.

If she'd been born a boy instead of a girl, she'd probably have equaled, or outstripped, Rose thought, her father's eminence. With her courage, her vitality, her fine penetrating intelligence, she'd have managed to win her way out of this stagnant little back-water of life. But, having been born a girl, brought up helpless, as became the daughter of the circuit judge, and then having had this support wrenched from under her at the critical moment, there had been nothing for her but—hats.

She'd never gone sour, at that; never, apparently, wasted any hours in repining. She'd made, after a fashion, a career of hats; had risen on them, to a position of acknowledged social consequence. There must have been disquieting echoes in her, rhythms that answered to the pulsation of an ampler life. She never could hope to get out into it, she undoubtedly knew, but she took every opportunity she could get for a glimpse at it. Rose's incursion into her life must have been a godsend to her.

She probably pieced together a pretty good picture of Rose, too. But she did this piecing in silence and kept her surmises to herself.

In a material way, her adoption of Rose was an immense success. Centropolis, when it learned the news, was thunder-struck. For a matter of hours, one might say, the town held its breath. Then it began to talk. The women began asking questions: What did the actress look like? The men offered lame descriptions. Rose had been seen, apparently, that morning on Main Street, by the entire male population, but their descriptions weren't satisfactory. Curiosity must be assuaged! But Rose never went into the stores on Main Street; never patronized the picture-show, and even had these glimpses been afforded, they'd have been pretty unsatisfactory. There was only one real way of discovering what the creature was like; discovering for yourself, that is—and hearsay evidence is notoriously unreliable; that was to buy a hat of Lizzie Gibbons.

The first daring adventurer was Agatha Stebbins. Agatha found, you will remember, the hat Rose had already designed for her. And, as Miss Gibbons caustically disclaimed the authorship of it ("I'd never have made you up a thing like that, you can believe!") and as Miss Stebbins, after a moment's hesitation, decided she adored it, another inducement, though perhaps a superfluous one, was offered for visits to the atelier.

"Of course she isn't what you could call genteel," Miss Stebbins explained, parading her acquisition, "and she's never had any advantages. And as to her moral character, I suppose the less said the better. Lizzie Gibbons can settle that question with her own conscience. But when it comes to hats she's got more gimp in her little finger than Lizzie's got in both hands. Dear, no! She's not what I call pretty. Not with a mouth like that. Of course the men. . ."

So Miss Gibbons' spring business was distended to unrecognizable proportions. Rose fitted on hats in the show-room during business hours and took a mischievous delight in the assumption of the intangible manner of a perfect shop-assistant; in saying "Yes, madam," and "No, madam," and "Will you try this, madam?" with a perfection of politeness that baffled the most determined curiosity. Miss Gibbons got as much fun out of it as she did.

The hours in the workroom were pleasant ones, too, with their perpetual reminder that the creative power that had deserted her last January, had come back. The little problems were ludicrously easy, of course but they stimulated a pleasant sense of reserve power.

She couldn't, of course, have stayed in Centropolis indefinitely. In time, that feeling of mounting energy would have driven her out in search of something that would test it.

But, when Galbraith's letter came, it took her a little aback. Miss Gibbons had brought it in; because Rose, even then, didn't go to the post-office. Miss Gibbons watched her tear open the big envelope addressed to Rose in the handwriting that always went with the California post-mark, and saw her take another unopened letter out of it. She saw the girl's face set itself in a sudden gravity; watched her with a hungry misgiving, while she read the enclosure, and felt the misgiving mount to an unhappy certainty, when Rose put it away without comment.

But Rose wasn't certain, or she felt that night when she went to bed that she was not. Galbraith's letter frightened her a little. It was a dictated letter, very stiff, wholly businesslike. It offered to make her his personal assistant at a salary of fifty dollars a week. He summarized in rather formidable terms, what her duties would be. He wished her to report to him promptly, July first, and to telegraph him at her earliest convenience, whether she accepted his offer. There was no explanation of his long delay in sending for her.

Rose had no illusions as to what its acceptance would mean. It would mean gripping life again with the full strength of both hands. It would mean many anxious days and sleepless nights. It would mean spurring herself to a high degree of competency. You didn't get fifty dollars a week for anything that was easy to do. She knew that now, by hard experience. And then the transplantation to New York would mean an end of the cool healing peace of her present life. Things would begin happening to her that she couldn't foresee nor control. Feelings would begin happening to her; the kind of feelings that scorched and terrified you. They wouldn't happen to her here in Centropolis.

She fell asleep that night under the persuasion that the thing wasn't decided; that the safe, quiet, peaceful way was still open to her. But when she awakened in the morning, she knew it was not.

"I surmise," said Miss Gibbons that morning at breakfast, "that you're figuring to go away."

Rose smiled and sighed. "I don't know how you guess things like that," she said, "but it's true. I must be in New York on the first of July."

"Well, the sooner the quicker," said Miss Gibbons dryly. "You came all at once and I guess it's just as well you should go the same way. I guess neither of us is sorry you came, and I hope you'll never be sorry you went."

That was her nearest approach to an affectionate farewell. Rose managed to express her affection and gratitude a little more adequately, but not much. "It isn't the end of us, you know," she concluded. "You're coming to see me in New York."

Miss Gibbons smiled with good-humored skepticism at that.

Rose telegraphed Galbraith that morning, and she took the noon train for St. Louis. She needed a day or two there to make the modest supplements to her wardrobe that her savings permitted.

BOOK IV
THE REAL ADVENTURE

I

The Tune Changes

John Williamson's doctor packed him off to Carlsbad just about the time that Rose achieved the conquest of Centropolis (along in April, 1914, that was). Violet and their one child, a girl of twelve, went along with him to keep him company; at rather long range, it seemed, because they were both in Paris on the first of August, when the war broke out, and John spent six frantic days getting into Switzerland and out again into France, before his attempt to join them was successful. They had run the full gamut of refugees' experiences, by the time they got to England and secured accommodations on a liner to New York, and the tale got an added touch from the stratagem Violet employed in successfully bringing off all her new French frocks.

It took just two hours' steady talking to tell the story, and Violet figured that during the first week after her return to Chicago, she told it on an average of three times a day. So that by the time she could manage a day for motoring out to Lake Forest to see Constance Crawford, she was ready to talk about something else.

Constance had lately had her fourth—and she asserted, last—baby, and wasn't seeing anybody yet, except intimates, one at a time; and she relaxed a little deeper, with a sigh of relief, into her cushioned chair, when Violet said:

"The same things happened to us that happened to everybody else, so you don't have to hear them. Oh, it was nice, in a way, being separated from poor John when the thing happened, because—well, he hasn't got over it yet. He's still more as he was when we were first engaged, than he's ever been since. And at thirty-seven that's something! And then it's a satisfaction about the clothes. It seems as if I must have had a premonition that something was going to happen, because I bought absolutely everything I wanted.

"Of course it was an awful moment when John said we couldn't take anything but hand-luggage. But I got three perfectly enormous straw-telescopes—you know the kind—about four feet long, and then we left everything else behind, except a tooth-brush and a comb apiece. And what with that and the biggest hat box in the world—my, but it's lucky hats are small!—we managed it.

"But all the stuff about having your automobile taken away and riding in a cart, and thinking you're going to be arrested as a spy, and living for days on milk-chocolate and *vin ordinaire*, you've heard it all a hundred times already, so we'll talk about something else."

"I never heard anything so heroic in my life," Constance said. "But you don't need to be, because I'm perishing for details.—Unless," she went on, "it isn't heroism at all, but something else you want to talk about."

"Just my luck!" said Violet. "I thought I was going to get away with that. There *is* something I'm frantic with curiosity about, and you're the first person I've seen I could ask. I spent two hours trying to get up my courage with Frederica, but I couldn't. Do you know anything about them—Rose and Rodney? Does any one know anything about her since she disappeared from the Globe?"

"Why, I fancy *they* do," said Constance, "Rodney and Frederica. I don't know just why I think so. Frank sees Rodney every day or two at lunch time at the club; says he seems all right. He's working terribly hard. And the money he's making! Frank says he's a regular robber in the fees he asks—and gets. He says he speaks of Rose once in a while, and not—at least not exactly, as if she were dead. You know what I mean! Just in that maddening, matter-of-course way, as if everybody knew all about her.

"Frederica won't talk about her at all. I mean, she won't start the subject, and nobody has the nerve to start it with her. Freddy can be like that, you know. She'd make a perfectly wonderful queen—did you ever think of that? Of England. Harriet's the only one who'd talk, and of course she's gone back. You knew that, didn't you? Oh, but naturally, since you've talked to Freddy."

Violet nodded. "It all sounded so exactly like Harriet," she said, "as Freddy told about it. No confidences, no flutters. She didn't even seem interested until the day England went in. And then at lunch that day, she said to Frederica, 'I've just cabled Tony that I'm coming back on the next boat. And I telephoned Rodney just now, to find out what the next boat for Genoa was, or Naples, and get me a stateroom. Lend me Marie, will you, to help pack? Because I'll probably have to take the five-thirty.' Harriet all over. Well, on the whole, I'm glad."

"Oh, yes," said Constance. "She'd always be at a loose end in this country. She doesn't believe in divorce. She might, of course, if she fell in love with another man over here. But that's not likely to happen. And she can't stand America any more. So even an unsuccessful marriage over there, especially if Italy gets drawn into the war, and her man gets. . ."

"Constance!" cried Violet, horrified.

"Oh, not necessarily killed," Constance went on. "Crippled or something, or even if he really got interested in the profession of being a soldier. She's done well to go back to him."

"Anyway, that wasn't what I meant," said Violet. "I meant I was glad for Rodney and—Rose. Mind you, I don't *know* a single thing. But I've just got a hunch that with Harriet off the board, it will be a little more possible for those two to get together."

Constance looked at her intently. "You've changed your tune," she said. "I thought you were through with Rose for good and all. I thought what you were rooting for was a divorce and a fresh start for Rodney."

"I thought so, too," said Violet, "until I saw her."

"Saw her!" Constance cried. "Where? When?"

"In New York on the way home," said Violet.

"Well—tell me all about it," said Constance, when she saw Violet wasn't going on of her own accord. "You, pretending you wanted to know about everything, and pretending to be a heroine for not telling me all about being a refugee! What is she doing? What did she look like? What did she say?"

"You've changed your tune, too," said Violet. "Because you were through with her just as much as I was. You didn't want to hear anything more about her. Of course she could ran away and go on the stage if she liked, you said, but she'd better not try to come back."

Constance pointed out that she hadn't, as yet, expressed the hope that Rodney would make it up with her. But she pleaded guilty to a strong curiosity.

"Well, I can't tell you much," said Violet. "John and I were coming down Fifth Avenue in a taxi one afternoon, and were stopped by the traffic at Forty-fourth Street. And right there, in another taxi, was Rose. I didn't see her till just as we got the whistle to go ahead. I was so surprised I could only grab John and tell him to look. I did shriek at her at last, and she saw us and lighted up and smiled. Just that old smile of hers, you know. But her car was turning west, down past Sherry's, and we were going straight ahead and we weren't quick enough to tell the chauffeur to turn, too. We did turn on Forty-third and came around the block, and of course we missed her.

"We went to three musical shows in the next two days, in the hope of spotting her in the chorus. But she wasn't in any of them, and then I simply dragged John home. There was no way of finding her of course, nor of her finding us, because John's given up the Holland House at last and taken to the Vanderbilt. But it was rather maddening."

"Well, I don't know," said Constance. "Oh, yes, maddening of course, because one would be curious. But that sort of curiosity might prove pretty expensive if you gratified it. Talk about the clutch of a drowning person! It's nothing to the clutch of a *déclassée* woman. And if she's been somebody once who really mattered, and somebody you were really fond of. . . Because it *is* no use. They can't ever come back."

Violet stirred in her chair. "Of course we're all perfectly good Christians," she observed ironically. "And once a week we say 'Forgive us our debts,' besides teaching it to the kids."

Constance broke in on her hotly. "Oh, come, Violet! You know it's not a question of forgiveness. I don't claim any moral superiority over Rose. I'm just talking about her social possibility. A person who does an outrageous thing, knowing it's outrageous, just because he—or she—wants to do it, can be downright immoral without being impossible. But a person who's done the other sort of thing, a shabby thing—and what Rose did was shabby—will always be on the defensive about it. They can't let it alone. They're always making references you can't ignore; always seeing references in perfectly harmless things that other people say. And the only society where they're ever happy, is that of a lot of other people with shady, shabby things that *they're* on the defensive about. And they all get together and call it Bohemia. And they sprawl around in studios and talk about sex and try to feel superior and emancipated. Well, maybe they are. All I say is they don't belong with us. Oh, you know it's true! You hate that as much as I do."

"Oh, yes," said Violet. "Only, since I've seen Rose—even for that minute—it doesn't seem possible to apply it to her. You know, I don't believe she's on the stage any more."

Constance asked with good-humored satire, "Why? From the way she looked in the taxi-cab?"

"Yes," said Violet. "Just from that. There she was in an open taxi, on Fifth Avenue, at half past four in the afternoon, and she didn't look somehow, as if how she looked mattered. She wasn't on parade a bit. She looked smart and successful, but busy. Not exactly irritated at being held up in the block, but keen to get out of it. The way Frank or John would look on the way to a directors' meeting. And the way she smiled when she saw us. . . It's not quite exactly her old smile, either, but it's just as fascinating. It pleased her to see us all right. But as for her caring a rap what we thought—well, you couldn't imagine it. Defensive indeed! And poor old John just about went out of his head with disappointment when we lost her."

"Oh, I'll never deny she's a charmer," said Constance. "All the same. . ."

"You wait till you see her!" said Violet.

Violet's report of the glimpse she had had of Rose, together with what were felt to be the rather amusingly extravagant set of deductions she had made from it, spread in diminishing ripples of discussion through all their circle. And then, concentrically, into wider circles. Most of their own intimate group took Constance's attitude. Forced to concede a lively curiosity as to what had become of Rose, they still professed that the way of discretion lay not in gratifying it; at least not at first-hand. When they were in New York, they kept an eye open for a sight of her, on the stage and elsewhere, and an alert ear for news, finding a sort of fearful joy in wondering what they would do if an encounter took place. They were mildly derisive with Violet over her *volte-face*.

Secretly, Violet was a good deal closer to agreeing with them than she'd admit. For, as the effect of her encounter lost its vividness, with the recession of the encounter itself, she began to suspect that she had gone unwarranted lengths in her interpretations from it. But under fire, she stuck to her guns. Her husband, who delighted in her public attitude, was amazed when she rounded upon him in their domestic sanctuary, and emphatically took the other side. In his disgust, he made a very penetrating observation, whose cogency Violet realized, though she loftily ignored it at the time it was uttered. But three or four nights later, at an opera dinner at the Heaton-Duncans, she fired it off shamelessly, as a shot out of her own locker.

"It's all very well," she exploded, "to say that Rose can't come back. But as a matter of fact she's never been out of it. At least the hole she left has never closed up. You all agree that she's to be forgotten and treated as a regrettable incident, but you keep on talking about her. It's like Roosevelt. There she is all the time."

She didn't dare catch John's eye for the next twenty minutes, but she knew precisely, without looking, the exasperated quality of his stare.

It was true. They couldn't let her alone. Speculation flared up again, and this time with a justifiable basis, when it became known that Rodney had bought the McCrea house; bought it outright, for cash, with its complete contents.

Of course everybody knew that Rodney was getting rich. And he was doing it, as Frank Crawford pointed out to Constance, with precisely the same contemptuous disregard of money that he had shown before his marriage.

"He doesn't care what he charges, and he didn't care then. Only then it was out of the little end of the horn, and now it's out of the big. And the thing that seems to make him particularly wild is that the higher the price he puts on his opinions, the more people there are who think that nobody's opinion but his is any good. So he just grins at them and goes up another notch. He's no better a lawyer, he says, than he was when his practise brought him in ten thousand a year. Of course he is a better lawyer. He's getting better all the time. He does deliver the goods. And fighting out these great big cases really educates a man. You can't be really first-class unless you've got first-class things to do. And down inside Rodney knows that as well as anybody.

"Only, with all his money, after the way he's talked about that house— the way he's damned it and made fun of it, what did he want to go and buy it for?"

Constance had an idea he'd got it at a bargain. The McCreas had made a flying trip home just to sell it. Their investments had gone off, it seemed, still further, and besides, Florence had at last found something in the world to be in earnest about, and that was in France; the American hospital. Florence had already taken an emergency training course in nursing. Her husband, whose one marked talent was that of a chauffeur, was going to drive a motor ambulance, and they were both on fire to get back to Paris into the thick of things. Almost any round sum, in absolutely spot cash, would satisfy them. So Rodney, too busy with other things to take the trouble to invest his money, would have been in a position to get the house cheap. It was Constance's opinion that he had.

"Do you know anybody in the world," her husband demanded, "less likely to be interested in a bargain than Rodney? Or to pick a thing up because it is cheap?"

"Well, then," Constance said, "you must think he's expecting Rose, sometime or other, to come back to him. Because if he meant to get a divorce and marry some one else, he certainly wouldn't want to live in that house with her. He'd want as few reminders as possible, not as many. And yet, it was Rose herself, according to Harriet, who was so anxious, toward the last, to get rid of the place. So there you are! It's a mystery any way you take it."

John Williamson said he understood, though when Violet pressed him for an explanation he was a little vague.

"Why," he said, "it's just a polite way of telling us all to go to the devil. He knows we're all talking our heads off about him, and sympathizing with him, and wondering what he's going to do, and he buys that house to serve notice that he's going to stay put. Business as usual at the old stand. I shouldn't be surprised if he meant the same message for Rose. That is to say, that the place will always be there for her to come back to."

Outside their immediate circle, no such imaginative explanations were resorted to. Rose was coming back of course. And the interesting theme for speculation was what would happen to her when she did. Would she try to take her old place; ignore the past; treat that outrageous escapade with the Globe chorus as if it had never happened? And if she did try to do that, could she succeed? It all depended on what a few people did. If they, the three or four supremely right ones, were to acquiesce in this treatment of the situation, Rose could, more or less, get away with it. Although even then, things could never be quite the same.

But the sterility of these speculations gradually became apparent as the winter months slipped away and Rose did not come back. It was felt, though such a feeling would have looked absurd if put into words, that by failing to come when the stage was set for her, as by Rodney's act in purchasing the McCrea house it was, missing her cue like that, letting them, with such a lot of solemn thought, discuss and prepare their attitudes toward her, all in vain, she had, somehow, aggravated her original offense in running away.

And, just as suddenly as they had begun talking about her, they stopped. Rodney and the twins, living alone in the perfect house, under the ministrations of a housekeeper, a head nurse and an undiminished corps of servants, came to be accepted as a fact that could be mentioned without any string of commiserations tied to it. Their world wagged on as usual. If, as John Williamson said, the hole where Rose had been torn out of it had never been closed up, people managed to walk around the edge of it with an apparently complete unawareness that it was there. There were fresher themes for gossip:

Hermione Woodruff's amazing marriage, for example, to a dapper little futurist painter named Bunting, ten years, the uncharitable said, younger than she was. And then the Randolphs! After all the thrilling events of their romance, were they drifting on the reefs? There were straws that indicated the wind was blowing that way.

This was the state of things when Jimmy Wallace threw his bomb.

There was always a warm, corner in Jimmy Wallace's bachelor heart for youth, and innocence, and enthusiasm. Especially for young girls who were innocent and enthusiastic. But since he suspected himself of a tendency to idealize these qualities, even to sentimentalize upon them, he generally kept a cautious distance off. Rose, with the bloom that was on her, and the glow that radiated from her the night he was introduced to her at a dinner party at the Williamsons', had struck him—he was unconscious of this mental process no doubt—as a person whom it would be difficult, at close range, to remain quite level-headed about.

Consequently, though his and Rodney's common friendship for the Lakes had drawn him rather intimately into their circle, his attitude toward Rose herself throughout had remained deliberately detached and impersonal. He was not in the least priggish about it. He was quite willing to let it appear that he liked her and to admit that she liked him. But their talk had always been not only objective, but about objects comparatively remote; chorus-girls, for example, and Norse sagas, to take at random two of his wide assortment of hobbies.

He never felt himself in any danger of idealizing Violet Williamson or Bella Forrester, and they, along with their respective husbands, were the nearest approach to intimates he had in that segment of society which gets itself spelled with a capital S.

Violet's attitude toward Rose, as revealed to him at the little dinner following the Williamsons' discovery of Rose in the Globe chorus, had not in the least surprised him. For, with her husband he had recognized in her biting contempt of the thing the girl had done, the typical attitude of her class. He didn't do Society very much, but he dipped expertly now and then. He understood the class—loyalty that is woven into all their traditions, and knew how violently it was outraged by Rose's inexplicable bolt.

But, as I said, he went home after that dinner, rather mournful over Violet's failure to see an aspect of the thing which, it seemed to him, should have been apparent to anybody: this was Rose's courage in actually doing the thing. The idea that had evidently prompted the act was a perfectly familiar guest at their tea-tables. Rose wouldn't have had to go to "that votes-for-women mother of hers" to pick up the notion of the desirability of economic independence for women. But, instead of playing with the idea, Rose had gripped it in both hands and gone through with it; and at what cost of resolution and courage Jimmy was perhaps the only one of her friends capable of forming an adequate conception. But he'd have thought that even Violet might be expected to see that a mere petulant restlessness wouldn't have carried her through; might have admitted, if only in parenthesis, the gameness the girl had shown.

She'd made no attempt to get the cards stacked in her favor, as she might so easily have done. She must have thought of coming to him for advice and help; must have known how gladly he'd give it. A note from him to Goldsmith would have spared her untold terrors and uncertainties. Yet she had denied herself that help; gone ahead and done the thing on her own.

He could imagine the sort of test Galbraith had put her to before giving her a job at all. He'd seen inexperienced girls applying for positions in the chorus. He knew the sort of work that lay behind her advancement to the sextette. He knew that her presence there on the stage of the Globe the opening night, unrecognized by any one in the company as anybody except Doris Dane of nowhere, represented a solid achievement that a girl with Rose's background and training might be proud of.

For Jimmy it had stamped her, once and for all, as sterling metal; as one who, however mistaken her judgments, or misguided her actions—admitting for the sake of argument that they were misguided—must be taken seriously; admitted to be the real thing. She'd given indisputable guarantees of good faith.

There was no good, of course, getting warm over the flippant cynicisms of her former friends. There was no use even in trying to make them understand how the thing looked to him. But there crystallized in him a wish that he might some day see Rose's critics fluttering about her and, as it were, eating out of her hand. He used to amuse himself by arranging all sorts of extravagant settings for this picture. He never included Rodney in this vengeance, although he felt sure—indeed Rodney had practically admitted as much to him—that it had been her husband's disapproval, rather than the miscellaneous gossip of society at large, which had driven her from the security and promise of the Globe to the exiguities of a fly-by-night road company. Rodney never brought up the subject again after his return from Dubuque, though it soon became plain enough without that, that his journey had accomplished nothing.

Jimmy kept track of the company's route after that, through the list of bookings printed in his theater weekly, and when he learned that the tour had been abandoned, he dropped in one night at the Globe on the off-chance that she might have come back and got herself reinstated in the Number One company, which was still doing a prosperous business.

He didn't expect to find her there; hardly hoped to. A somewhat better chance was that he might find Alec McEwen in the lobby, and that if little Alec were properly primed with alcohol and led to a discussion of the collapse of the road company, he might volunteer some scrap of information about her.

Little Alec was found in the lobby, right enough, and properly primed in the bar next door, and he described very vigorously, the disgust of Block's brother-in-law over the lemon the astute partners had sold him; for real money, too. But not a word did little Alec offer about Rose.

It was Jimmy's practise to make two professional visits to New York every year; one in the autumn, one in the spring, in order that he might have interesting matters to write about when the local theatrical doings had been exhausted.

On his first trip after Rose's disappearance, he went faithfully to every musical show in New York, and, as far as Rose was concerned, drew blank. He'd have taken more active measures for finding her; would have made inquiries of people he knew, had it not been for a sort of morbid delicacy about interfering in a concern that not only was none of his, but that was supremely the concern of Rodney Aldrich, his friend.

But from his spring pilgrimage, he came back wearing a deep-lying and contented smile, and a few days later, after a talk over the telephone with Rodney, he headed a column of gossip about the theater, with the following paragraph:

"*Come On In*, as the latest of the New York revues is called, is much like all the others. It contains the same procession of specialty-mongers, the same cacophony of rag-time, the same gangway out into the audience which refreshes tired business men with a thrilling, worm's-eye view of dancing girls' knees *au naturel*. And up and down this straight and narrow pathway of the chorus there is the customary parade of the same haughty beauties of Broadway. Only in one item is there a deviation from the usual formula: the costumes. For several years past, the revues at this theater (the Columbian) have been caparisoned with the decadent colors and bizarre designs of the exotic Mr. Grenville Melton. I knew there had been a change for the better as soon as I saw the first number, for these dresses have the stimulating quality of a healthy and vigorous imagination, as well as a vivid decorative value. They are exceedingly smart, of course, or else they would never do for a Broadway revue, but they are also alive, while those of Mr. Melton were invariably sickly. Curiously enough, the name of the new costume designer has a special interest for Chicago. She is Doris Dane, who participated in *The Girl Up-stairs* at the Globe. Miss Dane's stage experience here was brief, but nevertheless her striking success in her new profession will probably cause the formation of a large and enthusiastic 'I-knew-her-when' club."

Jimmy expected to produce an effect with it. But what he did produce exceeded his wildest anticipations. The thing came out in the three o'clock edition, and before he left the office that afternoon (he stayed a little late, it is true, and it wasn't his "At home" to press agents either) he had received, over the telephone, six invitations to dinner; three of them for that night.

He declined the first two on the ground of an enormous press of work incident to his fresh return from a fortnight in New York. But when Violet called up and said, with a reference to a previous engagement that was shamelessly fictitious:

"Jimmy, you haven't forgotten you're dining with us tonight, have you? It's just us, so you needn't dress," he answered:

"Oh, no, I've got it down on my calendar all right. Seven-thirty?"

Violet snickered and said: "You wait!—Or rather, don't wait. Make it seven."

Jimmy was glad to be let off that extra half-hour of waiting. He was impatient for the encounter with Violet—a state of mind most rare with him. He meant to wring all the pleasure out of it he could by way of compensating himself for that other dinner when Violet had decided that all Rodney's most intimate friends ought really to be told what Rose had done, in order that they might be scrupulous enough in avoiding subjects which he might take as a reference to his disgrace.

Violet said, the moment he appeared in the drawing-room doorway, "John made me swear not to let you tell me a word until he came in. He's simply burbling. He's out in the pantry now mixing some extra-special cocktails—with his own hands, you know—to celebrate the event. But there's one thing he won't mind your telling me, and that's her address. I'm simply perishing to write her a note and tell her how glad we are."

Jimmy made a little gesture of regret. He'd have spoken too, but she didn't give him time.

"You don't mean to tell me," she cried, "that you didn't find out where she lived while you were right there in New York!"

John came in just then with the cocktails and Violet, turning to him tragically, repeated, "He doesn't even know where she lives!"

"Oh, I'm a boob, I know," said Jimmy. "Give me a cocktail. A telephone's the driest thing in the world to talk into. But, as I told the other five. . ."

Violet frowned as she echoed, "The other five—what?"

Jimmy turned to John Williamson with a perfectly electric grin.

"The other five of Rose Aldrich's friends—and yours," he said, "who called me up this afternoon and invited me to dinner, and asked for her address so that they could write her notes and tell her how glad they were."

John said, "Whoosh!" all but upset his tray and slammed it down on the piano, in order to leave himself free to jubilate properly. With solemn joy he ceremoniously shook hands with Jimmy.

Violet stood looking at them thoughtfully. A little flush of color was coming up into her face.

"You two men," she said, "are trying to act as if I weren't in this; as if I weren't just as glad as you are, and hadn't as good a right to be. John here," this was to Jimmy, "has been gloating ever since he came home with the paper. And you. . . Did you mean me by that snippy little thing you said about the 'I-knew-her-when' club? Oh, it was fair enough. I'm glad you said it. Because some people we know have been downright catty about her. But you both know perfectly well that I've stood up for her ever since last fall when we came through New York."

John grinned. "When you saw her," he pointed out, "riding down Fifth Avenue in a taxi, in an expensive dress. . ."

"It wasn't. I didn't see what she had on. I just saw that she looked. . ."

"Successful," John interrupted. But, meeting her eye, he apologized hastily and withdrew the word. His gale of spirits had blown him a little too far.

"I saw," said Violet with dignity, "that she looked busy and cheerful, as if she knew, in her own mind, that she was all right. And I was glad for her, and for us. Because you can say what you like, you can't do anything with the people who have made mistakes and know it, and are always on the defensive about them. When I saw she didn't feel like that, that was enough for me. And," she fairly impaled John Williamson now with her eye, "and you know it."

It was an able summary of her public attitude since the encounter on Fifth Avenue, and her look at her husband relegated any private observations of hers at variance with it into the limbo, not of things forgotten, but of things undone, unsaid, dissolved by the sheer force of their unfitness to exist, into the breath that begot them.

"You're quite right about it," said Jimmy. "We men are sentimentalists, as long as things don't come home. But when they do, we're as uncomfortable about penitents as anybody, and we give them as wide a berth."

"You're my friend, Jimmy," she said. "There's dinner! But you won't be allowed to eat. You'll have to begin at the beginning and tell us all about her! Though I don't see," she went on, "how you can know very much more than you put in the paper, if you didn't even find out where she lived."

Jimmy, his effect produced, his long meditated vengeance completed by the flare of color he'd seen come up in Violet's cheeks, settled down seriously to the telling of his tale, stopping occasionally to bolt a little food just before his plate was snatched away from him, but otherwise without intermission.

He'd suspected nothing about the costumes on that opening night of *Come On In*, until a realization of how amazingly good they were, made him search his program. The line "Costumes by Dane," had lighted up in his mind a wild surmise of the truth, though he admitted it had seemed almost too good to be true. Because the costumes were really wonderful. He tried to tell them how wonderful they were, but Violet seemed to regard this as a digression. She wanted facts.

"Anyhow," he put in in confirmation, "there wasn't a single paper the next day that didn't feature the costumes in speaking of the performance. They were the one unqualified hit of the show."

He cast about in his mind, he said, for some way of finding out who Dane really was. And having learned that Galbraith was putting on the show at the Casino, and having reflected that he was as likely to know about Rose as anybody, he looked him up.

"Galbraith, you know," he explained, "is the man who put on *The Girl Up-stairs* here at the Globe, winter before last."

Galbraith proved a mine of information—no, not a mine, because you had to dig to get things out of a mine. Galbraith was more like one of those oil-wells that is technically known as a gusher. He simply spouted facts about Rose and couldn't be stopped. She was his own discovery. He'd seen her possibilities when she designed and executed those twelve costumes for the sextette in *The Girl Up-stairs*. He'd brought her down to New York to act as his assistant. She worked for Galbraith the greater part of last season. Jimmy had never known of anybody having just that sort of job before. Galbraith, busy with two or three productions at once, had put over a lot of the work of conducting rehearsals on her shoulders. He'd get a number started, having figured out the maneuvers the chorus were to go through, the steps they'd use and so on, and then Rose would actually take his place; would be in complete charge of the rehearsal as the director's representative, while he was off doing something else.

It must have been an extraordinarily interesting job, Jimmy thought, and evidently she'd got away with it, since Galbraith spoke of the loss of her with unqualified regret.

The costuming, last season, had been a side issue, at the beginning at least, but she'd done part of the costumes for one of his productions, and they were so strikingly successful that Abe Shuman had simply snatched her away from him.

"The funny thing is the way she does them," Jimmy said. "Everybody else who designs costumes, just draws them; dinky little water-colored plates, and the plates are sent out to a company like The Star Costume Company, and they execute them. But Rose can't draw a bit. She got a manikin—not an ordinary dressmaker's form, but a regular painter's manikin with legs, and made her costumes on the thing; or at least cut out a sort of pattern of them in cloth. But somehow or other, the designing of them and the execution are more mixed up together by Rose's method than by the orthodox one. She wanted to get some women in to sew for her, and see the whole job through herself; deliver the costumes complete, and get paid for them. But it seems that the

Shumans, on the side, owned The Star Company and raked off a big profit on the costumes that way. I don't know all the details. I don't know that Galbraith did. But, anyhow, the first thing anybody knew, Rose had financed herself. She got one of those rich young bachelor women in New York to go into the thing with her, and organized a company, and made Abe Shuman an offer on all the costumes for *Come On In*. Galbraith thinks that Abe Shuman thought she was sure to lose a lot of money on it and go broke and that then he could put her to work at a salary, so he gave her the job.

"But she didn't lose. She evidently made a chunk out of it, and her reputation at the same time."

Violet was immensely thrilled by this recital. "Won't she be perfectly wonderful," she exclaimed, "for the Junior League show, when she comes back!"

Jimmy found an enormous satisfaction in saying, "Oh, she'll be too expensive for you. She's a regular robber, she says."

"She *says*!" cried Violet. "Do you mean you've talked with her?"

"Do you think I'd have come hack from New York without?" said Jimmy. "Galbraith told me to drop in at the Casino that same afternoon. Some of the costumes were to be tried on, and either 'Miss Dane' or some one of her assistants would be there. Probably she herself, though he knew she was dreadfully busy.

"Well, and she came. I almost fell over her out there in the dark, because of course the auditorium wasn't lighted at all. I'll admit she rather took my breath, just glancing up at me, and peering to make out who I was, and then her face going all alight with that smile of hers. I didn't know what to call her, and was stammering over a mixture of Miss Dane and Mrs. Aldrich, when she laughed and held out a hand to me and said she didn't remember whether I'd ever called her Rose or not, but she'd like to hear some one call her that, and wouldn't I begin."

"And of course," said Violet, "you fell in love with her on the spot."

"No, that wasn't the spot," said Jimmy. "It was where she stood on the Globe stage, the opening night of *The Girl Up-stairs*, when she caught my eye and gave a sort of little gasp, and then went on with her dance as if nothing had happened that mattered to her. I saw then that she had more sand than I knew was in the world."

"And all your pretending that night you were here, then," said Violet, "all that stuff about an amazing resemblance and a working hypothesis. . ."

"All bunk," said Jimmy. "I'd have gone a lot further if there'd been any use."

"All right," said Violet. "I'll forgive you, if you'll tell me every word she said."

Jimmy explained that there hadn't been any chance to talk much. The costumes began coming up on the stage just then (on chorus-girls, of course) and she was up over the runway in a minute, talking them over with Galbraith. "When she'd finished, she came down to me again for a minute, but it was hardly longer than that really. She said she wished she might see me again, but that she couldn't ask me to come to the studio, because it was a perfect bedlam, and that there was no use asking me to come to her apartment, because she was never there herself these days, except for about seven hours a night of the hardest kind of sleep. If I could stay around till her rush was over. . . But then, of course, she knew I couldn't."

"And you never thought of asking her," Violet wailed, "where the apartment was, so that the rest of us, if we were in New York, could look her up, or write to her from here?"

"No," said Jimmy. "I never thought of asking for her address. But it's the easiest thing in the world to get it. Call up Rodney. He knows. That's what I told the other five."

"What makes you think he knows?" Violet demanded. "We thought he knew about that other thing, but I don't believe he did."

"Well, for one thing," said Jimmy, "when Rose was asking for news of all of you, she said 'I hear from Rodney regularly. Only he doesn't tell me much gossip.'"

"*Hears* from him!" gasped Violet. "*Regularly!*" She was staring at Jimmy in a dazed sort of way. "Well, does she write to him? Has she made it up with him? Is she coming back?"

"I suppose you can just hear me asking her all those questions? Casually, in the aisle of a theater, while she was getting ready for a running jump into a taxi?"

The color came up into Violet's face again. There was a maddening sort of jubilant jocularity about these men, the looks and almost winks they exchanged, the distinctly saucy quality of the things they said to her.

"Of course," she said coolly, "if Rose had told me that she heard from Rodney regularly, although he didn't send her much of the gossip, I shouldn't have had to ask her those questions I'd have known from the way she looked and the way her voice sounded, whether she was writing to Rodney or not and whether she meant to come back to him or not; whether she was ready to make it up if he was—all that. Any woman who knew her at all would. Only a man, perfectly infatuated, grinning. . . See if you can't tell what she looked like and how she said it."

Jimmy, meek again, attempted the task.

"Well," he said, "she didn't look me in the eye and register deep meanings or anything like that. I don't know where she looked. As far as the inflection of her voice went, it was just as casual as if she'd been telling me what she'd had for lunch. But the quality of her voice just— richened up a bit, as if the words tasted good to her. And she smiled just barely as if she knew I'd be staggered and didn't care a damn. There you are! Now interpret unto me this dream, oh, Joseph."

Violet's eyes were shining. "Why, it's as plain!" she said. "Can't you see that she's just waiting for him; that she'll come like a shot the minute he says the word? And there he is, eating his heart out for her, and in his rage charging poor John perfectly terrific prices for his legal services, when all he's got to do is to say 'please,' in order to be happy."

There was a little silence after that. Then:

"Don't you suppose," she went on, "there's something we can do?"

A supreme contentment always made John Williamson silent. He'd been beaming at Jimmy all through the dinner, guarding him tenderly against interruptions, with pantomimic instructions to the servants. If the vague look in Jimmy's eyes suggested the want of a cigarette, John nodded one up for him. He didn't ask a question. Evidently, between Jimmy and Violet, the story was being elicited to his satisfaction. But it was amazing how quickly that last words of his wife's snatched him out of that beatific abstraction.

"No, there is not," he said.

The tone of his voice was a good deal more familiar to his fellow directors in some of his enterprises, than it was to his wife. She looked at him as if she couldn't quite believe she'd understood.

"There is not what?" she asked.

"There is not a thing that we can do or are going to do about Rose and Rodney. We did something once before and made a mess of it. This time we're going to let them alone. They're both of age and of sound mind, and they've got each other's addresses. If they want to get together again, they will."

"I've had a perfectly bang-up evening," said Jimmy to Violet a little later when he took his leave.

"I know you have," she said dryly. Then, with a change of manner, "But I have, too, Jimmy. You believe that, don't you?"

"Sure I do," he said, and shook hands with her all over again. Violet was a good sort.

Riding home in the elevated train, Jimmy Wallace hummed what he conceived to be a tune. And when he did that. . . !

II

A Broken Parallel

None of the speculative explanations Rodney's friends advanced for his having bought that precious solemn house of the McCreas, together with all its rarified esthetic furniture, exactly covered the ground. He didn't buy it in the expectation that Rose was coming back to live in it, and still less with the even remote notion of finding a successor to her. He hadn't bought it because it was a bargain. He had very little idea whether it was a bargain or not. And if there was a grain of truth in John Williamson's explanation, Rodney was only vaguely aware of it.

He'd have said, if he'd set about formulating an explanation, that he bought the house as a result of eliminating the alternatives to buying it. Florence meant to sell it to somebody, and if he didn't buy it, he'd have to move out. Rather disingenuously, he represented to himself that his dislike of moving out sprang from the trouble that would be involved in finding some other place to live in, furnishing it, reorganizing his establishment. Really, he hadn't time for that. Frederica would have done it for him in a minute, but he ignored that possibility.

Down underneath these shallow practical considerations, lay the fact that such a reorganization would have been a tacit acknowledgment of defeat; not only an acknowledgment to the world, which he'd have liked to pretend didn't matter much, but an acknowledgment of defeat to himself. What he had been trying to do ever since his return from that maddening talk with Rose in Dubuque, had been just to sit tight; to go on living a day at a time; to take the future in as small doses as he could manage.

Had he been the sort of person who finds comfort in mottoes, he'd have laid in a stock, such as, "Sufficient unto the day is the evil thereof"; "Holdfast is the only dog"; "Don't cross your bridges until you come to them." As the period between the night of his discovery of Rose on the Globe stage and the day of his return from Dubuque receded, and as the fierceness of the pain of it died away again (because such pains do die away. They can't keep screwed up into an ecstasy of torment forever) the part he'd played in the events of it, seemed to him less and less worthy of the sort of man he'd always considered himself to be; a self-controlled, self-disciplined adult. He'd acted for a while there, with the savage egotism of a distracted boy; thrown his dignity to the winds; made a holy show of himself. Well, that period was over at all events. Whatever the future might confront him with, he could promise himself, he thought, to keep his head.

But for a while, he didn't want to be confronted with anything, let alone to start anything; not until he could get his breath; not until he had time to think everything out; discover, if possible, where the whole miserable trouble had begun. He'd go back to the beginning, sometime, and try to work it all out. It went, probably, a long way back of the night when that hasty speech of his about not jeopardizing the children's lives to gratify his wife's whims had set the match to her resolution to leave him and the babies and live a life for herself.

But, though he told himself every day that he must begin ordering his old memories, analyzing them, in search of the clue, he didn't begin the process. Spiritually, he just held himself rigidly still. He might have compared himself to a man standing off a pack of wolves, knowing that his slightest move would precipitate a rush upon him. Or, perhaps more nearly, to a man just recovering consciousness after an accident, afraid to stir lest the smallest movement might reveal more serious injuries than he suspected.

His mind had never worked so brilliantly as it was working now. The problems involved in his clients' affairs were child's play to him. He took them apart and put them together again with a careless, confident, infallible perspicacity that amazed his colleagues and his opponents. And, as Frank Crawford had pointed out, he took a savagely contemptuous pleasure in making those clients pay through the nose.

But he could look neither back at Rose, nor forward to her. He could not, by any stretch of resolution, have nerved himself to the point of giving up that house that had nearly all his memories of her associated with it. There hadn't been a change of a single piece of furniture in it since she went away. Her bedroom and her dressing-room were just as she had left them. Her clothes were just as they had been left after the packing of that small trunk. She might have been off spending a week-end somewhere.

The attitude couldn't be kept up forever, he knew. Some time or other he'd have to cross the next bridge; come to some more definite understanding with Rose than that inconclusive ridiculous scene there in Dubuque had left him with. (*What* a fool he had been that day!) There were the twins coming along. For the present, their nurse (It wasn't Mrs. Ruston. He'd taken the first reasonable excuse for supplanting her.) and the pretty little snub-nosed nurse-maid Rose had liked, could supply their wants well enough. But the time wasn't so far ahead when they'd need a mother. What would he do then; let Rose have them half the time and keep them half the time himself? He'd read a perfectly beastly book once,—he couldn't remember the title of it—about a child who had been brought up that way. But, at all events, he needn't do anything yet.

Meanwhile, it healed his lacerated pride to march along and keep the routine going. It was with a perfectly immense relief that he snatched at the chance to buy the McCrea house, and by so doing make the permanency of his way of life a little more secure. He could keep what he had, anyway. And he could show the world, and Rose, that he wasn't the broken frantic creature he knew she'd seen, and suspected it had glimpsed. John Williamson's explanation wasn't altogether wrong.

Perhaps, had it been possible for Jimmy Wallace to tell him, just as he told Violet and John Williamson, how Rose's voice "richened up as if the words tasted good to her," when she mentioned the fact that she heard from her husband "regularly but not much," he might have drawn the same favorable augury from it that Violet did. But from her answering communications, though he drew comfort, he got no hope.

It was Rose herself who began this correspondence, within a month of her arrival in New York. And Rodney, when he finished reading her letter, tore it to pieces and flung it into the fire, in a transport of disappointment and anger. The sight of her writing on the envelope had brought his heart into his mouth, of course. And when his shaking fingers had got it open and he saw that it indeed contained a letter from her, beginning "Dear Rodney," and signed "Rose," the wild surge of hope that swept over him actually turned him giddy, so that it was two or three minutes before he could read it.

But the thing ran like another instalment of the talk they had had in Dubuque. She knew he had been distressed over the shabbiness of her surroundings, knocking about with that road company, and she was afraid that in spite of the assurance she had then given him, he was still worried about her. She was sure he'd be glad to know that she'd quit the stage for good, as an active performer on it, at least; that she was earning an excellent salary, fifty dollars a week, doing a highly congenial kind of work that had good prospects of advancement in it. She had a very comfortable little apartment (she gave him the address of it) and was living in a way that—she had written "even Harriet," but scratched this out—Frederica, for example, would consider entirely respectable. So he needn't feel another moment's anxiety about her. She'd have written sooner, but had wanted to get fully settled in her new job and be sure she was going to be able to keep it, in order that she might have something definitely reassuring to tell him. And she hoped he and the babies were well.

It was not until hours afterward, when the letter was an indistinguishable fluff of white ash in the fireplace, that it occurred to him that it had no satirical intent whatever and that the purpose of it had been, quite simply, what it had pretended to be; namely, to reassure him and put an end to his anxieties.

As he had read it in the revulsion from that literally sickening hope of his, it had seemed about the most mordant piece of irony that had ever been launched against him. The assumption of it had seemed to be that he was the most pitiable snob in the world; that all he'd cared for had been that she'd disgraced him by going on the stage. He'd be glad to know that she was once more "respectable."

Well—this was the question which, as I said, he did not ask himself until hours later—wasn't she justified in believing that? Certainly that night, in her little room on North Clark Street, he'd given her reason enough for thinking so. But later, in Dubuque—well, hadn't he quoted Harriet to her? Hadn't he offered to help her as a favor to himself, because he couldn't endure it that she should live like this? Had he exhibited anything to her at all in their two encounters, but an uncontrolled animal lust and a perfectly contemptible vanity?

He bitterly regretted having destroyed the letter. But the tone of it, he was sure, except for that well merited jibe about Harriet, which had been erased, was kindly. Yet he had acted once more, like a spoiled child about it.

Could he write and thank her? In Dubuque she had asked him not to come back. Did that prohibition cover writing? Her letter did not explicitly revoke it. She asked him no questions. But he remembered now a post-script, which, at the time of reading, he'd taken merely as a final barb of satire. "I am still Doris Dane down here, of course," it had read. If she hadn't meant that for a sneering assurance that his precious name wasn't being taken in vain—and had he ever heard Rose sneer at anybody?—what could have been the purpose of it except to make sure that a letter from him wouldn't come addressed "Rose Aldrich," and so fail to be delivered to her.

It was due only to luck that, in his first disappointment, he hadn't destroyed her address with the letter. But she had duplicated it on the flap of the envelope, and the envelope was not thrown in the fire.

He spent hours composing a reply. And the thing he finally sent off, once it was committed to the post, seemed quite the worst of all his efforts. His impulse was to send another on the heels of it. But he waited a week, then wrote again. And this time, the stiffness of self-consciousness was not quite so paralyzing. He managed to give her a little real information about the condition of the twins and the household. About himself, he stated that he was well, though busier than he liked to be.

He experienced a very vague, faint satisfaction, two days later, over the reflection that this letter was in her hands, and he came presently to the audacious resolution that until she forbade him, he would go on writing to her every week. She'd see that she needn't answer and it would no doubt add something—how much he didn't dare to try to estimate—to her happiness, to know that all was going well in the home that she had left.

She began pretty soon to answer these letters with stiff little notes, strictly limited to a bulletin of her own activities and a grateful acknowledgment of the latest one he had sent her. Invariably, every Tuesday morning, one of these notes arrived. And this state of things continued, unchanged, for months.

He experienced a bewildering mixture of emotions over these letters of hers. They drove him, sometimes, into outbursts of petulant rage. Often the knowledge that one of them was to be expected in the morning, delivered him up, against all the resistance he could make, to a flood of tormenting memories of her. And across the mood the letter would find him in, its cool little commonplaces would sting like the cut of a whip.

The mere facts her letters recounted aroused contradictory emotions in him, too. They all spelled success and assurance, and almost from week to week they marked advancement. The first effect of this was always to make his heart sink; to make her seem farther away from him; to make the possibility of any future need of him that would give him his opportunity, seem more and more remote. The other feeling, whose glow he was never conscious of till later—a feeling so surprising and irrational that he could hardly call it by name, was pride. What in God's name had he to be proud of? Was she a possession of his? Could he claim any credit for her success? But the glow persisted in spite of these questions.

His satisfaction in his own letters to her was less mixed. They must, he thought, gradually be restoring in her mind, the image of himself as a man who, as Harriet said, could take his medicine without making faces; who could endure pain and punishment without howling about it. Perhaps, in time, those letters would obliterate the memory of the vain beast he'd been that night. . .

If Rodney had done an unthinkable thing; if he had kept copies of his letters to Rose, along with her answers, in a chronological file the way Miss Beach kept his business correspondence, he would have made the discovery that the stiffness of them had gradually worn away and that they were now a good deal more than mere *pro forma* bulletins. There had crept into them, so subtly and so gently that between one of them and the next no striking difference was to be observed, a friendliness, quite cool, but wonderfully firm. She was frankly jubilant over the success of her costumes in *Come On In* and she enclosed with her letter a complete set of newspaper reviews of the piece. They reached him a day or two before Jimmy Wallace telephoned, and this fact perhaps had something to do with the gruff good humor with which he told Jimmy to go as far as he liked in his newspaper paragraph.

It was a week later that she wrote:

"I met James Randolph coming up Broadway yesterday afternoon, about five o'clock. I had a spare half-hour and he said he had nothing else but spare half-hours; that was what he'd come to New York for. So we turned into the Knickerbocker and had tea. He's changed, somehow, since I saw him last; as brilliant as ever, but rather—lurid. Do you suppose things are going badly between him and Eleanor? I'd hate to think that, but I shouldn't be surprised. He spoke of calling me up again, but this morning, instead, I got a note from him saying he was going back to Chicago. He told me he hadn't seen you forever. Why don't you drop in on him?"

It was quite true that Rodney had seen very little of the Randolphs since Rose went away. His liking for James had always been an affair of the intelligence. The doctor's mind, with its powers of dissecting and coordinating the phenomena of every-day life, its luminous flashes, its readiness to go all the way through to the most startling conclusions, had always so stimulated and attracted his own, that he'd never stopped to ask whether or not he liked the rest of the man that lay below the intelligence.

When it came to confronting his friends, in the knowledge that they knew that Rose had left him for the Globe chorus, he found that James Randolph was one he didn't care to face. He knew too damned much. He'd be too infernally curious; too full of surmises, eager for experiments.

The Rodney of a year before, intact, unscarred, without, he'd have said, a joint in his harness, could afford to enjoy with no more than a deprecatory grin, the doctor's outrageous and remorseless way of pinning out on his mental dissecting board, anything that came his way. The Rodney who came back from Dubuque couldn't grin. He knew too much of the intimate agony that produced those interesting lesions and abnormalities. Even in the security, if it could have been had, that his own situation wouldn't be scientifically dissected and discussed, he'd still have wanted to keep away from James Randolph.

But Rose's letter put a different face on the matter. He felt perfectly sure that Randolph hadn't been analyzing her during that spare half-hour at the Knickerbocker. The shoe, it appeared, had been on the other foot. The fact that she'd put him, partly at least, in possession of what she had observed and what she guessed, gave him a sort of shield against the doctor. He told himself that his principal reason for going was to get a little bit more information about Rose than her letters provided him with. But the anticipation he dwelt on with the greatest pleasure, really, was of saying, "Oh, yes. Rose wrote that she'd seen you."

So one evening, after keeping up the pretense through his solitary dinner and the cigar that followed it, that he meant presently to go up to his study and correct galley proofs on an enormous brief, he slipped out about nine o'clock, and walked around to the Randolphs' new house.

This latest venture of Eleanor's had attracted a good deal of comment among her friends. Somebody called it, with a rather cruel *double entendre*, Bertie Willis' last word. In the obvious sense of the phrase, this was true. Eleanor had given him a free hand, and he had gone his limit. He'd been working slowly backward from Jacobean, through Tudor. But this thing was perfect Perpendicular. You could, as John Williamson said, kid yourself into the notion, when you walked under the keel-shaped arch to their main doorway, that you were going to church. And the style was carried out with inexorable rigor, down to the most minute details. But since everybody knew that the latest thing, the inevitably coming thing, was the pure unadulterated ugliness of Georgian, a style that Bertie had opposed venomously (because he couldn't build it, the uncharitable said); and because even Bertie's carefully preserved youth was felt to have gone a little stale and it was no longer fashionable to consider his charms irresistible, the phrase, "his last word," was instantly understood, as I said, to have a secondary sense.

No one, of course, could tell Eleanor anything about what the coming styles were going to be, in architecture or anything else. She was one of these persons with simply a sixth sense for fashions, and her having gone to Bertie Willis, instead of to young Mellish of the historic New York firm, McCleod, Hill, Stone & Black, who was doing such delightfully hideous things in Georgian, caused, among her friends, a good deal of comment. Her explanation that medicine was a medieval profession and that she had to have a medieval house to go with James, was felt to be a mere evasion.

It was recognized that one had to flirt with Bertie while he was building her house. And in the days when everybody else had been doing it, too, it didn't matter. But now that the celebrated *hareem* had ceased to exist, it was felt that one would do well to be a little careful; at least, to put a more or less summary end to the flirtation when the house was finished. But Eleanor hadn't done that. She was playing with him more exclusively than ever.

Rodney hadn't been in the house before, and he reflected, as he stood at the door, after ringing the bell, that his own house was quite meek and conventional alongside this. The grin that this consideration afforded him, was still on his lips when, a servant having opened the door, he found himself face to face with the architect.

Bertie, top-coated and hat in hand, was waiting for Eleanor, who was coming down the stairs followed by a maid with her carriage coat. He returned Rodney's nod pretty stiffly, as was natural enough, since Rodney's grin had distinctly brightened up at sight of him.

Eleanor said, rather negligently, "Hello, Rod. We're just dashing off to the Palace to see a perfectly exquisite little dancer Bertie's discovered down there. She comes on at half past nine, so we've got to fly. Want to come?"

"No," Rodney said. "I came over to see Jim. Is he at home?"

The maid was holding out the coat for Eleanor's arms, Bertie was fussing around ineffectually, hooking his stick over his left arm to give him a free right hand to do something with, he didn't quite know what. But Eleanor, at Rodney's question, just stood for a second quite still. She wasn't looking at anybody, but the expression in her eyes was sullen.

"Yes, he's at home," she said at last.

"Busy, I suppose;" said Rodney. Her inflection had dictated this reply.

"Yes, he's busy," she repeated absently and in a tone still more coldly hostile, though Rodney perceived that the hostility was not meant for him. And so plainly did the tone and the look and the arrested attitude proclaim that she was following out a train of thought and hadn't as yet got to the end of it, that he stood as still as she was.

Bertie, irreproachably correct as always, settled his shoulders inside his coat, and took his stick in his right hand again. Eleanor now looked around at him.

"Wait two minutes," she said, "if you don't mind." Then, to Rodney, "Come along." And she led the way up the lustrous, velvety teakwood stair.

He followed her. But arrived at the drawing-room floor, he protested. "Look here!" he said. "If Jim's busy. . ."

"You've never been in here before, have you?" she asked. "How's Rose? Jim saw her, you know, in New York."

"Yes," he said. "Rose wrote to me she'd seen him, and I thought I'd drop around for a chat. But if he's busy. . ."

"Oh, don't be *too* dense, Rodney!" she said. "A man has to be busy when he's known to be in the house and won't entertain his wife's guests. Go up one flight more and to the door that corresponds to that one. It won't do you any good to knock. He'll either not answer or else tell you to go to hell. Just sing out who you are and go right in."

She gave him a nod and a hard little smile, and went down-stairs again to Bertie.

Rodney stood where she had left him, in two minds whether to carry out her instructions or to wait until he heard her and Bertie go out and then quietly follow them. It was a beastly situation, dragged into a family quarrel like that; forced to commit an intrusion that was so plainly labeled in advance. And on the other hand, it was a decidedly interesting situation. If Eleanor was as reckless as that with facts most women keep to themselves as long as possible, what would her outspoken husband be. But if he were full of his grievances, he probably wouldn't talk about Rose.

What really determined his action was Eleanor's discovery, or pretended discovery down in the hall below, that her gloves weren't what she wanted and her instructions to the maid to go up and get her a fresh pair. It would be too ridiculous to be caught there— lurking.

So he mounted the next flight, found the door Eleanor had indicated, knocked smartly on it, and to forestall his getting told to go to hell, sang out at the same time, "This is Rodney Aldrich. May I come in?"

"Come in, of course," Randolph called. "I'm glad to see you," he added, coming to meet his guest. "But do you mind telling me how the devil you got in here? Some poor wretch will lose his job, you know, if Eleanor finds out about this. When I'm in this room, sacred to reflection and research, it's a first-class crime to let me be disturbed."

It didn't need his sardonic grin to point the satire of his words. The way he had uttered "sacred to reflection and research," was positively savage.

Rodney said curtly, "Eleanor sent me up herself. I didn't much want to come, to tell the truth, when I heard you were busy."

"Eleanor!" her husband repeated. "I thought she'd gone out—with her poodle."

Rodney said, with unconcealed distaste, "They were on the point of going out when I came in. That's how Eleanor happened to see me."

With a visible effort, Randolph recovered a more normal manner. "I'm glad it happened that way," he said. "Get yourself a drink. You'll find anything you want over there, I guess, and something to smoke; then we'll sit down and have an old-fashioned talk."

The source of drinks he indicated was a well-stocked cellarette at the other side of the room. But Rodney's eye fell first on a decanter and siphon on the table, within reach of the chair Randolph had been sitting in. His host's glance followed his.

"This is Bourbon I've got over here," he added. "I suppose you prefer Scotch."

"I don't believe I want anything more to drink just now," Rodney said. And as he turned to the smoking table to get a cigar, Randolph allowed himself another sardonic grin.

The preliminaries were gone through rather elaborately; chairs drawn up and adjusted, ash-trays put within reach; cigars got going satisfactorily. But the talk they were supposed to prepare the way for didn't at once begin.

Randolph took another stiffish drink and settled back into a dull sullen abstraction.

Rodney wanted to say, "I hear from Rose you had a little visit with her in New York." But, with his host's mood what it was, he shrank from introducing that topic. Finally, for the sake of saying something, he remarked:

"This is a wonderful room, isn't it?"

Randolph roused himself. "Never been in here before?" he asked.

"I've never been in the house before, I'm ashamed to say."

"What!" Randolph cried. "My God! Well, then, come along."

Rodney resisted a little. He was comfortable. They could look over the house later. But Randolph wouldn't listen.

"That's the first thing to do," he insisted. "Indispensable preliminary. You can't enjoy the opera without a libretto. Come along."

It was a remarkable house. Before the first fifteen minutes of their inspection were over, Rodney had come to the conclusion that though Bertie Willis might be an ass, was indeed an indisputable ass, he was no fool. It was almost uncannily clever, the way all the latest devices for modern comfort wore, so demurely, the mask of a perfectly consistent medievalism. And there were some effects that were really magnificent. The view of the drawing-room, for instance, from the recessed dais at the far end of it, where the grand piano stood—a piano that contrived to look as if it might have been played upon by the second wife of Henry VIII,—down toward the magnificent stone chimney at the other; the octagonal dining-room with the mysterious audacity of its lighting; the kitchen with its flag floor (only they were not flags, but an artful linoleum), its great wrought-iron chains and hoods beneath which all the cooking was done—by electricity.

Randolph took him over the whole thing from bottom to top. Through it all, he kept up the glib patter of a showman; the ironic intent of it becoming more and more marked all the while.

They brought up at last in the study they had started from.

"Oh, but wait a moment!" Randolph said. "Here's two more rooms for you to see."

The first one explained its purpose at a glance, with a desk and typewriter, and filing cabinets around the walls.

"Rubber floor," Randolph pointed out, "felt ceiling; absolutely sound-proof. Here's where my stenographer sits all day, ready,—like a fireman. And this," he concluded, leading the way to the other room, "is the holy of holies."

It had a rubber floor, too, and Rodney supposed, a felt ceiling. But its only furniture was one straight-back chair and a canvas cot.

"Sound-proof too," said Randolph. "But sounding-boards or something in all the walls. I press this button, start a dictaphone, and talk in any direction, anywhere. It's all taken down. Here's where I'm supposed to think, make discoveries, and things. No distractions. One hundred per cent. efficient. My God! I tried it for a while. Felt like a fool actor in a Belasco play. Do you remember? The one with the laboratory and the doctor?"

They went back into the study.

"Clever beasts, though—poodles," he remarked, as he nodded Rodney to his chair and poured himself another drink. "Learn their tricks very nicely. But good Heavens, Aldrich, think of him as a man! Think what our American married women are up against, when they want somebody to play off against their husbands and have to fall back on tired little beasts like that. In all the older countries there are plenty of men, real men who've got something, that a married woman can fall back on. But think of a woman of Eleanor's attractions having to take up a thing like that. There's nothing else for her. Would *you* come around and hold her hand and make love to her, or any other man like you? Not once in a thousand times. Eleanor doesn't mean anything. She's trying to make me jealous. That's her newest experiment. But it's downright pitiful, I say."

Rodney got up out of his chair. It wasn't a possible conversation.

"I'll be running along, I think," he said. "I've a lot of proof to correct tonight, and you've got work of your own, I expect."

"Sit down again," said Randolph sharply. "I'm just getting drunk. But that can wait. I'm going to talk. I've got to talk. And if you go, I swear I'll call up Eleanor's butler and talk to him. You'll keep it to yourself, anyway."

He added, as Rodney hesitated, "I want to tell you about Rose. I saw her in New York, you know."

Rodney sat down again. "Yes," he said, "so she wrote. Tell me how she looked. She's been working tremendously hard, and I'm a little afraid she's overdoing it."

"She looks," Randolph said very deliberately, "a thousand years old." He laughed at the sharp contraction of Rodney's brows. "Oh, not like that! She's as beautiful as ever. More. Facial planes just a hair's breadth more defined perhaps—a bit more of what that painter Burton calls edge. But not a line, not a mark. Her skin's still got that bloom on it, and she still flushes up when she smiles. She's lost five pounds, perhaps, but that's just condition. And vitality! My God!—But a thousand years old just the same."

"I'd like to know what you mean by that," said Rodney. He added, "if you mean anything," but the words were unspoken.

Randolph did mean something.

"Why, look here," he said. "You know what a kid she was when you married her. Schoolgirl! I used to tell her things and she'd listen, all eyes—holding her breath! Until I felt almost as wise as she thought I was. She was always game, even then. If she started a thing, she saw it through. If she said, 'Tell it to me straight,' why she took it, whatever it might be, standing up. She wasn't afraid of anything. Courage of innocence. Because she didn't know.

"Well, she's courageous now, because she knows. She's been through it all and beaten it all, and she knows she can beat it again. She understands—I tell you—everything.

"Why, look here! We all but ran into each other on the corner, there, of Broadway and Forty-second Street; shook hands, said howdy-do. How long was I here for? Was Eleanor with me? And so on. If I had a spare half-hour, would I come in and have tea with her at the Knickerbocker? She'd nodded at two or three passing people while we stood there. And then somebody said, 'Hello, Dane,' and stopped. A miserable, shabby, shivering little painted thing. Rose said, 'Hello,' and asked how she was getting along. Was she working now? She said no; did Rose know of anything? Rose said, 'Give me your address and if I can find anything, I'll let you know.' The horrible little beast told where she lived and went away. Rose didn't say anything to me, except that she was somebody who'd been out in a road company with her. But there was a look in her eyes. . . ! Oh, she knew—everything. Knew what that kid was headed for. Knew there was nothing to be done about it. She had no flutters about it, didn't pull a long face, didn't, as I told you, say a word. But there was a look in her eyes, behind her eyes, somehow, that understood and *faced*—God!—everything. And then we went in and had our tea.

"I had a thousand curiosities about her. I'd have found out anything I could. But it was she who did the finding out. Beyond inquiring about you, how lately I'd seen you, and so on, she hardly asked a question; talked about indifferent things: New York, the theaters, how we passed the time out here, I don't know what. But pretty soon I saw that she understood me, saw right into me like through an open window into a lighted room. As easily as that. She knew what was the matter with me; knew what I'd made of myself. And by God, Aldrich, she didn't even despise me!

"I came back here to kick this damned thing to pieces, give myself a fresh start. And when I got here, I hadn't the sand. I get drunk instead."

He poured himself another long drink and sipped it slowly. "Everybody knows," he said at last, "that prostitutes almost invariably take to drugs or drink. But I know why they do."

That remark stung Rodney out of his long silence. During the whole of Randolph's recital of his encounter with Rose, he'd never once lifted his eyes from the gray ash of his cigar, and the violet filament of smoke that arose from it. He didn't want to look at Randolph, nor think about him. Just wanted to remember every word he said, so that he could carry the picture away intact. Now that the picture was finished, he wanted to get out of that room, with it; out into the dark and loneliness of the streets, where he could walk and think.

There was something peculiarly horrifying to him in the exhibition Randolph was making of himself. He'd never in his life taken a drink, except convivially, and then he took as little as would pass muster. He'd always found it hard to be sensibly tolerant of the things men said and did in liquor, even when their condition had overtaken them unawares. Going off alone and deliberately fuddling one's self as a means of escaping unpleasant realities, struck him as an act of the basest cowardice. Whether Randolph's revelation of himself were true or distorted by alcohol, didn't seem much to matter. But for that picture of Rose, he'd have gone long ago and left the man to his bemused reflections. Only. . .

He'd said that Rose understood everything and didn't despise him. A drunken fancy likely enough. She had seen something though. Her letter proved that. And having seen it, she'd asked him to drop in on the doctor for a visit. Did she mean she wanted him to try to help?

He tried, though not very successfully, to conceal his violent disrelish of the task, when he said:

"Look here, Jim! What the devil is the matter with you? Are you sober enough to tell me?"

Randolph put down his glass. "I have told you," he said. "It's a thing that can be told in one word. I'm a prostitute. I'm Eleanor's kept man. Well kept, oh, yes. Beautifully kept. I'm nothing in God's world but a possession of hers! A trophy of sorts, an ornament. I'm something she's made. I have a hell of a big practise. I'm the most fashionable doctor in Chicago. They come here, the women, damn them, in shoals. That's Eleanor's doing. I'm a faker, a fraud, a damned actor. I pose for them. I play up. I give them what they want. And that's her doing. They go silly about me; fancy they're in love with me. That's what she wants them to do. It increases my value for her as a possession.

"I haven't done a lick of honest work in the last year. I can't work. She won't let me work. She—smothers me. Wherever I turn, there she is, smoothing things out, trying to making it easy, trying to anticipate my wants. I've only one want. That's to be let alone. She can't do that. She's insatiable. She can't help it. There's something drives her on so that she never can feel sure that she possesses me completely enough. There's always something more she's trying to get, and I'm always trying to keep something away from her, and failing.

"And why? Do you want to know why, Aldrich? That's the cream of the thing. Because we're so damnably in love with each other. She wants me to live on her love. To have nothing else to live on. Do you know why she won't have any children? Because she's jealous of them. Afraid they'd get between us. She tries to make me jealous with that poodle of hers—and she succeeds. With that! I'd like to wring his neck.

"Do you want to know what my notion of Heaven is? It would be to go off alone, with one suit of clothes in a handbag, oh, and fifty or a hundred dollars in my pocket—I wouldn't mind that; I don't want to be a tramp—to some mining town, or mill town, or slum, where I could start a general practise; where the things I'd get would be accident cases, confinement cases; real things, urgent things, that night and day are all alike to. I'd like to start again and be poor; get this stink of easy money out of my nostrils. I'd like to see if I could make good on my own; have something I could look at and say, 'That's mine. I did that. I had to sweat for it.'

"I've been thinking about that for two years. It makes quite a fancy-picture. There are a million details I can fill into it. A rotten little office over a drug-store somewhere; people coming in with real ills, and I curing them up and charging them a dollar, and sending them away happy. I smoke a pipe because I can't afford cigars; get my meals at lunch-counters. I sit up here—in this room—and think about it.

"I came back from New York, after that look at Rose, meaning to do it; meaning to talk it out with Eleanor and tell her why, and then go. Well, I talked. Talk's cheap. But I didn't go. I'll never go. I'll go on getting softer and more of a fake; more dependent. And Eleanor will go on eating me up, until the last thing in me that's me myself, is gone. And then, some day, she'll look at me and see that I'm nothing. That I have nothing left to love her with."

Then, with suddenly thickened speech (an affectation, perhaps) he looked up at Rodney and demanded:

"What the hell are you looking so s-solemn about? Can't you take a joke? Come along and have another drink. The night's young."

"No," Rodney said, "I'm going. And you'd better get to bed."

"A couple more drinks," Randolph said, "to put the cap on a jolly evening. Always get drunk th-thoroughly. Then in the morning, you wake up a wiser man. Wise enough to forget what a damned fool you've been. You don't want to forget that, Aldrich. You've been drunk and you've talked like a damned fool. And I've been drunk and I've talked like a damned fool. But we'll both be wiser in the morning."

Rodney walked home that night like a man dazed. The vividness of one blazing idea blinded him. The thing that Randolph had seen and lacked the courage to do; the thing Rodney despised him for a coward for having failed to do, that thing Rose had done. Line by line, the parallel presented itself to him, as the design comes through in a half-developed photographic plate.

Without knowing it, yielding to a blind, unscrutinized instinct, he'd wanted Rose to live on his love. He'd tried to smooth things out for her, anticipate her wants. He'd wanted her soft, helpless, dependent. As a trophy? That was what Randolph had said. Had he been as bad as that? From what other desire of his than that could have come the sting of exasperation he'd always felt when she'd urged him to let her work for him; help him to economize, dust and make beds, so that he could go on writing his book? She'd seen, even then, something he'd been blind to—something he'd blinded himself to; that love, by itself, was not enough. That it could poison, as well as feed.

And, seeing, she had the courage. . . He pressed his hands against his eyes.

When there could be friendship as well as love between them, she said, she'd come back. Would she come back now, even for his friendship? He doubted it. Dared not hope. There came up before him that face of frozen agony that had confronted him in the room on Clark Street, and he remembered what she'd said then—with a shudder—about it all ending "like this." Ending!

His love had played her false; had tried, instinctively, to smother her, and defeated at that, had outraged and tortured her. She couldn't possibly look at it any way but that. And now that she was free, self-discovered, victorious, was it likely she would submit to its blind caprices again? The thing Randolph had said was his notion of Heaven, she'd triumphantly attained. Wouldn't it be her notion of Heaven too?

But she had won, among the rest of her spoils of victory, the thing she had originally set out to get. His friendship and respect. Friendship, he remembered her saying, was a thing you had to earn. When you'd earned it, it couldn't be withheld from you. Well, it was right she should be told that; made to understand it to the full. He couldn't ask her to come back to him. But she must know that her respect was as necessary now to him, as she'd once said his was to her. He must tell her that. He must see her and tell her that.

He stopped abruptly in his walk. His bones, as the Psalmist said, turned to water. How should he confront that gaze of hers, which knew so much and understood so deeply—he with the memory of his two last ignominious encounters with her, behind him?

III

FRIENDS

Except for the vacuum where the core and heart of it all ought to have been, Rose's life in New York during the year that put her on the high road to success as a designer of costumes for the theater, was a good life, broadening, stimulating, seasoning. It rested, to begin with, on a foundation of adequate material comfort which the unwonted physical privations of the six months that preceded it—the room on Clark Street, the nightmare tour on the road, and even the little back room in Miss Gibbons' apartment over the drug-store in Centropolis—made seem like positive luxury.

After a preliminary fortnight in a little hotel off Washington Square, which she had heard Jane Lake speak of once as a possible place for a respectable young woman of modest means to live in, she found an apartment in Thirteenth Street, not far west of Sixth Avenue. It was in a quiet block of old private residences. But this building was clean and new, with plenty of white tile and modern plumbing, and an elevator. Her apartment had two rooms in it, one of them really spacious to poor Rose after what she'd been taking for granted lately, besides a nice white bathroom and a kitchenette. She paid thirty-seven dollars a month for it, and five dollars a month for a share in a charwoman who came in every day and made her bed and washed up dishes.

The extensiveness of this domestic establishment frightened her a little at first. But she reassured herself with the reflection that under the rule Gertrude Morse had quoted to her, one week's pay for one month's rent, she still had a comfortable margin. She furnished it a bit at a time, with articles chosen in the order of their indispensability, and she went on, during the summer, to buy some things which were not indispensable at all. But not very many. Like most persons with a highly specialized creative talent for one form of beauty (in her case this was clothes) she was more or less indifferent about others. Witness how little interest she had taken in the labored beauties of Florence McCrea's house, even in the unthinking days before she had begun worrying about the expense of that establishment. Her indifference had always made Portia boil. Also it may be noted, that Florence McCrea herself, always went about looking a perfect frump.

So that, by the time Rose's apartment was furnished to the point of adequate comfort and decency, she took it for granted and stopped there. For her, the temptations of old brass, mezzo-tints, and Italian majolica—Fourth Avenue generally—simply did not exist.

She bought real china to eat her breakfasts out of, and the occasional suppers she had at home. She had had enough of thick cups and plates in the last six months to last her the rest of her life. And it is probable that she ate up, literally, the margin she had under Gertrude Morse's rule, in somewhat better restaurants than she need have patronized.

She did save money though, and put it away in a safe bank. But she never saved quite so much as she was always meaning to, and she carried along, for months after she went to work for Galbraith, an almost guilty sense of luxury. In spite of the fact that she was working very hard and of the further fact that her hours of labor were largely coincident with the leisure hours of other people, she made a good many friends. The first of these was Gertrude Morse, and it was through her, directly or indirectly, that she acquired the others.

Gertrude was Abe Shuman's confidential secretary and you can get a fairly good working notion of her by conceiving the type of person likely to be found in the borderland of theatrical enterprises, and then, in all respects, taking the exact antithesis of it. She was a brisk, prim-mannered, snub-nosed little thing, who wore her hair brushed down as flat as possible and showed an affection for mannish clothes. She had a level head, a keen and rather biting wit, which had the effect of making her constant acts of kindness always unexpected; and an education which, in her surroundings, seemed almost fantastic. She was a Radcliff Master of Arts.

Every one who had any dealings with Abe Shuman perforce knew Gertrude, and Rose got acquainted with her the first day. Galbraith introduced them in Shuman's office, and Rose found herself being investigated by a bright, penetrating and decidedly complex look which she interpreted—pretty accurately as she found out later—as saying, "Well, you're about what I expected; ornamental and enthusiastic; just what an otherwise sane and successful man of fifty would pick out for an 'assistant.' Aren't they just children at that age! But you're welcome. They deserve it. Good luck to you!"

But when Rose returned the look with a comprehending smile which said good-naturedly, "All right! You wait and see," Gertrude's expression altered into a frankly questioning frown. Two or three days later she dropped in at a rehearsal, ostensibly with a message from Shuman to Galbraith. He was on the point of leaving and had turned over the rehearsal to Rose. Gertrude, when he had gone, settled down comfortably in the back of the auditorium and watched through a solid hour, obviously under instructions from Abe to bring back a report as to whether Galbraith's infatuation should be tolerated or suppressed. At the end of the hour, during a brief lull in the rehearsal, she came down the aisle and stopped beside Rose who still had her eye on the stage.

"I apologize," she said.

Rose grinned around at her. It was not necessary to ask what for. "Much obliged," she said.

"I didn't know that a woman could do that," Gertrude went on. "Didn't think she'd have the—drive. But you've got it, all right. I don't suppose you've got an idea when you'll be free for lunch?"

Rose hadn't, but it was not many days before they got together for that meal at a business woman's club down on Fortieth Street, and from then on their acquaintance progressed rapidly. She helped Rose find the little apartment on Thirteenth Street, entertaining her during the search with a highly instructive disquisition on the social topography of New York, and on the following Sunday she ran in, she said, to see if she could help her get settled. There was no settling to do, but she sat down and talked—most of the time—for an hour or so. It was a theory of Gertrude's that the way to find out about people was to talk to them.

"You can't tell much," she used to say, "by the things people say to you. Perhaps they've just heard somebody else say them. Maybe they've got a repertory that it will take you weeks to get to the end of. Or they may not be able to show you at all what's really inside them. But from how they take the things you say to them—the things they light up at and the things they look blank about, the things they're too anxious to show you they understand, and the things they dare admit they never heard of—you can tell every time. Find out all you want to know about anybody in an hour!"

Rose, it seemed, reacted satisfactorily to her tests, since she was introduced as rapidly thereafter as their scanty leisure made possible, to Gertrude's more immediate circle of friends.

During that first winter, she enjoyed them immensely. They were all interesting; all "did things"; widely various things, yet, somehow, related. There was a red-haired fire-brand whose specialty seemed to be bailing out girls arrested for picketing and whose Sunday diversion consisted in going down to Paterson, New Jersey, making the police ridiculous and unhappy for an hour or so, delivering herself of a speech in defiance of their preventive efforts and finally escaping arrest by a hair's breadth. They got her finally but since she enjoyed the privilege of addressing as Uncle a man whose name was uttered with awe about the corner of Broad Street and Exchange Place, they had to let her go.

There was a young woman lawyer, associated with Gertrude in an organization for getting jobs for girls who had just been let out of jail, a level-headed enterprise, which by conserving its efforts for those who really wished to benefit by them, managed to accomplish a good deal. One of their circle was associate editor of a popular magazine and another wrote short stories, mostly about shop-girls. The last one of them for Rose to meet, she having been out of town all summer, was Alice Perosini. She was the daughter of a rich Italian Jew, a beautiful—really a wonderful person to look at—but a little unaccountable, especially with the gorgeous clothes she wore, in their circle. Rose took her time about deciding that she liked her but ended by preferring her to all the rest. She never talked much; would smoke and listen, making most of her comments in pantomime, but she had a trick of capping a voluble discussion with a hard-chiseled phrase which, whether you felt it precisely fitted or not, you found it difficult to escape from.

What forced Rose to a realization of her preference for Alice was the impulse to tell her who she really was and the suddenly following reflection that she never had wanted to tell any of the others; that she had taken care to avoid all reference to the husband and the babies she had fled from in search of a life of her own.

She never tried to explain to herself the feeling that imposed this reticence on her, until the discovery that it didn't exist toward Alice. She couldn't have feared that they would not approve of what she had done; it squared so exactly with all their ideas. Indeed the one real bond between them was a common revolt against the traditional notion that the way for a woman to effect her will in the world was by "influencing" a man. They wanted to hold the world in their own hands. They contemned the "feminine" arts of cajolery. They wanted no odds from anybody. There wasn't a real man-hater in the crowd, they were too normal and healthy for that. But they didn't talk much about men; never, as far as Rose knew, about men—as such. Was the topic suppressed, she wondered, or was it just that they didn't think about them?

That question made her realize how little she knew of any of them; how limited was the range of their intercourse. It was as if they met in a sort of mental gymnasium, fenced with one another, did callisthenics. Oh, that was going too far, of course; it was more real than that. But it was true that it was only their minds that met. And it seemed to be true that in the realm of mind they were content to live. Had they, like herself, deep labyrinthine, half-lit caverns down underneath those north-lighted, logically ordered apartments where Rose always found them? If they had they never let her or one another suspect it.

They'd be capable of deciding the great issue between herself and Rodney, if ever they were told the story, in a half dozen brisk sentences. Rose would be held to have been right and Rodney wrong, demonstrably. Rose, illogically, perhaps, shrank from that conclusion or at least from having it reached that way. There was more to it than that. There were elements in the situation they wouldn't know how to allow for.

But Alice Perosini, she thought, was different. She'd be able to make some of those allowances. Rose didn't tell her the story but she felt that at a pinch she could and this feeling was enough to establish Alice on a different basis from the others. It was with Alice that she discussed the more personal sort of problems that arose in connection with her new job. (One of these, as you are to be told, was highly personal.) And when the question came up of finding the capital that would enable her to make the Shumans a bid on all the costumes for *Come On In* it was Alice, who, with all the sang-froid in the world, sketched out the articles of partnership and brought her in a certified check for three thousand dollars.

The fact that they had become partners served, somehow, to divert a relation between them which might otherwise have developed into a first-class friendship. Not that they quarreled or even disappointed each other in the close contacts of the day's work. They were admirably complementary. Alice had the business acumen, the executive grasp, the patient willingness to master details, which were needed to set Rose free for the more imaginative part of the enterprise. Both were immensely determined on success. Alice couldn't have been keener about it if every cent she had in the world had been embarked in the business.

But at the end of the day's work they tended to fly apart rather than to stick together. Both were charged with the same kind of static electricity. It was an instinct they were sensible enough to follow. Both realized that they were more efficient as partners from not going too intimately into each other's outside affairs.

But when the winter had passed and the early spring had brought its triumph, with the success of her costumes in *Come On In*, and when the inevitable reaction from the burst of energy that had won that triumph had taken possession of her, Rose found herself in need of a friendship that would grip deeper, understand more. And with the realization of the need of it she found she had it. It was a friendship that had grown in the unlikeliest soil in the world, the friendship of a man who had wanted to be her lover. The man was John Galbraith.

For the first month after she came to New York to work for him she had found Galbraith a martinet. She never once caught that twinkling gleam of understanding in his eye that had meant so much to her during the rehearsals of *The Girl Up-stairs*. His manner toward her carried out the tone of the letter she'd got from him in Centropolis. It was stiff, formal, severe. He seldom praised her work and never ungrudgingly. His censure was rare too, to be sure, but this obviously was because Rose almost never gave him an excuse for it. Of course she was up to her work, but, well, she had better be. This, in a nutshell, was his attitude toward her. Nothing but the undisputable fact that she was up to her work (Gertrude was comforting here, with her reticent but convincing reports of Abe Shuman's satisfaction with her) kept Rose from losing confidence. Even as it was, working for Galbraith in this mood gave her the uneasy sensation one experiences when walking abroad under a sultry overcast sky with mutterings and flashes in it. And then one night the storm broke.

They had lingered in the theater after the dismissal of a rehearsal, to talk over a change in one of the numbers Rose had been working on. It refused to come out satisfactorily. Rose thought she saw a way of doing it that would work better and she had been telling him about it. Eagerly, at first, and with a limpid directness which, however, became clouded and troubled when she felt he wasn't paying attention. It was a difficulty with him she had encountered before. Some strong preoccupation she could neither guess the nature of nor lure him away from.

But tonight after an angry turn down the aisle and back he suddenly cried out, "I don't know. I don't know what you've been talking about. I don't know and I don't care." And then confronting her, their faces not a foot apart, for by now she had got to her feet, his hands gripped together and shaking, his teeth clenched, his eyes glowing there in the half-light of the auditorium, almost like an animal's, he demanded, "Can't you see what's the matter with me? Haven't you seen it yet? My God!"

Of course she saw it now, plainly enough. She sat down again, managing an air of deliberation about it, and gripped the back of the orchestra chair in front of her. He remained standing over her there in the aisle.

When the heightening tension of the silence that followed this outburst had grown absolutely unendurable she spoke. But the only thing she could find to say was almost ludicrously inadequate.

"No, I didn't see it until now. I'm sorry."

"You didn't see it," he echoed. "I know you didn't. You've never seen me at all, from the beginning, as anything but a machine. But why haven't you? You're a woman. If I ever saw a woman in my life you're one all the way through. Why couldn't you see that I was a man? It isn't because I've got gray hair, nor because I'm fifty years old. You aren't like that. I don't believe you're like that. But even back there in Chicago, the night we walked down the avenue from Lessing's store—or the night we had supper together after the show. . ."

"I suppose I ought to have seen," she said dully. "Ought to have known that that was all there was to it. That there couldn't be anything else in the world. But I didn't."

"Well, you see it now," he said savagely fairly, and strode away up the aisle and then back to her. He sat down in the seat in front of her and turned around. "I want to see your face," he said. "There's something I've got to know. Something you've got to tell me. You said once, back there in Chicago, that there was only one person who really mattered to you. I want to know who that one person is. What he is. Whether he's still the one person who really matters. If he isn't I'll take my chance. I'll make you love me if it's the last thing I ever do in the world."

Remembering the scene afterward Rose was a little surprised that she'd been able to answer him as she did, without a hesitation or a stammer, and with a straight gaze that held his until she had finished.

"The only person in the world," she said, "who ever has mattered to me, or ever will matter, is my husband. I fell in love with him the day I met him. I was in love with him when I left him. I'm in love with him now. Everything I do that's any good is just something he might be proud of if he knew it. And every failure is just something I hope I could make him understand and not despise me for. It's months since I've seen him but there isn't a day, there isn't an hour in a day, when I don't think about him and—want him. I don't know whether I'll ever see him again but if I don't it won't make any difference with that. That's why I didn't see what I might have seen about you. It wasn't possible for me to see. I'd never have seen it if you hadn't told me in so many words, like this. Do you see now?"

He turned away from her with a nod and put his hands to his face. She waited a moment to see whether he had anything else to say, for the habit of waiting for his dismissal was too strong to be broken even in a situation like this. But finding that he hadn't she rose and walked out of the theater.

There was an hour after she had gained the haven of her own apartment, when she pretty well went to pieces. So this was all, was it, that she owed her illusory appearance of success to? The amorous desires of a man old enough to be her father! Once more, she blissfully and ignorantly unsuspecting all the while, it was love that had made her world go round. The same long-circuited sex attraction that James Randolph long ago had told her about. But for that attraction she'd never have got this job in New York, never have had the chance to design those costumes for Goldsmith and Block. Never, in all probability, have got even that job in the chorus of *The Girl Up-stairs*. All she'd accomplished in that bitter year since she left Rodney had been to make another man fall in love with her!

But she didn't let herself go like that for long. The situation was too serious for the indulgence of an emotional sprawl. Here she was in an apartment that cost her thirty-seven dollars a month. She'd got to earn a minimum of thirty dollars a week to keep on with it. Of course she couldn't go on working for Galbraith. The question was, what could she do? Well, she could do a good many things. Whatever Galbraith's motives had been in giving her her chance, she had taken that chance and made the most of it. Gertrude Morse knew what she could do. For that matter, so did Abe Shuman himself. The thing to do now was to go to bed and get a night's sleep and confront the situation with a clear mind in the morning.

It was a pretty good indication of the way she had grown during the last year that she was able to conquer the shuddering revulsion that had at first swept over her, get herself in hand again, eat a sandwich and drink a glass of milk, re-read a half dozen chapters of Albert Edwards' *A Man's World*, and then put out her light and sleep till morning.

It was barely nine o'clock when Galbraith called her up on the telephone. She hadn't had her breakfast yet and had not even begun to think out what the day's program must be.

He apologized for calling her so early. "I wanted to be sure of catching you," he said, "before you did anything. You haven't yet, have you? Not written to Shuman throwing up your job, or anything like that?"

Even over the telephone his manner was eloquent with relief when she told him she had not. "I want to talk with you," he said. "It's got to be somewhere where we won't be interrupted." He added, "I shan't say again what I said last night. You'll find me perfectly reasonable."

Somehow his voice carried entire conviction. The man she visualized at the other telephone was neither the distracted pleader she had left last night, nor the martinet she had been working for during the last month here in New York, but the John Galbraith she had known in Chicago.

"All right," she said, "I don't know any better place than here in my apartment, if that's convenient for you."

"Yes," he said, "that's all right. When may I come? The sooner the better of course."

"Can you give me an hour?" she asked, and he said he could.

It occurred to her, as the moment of his arrival drew near, that she might better have thought twice before appointing their meeting here in her apartment. Discretion perhaps would have suggested a more neutral rendezvous. But she didn't take this consideration very seriously and with the first real look she got into his face after she had let him in, she dismissed it utterly. They shook hands and said, "Good morning," and she asked him to sit down, all as if nothing had happened the night before. But he wasted no time in getting to the point.

"There's one idea you'll have got, from what I said last night, that's a mistake and that's got to be set right before we go any further. That is, that you owe your position here, as my assistant, to the fact that I'd fallen in love with you. That's not true. In fact, it's the opposite of the truth. That feeling of mine has worked against you instead of for you. I'll have to explain that a little to make you understand it. And if you won't mind I'll have to talk pretty straight." She gave him a nod of assent, but he did not immediately go on. It was a reflective pause, not an embarrassed one.

"I've always despised," he said, "a man who mixed up his love-affairs with his business. In my business, perhaps, there's a certain temptation to do that and I've always been on guard against it. I've had love-affairs, more or less, all along. But in my vacations. You can't do decent honest work when your mind's on that sort of thing, and I care more about my work than anything else.

"Well, that night in Chicago, after the opening of *The Girl Up-stairs*, when I took you out to supper, I didn't know what I wanted. That's the truth. I'd been fighting my interest in you, my personal interest that is, calling myself all kinds of an old fool. I'd never had a thing get me like that before and I didn't know what to make of it. Well, the business was over, of course. I was entitled to a little vacation. I suppose, that night, if you'd shown the least sense of how I felt, even if it was just by seeming frightened, I might have flared up and made love to you. But you didn't see it at all. You had some sort of—fence around you that held me off. And for a while you even made me forget that I was in love with you. Forget that you were anything but the cleverest person I had known at catching my ideas and putting them over. I saw how enormously valuable you'd be to me, in this job you've got now, and I offered it to you.

"And then, all in a wave the other feeling came back. On my way to New York I decided that as long as I felt like that I'd have nothing more to do with you. A man couldn't possibly do any decent work with a woman he was in love with, either after he'd got her or while he was trying to get her. That's why you didn't hear from me within a month after I'd got back to New York. But as time went on I forgot how strong my feeling had been. I decided. I'd got over it. I'd been looking for some one else to take the place I'd designed for you and I couldn't find anybody.

"I might have got a man, but I didn't want a man, because if he were clever enough to be any good he'd be out after my job from the very first day. It would suit Abe Shuman down to the ground to have me teach a man all I know in two years and then put him in my place at half my pay. As for women, well, I've never seen a woman yet with just your combination of qualities, your drive and your knack. So I persuaded myself that it would be all right. That I could get along without thinking about you the other way. And I sent for you.

"But the minute I saw you I knew I'd have to look out. I've tried to; you know that. I've been treating you like a sweep since you've been down here. I didn't mean to but I couldn't help it. I was in such a rage with myself for going on like a sentimental fool about you. And the way you took it, always good-humored and never afraid, made me all the more ashamed of myself and all the more in love with you. And so last night I burst. In a way I'm glad I did. I think perhaps it will clear the air. But I'll come to that later. I want to know now whether you're convinced that what I said is true. That the fact that I fell in love with you has been against you and not in your favor."

"Yes," Rose said, "I'm convinced of that and I want to thank you for telling me. Because the other feeling was pretty—discouraging."

"All right," he said with a nod, "that's understood. Now, here's my proposition. That you go on working for me exactly as if nothing had happened."

"Oh, but that's impossible!" she said, and when he put in "Why is it?" she told him he had just said so himself. That it was impossible for a man to do decent work with a woman he was in love with.

"That's what I thought last night when I blew up," he admitted, "but I've got things a bit straighter since. In the first place, we have been doing decent work all this last month. We've been doing, between us, the work of two high-priced directors."

She said, "Yes, but I didn't know. . ."

"Understanding's better than ignorance," he interrupted, "any time. Between people of sense, that is. We'd get on better together, not worse. Look at us now. We're talking together sensibly enough, aren't we? And we're here in your sitting-room, talking about the fact that I fell in love with you. Couldn't we talk just as sensibly in the theater, about whether a song or number was in the right place or not? Of course we could."

The truth of this argument rather stumped Rose. It didn't seem reasonable, but it was true. Instead of embarrassing and distressing her, this talk with Galbraith was doing her good, restoring her confidence. The air between them was easier to breathe than it had been for weeks.

"You seem different this morning, somehow," she said.

"Why," he told her, "I am different. Permanently different toward you. I am convinced of it. I don't pretend to understand it myself, but somehow—I'm relieved. For one thing, I never wanted to fall in love with you. It was quite against my will that I did it. And then I've always been tortured with curiosity about you. I've wondered. Were you as unconscious of me as you seemed? Was it possible that you didn't know. And if you did know, was it possible that you were—waiting? That it only needed a word of mine to put everything between us on a different basis? I couldn't get rid of that idea. It kept nagging at me. But after what you told me last night—and you certainly told it straight—that idea's exploded. What you said explains everything about you. I know now that I haven't a chance in the world. From now on, I imagine, I'll be able to treat you like a human being. Well, are you willing to try it?"

Up to now they'd been sitting quietly in their two chairs with most of the width of the room between them. But at this last question of his she got up and walked over to the window.

"I don't know," she said at last. "It seems dangerous, somehow; like courting trouble. I know. . ." She hesitated, but then decided to say what was in her mind. "I know how terribly strong those feelings are and I've found out how little they've got to do with what it's so easy to decide is reasonable." Now she turned and faced him.

"Don't you think it would be more sensible for me to find another job? So that we could—well, take a fresh start?"

"Child," he said, "don't you know there's no such thing in the world as a fresh start? Or a new leaf? That's a comfortable delusion for cowards. The situation's in a mess, is it? All right, run away. Begin again with a clean slate. But the first thing written down on that slate is that you've just run away. Besides, suppose you do get another job, working, say, for another director. How do you know that he won't fall in love with you?"

That last sentence went by unheard. She was staring at him, almost in consternation. "That's true," she said. "That's perfectly true. That about running away. I—I never thought of it before." She went back to her chair and dropped into it rather limply. She sat there through a long silence, still thinking over his words and apparently almost frightened over her own implications from them.

At last he said, "You've no cause for worry over that, I should think. I don't believe you've ever run away from anything yet."

"I don't know," she answered thoughtfully. "I don't know whether I did or not."

"Well," he came out at last, getting to his feet, "how about it? What shall we do this time? Shall we tackle the situation and try to make the best of it, or. . ."

"Yes, that's what we'll do," she said. "And, well, I'm much obliged to you for putting me right."

"I made all the trouble in the first place," said Galbraith, with a rueful sort of grin. "It was up to me to think of something."

And after the elevator she'd escorted him to had carried him down, she stood there in the hallway smiling, with the glow of a quite new friendliness for him warming her heart.

It was natural, of course, that the relation between them after that day should not prove quite so simple and manageable a thing as it had looked that morning. There were breathless days when the storm visibly hung in the sky; there were strained, stiff, self-conscious moments of rigidly enforced politeness. Things got said despite his resolute repression that had, as resolutely, to be ignored.

But in the intervals of these failures there emerged, and endured unbroken for longer periods, the new thing they sought—genuine friendliness, partnership.

It was just after Christmas that Abe Shuman took her away from him and put her to work exclusively on costumes. And the swift sequence of events within a month thereafter launched her in an independent business; the new partnership with Alice Perosini, with the details of which, through Jimmy Wallace, you are already sufficiently acquainted. By the time that happened the friendship had gone so far that Rose's chief reluctance in making the change sprang from a fear that the change would interrupt it.

But the thing worked the other way. Released from the compulsory relation of employer and employee, they frankly sought each other as friends, and found that they got more out of a half-hour together over a hasty lunch than a whole day's struggle over a common task had given them.

There were long stretches of days, of course, when they saw nothing of each other, and Rose, so long as she had plenty to do, was never conscious of missing him. She never, in the course of her own day's work, made an unconscious reference to him, as she was always making them to Rodney. But the prospect of an empty Sunday morning, for instance, was always enormously brightened if he called up to say that it was empty for him, too, and shouldn't they go for a walk or a ferry ride somewhere.

He did the greater part of the talking. Told her, a good deal to his own surprise, stories of his early life in London—a chapter he'd never been willing to refer to, except in the vaguest terms, to anybody else. He told her, too, with more and more freedom and explicitness, as he discovered how straight and honest her mind was, how eager it was for facts instead of for sentimental refractions of them, about certain emotional adventures of his as he was emerging into manhood, and of the marks they had left on him.

All told, she learned more about men, as such, from him than ever she had learned, consciously at least, from Rodney. She'd never been able to regard her husband as a specimen. He was Rodney, *sui generis*, and it had never occurred to her either to generalize from him to other men, or to explain any of the facts she had noted about him, on the mere ground of his masculinity. She began doing that now a little, and the exercise opened her eyes.

In many ways Galbraith and her husband were a good deal alike. Both were rough, direct, a little remorseless, and there was in both of them, right alongside the best and finest and clearest things they had, an unaccountable vein of childishness. She'd never been willing to call it by that name in Rodney. But when she saw it in Galbraith, too, she wondered. Was that just the man of it? Were they all like that; at least all the best of them? Did a man, as long as he lived, need somebody in the rôle of—mother? The thought all but suffocated her.

She did not return Galbraith's confidences with any detailed account of her own life, and the one great emotional experience of it that seemed to have absorbed all the rest and drawn it up into itself. But she had a comforting sense that, scanty as was the framework of facts he had to go on, he knew, somehow, all about it; all the essentials of it; knew infinitely more about her than Alice Perosini did, although from time to time she had told Alice a good deal.

Spring came on them with a rush that year; swept a vivid flush of green over the parks and squares, all in a day; pumped the sap up madly into the little buds, so that they could hardly swell fast enough, and burst at last into a perfectly riotous fanfare through the shrubberies. It pumped blood, too, as well as sap, and made hearts flutter to strange irregular rhythms with the languorous insolence of its perfumes, and the soft caressing pressures of its south wind.

It worried Rose nearly mad. She was bound to have gone slack anyway; to have experienced the well-earned, honest lassitude of a finished struggle and an achieved victory. Dane & Company had any amount of work in sight, to be sure—a success of such triumphant proportions as they had had with *Come On In*, made that inevitable— but it would be months before any of the new work was wanted.

Alice, who could see plainly enough that something was the matter, kept urging Rose to run away somewhere for a long vacation. Why not, if it came to that, put in a few weeks in London and Paris? She was almost sure to pick up some valuable ideas over there. Rose declined that suggestion almost sharply. If she'd had any practical training as a nurse, she'd go over to Paris and stay, but to use that magnificently courageous tragic city as a source of ideas for a Shuman *revue* was out of the question. As for the quiet place in the Virginia mountains, which Alice had suggested as an alternative, Rose would die of ennui there within three days. The only thing to do was to stick to her routine as well as she could, and worry along.

These weren't reasons that she gave Alice, they were excuses. The reason, which she tried to avoid stating, even to herself, was that she couldn't bear the thought of going one step farther away from Rodney than she was already.

A letter from him was always in the first Saturday morning delivery and she never left for her atelier till she got it. She had perceived, what he had not, the steadily growing friendliness of these letters. It wasn't a made-up thing, either. He was not telling her things because he thought she'd like to be told, but because it had insensibly become a need of his to tell her.

A year ago those letters would have made her wildly happy; would have filled her with the confidence that the end she sought was in sight at last. Now they drove her half mad with disappointment. She never opened one of those dearly familiar envelopes without the irrepressible hope that it contained a love-letter; a passionate demand that she come back to him; leave all she had and come back to him; his woman to her man. And her disappointment and inconsistency bewildered her.

Her two chance encounters, first with Jimmy Wallace in the theater, and later with James Randolph, made her restlessness more nearly unendurable. The thought that they were going back to Chicago and would, no doubt, within a few days after their talks with her, see and talk with him, was like the cup of Tantalus. And if she could encounter them by chance, like that, why mightn't she encounter him? Why mightn't he come to New York on business? She never walked anywhere, nowadays, without watching for him.

She didn't yield, passively, to these thoughts and feelings. She fought them relentlessly, methodically. She went to a women's gymnasium every evening, threw a medicine ball around for a while, and then played a hard game of squash, in the sometimes successful attempt to get tired enough so that she'd have to sleep. Also she tried riding in the park, mornings, but that didn't work so well, and she gave it up.

There came a Saturday morning, toward the end of May, which brought no letter from Rodney, and she stayed in all day, from one delivery to the next, waiting for it. She tried to disguise her excitement over its failure to arrive, as a fear lest something might have gone wrong with him or with the twins, but did not succeed. If anything had gone wrong she knew she'd have heard. The thing that kept clutching at her heart was hope. The hope that the letter wouldn't come at all; that there'd be a telephone call instead—and Rodney's voice.

The telephone did ring just before noon, but the voice was Galbraith's. He wanted to know if she wouldn't come over to his Long Island farm the following morning and spend the day.

She had visited the place two or three times and had always enjoyed it immensely there. It wasn't much of a farm, but there was a delightful old Revolutionary farmhouse on it, with ceilings seven feet high and casement windows, and the floors of all the rooms on different levels; and Galbraith, there, was always quite at his best. His sister and her husband, whom he had brought over from England when he bought the place, ran it for him. They were the simplest sort of peasant people who had hardly stirred from their little Surrey hamlet until that meteoric brother of theirs had summoned them on their breath-taking voyage to America, and for whom now, on this little Long Island farm, New York might have been almost as far away as London. Mrs. Flaxman did all the work of the house and farmyard without the aid of a servant, and her husband raised vegetables for the New York market.

What the pair really thought of the life John Galbraith led, or of the guests he sometimes brought out for week-end visits, no one knew. But the pleasant sort of homely hospitality one always found there was extremely attractive to Rose, and with Rodney's regular Saturday letter at hand she'd have accepted the invitation eagerly. As it was, she answered almost shortly that she couldn't come. Then, contrite, she hastened to dilute her refusal with an elaboration of regrets and hastily contrived reasons.

"All right," he said good-humoredly, "I shan't ask any one else, but if you happen to change your mind call me on the phone in the morning. Tell me what train you're coming down on and I'll meet you."

She didn't expect to change her mind, but a phonograph did it for her. This instrument was domesticated across the court somewhere—

she had never bothered to discover just which pair of windows the sound of it issued from—and it was addicted to fox-trots, comic recitations in negro dialect, and the melodies of Mr. Irving Berlin. It was jolly and companionable and Rose regarded it as a friend. But on this Saturday night, perversely enough, perhaps because its master was in Pittsburgh on a business trip and hadn't come home as expected, the thing turned sentimental. It sang *I'm on My Way to Mandalay*, under the impression that Mandalay was an island somewhere. It played *The Rosary*, done as a solo on the cornet; and over and over again it sang, with the thickest, sirupiest sentiment that John McCormack at his best is capable of,

> *"Just a little love, a li—ttle kiss,*
> *Just an hour that holds a world of bliss,*
> *Eyes that tremble like the stars above me,*
> *And the little word that says you love me."*

It was a song that had tormented Rose before with the abysmal fatuity of its phrases, its silly sloppy melody, and yet—this was the infuriating thing—the way it had of getting into her, somehow, reaching bare nerves and setting them all aquiver.

Tonight it broke her down. She closed the windows, despite the sultriness of the night, but the tune, having once got in, couldn't be shut out. Whether she heard it or only fancied she did, didn't matter. The words bored their way into her brain.

> *"Just a little love, a little kiss,*
> *I would give you all my life for this,*
> *As I hold you fast and bend above you. . ."*

It was a white night for Rose. The morning sun had been streaming into her bedroom for an hour before she finally fell asleep. And at nine o'clock, when she wakened, she heard the phonograph going again. It was now on its way to Mandalay, but John McCormack was no doubt waiting in the background. She went to the telephone and called up Galbraith, telling him she'd come by the first train she could get.

He met her with a dog-cart and a fat pony, and when they had jogged their way to their destination they spent what was left of the morning looking over the farm. Then there was a midday farm dinner that Rose astonished herself by dealing with as it deserved and by feeling sleepy at the conclusion of. Galbraith caught her biting down a yawn and packed her off to the big Gloucester swing in the veranda, the one addition he'd built on the place, for a nap; and obediently she did as he bade her.

Coming into the veranda about four o'clock, and finding her awake, he suggested that they go for a walk. She had dressed, in anticipation of this, in a short skirt and heavy walking boots, so they set out across the fields. Two hours later, having swung her legs over a stone wall that had a comfortably inviting flat top, she remained sitting there and let her gaze rest, unfocused, on the pleasant farm land that lay below them.

After a glance at her he leaned back against the wall at her side and began filling his pipe. She dropped her hand on his nearer shoulder. After all these months of friendship it was the first approach to a caress that had passed between them.

"You're a good friend," she said, and then the hand that had rested on him so lightly suddenly gripped hard. "And I guess I need one," she ended.

He went on filling his pipe. "Anything special you need one for?" he asked quietly.

She gave a ragged little laugh. "I guess not. Just somebody strong and steady to hold on to like this."

"Well," he said very deliberately, "you want to realize this: You say I'm a friend and I am, but if there is anything in this friendship which can be of use to you you're entitled to it; to everything there is in it. Because you made it."

"One person can't make a friendship," she said. "Even two people can't. It's got to—grow out of them somehow."

He assented with a nod. "But in this case who gave it a chance to grow? Where would it have been if I'd had my way? If you hadn't pulled me up and set me straight?"

"For that matter," she said, "where would it have been if I had had mine? If I'd run away and tried for a fresh start, as I'd have done if you hadn't set me right?"

"Make it so," he said. "Say we've equal rights in it. Still you needn't worry about my not getting my share of the benefits."

"You *are* content with it, aren't you? Like this? I haven't—cheated? Used you? It's easy for a woman to do that, I think. It isn't. . . ?" She asked that last question by taking her hand off his shoulder.

"No, put it back," he said. "It's all right." He smoked in silence for a minute; then went on. "Why, 'content' is hardly the word for it. When I think what it was I wanted and what you've given me instead. . . ! It wasn't self-denial or any other high moral principle that kept me from flaring up when you took hold of me just now. It's because I've got a better thing. Something I wouldn't trade for all the love in the world. 'Content'!"

"I'd like to believe it was a better thing," she said; "but I'm afraid I can't."

"Neither could I when I was—how old are you?—twenty-four. Perhaps when you're fifty-one you can."

"I suppose so," she said absently. "Perhaps if it were a question of choosing between a love that hadn't any friendship in it and a friendship. . . But it *can't* be like that!—Can it? Can't one have both? Can't a man—love a woman and be her friend and partner all at the same time?"

"I can't answer for every man," he said reflectively. "There are all kinds of men. And that's not mentioning the queers, who aren't real men at all. Take a dozen sound, normal, healthy men and if you could find out the truth about them, which it would be pretty hard to do, you'd find immense differences in their wants, habits, feelings; in the way things *took* them. But I've a notion that nine out of the dozen, if you could get down to the actual bedrock facts about them, would own up that if they were in love with a woman—really, you know, all the way—they wouldn't want her for a partner, and wouldn't be able to see her as a friend. That's just a guess, of course. But there's one thing I know, and that is that I couldn't."

She gave a little shiver. "*Oh*, what a mess it is!" she said. "What a perfectly hopeless blunder it is!" She slid down from the wall. "Come; let's walk."

He fell in beside her and they tramped sturdily along for a while in silence. At last she said, "Can you tell me why? Suppose there hadn't been any one else with me; suppose I'd felt toward you the way you did toward me, then; why couldn't you have gone on being my friend and partner as well as my lover? You'd have known I was worth it; have known I understood the things you were interested in and—yes, and was able to help you to work them out. Why would all that have had to go?"

"Oh, I don't know that I can explain it," he said. "But I don't think I'd call it a blunder that a strip of spring steel can't bend in your fingers like copper and still go on being a spring. You see, a man wants his work and then he wants something that isn't his work; that's altogether apart from his work; doesn't remind him of it. Love's about as far away as anything he can get. So that the notion of our working ourselves half to death over the same job, and then going home together. . ."

"Yes," she admitted. "I can see that. But that doesn't cover friendship."

He owned that it didn't. "But when I'm in love with a woman—this isn't a fact I'm proud of, but it's true—I'm jealous of her. Not of other men alone, though I'm that, too, but jealous of everything. I want to be all around her. I want to be everything to her. I want her to think there's nobody like me; that nobody else could be right and I be wrong. And I want to be able to think the same of her. I want her to hide, from me, the things about herself that I wouldn't like. When I ask her what she thinks about something, I want her to say—what I want her to think. I know what I want her to think, and if she doesn't say it she hurts my feelings."

He thought it over a bit longer and then went on. "No, I've been in love with women I could suspect of anything. Women I thought were lying to me, cheating me; women I've hated; women I've known hated me. But I've never been in love with a woman who was my friend. I'd never figured it out before, but it's so."

In the process of figuring it out he'd more or less forgotten Rose. He had been tramping along communing with his pipe; thinking aloud. If he'd been watching her face he wouldn't have gone so far.

"Well, if it's like that," she said, and the quality of her voice drew his full attention instantly—"if love has to be like that, then the game doesn't seem worth going on with. You can't live with it, and you can't live—without it." Her voice dropped a little, but gained in intensity. "At least I can't. I don't believe I can." She stopped and faced him. "What can one do?" she demanded. "Wait, I suppose you'll say, till you're fifty. Well, you're fifty, and the thing can still torment you; spring on you when you aren't looking; twist you about." She turned away with a despairing gesture and stood gazing out, tear-blinded, over the little valley the hilltop they had reached commanded.

"You want to remember this," he said at last. "I've been talking about myself. I haven't even pretended to guess for more than nine of those twelve men. That leaves three who are, I am pretty sure, different. I might have been different myself, a little anyway, if I'd got a different sort of start. If my first love-affair had been an altogether different thing. If it had been the kind that gave me a home and kids. So you don't want to take what I've said for anything more than just the truth about me. And I'm not, thank God, a fair sample."

He stood behind her, miserably helpless to say or do anything to comfort her. An instinct told him she didn't want his hands on her just then, and he couldn't unsay the things he had told her any further than he had already.

Presently she turned back to him, slid her hand inside his arm, and started down the road with him. "My love-affair brought me a home and—kids," she said. "There are two of them—twins—a year and a half old now; and I went off and left them; left him. And all I did it for was to make myself over, into somebody he could be friends with, instead of just—as I said then—his mistress. I'd never known a woman then who was a man's mistress, really, and I didn't see why he should be so angry over my using the word. I thought it was fair enough. And the day I left his house I came to you and got a job in the chorus in *The Girl Up-stairs*. I thought that by earning my own way, building a life that he didn't—surround, as you say—I could win his friendship. And have his love besides. I don't suppose you would have believed there could be such a fool in the world as I was to do that."

He took a while digesting this truly amazing statement of hers, a half-mile perhaps of steady silent tramping. But at last he said, "No, I wouldn't call you a fool. I call a fool a person who thinks he can get something for nothing. You didn't think that. You were willing to pay—a heavy price it must have been, too—for what you wanted. And I've an idea, you know, that you never really pay without getting something; though you don't always get what you expect. You've got something now. A knowledge of what you can do; of what you are worth; and I don't believe you'd trade it for what you had the day before you came to me for a job."

"I don't know," she said raggedly. "Perhaps. . ." A sob clutched at her throat and she did not try to conclude the sentence.

"As to whether you did right or wrong in leaving him," he went on, "you've got to figure it this way. It isn't fair to say, 'Knowing what I know now and being what I am now, but in the situation I was in then, I'd have done differently.' The thing you've got to take into account is, being what you were then, suppose you hadn't gone? You thought then that you were just his mistress, not knowing what a real mistress was like; and you thought that by going away you could make yourself his friend. You thought that was your great chance. Well, you couldn't have stayed without feeling that you had thrown away your chance; without knowing that you'd had your big thing to do and had been afraid to do it. And that knowledge would have gone a long way toward making you the thing you thought you were.

"Well, you did your big thing. And a person who's done that has stayed alive anyway; and he knows that when his next big thing comes along he'll do that too. I don't pretend that you'll always come out right in the end if you do the big thing, but I'm pretty sure of this; that you never come out at all if you refuse it."

His amazement over what she had done increased as he thought about it and was testified to every now and then by grunts and snorts and little exclamations, but he made no more articulate comment.

There was a seven-thirty train she thought she ought to take back to town and as their walk had led in that direction they finished it at the station, where he waited with her for the train to come in.

"It's been a good day," she said. "I feel as if you'd somehow pulled me through."

"And I," he said, "feel like a wind-bag. I've talked and talked; smug comfortable preaching."

"No, it's helped," she insisted. "Or something has. Just having you there, perhaps. I feel better, anyway."

But after she'd got her last look at him on the platform, when the train had carried her off, an observer, seeing the way the color faded out of her face, and the look in the eyes, which, so wide open and so unseeing, stared straight ahead, would have said that the benefit hadn't lasted long. There was about her the look of somber terror, just verging on panic, which you have seen in a child's face when he has been sent up-stairs to bed alone in the dark.

Fragments of Galbraith's talk came back to her. It was by ceasing to be her lover and her partner that he had become her friend. Rodney, it seemed from his letters, was becoming her friend too. Was it because he, too, had ceased to be her lover? if ever she stood face to face with him again would she search in vain for that look of hunger—of ages-old hunger and need—that she'd last seen when they stood face to face in her little room on Clark Street?

She walked down-town to her apartment from the Pennsylvania station end, though the natural effect of fatigue was to quicken her pace, and though she was indubitably tired, she walked slowly; slowly, and still more slowly. She found she dreaded going back to that apartment of hers and shutting herself in for the night, alone.

She found two corners of white projecting from under her door. And when she'd unlocked and opened it she stooped and picked them up, a visiting card and a folded bit of paper. She turned the card over and gave a little half-suffocated cry.

It was Rodney's card and on it he'd written, "Sorry to have missed you. I'll come back at eight."

Her shaking fingers fumbled pitifully over the folds of the note, but she got it open at last. It was from him too. It read:

Dear Rose:
    This is hard luck. I suppose you're off for a week-end somewhere. I want very much to see you. When you come back and have leisure for me, will you call me up? I know how busy you are so I'll wait until I hear from you.

                                      Rodney

Her heart felt like lead when she'd read it. Dazedly, a little giddily, she pulled her door shut, went into her room and sat down.

He was in New York! He'd been to see her this afternoon—and left a card! And the note he'd written after his second visit was what Howard West might have written, or any other quite casual, slightly over-polite acquaintance. And it was from Rodney to her!

She couldn't see him if he felt like that; couldn't stand it to see him if he felt like that! Bitterness, contempt, hatred, anything would be easier to bear than that. She was to call up his hotel, was she? Well, she wouldn't!

And then suddenly she spread the note open again and read it once more. Turned it over and scrutinized the reverse side of the paper, and uttered a little sobbing laugh. If he'd been as cool, unmoved, self-possessed, as that note had tried to sound, would he have forgotten to tell her at what hotel she was to call him up?

Then, with a gasp, she wondered how she *could* call him up. He'd think she knew where he was; he'd wait; and after he'd waited a while, in default of word from her, wouldn't he take her silence for an answer and go back to Chicago?

She clenched her hands at that and tried to think. Well, the obvious thing to do seemed to be the only one. She must try one hotel after another until she found him. After all, there probably weren't more than a dozen to choose among. It wouldn't be easy looking up numbers with everything dancing before her eyes like this, but if she took the likeliest ones first she mightn't have to go very far. And, indeed, at a third attempt she found him.

When the telephone girl switched her to the information desk, and the information clerk said, "Mr. Rodney Aldrich? Just a moment," and then; "Mr. Aldrich is in fifteen naught five," the dry contraction in her throat made it impossible for her to speak.

But the switchboard girl had evidently been listening in and plugged her through, because she heard the throb of another ring, a click of a receiver and then—then Rodney's voice.

She couldn't answer his first "Hello," and he said it again, sharply, "Hello, what is it?"

And then suddenly her voice came back. A voice that startled her with its distinctness. "Hello, Rodney," she said; "this is Rose."

There was a perfectly blank silence after that and, then the crisp voice of an operator somewhere—"Waiting?"

"Yes," she heard Rodney say, "get off the line." And then to her. "I came to see you this afternoon and again tonight."

"Yes, I know," she said. "I just this minute got in. Can't you come back again now?"

How in the world, she had wondered, could she manage her voice like that! From the way it sounded she might have been speaking to Alice Perosini; and yet her shaking hand could hardly hold the receiver. She heard him say:

"It's pretty late, isn't it? I don't want to. . . You'll be tired and. . ."

"It's not too late for me," she said, "only you might come straight along before it gets any later."

She managed to wait until she heard him say, "All right," before she hung up the receiver. Then a big racking sob, not to be denied any longer, pounced on her and shook her.

IV

Couleur-de-rose

The fact that the length of time it would take a taxi to bring him down from his hotel to her apartment was not enough to decide anything in, plan anything in, was no more than enough, indeed, to give her a chance to stop crying and wash her face, was a saving factor in the situation.

In the back of her mind, as with a hairpin or two she righted her hair and decided, glancing down over herself, against attempting to change even her tumbled blouse or her dusty boots, was an echoing consciousness of something Galbraith had said that afternoon—"And you know when your next big thing comes along you will do that too."

Without actually quoting those words to herself, she experienced a sudden confidence that was almost serene. In a few minutes now, not more than five, probably—she hoped not more than that—something incalculable, tremendous, was going to begin happening to her. A thing whose issue would in all likelihood determine the course of her whole life. There might be a struggle, a tempest, but she made no effort to foresee the nature of it. She just relaxed physical and spiritual muscles and waited. Only she hoped she wouldn't have to wait long.

No—there was the bell.

It was altogether fortunate for Rose that she had attempted no preparation, because the situation she found herself in when she'd opened the door for her husband, shaken hands with him, led him into her sitting-room and asked him to sit down, was one that the wildest cast of her imagination would never have suggested as a possible one for her and Rodney. And it lasted—recurred, at least, whenever they were together—almost unaltered, for two whole days.

It was his manner, she felt sure, that had created it; and yet, so prompt and automatic had been her response that she couldn't be sure, not for the first half-hour or so, anyway, that he wasn't attributing it to her. It wasn't so much the first words he said, when, opening her door, she saw him standing in the hallway, as it was his attitude; his rather formal attitude; the way he held his hat; the fact—this was absurd, of course, but she reconstructed the memory very clearly afterward—

that his clothes were freshly pressed. It was the slightly anxious, very determined attitude of an estimable and rather shy young man making his first call on a young lady, on whom he is desperately desirous of making a favorable impression.

What he said was something not very coherent about being very glad and its being very good of her, and almost simultaneously she gasped out that she was glad, and wouldn't he come in. She held out her hand to him, politely, and he, compensating for an imperceptible hesitation with a kind of clumsy haste, took it and released it almost as hastily. She showed him where to hang his coat and hat, conducted him into her sitting-room and invited him to sit down. And there they were.

And he was Rodney, and she was Rose! It was like an absurd dream.

For a while she talked desperately, under the same sort of delirious conviction one has in dreams that if he desists one moment from some grotesquely futile form of activity a cosmic disaster will instantly take place. A moment of silence between them would be, she felt, something unthinkably terrible. It was not a fear of what might emerge from such a silence, the sudden rending of veils and the confrontation of two realities; it was a dread, purely, of the silence itself. But the feeling did not last very long.

"Won't you smoke?" she asked suddenly; and hurried on when he hesitated, "I don't do it myself, but most of my friends do, and I keep the things." From a drawer in her writing-desk she produced a tin box of cigarettes. "They're your kind—unless you've changed," she commented, and went over to the mantel shelf for an ash-tray and a match-safe. The match-safe was empty and she left the room to get a fresh supply from her kitchenette.

On the inner face of her front door was a big mirror, and in it, as she came back through the unlighted passage, she saw her husband. He was sitting just as she'd left him, and as his face was partly turned away from her, it could not have been from the expression of it that she got her revelation. But she stopped there in the dark and caught her breath and leaned back against the wall and squeezed the tears out of her eyes.

Perhaps it was just because he was sitting so still, a thing it was utterly unlike him to do. The Rodney of her memories was always ranging about the rooms that confined him. Or the grip of the one hand she could see upon the chair-arm it rested on may have had something to do with it. But it was not, really, a consciously deductive process at all; just a clairvoyant look—*into* him, and a sudden, complete, utterly confident understanding.

He had come down here to New York to make another beginning. He meant to assert no rights, not even in their common memories, he would make no appeal. But something that he felt he had forfeited he was going to try to earn back. What was the thing he sought—her friendship, or her love? She knew! No plea that the inspired rhetoric of passion could be capable of could have convinced her of his love for her and of his need for her love as did the divine absurdity of this attempt of his to show her that she need give him—nothing. She knew. Oh, how she knew!

She stole back into her little kitchen and shut the door and leaned giddily against it, trying to get her breath to coming steadily again. At last she straightened up and wiped her eyes. A smile played across her lips; the smile of deep maternal tenderness. Then she picked up her box of matches and carried them to him in the sitting-room.

He stayed that first evening a little less than an hour, and when he got up to go, she made no effort to detain him. The thing had been, as its unbroken surface could testify, a highly successful first call. Before she let him go, though, she asked him how long he was going to be in New York, and on getting a very indeterminate answer that offered a minimum of "two or three days" and a maximum that could not even be guessed at, she said:

"I hope you're not going to be too dreadfully busy for us to see a lot of each other. I wish we might manage it once every day."

That shook him; for a moment, she thought the lightning was going to strike and stood very still holding her breath, waiting for it.

But he steadied himself, said he could certainly manage that if she could, and as the elevator came up in response to her ring, said that he would call her up in the morning at her office.

She puzzled a little during the intermittent processes of undressing, over why she had let him go like that. She found it easy to name some of the things that were *not* the reason. It was not—oh, a thousand times it was not!—that she wasn't quite sure of him. There was no expressing the completeness of her certainty that, with a look, a sudden holding out of the hands to him, the release of one little love-cry from her lips, a half-articulate, "Come and take me, Roddy! That's all I want!" she could have shattered, annihilated, that brittle restraint of his; released the full tempest of his passion; found herself—lost herself—in his embrace.

Certainly it was no doubt of that that had held her back. And, no more than doubt, was it pride or modesty. The one thing her whole being was crying out for was a complete surrender to him.

But the real reason seemed rather absurd, when she tried to state it to herself. She had felt that it would be a *brutal* thing to do. Really, her feeling toward him was that of a mother toward a child who, having, he thinks, merited her displeasure, offers her, by way of atonement, some dearly prized possession; an iron fire-engine, a woolly sheep. What mother wouldn't accept an offering like that gravely!

This thing that Rodney had offered her, the valiant, heart breaking pretense that she needn't give him anything—to her, whose aching need was to give him everything she had!—was just as absurd as the child's toy could have been. But it had cost him. . . Oh, what must it not have cost him in struggle and sacrifice, to construct that pitiful, transparent pretense!—to maintain that manner! And the struggle and the sacrifice must not be cheapened, made absurd by a sudden shattering demonstration that they'd been unnecessary. His pretense must be melted, not shattered. And until it could be melted, that aching need of hers must wait.

And then she realized that the ache was gone—the tormenting restless hunger for him that had been nagging at her ever since the first rush of spring was somehow appeased. She'd have said, twenty-four hours ago, that to be with him, have him near her, in any other relation than that of her lover, would be unendurable. Twenty-four hours ago! She thought of that as she was winding her watch. It seemed incredible that it was no longer than that since the saccharine little sob in John McCormack's voice as he had sung "Just a little love, a li-ttle ki-iss," had driven her frantic.

She turned out her light and opened her bedroom window. The phonograph across the court was going again. But now, evidently, its master had come back from Pittsburgh, for it was singing lustily, "That's why I wish again that I was in Michigan, back on the farm."

Rose smiled her old wide smile, and cuddled her cheek into the pillow. She was the happiest person in the world.

When he called her up the next morning, she asked him to come down to the premises of Dane & Company (it was a loft on lower Fifth Avenue) about noon and go out to lunch with her, and she made no secret of her motive in selecting their rendezvous. "I'd like to have you see what our place is like;" she said, "though it isn't like anything much just now, between seasons this way. Still you can get an idea."

He said he would be immensely interested to see the place, and from the cadence of his voice was apparently prepared to let the conversation end there. But she prolonged it a little.

"Do you hear from—Chicago while you're down here, Roddy?" she asked. "Whether everything's all right—at home, I mean?"

It was a second or two before he answered, but when he did, his voice was perfectly steady.

"Yes," he said. "I get a night-letter every morning from Miss French. (This was Mrs. Ruston's successor.) It's—everything's all right."

"Good-by, then, till noon," she said. And if he could have seen the smile that was on her lips, and the brightness that was in her eyes as she said it. . . !

It was a part, you see, of his Quixotic determination to make no claims, that he had not said a word, during his evening call, about the twins—her babies!

On the stroke of twelve his card was brought to her, and she went out into their bare little waiting-room to meet him.

"We aren't a regular dressmaking establishment, you see," she said. "The people we have to impress aren't the ones we make the clothes for. So we can be as shabby down here as we please, and Alice says—Alice Perosini, you know—that our shabbiness really does impress them. Shows we don't care what they think.

"You're sure you've plenty of time to see around in?" she went on. "That it won't cut into your time for lunch?"

He made it plain that he had plenty of time, and she took him into her own studio, a big north-lighted room at the back of the building, with the painter's manikins that Jimmy Wallace had told about, standing about in it, and some queer-looking electric-light fixtures suggestive of the stage; a big tin-lined box with half a dozen powerful tungsten lamps in it, and grooves in the mouth of it for the reception of colored slides. And a sort of search-light that swung on a pivot. There was a high cutting-table with a deep indentation in it, in which Rose could stand with her work all around her. On a shelf in a corner he noticed two or three little figures twelve inches high or so that he'd have thought of as dolls had it not been that their small heads gave them the scale of adults. Rose followed his glance.

"I play with those," she said. "Dress them in all sorts of things—tissue-paper mostly. It seems easier to catch an idea small in the tips of my fingers, and then let it grow up. You have to find out for yourself how you can do things, don't you?"

Then she took him out into the workroom, where there were more cutting-tables and power-driven sewing-machines.

"'It never rains but it pours,' is the motto of this business," she told him. "Nobody ever knows what he wants until the very last minute, and then he wants it the next, and everybody wants it at once. And then this place is like a madhouse. We simply go out of our heads. It was like that when Jimmy Wallace was down here. I hadn't a minute for him."

She added deliberately, "I'm glad you didn't come down then," and went swiftly on to explain to him a sort of pantograph arrangement which could be set with reference to the measurements of the manikin Rose had designed the costume upon, and those of the girl who was going to wear it, so that the pattern for the costume itself, as distinct from Rose's master-pattern, was cut almost automatically to fit.

"It's not really automatic, of course," she said. "No costume's done until I have seen it on the girl who's going to wear it. But it does save time."

Alice Perosini came in just then, and a breath-taking spectacle she'd have been to most men in the frock she had on. But it was not Rodney who gasped. It was Alice herself who almost did, when Rose introduced him to her, without explanations, as Mr. Aldrich and said she was going out to lunch with him.

"And there's no telling when I'll be back," she added, "so if there's anything to talk about, you'd better seize the chance and tell me now."

Alice couldn't be blamed if her face was a study. She knew that Aldrich was the name of Rose's abandoned husband, and it would have been natural to believe that this highly impressive-looking person, whom Rose so casually introduced, was he. But the matter-of-fact way in which Rose was trotting him about the shop, and spoke of carrying him off to lunch, seemed to make such a conclusion fantastic.

There was nothing casual about the man, though, she reflected afterward. He'd taken his part, adequately and politely, of course, in the introduction and the fragmentary word or two of small-talk that had followed it, but Alice doubted if he'd really seen her at all. And when a man didn't see Alice—this was a line of reasoning she was quite candidly capable of—it meant an intensity of preoccupation that one might call monstrous—portentous, anyway.

Rose asked him if he minded the Brevoort, which was near by and airy, on a warm spring day like this, and he assented to it with enthusiasm. He hadn't been there in years, he said. She wished, a little later, that she had thought twice and had taken him somewhere else, where she wasn't quite so obviously well acquainted. The cordial salutation of the head waiter, the number of people who nodded at her from this table or that, might well have been dispensed with on an occasion like this. And the climax was when the table waiter, well accustomed to having her bring guests of either sex to lunch with her, and on confidential terms with her gustatory preferences, handed her a menu—as a matter of form—told her what he thought she'd like today, and, getting out his pencil and his card, prepared to write it down. She saw Rodney looking pretty blank, so she checked the waiter and said:

"I think I *did* ask you to lunch with me, but if you'd rather I lunched with you. . . You can have it whichever way you like."

He hesitated just an instant; then said he'd like to lunch with her. And somehow their eyes met over that in a way that, once more, made Rose hold her breath. But the lightning didn't strike that time.

Even so, their hour wasn't wasted on the polite topics of custom-made conversation, as, for a while, she had feared it would be; because he asked her, presently—and she could see he really wanted to know—how she had got started in this costuming business. It was evidently a thing she had a genius for, but how had she found it out, and how had she worked out that technique which, even to the eyes of his ignorance, was clearly extraordinary?

And Rose, beginning a little timidly, because she knew there were rocks ahead for him, told him the tale that had its beginning in Lessing's store; the story of Mrs. Goldsmith and her bad taste, of the Poiret model that had suggested her great idea, of the offer she had made Galbraith, the way she had bought her dressmaker's form and her bolts of paper-cambric out of the Christmas rush, and had cut out her patterns in the dead of nights after rehearsals, up in her little room on Clark Street. She told him of the wild rush with which the costumes themselves got made down under the stage at the Globe; of Galbraith's enthusiasm, of the bargain she'd driven with Goldsmith and Block—the unwittingly good bargain that had left her a profit of over two hundred dollars. She told him how Goldsmith and Block had driven a good bargain of their own, hiring her at her chorus-girl's salary for the last two delirious weeks; how insanely hard she'd worked, and how, at last, after the opening performance, Galbraith had offered her a job in New York when he should be ready for her.

Somehow, while she told it, though it was only occasionally that she glanced up at him—somehow, as she told it, she seemed to be hearing it with his ears—to be thinking, actually, the very thoughts that were going through his mind.

The central cord of it all, that everything else depended from, was, she knew, the reflection that this triumphant narrative he was listening to now, had been waiting on her lips to be told to him that night in the room on Clark Street, and that the smoking smoldering fires of his outraged pride and masculine sense of possession, had made the telling impossible—had made everything impossible but that dull outcry of hers that it had ended—like this.

But he never winced. Indeed, now and then when she tried to run ahead in a way to elide this incident or that, he asked questions that brought out all the details, and at the end he said with undisguised gravity, but quite steadily:

"So after the play opened you were just waiting for Galbraith to send for you. Why—why did you go on the road, instead of to New York?"

"He hadn't sent for me yet, and I'd made up my mind, by that time, that he meant not to. And I was too tired just then to come down here and try for anything else. I went on the road for a sort of rest-cure."

He sat for a good while after that in a reflective silence. And, at the end of it, deliberately introduced a new and entirely harmless topic of conversation. She knew why he did that. She understood now that there was more on his program than his manner last night had indicated. That had been a preliminary, but the past wasn't to be ignored forever. A time was coming when the issue between them should be brought up and settled. But the time was not now, nor the place this crowded restaurant.

She was perfectly docile to his new conversational lead, but the fact that she yielded, that she knew it would be beyond her powers to force that issue until he was ready for it, thrilled her—brought the blood into her cheeks. The thing he was doing might be absurd, but his way of doing it was not absurd. He had changed, somehow, or something had changed between them. She engaged all his powers. If there should be a struggle now, his mind would not betray him.

Just before they left the restaurant he asked her if she would dine with him some night and go to a show afterward, and when she said she would he asked what night would be convenient to her.

Her inflection was perfectly demure and even casual, but nothing could keep the sudden "richening" that Jimmy Wallace had tried to describe out of her voice, and the light of mischief danced openly in her eyes when she said:

"Why, tonight's all right for me." She added, "If that's not too soon for you."

He flushed and dropped his hands from the edge of the table where they'd been resting, but he answered evenly enough:

"No, it's not too soon for me."

And then force of habit betrayed Rose into a stupid blunder that almost precipitated a small quarrel.

"Tell me what you'd like to see," she said, "and I'll telephone for the seats."

Then, at his horrified stare, she gasped out an explanation. "Roddy, I didn't mean *buy* the seats! I don't have to buy seats at any theater. And at this time of year they're so glad to have somebody to give them to that it seems sort of—wicked to pay real money."

"It's my mistake," he said. "Naturally, going to the theater wouldn't be much of a—treat to you. I'd forgotten that."

"Going with *you* would be a treat to me," she said earnestly. "That's why I didn't think about the other part of it. But I needn't have been so stupid as that. Will you forget I said it, please?"

He smiled now at himself, the first smile of genuine amusement she had seen on his lips for—how long?

"And I needn't have been quite so horrified," he admitted. "All the same, I hope I may manage to hit on a restaurant up-town somewhere, where the waiter won't hand you the check."

It was on this note that he parted from her at Dane & Company's doorway.

But the ice didn't melt so fast as she had expected it would, and she went to bed that night, after he'd brought her home in a taxi and, having told the chauffeur to wait, formally escorted her to her elevator, in a state of mind not quite so serenely happy as that of the night before. She had held her breath a good many times during the dinner, and even in the theater, where certain old memories and associations sprang at them both, as it were, from ambush. But always, at the breaking point, he managed to summon up unexpected reserves for resistance, intrenched himself in the manner of his first call.

Rose both smiled and wept over her review of this evening, and was a long while getting off to sleep. She felt she couldn't stand this state of things much longer.

But it was not required of her. With the last of the next day's light, the ice broke up and the floods came.

She had taken him to a studio tea in the upper sixties just off West End Avenue, the proprietors of the studio being a tousled, bearded, blond anarchist of a painter and his exceedingly pretty, smart, frivolous-looking wife—who had more sense than she was willing to let appear. They had lived in Paris for years, but the fact that he had a German-sounding name had driven them back to New York. It was through Gertrude that Rose had got acquainted with them—she having wrung from Abe Shuman permission for the painter to prowl around back-stage and make notes for a series of queerly lighted pictures of chorus-girls and dancers—"Degas—and then some," as his admirers said. Gertrude was at the tea and two or three others. It wasn't a party.

The two men had instinctively drawn controversial swords almost at sight of each other and for the hour and a half that they were together the combat raged mightily, to the unmixed satisfaction of both participants. The feelings of the bystanders were perhaps more diverse, but Rose, at least, enjoyed herself thoroughly, not only over seeing her husband's big, formidable, finely poised mind in action again, but over a change that had taken place in the nature of some of his ideas. The talk, of course, ranged everywhere: Socialism, feminism, law and its crimes, art and the social mind. Gertrude took a hand in it now and then, and it was something Rodney said to her, in answer to a remark about dependent wives, that really made Rose sit up.

"Wives aren't dependents," he said, "except as they let their husbands make them think they are. Or only in very rare cases. Certainly I don't know of a wife who doesn't render her husband valuable economic services in exchange for her support. I can hardly imagine one. Of course if they don't recognize that these services are valuable, they can be made to feel dependent all right."

Gertrude demurred. She was willing to admit that a wife who took care of a husband's house, cooked his meals, brought up his children, did him an economic service and that if she didn't feel that she was earning her way in the world it was because she had been imposed on. But here in New York, anyway—she didn't know how it might be out in Chicago—one didn't have to resort to his imagination to conjure up a wife who rendered none of these services whatever. "They live, thousands of them, in smart up-town apartments, don't do a lick of work, choke up Fifth Avenue with their limousines in the afternoon, dress like birds of paradise, or as near to it as they can come, dine with their husbands in the restaurants, go to the first nights, eat lobster Newburg afterward, and spend the next morning in bed getting over it. Those that can't afford that kind of life scrape along giving the best imitation of it they know how. Thousands of them—thousands and thousands. If they aren't dependents. . ."

"They're not, though," said Rodney. "Not a bit of it. They're giving their husbands an economic service of a peculiarly indispensable sort. The first requisite for success to the husbands of women who live like that is the appearance of success. Their status, their front, is the one thing they can't do without. Well, and it's a curious fact that a man can't keep up his own front. If he tries to dress extravagantly, wear diamonds, spend his money on himself, he doesn't look prosperous. He looks a fool. People won't take him seriously. If he can get a wife who's ornamental, who has attractive manners, who can convey the appearance of being expensive without being vulgar, she's of a perfectly enormous economic advantage to him. She'd only have to quit buying the sort of clothes he could parade her in, and begin spoiling her looks with a menial domestic routine, to draw howls of protest from him. Only, so long as she doesn't call his bluff, she leaves him free to think that he's doing it all for her and that except for her extravagance—extravagance, mind you, that nine times out of ten he's absolutely rammed down her throat—he'd be as rich, really, as he has to try to pretend he is. He tells her so, with perfect sincerity—and she believes it." Rose enjoyed the look in Gertrude's face as she listened to that.

It was half past six or thereabout when they left the studio, and the late May afternoon was at its loveliest. It was the sort of day, as Rodney said, that convicted you, the minute you came out of it, of abysmal folly in having wasted any of it indoors.

"I want to walk," said Rose, "after that tea, if I'm ever to want any dinner."

He nodded a little absently, she thought, and fell in step beside her. There was no mention at any time, of their destination.

It was a good while before Rose got the key to his preoccupation. They had turned into the park at Sixty-sixth Street, and were half-way over to the Fifth Avenue corner at Fifty-ninth, before he spoke out.

"On a day like this," he said, "to have sat there for two or three mortal hours arguing about stale ideas! Threshing over the straw—almost as silly an occupation as chess—when we might have been out here, being alive! But it must have seemed natural to you to hear me going on like that." And then with a burst, before she could speak:

"You must remember me as the most blindly opinionated fool in the world!"

She caught her breath, then said very quietly, with a warm little laugh in her voice, "That's not how I remember you, Rodney."

She declined to help him when he tried to scramble back to the safe shores of conventional conversation. That sort of thing had lasted long enough. She just walked along in step with him and, for her part, in silence. It wasn't long before he fell silent too.

A thing that Rose hadn't counted on was the effect produced on both of them just by walking along like this together, side by side, in step. Just the rhythm of it established a sort of communion—and it was a communion fortified by many associations. Practically the whole of their courtship, from the day when he dropped off the street-car with her in the rain and walked her over to the elevated and kept her note-books, down to the day on the bridge over the Drainage Canal in the swirl of that March blizzard, when she'd felt his first embrace, had been on foot like this, tramping along side by side; miles and miles and miles, as she'd told her mother. And there had been other walks since. Do you remember the last time they had walked together? It was from the stage door of the Globe theater to her little room on North Clark Street. Rose remembered it and she felt sure that he did. The same singing wire of memories and associations that had vibrated between them then was vibrating between them now and drawing up palpably tighter with every half-mile they walked. Their pace quickened a little.

Straight down Fifth Avenue they walked to the corner of Thirteenth Street, and then west. And when they stopped and faced each other in the entrance to the gray brick building where Rose's apartment was, it was at the end of a mile or more of absolutely unbroken silence. And facing each other there, all that was said between them was her:

"You'll come in, won't you?" and his, "Yes."

But the gravity with which she'd uttered the invitation and the tenseness of his acceptance of it, the square look that passed between them, marked an end of something and the beginning of something new.

She left him in her sitting-room while she went through into her bedroom to take off her hat and jacket and take a glance into her mirror. When she came back, she found him standing at her window looking out. He didn't turn when she came in, but almost immediately he began speaking. She went rather limp at the sound of his voice and dropped down on a cushioned ottoman in front of the fireplace, and squeezed her hands together between her knees.

"I don't know how much you will have understood," he began, "probably a good deal. You told me in Dubuque—as you were quite right to tell me—that I mustn't come back to you. And now I've disobeyed you and come. What I hope you will have guessed is that I wouldn't have come except that I'd something to tell you—something different from the—idiocies I tormented you with in Dubuque;—something I felt you were entitled to be told. But I felt—this is what you won't have understood—I felt that I hadn't any right to speak to you at all, about anything vital, about anything that concerned us, until I'd given you some sort of guarantee—until I'd shown you that I was a person it was possible to deal reasonably with."

She smiled, then pressed her hands suddenly to her eyes.

"I understood," she said.

"Well, then. . ." But he didn't at once go on. Stood there a while longer at the window, then crossed the room and brought up before her book-shelves, staring blindly at the titles. He hadn't looked at her even as he crossed the room.

"Oh, it's a presumptuous thing to try to say," he broke out at last, "a pitifully unnecessary thing to say, because you must know it without my telling you. But when you went away you said—you said it was because you hadn't—my—friendship! You said that was the thing you wanted and that you were going to try to earn it. And in Dubuque you told me that I'd evidently never be able to understand that you could have been happy in that room on Clark Street, that I'd wanted to 'rescue' you from; that I'd never be able to see that the thing you were doing there was a fine thing, worth doing, entitled to my respect. Well, the things I'd been saying to you and the things I'd been doing, justified you in thinking that. But what I've come down here to say is—is that now—at last—I do see it."

She would have spoken then if she could have commanded her voice, and as it was, the sound she made conveyed her intention to him, for he turned on her quickly as if to interrupt the unspoken words, and went on with an almost savage bitterness.

"Oh, I'm under no illusions about it. I had my chance to see, when seeing would have meant something to you—helped you. When any one but the blindest sort of fool would have seen. I didn't. Now, when the thing is patent for the world to see—now that Violet Williamson has seen it and Constance, and God knows who of the rest of them, who were so tactful and sympathetic about my 'disgrace'—now that you've won your fight without any help from me. . . Without any help! In spite of every hindrance that my idiocy could put in your way! Now, after all—I come and tell you that you've earned the thing you've set out to get."

There was a little silence after that. She got up and took the post he had abandoned at the window.

"Why did you do it, Roddy?" she asked. "I mean, why did you want to come and tell me?"

"Why, in the first place," he said, "I wanted to get back a little of my self-respect. I couldn't get that until I'd told you."

This time the silence was longer.

"What else did you want?" she asked. "What—in the second place?"

"I don't know why I put it like that," he said. "Please don't think. . . I can't bear to have you think that I came down here to—ask anything of you—anything in the way of a reward for having seen what is so plain to every one. I haven't any—claim at all. I want to earn your friendship. It's the biggest thing I've got to hope for. But I've no idea that you can hand it out to me ready-made. I believe you'd do it if you could. But you said once, yourself, that it wasn't a thing that could be given. It was a thing that had to be earned. And you were right about that, as you were about so many other things. Well, I'm going to try to earn it." "Is that—all you want?" she asked, and then hearing the little gasp he gave, she swung round quickly and looked at him. It was pretty dark in the room, but his face in the dusk seemed to have whitened.

"Is friendship all you want of me, Roddy?" she asked again.

She stood there waiting, a full minute, in silence. Then she said, "You don't have to tell me that. Because I know. Oh—oh, my dear, how well I know!"

He didn't come to her; just stood there, gripping the corner of her bookcase and staring at her silhouette, which was about all he could see of her against the window. At last he said, in a strained dry voice she'd hardly have known for his:

"If you know that—if I've let you see that, then I've done just about the last despicable thing there was left for me to do. I've come down here and—made you feel sorry for me. So that with that—divine—kindliness of yours, you're willing to give me—everything."

He straightened up and came a step nearer. "Well, I won't have it, I tell you! I don't know how you guessed. If I'd dreamed I was betraying that to you. . . ! Don't I know—it's burnt into me so that I'll never forget—what the memory of my love must be to you—the memory of the hideous things it's done to you. And now, after all that—after you've won your fight—alone—and stand where you stand now—for me to come begging! And take a gift like that! I tell you it *is* pity. It can't be anything else."

There was another minute of silence, and then he heard her make a little noise in her throat, a noise that would have been a sob had there not been something like a laugh in it. The next moment she said, "Come over here, Roddy," and as he hesitated, as if he hadn't understood, she added, "I want you to look at me. Over here by the window, where there's light enough to see me by."

He came wonderingly, very slowly, but at last, with her outstretched hand she reached him and drew him around between her and the window.

"Look into my face," she commanded. "Look into my eyes; as far in as you can. Is it—oh, my dearest"—the sob of pure joy came again—"is it pity that you see?"

She'd had her hands upon his shoulders, but now they clasped themselves behind his head. Her vision of him had swum away in a blur, and without the support she got from him she'd have been swaying giddily.

"Roddy, old man," she said, "if I hadn't seen—in the first—ten minutes, the thing you—meant so hard I shouldn't see—I think it would have—killed me. If I hadn't seen that you loved me—after all; after everything. After all the tortures you'd suffered, through me. Because that's all I want—in the world."

At that he put his arms around her and pulled her up to him. But the manner of it was so different from his old embraces that presently she drew him around so that what little light there was fell on his face, and searched it thoughtfully.

"You *do* believe me, Roddy, don't you—that there isn't any pity about it? There isn't any room for pity. There's nothing in me at all but just a great big—want of you. Don't you understand that?"

He did understand it with his mind, but he was a little dazed, like one who has stood too near where the lightning struck. The hope he had kept buried alive so long—buried alive because it wouldn't die—could not be brought out into a blinding glory like this without shrinking—pain—exquisite terrifying pain.

The knowledge she had acquired by her own suffering stood her in good stead now. She did not mistake, as the Rose he had married might have done, the weakness of his response for coldness—indifference.

She went back and began making love to him more gently; released herself from his arms, led him over to her one big chair, and made him sit down in it, settled herself upon the arm of it and contented herself with one of his hands. Presently he took one of hers, bent his face down over it and brushed the back of it with his lips.

The timidity of that caress, with all it revealed to her, was too much for her. She swallowed one sob, and another, but the next one got away from her and she broke out in a passionate fit of weeping.

That roused him from his daze a little, and he pulled her down in his arms—held her tight—comforted her.

When she got herself in hand again, she got up, went away to wash her face, and coming back in the room again, lighted a reading-lamp and drew down the blinds.

"Rose," he said presently, "what are we going to do?"

She knew she was not answering the true intent of his question when she said:

"Well, for one thing we can get a little supper. I don't know what we've got to eat, but we won't care—tonight."

There was a ring of decision in his voice that startled her a little when he said:

"No, we won't do that tonight. We'll go out somewhere to a restaurant."

Their eyes met—unwavering.

"Yes," she said, "that's what we'll do."

They didn't talk much across the table in the deserted little Italian restaurant they went to. Neither of them afterward could remember anything they'd said. They ate their meal in a sort of grave contented happiness that was reaching down deeper and deeper into them every minute, and they walked back to the gray brick building in Thirteenth Street, arm in arm, hand in hand, in silence. But when she stopped there, he said:

"Let's walk a little farther, Rose. There are things we've got to decide, and—and I'm not going in with you again tonight."

She caught her breath at that, and her hand tightened its hold on his. But she walked on with him.

He said, presently, "You understand, don't you?"

She answered, "Oh, my dear!—yes." But she added, a little shakily, "I wish we had a magic-carpet right here, that we could fly home on."

Then they walked a while in silence.

At last he said: "There's this we can do. I can go back to my hotel tonight, and tell them that I'm expecting you—that I'm expecting my wife to join me there. Tomorrow? And then I can come and get you and bring you there. It's not home, and it's not the place I'd choose for—for a honeymoon, but. . ."

The way she echoed the word set him thinking. But before his thoughts had got to their destination she said:

"Shall we make it a real honeymoon, Roddy—make it as complete as we can? Forget everything and let all the world be. . ."

He supplied a word for her, "Rose-color?"

She accepted it with a caressing little laugh, ". . . for a while?"

"That's what I was fumbling for," he said, "but I can't think very straight tonight. I've got it now, though. That cottage we had—before the twins were born—down on the Cape. There won't be a soul there this time of the year. We'd have the world to ourselves."

"Yes," she said, "for a little while, we'd want it like that. But after a while—after a day or two, could we have the babies? Could the nurse bring them on to me and then go straight back, so that I could have them—and you, altogether?"

He said, "You darling!" But he couldn't manage more than that.

A little later he suggested that they could get the place by telegraph and could set out for it tomorrow.

She laughed and asked, "Will you let me be as silly as I like for once? Will you give me a week—well, till Saturday; that would do—to get ready in?"

"Get ready?" he echoed.

"Clothes and thinks," she said. "A—trousseau, don't you see? I've been so busy making clothes for other people that I've got just about nothing myself. And I'd like. . . But I don't really care, Roddy. I'll go with you tomorrow, 'as is,' if you want me to."

"No," he said. "We'll do it the other way."

And then he took her back to the gray brick entrance and, just out of range of the elevator man, kissed her good night.

"But will you telephone to me as soon as you wake up in the morning, so that I'll know it's true?"

She nodded. Then her eyes went wide and she clung to him.

"*Is* it true, Roddy? Is it possible for a thing to come back like that? Are we really the old Rodney and Rose, planning our honeymoon again? It wasn't quite three years ago. Three years next month. Will it be like that?"

"Not like that, perhaps," he said, "exactly. It will be better by all we've learned and suffered since."

V

The Beginning

There was a sense in which this prediction of Rodney's about their honeymoon was altogether true, They had great hours—hours of an emotional intensity greater than any they had known during that former honeymoon, greater by all they had learned and suffered since— hours that repaid all that suffering, and could not have been captured at any smaller price. There were hours when the whole of their two selves literally seemed transfused into one essence; when there was nothing of either of them that was not the other; when all their thoughts, impulses, desires, flowered spontaneously out of a common mind. There was no precalculating these experiences. They came upon them, seized them, carried them off.

One of these, that neither of them will ever forget, came at the end of a long tramp through the dawn of their second day. They had been swinging along in almost unbroken silence through the gray mist, had mounted a little hillock and halted, hand in hand, as the first lance of sunlight transfixed and flushed the still vaporous air, and it had seemed to them, as they watched, breathless, while the sun mounted, that the whole of the life that lay before them was a track of gold like that which blazed across the sea, leading to an intolerable glory.

And there were other hours of equally memorable transfiguration, which their surroundings had nothing whatever to do with—hours lighted only by the flame that flared up from their two selves.

But life, of course, can not be made up of hours like that. No sane person can even want to live in a perpetual ecstasy. What makes a mountain peak is the fall away into the surrounding valleys.

In their valleys of commonplace, every-day existence—and these occurred even in their first days together—they were stiff, shy, self- conscious with each other. And their attempt to ignore this fact only made the self-consciousness the worse. It troubled and bewildered both of them.

Rose's misgiving had been justified. They weren't the old Rodney and Rose. Those two splendid careless savages, who had lived for a fortnight on an island in the midst of Martin Whitney's carefully preserved solitude in Northern Wisconsin, accepting the gifts of the gods with such joyous confidence that none of them could ever turn bitter, those two zestful children, had ceased to exist.

John Galbraith had spoken truth when he said there was no such thing as a fresh start. For good or evil, you were the product of your yesterdays. The nightmare tour on the road with *The Girl Up-stairs* company was a part of Rose; the day in Centropolis, the night when Galbraith had made love to her. The hour in the University Club, when Rodney's heart had first shrunk from an unacknowledged fear; the days and weeks of humiliation and distress that had succeeded it, were a part of him—an ineffaceable part.

So it was natural enough—though not, therefore, the less distressing—that Rose should note, with wonder, a tendency in him to revert to the manner which had characterized his first call on her in New York; a tendency to be—of all things—polite. He didn't swear any more, nor contradict. He chose his words, got up when she did, picked up things she dropped. And when she was quite sure she was safe from discovery, she sometimes wept forlornly, for the rough, outrageous, absent-minded, imperious lover of the old days.

She did not know that she was different too—as remote from the girl she had been during the first six months of their marriage—the girl who, "all eyes," had held her breath while Doctor Randolph told her things; the girl who had smiled over Bertie Willis' love-making, because she didn't know that such things happened except in books—as he was from the old Rodney. Even Violet had seen, in the glimpse she'd caught across two taxicabs, that her smile was somehow different, and James Randolph had come back from his tea with her in the Knickerbocker, saying that she was a thousand years old.

So it was not wonderful that Rodney should have found a new mystery in her; nor that, seeing in her look, sometimes—especially when it was not meeting his own—the reflections of a thousand experiences he had not shared with her, he should have felt that she was a long way off. And his heart ached for the old Rose, whom he had so completely "surrounded"—the Rose who had consulted him about the menus for her dinners, who had brought him all her little troubles; who had tried—bless her!—to study law, and had stolen into court to hear his argument, so that she could talk with him. Whatever the future might have for him, it would never bring that Rose back.

The arrival of the twins, in the convoy of a badly flustered—and, to tell the truth, a somewhat scandalized—Miss French, simplified the situation a little—by complicating it! They absolutely enforced a routine. They had needs that must be met on the minute. And they gave Rose and Rodney so many occupations that the contemplation of their complicated states of mind was much abridged.

But even her babies brought Rose a disappointment along with them. From the time of the receipt of Miss French's telegram acknowledging Rodney's and telling them what train she and the twins would take, Rose had been telling off the hours in mounting excitement. The two utterly adorable little creatures, as the pictures of them in Rodney's pocketbook showed them to be, who were, miraculously—incredibly—hers, were coming to bring motherhood to her; a long-deferred payment for the labor and the agony with which she had borne them; the realization of half-forgotten hopes that had, during the period of her pregnancy, been the mainstay of her life. There was now no Mrs. Ruston, no Harriet, no plausible physician to keep them away from her. Rose had a smile of tender pity for the memory of the girl who had struggled so ineffectually and yet with such heart-breaking earnestness to break the filaments of the web they'd spun around her.

No, it wouldn't be like that now. Rodney had agreed explicitly that Miss French was to be allowed to stay only as long as Rose wanted her; only for the few days—or hours—she would need for making herself mistress of their régime. Then the nurse was to be sent away on a vacation and Rose should have her children to herself.

She didn't go to Boston with Rodney to meet them; nor even to the station; stayed in the cottage, ostensibly to see to it, up to the very last minute, that the fires were right (June had come in cold and rainy) and in general to be ready on the moment to produce anything that their rather unforeseeable needs might call for. Her real reason was a shrinking from having her first meeting with them in the confusion of arrival on a station platform, under the eyes of the world, amid the distractions of things like luggage.

Rodney understood this well enough, and arriving at the cottage, he clambered out of the wagon with them and carried them both straight in to Rose, leaving the nurse and the bewildering paraphernalia of travel for a second trip.

Rose, in the passionate surge of gratified desire that came with the sight of them, caught them from him, crushed them up tight against her breast—and frightened them half to death. So that without dissimulation, they howled and brought Miss French flying to the rescue.

Rose didn't make a tragedy of it; managed a smile at herself, though she suspected she'd cry when she got the chance, and subjected her ideas to an instantaneous revision. They were—*persons*, those two funnily indignant little mites, with their own ideas, their own preferences, and the perfectly adequate conviction of being entitled to them. How would she herself have liked it, to have a total stranger, fifteen feet high or so, snatch at her like that?

She was rather apologetic all day, and got her reward; especially from the boy, who was an adventurous and rather truculent baby, much she fancied, as his father must once have been, and who took to her more quickly than the girl did. Indeed, the second Rodney fell in love with her almost as promptly as his father had done before him. But little Portia wasn't very far behind. Two days sufficed for the conquest of the pair of them.

The really disquieting discovery awaited the time when the wire-edge of novelty about this adventure in motherhood had worn off; when she could bathe them, dress them, feed them their very strictly regimented meals, without being spurred to the highest pitch of alertness by the fear of making a mistake—forgetting something, like the juice of a half orange at ten o'clock in the morning, the omission of which might have—who knew what disastrous consequences!

That attitude can't last any woman long, and Rose, with her wonderfully clever hands, her wits trained—as the wits of persons who had worked for John Galbraith were always trained—not to be told the same thing twice, her pride keeping in sharp focus the determination that Rodney should see that she could be as good a nurse as Miss French—Rose wore off that nervous tenseness over her new job very quickly. Within a week she had a routine established that was noiseless—frictionless.

But do you remember how aghast she was over the forty weeks John Galbraith had talked about as the probable run of *The Girl Up-stairs*; her consternation over the idea of just going on doing the same thing over and over again, "around and round, like a horse at the end of a pole"? What she would like to do, she had told him, now that this was done, was to begin on something else.

Well, it was with something the same feeling of consternation that, having thrown herself heart and soul into the task of planning and setting in motion a routine for two year-and-a-half-old babies, she found herself straightening up and saying "What next?" And realizing, that as far as this job was concerned, there was no "next." The supreme merit of her care, from now on, would be—barring emergencies—the placid continuation of that routine. There were no heroics about motherhood—save in emergency, once more. It was a question of remembering a hundred trivial details, and executing them in the same way every day. It was a question of doing a thousand little services, not one of which was serious enough to occupy her mind, every one of which was capable of being done almost automatically—but not quite! The whole of the attention was never quite taken, and yet it was never, all the way around the clock, entirely left free. And her love for them, which had become almost as intense and overmastering a thing as her love for her husband, could never be expressed fully, as was her love for him. It would be cruelly unfair, she recognized that, to emotionalize over them—force them.

It was a fine relation. It was, perhaps, the very finest in the world. But as a job, it wasn't so satisfactory. Four-fifths of it, anyway, could be done with better results for the children by a placid, unimaginative, tolerably stupid person, who had no stronger feeling for them than the mild temporary affection they could excite in any one not a monster. And the other fifth of it wasn't strictly a job at all.

On the whole, then, leaving their miraculous hours out of the account—and, being incommensurable, imponderable, they couldn't be included in an inventory—their honeymoon, considered as an attempt to revisit Arcady, to seize a golden day that looked neither toward the past nor toward the future, complete in itself, perfect—was a failure.

It was not until, pretty ruefully, they acknowledged this, tore up their artificial resolution not to look at the future, and deliberately set themselves to the contemplation of a life that would have to take into account complex and baffling considerations, that their honeymoon became a success. It was well along in their month that this happened.

Rose had spent a maddening sort of day, a day that had been all edges, trying not to let herself feel hurt over fantastic secondary meanings which it was possible to attach to some of the things Rodney had said, frying to be cheerful and sensible, and to ignore the patent fact that his cheerfulness was as forced and unnatural a thing as hers. The children—as a rule the best-behaved little things in the world—had been refractory. They'd refused to take their morning nap for some reason or other, and had been fractious ever since. So, after their supper, when they'd finally gone off to sleep, and Rose had rejoined Rodney in the sitting-room, she was in a state where it did not take much to set her off.

It was not much that did; nothing more, indeed, than the fact that she found her husband brooding in front of the fire, and that the smile with which he greeted her was a little too quick and bright and mechanical, and that it soon faded out. The Rodney of her memories had never done things like that. If you found him sitting in a chair, you found him reading a book. When he was thinking something out he tramped back and forth, twisted his face up, made gestures! That habit couldn't have changed. It was just that he wasn't being natural with her! Couldn't feel at home with her! Before she knew it, she was crying.

He asked, in consternation, what the matter was. What had happened?

"Nothing," she said. "Absolutely nothing. Really."

"Then it's just—that you're not happy. With me, like this." He brought that out gravely, a word at a time; as though they hurt.

"Are you happy? With me—like this?" she countered.

It was a question he could not answer categorically and she did not give him time for anything else. "What's the matter with us, Roddy?" she demanded. "We ought to be happy. We meant to be. We said that we'd been through a lot, and that probably there was a lot mere to go through—in the way of working things out, at least—and that we'd take a month just for nothing but to be happy in—just for pure joy." Her voice broke in a sob over that. "And here we are—like this!"

"It hasn't all been like this," he said. "There have been hours, a day or two, that I'd go through the whole thing for, again, if necessary."

She nodded assent to that. "But the rest of the time!" she cried. "Why can't we be—comfortable together? Why. . . Roddy, why can't you be natural with me? Like your old self. Why don't you roar at me any more? And swear when you run into things? I've never seen you formal before—not with anybody. Not even with strangers. And now you're formal with me."

The rueful grin with which he acknowledged the truth of this indictment was more like him, and it cheered her immensely. She answered it with one of her own, dried her eyes and asked again, more collectedly:

"Well, can you tell me why?"

"Why, it seemed to me," he said, "that it was you who were different. And you have changed, of course, down inside, more than I have. You've been through things in the last year and a half; found out things that I know nothing about, except as I have read about them in books. I've never had to ask a stranger for a job. I've never been—brought to bay, the way you were in that damned town of Centropolis (I'd like to burn it). And other things—horrible things, have—have come so near you, that if it hadn't been for that—white flame of yours, they'd have marked you. When I think of those things I feel like a schoolboy beside you. You've no idea how—how innocent a man can be, Rose. That's not the tradition, but it's true. So, when I remember how things used to be between us, how I used to be the one who knew things, and how I preached and spouted, I get to feeling that the man you remember must look to you now, like—well, like a schoolboy. Showing off."

She stared at him incredulously. "But that's downright morbid," she said. "You don't have to go—into the gutter to learn things. And what you say about innocence. . . A man can't keep his innocence by being ignorant, Roddy. If he's kept it, he must have—fought for it. I know that."

She was still deeply disturbed. "It's horrible that I should make you feel like that," she concluded.

"It isn't you," he told her. "It's just—the situation. I can't help feeling that I'm taken—on approval. Oh, it's *got* to be like that! There are things that, with all the forgiveness in the world, you can't forget. And until you have seen that I am different, that I have made myself different. . ."

"What things?" she demanded.

"Well—a thing," he amended. "You know what I mean. The night I came to the stage door of the Globe for you."

She colored at that, and then, to his amazement, she smiled.

"I've been such a coward about that," she said. "I've tried to tell you a dozen times up here, and I've been afraid you'd be—shocked. I expect you will be, now. But I've got to tell you just the same.

"Roddy, when you were talking to me, there in the hotel at Dubuque, telling me how horrified you were over that, it came over me all at once that I had nothing to forgive; that if the thing was a fault at all, it was mine as much as yours, and that it wasn't so much of a fault as an—accident. You couldn't help hating me, and you couldn't help loving me. And you did both at once. And I, when I could have told you something that would have made you—well, hate me less, anyhow—didn't take the trouble. I said to myself then that it was too bad it happened, but that it wasn't, at least, your fault. And I was afraid to tell you so.

"But, Roddy, during these last months, down here in New York, I've been—glad it happened. It's been something to hold on to, that your love of me was strong enough, so that the hate couldn't kill it. It helped me to hope that it would be strong enough, some day or other, to bring you back to me. And without that hope, I couldn't have gone on. It's what I have lived on. The only thing that any of my—successes has meant has been that perhaps it brought that nearer."

She gave a shaky laugh. "On approval!" Her eyes filled again. "Roddy, you can't mean that."

She came over and sat down in his lap, and slid her arm around his neck.

"This is where we'll begin!" she said. "That I'll never—whatever happens—walk out on you again. Whether things go well or badly with us, we'll work it out, somehow, together."

It was not until she heard the long shuddering sigh he drew at that, and felt him go limp under her, that she realized how genuine his fear had been—the perfectly preposterous fear that if their new experiment didn't come up to her anticipation she'd tell him so, and leave him once more. This time for good.

It was a good while before they took up a rational discussion again, but at last she said:

"It will take working out, though. We've been shirking that. Hadn't we better begin?"

He assented. "Only, you'll have to get up," he said, "and sit down somewhere else. Out of reach."

She smiled as she obeyed him. "It's hard for a woman to remember," she said, "that a man can't think about other things when he's making love, and can't think about the person he's in love with when he's doing other things. Because, that's about the easiest thing a woman does."

She saw by the expression that went over his face that her remark had chilled him a little. He didn't like to think of her as "a woman," nor as of his relation to her as accounted for by the fact that he was "a man." He'd generalize fast enough about the world at large, but it would always be hard for him to include her and himself in his generalizations.

"Well," he said when he'd got his pipe alight, "it's the first question I asked you after—after I got my eyes open: What are we going to do?"

"I told Alice Perosini," she said, "the day before we left to come up here, that I'd come back in a month, and that I'd stay until I'd finished all the work that we were contracted for. I felt I had to do that. It would have been so beastly unfair not to. You understand, don't you?"

"Of course," he said. "You couldn't consider anything else. But then what?"

"Then," she said after a silence, "then, if it's what you want me to do, Roddy, I'll come back to Chicago—for good."

"Give up your business, you mean?" he asked quickly.

She nodded. "It can't be done out there," she said. "All the big productions that there's any money in are made in New York. I'll come back and just be your wife. I'll keep your house and mother the children, and—what was it you said to Gertrude?—maintain your status, if you don't think I'm spoiled for that."

That last phrase, though, was said with a smile, which he answered with one of his own and threw in in parenthesis, "You ought to hear Violet go on, and Constance." But with an instant return to seriousness, he said:

"I've not asked that, Rose. I wouldn't dream of asking it!"

"I know," she said. "It's a thing I'm glad you let me give—unasked. But I mean it, Roddy. I've meant it from the first, when I told you you were all I wanted. There wasn't any string tied to that."

"I know," he said. "But all the same, it wouldn't work, Rose."

"There's a real job there," she persisted, "just in being successfully the wife of a successful man. I can see that now. I never saw it when it was my job. Hardly caught a glimpse of it. I didn't even see my bills; let you pay them down at the office, with all your own work that you had to do."

"It wasn't me," he said. "It was Miss Beach."

She stared at that and gave a short laugh. "If I'd known that. . . !" she said.

Then she came back to the point.

"It is a real job, and I think I could learn to do it pretty well. And of course a wife's the only person who can do it properly."

Still he shook his head. But he hadn't, as yet, any reasoned answer to make, except as before, that it wouldn't work.

"I shouldn't mind the money end of it," she said. "I mean living on yours. I know I can earn my way, and I know you know it. So that wouldn't matter. I'd never feel like a beggar again, Roddy."

"I know," he agreed. "But that isn't it. It isn't a question of what you'd like to be, or are willing to be. It's a question of what you are. You're something more than just my wife. You've got certain talents—certain proved capacities. That's as true as that I am something besides—just your husband. There you are! Try it on the other way around. Suppose I should offer to give up my practise and come down here to live with you—be just your husband and, say, your business manager. You can see that that's preposterous. Or, for that matter, we could both quit. I've made a devil of a lot of money lately. I've an income from my investments of from twenty-five to thirty thousand a year that we could live on, and not do a blessed thing but be husband and wife to each other. Like the McCreas. But it wouldn't work. You've got to be what you are, that's the point, and somehow or other, cut your life to fit. I expect that's one of the things that's been the trouble with us down here. We've both been trying so damned hard to *be* something. And that won't work."

"What will work then?" she asked. And this was a question he couldn't answer.

"We've just got to go ahead," he said at last, "and see what happens. Perhaps you can work it out so that you can do part of your work at home. We could move the nursery and give you Florence's old studio. And then it would do if you only came down here for your two big seasons—fall and spring."

"That doesn't seem fair to you," she protested. "You deserve a real wife, Roddy; not somebody dashing in and dashing out."

"I don't deserve anything I can't get," he said. "I'd rather have a part interest in you than to possess, lock, stock and barrel, any other woman I can think of."

She came back to him again and settled down in his arms.

"You used to possess me, lock, stock and barrel," she said. "You can do it again, if you'll say the word, Rodney."

He shook his head. "That's just what I can't do," he told her. "That's gone and we'll never get it back. And I don't believe I'd have it back if I could. For one thing, you can't possess without being possessed. I know that back in those days you're talking about I used to try to fight you out of my thoughts. Used to stay down late at the office, not working, just—trying not to think about you. Trying to save out part of myself from being—saturated with you. It was the fact that I was so terribly important to you that used to make me feel like that; the fact of your—dependence—I don't mean for money—on me. I used to think— it wasn't your lover that thought that; it was the other man—that it would be a perfectly wonderful relief to me if you could just get some interest that left me out. And all the while the lover in me was trying to have all of you there was. It's a hard thing to talk sense about."

"A man told me," Rose said, "—John Galbraith told me, that he couldn't be a woman's friend and her lover at the same time, any more than a steel spring could be made soft so that it would bend in your fingers like copper, and still be a spring. He said that was true of him, anyway, and he felt sure it was true of nine men out of a dozen. Do you think it's true? Have we got to decide which we'll be?"

"We can't decide," he said with an impatient laugh. "That's just what I've been telling you. We've got to take what we can get. We've got to work out the relation between ourselves that is *our* relation—the Rose and Rodney relation. It'll probably be a little different from any other. There'll be friendship in it, and there'll be love in it. Imagine our 'deciding' that we wouldn't be lovers! But I guess that what Galbraith said was true to this extent: that each of those will be more or less at the expense of the other. It won't spring quite so well, and it will bend a little."

She was still disposed to rebel at this conclusion. "I don't see why it has to be that way," she insisted. "Why it can't be a perfect thing instead of just a compromise. Why being friends and partners shouldn't make us better lovers, and why being lovers shouldn't make us better friends."

"Like the doctrine of the Trinity," he murmured. "'Three in one; one in three. Without confounding the persons nor dividing the substance.' It's a wonderful idea, certainly."

"Well, then," she demanded, "isn't it what we ought to try for? The very best there is?"

"'That's what they tell us," he admitted. "'Aim high,' they say. I'm not sure it isn't better sense to aim at something you can hit. Why, look at us, these last three weeks! We said we were going to have a month of pure happiness. One hundred per cent. pure. We waked up every morning telling ourselves we'd got to be happy, and we made ourselves miserable every night wondering if we'd been happy enough."

"I'm glad you were miserable, too," she said. "I was *so* ashamed of myself for being."

After a while he said, "Here's what we've got to build on: Whatever else it may or may not be, this relation between us is a permanent thing. We've lived with each other and without each other, and we know which we want. If we find it has its limitations and drawbacks we needn't worry. Just go ahead and make the best of it we can. There's no law that decrees we've got to be happy. When we *are* happy it'll be so much to the good. And when we aren't. . ."

She gave a contented little laugh and cuddled closer down against him. "You talk like Solomon in all his solemnity," she said. "But you can't imagine that we're going to be unhappy. Really."

His answer was that perhaps he couldn't imagine it, but that he knew it, just the same. "Even an ordinary marriage isn't any too easy; a marriage, I mean, where it's quite well understood which of the parties to it shall always submit to the other; and which of them is the important one who's always to have the right of way. There's generally something perfectly unescapable that decides that question. But with us there isn't. So the question who's got to give in will have to be decided on its merits every time a difference arises."

She burlesqued a look of extreme apprehension. She was deeply and utterly content with life just then. But he wouldn't be diverted.

"There's another reason," he went on. "I've a notion that the thing we're after is about the finest thing there is. If that's so, we'll have to pay for it, in one way or another. But we aren't going to worry about it. We'll just go ahead—and see what happens."

"Do you remember when you said that before?" asked Rose. "You told me that marriage was an adventure anyway, and that the only thing to do was to try it—and see what happened."

He grunted. "The real adventure's just begun," he said.

"Anyhow," she murmured drowsily, "you can talk to me again. Just as if we weren't married."

AND THERE IS JUST ABOUT where they stand today—at the beginning, or hardly past the beginning, of what he spoke of as their real adventure; they are going forward prepared to make the best of it and see what happens.

What did happen within two or three days after this last conversation of theirs that I have chronicled was that Rose went back with Rodney and the twins to Chicago, stayed there only until Miss French could be summoned back from her vacation, and then went on to New York to a badly worried Alice and the now extremely urgent affairs of Dane & Company.

Summer is a slack time for a lawyer, of course, since judges are gentlemen who like long vacations. So Rodney persuaded Rose to take a bigger apartment in the same building and to put a card in the mailbox that would account for him as well as for herself. He came down pretty often, and always had, it must be owned, a rather hard time of it. The spectacle of Rose driving along an ungodly number of hours a day while he idled about doing nothing was one he found it hard to get used to. It didn't altogether reconcile him to it to have her point out that there were times when he drove like that. They had two or three good Sundays, though; one of them out on Long Island with John Galbraith—a meeting and the beginning of a friendship that Rose had been very keen to bring about.

Her work ended with a terrific climax in September, just about as his began, and Rose came back to Chicago, spent a joyous month with the twins and with the little of Rodney his office could spare of him. Then, taking the babies and their nurse with her, she went out to California to see her mother and Portia.

Without any special incentive, just the natural desire of a daughter and a sister for reunion after so long a parting would have taken her there.

But Rose had a special incentive. She wanted to talk to Portia. They hadn't had a real talk since that devastating day—ages ago—when, yielding to an impulse of passionate self-revelation, Portia had exhibited her great sacrifice and her equally great, though thwarted desire; had said to Rose, "I am the branch they cut off so that you could grow. You're living my life as well as yours. The only thing I ever could hate you for would be for failing." She wanted to tell Portia how the life she had given up the chance of living had grown in her sister's trust. She wanted Portia's, "Well done."

Also, as a practical matter of justice, she wanted to repay, as far as money could repay—what Portia, at such a cost, had given her. It was a project that had often been in her thoughts; at first, just as a dream, latterly, as a realizable hope.

Considered just as a visit to her mother and sister, the journey to California was a success. Her mother, especially, got a vast satisfaction out of the twins, and Rose herself an equal satisfaction out of seeing how happy and content she was.

She was writing a book—a sort of autobiography. Not that her life, as she modestly said, was worth writing about, but that the progress of the Cause she had devoted her life to could hardly be illustrated in a better way than with an account of that life; of the ideas she had found current in her girlhood; of the long struggle by means of which those ideas had become modified; and, last and most important, of the danger lest, now that the old fixed ideas had become fluid, they should flow in the wrong direction. Portia was acting as her amanuensis—faithful, competent, devoted, and just as of old—or perhaps more so, Rose couldn't be sure—ironic; a little acrid.

Mrs. Stanton's attitude toward Rose's own adventure perplexed and amused her a little. She'd half expected to be embarrassed with approbation. She was prepared to deprecate a little the idea that by the example of her revolt and her attained independence she had done a service to the great Cause. She didn't feel at all sure that she had; couldn't believe that she and Rodney, with all their struggles, had settled anything; and she had hesitated as to how far she could convey that doubt to her mother.

But she might have spared her pains. Mrs. Stanton's attitude, while it fell short of "the less said the better," was one, at least, of suspended judgment. She couldn't, conceivably, ever have left Henry Stanton. She couldn't, evidently, understand why Rose mightn't have done her wifely duty and been content with that. She felt it incumbent on women to demonstrate to men that the new liberties they sought would not, when granted, lead them to disregard the ties that were the essential foundations of Christian society. But Rose belonged to the new generation—a generation that confronted, no doubt, new problems, and would have to solve them for itself.

This suited Rose well enough. What she wanted from her mother, anyway, was just the old look of love and trust and confidence. And she got that abundantly.

The thing she wanted from Portia she didn't get. As long as any one else was by—her mother, or Miss French in charge of the twins—she and Portia chatted easily, on the best of terms. But, left alone with her—as it seemed to Rose she actually took pains not to be—Portia's manner took on that old ironic aloofness that had always silenced her when she was a girl. She made at last a resolute effort to break through.

"One of the things I came out for," she said, "was to talk to you—talk it all out with you. I want to know what sort of job you think I've made of it."

"You've evidently made a good job of the costume business," said Portia. "I read that little article about you in *Vanity* about a month ago. That didn't seem to leave much doubt as to who's who."

"I don't mean that," said Rose. "I mean what sort of job of it altogether; of the—of the life that's yours as well as mine."

She stopped there and waited, but all the assent she got from Portia was that she forbore to change the subject. They were sitting in the study which her mother had just abandoned for her afternoon nap, and Portia had busied herself sorting over the litter of papers her mother's activities always left.

"I want to tell you all about it," Rose said. "I'd like to tell you every smallest thing about it, if it were possible, so that you could—remember it as I do."

She tried to do this; to give her sister—not a narrative (her letters, after all, had put Portia in possession of the outlines of the story)—but at least an interpretation of it that would go to the bottom; things she couldn't write in her letters, the actuating desires and hopes that lay behind the things she'd done. But the attempt collapsed. She was talking in a vacuum. Her phrases grew more disjointed until she felt that they were meaningless. At least, scrambling back to solid ground again, she told Portia that she wanted to pay back to her the cost of her education, as well as that could be calculated, and of her trousseau.

Portia's negative of this proposition was as keen and straight as a knife-edge. The thing wasn't to be discussed; not to be considered for an instant. "We're perfectly well off, mother and I. We're living easily within our income out here, and—we're as contented as possible." The cadence of those last three words had a finality about it that closed the subject.

Portia didn't want to share, vicariously, in the life she'd made possible for Rose. The branch had withered indeed and didn't want the pain of feeling the sap struggling up under its bark again. The ashes had better be left banked up about the fading coal. The silence was like the click of a closing door. Then Portia said:

"What does the North Side bunch think of you now you've come back? And those Lake Forest friends of yours? They must have been hideously scandalized. Are they going to forgive you?"

"Oh, they're lovely to me," said Rose. "The only one I've lost out with is Frederica. She'll be a long time making it up with me, if she ever does."

"She saw what Rodney went through while you were away, I expect," Portia suggested.

"That, of course," said Rose. "And then—well, my going away like that, especially as she began to see what the idea was, must have seemed a sort of criticism on her own way of life, which she's every reason to feel perfectly satisfied with. And that, after she'd let herself get really fond of me, and had brought me up by hand—which is what she did that first season, must be pretty hard to forgive. She has forgiven me, of course. She's a dear. But we've—sort of got to begin again."

Portia wanted to know about all the others: that pretty Williamson woman, and a few more whose names she remembered.

Rose told her; showed a feverish interest in the rather indifferent topic just to bury the memory of the one that had failed so dismally. She described a dinner or two she had been to since her return, and told of the little triumph that had been made for her on the occasion of the Chicago opening of *Come On In*. Everybody had been there and the Crawfords had given a supper dance for her at the Blackstone afterward. And driving in the last nail, she told of the feeble little witticism old Mrs. Crawford had made apropos of her return—a remark whose tinge of malice was so mild that it was felt by all to constitute an official sanction of her social rehabilitation.

Portia honestly enjoyed all that, but Rose went back to the hotel feeling pretty blue. (They were stopping at the hotel. The twins alone, to say nothing of Miss French and herself, would have been too much for the modest confines of the bungalow.) She wished she could have a good long talk, tonight, with Rodney.

She had a sense of somebody, away up above all mundane affairs—not responsible for them, perhaps, but capable, at all events, of thoroughly taking them in—smiling at them all with a sort of ferocious cynicism. In the foreground of this impression were the good friends—the really good friends she had just been telling Portia about, who had taken her back with so warm a welcome—because she'd succeeded; got away with it!

It was with a deeper feeling of melancholy that she thought of Portia and her mother. Portia, who had fought so gallantly and deserved so much, thwarted, withered, huddling her ashes around her so that her coal of fire might never be fanned into flame again. Her mother, living gently in the afterglow of an outworn gospel. Must every one come to an end like that when some initial store of energy was spent? Begin walling himself in against life? Stuffing new experiences into pigeonholes, unscrutinized? Would the time come when little Portia would have to begin treating *her* with the same tender-patronage that

Rose felt now for her mother? Would little Portia, some day, smile over her like that, and wonder whether she'd ever—really lived?

She did wish she could have a talk with Rodney.

The telephone switchboard in the lobby gave her an idea. It was five o'clock, now; seven in Chicago. He'd just be sitting down to dinner, all by himself, poor dear, most likely, and wishing for a talk with her. Well, why not?

She rather electrified the hotel office when she put in that call. The whole place wore an important air for the next half-hour. She went up to her room to wait for it, and before the line was put through she thought of something that would have prevented her doing it if she'd thought in time. He'd probably think something horrible had happened to one of them. So the moment she heard his voice—it was faint and far-away but clear enough that she could detect the straining urgency of it—she said:

"It's all right, Roddy. There isn't a thing the matter. Did I frighten you half to death?"

He said, "Thank God!" And then, "I don't suppose it was two minutes I waited for your voice, but it seemed a year. What is it?"

"I'm ashamed to tell you, after a scare like that. It's nothing, Roddy. Just to hear you say hello. It seems a pretty unjust sort of world, tonight, and I wanted to be reminded that you were in it. That's all."

She had to say it all over again before she could make him believe he'd heard her straight, and by that time she was feeling pretty foolish over the impulse she had yielded to. But just the sound of his good big laugh, when he understood, was worth it.

"You aren't running it, you know," he told her. "Leave the worry to the Authorities. I can't philosophize any better than that at twenty dollars a minute. I wish you were here."

"I wish so too," she said. "I will be next week."

When she had hung up the receiver, she had to squeeze the tears out of her eyes before she could see to do anything else. But it was with her own smile that she contemplated what she meant to do next. She went into the adjoining room, relegated Miss French to the side lines and undressed the twins herself.

The twins adored her and had the most ineffably delicious ways of showing it. But an added attraction for Rose resided in the fact that this incursion of hers always—just a little—annoyed Miss French. Clever as the nurse was about handling the twins, she could not manage even the pretense to that professional superiority which is the prerogative of nurses toward mothers. Rose, with those highly trained hands of hers, a twin in each of them, could exhibit a dazzling virtuosity that left Miss French nowhere.

A Note About the Author

Henry Kitchell Webster (1875–1932) was an American novelist and short story writer. Born in Evanston, Illinois, Webster graduated from Hamilton College in 1897 before taking a job as a teacher at Union College in Schenectady, New York. Alongside coauthor Samuel Merwin, Webster found early success with such novels as *The Short Line War* (1899) and *Calumet "K"* (1901), the latter a favorite of Ayn Rand's. Webster's stories, often set in Chicago, were frequently released as serials before appearing as bestselling novels, a formula perfected by the author throughout his hugely successful career. By the end of his life, Webster was known across the United States as a leading writer of mystery, science fiction, and realist novels and stories.

A Note from the Publisher

Spanning many genres, from non-fiction essays to literature classics to children's books and lyric poetry, Mint Edition books showcase the master works of our time in a modern new package. The text is freshly typeset, is clean and easy to read, and features a new note about the author in each volume. Many books also include exclusive new introductory material. Every book boasts a striking new cover, which makes it as appropriate for collecting as it is for gift giving. Mint Edition books are only printed when a reader orders them, so natural resources are not wasted. We're proud that our books are never manufactured in excess and exist only in the exact quantity they need to be read and enjoyed.

bookfinity™

Discover more of your favorite classics with Bookfinity™.

- Track your reading with custom book lists.
- Get great book recommendations for your personalized Reader Type.
- Add reviews for your favorite books.
- AND MUCH MORE!

Visit **bookfinity.com** and take the fun Reader Type quiz to get started.

Enjoy our classic and modern companion pairings!